VIRAGO MO
CLASSICS
491

Daphne du Maurier (1907–89) was born in London, into a family with a rich literary heritage. Her father, Sir Gerald du Maurier, was a prominent actor and theatre manager, while her grandfather, George du Maurier, was a renowned author and illustrator. A voracious reader, she developed a love of storytelling and imaginary worlds from an early age, including creating a male alter ego for herself. She began writing short stories and articles in 1928, and achieved widespread recognition in 1931 with her first novel, *The Loving Spirit*. A biography and three other novels followed, including *Jamaica Inn*, but it was her 1938 novel *Rebecca* that catapulted du Maurier into international fame. An instant bestseller, it made her one of the most popular authors of her day and was adapted into an acclaimed film by Alfred Hitchcock. Besides novels, du Maurier published short stories, most famously *The Birds* and *Don't Look Now*, plays and biographies, many of which have been adapted for film, television and the stage, and in 1969 she was awarded a DBE.

In 1932, she married Major Frederick Browning, with whom she had three children. She lived most of her life in Cornwall, which provided the atmospheric setting for many of her books. When she died in 1989, she left behind a remarkable literary legacy, and remains one of the most influential and beloved authors of the twentieth century.

DAPHNE DU MAURIER

AFTER MIDNIGHT

Introduced by Stephen King

VIRAGO MODERN
CLASSICS

VIRAGO

The Apple Tree, The Birds and Monte Verità were first published in
The Apple Tree: A Short Novel and Several Long Stories in 1952 by Victor Gollancz Ltd
Published in 2004 by Virago Press

The Alibi, The Blue Lenses, Ganymede and The Pool were first published in
The Breaking Point in 1959 by Victor Gollancz Ltd
Published in 2009 by Virago Press

The Breakthrough, Don't Look Now and Not After Midnight were first published in
Not After Midnight, and Other Stories in 1971 by Victor Gollancz Ltd
Published in 2015 by Virago Press

Leading Lady and Split Second were first published in
The Rendezvous and Other Stories in 1980 by Victor Gollancz Ltd
Published in 2005 by Virago Press

The Doll was first published in *The Doll* in 2004 by Virago Press

This edition published in 2025 by Virago Press

1 3 5 7 9 10 8 6 4 2

Copyright © The Chichester Partnership
Introduction copyright © Stephen King
Illustrations by Joe McLaren

A CIP catalogue record for this book
is available from the British Library.

Hardback ISBN 978-0-349-01954-3
Independent bookshop hardback 978-0-349-02063-1

Typeset in Bembo Std by Palimpsest Book Production Ltd, Falkirk, Stirlingshire
Printed and bound in Great Britain by Clays Ltd, Elcograf S.p.A.

Papers used by Virago are from well-managed forests and other responsible sources.

MIX
Paper | Supporting
responsible forestry
FSC
www.fsc.org
FSC® C104740

Virago Press
An imprint of
Little, Brown Book Group
Carmelite House
50 Victoria Embankment
London EC4Y 0DZ

The authorised representative
in the EEA is
Hachette Ireland
8 Castlecourt Centre,
Dublin 15, D15 YF6A, Ireland
(email: info@hbgi.ie)

An Hachette UK Company
www.hachette.co.uk

www.littlebrown.co.uk

Contents

After Midnight: An Appreciation

By Stephen King

'Last night I dreamt I went to Manderley again.'

It's one of the most well-known first lines ever written in a novel. Certainly the most memorable; I used it myself as an epigram in my novel, *Bag of Bones*. Daphne du Maurier (1907–1989) also wrote what may be the best first line in a tale of the uncanny and outré. Her classic story 'The Birds' opens with this: 'On December the third the wind changed overnight and it was winter.' Short, chilly and to the point. It could almost be a weather report.

It works so well at the outset of the gripping tale that follows, in which every species of bird attacks humankind, because it's flat, declarative and realistic. Du Maurier can gin up horror when she wants – see 'The Doll', 'The Blue Lenses' and the shocking final two pages of 'Don't Look Now' – but knows that what's wanted here to instil belief (and suspense) is a tone that's closer to reportage than narration.

The film version of 'The Birds', overloaded with a love-match between Hollywood pretty people (Rod Taylor as Mitch, Tippi Hedren as Melanie) to go with the bird attacks, bears almost no resemblance to du Maurier's story. The setting is sunny Bodega Bay instead of cold and overcast Cornwall, and the number of characters has been expanded. (Only notable among these is ornithologist Ethel Bundy, who explains to

Melanie that birds would never attack because 'their brain pans are not big enough'.) Du Maurier's story is, by contrast, almost claustrophobic, focusing on Nat Hocken and his family, who take refuge from the air assault in their cottage. It's more like *The Siege of Trencher's Farm* by Gordon Williams (which became the movie *Straw Dogs*).

The only real similarity between the story and the movie lies in their endings. In the film, Mitch and Melanie escape while thousands of roosting birds are resting between attacks. What happens later is up to the viewer to guess. The conclusion of the du Maurier story is even more chilling in its flat narration. After smoking his last cigarette, Nat tries the wireless and finds it silent. 'He threw the empty packet on the fire, and watched it burn.'

This final line is as quietly terrible, yet as matter-of-fact, as the one that opens the story. What happens to Nat, his wife and his children? We don't know. Du Maurier doesn't care, and she's right not to care. What she gives us is that last cigarette, which carries its own freight of firing-squad symbolism, and the burning packet. She tells us, in effect, *decide for yourself*. This is the essence of her unsettling genius, and here are twelve other examples of that genius.

I am impatient with the idea of 'spoilers', a term that's come into vogue along with other unpleasant side-effects of the internet in general and social media in particular. I find 'You spoiled it!' to be, in general, the cry of spoiled people. I'd argue you can rarely spoil a good story, because the joy is in the journey rather than the arrival.

The stories in *After Midnight* are a notable exception to that rule. In an afterword I could discuss the startling resolutions of certain stories in detail, having made the fair assumption that you have read them on your way to my essay. In a foreword, that won't work – not with these tales. To talk about any of them at length would destroy their effect. Suffice it to say that you are in the hands of a master storyteller. A *diabolical* one, at that.

The line-by-line quality of du Maurier's writing is astonishing, given how prolific she was: seventeen novels, six biographies, three plays and dozens of short stories. Those which follow are among her best. She is particularly good at quick-sketch characterisation. Midge, from 'The Apple Tree', is a masterpiece of passive-aggressive behaviour, a woman whose chief talent seems to be making her husband's life miserable. Not in any big way – she's not a thief, drug-addict or adulterer – but in a series of small nips that draw trickles of blood. She may or may not be aware of what she's doing. Either way, consciously or unconsciously, she is exerting control.

The narrator of 'The Apple Tree' (unnamed, like so many of du Maurier's characters, including the second Mrs de Winter of *Rebecca*) is a gentleman who gives his wife the newspaper first. She returns it crumpled and folded and out of order. The birth of a child to mutual friends is noted by Midge with dismay, whether a boy or a girl; she sees the drawbacks to both sexes. Although the couple has a maid, Midge 'would labour past him, stooping under the weight of the laden tray'. Stooping ostentatiously, one assumes – 'Look at me, how I must bear my woman's burden.'

The sighing, martyred Midge passes away, but her widowed husband remains in her thrall, associating an ugly apple tree with 'poor Midge', and the smaller, more shapely apple tree in its shadow with a laughing, cheerful farm girl named May, who Midge's husband once kissed (and who died in a motor-bike accident). Du Maurier describes the 'Midge-tree' this way: 'The moon shone upon the withered branches, and they looked like skeleton's arms raised in supplication. Frozen arms, stiff and numb with pain.'

Poor Midge, indeed!

Is the ugly apple tree, with its sour, mealy fruit, a kind of revenant, or does the narrator – a bit of a fussbudget, far from perfect himself – simply find it psychologically impossible to escape his dead wife's influence? Du Maurier doesn't say. She is deft enough to have it both ways, which is the case with many of these stories.

A few, like 'Monte Verità', feature doomed romance; at least one ('The Breakthrough') deals with telepathy, telekinesis and even envisions our current fixation with AI; the best of them inhabit a murky borderland between what may be supernatural or could be no more than overactive imaginations stressed into malignancy. The best of these 'twilight zone' stories are probably 'The Blue Lenses' and 'The Pool'.

In the former, following an eye operation, Marda West begins seeing people with the heads of animals which reflect the personalities of the people to whom those heads belong; the revelation that her husband has the head of a vulture is especially creepy.

In the latter, a young girl believes she sees a whole other plane of existence, guarded by a woman commanding a turnstile at the bottom of a scummy woodland pool. Deborah longs to visit that world, which almost leads to her death. Her glimpses of this underwater alternate reality, visited by streams of people, end with her delicately described first menstrual period ('Have you got a pain? It's usual, the first time'). This marks her entry into adulthood, where vivid imagination – or possibly that actual other world – is no longer allowed or accessible. There is an exquisite specificity to Deborah's imaginings, which makes the story particularly haunting.

Why is this an appreciation rather than a scholarly foreword? The answer is simple: I love these stories, and love defies scholarly analysis. I love their clarity, I love their often grim view of human nature, I love du Maurier's prodigious talent and narrative ability.

There is a reason why collections of short stories are, as a rule, less popular than novels. With a novel, you settle in with a cast of characters for what may be a day or two (if you're a fast reader like my wife) or a week or more (if you're a slow reader, like me). When it comes to short stories, even novellas like 'Monte Verità', the reader has to create a fictional world in his or her imagination, then disassemble it, move on to the next fictional world and build that one. That can be hard work. It's not with these stories.

I found myself enjoying each one – immersing myself in them – yet eager to discover the next. Because I trust the storyteller and know that while each story may vary in tone and cast of characters, I will certainly find much to enjoy and think about. Entering these worlds is a pleasure rather than an effort. Sometimes the build-up can be slow, but 'there are violins', as some critic or other said about Robert Bloch's *Psycho*. (That is certainly true of Bernard Herrmann's music for the film version, which is almost all violins.) Meaning that even when things seem relatively innocuous, you sense the shadows gathering. This is a gift few writers have.

'Ganymede' deals with latent homosexuality – 'the love that dare not speak its name', in the words of Lord Alfred Douglas. Du Maurier approaches this subject with appropriate tact, of course; when the story was published in *The Breaking Point* (1959), homosexuality between consenting adults was still illegal in Great Britain. The narrator, a self-proclaimed classical scholar, is a prissy naif who can't bear the idea of vulgarity, or what he terms *unsavouriness*. He thinks, 'The word unsavoury suggests a lack of personal cleanliness: unchanged linen, bed-sheets hanging to dry, the fluff off combs, torn packets in waste-paper baskets.' Is this perfect, or what?

The narrator's love object turns out to have a mind that's a bad match for his classical beauty. When the narrator asks Ganymede what he would buy if he could have anything connected with the English language, he is expecting – hoping, at least – that the youth might pick something like the plays of Shakespeare (or at least the sonnets). Instead, this beautiful boy, after giving the question due consideration, says he would like a long-playing record by Elvis Presley or Johnnie Ray. Perhaps this doesn't qualify as 'unsavoury', but it's certainly vulgar.

Du Maurier's horrors – and some of these stories are quite nasty – are described with a calm rationality that makes them true nightmare fuel. In 'The Alibi', Mr Fenton has a sudden, terrible epiphany when he is 'seized with the overwhelming, indeed appalling impression that . . . all the other people walking along the Embankment or crossing the bridge were minute, dangling puppets manipulated by a string'. He decides to murder one or two of these puppets, chosen almost at random. 'I have come to strangle you,' he thinks about Anna Kaufman, his new landlady, at the same time taking off his hat (as a gentleman should). 'You and your child.' The outcome is particularly awful for both Fenton and the woman he means to murder. When I finished, I could almost hear the gruesome host of the *Tales from the Crypt* series cackling, 'Irony, kiddies! It's good for your blood!'

Every story here possesses what I call *the gotta*, meaning you *gotta* keep going. Gotta find out what happens next, from Nat Hocken nailing up his windows to keep out the rampaging birds to Mrs Ellis, who goes out for a brief walk and finds another family living in her house when she returns (this particular chiller, titled 'Split Second', was originally published in *Today's Woman for Young Wives*). Better you discover each gotta for yourself.

Some stories have a sexual tingle. The most overtly sexual is 'The Doll', where a woman named Rebecca (*That* Rebecca? Who is to say it's not?) fascinates another of du Maurier's unnamed narrators. Rebecca is frightening, with her 'great wide fanatical eyes like a saint, the narrow mouth that hid [her] teeth, sharp and white as ivory, and [her] halo of savage hair, electric, dark, uncontrolled'. I am particularly taken with that halo of savage hair, which should not work (hair cannot be savage, any more than waves can be angry) but somehow does.

Rebecca has a secret lover named Julio. The narrator describes Julio, who seems to be about sixteen, this way: 'His face was the most evil thing I have ever seen. It was ashen pale in colour, and the mouth was a crimson gash, sensual and depraved. The nose was thin . . . the eyes were cruel, gleaming and narrow, and curiously still. They seemed to stare right through one – the eyes of a hawk.'

Du Maurier doesn't come right out and say that Rebecca is having a sexual relationship with Julio, but it's strongly implied . . . and the narrator clearly believes it. What makes this particularly perverse is the fact that Julio is not human (at least *probably* not), but a mannequin.

There. I have given away, at least in this story, a secret that should have been Daphne du Maurier's to impart, but only because the title allows the reader to see it coming. I will give away no more, and I only told this one because knowing doesn't affect readers admiring the story's careful construction . . . and its daring. Written in 1928, 'The Doll' was for many years presumed lost. Because of the subject matter, du Maurier, then just twenty-one years old, may have been persuaded to hold it back, lest it damage her reputation at a time when sexual matters were best left *sub rosa*. It was finally published in a book of previously rejected stories, aptly titled *The Editor Regrets*.

I have said quite enough. It's time for you to take Daphne du Maurier's hand and let her lead you into the dark. Her talent is a bright light that will guide you. These remarkable stories await. I envy your discoveries.

And your discomfort.

AFTER MIDNIGHT

The Blue Lenses

This was the day for the bandages to be removed and the blue lenses fitted. Marda West put her hand up to her eyes and felt the crêpe binder, and the layer upon layer of cotton-wool beneath. Patience would be rewarded at last. The days had passed into weeks since her operation, and she had lain there suffering no physical discomfort, but only the anonymity of darkness, a negative feeling that the world and the life around was passing her by. During the first few days there had been pain, mercifully allayed by drugs, and then the sharpness of this wore down, dissolved, and she was left with a sense of great fatigue, which they assured her was reaction after shock. As for the operation itself, it had been successful. Here was definite promise. A hundred per cent successful.

'You will see,' the surgeon told her, 'more clearly than ever before.'

'But how can you tell?' she urged, desiring her slender thread of faith to be reinforced.

1

'Because we examined your eyes when you were under the anaesthetic,' he replied, 'and again since, when we put you under for a second time. We would not lie to you, Mrs West.'

This reassurance came from them two or three times a day, and she had to steel herself to patience as the weeks wore by, so that she referred to the matter perhaps only once every twenty-four hours, and then by way of a trap, to catch them unawares. 'Don't throw the roses out. I should like to see them,' she would say, and the day-nurse would be surprised into the admission, 'They'll be over before you can do that.' Which meant that she would not see this week.

Actual dates were never mentioned. Nobody said, 'On the fourteenth of the month you will have your eyes.' And the subterfuge continued, the pretence that she did not mind and was content to wait. Even Jim, her husband, was now classed in the category of 'them', the staff of the hospital, and no longer treated as a confidant.

Once, long ago, every qualm and apprehension had been admitted and shared. This was before the operation. Then, fearful of pain and blindness, she had clung to him and said, 'What if I never see again, what will happen to me?' picturing herself as helpless and maimed. And Jim, whose anxiety was no less harsh than hers, would answer, 'Whatever comes, we'll go through it together.'

Now, for no known reason except that darkness, perhaps, had made her more sensitive, she was shy to discuss her eyes with him. The touch of his hand was the same as it had ever been, and his kiss, and the warmth of his voice; but always, during these days of waiting, she had the seed of fear that he, like the staff at the hospital, was being too kind. The kindness of those who knew towards the one who must not be told. Therefore, when at last it happened, when at his evening visit the surgeon said, 'Your lenses will be fitted tomorrow,' surprise was greater than joy. She could not say anything, and he had left the room before she could thank him. It was really true. The long agony had ended. She permitted herself only a last feeler, before the day-nurse went off duty – 'They'll take some getting used to, and hurt a bit at first?' – her statement of fact put as a careless question. But the voice of the woman who had tended her through so many weary days replied, 'You won't know you've got them, Mrs West.'

Such a calm, comfortable voice, and the way she shifted the pillows and held the glass to the patient's lips, the hand smelling faintly of the Morny French Fern soap with which she washed her, these things gave confidence and implied that she could not lie.

'Tomorrow I shall see you,' said Marda West, and the nurse, with the cheerful laugh that could be heard sometimes down the corridor outside, answered, 'Yes, I'll give you your first shock.'

It was a strange thought how memories of coming into the nursing-home were now blunted. The staff who had received her were dim shadows, the room assigned to her, where she still lay, like a wooden box built only to entrap. Even the surgeon, brisk and efficient during those two rapid consultations when he had recommended an immediate operation, was a voice rather than a presence. He gave his orders and the orders were carried out, and it was difficult to reconcile this bird-of-passage with the person who, those several weeks ago, had asked her to surrender herself to him, who had in fact worked this miracle upon the membranes and the tissues which were her living eyes.

'Aren't you feeling excited?' This was the low, soft voice of her night-nurse, who, more than the rest of them, understood what she had endured. Nurse Brand, by day, exuded a daytime brightness; she was a person of sunlight, of bearing in fresh flowers, of admitting visitors. The weather she described in the world outside appeared to be her own creation. 'A real scorcher,' she would say, flinging open windows, and her patient would sense the cool uniform, the starched cap, which somehow toned down the penetrating heat. Or else she might hear the steady fall of rain and feel the slight chill accompanying it. 'This is going to please the gardeners, but it'll put paid to Matron's day on the river.'

Meals, too, even the dullest of lunches, were made to appear delicacies through her method of introduction. 'A morsel of brill *au beurre*?' she would suggest happily, whetting reluctant appetite, and the boiled fish that followed must be eaten, for all its taste-lessness, because otherwise it would seem to let down Nurse Brand, who had recommended it. 'Apple fritters – you can manage two, I'm sure,' and the tongue began to roll the imaginary fritter, crisp as a flake and sugared, which in reality had a languid, leathery substance. And so her cheerful optimism brooked no discontent – it would be offensive to complain, lacking in back-bone to admit, 'Let me just lie. I don't want anything.'

The night brought consolation and Nurse Ansel. She did not expect courage. At first, during pain, it had been Nurse Ansel who had administered the drugs. It was she who had smoothed the pillows and held the glass to the parched lips. Then, with the passing weeks, there had been the gentle voice and the quiet encouragement. 'It will soon pass. This waiting is the worst.' At night the patient had only to touch the bell, and in a moment Nurse Ansel was by the bed. 'Can't sleep? I know, it's wretched for you. I'll give you just two and a half grains, and the night won't seem so long.'

How compassionate, that smooth and silken voice. The imag-ination, making fantasies through enforced rest and idleness, pictured some reality with Nurse Ansel that was not hospital – a holiday abroad, perhaps, for the three of them, and Jim playing golf with an unspecified male companion, leaving her,

Marda, to wander with Nurse Ansel. All she did was faultless. She never annoyed. The small shared intimacies of night-time brought a bond between nurse and patient that vanished with the day, and when she went off duty, at five minutes to eight in the morning, she would whisper, 'Until this evening,' the very whisper stimulating anticipation, as though eight o'clock that night would not be clocking-in but an assignation.

Nurse Ansel understood complaint. When Marda West said wearily, 'It's been such a long day,' her answering 'Has it?' implied that for her too the day had dragged, that in some hostel she had tried to sleep and failed, that now only did she hope to come alive.

It was with a special secret sympathy that she would announce the evening visitor. 'Here is someone you want to see, a little earlier than usual,' the tone suggesting that Jim was not the husband of ten years but a troubadour, a lover, someone whose bouquet of flowers had been plucked in an enchanted garden and now brought to a balcony. 'What gorgeous lilies!', the exclamation half a breath and half a sigh, so that Marda West imagined exotic dragon-petalled beauties growing to heaven, and Nurse Ansel, a little priestess, kneeling. Then, shyly, the voice would murmur, 'Good evening, Mr West. Mrs West is waiting for you.' She would hear the gentle closing of the door, the tip-toeing out with the lilies and the almost sound-less return, the scent of the flowers filling the room.

It must have been during the fifth week that Marda West had tentatively suggested, first to Nurse Ansel and then to her husband, that perhaps when she returned home the night-nurse might go with them for the first week. It would chime with Nurse Ansel's own holiday. Just a week. Just so that Marda West could settle to home again.

'Would you like me to?' Reserve lay in the voice, yet promise too.

5

'I would. It's going to be so difficult at first.' The patient, not knowing what she meant by difficult, saw herself as helpless still, in spite of the new lenses, and needing the protection and the reassurance that up to the present only Nurse Ansel had given her. 'Jim, what about it?'

His comment was something between surprise and indulgence. Surprise that his wife considered a nurse a person in her own right, and indulgence because it was the whim of a sick woman. At least, that was how it seemed to Marda West, and later, when the evening visit was over and he had gone home, she said to the night-nurse, 'I can't make out whether my husband thought it a good idea or not.'

The answer was quiet yet reassuring. 'Don't worry. Mr West is reconciled.'

But reconciled to what? The change in routine? Three people round the table, conversation, the unusual status of a guest who, devoting herself to her hostess, must be paid? (Though the last would not be mentioned, but glossed over at the end of a week in an envelope.)

'Aren't you feeling excited?' Nurse Ansel, by the pillow, touched the bandages, and it was the warmth in the voice, the certainty that only a few hours now would bring revelation, which stifled at last all lingering doubt of success. The operation had not failed. Tomorrow she would see once more.

'In a way,' said Marda West, 'it's like being born again. I've forgotten how the world looks.'

'Such a wonderful world,' murmured Nurse Ansel, 'and you've been patient for so long.'

The sympathetic hand expressed condemnation of all those who had insisted upon bandages through the waiting weeks. Greater indulgence might have been granted had Nurse Ansel herself been in command and waved a wand.

'It's queer,' said Marda West, 'tomorrow you won't be a voice to me any more. You'll be a person.'

'Aren't I a person now?'

A note of gentle teasing, of pretended reproach, which was all part of the communication between them, so soothing to the patient. This must surely, when sight came back, be forgone.

'Yes, of course, but it's bound to be different.'

'I don't see why.'

Even knowing she was dark and small – for so Nurse Ansel had described herself – Marda West must be prepared for surprise at the first encounter, the tilt of the head, the slant of the eyes, or perhaps some unexpected facial form like too large a mouth, too many teeth.

'Look, feel . . .' and not for the first time Nurse Ansel took her patient's hand and passed it over her own face, a little embarrassing, perhaps, because it implied surrender, the patient's hand a captive. Marda West, withdrawing it, said with a laugh, 'It doesn't tell me a thing.'

'Sleep, then. Tomorrow will come too soon.' There came the familiar routine of the bell put within reach, the last-minute drink, the pill, and then the soft, 'Good night, Mrs West. Ring if you want me.'

'Thank you. Good night.'

There was always a slight sense of loss, of loneliness, as the door closed and she went away, and a feeling of jealousy, too, because there were other patients who received these same mercies, and who, in pain, would also ring their bells. When she awoke – and this often happened in the small hours – Marda West would no longer picture Jim at home, lonely on his pillow, but would have an image of Nurse Ansel, seated perhaps by someone's bed, bending to give comfort, and this alone would make her reach for the bell, and press her thumb upon it, and say, when the door opened, 'Were you having a nap?'

'I never sleep on duty.'

She would be seated, then, in the cubby-hole midway along the passage, perhaps drinking tea or entering particulars of charts into a ledger. Or standing beside a patient, as she now stood beside Marda West.

'I can't find my handkerchief.'

'Here it is. Under your pillow all the time.'

A pat on the shoulder (and this in itself was a sort of delicacy), a few moments of talk to prolong companionship, and then she would be gone, to answer other bells and other requests.

'Well, we can't complain of the weather!' Now it was the day itself, and Nurse Brand coming in like the first breeze of morning, a hand on a barometer set fair. 'All ready for the great event?' she asked. 'We must get a move on, and keep your prettiest nightie to greet your husband.'

It was her operation in reverse. This time in the same room, though, and not a stretcher, but only the deft hands of the surgeon with Nurse Brand to help him. First came the disappearance of the crêpe, the lifting of the bandages and lint, the very slight prick of an injection to dull feeling. Then he did something to her eyelids. There was no pain. Whatever he did was cold, like the slipping of ice where the bandages had been, yet soothing too.

'Now, don't be disappointed,' he said. 'You won't know any difference for about half an hour. Everything will seem shadowed. Then it will gradually clear. I want you to lie quietly during that time.'

'I understand. I won't move.'

The longed-for moment must not be too sudden. This made sense. The dark lenses, fitted inside her lids, were temporary for the first few days. Then they would be removed and others fitted.

'How much shall I see?' The question dared at last.

'Everything. But not immediately in colour. Just like wearing sunglasses on a bright day. Rather pleasant.'

His cheerful laugh gave confidence, and when he and Nurse Brand had left the room she lay back again, waiting for the fog to clear and for that summer day to break in upon her vision, however subdued, however softened by the lenses.

Little by little the mist dissolved. The first object was angular, a wardrobe. Then a chair. Then, moving her head, the gradual forming of the window's shape, the vases on the sill, the flowers Jim had brought her. Sounds from the street outside merged with the shapes, and what had seemed sharp before was now in harmony. She thought to herself, 'I wonder if I can cry? I wonder if the lenses will keep back tears,' but, feeling the blessing of sight restored, she felt the tears as well, nothing to be ashamed of – one or two which were easily brushed away.

All was in focus now. Flowers, the wash-basin, the glass with the thermometer in it, her dressing-gown. Wonder and relief were so great that they excluded thought.

'They weren't lying to me,' she thought. 'It's happened. It's true.'

The texture of the blanket covering her, so often felt, could now be seen as well. Colour was not important. The dim light caused by the blue lenses enhanced the charm, the softness of all she saw. It seemed to her, rejoicing in form and shape, that colour would never matter. There was time enough for colour. The blue symmetry of vision itself was all-important. To see, to feel, to blend the two together. It was indeed rebirth, the discovery of a world long lost to her.

There seemed to be no hurry now. Gazing about the small room and dwelling upon every aspect of it was richness, some-thing to savour. Hours could be spent just looking at the room and feeling it, travelling through the window and to the windows of the houses opposite.

'Even a prisoner,' she decided, 'could find comfort in his cell if he had been blinded first, and had recovered his sight.'

She heard Nurse Brand's voice outside, and turned her head to watch the opening door.

'Well . . . are we happy once more?'

Smiling, she saw the figure dressed in uniform come into the room, bearing a tray, her glass of milk upon it. Yet, incongruous, absurd, the head with the uniformed cap was not a woman's head at all. The thing bearing down upon her was a cow . . . a cow on a woman's body. The frilled cap was perched upon wide horns. The eyes were large and gentle, but cow's eyes, the nostrils broad and humid, and the way she stood there, breathing, was the way a cow stood placidly in pasture, taking the day as it came, content, unmoved.

'Feeling a bit strange?'

The laugh was a woman's laugh, a nurse's laugh, Nurse Brand's laugh, and she put the tray down on the cupboard beside the bed. The patient said nothing. She shut her eyes, then opened them again. The cow in the nurse's uniform was with her still.

'Confess now,' said Nurse Brand, 'you wouldn't know you had the lenses in, except for the colour.'

It was important to gain time. The patient stretched out her hand carefully for the glass of milk. She sipped the milk slowly. The mask must be worn on purpose. Perhaps it was some kind of experiment connected with the fitting of the lenses – though how it was supposed to work she could not imagine. And it was surely taking rather a risk to spring such a surprise, and, to people weaker than herself who might have undergone the same operation, downright cruel?

'I see very plainly,' she said at last. 'At least, I think I do.'

Nurse Brand stood watching her, with folded arms. The broad uniformed figure was much as Marda West had imagined it, but that cow's head tilted, the ridiculous frill of the cap perched on the horns . . . where did the head join the body, if mask it in fact was?

'You don't sound too sure of yourself,' said Nurse Brand. 'Don't say you're disappointed, after all we've done for you.'

The laugh was cheerful, as usual, but she should be chewing grass, the slow jaws moving from side to side.

'I'm sure of myself,' answered her patient, 'but I'm not so sure of you. Is it a trick?'

'Is what a trick?'

'The way you look . . . your . . . face?'

Vision was not so dimmed by the blue lenses that she could not distinguish a change of expression. The cow's jaw distinctly dropped.

'Really, Mrs West!' This time the laugh was not so cordial. Surprise was very evident. 'I'm as the good God made me. I dare say he might have made a better job of it.'

The nurse, the cow, moved from the bedside towards the window and drew the curtains more sharply back, so that the full light filled the room. There was no visible join to the mask: the head blended to the body. Marda West saw how the cow, if she stood at bay, would lower her horns.

'I didn't mean to offend you,' she said, 'but it *is* just a little strange. You see . . .'

She was spared explanation because the door opened and the surgeon came into the room. At least, the surgeon's voice was recognizable as he called, 'Hullo! How goes it?', and his figure in the dark coat and the sponge-bag trousers was all that an eminent surgeon's should be, but . . . that terrier's head, ears pricked, the inquisitive, searching glance? In a moment surely he would yap, and a tail wag swiftly?

11

This time the patient laughed. The effect was ludicrous. It must be a joke. It was, it had to be; but why go to such expense and trouble, and what in the end was gained by the deception? She checked her laugh abruptly as she saw the terrier turn to the cow, the two communicate with each other soundlessly. Then the cow shrugged its too ample shoulders.

'Mrs West thinks us a bit of a joke,' she said. But the nurse's voice was not over-pleased.

'I'm all for that,' said the surgeon. 'It would never do if she took a dislike to us, would it?'

Then he came and put his hand out to his patient, and bent close to observe her eyes. She lay very still. He wore no mask either. None, at least, that she could distinguish. The ears were pricked, the sharp nose questing. He was even marked, one ear black, the other white. She could picture him at the entrance to a fox's lair, sniffing, then quick on the scent scuffing down the tunnel, intent upon the job for which he was trained.

'Your name ought to be Jack Russell,' she said aloud.

'I beg your pardon?'

He straightened himself but still stood beside the bed, and the bright eye had a penetrating quality, one ear cocked.

'I mean,' Marda West searched for words, 'the name seems to suit you better than your own.'

She felt confused. Mr Edmund Greaves, with all the letters after him on the plate in Harley Street, what must he think of her?

'I know a James Russell,' he said to her, 'but he's an orthopaedic surgeon and breaks your bones. Do you feel I've done that to you?'

His voice was brisk, but he sounded a little surprised, as Nurse Brand had done. The gratitude which was owed to their skill was not forthcoming.

'No, no, indeed,' said the patient hastily, 'nothing is broken at all, I'm in no pain. I see clearly. Almost too clearly, in fact.'

'That's as it should be,' he said, and the laugh that followed resembled a short sharp bark.

'Well, nurse,' he went on, 'the patient can do everything within reason except remove the lenses. You've warned her, I suppose?'

'I was about to, sir, when you came in.'

Mr Greaves turned his pointed terrier nose to Marda West.

'I'll be in on Thursday,' he said, 'to change the lenses. In the meantime, it's just a question of washing out the eyes with a solution three times a day. They'll do it for you. Don't touch them yourself. And above all don't fiddle with the lenses. A patient did that once and lost his sight. He never recovered it.'

'If you tried that,' the terrier seemed to say, 'you would get what you deserved. Better not make the attempt. My teeth are sharp.'

'I understand,' said the patient slowly. But her chance had gone. She could not now demand an explanation. Instinct warned her that he would not understand. The terrier was saying something to the cow, giving instructions. Such a sharp staccato sentence, and the foolish head nodded in answer. Surely on a hot day the flies would bother her – or would the frilled cap keep insects away?

As they moved to the door the patient made a last attempt.

'Will the permanent lenses,' she asked, 'be the same as these?'

'Exactly the same,' yapped the surgeon, 'except that they won't be tinted. You'll see the natural colour. Until Thursday, then.'

He was gone, and the nurse with him. She could hear the murmur of voices outside the door. What happened now? If it was really some kind of test, did they remove their masks instantly? It seemed to Marda West of immense importance that she should find this out. The trick was not truly fair: it was a misuse of confidence. She slipped out of bed and went to the door. She could hear the surgeon say, 'One and a half grains. She's a little overwrought. It's the reaction, of course.'

Bravely, she flung open the door. They were standing there in the passage, wearing the masks still. They turned to look at her, and the sharp bright eyes of the terrier, the deep eyes of the cow, both held reproach, as though the patient, by confronting them, had committed a breach of etiquette.

'Do you want anything, Mrs West?' asked Nurse Brand.

Marda West stared beyond them down the corridor. The whole floor was in the deception. A maid, carrying dust-pan and brush, coming from the room next door, had a weasel's head upon her small body, and the nurse advancing from the other side was a little prancing kitten, her cap coquettish on her furry curls, the doctor beside her a proud lion. Even the porter, arriving at that moment in the lift opposite, carried a boar's head between his shoulders. He lifted out luggage, uttering a boar's heavy grunt.

The first sharp prick of fear came to Marda West. How could they have known she would open the door at that minute? How could they have arranged to walk down the corridor wearing masks, the other nurses and the other doctor, and the maid appear out of the room next door, and the porter come up in the lift? Something of her fear must have shown in her face, for Nurse Brand, the cow, took hold of her and led her back into her room.

'Are you feeling all right, Mrs West?' she asked anxiously.

Marda West climbed slowly into bed. If it was a conspiracy what was it all for? Were the other patients to be deceived as well?

'I'm rather tired,' she said. 'I'd like to sleep.'

'That's right,' said Nurse Brand, 'you got a wee bit excited.'

14

She was mixing something in the medicine glass, and this time, as Marda West took the glass, her hand trembled. Could a cow see clearly how to mix medicine? Supposing she made a mistake?

'What are you giving me?' she asked.

'A sedative,' answered the cow.

Buttercups and daisies. Lush green grass. Imagination was strong enough to taste all three in the mixture. The patient shuddered. She lay down on her pillow and Nurse Brand drew the curtains close.

'Now just relax,' she said, 'and when you wake up you'll feel so much better.' The heavy head stretched forward – in a moment it would surely open its jaws and moo.

The sedative acted swiftly. Already a drowsy sensation filled the patient's limbs.

Soon peaceful darkness came, but she awoke, not to the sanity she had hoped for, but to lunch brought in by the kitten. Nurse Brand was off duty.

'How long must it go on for?' asked Marda West. She had resigned herself to the trick. A dreamless sleep had restored energy and some measure of confidence. If it was somehow necessary to the recovery of her eyes, or even if they did it for some unfathomable reason of their own, it was their business.

'How do you mean, Mrs West?' asked the kitten, smiling. Such a flighty little thing, with its pursed-up mouth, and even as it spoke it put a hand to its cap.

'This test on my eyes,' said the patient, uncovering the boiled chicken on her plate. 'I don't see the point of it. Making yourselves such guys. What is the object?'

The kitten, serious, if a kitten could be serious, continued to stare at her. 'I'm sorry, Mrs West,' she said, 'I don't follow you. Did you tell Nurse Brand you couldn't see properly yet?'

'It's not that I can't see,' replied Marda West. 'I see perfectly well. The chair is a chair. The table is a table. I'm about to eat boiled chicken. But why do you look like a kitten, and a tabby kitten at that?'

Perhaps she sounded ungracious. It was hard to keep her voice steady. The nurse – Marda West remembered the voice, it was Nurse Sweeting, and the name suited her – drew back from the trolley-table.

'I'm sorry,' she said, 'if I don't come up to scratch. I've never been called a cat before.'

Scratch was good. The claws were out already. She might purr to the lion in the corridor, but she was not going to purr to Marda West.

'I'm not making it up,' said the patient. 'I see what I see. You are a cat, if you like, and Nurse Brand's a cow.'

This time the insult must sound deliberate. Nurse Sweeting had fine whiskers to her mouth. The whiskers bristled.

'If you please, Mrs West,' she said, 'will you eat your chicken, and ring the bell when you are ready for the next course?'

She stalked from the room. If she had a tail, thought Marda West, it would not be wagging, like Mr Greaves's, but twitching angrily.

No, they could not be wearing masks. The kitten's surprise and resentment had been too genuine. And the staff of the hospital could not possibly put on such an act for one patient, for Marda West alone – the expense would be too great. The fault must lie in the lenses, then. The lenses, by their very nature, by some quality beyond the layman's understanding, must transform the person who was perceived through them.

A sudden thought struck her, and pushing the trolley-table aside she climbed out of bed and went over to the dressing-table. Her own face stared back at her from the looking-glass. The dark lenses concealed the eyes, but the face was at least her own.

'Thank heaven for that,' she said to herself, but it swung

16

her back to thoughts of trickery. That her own face should seem unchanged through the lenses suggested a plot, and that her first idea of masks had been the right one. But why? What did they gain by it? Could there be a conspiracy amongst them to drive her mad? She dismissed the idea at once – it was too fanciful. This was a reputable London nursing-home, and the staff was well known. The surgeon had operated on royalty. Besides, if they wanted to send her mad, or kill her even, it would be simple enough with drugs. Or with anaesthetics. They could have given her too much anaesthetic during the operation, and just let her die. No one would take the round-about way of dressing up staff and doctors in animals' masks.

She would try one further proof. She stood by the window, the curtain concealing her, and watched for passers-by. For the moment there was no one in the street. It was the lunch-hour, and traffic was slack. Then, at the other end of the street, a taxi crossed, too far away for her to see the driver's head. She waited. The porter came out from the nursing-home and stood on the steps, looking up and down. His boar's head was clearly visible. He did not count, though. He could be part of the plot. A van drew near, but she could not see the driver . . . yes, he slowed as he went by the nursing-home and craned from his seat, and she saw the squat frog's head, the bulging eyes.

Sick at heart, she left the window and climbed back into bed. She had no further appetite and pushed away her plate, the rest of the chicken untasted. She did not ring her bell, and after a while the door opened. It was not the kitten. It was the little maid with the weasel's head.

'Will you have plum tart or ice cream, madam?' she asked.

Marda West, her eyes half-closed, shook her head. The weasel, shyly edging forward to take the tray, said, 'Cheese, then, and coffee to follow?'

17

The head joined the neck without any fastening. It could not be a mask, unless some designer, some genius, had invented masks that merged with the body, blending fabric to skin.

'Coffee only,' said Marda West.

The weasel vanished. Another knock on the door and the kitten was back again, her back arched, her fluff flying. She plonked the coffee down without a word, and Marda West, irritated — for surely, if anyone was to show annoyance, it should be herself? — said sharply, 'Shall I pour you some milk in the saucer?'

The kitten turned. 'A joke's a joke, Mrs West,' she said, 'and I can take a laugh with anyone. But I can't stick rudeness.'

'Miaow,' said Marda West.

The kitten left the room. No one, not even the weasel, came to remove the coffee. The patient was in disgrace. She did not care. If the staff of the nursing-home thought they could win this battle, they were mistaken. She went to the window again. An elderly cod, leaning on two sticks, was being helped into a waiting car by the boar-headed porter. It could not be a plot. They could not know she was watching them. Marda went to the telephone and asked the exchange to put her through to her husband's office. She remembered a moment afterwards that he would still be at lunch. Nevertheless, she got the number, and as luck had it he was there.

'Jim . . . Jim, darling.'

'Yes?'

The relief to hear the loved familiar voice. She lay back on the bed, the receiver to her ear.

'Darling, when can you get here?'

'Not before this evening, I'm afraid. It's one hell of a day, one thing after another. Well, how did it go? Is everything OK?'

'Not exactly.'

'What do you mean? Can't you see? Greaves hasn't bungled it, has he?'

How was she to explain what had happened to her? It sounded so foolish over the telephone.

'Yes, I can see. I can see perfectly. It's just that . . . that all the nurses look like animals. And Greaves, too. He's a fox terrier. One of those little Jack Russells they put down the foxes' holes.'

'What on earth are you talking about?'

He was saying something to his secretary at the same time, something about another appointment, and she knew from the tone of his voice that he was very busy, very busy, and she had chosen the worst time to ring him up. 'What do you mean about Jack Russell?' he repeated.

Marda West knew it was no use. She must wait till he came. Then she would try to explain everything, and he would be able to find out for himself what lay behind it.

'Oh, never mind,' she said. 'I'll tell you later.'

'I'm sorry,' he told her, 'but I really am in a tearing hurry. If the lenses don't help you, tell somebody. Tell the nurses, the Matron.'

'Yes,' she said, 'yes.'

Then she rang off. She put down the telephone. She picked up a magazine, one left behind at some time or other by Jim himself, she supposed. She was glad to find that reading did not hurt her eyes. Nor did the blue lenses make any difference, for the photographs of men and women looked normal, as they had always done. Wedding groups, social occasions, débutantes, all were as usual. It was only here, in the nursing-home itself and in the street outside, that they were different.

It was much later in the afternoon that Matron called in to have a word with her. She knew it was Matron because of her clothes. But inevitably now, without surprise, she observed the sheep's head.

19

'I hope you're quite comfortable, Mrs West?'

A note of gentle inquiry in the voice. A suspicion of a baa?

'Yes, thank you.'

Marda West spoke guardedly. It would not do to ruffle the Matron. Even if the whole affair was some gigantic plot, it would be better not to aggravate her.

'The lenses fit well?'

'Very well.'

'I'm so glad. It was a nasty operation, and you've stood the period of waiting so very well.'

That's it, thought the patient. Butter me up. Part of the game, no doubt.

'Only a few days, Mr Greaves said, and then you will have them altered and the permanent ones fitted.'

'Yes, so he said.'

'It's rather disappointing not to observe colour, isn't it?'

'As things are, it's a relief.'

The retort slipped out before she could check herself. The Matron smoothed her dress. And if you only knew, thought the patient, what you look like, with that tape under your sheep's chin, you would understand what I mean.

'Mrs West . . .' The Matron seemed uncomfortable, and turned her sheep's head away from the woman in the bed. 'Mrs West, I hope you won't mind what I'm going to say, but our nurses do a fine job here and we are all very proud of them. They work long hours, as you know, and it is not really very kind to mock them, although I am sure you intended it in fun.'

Baa . . . Baa . . . Bleat away. Marda West tightened her lips.

'Is it because I called Nurse Sweeting a kitten?'

'I don't know what you called her, Mrs West, but she was quite distressed. She came to me in the office nearly crying.'

Spitting, you mean. Spitting and scratching. Those capable little hands are really claws.

'It won't happen again.'

She was determined not to say more. It was not her fault. She had not asked for lenses that deformed, for trickery, for make believe.

'It must come very expensive,' she added, 'to run a nursing-home like this.'

'It is,' said the Matron. Said the sheep. 'It can only be done because of the excellence of the staff, and the cooperation of all our patients.'

The remark was intended to strike home. Even a sheep can turn.

'Matron,' said Marda West, 'don't let's fence with each other. What is the object of it all?'

'The object of what, Mrs West?'

'This tomfoolery, this dressing up.' There, she had said it. To enforce her argument she pointed at the Matron's cap. 'Why pick on that particular disguise? It's not even funny.'

There was silence. The Matron, who had made as if to sit down to continue her chat, changed her mind. She moved slowly to the door.

'We, who were trained at St Hilda's, are proud of our badge,' she said. 'I hope, when you leave us in a few days, Mrs West, that you will look back on us with greater tolerance than you appear to have now.'

She left the room. Marda West picked up the magazine she had thrown down, but the matter was dull. She closed her eyes. She opened them again. She closed them once more. If the chair had become a mushroom and the table a haystack, then the blame could have been put on the lenses. Why was it only people had changed? What was so wrong with people? She kept her eyes shut when her tea was brought her, and when the voice said pleasantly, 'Some flowers for you, Mrs West,' she did not even open them, but waited for the owner of the voice to leave the room. The flowers were carnations. The card was Jim's. And the message on it said, 'Cheer up. We're not as bad as we seem.'

She smiled, and buried her face in the flowers. Nothing false about them. Nothing strange about the scent. Carnations were carnations, fragrant, graceful. Even the nurse on duty who came to put them in water could not irritate her with her pony's head. After all, it was a trim little pony, with a white star on its forehead. It would do well in the ring. 'Thank you,' smiled Marda West.

The curious day dragged on, and she waited restlessly for eight o'clock. She washed and changed her nightgown, and did her hair. She drew her own curtains and switched on the bedside lamp. A strange feeling of nervousness had come upon her. She realized, so strange had been the day, that she had not once thought about Nurse Ansel. Dear, comforting, bewitching Nurse Ansel. Nurse Ansel, who was due to come on duty at eight. Was she also in the conspiracy? If she was, then Marda West would have a showdown. Nurse Ansel would never lie. She would go up to her, and put her hands on her shoulders, and take the mask in her two hands, and say to her, 'There, now take it off. You won't deceive me.' But if it was the lenses, if all the time it was the lenses that were at fault, how was she to explain it?

She was sitting at the dressing-table, putting some cream on her face, and the door must have opened without her being aware; but she heard the well-known voice, the soft beguiling voice, and it said to her, 'I nearly came before. I didn't dare. You would have thought me foolish.' It slid slowly into view, the long snake's head, the twisting neck, the pointed barbed tongue swiftly thrusting and swiftly withdrawn, it came into view over her shoulders, through the looking-glass.

Marda West did not move. Only her hand, mechanically,

continued to cream her cheek. The snake was not motionless: it turned and twisted all the time, as though examining the pots of cream, the scent, the powder.

'How does it feel to see yourself again?'

Nurse Ansel's voice emerging from the head seemed all the more grotesque and horrible, and the very fact that as she spoke the darting tongue spoke too paralysed action. Marda West felt sickness rise in her stomach, choking her, and suddenly physical reaction proved too strong. She turned away, but as she did so the steady hands of the nurse gripped her, she suffered herself to be led to her bed, she was lying down, eyes closed, the nausea passing.

'Poor dear, what have they been giving you? Was it the sedative? I saw it on your chart,' and the gentle voice, so soothing and so calm, could only belong to one who understood. The patient did not open her eyes. She did not dare. She lay there on the bed, waiting.

'It's been too much for you,' said the voice. 'They should have kept you quiet, the first day. Did you have visitors?'

'No.'

'Nevertheless, you should have rested. You look really pale. We can't have Mr West seeing you like this. I've half a mind to telephone him to stay away.'

'No . . . please, I want to see him. I must see him.'

Fear made her open her eyes, but directly she did so the sickness gripped her again, for the snake's head, longer than before, was twisting out of its nurse's collar, and for the first time she saw the hooded eye, a pin's head, hidden. She put her hand over her mouth to stifle her cry.

A sound came from Nurse Ansel, expressing disquiet.

'Something has turned you very sick,' she said. 'It can't be the sedative. You've often had it before. What was the dinner this evening?'

23

'Steamed fish. I wasn't hungry.'

'I wonder if it was fresh. I'll see if anyone has complained. Meanwhile, lie still, dear, and don't upset yourself.'

The door quietly opened and closed again, and Marda West, disobeying instructions, slipped from her bed and seized the first weapon that came to hand, her nail-scissors. Then she returned to her bed again, her heart beating fast, the scissors concealed beneath the sheet. Revulsion had been too great. She must defend herself, should the snake approach her. Now she was certain that what was happening was real, was true. Some evil force encompassed the nursing-home and its inhabitants, the Matron, the nurses, the visiting doctors, her surgeon – they were all caught up in it, they were all partners in some gigantic crime, the purpose of which could not be understood. Here, in Upper Watling Street, the malevolent plot was in process of being hatched, and she, Marda West, was one of the pawns; in some way they were to use her as an instrument.

One thing was very certain. She must not let them know that she suspected them. She must try and behave with Nurse Ansel as she had done hitherto. One slip, and she was lost. She must pretend to be better. If she let sickness overcome her, Nurse Ansel might bend over her with that snake's head, that darting tongue.

The door opened and she was back. Marda West clenched her hands under the sheet. Then she forced a smile.

'What a nuisance I am,' she said. 'I felt giddy, but I'm better now.'

The gliding snake held a bottle in her hand. She came over to the wash-basin and, taking the medicine-glass, poured out three drops.

'This should settle it, Mrs West,' she said, and fear gripped the patient once again, for surely the words themselves constituted a threat. 'This should settle it' – settle what? Settle her finish? The liquid had no colour, but that meant nothing. She took the medicine-glass handed to her, and invented a subter-fuge.

'Could you find me a clean handkerchief, in the drawer there?'

'Of course.'

The snake turned its head, and as it did so Marda West poured the contents of the glass on to the floor. Then fascin-ated, repelled, she watched the twisting head peer into the contents of the dressing-table drawer, search for a handkerchief, and bring it back again. Marda West held her breath as it drew near the bed, and this time she noticed that the neck was not the smooth glow-worm neck that it had seemed on first encounter, but had scales upon it, zig-zagged. Oddly, the nurse's cap was not ill-fitting. It did not perch incongruously as had the caps of kitten, sheep and cow. She took the handkerchief.

'You embarrass me,' said the voice, 'staring at me so hard. Are you trying to read my thoughts?'

Marda West did not answer. The question might be a trap.

'Tell me,' the voice continued, 'are you disappointed? Do I look as you expected me to look?'

Still a trap. She must be careful. 'I think you do,' she said slowly, 'but it's difficult to tell with the cap. I can't see your hair.'

Nurse Ansel laughed, the low, soft laugh that had been so alluring during the long weeks of blindness. She put up her hands, and in a moment the whole snake's head was revealed, the flat, broad top, the tell-tale adder's V. 'Do you approve?' she asked.

Marda West shrank back against her pillow. Yet once again she forced herself to smile.

'Very pretty,' she said, 'very pretty indeed.'

The cap was replaced, the long neck wriggled, and then,

deceived, it took the medicine-glass from the patient's hand and put it back upon the wash-basin. It did not know everything.

'When I go home with you,' said Nurse Ansel, 'I needn't wear uniform – that is, if you don't want me to. You see, you'll be a private patient then, and I your personal nurse for the week I'm with you.'

Marda West felt suddenly cold. In the turmoil of the day she had forgotten the plans. Nurse Ansel was to be with them for a week. It was all arranged. The vital thing was not to show fear. Nothing must seem changed. And then, when Jim arrived, she would tell him everything. If he could not see the snake's head as she did – and indeed, it was possible that he would not, if her hypervision was caused by the lenses – he must just understand that for reasons too deep to explain she no longer trusted Nurse Ansel, could not, in fact, bear her to come home. The plan must be altered. She wanted no one to look after her. She only wanted to be home again, with him.

The telephone rang on the bedside-table and Marda West seized it, as she might seize salvation. It was her husband.

'Sorry to be late,' he said. 'I'll jump into a taxi and be with you right away. The lawyer kept me.'

'Lawyer?' she asked.

'Yes, Forbes & Millwall, you remember, about the trust fund.'

She had forgotten. There had been so many financial discussions before the operation. Conflicting advice, as usual. And finally Jim had put the whole business into the hands of the Forbes & Millwall people.

'Oh, yes. Was it satisfactory?'

'I think so. Tell you directly.'

He rang off, and looking up she saw the snake's head watching her. No doubt, thought Marda West, no doubt you would like to know what we were saying to one another.

'You must promise not to get too excited when Mr West comes.' Nurse Ansel stood with her hand upon the door.

'I'm not excited. I just long to see him, that's all.'

'You're looking very flushed.'

'It's warm in here.'

The twisting neck craned upward, then turned to the window. For the first time Marda West had the impression that the snake was not entirely at its ease. It sensed tension. It knew, it could not help but know, that the atmosphere had changed between nurse and patient.

'I'll open the window just a trifle at the top.'

If you were all snake, thought the patient, I could push you through. Or would you coil yourself round my neck and strangle me?

The window was opened, and pausing a moment, hoping perhaps for a word of thanks, the snake hovered at the end of the bed. Then the neck settled in the collar, the tongue darted rapidly in and out, and with a gliding motion Nurse Ansel left the room.

Marda West waited for the sound of the taxi in the street outside. She wondered if she could persuade Jim to stay the night in the nursing-home. If she explained her fear, her terror, surely he would understand. She would know in an instant if he had sensed anything wrong himself. She would ring the bell, make a pretext of asking Nurse Ansel some question, and then, by the expression on his face, by the tone of his voice, she would discover whether he saw what she saw herself.

The taxi came at last. She heard it slow down, and then the door slammed and, blessedly, Jim's voice rang out in the street below. The taxi went away. He would be coming up in the lift. Her heart began to beat fast, and she watched the door. She heard his footstep outside, and then his voice again – he must be saying something to the snake. She would know at once if he had seen the head. He would come into the room either startled, not believing his eyes, or laughing, declaring it a joke, a pantomime. Why did he not hurry? Why must they linger there, talking, their voices hushed?

The door opened, the familiar umbrella and bowler hat the first objects to appear round the corner, then the comforting burly figure, but – God . . . no . . . please God, not Jim too, not Jim, forced into a mask, forced into an organization of devils, of liars . . . Jim had a vulture's head. She could not mistake it. The brooding eye, the blood-tipped beak, the flabby folds of flesh. As she lay in sick and speechless horror, he stood the umbrella in a corner and put down the bowler hat and the folded overcoat.

'I gather you're not too well,' he said, turning his vulture's head and staring at her, 'feeling a bit sick and out of sorts. I won't stay long. A good night's rest will put you right.'

She was too numb to answer. She lay quite still as he approached the bed and bent to kiss her. The vulture's beak was sharp.

'It's reaction, Nurse Ansel says,' he went on, 'the sudden shock of being able to see again. It works differently with different people. She says it will be much better when we get you home.'

We . . . Nurse Ansel and Jim. The plan still held, then.

'I don't know,' she said faintly, 'that I want Nurse Ansel to come home.'

'Not want Nurse Ansel?' He sounded startled. 'But it was you who suggested it. You can't suddenly chop and change.'

There was no time to reply. She had not rung the bell, but Nurse Ansel herself came into the room. 'Cup of coffee, Mr West?' she said. It was the evening routine. Yet tonight it sounded strange, as though it had been arranged outside the door.

'Thanks, Nurse, I'd love some. What's this nonsense about not coming home with us?' The vulture turned to the snake, the snake's head wriggled, and Marda West knew, as she watched them, the snake with darting tongue, the vulture with his head hunched between his man's shoulders, that the plan for Nurse Ansel to come home had not been her own after all; she remembered now that the first suggestion had come from Nurse Ansel herself. It had been Nurse Ansel who had said that Marda West needed care during convalescence. The suggestion had come after Jim had spent the evening laughing and joking and his wife had listened, her eyes bandaged, happy to hear him. Now, watching the smooth snake whose adder's V was hidden beneath the nurse's cap, she knew why Nurse Ansel wanted to return with her, and she knew too why Jim had not opposed it, why in fact he had accepted the plan at once, had declared it a good one.

The vulture opened its blood-stained beak. 'Don't say you two have fallen out?'

'Impossible.' The snake twisted its neck, looked sideways at the vulture, and added, 'Mrs West is just a little bit tired tonight. She's had a trying day, haven't you, dear?'

How best to answer? Neither must know. Neither the vulture, nor the snake, nor any of the hooded beasts surrounding her and closing in, must ever guess, must ever know.

'I'm all right,' she said. 'A bit mixed-up. As Nurse Ansel says, I'll be better in the morning.'

The two communicated in silence, sympathy between them. That, she realized now, was the most frightening thing of all. Animals, birds and reptiles had no need to speak. They moved, they looked, they knew what they were about. They would not destroy her, though. She had, for all her bewildered terror, the will to live.

'I won't bother you,' said the vulture, 'with these documents

29

tonight. There's no violent hurry anyway. You can sign them at home.'

'What documents?'

If she kept her eyes averted she need not see the vulture's head. The voice was Jim's, steady and reassuring.

'The trust fund papers Forbes & Millwall gave me. They suggest I should become a co-director of the fund.'

The words struck a chord, a thread of memory belonging to the weeks before her operation. Something to do with her eyes. If the operation was not successful she would have difficulty in signing her name.

'What for?' she asked, her voice unsteady. 'After all, it is my money.'

He laughed. And, turning to the sound, she saw the beak open. It gaped like a trap, and then closed again.

'Of course it is,' he said. 'That's not the point. The point is that I should be able to sign for you, if you should be ill or away.'

Marda West looked at the snake, and the snake, aware, shrank into its collar and slid towards the door. 'Don't stay too long, Mr West,' murmured Nurse Ansel. 'Our patient must have a real rest tonight.'

She glided from the room and Marda West was left alone with her husband. With the vulture.

'I don't propose to go away,' she said, 'or be ill.'

'Probably not. That's neither here nor there. These fellows always want safeguards. Anyway, I won't bore you with it now.'

Could it be that the voice was over-casual? That the hand, stuffing the document into the pocket of the greatcoat, was a claw? This was a possibility, a horror, perhaps, to come. The bodies changing too, hands and feet becoming wings, claws, hoofs, paws, with no touch of humanity left to the people about her. The last thing to go would be the human voice.

When the human voice went, there would be no hope. The jungle would take over, multitudinous sounds and screams coming from a hundred throats.

'Did you really mean that,' Jim asked, 'about Nurse Ansel?'

Calmly she watched the vulture pare his nails. He carried a file in his pocket. She had never thought about it before – it was part of Jim, like his fountain pen and his pipe. Yet now there was reasoning behind it: a vulture needed sharp claws for tearing its victim.

'I don't know,' she said. 'It seemed to me rather silly to go home with a nurse, now that I can see again.'

He did not answer at once. The head sank deeper between the shoulders. His dark city suit was like the humped feathers of a large brooding bird. 'I think she's a treasure,' he said. 'And you're bound to feel groggy at first. I vote we stick to the plan. After all, if it doesn't work we can always send her away.'

'Perhaps,' said his wife.

She was trying to think if there was anyone left whom she could trust. Her family was scattered. A married brother in South Africa, friends in London, no one with whom she was intimate. Not to this extent. No one to whom she could say that her nurse had turned into a snake, her husband into a vulture. The utter hopelessness of her position was like damnation itself. This was her hell. She was quite alone, coldly conscious of the hatred and cruelty about her.

'What will you do this evening?' she asked quietly.

'Have dinner at the club, I suppose,' he answered. 'It's becoming rather monotonous. Only two more days of it, thank goodness. Then you'll be home again.'

Yes, but once at home, once back there, with a vulture and a snake, would she not be more completely at their mercy than she was here?

'Did Greaves say Thursday for certain?' she asked.

'He told me so this morning, when he telephoned. You'll have the other lenses then, the ones that show colour.'

The ones that would show the bodies too. That was the explanation. The blue lenses only showed the heads. They were the first test. Greaves, the surgeon, was in this too, very naturally. He had a high place in the conspiracy – perhaps he had been bribed. Who was it, she tried to remember, who had suggested the operation in the first place? Was it the family doctor, after a chat with Jim? Didn't they both come to her together and say that this was the only chance to save her eyes? The plot must lie deep in the past, extend right back through the months, perhaps the years. But, in heaven's name, for what purpose? She sought wildly in her memory to try to recall a look, or sign, or word which would give her some insight into this dreadful plot, this conspiracy against her person or her sanity.

'You look pretty peaky,' he said suddenly. 'Shall I call Nurse Ansel?'

'No . . .' It broke from her, almost a cry.

'I think I'd better go. She said not to stay long.'

He got up from the chair, a heavy, hooded figure, and she closed her eyes as he came to kiss her good night. 'Sleep well, my poor pet, and take it easy.'

In spite of her fear she felt herself clutch at his hand.

'What is it?' he asked.

The well-remembered kiss would have restored her, but not the stab of the vulture's beak, the thrusting blood-stained beak. When he had gone she began to moan, turning her head upon the pillow.

'What am I to do?' she said. 'What am I to do?'

The door opened again and she put her hand to her mouth. They must not hear her cry. They must not see her cry. She pulled herself together with a tremendous effort.

'How are you feeling, Mrs West?'

The snake stood at the bottom of the bed, and by her side the house physician. She had always liked him, a young pleasant man, and although like the others he had an animal's head it did not frighten her. It was a dog's head, an Aberdeen's, and the brown eyes seemed to quiz her. Long ago, as a child, she had owned an Aberdeen.

'Could I speak to you alone?' she asked.

'Of course. Do you mind, nurse?' He jerked his head at the door, and she had gone. Marda West sat up in bed and clasped her hands.

'You'll think me very foolish,' she began, 'but it's the lenses. I can't get used to them.'

He came over, the trustworthy Aberdeen, head cocked in sympathy.

'I'm sorry about that,' he said. 'They don't hurt you, do they?'

'No,' she said, 'no, I can't feel them. It's just that they make everyone look strange.'

'They're bound to do that, you know. They don't show colour.' His voice was cheerful, friendly. 'It comes as a bit of a shock when you've worn bandages so long,' he said, 'and you mustn't forget you were pulled about quite a bit. The nerves behind the eyes are still very tender.'

'Yes,' she said. His voice, even his head, gave her confidence. 'Have you known people who've had this operation before?'

'Yes, scores of them. In a couple of days you'll be as right as rain.' He patted her on the shoulder. Such a kindly dog. Such a sporting, cheerful dog, like the long-dead Angus. 'I'll tell you another thing,' he continued. 'Your sight may be better after this than it's ever been before. You'll actually see more clearly in every way. One patient told me that it was as though she had been wearing spectacles all her life, and then, because of the operation, she realized she saw all her friends and her family as they really were.'

'As they really were?' She repeated his words after him.

'Exactly. Her sight had always been poor, you see. She had thought her husband's hair was brown, but in reality it was red, bright red. A bit of a shock at first. But she was delighted.'

The Aberdeen moved from the bed, patted the stethoscope on his jacket, and nodded his head. 'Mr Greaves did a wonderful job on you, I can promise you that,' he said. 'He was able to strengthen a nerve he thought had perished. You've never had the use of it before – it wasn't functioning. So who knows, Mrs West, you may have made medical history. Anyway, sleep well and the best of luck. See you in the morning. Good night.' He trotted from the room. She heard him call good night to Nurse Ansel as he went down the corridor.

The comforting words had turned to gall. In one sense they were a relief, because his explanation seemed to suggest there was no plot against her. Instead, like the woman patient before her with the deepened sense of colour, she had been given vision. She used the words he had used himself. Marda West could see people as they really were. And those whom she had loved and trusted most were in truth a vulture and a snake . . .

The door opened and Nurse Ansel, with the sedative, entered the room.

'Ready to settle down, Mrs West?' she asked.

'Yes, thank you.'

There might be no conspiracy, but even so all trust, all faith, were over.

'Leave it with a glass of water. I'll take it later.'

She watched the snake put the glass on the bedside table. She watched her tuck in the sheet. Then the twisting neck peered closer and the hooded eyes saw the nail-scissors half-hidden beneath the pillow.

'What have you got there?'

The tongue darted and withdrew. The hand stretched out for the scissors. 'You might have cut yourself. I'll put them away, shall I, for safety's sake?'

Her one weapon was pocketed, not replaced on the dressing-table. The very way Nurse Ansel slipped the scissors into her pocket suggested that she knew of Marda West's suspicions. She wanted to leave her defenceless.

'Now, remember to ring your bell if you want anything.'

'I'll remember.'

The voice that had once seemed tender was over-smooth and false. How deceptive are ears, thought Marda West, what traitors to truth. And for the first time she became aware of her own new latent power, the power to tell truth from false-hood, good from evil.

'Good night, Mrs West.'

'Good night.'

Lying awake, her bedside clock ticking, the accustomed traffic sounds coming from the street outside, Marda West decided upon her plan. She waited until eleven o'clock, an hour past the time when she knew that all the patients were settled and asleep. Then she switched out her light. This would deceive the snake, should she come to peep at her through the window-slide in the door. The snake would believe that she slept. Marda West crept out of bed. She took her clothes from the wardrobe and began to dress. She put on her coat and shoes and tied a scarf over her head. When she was ready she went to the door and softly turned the handle. All was quiet in the corridor. She stood there motionless. Then she took one step across the threshold and looked to the left, where the nurse on duty sat. The snake was there. The snake was sitting crouched over a book. The light from the ceiling shone upon her head, and there could be no mistake. There were the trim uniform, the white starched front, the stiff collar, but rising from the collar the twisting neck of the snake, the long, flat, evil head.

Marda West waited. She was prepared to wait for hours. Presently the sound she hoped for came, the bell from a patient. The snake lifted its head from the book and checked the red light on the wall. Then, slipping on her cuffs, she glided down the corridor to the patient's room. She knocked and entered. Directly she had disappeared Marda West left her own room and went to the head of the staircase. There was no sound. She listened carefully, and then crept downstairs. There were four flights, four floors, but the stairway itself was not visible from the cubby-hole where the night nurses sat on duty. Luck was with her.

Down in the main hall the lights were not so bright. She waited at the bottom of the stairway until she was certain of not being observed. She could see the night-porter's back – his head was not visible, for he was bent over his desk – but when it straightened she noticed the broad fish face. She shrugged her shoulders. She had not dared all this way to be frightened by a fish. Boldly she walked through the hall. The fish was staring at her.

'Do you want anything, madam?' he said.

He was as stupid as she expected. She shook her head.

'I'm going out. Good night,' she said, and she walked straight past him, out of the swing-door, and down the steps into the street. She turned swiftly to the left, and, seeing a taxi at the further end, called and raised her hand. The taxi slowed and waited. When she came to the door she saw that the driver had the squat black face of an ape. The ape grinned. Some instinct warned her not to take the taxi.

'I'm sorry,' she said. 'I made a mistake.'

The grin vanished from the face of the ape. 'Make up your mind, lady,' he shouted, and let in his clutch and swerved away.

Marda West continued walking down the street. She turned right, and left, and right again, and in the distance she saw the lights of Oxford Street. She began to hurry. The friendly traffic drew her like a magnet, the distant lights, the distant men and women. When she came to Oxford Street she paused, wondering of a sudden where she should go, whom she could ask for refuge. And it came to her once again that there was no one, no one at all; because the couple passing her now, a toad's head on a short black body clutching a panther's arm, could give her no protection, and the policeman standing at the corner was a baboon, the woman talking to him a little prinked-up pig. No one was human, no one was safe, the man a pace or two behind her was like Jim, another vulture. There were vultures on the pavement opposite. Coming towards her, laughing, was a jackal.

She turned and ran. She ran, bumping into them, jackals, hyenas, vultures, dogs. The world was theirs, there was no human left. Seeing her run they turned and looked at her, they pointed, they screamed and yapped, they gave chase, their footsteps followed her. Down Oxford Street she ran, pursued by them, the night all darkness and shadow, the light no longer with her, alone in an animal world.

'Lie quite still, Mrs West, just a small prick, I'm not going to hurt you.'

She recognized the voice of Mr Greaves, the surgeon, and dimly she told herself that they had got hold of her again. She was back at the nursing-home, and it did not matter now – she might as well be there as anywhere else. At least in the nursing-home the animal heads were known.

They had replaced the bandages over her eyes, and for this she was thankful. Such blessed darkness, the evil of the night hidden.

'Now, Mrs West, I think your troubles are over. No pain and no confusion with these lenses. The world's in colour again.'

The bandages were being lightened after all. Layer after layer removed. And suddenly everything was clear, was day, and the face of Mr Greaves smiled down at her. At his side was a rounded, cheerful nurse.

'Where are your masks?' asked the patient.

'We didn't need masks for this little job,' said the surgeon. 'We were only taking out the temporary lenses. That's better, isn't it?'

She let her eyes drift round the room. She was back again all right. This was the shape, there was the wardrobe, the dressing-table, the vases of flowers. All in natural colour, no longer veiled. But they could not fob her off with stories of a dream. The scarf she had put round her head before slipping away in the night lay on the chair.

'Something happened to me, didn't it?' she said. 'I tried to get away.'

The nurse glanced at the surgeon. He nodded his head.

'Yes,' he said, 'you did. And, frankly, I don't blame you. I blame myself. Those lenses I inserted yesterday were pressing upon a tiny nerve, and the pressure threw out your balance. That's all over now.'

His smile was reassuring. And the large warm eyes of Nurse Brand – it must surely be Nurse Brand – gazed down at her in sympathy.

'It was very terrible,' said the patient. 'I can never explain how terrible.'

'Don't try,' said Mr Greaves. 'I can promise you it won't happen again.'

The door opened and the young physician entered. He too was smiling. 'Patient fully restored?' he asked.

'I think so,' said the surgeon. 'What about it, Mrs West?'

Marda West stared gravely at the three of them, Mr Greaves, the house physician and Nurse Brand, and she wondered what palpitating wounded tissue could so transform three individuals into prototypes of an animal kingdom, what cell linking muscle to imagination.

'I thought you were dogs,' she said. 'I thought you were a hunt terrier, Mr Greaves, and that you were an Aberdeen.'

The house physician touched his stethoscope and laughed.

'But I am,' he said, 'it's my native town. Your judgement was not wholly out, Mrs West. I congratulate you.'

Marda West did not join in the laugh.

'That's all right for you,' she said. 'Other people were not so pleasant.' She turned to Nurse Brand. 'I thought you were a cow,' she said, 'a kind cow. But you had sharp horns.'

This time it was Mr Greaves who took up the laugh. 'There you are, nurse,' he said, 'just what I've often told you. Time they put you out to grass and to eat the daisies.'

Nurse Brand took it in good part. She straightened the patient's pillows and her smile was benign. 'We get called some funny things from time to time,' she said. 'That's all part of our job.'

The doctors were moving towards the door, still laughing, and Marda West, sensing the normal atmosphere, the absence of all strain, said, 'Who found me, then? What happened? Who brought me back?'

Mr Greaves glanced back at her from the door. 'You didn't get very far, Mrs West, and a damn good job for you, or you mightn't be here now. The porter followed you.'

'It's all finished with now,' said the house physician, 'and the episode lasted five minutes. You were safely in your bed before any harm was done, and I was here. So that was that. The person who really had the full shock was poor Nurse Ansel when she found you weren't in your bed.'

39

Nurse Ansel . . . The revulsion of the night before was not so easily forgotten. 'Don't say our little starlet was an animal too?' smiled the house doctor. Marda West felt herself colour. Lies would have to begin. 'No,' she said quickly, 'no, of course not.'

'Nurse Ansel is here now,' said Nurse Brand. 'She was so upset when she went off duty that she wouldn't go back to the hostel to sleep. Would you care to have a word with her?'

Apprehension seized the patient. What had she said to Nurse Ansel in the panic and fever of the night? Before she could answer the house doctor opened the door and called down the passage.

'Mrs West wants to say good morning to you,' he said. He was smiling all over his face. Mr Greaves waved his hand and was gone, Nurse Brand went after him, and the house doctor, saluting with his stethoscope and making a mock bow, stepped back against the wall to admit Nurse Ansel. Marda West stared, then tremulously began to smile, and held out her hand.

'I'm sorry,' she said, 'you must forgive me.'

How could she have seen Nurse Ansel as a snake! The hazel eyes, the clear olive skin, the dark hair trim under the frilled cap. And that smile, that slow, understanding smile.

'Forgive you, Mrs West?' said Nurse Ansel. 'What have I to forgive you for? You've been through a terrible ordeal.'

Patient and nurse held hands. They smiled at one another. And, oh heaven, thought Marda West, the relief, the thankfulness, the load of doubt and despair that was swept away with the new-found sight and knowledge.

'I still don't understand what happened,' she said, clinging to the nurse. 'Mr Greaves tried to explain. Something about a nerve.'

Nurse Ansel made a face towards the door. 'He doesn't know himself,' she whispered, 'and he's not going to say either, or he'll find himself in trouble. He fixed those lenses too deep, that's all. Too near a nerve. I wonder it didn't kill you.'

She looked down at her patient. She smiled with her eyes. She was so pretty, so gentle. 'Don't think about it,' she said. 'You're going to be happy from now on. Promise me?'

'I promise,' said Marda West.

The telephone rang, and Nurse Ansel let go her patient's hand and reached for the receiver. 'You know who this is going to be,' she said. 'Your poor husband.' She gave the receiver to Marda West.

'Jim . . . Jim, is that you?'

The loved voice sounding so anxious at the other end. 'Are you all right?' he said. 'I've been through to Matron twice, she said she would let me know. What the devil has been happening?'

Marda West smiled and handed the receiver to the nurse.

'You tell him,' she said.

Nurse Ansel held the receiver to her ear. The skin of her hand was olive smooth, the nails gleaming with a soft pink polish.

'Is that you, Mr West?' she said. 'Our patient gave us a fright, didn't she?' She smiled and nodded at the woman in the bed. 'Well, you don't have to worry any more. Mr Greaves changed the lenses. They were pressing on a nerve, and everything is now all right. She can see perfectly. Yes, Mr Greaves said we could come home tomorrow.'

The endearing voice blended to the soft colouring, the hazel eyes. Marda West reached once more for the receiver.

'Jim, I had a hideous night,' she said. 'I'm only just beginning to understand it now. A nerve in the brain . . .'

'So I gather,' he said. 'How damnable. Thank God they traced it. That fellow Greaves can't have known his job.'

'It can't happen again,' she said. 'Now the proper lenses are in, it can't happen again.'

'It had better not,' he said, 'or I'll sue him. How are you feeling in yourself?'

'Wonderful,' she said, 'bewildered, but wonderful.'

41

'Good girl,' he said. 'Don't excite yourself. I'll be along later.'

His voice went. Marda West gave the receiver to Nurse Ansel, who replaced it on the stand.

'Did Mr Greaves really say I could go home tomorrow?' she asked.

'Yes, if you're good.' Nurse Ansel smiled and patted her patient's hand. 'Are you sure you still want me to come with you?' she asked.

'Why, yes,' said Marda West. 'Why, it's all arranged.'

She sat up in bed and the sun came streaming through the window, throwing light on the roses, the lilies, the tall-stemmed iris. The hum of traffic outside was close and friendly. She thought of her garden waiting for her at home, and her own bedroom, her own possessions, the day-by-day routine of home to be taken up again with sight restored, the anxiety and fear of the past months put away for ever.

'The most precious thing in the world,' she said to Nurse Ansel, 'is sight. I know now. I know what I might have lost.'

Nurse Ansel, hands clasped in front of her, nodded her head in sympathy. 'You've got your sight back,' she said, 'that's the miracle. You won't ever lose it now.'

She moved to the door. 'I'll slip back to the hostel and get some rest,' she said. 'Now I know everything is well with you I'll be able to sleep. Is there anything you want before I go?'

'Give me my face-cream and my powder,' said the patient, 'and the lipstick and the brush and comb.'

Nurse Ansel fetched the things from the dressing-table and put them within reach upon the bed. She brought the hand-mirror, too, and the bottle of scent, and with a little smile of intimacy sniffed at the stopper. 'Gorgeous,' she murmured. 'This is what Mr West gave you, isn't it?'

Already, thought Marda West, Nurse Ansel fitted in. She saw herself putting flowers in the small guest-room, choosing the

42

right books, fitting a portable wireless in case Nurse Ansel should be bored in the evenings.

'I'll be with you at eight o'clock.'

The familiar words, said every morning now for so many days and weeks, sounded in her ear like a melody, loved through repetition. At last they were joined to the individual, the person who smiled, the one whose eyes promised friendship and loyalty.

'See you this evening.'

The door closed. Nurse Ansel had gone. The routine of the nursing-home, broken by the fever of the night before, resumed its usual pattern. Instead of darkness, light. Instead of negation, life.

Marda West took the stopper from the scent-bottle and put it behind her ears. The fragrance filtered, becoming part of the warm, bright day. She lifted the hand-mirror and looked into it. Nothing changed in the room, the street noises penetrated from outside, and presently the little maid who had seemed a weasel yesterday came in to dust the room. She said, 'Good morning,' but the patient did not answer. Perhaps she was tired. The maid dusted, and went her way.

Then Marda West took up the mirror and looked into it once more. No, she had not been mistaken. The eyes that stared back at her were doe's eyes, wary before sacrifice, and the timid deer's head was meek, already bowed.

Don't Look Now

'Don't look now,' John said to his wife, 'but there are a couple of old girls two tables away who are trying to hypnotise me.'

Laura, quick on cue, made an elaborate pretence of yawning, then tilted her head as though searching the skies for a non-existent aeroplane.

'Right behind you,' he added. 'That's why you can't turn round at once – it would be much too obvious.'

Laura played the oldest trick in the world and dropped her napkin, then bent to scrabble for it under her feet, sending a shooting glance over her left shoulder as she straightened once again. She sucked in her cheeks, the first tell-tale sign of suppressed hysteria, and lowered her head.

'They're not old girls at all,' she said. 'They're male twins in drag.'

Her voice broke ominously, the prelude to uncontrolled laughter, and John quickly poured some more chianti into her glass.

'Pretend to choke,' he said, 'then they won't notice. You know what it is – they're criminals doing the sights of Europe, changing sex at each stop. Twin sisters here on Torcello. Twin brothers tomorrow in Venice, or even tonight, parading arm-in-arm across the Piazza San Marco. Just a matter of switching clothes and wigs.'

'Jewel thieves or murderers?' asked Laura.

'Oh, murderers, definitely. But why, I ask myself, have they picked on me?'

The waiter made a diversion by bringing coffee and bearing away the fruit, which gave Laura time to banish hysteria and regain control.

'I can't think,' she said, 'why we didn't notice them when we arrived. They stand out to high heaven. One couldn't fail.'

'That gang of Americans masked them,' said John, 'and the bearded man with a monocle who looked like a spy. It wasn't until they all went just now that I saw the twins. Oh God, the one with the shock of white hair has got her eye on me again.'

Laura took the powder compact from her bag and held it in front of her face, the mirror acting as a reflector.

'I think it's me they're looking at, not you,' she said. 'Thank heaven I left my pearls with the manager at the hotel.' She paused, dabbing the sides of her nose with powder. 'The thing is,' she said after a moment, 'we've got them wrong. They're neither murderers nor thieves. They're a couple of pathetic old retired schoolmistresses on holiday, who've saved up all their lives to visit Venice. They come from some place with a name like Walabanga in Australia. And they're called Tilly and Tiny.'

Her voice, for the first time since they had come away, took on the old bubbling quality he loved, and the worried frown between her brows had vanished. At last, he thought, at last she's beginning to get over it. If I can keep this going, if we can pick up the familiar routine of jokes shared on holiday and at home, the ridiculous fantasies about people at other tables, or staying in the hotel, or wandering in art galleries and churches, then everything will fall into place, life will become as it was before, the wound will heal, she will forget.

'You know,' said Laura, 'that really was a very good lunch. I did enjoy it.'

Thank God, he thought, thank God . . . Then he leant forward, speaking low in a conspirator's whisper. 'One of them is going to the loo,' he said. 'Do you suppose he, or she, is going to change her wig?'

'Don't say anything,' Laura murmured. 'I'll follow her and find out. She may have a suitcase tucked away there, and she's going to switch clothes.'

She began to hum under her breath, the signal, to her husband, of content. The ghost was temporarily laid, and all because of the familiar holiday game, abandoned too long, and now, through mere chance, blissfully recaptured.

'Is she on her way?' asked Laura.

'About to pass our table now,' he told her.

Seen on her own, the woman was not so remarkable. Tall, angular, aquiline features, with the close-cropped hair which was fashionably called an Eton crop, he seemed to remember, in his mother's day, and about her person the stamp of that particular generation. She would be in her middle sixties, he supposed, the masculine shirt with collar and tie, sports jacket, grey tweed skirt coming to mid-calf. Grey stockings and laced black shoes. He had seen the type on golf-courses and at dogshows – invariably showing not sporting breeds but pugs – and if you came across them at a party in somebody's house they were quicker on the draw with a cigarette-lighter than he was himself, a mere male, with pocket-matches. The general belief that they kept house with a more feminine, fluffy companion was not always true. Frequently they boasted, and adored, a golfing husband. No, the striking point about this particular individual was that there were two of them. Identical twins cast in the same mould. The only difference was that the other one had whiter hair.

'Supposing,' murmured Laura, 'when I find myself in the *toilette* beside her she starts to strip?'

'Depends on what is revealed,' John answered. 'If she's hermaphrodite, make a bolt for it. She might have a hypodermic syringe concealed and want to knock you out before you reached the door.'

Laura sucked in her cheeks once more and began to shake. Then, squaring her shoulders, she rose to her feet. 'I simply must not laugh,' she said, 'and whatever you do, don't look at me when I come back, especially if we come out together.' She picked up her bag and strolled self-consciously away from the table in pursuit of her prey.

John poured the dregs of the chianti into his glass and lit a cigarette. The sun blazed down upon the little garden of the restaurant. The Americans had left, and the monocled man, and the family party at the far end. All was peace. The identical twin was sitting back in her chair with her eyes closed. Thank heaven, he thought, for this moment at any rate, when relaxation was possible, and Laura had been launched upon her foolish, harmless game. The holiday could yet turn into the cure she needed, blotting out, if only temporarily, the numb despair that had seized her since the child died.

'She'll get over it,' the doctor said. 'They all get over it, in time. And you have the boy.'

'I know,' John had said, 'but the girl meant everything. She always did, right from the start, I don't know why. I suppose it was the difference in age. A boy of school age, and a tough one at that, is someone in his own right. Not a baby of five. Laura literally adored her. Johnnie and I were nowhere.'

'Give her time,' repeated the doctor, 'give her time. And anyway, you're both young still. There'll be others. Another daughter.'

So easy to talk . . . How replace the life of a loved lost child with a dream? He knew Laura too well. Another child, another girl, would have her own qualities, a separate identity, she might even induce hostility because of this very fact. A usurper in the cradle, in the cot, that had been Christine's. A chubby, flaxen replica of Johnnie, not the little waxen darkhaired sprite that had gone.

He looked up, over his glass of wine, and the woman was staring at him again. It was not the casual, idle glance of someone at a nearby table, waiting for her companion to return, but something deeper, more intent, the prominent, light blue eyes oddly penetrating, giving him a sudden feeling of discomfort. Damn the woman! All right, bloody stare, if you must. Two can play at that game. He blew a cloud of cigarette smoke into the air and smiled at her, he hoped offensively. She did not register. The blue eyes continued to hold his, so that he was obliged to look away himself, extinguish his cigarette, glance over his shoulder for the waiter and call for the bill. Settling this, and fumbling with the change, with a few casual remarks about the excellence of the meal, brought composure, but a prickly feeling on his scalp remained, and an odd sensation of unease. Then it went, as abruptly as it had started, and stealing a furtive glance at the other table he saw that her eyes were closed again, and she was sleeping, or dozing, as she had done before. The waiter disappeared. All was still.

Laura, he thought, glancing at his watch, is being a hell of a time. Ten minutes at least. Something to tease her about, anyway. He began to plan the form the joke would take. How

49

the old dolly had stripped to her smalls, suggesting that Laura should do likewise. And then the manager had burst in upon them both, exclaiming in horror, the reputation of the restaurant damaged, the hint that unpleasant consequences might follow unless . . . The whole exercise turning out to be a plant, an exercise in blackmail. He and Laura and the twins taken in a police launch back to Venice for questioning. Quarter of an hour . . . Oh, come on, come on . . .

There was a crunch of feet on the gravel. Laura's twin walked slowly past, alone. She crossed over to her table and stood there a moment, her tall, angular figure interposing itself between John and her sister. She was saying something, but he couldn't catch the words. What was the accent, though – Scottish? Then she bent, offering an arm to the seated twin, and they moved away together across the garden to the break in the little hedge beyond, the twin who had stared at John leaning on her sister's arm. Here was the difference again. She was not quite so tall, and she stooped more – perhaps she was arthritic. They disappeared out of sight, and John, becoming impatient, got up and was about to walk back into the hotel when Laura emerged.

'Well, I must say, you took your time,' he began, and then stopped, because of the expression on her face.

'What's the matter, what's happened?' he asked.

He could tell at once there was something wrong. Almost as if she were in a state of shock. She blundered towards the table he had just vacated and sat down. He drew up a chair beside her, taking her hand.

'Darling, what is it? Tell me – are you ill?'

She shook her head, and then turned and looked at him. The dazed expression he had noticed at first had given way to one of dawning confidence, almost of exaltation.

'It's quite wonderful,' she said slowly, 'the most wonderful

50

thing that could possibly be. You see, she isn't dead, she's still with us. That's why they kept staring at us, those two sisters. They could see Christine.'

Oh God, he thought. It's what I've been dreading. She's going off her head. What do I do? How do I cope?

'Laura, sweet,' he began, forcing a smile, 'look, shall we go? I've paid the bill, we can go and look at the cathedral and stroll around, and then it will be time to take off in that launch again for Venice.'

She wasn't listening, or at any rate the words didn't penetrate.

'John, love,' she said, 'I've got to tell you what happened. I followed her, as we planned, into the *toilette* place. She was combing her hair and I went into the loo, and then came out and washed my hands in the basin. She was washing hers in the next basin. Suddenly she turned and said to me, in a strong Scots accent, "Don't be unhappy any more. My sister has seen your little girl. She was sitting between you and your husband, laughing." Darling, I thought I was going to faint. I nearly did. Luckily, there was a chair, and I sat down, and the woman bent over me and patted my head. I'm not sure of her exact words, but she said something about the moment of truth and joy being as sharp as a sword, but not to be afraid, all was well, but the sister's vision had been so strong they knew I had to be told, and that Christine wanted it. Oh John, don't look like that. I swear I'm not making it up, this is what she told me, it's all true.'

The desperate urgency in her voice made his heart sicken. He had to play along with her, agree, soothe, do anything to bring back some sense of calm.

'Laura, darling, of course I believe you,' he said, 'only it's a sort of shock, and I'm upset because you're upset . . .'

'But I'm not upset,' she interrupted. 'I'm happy, so happy that I can't put the feeling into words. You know what it's been like all these weeks, at home and everywhere we've been on holiday, though I tried to hide it from you. Now it's lifted, because I know, I just know, that the woman was right. Oh Lord, how awful of me, but I've forgotten their name – she did tell me. You see, the thing is that she's a retired doctor, they come from Edinburgh, and the one who saw Christine went blind a few years ago. Although she's studied the occult all her life and been very psychic, it's only since going blind that she has really seen things, like a medium. They've had the most wonderful experiences. But to describe Christine as the blind one did to her sister, even down to the little blue-and-white dress with the puff sleeves that she wore at her birthday party, and to say she was smiling happily . . . Oh, darling, it's made me so happy I think I'm going to cry.'

No hysteria. Nothing wild. She took a tissue from her bag and blew her nose, smiling at him. 'I'm all right, you see, you don't have to worry. Neither of us need worry about anything any more. Give me a cigarette.'

He took one from his packet and lighted it for her. She sounded normal, herself again. She wasn't trembling. And if this sudden belief was going to keep her happy he couldn't possibly begrudge it. But . . . but . . . he wished, all the same, it hadn't happened. There was something uncanny about thought-reading, about telepathy. Scientists couldn't account for it, nobody could, and this is what must have happened just now between Laura and the sisters. So the one who had been staring at him was blind. That accounted for the fixed gaze. Which somehow was unpleasant in itself, creepy. Oh hell, he thought, I wish we hadn't come here for lunch. Just chance, a flick of a coin between this, Torcello, and driving to Padua, and we had to choose Torcello.

'You didn't arrange to meet them again or anything, did you?' he asked, trying to sound casual.

'No, darling, why should I?' Laura answered. 'I mean, there was nothing more they could tell me. The sister had had her wonderful vision, and that was that. Anyway, they're moving on. Funnily enough, it's rather like our original game. They *are* going round the world before returning to Scotland. Only I said Australia, didn't I? The old dears . . . Anything less like murderers and jewel thieves.'

She had quite recovered. She stood up and looked about her. 'Come on,' she said. 'Having come to Torcello we must see the cathedral.'

They made their way from the restaurant across the open piazza, where the stalls had been set up with scarves and trinkets and postcards, and so along the path to the cathedral. One of the ferry-boats had just decanted a crowd of sightseers, many of whom had already found their way into Santa Maria Assunta. Laura, undaunted, asked her husband for the guide-book, and, as had always been her custom in happier days, started to walk slowly through the cathedral, studying mosaics, columns, panels from left to right, while John, less interested, because of his concern at what had just happened, followed close behind, keeping a weather eye alert for the twin sisters. There was no sign of them. Perhaps they had gone into the church of Santa Fosca close by. A sudden encounter would be embarrassing, quite apart from the effect it might have upon Laura. But the anonymous, shuffling tourists, intent upon culture, could not harm her, although from his own point of view they made artistic appreciation impossible. He could not concentrate, the cold clear beauty of what he saw left him untouched, and when Laura touched his sleeve, pointing to the mosaic of the Virgin and Child standing above the frieze of the Apostles, he nodded in sympathy yet saw nothing, the long, sad face of the Virgin infinitely remote, and turning on sudden impulse stared back over the heads of the tourists towards the door, where frescoes of the blessed and the damned gave themselves to judgement.

The twins were standing there, the blind one still holding on to her sister's arm, her sightless eyes fixed firmly upon him. He felt himself held, unable to move, and an impending sense of doom, of tragedy, came upon him. His whole being sagged, as it were, in apathy, and he thought, 'This is the end, there is no escape, no future.' Then both sisters turned and went out of the cathedral and the sensation vanished, leaving indignation in its wake, and rising anger. How dare those two old fools practise their mediumistic tricks on him? It was fraudulent, unhealthy; this was probably the way they lived, touring the world making everyone they met uncomfortable. Give them half a chance and they would have got money out of Laura – anything.

He felt her tugging at his sleeve again. 'Isn't she beautiful? So happy, so serene.'

'Who? What?' he asked.

'The Madonna,' she answered. 'She has a magic quality. It goes right through to one. Don't you feel it too?'

'I suppose so. I don't know. There are too many people around.'

She looked up at him, astonished. 'What's that got to do with it? How funny you are. Well, all right, let's get away from them. I want to buy some postcards anyway.'

Disappointed, she sensed his lack of interest, and began to thread her way through the crowd of tourists to the door.

'Come on,' he said abruptly, once they were outside, 'there's plenty of time for postcards, let's explore a bit,' and he struck off from the path, which would have taken them back to the centre where the little houses were, and the stalls, and the drifting crowd of people, to a narrow way amongst uncultivated ground, beyond which he could see a sort of cutting, or canal.

The sight of water, limpid, pale, was a soothing contrast to the fierce sun above their heads.

'I don't think this leads anywhere much,' said Laura. 'It's a bit muddy, too, one can't sit. Besides, there are more things the guidebook says we ought to see.'

'Oh, forget the book,' he said impatiently, and, pulling her down beside him on the bank above the cutting, put his arms round her.

'It's the wrong time of day for sight-seeing. Look, there's a rat swimming there the other side.'

He picked up a stone and threw it in the water, and the animal sank, or somehow disappeared, and nothing was left but bubbles.

'Don't,' said Laura. 'It's cruel, poor thing,' and then suddenly, putting her hand on his knee, 'Do you think Christine is sitting here beside us?'

He did not answer at once. What was there to say? Would it be like this forever?

'I expect so,' he said slowly, 'if you feel she is.'

The point was, remembering Christine before the onset of the fatal meningitis, she would have been running along the bank excitedly, throwing off her shoes, wanting to paddle, giving Laura a fit of apprehension. 'Sweetheart, take care, come back . . .'

'The woman said she was looking so happy, sitting beside us, smiling,' said Laura. She got up, brushing her dress, her mood changed to restlessness. 'Come on, let's go back,' she said.

He followed her with a sinking heart. He knew she did not really want to buy postcards or see what remained to be seen; she wanted to go in search of the women again, not necessarily to talk, just to be near them. When they came to the open place by the stalls he noticed that the crowd of tourists had thinned, there were only a few stragglers left, and the sisters were not amongst them. They must have joined the main body who had come to Torcello by the ferry-service. A wave of relief seized him.

'Look, there's a mass of postcards at the second stall,' he said quickly, 'and some eye-catching head scarves. Let me buy you a head scarf.'

'Darling, I've so many!' she protested. 'Don't waste your lire.'

'It isn't a waste. I'm in a buying mood. What about a basket? You know we never have enough baskets. Or some lace. How about lace?'

She allowed herself, laughing, to be dragged to the stall. While he rumpled through the goods spread out before them, and chatted up the smiling woman who was selling her wares, his ferociously bad Italian making her smile the more, he knew it would give the body of tourists more time to walk to the landing stage and catch the ferry-service, and the twin sisters would be out of sight and out of their life.

'Never,' said Laura, some twenty minutes later, 'has so much junk been piled into so small a basket,' her bubbling laugh reassuring him that all was well, he needn't worry any more, the evil hour had passed. The launch from the Cipriani that had brought them from Venice was waiting by the landing-stage. The passengers who had arrived with them, the Americans, the man with the monocle, were already assembled. Earlier, before setting out, he had thought the price for lunch and transport, there and back, decidedly steep. Now he grudged none of it, except that the outing to Torcello itself had been one of the major errors of this particular holiday in Venice. They stepped down into the launch, finding a place in the open, and the boat chugged away down the canal and into the lagoon. The ordinary ferry had gone before, steaming towards Murano, while their own craft headed past San

Francesco del Deserto and so back direct to Venice.

He put his arm around her once more, holding her close, and this time she responded, smiling up at him, her head on his shoulder.

'It's been a lovely day,' she said. 'I shall never forget it, never. You know, darling, now at last I can begin to enjoy our holiday.'

He wanted to shout with relief. It's going to be all right, he decided, let her believe what she likes, it doesn't matter, it makes her happy. The beauty of Venice rose before them, sharply outlined against the glowing sky, and there was still so much to see, wandering there together, that might now be perfect because of her change of mood, the shadow having lifted, and aloud he began to discuss the evening to come, where they would dine – not the restaurant they usually went to, near the Fenice theatre, but somewhere different, somewhere new.

'Yes, but it must be cheap,' she said, falling in with his mood, 'because we've already spent so much today.'

Their hotel by the Grand Canal had a welcoming, comforting air. The clerk smiled as he handed over their key. The bedroom was familiar, like home, with Laura's things arranged neatly on the dressing-table, but with it the little festive atmosphere of strangeness, of excitement, that only a holiday bedroom brings. This is ours for the moment, but no more. While we are in it we bring it life. When we have gone it no longer exists, it fades into anonymity. He turned on both taps in the bathroom, the water gushing into the bath, the steam rising. 'Now,' he thought afterwards, 'now at last is the moment to make love,' and he went back into the bedroom, and she understood, and opened her arms and smiled. Such blessed relief after all those weeks of restraint.

'The thing is,' she said later, fixing her ear-rings before the looking-glass, 'I'm not really terribly hungry. Shall we just be dull and eat in the dining-room here?'

'God, no!' he exclaimed. 'With all those rather dreary couples at the other tables? I'm ravenous. I'm also gay. I want to get rather sloshed.'

'Not bright lights and music, surely?'

'No, no . . . some small, dark, intimate cave, rather sinister, full of lovers with other people's wives.'

'H'm,' sniffed Laura, 'we all know what *that* means. You'll spot some Italian lovely of sixteen and smirk at her through dinner, while I'm stuck high and dry with a beastly man's broad back.'

They went out laughing into the warm soft night, and the magic was about them everywhere. 'Let's walk,' he said, 'let's walk and work up an appetite for our gigantic meal,' and inevitably they found themselves by the Molo and the lapping gondolas dancing upon the water, the lights everywhere blending with the darkness. There were other couples strolling for the same sake of aimless enjoyment, backwards, forwards, purposeless, and the inevitable sailors in groups, noisy, gesticulating, and dark-eyed girls whispering, clicking on high heels.

'The trouble is,' said Laura, 'walking in Venice becomes compulsive once you start. Just over the next bridge, you say, and then the next one beckons. I'm sure there are no restaurants down here, we're almost at those public gardens where they hold the Biennale. Let's turn back. I know there's a restaurant somewhere near the church of San Zaccaria, there's a little alley-way leading to it.'

'Tell you what,' said John, 'if we go down here by the Arsenal, and cross that bridge at the end and head left, we'll come upon San Zaccaria from the other side. We did it the other morning.'

'Yes, but it was daylight then. We may lose our way, it's not very well lit.'

'Don't fuss. I have an instinct for these things.'

They turned down the Fondamenta dell'Arsenale and crossed the little bridge short of the Arsenal itself, and so on past the church of San Martino. There were two canals ahead, one bearing right, the other left, with narrow streets beside them. John hesitated. Which one was it they had walked beside the day before?

'You see,' protested Laura, 'we shall be lost, just as I said.'

'Nonsense,' replied John firmly. 'It's the left-hand one, I remember the little bridge.'

The canal was narrow, the houses on either side seemed to close in upon it, and in the daytime, with the sun's reflection on the water and the windows of the houses open, bedding upon the balconies, a canary singing in a cage, there had been an impression of warmth, of secluded shelter. Now, ill-lit, almost in darkness, the windows of the houses shuttered, the water dank, the scene appeared altogether different, neglected, poor, and the long narrow boats moored to the slippery steps of cellar entrances looked like coffins.

'I swear I don't remember this bridge,' said Laura, pausing, and holding on to the rail, 'and I don't like the look of that alley-way beyond.'

'There's a lamp halfway up,' John told her. 'I know exactly where we are, not far from the Greek quarter.'

They crossed the bridge, and were about to plunge into the alley-way when they heard the cry. It came, surely, from one of the houses on the opposite side, but which one it was impossible to say. With the shutters closed each one of them seemed dead. They turned, and stared in the direction from which the sound had come.

'What was it?' whispered Laura.

'Some drunk or other,' said John briefly. 'Come on.'

Less like a drunk than someone being strangled, and the choking cry suppressed as the grip held firm.

'We ought to call the police,' said Laura.

'Oh, for heaven's sake,' said John. Where did she think she was – Piccadilly?

'Well, I'm off, it's sinister,' she replied, and began to hurry away up the twisting alley-way. John hesitated, his eye caught by a small figure which suddenly crept from a cellar entrance below one of the opposite houses, and then jumped into a narrow boat below. It was a child, a little girl – she couldn't have been more than five or six – wearing a short coat over her minute skirt, a pixie hood covering her head. There were four boats moored, line upon line, and she proceeded to jump from one to the other with surprising agility, intent, it would seem, upon escape. Once her foot slipped and he caught his breath, for she was within a few feet of the water, losing balance; then she recovered, and hopped on to the furthest boat. Bending, she tugged at the rope, which had the effect of swinging the boat's after-end across the canal, almost touching the opposite side and another cellar entrance, about thirty feet from the spot where John stood watching her. Then the child jumped again, landing upon the cellar steps, and vanished into the house, the boat swinging back into mid-canal behind her. The whole episode could not have taken more than four minutes. Then he heard the quick patter of feet. Laura had returned. She had seen none of it, for which he felt unspeakably thankful. The sight of a child, a little girl, in what must have been near danger, her fear that the scene he had just witnessed was in some way a sequel to the alarming cry, might have had a disastrous effect on her overwrought nerves.

'What are you doing?' she called. 'I daren't go on without you. The wretched alley branches in two directions.'

'Sorry,' he told her. 'I'm coming.'

He took her arm and they walked briskly along the alley, John with an apparent confidence he did not possess.

'There were no more cries, were there?' she asked.

'No,' he said, 'no, nothing. I tell you, it was some drunk.'

The alley led to a deserted *campo* behind a church, not a church he knew, and he led the way across, along another street and over a further bridge.

'Wait a minute,' he said. 'I think we take this right-hand turning. It will lead us into the Greek quarter – the church of San Georgio is somewhere over there.'

She did not answer. She was beginning to lose faith. The place was like a maze. They might circle round and round forever, and then find themselves back again, near the bridge where they had heard the cry. Doggedly he led her on, and then surprisingly, with relief, he saw people walking in the lighted street ahead, there was a spire of a church, the surroundings became familiar.

'There, I told you,' he said. 'That's San Zaccaria, we've found it all right. Your restaurant can't be far away.'

And anyway, there would be other restaurants, somewhere to eat, at least here was the cheering glitter of lights, of movement, canals beside which people walked, the atmosphere of tourism. The letters 'Ristorante', in blue lights, shone like a beacon down a left-hand alley.

'Is this your place?' he asked.

'God knows,' she said. 'Who cares? Let's feed there anyway.'

And so into the sudden blast of heated air and hum of voices, the smell of pasta, wine, waiters, jostling customers, laughter. 'For two? This way, please.' Why, he thought, was one's British nationality always so obvious? A cramped little table and an enormous menu scribbled in an indecipherable mauve biro, with the waiter hovering, expecting the order forthwith.

'Two very large camparis, with soda,' John said. '*Then* we'll study the menu.'

He was not going to be rushed. He handed the bill of fare

to Laura and looked about him. Mostly Italians – that meant the food would be good. Then he saw them. At the opposite side of the room. The twin sisters. They must have come into the restaurant hard upon Laura's and his own arrival, for they were only now sitting down, shedding their coats, the waiter hovering beside the table. John was seized with the irrational thought that this was no coincidence. The sisters had noticed them both, in the street outside, and had followed them in. Why, in the name of hell, should they have picked on this particular spot, in the whole of Venice, unless . . . unless Laura herself, at Torcello, had suggested a further encounter, or the sister had suggested it to her? A small restaurant near the church of San Zaccaria, we go there sometimes for dinner. It was Laura, before the walk, who had mentioned San Zaccaria . . .

She was still intent upon the menu, she had not seen the sisters, but any moment now she would have chosen what she wanted to eat, and then she would raise her head and look across the room. If only the drinks would come. If only the waiter would bring the drinks, it would give Laura something to do.

'You know, I was thinking,' he said quickly, 'we really ought to go to the garage tomorrow and get the car, and do that drive to Padua. We could lunch in Padua, see the cathedral and touch St Antony's tomb and look at the Giotto frescoes, and come back by way of those various villas along the Brenta that the guidebook cracks up.'

It was no use, though. She was looking up, across the restaurant, and she gave a little gasp of surprise. It was genuine. He could swear it was genuine.

'Look,' she said. 'how extraordinary! How really amazing!'

'What?' he said sharply.

'Why, there they are. My wonderful old twins. They've seen

us, what's more. They're staring this way.' She waved her hand, radiant, delighted. The sister she had spoken to at Torcello bowed and smiled. False old bitch, he thought. I know they followed us.

'Oh, darling, I must go and speak to them,' she said impulsively, 'just to tell them how happy I've been all day, thanks to them.'

'Oh, for heaven's sake!' he said. 'Look, here are the drinks. And we haven't ordered yet. Surely you can wait until later, until we've eaten?'

'I won't be a moment,' she said, 'and anyway I want scampi, nothing first. I told you I wasn't hungry.'

She got up, and, brushing past the waiter with the drinks, crossed the room. She might have been greeting the loved friends of years. He watched her bend over the table and shake them both by the hand, and because there was a vacant chair at their table she drew it up and sat down, talking, smiling. Nor did the sisters seem surprised, at least not the one she knew, who nodded and talked back, while the blind sister remained impassive.

'All right,' thought John savagely, 'then I *will* get sloshed,' and he proceeded to down his campari and soda and order another, while he pointed out something quite unintelligible on the menu as his own choice, but remembered scampi for Laura. 'And a bottle of Soave,' he added, 'with ice.'

The evening was ruined anyway. What was to have been an intimate, happy celebration would now be heavy-laden with spiritualistic visions, poor little dead Christine sharing the table with them, which was so damned stupid when in earthly life she would have been tucked up hours ago in bed. The bitter taste of the campari suited his mood of sudden self-pity, and all the while he watched the group at the table in the opposite corner, Laura apparently listening while the more active sister held forth and the blind one sat silent, her formidable sightless eyes turned in his direction.

'She's phoney,' he thought, 'she's not blind at all. They're both of them frauds, and they could be males in drag after all, just as we pretended at Torcello, and they're after Laura.'

He began on his second campari and soda. The two drinks, taken on an empty stomach, had an instant effect. Vision became blurred. And still Laura went on sitting at the other table, putting in a question now and again, while the active sister talked. The waiter appeared with the scampi, and a companion beside him to serve John's own order, which was totally unrecognisable, heaped with a livid sauce.

'The signora does not come?' enquired the first waiter, and John shook his head grimly, pointing an unsteady finger across the room.

'Tell the signora,' he said carefully, 'her scampi will get cold.'

He stared down at the offering placed before him, and prodded it delicately with a fork. The pallid sauce dissolved, revealing two enormous slices, rounds, of what appeared to be boiled pork, bedecked with garlic. He forked a portion to his mouth and chewed, and yes, it was pork, steamy, rich, the spicy sauce having turned it curiously sweet. He laid down his fork, pushing the plate away, and became aware of Laura, returning across the room and sitting beside him. She did not say anything, which was just as well, he thought, because he was too near nausea to answer. It wasn't just the drink, but reaction from the whole nightmare day. She began to eat her scampi, still not uttering. She did not seem to notice he was not eating. The waiter, hovering at his elbow, anxious, seemed aware that John's choice was somehow an error, and discreetly removed the plate. 'Bring me a green salad,' murmured John, and even then Laura did not register surprise, or, as she might have done in more normal circumstances, accuse him of having had too much to drink. Finally, when she had finished her scampi and was sipping her wine, which John had waved away, to nibble at his salad in small mouthfuls like a sick rabbit, she began to speak.

'Darling,' she said, 'I know you won't believe it, and it's rather frightening in a way, but after they left the restaurant in Torcello the sisters went to the cathedral, as we did, although we didn't see them in that crowd, and the blind one had another vision. She said Christine was trying to tell her something about us, that we should be in danger if we stayed in Venice. Christine wanted us to go away as soon as possible.'

So that's it, he thought. They think they can run our lives for us. This is to be our problem from henceforth. Do we eat? Do we get up? Do we go to bed? We must get in touch with the twin sisters. They will direct us.

'Well?' she said. 'Why don't you say something?'

'Because,' he answered, 'you are perfectly right, I don't believe it. Quite frankly, I judge your old sisters as being a couple of freaks, if nothing else. They're obviously unbalanced, and I'm sorry if this hurts you, but the fact is they've found a sucker in you.'

'You're being unfair,' said Laura. 'They are genuine, I know it. I just know it. They were completely sincere in what they said.'

'All right. Granted. They're sincere. But that doesn't make them well-balanced. Honestly, darling, you meet that old girl for ten minutes in a loo, she tells you she sees Christine sitting beside us — well, anyone with a gift for telepathy could read your unconscious mind in an instant — and then, pleased with her success, as any old psychic expert would be, she flings a further mood of ecstasy and wants to boot us out of Venice. Well, I'm sorry, but to hell with it.'

The room was no longer reeling. Anger had sobered him.

65

If it would not put Laura to shame he would get up and cross to their table, and tell the old fools where they got off.

'I knew you would take it like this,' said Laura unhappily. 'I told them you would. They said not to worry. As long as we left Venice tomorrow everything would come all right.'

'Oh, for God's sake,' said John. He changed his mind, and poured himself a glass of wine.

'After all,' Laura went on, 'we have really seen the cream of Venice. I don't mind going on somewhere else. And if we stayed − I know it sounds silly, but I should have a nasty nagging sort of feeling inside me, and I should keep thinking of darling Christine being unhappy and trying to tell us to go.'

'Right,' said John with ominous calm, 'that settles it. Go we will. I suggest we clear off to the hotel straight away and warn the reception we're leaving in the morning. Have you had enough to eat?'

'Oh dear,' sighed Laura, 'don't take it like that. Look, why not come over and meet them, and then they can explain about the vision to you? Perhaps you would take it seriously then. Especially as you are the one it most concerns. Christine is more worried over you than me. And the extraordinary thing is that the blind sister says you're psychic and don't know it. You are somehow *en rapport* with the unknown, and I'm not.'

'Well, that's final,' said John. 'I'm psychic, am I? Fine. My psychic intuition tells me to get out of this restaurant now, at once, and we can decide what we do about leaving Venice when we are back at the hotel.'

He signalled to the waiter for the bill and they waited for it, not speaking to each other, Laura unhappy, fiddling with her bag, while John, glancing furtively at the twins' table, noticed that they were tucking into plates piled high with spaghetti, in very un-psychic fashion. The bill disposed of, John pushed back his chair.

'Right. Are you ready?' he asked.

'I'm going to say goodbye to them first,' said Laura, her mouth set sulkily, reminding him instantly, with a pang, of their poor lost child.

'Just as you like,' he replied, and walked ahead of her out of the restaurant, without a backward glance.

The soft humidity of the evening, so pleasant to walk about in earlier, had turned to rain. The strolling tourists had melted away. One or two people hurried by under umbrellas. This is what the inhabitants who live here see, he thought. This is the true life. Empty streets by night, the dank stillness of a stagnant canal beneath shuttered houses. The rest is a bright façade put on for show, glittering by sunlight.

Laura joined him and they walked away together in silence, and emerging presently behind the ducal palace came out into the Piazza San Marco. The rain was heavy now, and they sought shelter with the few remaining stragglers under the colonnades. The orchestras had packed up for the evening. The tables were bare. Chairs had been turned upside down.

The experts are right, he thought, Venice is sinking. The whole city is slowly dying. One day the tourists will travel here by boat to peer down into the waters, and they will see pillars and columns and marble far, far beneath them, slime and mud uncovering for brief moments a lost underworld of stone. Their heels made a ringing sound on the pavement and the rain splashed from the gutterings above. A fine ending to an evening that had started with brave hope, with innocence.

When they came to their hotel Laura made straight for the lift, and John turned to the desk to ask the night-porter for the key. The man handed him a telegram at the same time. John stared at it a moment. Laura was already in the lift. Then he opened the envelope and read the message. It was from the headmaster of Johnnie's preparatory school.

Johnnie under observation suspected appendicitis in city hospital here.
No cause for alarm but surgeon thought wise advise you.
Charles Hill

He read the message twice, then walked slowly towards the lift where Laura was waiting for him. He gave her the telegram. 'This came when we were out,' he said. 'Not awfully good news.' He pressed the lift button as she read the telegram. The lift stopped at the second floor, and they got out.

'Well, this decides it, doesn't it?' she said. 'Here is the proof. We have to leave Venice because we're going home. It's Johnnie who's in danger, not us. This is what Christine was trying to tell the twins.'

The first thing John did the following morning was to put a call through to the headmaster at the preparatory school. Then he gave notice of their departure to the reception manager, and they packed while they waited for the call. Neither of them referred to the events of the preceding day, it was not necessary. John knew the arrival of the telegram and the foreboding of danger from the sisters was coincidence, nothing more, but it was pointless to start an argument about it. Laura was convinced otherwise, but intuitively she knew it was best to keep her feelings to herself. During breakfast they discussed ways and means of getting home. It should be possible to get themselves, and the car, on to the special car train that ran from Milan through to Calais, since it was early in the season. In any event, the headmaster had said there was no urgency.

The call from England came while John was in the bathroom. Laura answered it. He came into the bedroom a few minutes later. She was still speaking, but he could tell from the expression in her eyes that she was anxious.

'It's Mrs Hill,' she said. 'Mr Hill is in class. She says they reported from the hospital that Johnnie had a restless night and the surgeon may have to operate, but he doesn't want to unless it's absolutely necessary. They've taken X-rays and the appendix is in a tricky position, it's not awfully straightforward.'

'Here, give it to me,' he said.

The soothing but slightly guarded voice of the headmaster's wife came down the receiver. 'I'm so sorry this may spoil your plans,' she said, 'but both Charles and I felt you ought to be told, and that you might feel rather easier if you were on the spot. Johnnie is very plucky, but of course he has some fever. That isn't unusual, the surgeon says, in the circumstances. Sometimes an appendix can get displaced, it appears, and this makes it more complicated. He's going to decide about operating this evening.'

'Yes, of course, we quite understand,' said John.

'Please do tell your wife not to worry too much,' she went on. 'The hospital is excellent, a very nice staff, and we have every confidence in the surgeon.'

'Yes,' said John, 'yes,' and then broke off because Laura was making gestures beside him.

'If we can't get the car on the train, I can fly,' she said. 'They're sure to be able to find me a seat on a plane. Then at least one of us would be there this evening.'

He nodded agreement. 'Thank you so much, Mrs Hill,' he said, 'we'll manage to get back all right. Yes, I'm sure Johnnie is in good hands. Thank your husband for us. Goodbye.'

He replaced the receiver and looked round him at the tumbled beds, suitcases on the floor, tissue-paper strewn. Baskets, maps, books, coats, everything they had brought with them in the car. 'Oh God,' he said, 'what a bloody mess. All this junk.' The telephone rang again. It was the hall porter to say he had succeeded in booking a sleeper for them both, and a place for the car, on the following night.

'Look,' said Laura, who had seized the telephone, 'could you book one seat on the midday plane from Venice to London today, for me? It's imperative one of us gets home this evening. My husband could follow with the car tomorrow.'

'Here, hang on,' interrupted John. 'No need for panic stations. Surely twenty-four hours wouldn't make all that difference?'

Anxiety had drained the colour from her face. She turned to him, distraught.

'It mightn't to you, but it does to me,' she said. 'I've lost one child, I'm not going to lose another.'

'All right, darling, all right . . .' He put his hand out to her but she brushed it off, impatiently, and continued giving directions to the porter. He turned back to his packing. No use saying anything. Better for it to be as she wished. They could, of course, both go by air, and then when all was well, and Johnnie better, he could come back and fetch the car, driving home through France as they had come. Rather a sweat, though, and the hell of an expense. Bad enough Laura going by air and himself with the car on the train from Milan.

'We could, if you like, both fly,' he began tentatively, explaining the sudden idea, but she would have none of it. 'That really *would* be absurd,' she said impatiently. 'As long as I'm there this evening, and you follow by train, it's all that matters. Besides, we shall need the car, going backwards and forwards to the hospital. And our luggage. We couldn't go off and just leave all this here.'

No, he saw her point. A silly idea. It was only — well, he was as worried about Johnnie as she was, though he wasn't going to say so.

'I'm going downstairs to stand over the porter,' said Laura. 'They always make more effort if one is actually on the spot. Everything I want tonight is packed. I shall only need my overnight case. You can bring everything else in the car.'

She hadn't been out of the bedroom five minutes before the telephone rang. It was Laura. 'Darling,' she said, 'it couldn't have worked out better. The porter has got me on a charter flight that leaves Venice in less than an hour. A special motor-launch takes the party direct from San Marco in about ten minutes. Some passenger on the charter flight cancelled. I shall be at Gatwick in less than four hours.'

'I'll be down right away,' he told her.

He joined her by the reception desk. She no longer looked anxious and drawn, but full of purpose. She was on her way. He kept wishing they were going together. He couldn't bear to stay on in Venice after she had gone, but the thought of driving to Milan, spending a dreary night in a hotel there alone, the endless dragging day which would follow, and the long hours in the train the next night, filled him with intolerable depression, quite apart from the anxiety about Johnnie. They walked along to the San Marco landing-stage, the Molo bright and glittering after the rain, a little breeze blowing, the postcards and scarves and tourist souvenirs fluttering on the stalls, the tourists themselves out in force, strolling, contented, the happy day before them.

'I'll ring you tonight from Milan,' he told her. 'The Hills will give you a bed, I suppose. And if you're at the hospital they'll let me have the latest news. That must be your charter party. You're welcome to them!'

The passengers descending from the landing-stage down into the waiting launch were carrying hand-luggage with Union Jack tags upon them. They were mostly middle-aged, with what appeared to be two Methodist ministers in charge. One of them advanced towards Laura, holding out his hand, showing a gleaming row of dentures when he smiled. 'You must be the lady joining us for the homeward flight,' he said. 'Welcome aboard, and to the Union of Fellowship. We are all delighted to make your acquaintance. Sorry we hadn't a seat for hubby too.'

Laura turned swiftly and kissed John, a tremor at the corner of her mouth betraying inward laughter. 'Do you think they'll break into hymns?' she whispered. 'Take care of yourself, hubby. Call me tonight.'

The pilot sounded a curious little toot upon his horn, and in a moment Laura had climbed down the steps into the launch and was standing amongst the crowd of passengers, waving her hand, her scarlet coat a gay patch of colour amongst the more sober suiting of her companions. The launch tooted again and moved away from the landing-stage, and he stood there watching it, a sense of immense loss filling his heart. Then he turned and walked away, back to the hotel, the bright day all about him desolate, unseen.

There was nothing, he thought, as he looked about him presently in the hotel bedroom, so melancholy as a vacated room, especially when the recent signs of occupation were still visible about him. Laura's suitcases on the bed, a second coat she had left behind. Traces of powder on the dressing-table. A tissue, with a lipstick smear, thrown in the waste-paper basket. Even an old tooth-paste tube squeezed dry, lying on the glass shelf above the wash-basin. Sounds of the heedless traffic on the Grand Canal came as always from the open window, but Laura wasn't there any more to listen to it, or to watch from the small balcony. The pleasure had gone. Feeling had gone.

John finished packing, and leaving all the baggage ready to be collected he went downstairs to pay the bill. The reception clerk was welcoming new arrivals. People were sitting on the terrace overlooking the Grand Canal reading newspapers, the pleasant day waiting to be planned.

John decided to have an early lunch, here on the hotel terrace, on familiar ground, and then have the porter carry the baggage to one of the ferries that steamed direct between San Marco and the Porta Roma, where the car was garaged. The fiasco meal of the night before had left him empty, and he was ready for the trolley of hors d'œuvres when they brought it to him, around midday. Even here, though, there was change. The head-waiter, their especial friend, was off-duty, and the table where they usually sat was occupied by new arrivals, a honeymoon couple, he told himself sourly, observing the gaiety, the smiles, while he had been shown to a small single table behind a tub of flowers.

'She's airborne now,' John thought, 'she's on her way,' and he tried to picture Laura seated between the Methodist ministers, telling them, no doubt, about Johnnie ill in hospital, and heaven knows what else besides. Well, the twin sisters anyway could rest in psychic peace. Their wishes would have been fulfilled.

Lunch over, there was no point in lingering with a cup of coffee on the terrace. His desire was to get away as soon as possible, fetch the car, and be en route for Milan. He made his farewells at the reception desk, and, escorted by a porter who had piled his baggage on to a wheeled trolley, made his way once more to the landing-stage of San Marco. As he stepped on to the steam-ferry, his luggage heaped beside him, a crowd of jostling people all about him, he had one momentary pang to be leaving Venice. When, if ever, he wondered, would they come again? Next year . . . in three years . . . Glimpsed first on honeymoon, nearly ten years ago, and then a second visit, *en passant*, before a cruise, and now this last abortive ten days that had ended so abruptly.

The water glittered in the sunshine, buildings shone, tourists in dark glasses paraded up and down the rapidly receding Molo, already the terrace of their hotel was out of sight as the ferry churned its way up the Grand Canal. So many impressions to seize and hold, familiar loved façades, balconies, windows, water lapping the cellar steps of decaying palaces, the little red house where d'Annunzio lived, with its garden – our house, Laura called it, pretending it was theirs – and too soon the ferry would be turning left on the direct route to the Piazzale Roma, so missing the best of the Canal, the Rialto, the further palaces.

Another ferry was heading downstream to pass them, filled with passengers, and for a brief foolish moment he wished he could change places, be amongst the happy tourists bound for Venice and all he had left behind him. Then he saw her. Laura, in her scarlet coat, the twin sisters by her side, the active sister with her hand on Laura's arm, talking earnestly, and Laura herself, her hair blowing in the wind, gesticulating, on her face a look of distress. He stared, astounded, too astonished to shout, to wave, and anyway they would never have heard or seen him, for his own ferry had already passed and was heading in the opposite direction.

What the hell had happened? There must have been a hold-up with the charter flight and it had never taken off, but in that case why had Laura not telephoned him at the hotel? And what were those damned sisters doing? Had she run into them at the airport? Was it coincidence? And why did she look so anxious? He could think of no explanation. Perhaps the flight had been cancelled. Laura, of course, would go straight to the hotel, expecting to find him there, intending, doubtless, to drive with him after all to Milan and take the train the following night. What a blasted mix-up. The only thing to do was to telephone the hotel immediately his ferry reached the Piazzale Roma and tell her to wait – he would return and fetch her. As for the damned interfering sisters, they could get stuffed.

The usual stampede ensued when the ferry arrived at the landing-stage. He had to find a porter to collect his baggage, and then wait while he discovered a telephone. The fiddling with change, the hunt for the number, delayed him still more. He succeeded at last in getting through, and luckily the reception clerk he knew was still at the desk.

'Look, there's been some frightful muddle,' he began, and explained how Laura was even now on her way back to the hotel – he had seen her with two friends on one of the ferry-services. Would the reception clerk explain and tell her to wait? He would be back by the next available service to collect her. 'In any event, detain her,' he said. 'I'll be as quick as I can.' The reception clerk understood perfectly, and John rang off.

Thank heaven Laura hadn't turned up before he had put through his call, or they would have told her he was on his way to Milan. The porter was still waiting with the baggage, and it seemed simplest to walk with him to the garage, hand everything over to the chap in charge of the office there and ask him to keep it for an hour, when he would be returning with his wife to pick up the car. Then he went back to the landing-station to await the next ferry to Venice. The minutes dragged, and he kept wondering all the time what had gone wrong at the airport and why in heaven's name Laura hadn't telephoned. No use conjecturing. She would tell him the whole story at the hotel. One thing was certain: he would not allow Laura and himself to be saddled with the sisters and become involved with their affairs. He could imagine Laura saying that they also had missed a flight, and could they have a lift to Milan?

Finally the ferry chugged alongside the landing-stage and he stepped aboard. What an anti-climax, thrashing back past the familiar sights to which he had bidden a nostalgic farewell such a short while ago! He didn't even look about him this time, he was so intent on reaching his destination. In San Marco there were more people than ever, the afternoon crowds walking shoulder to shoulder, every one of them on pleasure bent.

He came to the hotel and pushed his way through the swing door, expecting to see Laura, and possibly the sisters, waiting in the lounge to the left of the entrance. She was not there. He went to the desk. The reception clerk he had spoken to on the telephone was standing there, talking to the manager.

'Has my wife arrived?' John asked.

'No, sir, not yet.'

'What an extraordinary thing. Are you sure?'

'Absolutely certain, sir. I have been here ever since you telephoned me at a quarter to two. I have not left the desk.'

'I just don't understand it. She was on one of the *vaporettos* passing by the Accademia. She would have landed at San Marco about five minutes later and come on here.'

The clerk seemed nonplussed. 'I don't know what to say. The signora was with friends, did you say?'

'Yes. Well, acquaintances. Two ladies we had met at Torcello yesterday. I was astonished to see her with them on the *vaporetto*, and of course I assumed that the flight had been cancelled, and she had somehow met up with them at the airport and decided to return here with them, to catch me before I left.'

Oh hell, what was Laura doing? It was after three. A matter of moments from San Marco landing-stage to the hotel.

'Perhaps the signora went with her friends to their hotel instead. Do you know where they are staying?'

'No,' said John, 'I haven't the slightest idea. What's more, I don't even know the names of the two ladies. They were sisters, twins, in fact – looked exactly alike. But anyway, why go to their hotel and not here?'

The swing-door opened but it wasn't Laura. Two people staying in the hotel.

The manager broke into the conversation. 'I tell you what I will do,' he said. 'I will telephone the airport and check about the flight. Then at least we will get somewhere.' He smiled apologetically. It was not usual for arrangements to go wrong.

'Yes, do that,' said John. 'We may as well know what happened there.'

He lit a cigarette and began to pace up and down the entrance hall. What a bloody mix-up. And how unlike Laura, who knew he would be setting off for Milan directly after lunch – indeed, for all she knew he might have gone before. But surely, in that case, she would have telephoned at once, on arrival at the airport, had the flight been cancelled? The manager was ages telephoning, he had to be put through on some other line, and his Italian was too rapid for John to follow the conversation. Finally he replaced the receiver.

'It is more mysterious than ever, sir,' he said. 'The charter flight was not delayed, it took off on schedule with a full complement of passengers. As far as they could tell me, there was no hitch. The signora must simply have changed her mind.' His smile was more apologetic than ever.

'Changed her mind,' John repeated. 'But why on earth should she do that? She was so anxious to be home tonight.'

The manager shrugged. 'You know how ladies can be, sir,' he said. 'Your wife may have thought that after all she would prefer to take the train to Milan with you. I do assure you, though, that the charter party was most respectable, and it was a Caravelle aircraft, perfectly safe.'

'Yes, yes,' said John impatiently, 'I don't blame your arrangements in the slightest. I just can't understand what induced her to change her mind, unless it was meeting with these two ladies.'

The manager was silent. He could not think of anything to say. The reception clerk was equally concerned. 'Is it possible,' he ventured, 'that you made a mistake, and it was not the signora that you saw on the *vaporetto*?'

'Oh no,' replied John, 'it was my wife, I assure you. She was wearing her red coat, she was hatless, just as she left here. I saw her as plainly as I can see you. I would swear to it in a court of law.'

'It is unfortunate,' said the manager, 'that we do not know the name of the two ladies, or the hotel where they were staying. You say you met these ladies at Torcello yesterday?'

'Yes . . . but only briefly. They weren't staying there. At least, I am certain they were not. We saw them at dinner in Venice later, as it happens.'

'Excuse me . . .' Guests were arriving with luggage to check in, the clerk was obliged to attend to them. John turned in desperation to the manager. 'Do you think it would be any good telephoning the hotel in Torcello in case the people there knew the name of the ladies, or where they were staying in Venice?'

'We can try,' replied the manager. 'It is a small hope, but we can try.'

John resumed his anxious pacing, all the while watching the swing-door, hoping, praying, that he would catch sight of the red coat and Laura would enter. Once again there followed what seemed an interminable telephone conversation between the manager and someone at the hotel in Torcello.

'Tell them two sisters,' said John, 'two elderly ladies dressed in grey, both exactly alike. One lady was blind,' he added. The manager nodded. He was obviously giving a detailed description. Yet when he hung up he shook his head. 'The manager at Torcello says he remembers the two ladies well,' he told John, 'but they were only there for lunch. He never learnt their names.'

'Well, that's that. There's nothing to do now but wait.'

John lit his third cigarette and went out on to the terrace, to resume his pacing there. He stared out across the canal, searching the heads of the people on passing steamers, motorboats, even drifting gondolas. The minutes ticked by on his watch, and there was no sign of Laura. A terrible foreboding nagged at him that somehow this was prearranged, that Laura had never intended to catch the aircraft, that last night in the restaurant she had made an assignation with the sisters. Oh God, he thought, that's impossible, I'm going paranoiac . . . Yet why, why? No, more likely the encounter at the airport was fortuitous, and for some incredible reason they had persuaded Laura not to board the aircraft, even prevented her from doing so, trotting out one of their psychic visions, that the aircraft would crash, that she must return with them to Venice. And Laura, in her sensitive state, felt they must be right, swallowed it all without question.

But granted all these possibilities, why had she not come to the hotel? What was she doing? Four o'clock, half-past four, the sun no longer dappling the water. He went back to the reception desk.

'I just can't hang around,' he said. 'Even if she does turn up, we shall never make Milan this evening. I might see her walking with these ladies, in the Piazza San Marco, anywhere. If she arrives while I'm out, will you explain?'

The clerk was full of concern. 'Indeed, yes,' he said. 'It is very worrying for you, sir. Would it perhaps be prudent if we booked you in here tonight?'

John gestured, helplessly. 'Perhaps, yes, I don't know. Maybe . . .'

He went out of the swing-door and began to walk towards the Piazza San Marco. He looked into every shop up and down the colonnades, crossed the piazza a dozen times, threaded his way between the tables in front of Florian's, in front of Quadri's, knowing that Laura's red coat and the distinctive appearance of the twin sisters could easily be spotted, even amongst this milling crowd, but there was no sign of them. He joined the crowd of shoppers in the Merceria, shoulder to shoulder with idlers, thrusters, window-gazers, knowing instinctively that it was useless, they wouldn't be here. Why should Laura have deliberately missed her flight to return to Venice for such a purpose? And even if she had done so, for some reason beyond his imagining, she would surely have come first to the hotel to find him.

The only thing left to him was to try to track down the sisters. Their hotel could be anywhere amongst the hundreds of hotels and pensions scattered through Venice, or even across the other side at the Zattere, or further again on the Giudecca. These last possibilities seemed remote. More likely they were staying in a small hotel or pension somewhere near San Zaccaria handy to the restaurant where they had dined last night. The blind one would surely not go far afield in the evening. He had been a fool not to have thought of this before, and he turned back and walked quickly away from the brightly lighted shopping district towards the narrower, more cramped quarter where they had dined last evening. He found the restaurant without difficulty, but they were not yet open for dinner, and the waiter preparing tables was not the one who had served them. John asked to see the *padrone*, and the waiter disappeared to the back regions, returning after a moment or two with the somewhat dishevelled-looking proprietor in shirt-sleeves, caught in a slack moment, not in full tenue.

'I had dinner here last night,' John explained. 'There were two ladies sitting at that table there in the corner.' He pointed to it.

'You wish to book that table for this evening?' asked the proprietor.

'No,' said John. 'No, there were two ladies there last night, two sisters, due sorelle, twins, gemelle' – what was the right word for twins? – 'Do you remember? Two ladies, sorelle vecchie . . .'

'Ah,' said the man, 'si, si, signore, la povera signorina.' He put his hands to his eyes to feign blindness. 'Yes, I remember.'

'Do you know their names?' asked John. 'Where they were staying? I am very anxious to trace them.'

The proprietor spread out his hands in a gesture of regret. 'I am ver' sorry, signore, I do not know the names of the signorine, they have been here once, twice perhaps, for dinner, they do not say where they were staying. Perhaps if you come again tonight they might be here? Would you like to book a table?'

He pointed around him, suggesting a whole choice of tables that might appeal to a prospective diner, but John shook his head.

'Thank you, no. I may be dining elsewhere. I am sorry to have troubled you. If the signorine should come . . .' he paused, 'possibly I may return later,' he added. 'I am not sure.'

The proprietor bowed, and walked with him to the entrance. 'In Venice the whole world meets,' he said smiling. 'It is possible the signore will find his friends tonight. Arrivederci, signore.'

Friends? John walked out into the street. More likely kidnappers . . . Anxiety had turned to fear, to panic. Something had gone terribly wrong. Those women had got hold of Laura, played upon her suggestibility, induced her to go with them, either to their hotel or elsewhere. Should he find the

Consulate? Where was it? What would he say when he got there? He began walking without purpose, finding himself, as they had done the night before, in streets he did not know, and suddenly came upon a tall building with the word 'Questura' above it. This is it, he thought. I don't care, something has happened, I'm going inside. There were a number of police in uniform coming and going, the place at any rate was active, and, addressing himself to one of them behind a glass partition, he asked if there was anyone who spoke English. The man pointed to a flight of stairs and John went up, entering a door on the right where he saw that another couple were sitting, waiting, and with relief he recognised them as fellow-countrymen, tourists, obviously a man and his wife, in some sort of predicament.

'Come and sit down,' said the man. 'We've waited half an hour but they can't be much longer. What a country! They wouldn't leave us like this at home.'

John took the proffered cigarette and found a chair beside them.

'What's your trouble?' he asked.

'My wife had her handbag pinched in one of those shops in the Merceria,' said the man. 'She simply put it down one moment to look at something, and you'd hardly credit it, the next moment it had gone. I say it was a sneak thief, she insists it was the girl behind the counter. But who's to say? These Ities are all alike. Anyway, I'm certain we shan't get it back. What have you lost?'

'Suitcase stolen,' John lied rapidly. 'Had some important papers in it.'

How could he say he had lost his wife? He couldn't even begin . . .

The man nodded in sympathy. 'As I said, these Ities are all alike. Old Musso knew how to deal with them. Too many

Communists around these days. The trouble is, they're not going to bother with our troubles much, not with this murderer at large. They're all out looking for him.'

'Murderer? What murderer?' asked John.

'Don't tell me you've not heard about it?' The man stared at him in surprise. 'Venice has talked of nothing else. It's been in all the papers, on the radio, and even in the English papers. A grisly business. One woman found with her throat slit last week – a tourist too – and some old chap discovered with the same sort of knife wound this morning. They seem to think it must be a maniac, because there doesn't seem to be any motive. Nasty thing to happen in Venice in the tourist season.'

'My wife and I never bother with the newspapers when we're on holiday,' said John. 'And we're neither of us much given to gossip in the hotel.'

'Very wise of you,' laughed the man. 'It might have spoilt your holiday, especially if your wife is nervous. Oh well, we're off tomorrow anyway. Can't say we mind, do we, dear?' He turned to his wife. 'Venice has gone downhill since we were here last. And now this loss of the handbag really is the limit.'

The door of the inner room opened, and a senior police officer asked John's companion and his wife to pass through.

'I bet we don't get any satisfaction,' murmured the tourist, winking at John, and he and his wife went into the inner room. The door closed behind them. John stubbed out his cigarette and lighted another. A strange feeling of unreality possessed him. He asked himself what he was doing here, what was the use of it? Laura was no longer in Venice but had disappeared, perhaps forever, with those diabolical sisters. She would never be traced. And just as the two of them had made up a fantastic story about the twins, when they first spotted them in Torcello, so, with nightmare logic, the fiction would have basis in fact; the women were in reality disguised crooks, men with criminal intent who lured unsuspecting persons to some appalling fate. They might even be the murderers for whom the police sought. Who would ever suspect two elderly women of respectable appearance, living quietly in some second-rate pension or hotel? He stubbed out his cigarette, unfinished.

'This,' he thought, 'is really the start of paranoia. This is the way people go off their heads.' He glanced at his watch. It was half-past six. Better pack this in, this futile quest here in police headquarters, and keep to the single link of sanity remaining. Return to the hotel, put a call through to the prep school in England, and ask about the latest news of Johnnie. He had not thought about poor Johnnie since sighting Laura on the *vaporetto*.

Too late, though. The inner door opened, the couple were ushered out.

'Usual clap-trap,' said the husband sotto voce to John. 'They'll do what they can. Not much hope. So many foreigners in Venice, all of 'em thieves! The locals all above reproach. Wouldn't pay 'em to steal from customers. Well, I wish you better luck.'

He nodded, his wife smiled and bowed, and they had gone. John followed the police officer into the inner room.

Formalities began. Name, address, passport. Length of stay in Venice, etc., etc. Then the questions, and John, the sweat beginning to appear on his forehead, launched into his interminable story. The first encounter with the sisters, the meeting at the restaurant, Laura's state of suggestibility because of the death of their child, the telegram about Johnnie, the decision to take the chartered flight, her departure, and her sudden inexplicable return. When he had finished he felt as exhausted as if he had driven three hundred miles non-stop after a severe bout of 'flu. His interrogator spoke excellent English with a strong Italian accent.

'You say,' he began, 'that your wife was suffering the after-effects of shock. This had been noticeable during your stay here in Venice?'

'Well, yes,' John replied, 'she had really been quite ill. The holiday didn't seem to be doing her much good. It was only when she met these two women at Torcello yesterday that her mood changed. The strain seemed to have gone. She was ready, I suppose, to snatch at every straw, and this belief that our little girl was watching over her had somehow restored her to what appeared normality.'

'It would be natural,' said the police officer, 'in the circumstances. But no doubt the telegram last night was a further shock to you both?'

'Indeed, yes. That was the reason we decided to return home.'

'No argument between you? No difference of opinion?'

'None. We were in complete agreement. My one regret was that I could not go with my wife on this charter flight.'

The police officer nodded. 'It could well be that your wife had a sudden attack of amnesia, and meeting the two ladies served as a link, she clung to them for support. You have described them with great accuracy, and I think they should not be too difficult to trace. Meanwhile, I suggest you should return to your hotel, and we will get in touch with you as soon as we have news.'

At least, John thought, they believed his story. They did not consider him a crank who had made the whole thing up and was merely wasting their time.

'You appreciate,' he said, 'I am extremely anxious. These women may have some criminal design upon my wife. One has heard of such things . . . '

The police officer smiled for the first time. 'Please don't concern yourself,' he said. 'I am sure there will be some satisfactory explanation.'

All very well, thought John, but in heaven's name, what?

'I'm sorry,' he said, 'to have taken up so much of your time. Especially as I gather the police have their hands full hunting down a murderer who is still at large.'

He spoke deliberately. No harm in letting the fellow know that for all any of them could tell there might be some connection between Laura's disappearance and this other hideous affair.

'Ah, that,' said the police officer, rising to his feet. 'We hope to have the murderer under lock and key very soon.'

His tone of confidence was reassuring. Murderers, missing wives, lost handbags were all under control. They shook hands, and John was ushered out of the door and so downstairs. Perhaps, he thought, as he walked slowly back to the hotel, the fellow was right. Laura had suffered a sudden attack of amnesia, and the sisters happened to be at the airport and had brought her back to Venice, to their own hotel, because Laura couldn't remember where she and John had been staying. Perhaps they were even now trying to track down his hotel. Anyway, he could do nothing more. The police had everything in hand, and, please God, would come up with the solution. All he wanted to do right now was to collapse upon a bed with a stiff whisky, and then put through a call to Johnnie's school.

The page took him up in the lift to a modest room on the fourth floor at the rear of the hotel. Bare, impersonal, the shutters closed, with a smell of cooking wafting up from a courtyard down below.

'Ask them to send me up a double whisky, will you?' he said to the boy. 'And a ginger-ale,' and when he was alone he plunged his face under the cold tap in the wash-basin, relieved to find that the minute portion of visitor's soap afforded some measure of comfort. He flung off his shoes, hung his coat over the back of a chair and threw himself down on the bed. Somebody's radio was blasting forth an old popular song, now several seasons out of date, that had been one of Laura's favourites a couple of years ago. 'I love you, Baby . . .' He reached for the telephone, and asked the exchange to put through the call to England. Then he closed his eyes, and all the while the insistent voice persisted, 'I love you, Baby . . . I can't get you out of my mind.'

Presently there was a tap at the door. It was the waiter with his drink. Too little ice, such meagre comfort, but what desperate need. He gulped it down without the ginger-ale, and in a few moments the ever-nagging pain was eased, numbed, bringing, if only momentarily, a sense of calm. The telephone rang, and now, he thought, bracing himself for ultimate disaster, the final shock, Johnnie probably dying, or already dead. In which case nothing remained. Let Venice be engulfed . . .

The exchange told him that the connection had been made, and in a moment he heard the voice of Mrs Hill at the other end of the line. They must have warned her that the call came from Venice, for she knew instantly who was speaking.

'Hullo?' she said. 'Oh, I am so glad you rang. All is well. Johnnie has had his operation, the surgeon decided to do it at midday rather than wait, and it was completely successful. Johnnie is going to be all right. So you don't have to worry any more, and will have a peaceful night.'

'Thank God,' he answered.

'I know,' she said, 'we are all so relieved. Now I'll get off the line and you can speak to your wife.'

John sat up on the bed, stunned. What the hell did she mean? Then he heard Laura's voice, cool and clear.

'Darling? Darling, are you there?'

He could not answer. He felt the hand holding the receiver go clammy cold with sweat. 'I'm here,' he whispered.

'It's not a very good line,' she said, 'but never mind. As Mrs Hill told you, all is well. Such a nice surgeon, and a very sweet Sister on Johnnie's floor, and I really am happy about the way it's turned out. I came straight down here after landing at Gatwick – the flight O.K., by the way, but such a funny crowd, it'll make you hysterical when I tell you about them – and I went to the hospital, and Johnnie was coming round. Very dopey, of course, but so pleased to see me. And the Hills are being wonderful, I've got their spare-room, and it's only a short taxi-drive into the town and the hospital. I shall go to bed as soon as we've had dinner, because I'm a bit fagged, what with the flight and the anxiety. How was the drive to Milan? And where are you staying?'

John did not recognise the voice that answered as his own. It was the automatic response of some computer.

'I'm not in Milan,' he said. 'I'm still in Venice.'

'Still in Venice? What on earth for? Wouldn't the car start?'

'I can't explain,' he said. 'There was a stupid sort of mix-up . . .'

He felt suddenly so exhausted that he nearly dropped the receiver, and, shame upon shame, he could feel tears pricking behind his eyes.

'What sort of mix-up?' Her voice was suspicious, almost hostile. 'You weren't in a crash?'

'No . . . no . . . nothing like that.'

A moment's silence, and then she said, 'Your voice sounds very slurred. Don't tell me you went and got pissed.'

Oh Christ . . . If she only knew! He was probably going to pass out any moment, but not from the whisky.

'I thought,' he said slowly, 'I thought I saw you, in a *vaporetto*, with those two sisters.'

What was the point of going on? It was hopeless trying to explain.

'How could you have seen me with the sisters?' she said. 'You knew I'd gone to the airport. Really, darling, you are an idiot. You seem to have got those two poor old dears on the brain. I hope you didn't say anything to Mrs Hill just now.'

'No.'

'Well, what are you going to do? You'll catch the train at Milan tomorrow, won't you?'

'Yes, of course,' he told her.

'I still don't understand what kept you in Venice,' she said. 'It all sounds a bit odd to me. However . . . thank God Johnnie is going to be all right and I'm here.'

'Yes,' he said, 'yes.'

He could hear the distant boom-boom sound of a gong from the headmaster's hall.

'You had better go,' he said. 'My regards to the Hills, and my love to Johnnie.'

'Well, take care of yourself, darling, and for goodness' sake don't miss the train tomorrow, and drive carefully.'

The telephone clicked and she had gone. He poured the remaining drop of whisky into his empty glass, and sousing it with ginger-ale drank it down at a gulp. He got up, and crossing the room threw open the shutters and leant out of the window. He felt light-headed. His sense of relief, enormous, over-whelming, was somehow tempered with a curious feeling of unreality, almost as though the voice speaking from England had not been Laura's after all but a fake, and she was still in Venice, hidden in some furtive pension with the two sisters.

The point was, he *had* seen all three of them on the *vaporetto*. It was not another woman in a red coat. The women *had* been there, with Laura. So what was the explanation? That he was going off his head? Or something more sinister? The sisters, possessing, psychic powers of formidable strength, had seen him as their two ferries had passed, and in some inexplicable fashion had made him believe Laura was with them. But why, and to what end? No, it didn't make sense. The only explanation was that he had been mistaken, the whole episode an hallucination. In which case he needed psychoanalysis, just as Johnnie had needed a surgeon.

And what did he do now? Go downstairs and tell the management he had been at fault and had just spoken to his wife, who had arrived in England safe and sound from her charter flight? He put on his shoes and ran his fingers through his hair. He glanced at his watch. It was ten minutes to eight. If he nipped into the bar and had a quick drink it would be easier to face the manager and admit what had happened. Then, perhaps, they would get in touch with the police. Profuse apologies all round for putting everyone to enormous trouble.

He made his way to the ground floor and went straight to the bar, feeling self-conscious, a marked man, half-imagining everyone would look at him, thinking, 'There's the fellow with the missing wife.' Luckily the bar was full and there wasn't a face he knew. Even the chap behind the bar was an underling who hadn't served him before. He downed his whisky and glanced over his shoulder to the reception hall. The desk was momentarily empty. He could see the manager's back framed in the doorway of an inner room, talking to someone within. On impulse, coward-like, he crossed the hall and passed through the swing-door to the street outside.

'I'll have some dinner,' he decided, 'and then go back and face them. I'll feel more like it once I've some food inside me.'

He went to the restaurant nearby where he and Laura had dined once or twice. Nothing mattered any more, because she was safe. The nightmare lay behind him. He could enjoy his dinner, despite her absence, and think of her sitting down with the Hills to a dull, quiet evening, early to bed, and on the following morning going to the hospital to sit with Johnnie. Johnnie was safe, too. No more worries, only the awkward explanations and apologies to the manager at the hotel.

There was a pleasant anonymity sitting down at a corner table alone in the little restaurant, ordering vitello alla Marsala and half a bottle of Merlot. He took his time, enjoying his food but eating in a kind of haze, a sense of unreality still with him, while the conversation of his nearest neighbours had the same soothing effect as background music.

When they rose and left, he saw by the clock on the wall that it was nearly half-past nine. No use delaying matters any further. He drank his coffee, lighted a cigarette and paid his bill. After all, he thought, as he walked back to the hotel, the manager would be greatly relieved to know that all was well.

When he pushed through the swing-door, the first thing he noticed was a man in police uniform, standing talking to the manager at the desk. The reception clerk was there too. They turned as John approached, and the manager's face lighted up with relief.

'Eccolo!' he exclaimed. 'I was certain the signore would not be far away. Things are moving, signore. The two ladies have been traced, and they very kindly agreed to accompany the police to the Questura. If you will go there at once, this agente di polizia will escort you.'

John flushed. 'I have given everyone a lot of trouble,' he said. 'I meant to tell you before going out to dinner, but you were not at the desk. The fact is that I have contacted my wife. She did make the flight to London after all, and I spoke to her on the telephone. It was all a great mistake.'

The manager looked bewildered. 'The signora is in London?' he repeated. He broke off, and exchanged a rapid conversation in Italian with the policeman. 'It seems that the ladies maintain they did not go out for the day, except for a little shopping in the morning,' he said, turning back to John. 'Then who was it the signore saw on the *vaporetto*?'

John shook his head. 'A very extraordinary mistake on my part which I still don't understand,' he said. 'Obviously, I did not see either my wife or the two ladies. I really am extremely sorry.'

More rapid conversation in Italian. John noticed the clerk watching him with a curious expression in his eyes. The manager was obviously apologising on John's behalf to the policeman, who looked annoyed and gave tongue to this effect, his voice increasing in volume, to the manager's concern. The whole business had undoubtedly given enormous trouble to a great many people, not least the two unfortunate sisters.

'Look,' said John, interrupting the flow, 'will you tell the agente I will go with him to headquarters and apologise in person both to the police officer and to the ladies?'

The manager looked relieved. 'If the signore would take the trouble,' he said. 'Naturally, the ladies were much distressed when a policeman interrogated them at their hotel, and they offered to accompany him to the Questura only because they were so distressed about the signora.'

John felt more and more uncomfortable. Laura must never learn any of this. She would be outraged. He wondered if there were some penalty for giving the police misleading information involving a third party. His error began, in retrospect, to take on criminal proportions.

He crossed the Piazza San Marco, now thronged with after-dinner strollers and spectators at the cafés, all three orchestras going full blast in harmonious rivalry, while his companion kept a discreet two paces to his left and never uttered a word.

They arrived at the police station and mounted the stairs to the same inner room where he had been before. He saw immediately that it was not the officer he knew but another who sat behind the desk, a sallow-faced individual with a sour expression, while the two sisters, obviously upset – the active one in particular – were seated on chairs nearby, some underling in uniform standing behind them. John's escort went at once to the police officer, speaking in rapid Italian, while John himself, after a moment's hesitation, advanced towards the sisters.

'There has been a terrible mistake,' he said. 'I don't know how to apologise to you both. It's all my fault, mine entirely, the police are not to blame.'

The active sister made as though to rise, her mouth twitching nervously, but he restrained her.

'We don't understand,' she said, the Scots inflection strong. 'We said goodnight to your wife last night at dinner, and we have not seen her since. The police came to our pension more than an hour ago and told us your wife was missing and you had filed a complaint against us. My sister is not very strong. She was considerably disturbed.'

'A mistake. A frightful mistake,' he repeated.

He turned towards the desk. The police officer was addressing him, his English very inferior to that of the previous interrogator. He had John's earlier statement on the desk in front of him, and tapped it with a pencil.

'So?' he queried. 'This document all lies? You not speaka the truth?'

'I believed it to be true at the time,' said John. 'I could have sworn in a court of law that I saw my wife with these two ladies on a *vaporetto* in the Grand Canal this afternoon. Now I realise I was mistaken.'

'We have not been near the Grand Canal all day,' protested the sister, 'not even on foot. We made a few purchases in the Merceria this morning, and remained indoors all afternoon. My sister was a little unwell. I have told the police officer this a dozen times, and the people at the pension would corroborate our story. He refused to listen.'

'And the signora?' rapped the police officer angrily. 'What happen to the signora?'

'The signora, my wife, is safe in England,' explained John patiently. 'I talked to her on the telephone just after seven. She did join the charter flight from the airport, and is now staying with friends.'

'Then who you see on the *vaporetto* in the red coat?' asked the furious police officer. 'And if not these signorine here, then what signorine?'

'My eyes deceived me,' said John, aware that his English was likewise becoming strained. 'I think I see my wife and these ladies but no, it was not so. My wife in aircraft, these ladies in pension all the time.'

It was like talking stage Chinese. In a moment he would be bowing and putting his hands in his sleeves.

The police officer raised his eyes to heaven and thumped the table. 'So all this work for nothing,' he said. 'Hotels and pensiones searched for the signorine and a missing signora inglese, when here we have plenty, plenty other things to do. You maka a mistake. You have perhaps too much vino at mezzo giorno and you see hundred signore in red coats in hundred vaporetti.' He stood up, rumpling the papers on his desk. 'And you, signorine,' he said, 'you wish to make complaint against this person?' He was addressing the active sister.

'Oh no,' she said, 'no, indeed. I quite see it was all a mistake. Our only wish is to return at once to our pension.'

The police officer grunted. Then he pointed at John. 'You very lucky man,' he said. 'These signorine could file complaint against you – very serious matter.'

'I'm sure,' began John, 'I'll do anything in my power . . .'

'Please don't think of it,' exclaimed the sister, horrified. 'We would not hear of such a thing.' It was her turn to apologise to the police officer. 'I hope we need not take up any more of your valuable time,' she said.

He waved a hand of dismissal and spoke in Italian to the underling. 'This man walk with you to the pension,' he said. 'Buona sera, signorine,' and, ignoring John, he sat down again at his desk.

'I'll come with you,' said John. 'I want to explain exactly what happened.'

They trooped down the stairs and out of the building, the blind sister leaning on her twin's arm, and once outside she turned her sightless eyes to John.

'You saw us,' she said, 'and your wife too. But not today. You saw us in the future.'

Her voice was softer than her sister's, slower, she seemed to have some slight impediment in her speech.

'I don't follow,' replied John, bewildered.

He turned to the active sister and she shook her head at him, frowning, and put her finger on her lips.

'Come along, dear,' she said to her twin. 'You know you're very tired, and I want to get you home.' Then, sotto voce to John, 'She's psychic. Your wife told you, I believe, but I don't want her to go into trance here in the street.'

God forbid, thought John, and the little procession began to move slowly along the street, away from police headquarters, a canal to the left of them. Progress was slow, because of the blind sister, and there were two bridges. John was completely lost after the first turning, but it couldn't have mattered less. Their police escort was with them, and anyway, the sisters knew where they were going.

'I must explain,' said John softly. 'My wife would never forgive me if I didn't,' and as they walked he went over the whole inexplicable story once again, beginning with the telegram received the night before and the conversation with Mrs Hill, the decision to return to England the following day, Laura by air, and John himself by car and train. It no longer sounded as dramatic as it had done when he had made his statement to the police officer, when, possibly because of his conviction of something uncanny, the description of the two *vaporettos* passing one another in the middle of the Grand Canal had held a sinister quality, suggesting abduction on the part of the sisters, the pair of them holding a bewildered Laura captive. Now that neither of the women had any further menace for him he spoke more naturally, yet with great sincerity, feeling for the first time that they were somehow both in sympathy with him and would understand.

'You see,' he explained, in a final endeavour to make amends for having gone to the police in the first place, 'I truly believed I had seen you with Laura, and I thought . . .' he hesitated, because this had been the police officer's suggestion and not his, 'I thought that perhaps Laura had some sudden loss of memory, had met you at the airport, and you had brought her back to Venice to wherever you were staying.'

They had crossed a large square and were approaching a house at one end of it, with a sign 'Pensione' above the door. Their escort paused at the entrance.

'Is this it?' asked John.

'Yes,' said the sister. 'I know it is nothing much from the outside, but it is clean and comfortable, and was recommended by friends.' She turned to the escort. 'Grazie,' she said to him, 'grazie tanto.'

The man nodded briefly, wished them 'Buona notte,' and disappeared across the campo.

'Will you come in?' asked the sister. 'I am sure we can find you some coffee, or perhaps you prefer tea?'

'No, really,' John thanked her, 'I must get back to the hotel.

I'm making an early start in the morning. I just want to make quite sure you do understand what happened, and that you forgive me.'

'There is nothing to forgive,' she replied. 'It is one of the many examples of second sight that my sister and I have experienced time and time again, and I should very much like to record it for our files, if you will permit it.'

'Well, as to that, of course,' he told her, 'but I myself find it hard to understand. It has never happened to me before.'

'Not consciously, perhaps,' she said, 'but so many things happen to us of which we are not aware. My sister felt you had psychic understanding. She told your wife. She also told your wife, last night in the restaurant, that you were to experience trouble, danger, that you should leave Venice. Well, don't you believe now that the telegram was proof of this? Your son was ill, possibly dangerously ill, and so it was necessary for you to return home immediately. Heaven be praised your wife flew home to be by his side.'

'Yes, indeed,' said John, 'but why should I see her on the *vaporetto* with you and your sister when she was actually on her way to England?'

'Thought transference, perhaps,' she answered. 'Your wife may have been thinking about us. We gave her our address, should you wish to get in touch with us. We shall be here another ten days. And she knows that we would pass on any message that my sister might have from your little one in the spirit world.'

'Yes,' said John awkwardly, 'yes, I see. It's very good of you.' He had a sudden rather unkind picture of the two sisters putting on headphones in their bedroom, listening for a coded message from poor Christine. 'Look, this is our address in London,' he said. 'I know Laura will be pleased to hear from you.'

He scribbled their address on a sheet torn from his pocket-diary, even, as a bonus thrown in, the telephone number, and handed it to her. He could imagine the outcome. Laura springing it on him one evening that the 'old dears' were passing through London on their way to Scotland, and the least they could do was to offer them hospitality, even the spare-room for the night. Then a seance in the living-room, tambourines appearing out of thin air.

'Well, I must be off,' he said. 'Goodnight, and apologies, once again, for all that has happened this evening.' He shook hands with the first sister, then turned to her blind twin. 'I hope,' he said, 'that you are not too tired.'

The sightless eyes were disconcerting. She held his hand fast and would not let it go. 'The child,' she said, speaking in an odd staccato voice, 'the child . . . I can see the child . . .' and then, to his dismay, a bead of froth appeared at the corner of her mouth, her head jerked back, and she half-collapsed in her sister's arms.

'We must get her inside,' said the sister hurriedly. 'It's all right, she's not ill, it's the beginning of a trance state.'

Between them they helped the twin, who had gone rigid, into the house, and sat her down on the nearest chair, the sister supporting her. A woman came running from some inner room. There was a strong smell of spaghetti from the back regions. 'Don't worry,' said the sister, 'the signorina and I can manage. I think you had better go. Sometimes she is sick after these turns.'

'I'm most frightfully sorry . . .' John began, but the sister had already turned her back, and with the signorina was bending over her twin, from whom peculiar choking sounds were proceeding. He was obviously in the way, and after a final gesture of courtesy, 'Is there anything I can do?', which received no reply, he turned on his heel and began walking across the square. He looked back once, and saw they had closed the door.

What a finale to the evening! And all his fault. Poor old girls, first dragged to police headquarters and put through an interrogation, and then a psychic fit on top of it all. More likely epilepsy. Not much of a life for the other sister, but she seemed to take it in her stride. An additional hazard, though, if it happened in a restaurant or in the street. And not particularly welcome under his and Laura's roof should the sisters ever find themselves beneath it, which he prayed would never happen.

Meanwhile, where the devil was he? The square, with the inevitable church at one end, was quite deserted. He could not remember which way they had come from police head-quarters, there had seemed to be so many turnings.

Wait a minute, the church itself had a familiar appearance. He drew nearer to it, looking for the name which was some-times on notices at the entrance. San Giovanni in Bragora, that rang a bell. He and Laura had gone inside one morning to look at a painting by Cima da Conegliano. Surely it was only a stone's throw from the Riva degli Schiavoni and the open wide waters of the San Marco lagoon, with all the bright lights of civilisation and the strolling tourists? He remembered taking a small turning from the Schiavoni and they had arrived at the church. Wasn't that the alley-way ahead? He plunged along it, but halfway down he hesitated. It didn't seem right, although it was familiar for some unknown reason.

Then he realised that it was not the alley they had taken the morning they visited the church, but the one they had walked along the previous evening, only he was approaching it from the opposite direction. Yes, that was it, in which case it would be quicker to go on and cross the little bridge over the narrow canal, and he would find the Arsenal on his left and the street leading down to the Riva degli Schiavoni to his right. Simpler than retracing his steps and getting lost once more in the maze of back streets.

He had almost reached the end of the alley, and the bridge was in sight, when he saw the child. It was the same little girl with the pixie hood who had leapt between the tethered boats the preceding night and vanished up the cellar steps of one of the houses. This time she was running from the direction of the church the other side, making for the bridge. She was running as if her life depended on it, and in a moment he saw why. A man was in pursuit, who, when she glanced backwards for a moment, still running, flattened himself against a wall, believing himself unobserved. The child came on, scampering across the bridge, and John, fearful of alarming her further, backed into an open doorway that led into a small court.

He remembered the drunken yell of the night before which had come from one of the houses near where the man was hiding now. This is it, he thought, the fellow's after her again, and with a flash of intuition he connected the two events, the child's terror then and now, and the murders reported in the newspapers, supposedly the work of some madman. It could be coincidence, a child running from a drunken relative, and yet, and yet . . . His heart began thumping in his chest, instinct warning him to run himself, now, at once, back along the alley the way he had come – but what about the child? What was going to happen to the child?

Then he heard her running steps. She hurtled through the open doorway into the court in which he stood, not seeing him, making for the rear of the house that flanked it, where steps led presumably to a back entrance. She was sobbing as she ran, not the ordinary cry of a frightened child, but the panic-stricken intake of breath of a helpless being in despair. Were there parents in the house who would protect her, whom

100

he could warn? He hesitated a moment, then followed her down the steps and through the door at the bottom, which had burst open at the touch of her hands as she hurled herself against it.

'It's all right,' he called. 'I won't let him hurt you, it's all right,' cursing his lack of Italian, but possibly an English voice might reassure her. But it was no use – she ran sobbing up another flight of stairs, which were spiral, twisting, leading to the floor above, and already it was too late for him to retreat. He could hear sounds of the pursuer in the courtyard behind, someone shouting in Italian, a dog barking. This is it, he thought, we're in it together, the child and I. Unless we can bolt some inner door above he'll get us both.

He ran up the stairs after the child, who had darted into a room leading off a small landing, and followed her inside and slammed the door, and, merciful heaven, there was a bolt which he rammed into its socket. The child was crouching by the open window. If he shouted for help someone would surely hear, someone would surely come before the man in pursuit threw himself against the door and it gave, because there was no one but themselves, no parents, the room was bare except for a mattress on an old bed, and a heap of rags in one corner.

'It's all right,' he panted, 'it's all right,' and held out his hand, trying to smile.

The child struggled to her feet and stood before him, the pixie hood falling from her head on to the floor. He stared at her, incredulity turning to horror, to fear. It was not a child at all but a little thick-set woman dwarf, about three feet high, with a great square adult head too big for her body, grey locks hanging shoulder-length, and she wasn't sobbing any more, she was grinning at him, nodding her head up and down.

Then he heard the footsteps on the landing outside and the hammering on the door, and a barking dog, and not one voice but several voices, shouting, 'Open up! Police!' The creature fumbled in her sleeve, drawing a knife, and as she threw it at him with hideous strength, piercing his throat, he stumbled and fell, the sticky mess covering his protecting hands.

And he saw the *vaporetto* with Laura and the two sisters steaming down the Grand Canal, not today, not tomorrow, but the day after that, and he knew why they were together and for what sad purpose they had come. The creature was gibbering in its corner. The hammering and the voices and the barking dog grew fainter, and, 'Oh God,' he thought, 'what a bloody silly way to die . . .'

The Alibi

The Fentons were taking their usual Sunday walk along the Embankment. They had come to Albert Bridge, and paused, as they always did, before deciding whether to cross it to the gardens, or continue along past the houseboats; and Fenton's wife, following some process of thought unknown to him, said, 'Remind me to telephone the Alhusons when we get home to ask them for drinks. It's their turn to come to us.'

Fenton stared heedlessly at the passing traffic. His mind took in a lorry swinging too fast over the bridge, a sports car with a loud exhaust, and a nurse in a grey uniform, pushing a pram containing identical twins with round faces like Dutch cheeses, who turned left over the bridge to Battersea.

'Which way?' asked his wife, and he looked at her without recognition, seized with the overwhelming, indeed appalling impression that she, and all the other people walking along the Embankment or crossing the bridge, were minute, dangling

103

puppets manipulated by a string. The very steps they took were jerking, lopsided, a horrible imitation of the real thing, of what should be; and his wife's face – the china-blue eyes, the too heavily made-up mouth, the new spring hat set at a jaunty angle – was nothing but a mask painted rapidly by a master-hand, the hand that held the puppets, on the strip of lifeless wood, matchstick wood, from which these marionettes were fashioned.

He looked quickly away from her and down to the ground, hurriedly tracing the outline of a square on the pavement with his walking-stick, and pin-pointing a blob in the centre of the square. Then he heard himself saying, 'I can't go on.'

'What's the matter?' asked his wife. 'Have you got a stitch?'

He knew then that he must be on his guard. Any attempt at explanation would lead to bewildered stares from those large eyes, to equally bewildered, pressing questions; and they would turn on their tracks back along the hated Embankment, the wind this time mercifully behind them yet carrying them inexorably towards the death of the hours ahead, just as the tide of the river beside them carried the rolling logs and empty boxes to some inevitable, stinking mud-spit below the docks.

Cunningly he rephrased his words to reassure her. 'What I meant was that we can't go on beyond the houseboats. It's a dead-end. And your heels . . .' he glanced down at her shoes . . . 'your heels aren't right for the long trek round Battersea. I need exercise, and you can't keep up. Why don't you go home? It's not much of an afternoon.'

His wife looked up at the sky, low-clouded, opaque, and blessedly, for him, a gust of wind shivered her too thin coat and she put up her hand to hold the spring hat.

'I think I will,' she said, and then with doubt, 'Are you sure you haven't a stitch? You look pale.'

'No, I'm all right,' he replied. 'I'll walk faster alone.'

Then, seeing at that moment a taxi approaching with its
flag up, he hailed it, waving his stick, and said to her, 'Jump
in. No sense in catching cold.' Before she could protest he had
opened the door and given the address to the driver. There
was no time to argue. He hustled her inside, and as it bore
her away he saw her struggle with the closed window to call
out something about not being late back and the Alhusons.
He watched the taxi out of sight down the Embankment, and
it was like watching a phase of life that had gone forever.

He turned away from the river and the Embankment, and,
leaving all sound and sight of traffic behind him, plunged into
the warren of narrow streets and squares which lay between
him and the Fulham Road. He walked with no purpose but
to lose identity, and to blot from present thought the ritual of
the Sunday which imprisoned him.

The idea of escape had never come to him before. It was
as though something had clicked in his brain when his wife
made the remark about the Alhusons. 'Remind me to telephone
when we get home. It's their turn to come to us.' The drowning
man who sees the pattern of his life pass by as the sea engulfs
him could at last be understood. The ring at the front door,
the cheerful voices of the Alhusons, the drinks set out on the
sideboard, the standing about for a moment and then the sitting
down – these things became only pieces of the tapestry that
was the whole of his life-imprisonment, beginning daily with
the drawing-back of the curtains and early morning tea, the
opening of the newspaper, breakfast eaten in the small dining-
room with the gas-fire burning blue (turned low because of
waste), the journey by Underground to the City, the passing
hours of methodical office work, the return by Underground,
unfolding an evening paper in the crowd which hemmed him
in, the laying down of hat and coat and umbrella, the sound
of television from the drawing-room blending, perhaps, with

the voice of his wife talking on the phone. And it was winter, or it was summer, or it was spring, or it was autumn, because with the changing seasons the covers of the chairs and sofa in the drawing-room were cleaned and replaced by others, or the trees in the square outside were in leaf or bare.

'It's their turn to come to us,' and the Alhusons, grimacing and jumping on their string, came and bowed and disappeared, and the hosts who had received them became guests in their turn, jiggling and smirking, the dancing couples set to partners in an old-time measure.

Now suddenly, with the pause by Albert Bridge and Edna's remark, time had ceased; or rather, it had continued in the same way for her, for the Alhusons answering the telephone, for the other partners in the dance; but for him everything had changed. He was aware of a sense of power within. He was in control. His was the master-hand that set the puppets jiggling. And Edna, poor Edna, speeding home in the taxi to a predestined role of putting out the drinks, patting cushions, shaking salted almonds from a tin, Edna had no conception of how he had stepped out of bondage into a new dimension.

The apathy of Sunday lay upon the streets. Houses were closed, withdrawn.

'They don't know,' he thought, 'those people inside, how one gesture of mine, now, at this minute, might alter their world. A knock on the door, and someone answers – a woman yawning, an old man in carpet slippers, a child sent by its parents in irritation; and according to what I will, what I decide, their whole future will be decided. Faces smashed in. Sudden murder. Theft. Fire.' It was as simple as that.

He looked at his watch. Half-past three. He decided to work on a system of numbers. He would walk down three more streets, and then, depending upon the name of the third street in which he found himself, and how many letters it contained, choose the number of his destination.

He walked briskly, aware of mounting interest. No cheating, he told himself. Block of flats or United Dairies, it was all one. It turned out that the third street was a long one, flanked on either side by drab Victorian villas which had been pretentious some fifty years ago, and now, let out as flats or lodgings, had lost caste. The name was Boulting Street. Eight letters meant Number 8. He crossed over confidently, searching the front-doors, undaunted by the steep flight of stone steps leading to every villa, the unpainted gates, the lowering basements, the air of poverty and decay which presented such a contrast to the houses in his own small Regency square, with their bright front-doors and window-boxes.

Number 8 proved no different from its fellows. The gate was even shabbier, perhaps, the curtains at the long, ugly ground-floor window more bleakly lace. A child of about three, a boy, sat on the top step. White-faced, blank-eyed, tied in some strange fashion to the mud-scraper so that he could not move. The front door was ajar.

James Fenton mounted the steps and looked for the bell. There was a scrap of paper pasted across it with the words 'Out of Order'. Beneath it was an old-fashioned bell-pull, fastened with string. It would be a matter of seconds, of course, to unravel the knotted strap binding the child, carry him off under his arm down the steps, and then dispose of him according to mood or fancy. But violence did not seem to be indicated just yet: it was not what he wanted, for the feeling of power within demanded a longer term of freedom.

He pulled at the bell. The faint tinkle sounded down the dark hall. The child stared up at him, unmoved. Fenton turned away from the door and looked out on the street, at the plane tree coming into leaf on the pavement edge, the brown bark patchy yellow, a black cat crouching at its foot biting a wounded paw; and he savoured the waiting moment as delicious because of its uncertainty.

He heard the door open wider behind him and a woman's voice, foreign in intonation, ask, 'What can I do for you?'

Fenton took off his hat. The impulse was strong within him to say, 'I have come to strangle you. You and your child. I bear you no malice whatever. It just happens that I am the instrument of fate sent for this purpose.' Instead, he smiled. The woman was pallid, like the child on the steps, with the same expressionless eyes, the same lank hair. Her age might have been anything from twenty to thirty-five. She was wearing a woollen cardigan too big for her, and her dark, bunched skirt, ankle-length, made her seem squat.

'Do you let rooms?' asked Fenton.

A light came into the dull eyes, an expression of hope. It was almost as if this was a question she had longed for and had believed would never come. But the gleam faded again immediately, and the blank stare returned.

'The house isn't mine,' she said. 'The landlord let rooms once, but they say it's to be pulled down, with those on either side, to make room for flats.'

'You mean,' he pursued, 'the landlord doesn't let rooms any more?'

'No,' she said. 'He told me it wouldn't be worth it, not with the demolition order coming any day. He pays me a small sum to caretake until they pull the house down. I live in the basement.'

'I see,' he said.

It would seem that the conversation was at an end. Nevertheless Fenton continued to stand there. The girl or woman – for she could be either – looked past him to the child, bidding him to be quiet, though he hardly whimpered.

'I suppose,' said Fenton, 'you couldn't sublet one of the rooms in the basement to me? It could be a private arrangement between ourselves while you remain here. The landlord couldn't object.'

He watched her make the effort to think. His suggestion, so unlikely, so surprising coming from someone of his appearance, was something she could not take in. Since surprise is the best form of attack, he seized his advantage. 'I only need one room,' he said quickly, 'for a few hours in the day. I shouldn't be sleeping here.'

The effort to size him up was beyond her – the tweed suit, appropriate for London or the country, the trilby hat, the walking-stick, the fresh-complexioned face, the forty-five to fifty years. He saw the dark eyes become wider and blanker still as they tried to reconcile his appearance with his unexpected request.

'What would you want the room for?' she asked doubtfully.

There was the crux. To murder you and the child, my dear, and dig up the floor, and bury you under the boards. But not yet.

'It's difficult to explain,' he said briskly. 'I'm a professional man. I have long hours. But there have been changes lately, and I must have a room where I can put in a few hours every day and be entirely alone. You've no idea how difficult it is to find the right spot. This seems to me ideal for the purpose.' He glanced from the empty house down to the child, and smiled. 'Your little boy, for instance. Just the right age. He'd give no trouble.'

A semblance of a smile passed across her face. 'Oh, Johnnie is quiet enough,' she said. 'He sits there for hours, he wouldn't interfere.' Then the smile wavered, the doubt returned. 'I don't know what to say . . . We live in the kitchen, with the bedroom next to it. There *is* a room behind, where I have a few bits of furniture stored, but I don't think you would like it. You see, it depends what you want to do . . .'

Her voice trailed away. Her apathy was just what he needed. He wondered if she slept very heavily, or was even drugged. Those dark shadows under the eyes suggested drugs. So much the better. And a foreigner too. There were too many of them in the country.

'If you would only show me the room, I should know at once,' he said.

Surprisingly she turned, and led the way down the narrow, dingy hall. Switching on a light above a basement stair, murmuring a continual apology the while, she took Fenton below. This had been, of course, the original servants' quarters of the Victorian villa. The kitchen, scullery and pantry had now become the woman's living-room, kitchenette and bedroom, and in their transformation had increased in squalor. The ugly pipes, the useless boiler, the old range, might once have had some pretension to efficiency, with fresh white paint on the pipes and the range polished. Even the dresser, still in position and stretching nearly the full width of one wall, would have been in keeping some fifty years ago, with polished brass saucepans and a patterned dinner-service, while an overalled cook, bustling about with arms befloured, called orders to a minion in the scullery. Now the dirty cream paint hung in flakes, the worn linoleum was torn, and the dresser was bare save for odds and ends bearing no relation to its original purpose – a battered wireless set with trailing aerial, piles of discarded magazines and newspapers, unfinished knitting, broken toys, pieces of cake, a toothbrush, and several pairs of shoes. The woman looked about her helplessly.

'It's not easy,' she said, 'with a child. One clears up all the time.'

It was evident that she never cleared, that she had given in, that the shambles he observed was her answer to life's problems, but Fenton said nothing, only nodded politely, and smiled. He caught a glimpse of an unmade bed through a half-open door, bearing out his theory of the heavy sleeper – his ring at the bell must have disturbed her – but seeing his glance she shut the door hurriedly, and in a half-conscious effort to bring herself to order buttoned her cardigan and combed her hair with her fingers.

'And the room you do not use?' he asked.

'Oh, yes,' she replied, 'yes, of course . . .' vague and uncertain, as if she had forgotten her purpose in bringing him to the basement. She led the way back across the passage, past a coal cellar – useful, this, he thought – a lavatory with a child's pot set in the open door and a torn *Daily Mirror* beside it, and so to a further room, the door of which was closed.

'I don't think it will do,' she said sighing, already defeated. Indeed, it would not have done for anyone but himself, so full of power and purpose; for as she flung open the creaking door, and crossed the room to pull aside the strip of curtain made out of old wartime blackout material, the smell of damp hit him as forcibly as a sudden patch of fog beside the river, and with it the unmistakable odour of escaping gas. They sniffed in unison.

'Yes, it's bad,' she said. 'The men are supposed to come, but they never do.'

As she pulled the curtain to let in air the rod broke, the strip of material fell, and through a broken pane of the window jumped the black cat with the wounded paw which Fenton had noticed beneath the plane tree in front of the house. The woman shooed it ineffectually. The cat, used to its surroundings, slunk into a far corner, jumped on a packing-case and composed itself to sleep. Fenton and the woman looked about them.

'This would do me very well,' he said, hardly considering the dark walls, the odd L-shape of the room and the low ceiling. 'Why, there's even a garden,' and he went to the window and looked out upon the patch of earth and stones – level with his head as he stood in the basement room – which had once been a strip of paved garden.

'Yes,' she said, 'yes, there's a garden,' and she came beside him to stare at the desolation to which they both gave so false a name. Then with a little shrug she went on, 'It's quiet, as you see, but it doesn't get much sun. It faces north.'

'I like a room to face north,' he said abstractedly, already seeing in his mind's eye the narrow trench he would be able to dig for her body – no need to make it deep. Turning towards her, measuring the size of her, reckoning the length and breadth, he saw a glimmer of understanding come into her eye, and he quickly smiled to give her confidence.

'Are you an artist?' she said. 'They like a north light, don't they?'

His relief was tremendous. An artist. But of course. Here was the excuse he needed. Here was a way out of all difficulty.

'I see you've guessed my secret,' he answered slyly, and his laugh rang so true that it surprised even himself. He began to speak very rapidly. 'Part-time only,' he said. 'That's the reason I can only get away for certain hours. My mornings are tied down to business, but later in the day I'm a free man. Then my real work begins. It's not just a casual hobby, it's a passion. I intend to hold my own exhibition later in the year. So you understand how essential it is for me to find somewhere . . . like this.'

He waved his hand at the surroundings, which could offer no inducement to anyone but the cat. His confidence was infectious and disarmed the still doubtful, puzzled inquiry in her eyes.

'Chelsea's full of artists, isn't it?' she said. 'At least they say so, I don't know. But I thought studios had to be high up for getting the light?'

'Not necessarily,' he answered. 'Those fads don't affect me. And late in the day the light will have gone anyway. I suppose there is electricity?'

'Yes . . .' She moved to the door and touched a switch. A naked bulb from the ceiling glared through its dust.

'Excellent,' he said. 'That's all I shall need.'

He smiled down at the blank, unhappy face. The poor soul would be so much happier asleep. Like the cat. A kindness, really, to put her out of her misery.

'Can I move in tomorrow?' he asked.

Again the look of hope that he had noticed when he first stood at the front door inquiring for rooms, and then – was it embarrassment, just the faintest trace of discomfort, in her expression?

'You haven't asked about . . . the cost of the room,' she said.

'Whatever you care to charge,' he replied, and waved his hand again to show that money was no object. She swallowed, evidently at a loss to know what to say, and then, a flush creeping into the pallid face, ventured, 'It would be best if I said nothing to the landlord. I will say you are a friend. You could give me a pound or two in cash every week, what you think fair.'

She watched him anxiously. Certainly, he decided, there must be no third party interfering in any arrangement. It might defeat his plan.

'I'll give you five pounds in notes each week, starting today,' he said.

He felt for his wallet and drew out the crisp, new notes. She put out a timid hand, and her eyes never left the notes as he counted them.

'Not a word to the landlord,' he said, 'and if any questions are asked about your lodger say your cousin, an artist, has arrived for a visit.'

She looked up and for the first time smiled, as though his joking words, with the giving of the notes, somehow sealed a bond between them.

'You don't look like my cousin,' she said, 'nor much like the artists I have seen, either. What is your name?'

'Sims,' he said instantly, 'Marcus Sims,' and wondered why he had instinctively uttered the name of his wife's father, a solicitor dead these many years, whom he had heartily disliked.

'Thank you, Mr Sims,' she said. 'I'll give your room a clean-up in the morning.' Then, as a first gesture towards this intention, she lifted the cat from the packing-case and shooed it through the window.

'You will bring your things tomorrow afternoon?' she asked.

'My things?' he repeated.

'What you need for your work,' she said. 'Don't you have paints and so on?'

'Oh, yes . . . yes, naturally,' he said, 'yes, I must bring my gear.' He glanced round the room again. But there was to be no question of butchery. No blood. No mess. The answer would be to stifle them both in sleep, the woman and her child. It was much the kindest way.

'You won't have far to go when you need tubes of paint,' she said. 'There are shops for artists in the King's Road. I have passed them shopping. They have boards and easels in the window.'

He put his hand over his mouth to hide his smile. It was really touching how she had accepted him. It showed such trust, such confidence.

She led the way back into the passage, and so up the base-ment stair to the hall once more.

'I'm so delighted,' he said, 'that we have come to this arrange-ment. To tell you the truth, I was getting desperate.'

She turned and smiled at him again over her shoulder. 'So

was I,' she said. 'If you hadn't appeared . . . I don't know what I might not have done.'

They stood together at the top of the basement stair. What an amazing thing. It was an act of God that he had suddenly arrived. He stared at her, shocked.

'You've been in some trouble, then?' he asked.

'Trouble?' She gestured with her hands, and the look of apathy, of despair, returned to her face. 'It's trouble enough to be a stranger in this country, and for the father of my little boy to go off and leave me without any money, and not to know where to turn. I tell you, Mr Sims, if you had not come today . . .' she did not finish her sentence, but glanced towards the child tied to the foot-scraper and shrugged her shoulders. 'Poor Johnnie . . .' she said, 'it's not your fault.'

'Poor Johnnie indeed,' echoed Fenton, 'and poor you. Well, I'll do my part to put an end to your troubles, I assure you.'

'You're very good. Truly, I thank you.'

'On the contrary, I thank *you*.' He made her a little bow and, bending down, touched the top of the child's head. 'Good-bye, Johnnie, see you tomorrow.' His victim gazed back at him without expression.

'Good-bye, Mrs . . . Mrs . . . ?'

'Kaufman is the name. Anna Kaufman.'

She watched him down the steps and through the gate. The banished cat slunk past his legs on a return journey to the broken window. Fenton waved his hat with a flourish to the woman, to the boy, to the cat, to the whole fabric of the mute, drab villa.

'See you tomorrow,' he called, and set off down Boulting Street with the jaunty step of someone at the start of a great adventure. His high spirits did not even desert him when he arrived at his own front-door. He let himself in with his latchkey and went up the stairs humming some old song of thirty years ago. Edna, as usual, was on the telephone – he could hear the interminable conversation of one woman to another. The drinks were set out on the small table in the drawing-room. The cocktail biscuits were laid ready, and the dish of salted almonds. The extra glasses meant that visitors were expected. Edna put her hand over the mouthpiece of the receiver and said, 'The Alhusons will be coming. I've asked them to stay on for cold supper.'

Her husband smiled and nodded. Long before his usual time he poured himself a thimbleful of sherry to round off the conspiracy, the perfection, of the past hour. The conversation on the telephone ceased.

'You look better,' said Edna. 'The walk did you good.'

Her innocence amused him so much that he nearly choked.

2

It was a lucky thing that the woman had mentioned an artist's props. He would have looked a fool arriving the following afternoon with nothing. As it was, it meant leaving the office early, and an expedition to fit himself up with the necessary paraphernalia. He let himself go. Easel, canvases, tube after tube of paint, brushes, turpentine – what had been intended as a few parcels became bulky packages impossible to transport except in a taxi. It all added to the excitement, though. He must play his part thoroughly. The assistant in the shop, fired by his customer's ardour, kept adding to the list of paints; and, as Fenton handled the tubes of colour and read the names, there was something intensely satisfying about the purchase, and he allowed himself to be reckless, the very words chrome and sienna and terre-verte going to his head like wine. Finally he tore himself away from temptation, and climbed into a taxi with his wares. No. 8, Boulting Street, the unaccustomed address instead of his own familiar square added spice to the adventure.

It was strange, but as the taxi drew up at its destination the row of villas no longer appeared so drab. It was true that yesterday's wind had dropped, the sun was shining fitfully, and there was a hint in the air of April and longer days to come; but that was not the point. The point was that No. 8 had something of expectancy about it. As he paid his driver and carried the packages from the taxi, he saw that the dark blinds in the basement had been removed and makeshift curtains, tangerine-coloured and a shock to the eye, hung in their place. Even as he noted this the curtains were pulled back and the woman, the child in her arms, its face smeared with jam, waved up at him. The cat leapt from the sill and came towards him purring, rubbing an arched back against his trouser leg. The taxi drove away, and the woman came down the steps to greet him.

'Johnnie and I have been watching for you the whole afternoon,' she said. 'Is that all you've brought?'

'All? Isn't it enough?' he laughed.

She helped him carry the things down the basement stair, and as he glanced into the kitchen he saw that an attempt had been made to tidy it, besides the hanging of the curtains. The row of shoes had been banished underneath the dresser, along with the child's toys, and a cloth, laid for tea, had been spread on the table.

'You'll never believe the dust there was in your room,' she said. 'I was working there till nearly midnight.'

'You shouldn't have done that,' he told her. 'It's not worth it, for the time.'

She stopped before the door and looked at him, the blank look returning to her face. 'It's not for long, then?' she faltered. 'I somehow thought, from what you said yesterday, it would be for some weeks?'

'Oh, I didn't mean that,' he said swiftly. 'I meant that I shall make such a devil of a mess anyway, with these paints, there was no need to dust.'

Relief was plain. She summoned a smile and opened the door. 'Welcome, Mr Sims,' she said.

He had to give her her due. She had worked. The room did look different. Smelt different, too. No more leaking gas, but carbolic instead – or was it Jeyes? Disinfectant, anyway. The blackout strip had vanished from the window. She had even got someone in to repair the broken glass. The cat's bed – the packing-case – had gone. There was a table now against the wall, and two little rickety chairs, and an armchair also, covered with the same fearful tangerine material he had observed in the kitchen windows. Above the mantelpiece, bare yesterday, she had hung a large, brightly-coloured reproduction of a Madonna and Child, with an almanac beneath. The eyes of the Madonna, ingratiating, demure, smiled at Fenton.

'Well . . .' he began, 'well, bless me . . .' and to conceal his emotion, because it was really very touching that the wretched woman had taken so much trouble on what was probably one of her last days on this earth, he turned away and began untying his packages.

'Let me help you, Mr Sims,' she said, and before he could protest she was down on her knees struggling with the knots, unwrapping the paper and fixing the easel for him. Then together they emptied the boxes of all the tubes of colour, laid them out in rows on the table, and stacked the canvases against the wall. It was amusing, like playing some absurd game, and curiously she entered into the spirit of it although remaining perfectly serious at the same time.

'What are you going to paint first?' she asked, when all was fixed and even a canvas set up upon the easel. 'You have some subject in mind, I suppose?'

'Oh, yes,' he said, 'I've a subject in mind.' He began to smile, her faith in him was so supreme, and suddenly she smiled too and said, 'I've guessed your subject.'

He felt himself go pale. How had she guessed? What was she driving at?

'What do you mean, you've guessed?' he asked sharply.

'It's Johnnie, isn't it?'

He could not possibly kill the child before the mother – what an appalling suggestion. And why was she trying to push him into it like this? There was time enough, and anyway his plan was not yet formed . . .

She was nodding her head wisely, and he brought himself back to reality with an effort. She was talking of painting, of course.

'You're a clever woman,' he said. 'Yes. Johnnie's my subject.'

'He'll be good, he won't move,' she said. 'If I tie him up he'll sit for hours. Do you want him now?'

'No, no,' Fenton replied testily. 'I'm in no hurry at all. I've got to think it all out.'

Her face fell. She seemed disappointed. She glanced round the room once more, converted so suddenly and so surprisingly into what she hoped was an artist's studio.

'Then let me give you a cup of tea,' she said, and to save argument he followed her into the kitchen. There he sat himself down on the chair she drew forward for him, and drank tea and ate Bovril sandwiches, watched by the unflinching eyes of the grubby little boy.

'Da . . .' uttered the child suddenly, and put out its hand.

'He calls all men Da,' said his mother, 'though his own father took no notice of him. Don't worry Mr Sims, Johnnie.'

Fenton forced a polite smile. Children embarrassed him. He went on eating his Bovril sandwiches and sipping his tea.

The woman sat down and joined him, stirring her tea in an absent way until it must have been cold and unfit to drink.

119

'It's nice to have someone to talk to,' she said. 'Do you know, until you came, Mr Sims, I was so alone . . . The empty house above, no workmen even passing in and out. And this is not a good neighbourhood – I have no friends at all.'

Better and better, he thought. There'll be nobody to miss her when she's gone. It would have been a tricky thing to get away with had the rest of the house been inhabited. As it was, it could be done at any time of the day and no one the wiser. Poor kid, she could not be more than twenty-six or seven; what a life she must have led.

'. . . he just went off without a word,' she was saying. 'Three years only we had been in this country, and we moved from place to place with no settled job. We were in Manchester at one time, Johnnie was born in Manchester.'

'Awful spot,' he sympathized, 'never stops raining.'

'I told him, "You've got to get work,"' she continued, banging her fist on the table, acting the moment over again. 'I said, "We can't go on like this. It's no life for me, or for your child." And, Mr Sims, there was no money for the rent. What was I to say to the landlord when he called? And then, being aliens here, there is always some fuss with the police.'

'Police?' said Fenton, startled.

'The papers,' she explained, 'there is such trouble with our papers. You know how it is, we have to register. Mr Sims, my life has not been a happy one, not for many years. In Austria I was a servant for a time to a bad man. I had to run away. I was only sixteen then, and when I met my husband, who was not my husband then, it seemed at last that there might be some hope if we got to England . . .'

She droned on, watching him and stirring her tea the while, and her voice with its slow German accent, rather pleasing and lilting to the ear, was somehow soothing and a pleasant accompaniment to his thoughts, mingling with the ticking of the alarm clock on the dresser and the thumping of the little boy's spoon upon his plate. It was delightful to remind himself that he was not in the office, and not at home either, but was Marcus Sims the artist, surely a great artist, if not in colour at least in premeditated crime; and here was his victim putting her life into his hands, looking upon him, in fact, almost as her saviour – as indeed he was.

'It's queer,' she said slowly, 'yesterday I did not know you. Today I tell you my life. You are my friend.'

'Your sincere friend,' he said, patting her hand. 'I assure you it's the truth.' He smiled, and pushed back his chair.

She reached for his cup and saucer and put them in the sink, then wiped the child's mouth with the sleeve of her jumper. 'And now, Mr Sims,' she said, 'which would you prefer to do first? Come to bed, or paint Johnnie?'

He stared at her. Come to bed? Had he heard correctly?

'I beg your pardon?' he said.

She stood patiently, waiting for him to move.

'It's for you to say, Mr Sims,' she said. 'It makes no difference to me. I'm at your disposal.'

He felt his neck turn slowly red, and the colour mount to his face and forehead. There was no doubt about it, no misunderstanding the half-smile she now attempted, and the jerk of her head towards the bedroom. The poor wretched girl was making him some sort of offer, she must believe that he actually expected . . . wanted . . . It was appalling.

'My dear Madame Kaufman,' he began – somehow the Madame sounded better than Mrs, and it was in keeping with her alien nationality – 'I am afraid there is some error. You have misunderstood me.'

'Please?' she said, puzzled, and then summoned a smile again. 'You don't have to be afraid. No one will come. And I will tie up Johnnie.'

It was preposterous. Tie up that little boy . . . Nothing he had said to her could possibly have made her misconstrue the situation. Yet to show his natural anger and leave the house would mean the ruin of all his plans, his perfect plans, and he would have to begin all over again elsewhere.

'It's . . . it's extremely kind of you, Madame Kaufman,' he said. 'I do appreciate your offer. It's most generous. The fact is, unfortunately, I've been totally incapacitated for many years . . . an old war wound . . . I've had to put all that sort of thing out of my life long ago. Indeed, all my efforts go into my art, my painting, I concentrate entirely upon that. Hence my deep pleasure in finding this little retreat, which will make all the difference to my world. And if we are to be friends . . .'

He searched for further words to extricate himself. She shrugged her shoulders. There was neither relief nor disappointment in her face. What was to be, would be.

'That's all right, Mr Sims,' she said. 'I thought perhaps you were lonely. I know what loneliness can be. And you are so kind. If at any time you feel you would like . . .'

'Oh, I'll tell you immediately,' he interrupted swiftly. 'No question of that. But alas, I'm afraid . . . Well now, to work, to work.' And he smiled again, making some show of bustle, and opened the door of the kitchen. Thank heaven she had buttoned up the cardigan which she had so disastrously started to undo. She lifted the child from his chair and proceeded to follow him.

'I have always wanted to see a real artist at work,' she said to him, 'and now, lo and behold, my chance has come. Johnnie will appreciate this when he is older. Now, where would you like me to put him, Mr Sims? Shall he stand or sit? What pose would be best?'

It was too much. From the frying-pan into the fire. Fenton was exasperated. The woman was trying to bully him. He could not possibly have her hanging about like this. If that horrid little boy had to be disposed of, then his mother must be out of the way.

'Never mind the pose,' he said testily. 'I'm not a photographer. And if there is one thing I cannot bear, it's being watched when I work. Put Johnnie there, on the chair. I suppose he'll sit still?'

'I'll fetch the strap,' she said, and while she went back to the kitchen he stared moodily at the canvas on the easel. He must do something about it, that was evident. Fatal to leave it blank. She would not understand. She would begin to suspect that something was wrong. She might even repeat her fearful offer of five minutes ago . . .

He lifted one or two tubes of paint, and squeezed out blobs of colour on to the palette. Raw sienna. . . . Naples yellow. . . . Good names they gave these things. He and Edna had been to Siena once, years ago, when they were first married. He remembered the rose-rust brickwork, and that square – what was the name of the square? – where they held a famous horse-race. Naples yellow. They had never got as far as Naples. See Naples and die. Pity they had not travelled more. They had fallen into a rut, always going up to Scotland, but Edna did not care for the heat. Azure blue . . . made you think of the deepest, or was it the clearest, blue? Lagoons in the South Seas, and flying-fish. How jolly the blobs of colour looked upon the palette . . .

'So . . . be good, Johnnie.' Fenton looked up. The woman had secured the child to the chair, and was patting the top of his head. 'If there is anything you want you have only to call, Mr Sims.'

'Thank you, Madame Kaufman.'

She crept out of the room, closing the door softly. The artist must not be disturbed. The artist must be left alone with his creation.

'Da,' said Johnnie suddenly.

'Be quiet,' said Fenton sharply. He was breaking a piece of charcoal in two. He had read somewhere that artists drew in the head first with charcoal. He adjusted the broken end between his fingers, and pursing his lips drew a circle, the shape of a full moon, upon the canvas. Then he stepped back and half-closed his eyes. The odd thing was that it did look like the rounded shape of a face without the features . . . Johnnie was watching him, his eyes large. Fenton realized that he needed a much larger canvas. The one on the easel would only take the child's head. It would look much more effective to have the whole head and shoulders on the canvas, because he could then use some of the azure blue to paint the child's blue jersey.

He replaced the first canvas with a larger one. Yes, that was a far better size. Now for the outline of the face again . . . the eyes . . . two little dots for the nose, and a small slit for the mouth . . . two lines for the neck, and two more, rather squared like a coat-hanger, for the shoulders. It was a face all right, a human face, not exactly that of Johnnie at the moment, but given time . . . The essential thing was to get some paint on to that canvas. He simply must use some of the paint. Feverishly he chose a brush, dipped it in turpentine and oil, and then, with little furtive dabs at the azure blue and the flake white to mix them, he stabbed the result on to the canvas. The bright colour, gleaming and glistening with excess of oil, seemed to stare back at him from the canvas, demanding more. It was not the same blue as the blue of Johnnie's jersey, but what of that?

Becoming bolder, he sloshed on further colour, and now the blue was all over the lower part of the canvas in vivid streaks, making a strange excitement, contrasting with the charcoal face. The face now looked like a real face, and the patch of wall behind the child's head, which had been nothing but

124

a wall when he first entered the room, surely had colour to it after all, a pinkish-green. He snatched up tube after tube and squeezed out blobs; he chose another brush so as not to spoil the brush with blue on it . . . damn it, that burnt sienna was not like the Siena he had visited at all, but more like mud. He must wipe it off, he must have rags, something that wouldn't spoil . . . He crossed quickly to the door.

'Madame Kaufman?' he called. 'Madame Kaufman? Could you find me some rags?'

She came at once, tearing some undergarment into strips, and he snatched them from her and began to wipe the offending burnt sienna from his brush. He turned round to see her peeping at the canvas.

'Don't do that,' he shouted. 'You must never look at an artist's work in the first rough stages.'

She drew back, rebuffed. 'I'm sorry,' she said, and then, with hesitation, added, 'It's very modern, isn't it?'

He stared at her, and then from her to the canvas, and from the canvas to Johnnie.

'Modern?' he said. 'Of course it's modern. What did you think it would be? Like that?' He pointed with his brush to the simpering Madonna over the mantelpiece. 'I'm of my time. I see what I see. Now let me get on.'

There was not enough room on one palette for all the blobs of colour. Thank goodness he had bought two. He began squeezing the remaining tubes on to the second palette and mixing them, and now all was riot – sunsets that had never been, and unrisen dawns. The Venetian red was not the Doge's palace but little drops of blood that burst in the brain and did not have to be shed, and zinc white was purity, not death, and yellow ochre . . . yellow ochre was life in abundance, was renewal, was spring, was April even in some other time, some other place . . .

It did not matter that it grew dark and he had to switch on the light. The child had fallen asleep, but he went on painting. Presently the woman came in and told him it was eight o'clock. Did he want any supper? 'It would be no trouble, Mr Sims,' she said.

Suddenly Fenton realized where he was. Eight o'clock, and they always dined at a quarter to. Edna would be waiting, would be wondering what had happened to him. He laid down the palette and the brushes. There was paint on his hands, on his coat.

'What on earth shall I do?' he said in panic.

The woman understood. She seized the turpentine and a piece of rag, and rubbed at his coat. He went with her to the kitchen, and feverishly began to scrub his hands at the sink.

'In future,' he said, 'I must always leave by seven.'

'Yes,' she said, 'I'll remember to call you. You'll be back tomorrow?'

'Of course,' he said impatiently, 'of course. Don't touch any of my things.'

'No, Mr Sims.'

He hurried up the basement stair and out of the house, and started running along the street. As he went he began to make up the story he would tell Edna. He'd dropped in at the club, and some of the fellows there had persuaded him into playing bridge. He hadn't liked to break up the game, and never realized the time. That would do. And it would do again tomorrow. Edna must get used to this business of him dropping into the club after the office. He could think of no better excuse with which to mask the lovely duplicity of a secret life.

3

It was extraordinary how the days slipped by, days that had once dragged, that had seemed interminable. It meant several changes, of course. He had to lie not only to Edna, but at the office as well. He invented a pressing business that took him away in the early part of the afternoon, new contacts, a family firm. For the time being, Fenton said, he could really only work at the office half-time. Naturally, there would have to be some financial adjustment, he quite understood that. In the meantime, if the senior partner would see his way . . . Amazing that they swallowed it. And Edna, too, about the club. Though it was not always the club. Sometimes it was extra work at another office, somewhere else in the City; and he would talk mysteriously of bringing off some big deal which was far too delicate and involved to be discussed. Edna appeared content. Her life continued as it had always done. It was only Fenton whose world had changed. Regularly now each afternoon, at around half-past three, he walked through the gate of No. 8, and glancing down at the kitchen window in the basement he could see Madame Kaufman's face peering from behind the tangerine curtains. Then she would slip round to the back door by the strip of garden, and let him in. They had decided against the front door. It was safer to use the back. Less conspicuous.

'Good afternoon, Mr Sims.'

'Good afternoon, Madame Kaufman.'

No nonsense about calling her Anna. She might have thought . . . she might have presumed. And the title 'Madame' kept the right sense of proportion between them. She was really very useful. She cleaned the studio – they always alluded to his room as the studio – and his paintbrushes, and tore up fresh strips of rag every day, and as soon as he arrived she had a cup of tea for him, not like the stew they used to brew in the office, but piping hot. And the boy . . . the boy had become quite appealing. Fenton had felt more tolerant about him as soon as he had finished the first portrait. It was as though the boy existed anew through him. He was Fenton's creation.

It was now midsummer, and Fenton had painted his portrait many times. The child continued to call him Da. But the boy was not the only model. He had painted the mother too. And this was more satisfying still. It gave Fenton a tremendous sense of power to put the woman upon canvas. It was not her eyes, her features, her colouring – heavens above, she had little enough colouring! – but somehow her shape: the fact that the bulk of a live person, and that person a woman, could be transmuted by him upon a blank canvas. It did not matter if what he drew and painted bore no resemblance to a woman from Austria called Anna Kaufman. That was not the point. Naturally the silly soul expected some sort of chocolate-box representation the first time she acted as his model. He had soon shut her up, though.

'Do you really see me like that?' she asked, disconsolate.

'Why, what's wrong?' he said.

'It's . . . it's just that . . . you make my mouth like a big fish ready to swallow, Mr Sims.'

'A fish? What utter nonsense!' He supposed she wanted a cupid's bow. 'The trouble with you is that you're never satisfied. You're no different from any other woman.'

He began mixing his colours angrily. She had no right to criticize his work.

'It's not kind of you to say that, Mr Sims,' she said after a moment or two. 'I am very satisfied with the five pounds that you give me every week.'

'I was not talking about money,' he said.

'What were you talking about, then?'

He turned back to the canvas, and put just the faintest touch of rose upon the flesh part of the arm. 'What was I talking about?' he asked. 'I haven't the faintest idea. Women, wasn't it? I really don't know. And I've told you not to interrupt.'

'I'm sorry, Mr Sims.'

That's right, he thought. Stay put. Keep your place. If there was one thing he could not stand it was a woman who argued, a woman who was self-assertive, a woman who nagged, a woman who stood upon her rights. Because of course they were not made for that. They were intended by their Creator to be pliable, and accommodating, and gentle, and meek. The trouble was that they were so seldom like that in reality. It was only in the imagination, or glimpsed in passing or behind a window, or leaning from a balcony abroad, or from the frame of a picture, or from a canvas like the one before him now – he changed from one brush to another, he was getting quite dexterous at this – that a woman had any meaning, any reality. And then to go and tell him that he had given her a mouth like a fish . . .

'When I was younger,' he said aloud, 'I had so much ambition.'

'To be a great painter?' she asked.

'Why, no . . . not particularly that,' he answered, 'but to become great. To be famous. To achieve something outstanding.'

'There's still time, Mr Sims,' she said.

'Perhaps . . . perhaps . . .' The skin should not be rose, it should be olive, a warm olive. Edna's father had been the trouble, really, with his endless criticizing of the way they lived. Fenton had never done anything right from the moment they became engaged: the old man was always carping, always finding fault. 'Go and live abroad?' he had exclaimed. 'You can't make a decent living abroad. Besides, Edna wouldn't stand it. Away from her friends and all she's been accustomed to. Never heard of such a thing.'

Well, he was dead, and a good thing too. He'd been a wedge between them from the start. Marcus Sims . . . Marcus Sims the painter was a very different chap. Surrealist. Modern. The old boy would turn in his grave.

'It's a quarter to seven,' murmured the woman.

'Damn . . .' He sighed, and stepped back from the easel. 'I resent stopping like this, now it's so light in the evenings,' he said. 'I could go on for quite another hour, or more.'

'Why don't you?' she asked.

'Ah! Home ties,' he said. 'My poor old mother would have a fit.'

He had invented an old mother during the past weeks. Bedridden. He had promised to be home every evening at a quarter to eight. If he did not arrive in time the doctors would not answer for the consequences. He was a very good son to her.

'I wish you could bring her here to live,' said his model. 'It's so lonely when you've gone back in the evenings. Do you know, there's a rumour this house may not be pulled down after all. If it's true, you could take the flat on the ground floor, and your mother would be welcome.'

'She'd never move now,' said Fenton. 'She's over eighty. Very set in her ways.' He smiled to himself, thinking of Edna's face if he said to her that it would be more comfortable to sell the house they had lived in for nearly twenty years and take up lodgings in No. 8, Boulting Street. Imagine the upheaval! Imagine the Alhusons coming to Sunday supper!

'Besides,' he said, thinking aloud, 'the whole point would be gone.'

'What point, Mr Sims?'

He looked from the shape of colour on the canvas that

meant so much to him to the woman who sat there, posing with her lank hair and her dumb eyes, and he tried to remember what had decided him, those months ago, to walk up the steps of the drab villa and ask for a room. Some temporary phase of irritation, surely, with poor Edna, with the windy grey day on the Embankment, with the fact of the Alhusons coming to drinks. But the workings of his mind on that vanished Sunday were forgotten, and he knew only that his life had changed from then, that this small, confined basement room was his solace, and the personalities of the woman Anna Kaufman and the child Johnnie were somehow symbolic of anonymity, of peace. All she ever did was to make him tea and clean his brushes. She was part of the background, like the cat, which purred at his approach and crouched on the windowsill, and to which he had not as yet given a single crumb.

'Never mind, Madame Kaufman,' he said. 'One of these days we'll hold an exhibition, and your face, and Johnnie's, will be the talk of the town.'

'This year . . . next year . . . sometime . . . never. Isn't that what you say to cherry stones?' she said.

'You've got no faith,' he told her. 'I'll prove it. Just wait and see.'

She began once more the long, tedious story about the man she had fled from in Austria, and the husband who had deserted her in London – he knew it all so well by now that he could prompt her – but it did not bother him. It was part of the background, part of the blessed anonymity. Let her blab away, he said to himself, it kept her quiet, it did not matter. He could concentrate on making the orange she was sucking, doling out quarters to Johnnie on her lap, larger than life, more colourful than life, rounder, bigger, brighter.

And as he walked home along the Embankment in the evening – because the walk was no longer suggestive of the old Sunday but was merged with the new life as well – he would throw his charcoal sketches and rough drawings into the river. They were now transfigured into paint and did not matter. With them went the used tubes of colour, pieces of rag, and brushes too clogged with oil. He threw them from Albert Bridge and watched them float for a moment, or be dragged under, or drift as bait for some ruffled, sooty gull. All his troubles went with his discarded junk. All his pain.

4

He had arranged with Edna to postpone their annual holiday until mid-September. This gave him time to finish the self-portrait he was working upon, which, he decided, would round up the present series. The holiday in Scotland would be pleasant. Pleasant for the first time for years, because there would be something to look forward to on returning to London.

The brief mornings at the office hardly counted now. He scraped through the routine somehow, and never went back after lunch. His other commitments, he told his colleagues, were becoming daily more pressing: he had practically decided to break his association with the present business during the autumn.

'If you hadn't warned us,' said the senior partner drily, 'we should have warned you.'

Fenton shrugged his shoulders. If they were going to be unpleasant about it, the sooner he went the better. He might even write from Scotland. Then the whole of the autumn and winter could be given up to painting. He could take a proper studio: No. 8, after all, was only a makeshift affair. But a large studio, with decent lighting and a kitchenette off it – there were some in the process of being built, only a few streets away – that might be the answer to the winter. There he could really work. Really achieve something good, and no longer feel he was only a part-time amateur.

The self-portrait was absorbing. Madame Kaufman had found a mirror and hung it on the wall for him, so the start was easy enough. But he found he couldn't paint his own eyes. They had to be closed, which gave him the appearance of a sleeping man. A sick man. It was rather uncanny.

'So you don't like it?' Fenton observed to Madame Kaufman, when she came to tell him it was seven o'clock.

She shook her head. 'It gives me what you call the creeps,' she said. 'No, Mr Sims, it's not you.'

'A bit too advanced for your taste,' he said cheerfully. 'Avant-garde, I believe, is the right expression.'

He himself was delighted. The self-portrait was a work of art.

'Well, it will have to do for the time being,' he said. 'I'm off for my holiday next week.'

'You are going away?'

There was such a note of alarm in her voice that he turned to look at her.

'Yes,' he said, 'taking my old mother up to Scotland. Why?'

She stared at him in anguish, her whole expression changed. Anyone would think he had given her some tremendous shock.

'But I have no one but you,' she said. 'I shall be alone.'

'I'll give you your money all right,' he said quickly. 'You shall have it in advance. We shall only be away three weeks.'

She went on staring at him, and then, of all things, her eyes filled with tears and she began to cry.

'I don't know what I shall do,' she said. 'I don't know where I am to go.'

It was a bit thick. What on earth did she mean? What should she do, and where should she go? He had promised her the money. She would just go on as she always did. Seriously, if she was going to behave like this the sooner he found himself a studio the better. The last thing in the world he wanted was for Madame Kaufman to become a drag.

'My dear Madame Kaufman, I'm not a permanency, you know,' he said firmly. 'One of these days I shall be moving. Possibly this autumn. I need room to expand. I'll let you know in advance, naturally. But it might be worth your while to put Johnnie in a nursery school and get some sort of daily job. It would really work out better for you in the end.'

He might have beaten her. She looked stunned, utterly crushed.

'What shall I do?' she repeated stupidly, and then, as if she still could not believe it, 'When do you go away?'

'Monday,' he said, 'to Scotland. We'll be away three weeks.' This last very forcibly, so that there was no mistake about it. The trouble was that she was a very unintelligent woman, he decided as he washed his hands at the kitchen sink. She made a good cup of tea and knew how to clean the brushes, but that was her limit. 'You ought to take a holiday yourself,' he told her cheerfully. 'Take Johnnie for a trip down the river to Southend or somewhere.'

There was no response. Nothing but a mournful stare and a hopeless shrug.

The next day, Friday, meant the end of his working week. He cashed a cheque that morning, so that he could give her three weeks' money in advance. And he allowed an extra five pounds for appeasement.

When he arrived at No. 8 Johnnie was tied up in his old place by the foot-scraper, at the top of the steps. She had not done this to the boy for some time. And when Fenton let himself in at the back door in the basement, as usual, there was no wireless going and the kitchen door was shut. He opened it and looked in. The door through to the bedroom was also shut.

'Madame Kaufman . . . ?' he called. 'Madame Kaufman . . . ?'

She answered after a moment, her voice muffled and weak. 'What is it?' she said.

'Is anything the matter?'

Another pause, and then. 'I am not very well.'

'I'm sorry,' said Fenton. 'Is there anything I can do?'

'No.'

Well, there it was. A try-on, of course. She never looked well, but she had not done this before. There was no attempt to prepare his tea: the tray was not even laid. He put the envelope containing the money on the kitchen table.

'I've brought you your money,' he called. 'Twenty pounds altogether. Why don't you go out and spend some of it? It's a lovely afternoon. The air would do you good.'

A brisk manner was the answer to her trouble. He was not going to be blackmailed into sympathy.

He went along to the studio, whistling firmly. He found, to his shocked surprise, that everything was as he had left it the evening before. Brushes not cleaned, but lying clogged still on the messed palette. Room untouched. It really was the limit. He'd a good mind to retrieve the envelope from the kitchen table. It had been a mistake ever to have mentioned the holiday. He should have posted the money over the week-end, and enclosed a note saying he had gone to Scotland. Instead of which . . . this infuriating fit of the sulks, and neglect of her job. It was because she was a foreigner, of course. You just couldn't trust them. They always let you down in the long run.

He returned to the kitchen with his brushes and palette, the turpentine and some rags, and made as much noise as possible running the taps and moving about, so as to let her know that he was having to do all the menial stuff himself.

135

He clattered the teacup, too, and rattled the tin where she put the sugar. Not a sound, though, from the bedroom. Oh, damn it, he thought, let her stew . . .

Back in the studio, he pottered with the final touches to the self-portrait, but concentration was difficult. Nothing worked. The thing looked dead. She had ruined his day. Finally, an hour or more before his usual time, he decided to go home. He would not trust her to clean up, though, not after last night's neglect. She was capable of leaving everything untouched for three weeks.

Before stacking the canvases one behind the other he stood them up, ranged them against the wall, and tried to imagine how they would look hanging in an exhibition. They hit the eye, there was no doubt about it. You couldn't avoid them. There was something . . . well, something telling about the whole collection! He didn't know what it was. Naturally, he couldn't criticize his own work. But . . . that head of Madame Kaufman, for instance, the one she had said was like a fish, possibly there *was* some sort of shape to the mouth that . . . or was it the eyes, the rather full eyes? It was brilliant, though. He was sure it was brilliant. And, although unfinished, that self-portrait of a man asleep, it had significance.

He smiled in fantasy, seeing himself and Edna walking into one of those small galleries off Bond Street, himself saying casually, 'I'm told there's some new chap got a show on here. Very controversial. The critics can't make out whether he's a genius or a madman.' And Edna, 'It must be the first time you've ever been inside one of these places.' What a sense of power, what triumph! And then, when he broke it to her, the dawn of new respect in her eyes. The realization that her husband had, after all these years, achieved fame. It was the shock of surprise that he wanted. That was it! The shock of surprise . . .

Fenton had a final glance round the familiar room. The

136

canvases were stacked now, the easel dismantled, brushes and palette cleaned and wiped and wrapped up. If he should decide to decamp when he returned from Scotland – and he was pretty sure it was going to be the only answer, after Madame Kaufman's idiotic behaviour – then everything was ready to move. It would only be a matter of calling a taxi, putting the gear inside, and driving off.

He shut the window and closed the door, and, carrying his usual weekly package of what he called 'rejects' under his arm – discarded drawings and sketches and odds and ends – went once more to the kitchen and called through the closed door of the bedroom.

'I'm off now,' he said. 'I hope you'll be better tomorrow. See you in three weeks' time.'

He noticed that the envelope had disappeared from the kitchen table. She could not be as ill as all that.

Then he heard her moving in the bedroom, and after a moment or two the door opened a few inches and she stood there, just inside. He was shocked. She looked ghastly, her face drained of colour and her hair lank and greasy, neither combed nor brushed. She had a blanket wrapped round the lower part of her, and in spite of the hot, stuffy day, and the lack of air in the basement, was wearing a thick woollen cardigan.

'Have you seen a doctor?' he asked with some concern.

She shook her head.

'I would if I were you,' he said. 'You don't look well at all.' He remembered the boy, still tied to the scraper above. 'Shall I bring Johnnie down to you?' he suggested.

'Please,' she said.

Her eyes reminded him of an animal's eyes in pain. He felt disturbed. It was rather dreadful, going off and leaving her like this. But what could he do? He went up the basement stairs and through the deserted front hall, and opened the front door.

The boy was sitting there, humped. He couldn't have moved since Fenton had entered the house.

'Come on, Johnnie,' he said. 'I'll take you below to your mother.'

The child allowed himself to be untied. He had the same sort of apathy as the woman. What a hopeless pair they were, thought Fenton; they really ought to be in somebody's charge, in some sort of welfare home. There must be places where people like this were looked after. He carried the child downstairs and sat him in his usual chair by the kitchen table.

'What about his tea?' he asked.

'I'll get it presently,' said Madame Kaufman.

She shuffled out of her bedroom, still wrapped in the blanket, with a package in her hands, some sort of paper parcel, tied up with string.

'What's that?' he asked.

'Some rubbish,' she said, 'if you would throw it away with yours. The dustmen don't call until next week.'

He took the package from her and waited a moment, wondering what more he could do for her.

'Well,' he said awkwardly, 'I feel rather bad about this. Are you sure there is nothing else you want?'

'No,' she said. She didn't even call him Mr Sims. She made no effort to smile or hold out her hand. The expression in her eyes was not even reproachful. It was mute.

'I'll send you a postcard from Scotland,' he said, and then patted Johnnie's head. 'So long,' he added – a silly expression, and one he never normally used. Then he went out of the back door, round the corner of the house and out of the gate, and so along Boulting Street, with an oppressive feeling in his heart that he had somehow behaved badly, been lacking in sympathy, and that he ought to have taken the initiative and insisted that she see a doctor.

The September sky was overcast and the Embankment dusty, dreary. The trees in the Battersea gardens across the river had a dejected, faded, end-of-summer look. Too dull, too brown. It would be good to get away to Scotland, to breathe the clean, cold air.

He unwrapped his package and began to throw his 'rejects' into the river. A head of Johnnie, very poor indeed. An attempt at the cat. A canvas that had got stained with something or other and could not be used again. Over the bridge they went and away with the tide, the canvas floating like a matchbox, white and frail. It was rather sad to watch it drift from sight.

He walked back along the Embankment towards home, and then, before he turned to cross the road, realized that he was still carrying the paper parcel Madame Kaufman had given him. He had forgotten to throw it away with the rejects. He had been too occupied in watching the disappearance of his own debris.

Fenton was about to toss the parcel into the river when he noticed a policeman watching him from the opposite side of the road. He was seized with an uneasy feeling that it was against the law to dispose of litter in this way. He walked on self-consciously. After he had gone a hundred yards he glanced back over his shoulder. The policeman was still staring after him. Absurd, but it made him feel quite guilty. The strong arm of the law. He continued his walk, swinging the parcel nonchalantly, humming a little tune. To hell with the river – he would dump the parcel into one of the litter bins in Chelsea Hospital gardens.

He turned into the gardens and dropped the parcel into the first basket, on top of two or three newspapers and a pile of orange peel. No offence in that. He could see the damn fool of a bobby watching through the railings, but Fenton took good care not to show the fellow he noticed him. Anyone would think he was trying to dispose of a bomb. Then he walked swiftly home, and remembered, as he went up the stairs, that the Alhusons were coming to dinner. The routine dinner before the holiday. The thought did not bore him now as it had once. He would chat away to them both about Scotland without any sensation of being trapped and stifled. How Jack Alhuson would stare if he knew how Fenton spent his afternoons! He would not believe his ears!

'Hullo, you're early,' said Edna, who was arranging the flowers in the drawing-room.

'Yes,' he replied. 'I cleared up everything at the office in good time. Thought I might make a start planning the itinerary. I'm looking forward to going north.'

'I'm so glad,' she said. 'I was afraid you might be getting bored with Scotland year after year. But you don't look jaded at all. You haven't looked so well for years.'

She kissed his cheek and he kissed her back, well content. He smiled as he went to look out his maps. She did not know she had a genius for a husband.

The Alhusons had arrived and they were just sitting down to dinner when the front-door bell rang.

'Who on earth's that?' exclaimed Edna. 'Don't say we asked someone else and have forgotten all about them.'

'I haven't paid the electricity bill,' said Fenton. 'They've sent round to cut us off, and we shan't get the soufflé.'

He paused in the middle of carving the chicken, and the Alhusons laughed.

'I'll go,' said Edna. 'I daren't disturb May in the kitchen. You know the bill of fare by now, it *is* a soufflé.'

She came back in a few moments with a half-amused, half-puzzled expression on her face. 'It's not the electricity man,' she said, 'it's the police.'

'The police?' repeated Fenton.

Jack Alhuson wagged his finger. 'I knew it,' he said. 'You're for it this time, old boy.'

Fenton laid down the carving knife. 'Seriously, Edna,' he said, 'what do they want?'

'I haven't the faintest idea,' she replied. 'It's an ordinary policeman, and what I assumed to be another in plain clothes. They asked to speak to the owner of the house.'

Fenton shrugged his shoulders. 'You carry on,' he said to his wife. 'I'll see if I can get rid of them. They've probably come to the wrong address.'

He went out of the dining-room into the hall, but as soon as he saw the uniformed policeman his face changed. He recognized the man who had stared after him on the Embankment.

'Good evening,' he said. 'What can I do for you?'

. The man in plain clothes took the initiative.

'Did you happen to walk through Chelsea Hospital gardens late this afternoon, sir?' he inquired. Both men were watching Fenton intently, and he realized that denial would be useless.

'Yes,' he said, 'yes, I did.'

'You were carrying a parcel?'

'I believe I was.'

'Did you put the parcel in a litter basket by the Embankment entrance, sir?'

'I did.'

'Would you object to telling us what was in the parcel?'

'I have no idea.'

'I can put the question another way, sir. Could you tell us where you obtained the parcel?'

Fenton hesitated. What were they driving at? He did not care for their method of interrogation.

'I don't see what it has to do with you,' he said. 'It's not an offence to put rubbish in a litter basket, is it?'

'Not ordinary rubbish,' said the man in plain clothes.

Fenton looked from one to the other. Their faces were serious.

'Do you mind if I ask you a question?' he said.

'No, sir.'

'Do you know what was in the parcel?'

'Yes.'

'You mean the policeman here – I remember passing him on the beat – actually followed me, and took the parcel after I had dropped it in the bin?'

'That is correct.'

'What an extraordinary thing to do. I should have thought he would have been better employed doing his regular job.'

'It happens to be his regular job to keep an eye on people who behave in a suspicious manner.'

Fenton began to get annoyed. 'There was nothing suspicious in my behaviour whatsoever,' he declared. 'It so happens that I had been clearing up odds and ends in my office this afternoon, and it's rather a fad of mine to throw rubbish in the river on my way home. Very often I feed the gulls too. Today I was about to throw in my usual packet when I noticed the officer here glance in my direction. It occurred to me that perhaps it's illegal to throw rubbish in the river, so I decided to put it in the litter basket instead.'

The two men continued to stare at him.

'You've just stated,' said the man in plain clothes, 'that you didn't know what was in the parcel, and now you state that it was odds and ends from the office. Which statement is true?'

Fenton began to feel hunted.

'Both statements are true,' he snapped. 'The people at the office wrapped the parcel up for me today, and I didn't know what they had put in it. Sometimes they put in stale biscuits for the gulls, and then I undo it and throw the crumbs to the birds on my way home, as I told you.'

It wouldn't do, though. Their set faces said so, and he supposed it sounded a thin enough tale – a middle-aged man collecting rubbish so that he could throw it in the river on his way home from the office, like a small boy throwing twigs from a bridge to see them float out on the other side. But it was the best he could think of on the spur of the moment, and he would have to stick to it now. After all, it couldn't be a criminal action – the worst they could call him was eccentric.

The plain-clothes policeman said nothing but, 'Read your notes, Sergeant.'

The man in uniform took out his notebook and read aloud:

'At five minutes past six today I was walking along the Embankment and I noticed a man on the opposite pavement make as though to throw a parcel in the river. He observed me looking and walked quickly on, and then glanced back over his shoulder to see if I was still watching him. His manner was suspicious. He then crossed to the entrance to Chelsea Hospital gardens and, after looking up and down in a furtive manner, dropped the parcel in the litter bin and hurried away. I went to the bin and retrieved the parcel, and then followed the man to 14 Annersley Square, which he entered. I took the parcel to the station and handed it over to the officer on duty. We examined the parcel together. It contained the body of a premature new-born infant.'

He snapped the notebook to.

Fenton felt all his strength ebb from him. Horror and fear merged together like a dense, overwhelming cloud, and he collapsed on to a chair.

'Oh, God,' he said. 'Oh, God, what's happened . . . ?'

Through the cloud he saw Edna looking at him from the open door of the dining-room, with the Alhusons behind her. The man in plain clothes was saying, 'I shall have to ask you to come down to the station and make a statement.'

5

Fenton sat in the Inspector's room, with the Inspector of Police behind a desk, and the plain-clothes man, and the policeman in uniform, and someone else, a medical officer. Edna was there too – he had especially asked for Edna to be there. The Alhusons were waiting outside, but the terrible thing was the expression on Edna's face. It was obvious that she did not believe him. Nor did the policemen.

'Yes, it's been going on for six months,' he repeated. 'When I say "going on", I mean my painting has been going on, nothing else, nothing else at all . . . I was seized with the desire to paint . . . I can't explain it. I never shall. It just came over me. And on impulse I walked in at the gate of No. 8, Boulting Street. The woman came to the door and I asked if she had a room to let, and after a few moments' discussion she said she had – a room of her own in the basement – nothing to do with the landlord, we agreed to say nothing to the landlord. So I took possession. And I've been going there every afternoon for six months. I said nothing about it to my wife . . . I thought she wouldn't understand . . .'

He turned in despair to Edna, and she just sat there, staring at him.

'I admit I've lied,' he said. 'I've lied to everyone. I lied at home, I lied at the office. I told them at the office I had contacts with another firm, that I went there during the afternoon, and I told my wife – bear me out, Edna – I told my wife I was either kept late at the office or I was playing bridge at the club. The truth was that I went every day to No. 8, Boulting Street. Every day.'

He had not done anything wrong. Why did they have to stare at him? Why did Edna hold on to the arms of the chair?

'What age is Madame Kaufman? I don't know. About twenty-seven, I should think . . . or thirty, she could be any age . . . and she has the little boy, Johnnie . . . She is an Austrian, she has led a very sad life and her husband has left her . . . No, I never saw anyone in the house at all, no other men . . . I don't know, I tell you . . . I don't know. I went there to paint. I didn't go for anything else. She'll tell you so. She'll tell you the truth. I'm sure she is very attached to me . . . At least, no, I don't mean that; when I say attached I mean she is grateful for the money I pay her . . . that is, the rent, the five pounds for the room. There was absolutely nothing else between us, there couldn't have been, it was out of the question . . . Yes, yes, of course I was ignorant of her condition. I'm not very observant . . . it wasn't the sort of thing I would have noticed. And she did not say a word, not a word.'

He turned again to Edna. 'Surely you believe me?'

She said, 'You never told me you wanted to paint. You've never mentioned painting, or artists, all our married life.'

It was the frozen blue of her eyes that he could not bear.

He said to the Inspector, 'Can't we go to Boulting Street now, at once? That poor soul must be in great distress. She should see a doctor, someone should be looking after her. Can't we all go now, my wife too, so that Madame Kaufman can explain everything?'

And, thank God, he had his way. It was agreed they should go to Boulting Street. A police car was summoned, and he and Edna and two police officers climbed into it, and the Alhusons followed behind in their car. He heard them say something to the Inspector about not wanting Mrs Fenton to be alone, the shock was too great. That was kind, of course, but there need not be any shock when he could quietly and calmly explain the whole story to her, once they got home.

145

It was the atmosphere of the police station that made it so appalling, that made him feel guilty, a criminal.

The car drew up before the familiar house, and they all got out. He led the way through the gate and round to the back door, and opened it. As soon as they entered the passage the smell of gas was unmistakable.

'It's leaking again,' he said. 'It does, from time to time. She tells the men, but they never come.'

Nobody answered. He walked swiftly to the kitchen. The door was shut, and here the smell of gas was stronger still.

The Inspector murmured something to his subordinates. 'Mrs Fenton had better stay outside in the car with her friends.'

'No,' said Fenton, 'no, I want my wife to hear the truth.'

But Edna began to walk back along the passage with one of the policemen, and the Alhusons were waiting for her, their faces solemn. Then everybody seemed to go at once into the bedroom, into Madame Kaufman's bedroom. They jerked up the blind and let in the air, but the smell of gas was overpowering, and they leant over the bed and she was lying there asleep, with Johnnie beside her, both fast asleep. The envelope containing the twenty pounds was lying on the floor.

'Can't you wake her?' said Fenton. 'Can't you wake her and tell her that Mr Sims is here? Mr Sims.'

One of the policemen took hold of his arm and led him from the room.

When they told Fenton that Madame Kaufman was dead and Johnnie too, he shook his head and said, 'It's terrible . . . terrible . . . if only she'd told me, if only I'd known what to do . . .' But somehow the first shock of discovery had been so great, with the police coming to the house and the appalling contents of the parcel, that this fulfilment of disaster did not touch him in the same way. It seemed somehow inevitable.

146

'Perhaps it's for the best,' he said. 'She was alone in the world. Just the two of them. Alone in the world.'

He was not sure what everyone was waiting for. The ambulance, he supposed, or whatever it was that would take poor Madame Kaufman and Johnnie away. He asked, 'Can we go home, my wife and I?'

The Inspector exchanged a glance with the man in plain clothes, and then he said, 'I'm afraid not, Mr Fenton. We shall want you to return with us to the station.'

'But I've told you the truth,' said Fenton wearily. 'There's no more to say. I have nothing to do with this tragedy. Nothing at all.' Then he remembered his paintings. 'You haven't seen my work,' he said. 'It's all here, in the room next door. Please ask my wife to come back, and my friends too. I want them to see my work. Besides, now that this has happened I wish to remove my belongings.'

'We will take care of that,' said the Inspector.

The tone was noncommittal, yet firm. Ungracious, Fenton thought. The officious attitude of the law.

'That's all very well,' said Fenton, 'but they are my possessions, and valuable at that. I don't see what right you have to touch them.'

He looked from the Inspector to his colleague in plain clothes – the medical officer and the other policeman were still in the bedroom – and he could tell from their set expressions that they were not really interested in his work. They thought it was just an excuse, an alibi, and all they wanted to do was to take him back to the police station and question him still further about the sordid, pitiful deaths in the bedroom, about the body of the little, prematurely born child.

'I'm quite ready to go with you, Inspector,' he said quietly, 'but I make this one request – that you will allow me to show my work to my wife and my friends.'

147

The Inspector nodded at his subordinate, who went out of the kitchen, and then the little group moved to the studio, Fenton himself opening the door and showing them in.

'Of course,' he said, 'I've been working under wretched conditions. Bad light, as you see. No proper amenities at all. I don't know how I stuck it. As a matter of fact, I intended to move out when I returned from my holiday. I told the poor girl so, and it probably depressed her.'

He switched on the light, and as they stood there, glancing about them, noting the dismantled easel, the canvases stacked neatly against the wall, it struck him that of course these preparations for departure must seem odd to them, suspicious, as though he had in truth known what had happened in the bedroom behind the kitchen and had intended a getaway.

'It was a makeshift, naturally,' he said, continuing to apologize for the small room that looked so unlike a studio, 'but it happened to suit me. There was nobody else in the house, nobody to ask questions. I never saw anyone but Madame Kaufman and the boy.'

He noticed that Edna had come into the room, and the Alhusons too, and the other policeman, and they were all watching him with the same set expressions. Why Edna? Why the Alhusons? Surely they must be impressed by the canvases stacked against the wall? They must realize that his total output for the past five and a half months was here, in this room, only awaiting exhibition? He strode across the floor, seized the nearest canvas to hand, and held it up for them to see. It was the portrait of Madame Kaufman that he liked best, the one which – poor soul – she had told him looked like a fish.

'They're unconventional, I know that,' he said, 'not picture-book stuff. But they're strong. They've got originality.' He seized another. Madame Kaufman again, this time with Johnnie on her lap. 'Mother and child,' he said, half-smiling, 'a true

148

primitive. Back to our origins. The first woman, the first child.'

He cocked his head, trying to see the canvas as they would see it, for the first time. Looking up for Edna's approval, for her gasp of wonder, he was met by that same stony frozen stare of misunderstanding. Then her face seemed to crumple, and she turned to the Alhusons and said, 'They're not proper paintings. They're daubs, done anyhow.' Blinded by tears, she looked up at the Inspector. 'I told you he couldn't paint,' she said. 'He's never painted in his life. It was just an alibi, to get into the house with this woman.'

Fenton watched the Alhusons lead her away. He heard them go out of the back door and through the garden to the front of the house. 'They're not proper paintings, they're daubs,' he repeated. He put the canvas down on the ground with its face to the wall, and said to the Inspector, 'I'm ready to go with you now.'

They got into the police car. Fenton sat between the Inspector and the man in plain clothes. The car turned out of Boulting Street. It crossed two other streets, and came into Oakley Street and on towards the Embankment. The traffic lights changed from amber to red. Fenton murmured to himself, 'She doesn't believe in me – she'll never believe in me.' Then, as the lights changed and the car shot forward, he shouted, 'All right, I'll confess everything. I was her lover, of course, and the child was mine. I turned on the gas this evening before I left the house. I killed them all. I was going to kill my wife too when we got to Scotland. I want to confess that I did it . . . I did it . . . I did it . . .'

The Apple Tree

It was three months after she died that he first noticed the apple tree. He had known of its existence, of course, with the others, standing upon the lawn in front of the house, sloping upwards to the field beyond. Never before, though, had he been aware of this particular tree looking in any way different from its fellows, except that it was the third one on the left, a little apart from the rest and leaning more closely to the terrace.

It was a fine clear morning in early spring, and he was shaving by the open window. As he leant out to sniff the air, the lather on his face, the razor in his hand, his eye fell upon the apple tree. It was a trick of light, perhaps, something to do with the sun coming up over the woods, that happened to catch the tree at this particular moment; but the likeness was unmistakable.

He put his razor down on the window-ledge and stared. The tree was scraggy and of a depressing thinness, possessing none of the gnarled solidity of its companions. Its few branches, growing high up on the trunk like narrow shoulders on a tall body, spread themselves in martyred resignation, as though chilled by the fresh morning air. The roll of wire circling the tree, and reaching to about halfway up the trunk from the base, looked like a grey tweed skirt covering lean limbs; while the topmost branch, sticking up into the air above the ones below, yet sagging slightly, could have been a drooping head poked forward in an attitude of weariness.

How often he had seen Midge stand like this, dejected. No matter where it was, whether in the garden, or in the house, or even shopping in the town, she would take upon herself this same stooping posture, suggesting that life treated her hardly, that she had been singled out from her fellows to carry some impossible burden, but in spite of it would endure to the end without complaint. 'Midge, you look worn out, for heaven's sake sit down and take a rest!' But the words would be received with the inevitable shrug of the shoulder, the inevitable sigh, 'Someone has got to keep things going,' and straightening herself she would embark upon the dreary routine of unnecessary tasks she forced herself to do, day in, day out, through the interminable changeless years.

He went on staring at the apple tree. That martyred bent position, the stooping top, the weary branches, the few withered leaves that had not blown away with the wind and rain of the past winter and now shivered in the spring breeze like wispy hair; all of it protested soundlessly to the owner of the garden looking upon it, 'I am like this because of you, because of your neglect.'

He turned away from the window and went on shaving. It would not do to let his imagination run away with him and start building fancies in his mind just when he was settling at long last to freedom. He bathed and dressed and went down to breakfast. Egg and bacon were waiting for him on the hot-plate, and he carried the dish to the single place laid for him at the dining-table. *The Times*, folded smooth and new, was ready for him to read. When Midge was alive he had handed it to her first, from long custom, and when she gave it back to him after breakfast, to take with him to the study, the pages were always in the wrong order and folded crookedly, so that part of the pleasure of reading it was spoilt. The news, too, would be stale to him after she had read the worst of it aloud, which was a morning habit she used to take upon herself, always adding some derogatory remark of her own about what she read. The birth of a daughter to mutual friends would bring a click of the tongue, a little jerk of the head, 'Poor things, another girl,' or if a son, 'A boy can't be much fun to educate these days.' He used to think it psychological, because they themselves were childless, that she should so grudge the entry of new life into the world; but as time passed it became thus with all bright or joyous things, as though there was some fundamental blight upon good cheer.

'It says here that more people went on holiday this year than ever before. Let's hope they enjoyed themselves, that's all.' But no hope lay in her words, only disparagement. Then, having finished breakfast, she would push back her chair and sigh and say, 'Oh well . . .', leaving the sentence unfinished; but the sigh, the shrug of the shoulders, the slope of her long, thin back as she stooped to clear the dishes from the serving-table – thus sparing work for the daily maid – was all part of her long-term reproach, directed at him, that had marred their existence over a span of years.

Silent, punctilious, he would open the door for her to pass through to the kitchen quarters, and she would labour past him, stooping under the weight of the laden tray that there was no need for her to carry, and presently, through the half-open door,

153

he would hear the swish of the running water from the pantry tap. He would return to his chair and sit down again, the crumpled *Times*, a smear of marmalade upon it, lying against the toast-rack; and once again, with monotonous insistence, the question hammered at his mind, 'What have I done?'

It was not as though she nagged. Nagging wives, like mothers-in-law, were chestnut jokes for music-halls. He could not remember Midge ever losing her temper or quarrelling. It was just that the undercurrent of reproach, mingled with suffering nobly borne, spoilt the atmosphere of his home and drove him to a sense of furtiveness and guilt.

Perhaps it would be raining and he, seeking sanctuary within his study, electric fire aglow, his after-breakfast pipe filling the small room with smoke, would settle down before his desk in a pretence of writing letters, but in reality to hide, to feel the snug security of four safe walls that were his alone. Then the door would open and Midge, struggling into a raincoat, her wide-brimmed felt hat pulled low over her brow, would pause and wrinkle her nose in distaste.

'Phew! What a fug.'

He said nothing, but moved slightly in his chair, covering with his arm the novel he had chosen from a shelf in idleness.

'Aren't you going into the town?' she asked him.

'I had not thought of doing so.'

'Oh! Oh, well, it doesn't matter.' She turned away again towards the door.

'Why, is there anything you want done?'

'It's only the fish for lunch. They don't deliver on Wednesdays. Still, I can go myself if you are busy. I only thought . . .'

She was out of the room without finishing her sentence.

'It's all right, Midge,' he called, 'I'll get the car and go and fetch it presently. No sense in getting wet.'

Thinking she had not heard he went out into the hall. She

was standing by the open front door, the mizzling rain driving in upon her. She had a long flat basket over her arm and was drawing on a pair of gardening gloves.

'I'm bound to get wet in any case,' she said, 'so it doesn't make much odds. Look at those flowers, they all need staking. I'll go for the fish when I've finished seeing to them.'

Argument was useless. She had made up her mind. He shut the front door after her and sat down again in the study. Somehow the room no longer felt so snug, and a little later, raising his head to the window, he saw her hurry past, her raincoat not buttoned properly and flapping, little drips of water forming on the brim of her hat and the garden basket filled with limp michaelmas daisies already dead. His conscience pricking him, he bent down and turned out one bar of the electric fire.

Or yet again it would be spring, it would be summer. Strolling out hatless into the garden, his hands in his pockets, with no other purpose in his mind but to feel the sun upon his back and stare out upon the woods and fields and the slow winding river, he would hear, from the bedrooms above, the high-pitched whine of the Hoover slow down suddenly, gasp, and die. Midge called down to him as he stood there on the terrace.

'Were you going to do anything?' she said.

He was not. It was the smell of spring, of early summer, that had driven him out into the garden. It was the delicious knowledge that being retired now, no longer working in the City, time was a thing of no account, he could waste it as he pleased.

'No,' he said, 'not on such a lovely day. Why?'

'Oh, never mind,' she answered, 'it's only that the wretched drain under the kitchen window has gone wrong again. Completely plugged up and choked. No one ever sees to it, that's why. I'll have a go at it myself this afternoon.'

155

Her face vanished from the window. Once more there was a gasp, a rising groan of sound, and the Hoover warmed to its task again. What foolishness that such an interruption could damp the brightness of the day. Not the demand, nor the task itself – clearing a drain was in its own way a schoolboy piece of folly, playing with mud – but that wan face of hers looking out upon the sunlit terrace, the hand that went up wearily to push back a strand of falling hair, and the inevitable sigh before she turned from the window, the unspoken, 'I wish I had the time to stand and do nothing in the sun. Oh, well . . .'

He had ventured to ask once why so much cleaning of the house was necessary. Why there must be the incessant turning out of rooms. Why chairs must be lifted to stand upon other chairs, rugs rolled up and ornaments huddled together on a sheet of newspaper. And why, in particular, the sides of the upstairs corridor, on which no one ever trod, must be polished laboriously by hand, Midge and the daily woman taking it in turns to crawl upon their knees the whole endless length of it, like slaves of bygone days.

Midge stared at him, not understanding.

'You'd be the first to complain,' she said, 'if the house was like a pigsty. You like your comforts.'

So they lived in different worlds, their minds not meeting. Had it been always so? He did not remember. They had been married nearly twenty-five years and were two people who, from force of habit, lived under the same roof.

When he had been in business, it seemed different. He had not noticed it so much. He came home to eat, to sleep, and to go up by train again in the morning. But when he retired he became aware of her forcibly, and day by day his sense of her resentment, of her disapproval, grew stronger.

Finally, in that last year before she died, he felt himself engulfed in it, so that he was led into every sort of petty

156

deception to get away from her, making a pretence of going up to London to have his hair cut, to see the dentist, to lunch with an old business friend; and in reality he would be sitting by his club window, anonymous, at peace.

It was mercifully swift, the illness that took her from him. Influenza, followed by pneumonia, and she was dead within a week. He hardly knew how it happened, except that as usual she was overtired and caught a cold, and would not stay in bed. One evening, coming home by the late train from London, having sneaked into a cinema during the afternoon, finding release amongst the crowd of warm friendly people enjoying themselves – for it was a bitter December day – he found her bent over the furnace in the cellar, poking and thrusting at the lumps of coke.

She looked up at him, white with fatigue, her face drawn.

'Why, Midge, what on earth are you doing?' he said.

'It's the furnace,' she said, 'we've had trouble with it all day, it won't stay alight. We shall have to get the men to see it tomorrow. I really cannot manage this sort of thing myself.'

There was a streak of coal dust on her cheek. She let the stubby poker fall on the cellar floor. She began to cough, and as she did so winced with pain.

'You ought to be in bed,' he said, 'I never heard of such nonsense. What the dickens does it matter about the furnace?'

'I thought you would be home early,' she said, 'and then you might have known how to deal with it. It's been bitter all day, I can't think what you found to do with yourself in London.'

She climbed the cellar stairs slowly, her back bent, and when she reached the top she stood shivering and half closed her eyes.

'If you don't mind terribly,' she said, 'I'll get your supper right away, to have it done with. I don't want anything myself.'

'To hell with my supper,' he said, 'I can forage for myself. You go up to bed. I'll bring you a hot drink.'

'I tell you, I don't want anything,' she said. 'I can fill my hot-water bottle myself. I only ask one thing of you. And that is to remember to turn out the lights everywhere, before you come up.' She turned into the hall, her shoulders sagging.

'Surely a glass of hot milk?' he began uncertainly, starting to take off his overcoat; and as he did so the torn half of the ten-and-sixpenny seat at the cinema fell from his pocket on to the floor. She saw it. She said nothing. She coughed again and began to drag herself upstairs.

The next morning her temperature was a hundred and three. The doctor came and said she had pneumonia. She asked if she might go to a private ward in the cottage hospital, because having a nurse in the house would make too much work. This was on the Tuesday morning. She went there right away, and they told him on the Friday evening that she was not likely to live through the night. He stood inside the room, after they told him, looking down at her in the high impersonal hospital bed, and his heart was wrung with pity, because surely they had given her too many pillows, she was propped too high, there could be no rest for her that way. He had brought some flowers, but there seemed no purpose now in giving them to the nurse to arrange, because Midge was too ill to look at them. In a sort of delicacy he put them on a table beside the screen, when the nurse was bending down to her.

'Is there anything she needs?' he said. 'I mean, I can easily . . .' He did not finish the sentence, he left it in the air, hoping the nurse would understand his intention, that he was ready to go off in the car, drive somewhere, fetch what was required.

The nurse shook her head. 'We will telephone you,' she said, 'if there is any change.'

What possible change could there be, he wondered, as he

found himself outside the hospital? The white pinched face upon the pillows would not alter now, it belonged to no one.

Midge died in the early hours of Saturday morning.

He was not a religious man, he had no profound belief in immortality, but when the funeral was over, and Midge was buried, it distressed him to think of her poor lonely body lying in that brand-new coffin with the brass handles: it seemed such a churlish thing to permit. Death should be different. It should be like bidding farewell to someone at a station before a long journey, but without the strain. There was something of indecency in this haste to bury underground the thing that but for ill-chance would be a living breathing person. In his distress he fancied he could hear Midge saying with a sigh, 'Oh, well . . .' as they lowered the coffin into the open grave.

He hoped with fervour that after all there might be a future in some unseen Paradise and that poor Midge, unaware of what they were doing to her mortal remains, walked somewhere in green fields. But who with, he wondered? Her parents had died in India many years ago; she would not have much in common with them now if they met her at the gates of Heaven. He had a sudden picture of her waiting her turn in a queue, rather far back, as was always her fate in queues, with that large shopping bag of woven straw which she took everywhere, and on her face that patient martyred look. As she passed through the turnstile into Paradise she looked at him, reproachfully.

These pictures, of the coffin and the queue, remained with him for about a week, fading a little day by day. Then he forgot her. Freedom was his, and the sunny empty house, the bright crisp winter. The routine he followed belonged to him alone. He never thought of Midge until the morning he looked out upon the apple tree.

Later that day he was taking a stroll round the garden, and

he found himself drawn to the tree through curiosity. It had been stupid fancy after all. There was nothing singular about it. An apple tree like any other apple tree. He remembered then that it had always been a poorer tree than its fellows, was in fact more than half dead, and at one time there had been talk of chopping it down, but the talk came to nothing. Well, it would be something for him to do over the weekend. Axing a tree was healthy exercise, and apple wood smelt good. It would be a treat to have it burning on the fire.

Unfortunately wet weather set in for nearly a week after that day, and he was unable to accomplish the task he had set himself. No sense in pottering out of doors this weather, and getting a chill into the bargain. He still noticed the tree from his bedroom window. It began to irritate him, humped there, straggling and thin, under the rain. The weather was not cold, and the rain that fell upon the garden was soft and gentle. None of the other trees wore this aspect of dejection. There was one young tree – only planted a few years back, he recalled quite well – growing to the right of the old one and standing straight and firm, the lithe young branches lifted to the sky, positively looking as if it enjoyed the rain. He peered through the window at it, and smiled. Now why the devil should he suddenly remember that incident, years back, during the war, with the girl who came to work on the land for a few months at the neighbouring farm? He did not suppose he had thought of her in months. Besides, there was nothing to it. At weekends he had helped them at the farm himself – war work of a sort – and she was always there, cheerful and pretty and smiling; she had dark curling hair, crisp and boyish, and a skin like a very young apple.

He looked forward to seeing her, Saturdays and Sundays; it was an antidote to the inevitable news bulletins put on throughout the day by Midge, and to ceaseless war talk. He liked looking at the child – she was scarcely more than that, nineteen or so – in her slim breeches and gay shirts; and when she smiled it was as though she embraced the world.

He never knew how it happened, and it was such a little thing; but one afternoon he was in the shed doing something to the tractor, bending over the engine, and she was beside him, close to his shoulder, and they were laughing together; and he turned round, to take a bit of waste to clean a plug, and suddenly she was in his arms and he was kissing her. It was a happy thing, spontaneous and free, and the girl so warm and jolly, with her fresh young mouth. Then they went on with the work of the tractor, but united now, in a kind of intimacy that brought gaiety to them both, and peace as well. When it was time for the girl to go and feed the pigs he followed her from the shed, his hand on her shoulder, a careless gesture that meant nothing really, a half caress; and as they came out into the yard he saw Midge standing there, staring at them.

'I've got to go in to a Red Cross meeting,' she said. 'I can't get the car to start. I called you. You didn't seem to hear.'

Her face was frozen. She was looking at the girl. At once guilt covered him. The girl said good evening cheerfully to Midge, and crossed the yard to the pigs.

He went with Midge to the car and managed to start it with the handle. Midge thanked him, her voice without expression. He found himself unable to meet her eyes. This, then, was adultery. This was sin. This was the second page in a Sunday newspaper – 'Husband Intimate with Land Girl in Shed. Wife Witnesses Act.' His hands were shaking when he got back to the house and he had to pour himself a drink. Nothing was ever said. Midge never mentioned the matter. Some craven instinct kept him from the farm the next weekend, and then he heard that the girl's mother had been taken ill and she had been called back home.

He never saw her again. Why, he wondered, should he remember her suddenly, on such a day, watching the rain falling on the apple trees? He must certainly make a point of cutting down the old dead tree, if only for the sake of bringing more sunshine to the little sturdy one; it hadn't a fair chance, growing there so close to the other.

On Friday afternoon he went round to the vegetable garden to find Willis, the jobbing gardener, who came three days a week, to pay him his wages. He wanted, too, to look in the toolshed and see if the axe and saw were in good condition. Willis kept everything neat and tidy there – this was Midge's training – and the axe and saw were hanging in their accustomed place upon the wall.

He paid Willis his money, and was turning away when the man suddenly said to him, 'Funny thing, sir, isn't it, about the old apple tree?'

The remark was so unexpected that it came as a shock. He felt himself change colour.

'Apple tree? What apple tree?' he said.

'Why, the one at the far end, near the terrace,' answered Willis. 'Been barren as long as I've worked here, and that's some years now. Never an apple from her, nor as much as a sprig of blossom. We were going to chop her up that cold winter, if you remember, and we never did. Well, she's taken on a new lease now. Haven't you noticed?' The gardener watched him smiling, a knowing look in his eye.

What did the fellow mean? It was not possible that he had been struck also by that fantastic freak resemblance – no, it was out of the question, indecent, blasphemous; besides, he had put it out of his own mind now, he had not thought of it again.

'I've noticed nothing,' he said, on the defensive.

Willis laughed. 'Come round to the terrace, sir,' he said, 'I'll show you.'

They went together to the sloping lawn, and when they came to the apple tree Willis put his hand up and pulled down a branch within reach. It creaked a little as he did so, as though stiff and unyielding, and Willis brushed away some of the dry lichen and revealed the spiky twigs. 'Look there, sir,' he said, 'she's growing buds. Look at them, feel them for yourself. There's life here yet, and plenty of it. Never known such a thing before. See this branch too.' He released the first, and leant up to reach another.

Willis was right. There were buds in plenty, but so small and brown that it seemed to him they scarcely deserved the name, they were more like blemishes upon the twig, dusty and dry. He put his hands in his pockets. He felt a queer distaste to touch them.

'I don't think they'll amount to much,' he said.

'I don't know, sir,' said Willis, 'I've got hopes. She's stood the winter, and if we get no more bad frosts there's no knowing what we'll see. It would be some joke to watch the old tree blossom. She'll bear fruit yet.' He patted the trunk with his open hand, in a gesture at once familiar and affectionate.

The owner of the apple tree turned away. For some reason he felt irritated with Willis. Anyone would think the damned tree lived. And now his plan to axe the tree, over the weekend, would come to nothing.

'It's taking the light from the young tree,' he said. 'Surely it would be more to the point if we did away with this one, and gave the little one more room?'

He moved across to the young tree and touched a limb. No lichen here. The branches smooth. Buds upon every twig, curling tight. He let go the branch and it sprang away from him, resilient.

'Do away with her, sir,' said Willis, 'while there's still life in her? Oh no, sir, I wouldn't do that. She's doing no harm to

163

the young tree. I'd give the old tree one more chance. If she doesn't bear fruit, we'll have her down next winter.'

'All right, Willis,' he said, and walked swiftly away. Somehow he did not want to discuss the matter any more.

That night, when he went to bed, he opened the window wide as usual and drew back the curtains; he could not bear to wake up in the morning and find the room close. It was full moon, and the light shone down upon the terrace and the lawn above it, ghostly pale and still. No wind blew. A hush upon the place. He leant out, loving the silence. The moon shone full upon the little apple tree, the young one. There was a radiance about it in this light that gave it a fairy-tale quality. Small and lithe and slim, the young tree might have been a dancer, her arms upheld, poised ready on her toes for flight. Such a careless, happy grace about it. Brave young tree. Away to the left stood the other one, half of it in shadow still. Even the moonlight could not give it beauty. What in heaven's name was the matter with the thing that it had to stand there, humped and stooping, instead of looking upwards to the light? It marred the still quiet night, it spoilt the setting. He had been a fool to give way to Willis and agree to spare the tree. Those ridiculous buds would never blossom, and even if they did . . .

His thoughts wandered, and for the second time that week he found himself remembering the landgirl and her joyous smile. He wondered what had happened to her. Married probably, with a young family. Made some chap happy, no doubt. Oh, well . . . He smiled. Was he going to make use of that expression now? Poor Midge! Then he caught his breath and stood quite still, his hand upon the curtain. The apple tree, the one on the left, was no longer in shadow. The moon shone upon the withered branches, and they looked like skeleton's arms raised in supplication. Frozen arms, stiff and numb with pain. There was no wind, and the other trees were motionless; but there, in those topmost branches, something shivered and stirred, a breeze that came from nowhere and died away again. Suddenly a branch fell from the apple tree to the ground below. It was the near branch, with the small dark buds upon it, which he would not touch. No rustle, no breath of movement came from the other trees. He went on staring at the branch as it lay there on the grass, under the moon. It stretched across the shadow of the young tree close to it, pointing as though in accusation.

For the first time in his life that he could remember he drew the curtains over the window to shut out the light of the moon.

Willis was supposed to keep to the vegetable garden. He had never shown his face much round the front when Midge was alive. That was because Midge attended to the flowers. She even used to mow the grass, pushing the wretched machine up and down the slope, her back bent low over the handles.

It had been one of the tasks she set herself, like keeping the bedrooms swept and polished. Now Midge was no longer there to attend to the front garden and to tell him where he should work, Willis was always coming through to the front. The gardener liked the change. It made him feel responsible.

'I can't understand how that branch came to fall, sir,' he said on the Monday.

'What branch?'

'Why, the branch on the apple tree. The one we were looking at before I left.'

'It was rotten, I suppose. I told you the tree was dead.'

'Nothing rotten about it, sir. Why, look at it. Broke clean off.'

Once again the owner was obliged to follow his man up the slope above the terrace. Willis picked up the branch. The lichen upon it was wet, bedraggled looking, like matted hair.

'You didn't come again to test the branch, over the weekend, and loosen it in some fashion, did you, sir?' asked the gardener.

'I most certainly did not,' replied the owner, irritated. 'As a matter of fact I heard the branch fall, during the night. I was opening the bedroom window at the time.'

'Funny. It was a still night too.'

'These things often happen to old trees. Why you bother about this one I can't imagine. Anyone would think . . .'

He broke off; he did not know how to finish the sentence.

'Anyone would think that the tree was valuable,' he said.

The gardener shook his head. 'It's not the value,' he said. 'I don't reckon for a moment that this tree is worth any money at all. It's just that after all this time, when we thought her dead, she's alive and kicking, as you might say. Freak of nature, I call it. We'll hope no other branches fall before she blossoms.'

Later, when the owner set off for his afternoon walk, he saw the man cutting away the grass below the tree and placing new wire around the base of the trunk. It was quite ridiculous. He did not pay the fellow a fat wage to tinker about with a half-dead tree. He ought to be in the kitchen garden, growing vegetables. It was too much effort, though, to argue with him.

He returned home about half past five. Tea was a discarded meal since Midge had died, and he was looking forward to his armchair by the fire, his pipe, his whisky-and-soda, and silence.

The fire had not long been lit and the chimney was smoking. There was a queer, rather sickly smell about the living-room. He threw open the windows and went upstairs to change his heavy shoes. When he came down again the smoke still clung about the room and the smell was as strong as ever. Impossible to name it. Sweetish, strange. He called to the woman out in the kitchen.

'There's a funny smell in the house,' he said. 'What is it?'

The woman came out into the hall from the back.

'What sort of a smell, sir?' she said, on the defensive.

'It's in the living-room,' he said. 'The room was full of smoke just now. Have you been burning something?'

Her face cleared. 'It must be the logs,' she said. 'Willis cut them up specially, sir, he said you would like them.'

'What logs are those?'

'He said it was apple wood, sir, from a branch he had sawed up. Apple wood burns well, I've always heard. Some people fancy it very much. I don't notice any smell myself, but I've got a slight cold.'

Together they looked at the fire. Willis had cut the logs small. The woman, thinking to please him, had piled several on top of one another, to make a good fire to last. There was no great blaze. The smoke that came from them was thin and poor. Greenish in colour. Was it possible she did not notice that sickly rancid smell?

'The logs are wet,' he said abruptly. 'Willis should have known better. Look at them. Quite useless on my fire.'

The woman's face took on a set, rather sulky expression. 'I'm very sorry,' she said. 'I didn't notice anything wrong with them when I came to light the fire. They seemed to start well. I've always understood apple wood was very good for burning, and Willis said the same. He told me to be sure and see that you had these on the fire this evening, he had made a special job of cutting them for you. I thought you knew about it and had given orders.'

'Oh, all right,' he answered, abruptly. 'I dare say they'll burn in time. It's not your fault.'

He turned his back on her and poked at the fire, trying to separate the logs. While she remained in the house there was nothing he could do. To remove the damp smouldering logs and throw them somewhere round the back, and then light the fire afresh with dry sticks would arouse comment. He would have to go through the kitchen to the back passage where the kindling wood was kept, and she would stare at him, and come forward and say, 'Let me do it, sir. Has the fire gone out then?' No, he must wait until after supper, when she had cleared away and washed up and gone off for the night. Meanwhile, he would endure the smell of the apple wood as best he could.

He poured out his drink, lit his pipe and stared at the fire. It gave out no heat at all, and with the central heating off in the house the living-room struck chill. Now and again a thin wisp of the greenish smoke puffed from the logs, and with it seemed to come that sweet sickly smell, unlike any sort of wood smoke that he knew. That interfering fool of a gardener . . . Why saw up the logs? He must have known they were damp. Riddled with damp. He leant forward, staring more closely. Was it damp, though, that oozed there in a thin trickle from the pale logs? No, it was sap, unpleasant, slimy.

He seized the poker, and in a fit of irritation thrust it between the logs, trying to stir them to flame, to change that green smoke into a normal blaze. The effort was useless. The logs would not burn. And all the while the trickle of sap ran on to the grate and the sweet smell filled the room, turning his stomach. He took his glass and his book and went and turned on the electric fire in the study and sat in there instead.

It was idiotic. It reminded him of the old days, how he would make a pretence of writing letters, and go and sit in the study because of Midge in the living-room. She had a habit of yawning in the evenings, when her day's work was done; a habit of which she was quite unconscious. She would settle herself on the sofa with her knitting, the click-click of the needles going fast and furious; and suddenly they would start, those shattering yawns, rising from the depths of her, a prolonged 'Ah . . . Ah . . . Hi-Oh!' followed by the inevitable sigh. Then there would be silence except for the knitting needles, but as he sat behind his book, waiting, he knew that within a few minutes another yawn would come, another sigh.

A hopeless sort of anger used to stir within him, a longing to throw down his book and say, 'Look, if you are so tired, wouldn't it be better if you went to bed?'

Instead, he controlled himself, and after a little while, when he could bear it no longer, he would get up and leave the living-room, and take refuge in the study. Now he was doing the same thing, all over again, because of the apple logs. Because of the damned sickly smell of the smouldering wood.

He went on sitting in his chair by the desk, waiting for supper. It was nearly nine o'clock before the daily woman had cleared up, turned down his bed and gone for the night.

He returned to the living-room, which he had not entered since leaving it earlier in the evening. The fire was out. It had made some effort to burn, because the logs were thinner than they had been before, and had sunk low into the basket grate. The ash was meagre, yet the sickly smell clung to the dying embers. He went out into the kitchen and found an empty scuttle and brought it back into the living-room. Then he lifted the logs into it, and the ashes too. There must have been some damp residue in the scuttle, or the logs were still not dry, because as they settled there they seemed to turn darker than before, with a kind of scum upon them. He carried the scuttle down to the cellar, opened the door of the central heating furnace, and threw the lot inside.

He remembered then, too late, that the central heating had been given up now for two or three weeks, owing to the spring weather, and that unless he relit it now the logs would remain there, untouched, until the following winter. He found paper, matches, and a can of paraffin, and setting the whole alight closed the door of the furnace, and listened to the roar of flames. That would settle it. He waited a moment and then went up the steps, back to the kitchen passage, to lay and relight the fire in the living-room. The business took time, he had to find kindling and coal, but with patience he got the new fire started, and finally settled himself down in his arm-chair before it.

He had been reading perhaps for twenty minutes before he became aware of the banging door. He put down his book and listened. Nothing at first. Then, yes, there it was again. A rattle, a slam of an unfastened door in the kitchen quarters. He got up and went along to shut it. It was the door at the top of the cellar stairs. He could have sworn he had fastened it. The catch must have worked loose in some way. He switched on the light at the head of the stairs, and bent to examine the catch. There seemed nothing wrong with it. He was about to close the door firmly when he noticed the smell again. The sweet sickly smell of smouldering apple wood. It was creeping up from the cellar, finding its way to the passage above.

Suddenly, for no reason, he was seized with a kind of fear, a feeling of panic almost. What if the smell filled the whole house through the night, came up from the kitchen quarters to the floor above, and while he slept found its way into his bedroom, choking him, stifling him, so that he could not breathe? The thought was ridiculous, insane – and yet . . .

Once more he forced himself to descend the steps into the cellar. No sound came from the furnace, no roar of flames. Wisps of smoke, thin and green, oozed their way from the fastened furnace door; it was this that he had noticed from the passage above.

He went to the furnace and threw open the door. The paper had all burnt away, and the few shavings with them. But the logs, the apple logs, had not burnt at all. They lay there as they had done when he threw them in, one charred limb above another, black and huddled, like the bones of someone darkened and dead by fire. Nausea rose in him. He thrust his handkerchief into his mouth, choking. Then, scarcely knowing what he did, he ran up the steps to find the empty scuttle, and with a shovel and tongs tried to pitch the logs back into it, scraping for them through the narrow door of the furnace. He was retching in his belly all the while. At last the scuttle was filled, and he carried it up the steps and through the kitchen to the back door.

He opened the door. Tonight there was no moon and it was raining. Turning up the collar of his coat he peered about him in the darkness, wondering where he should throw the logs. Too wet and dark to stagger all the way to the kitchen garden and chuck them on the rubbish heap, but in the field behind the garage the grass was thick and long and they might lie there hidden. He crunched his way over the gravel drive, and coming to the fence beside the field threw his burden on to the concealing grass. There they could rot and perish, grow sodden with rain, and in the end become part of the mouldy earth; he did not care. The responsibility was his no longer. They were out of his house, and it did not matter what became of them.

He returned to the house, and this time made sure the cellar door was fast. The air was clear again, the smell had gone.

He went back to the living-room to warm himself before the fire, but his hands and feet, wet with the rain, and his stomach, still queasy from the pungent smoke, combined together to chill his whole person, and he sat there, shuddering.

He slept badly when he went to bed that night, and awoke in the morning feeling out of sorts. He had a headache, and an ill-tasting tongue. He stayed indoors. His liver was thoroughly upset. To relieve his feelings he spoke sharply to the daily woman.

'I've caught a bad chill,' he said to her, 'trying to get warm last night. So much for apple wood. The smell of it has affected my inside as well. You can tell Willis, when he comes tomorrow.'

She looked at him in disbelief.

'I'm sure I'm very sorry,' she said. 'I told my sister about the wood last night, when I got home, and that you had not fancied it. She said it was most unusual. Apple wood is considered quite a luxury to burn, and burns well, what's more.'

'This lot didn't, that's all I know,' he said to her, 'and I never want to see any more of it. As for the smell . . . I can taste it still, it's completely turned me up.'

Her mouth tightened. 'I'm sorry,' she said. And then, as she left the dining-room, her eye fell on the empty whisky bottle on the sideboard. She hesitated a moment, then put it on her tray.

'You've finished with this, sir?' she said.

Of course he had finished with it. It was obvious. The bottle was empty. He realized the implication, though. She wanted to suggest that the idea of apple-wood smoke upsetting him was all my eye, he had done himself too well. Damned impertinence.

'Yes,' he said, 'you can bring another in its place.'

That would teach her to mind her own business.

He was quite sick for several days, queasy and giddy, and finally rang up the doctor to come and have a look at him. The story of the apple wood sounded nonsense, when he told it, and the doctor, after examining him, appeared unimpressed.

'Just a chill on the liver,' he said, 'damp feet, and possibly something you've eaten combined. I hardly think wood smoke has much to do with it. You ought to take more exercise, if you're inclined to have a liver. Play golf. I don't know how I should keep fit without my weekend golf.' He laughed, packing up his bag. 'I'll make you up some medicine,' he said, 'and once this rain has cleared off I should get out and into the air. It's mild enough, and all we want now is a bit of sunshine to bring everything on. Your garden is farther ahead than mine. Your fruit trees are ready to blossom.' And then, before leaving the room, he added, 'You mustn't forget, you had a bad shock a few months ago. It takes time to get over these things. You're still missing your wife, you know. Best thing is to get out and about and see people. Well, take care of yourself.'

His patient dressed and went downstairs. The fellow meant well, of course, but his visit had been a waste of time. 'You're still missing your wife, you know.' How little the doctor understood. Poor Midge . . . At least he himself had the honesty to admit that he did not miss her at all, that now she was gone he could breathe, he was free, and that apart from the upset liver he had not felt so well for years.

During the few days he had spent in bed the daily woman had taken the opportunity to spring-clean the living-room. An unnecessary piece of work, but he supposed it was part of the legacy Midge had left behind her. The room looked scrubbed and straight and much too tidy. His own personal litter cleared, books and papers neatly stacked. It was an infernal nuisance, really, having anyone to do for him at all. It would not take much for him to sack her and fend for himself as best he could. Only the bother, the tie of cooking and washing up, prevented him. The ideal life, of course, was that led by a man out East, or in the South Seas, who took a native wife. No problem there. Silence, good service, perfect waiting, excellent cooking, no need for conversation; and then, if you wanted something more than that, there she was, young, warm, a companion for the dark hours. No criticism ever, the obedience of an animal to its master, and the light-hearted laughter of a child. Yes, they had wisdom all right, those fellows who broke away from convention. Good luck to them.

He strolled over to the window and looked out up the

sloping lawn. The rain was stopping and tomorrow it would be fine; he would be able to get out, as the doctor had suggested. The man was right, too, about the fruit trees. The little one near the steps was in flower already, and a blackbird had perched himself on one of the branches, which swayed slightly under his weight.

The rain-drops glistened and the opening buds were very curled and pink, but when the sun broke through tomorrow they would turn white and soft against the blue of the sky. He must find his old camera, and put a film in it, and photograph the little tree. The others would be in flower, too, during the week. As for the old one, there on the left, it looked as dead as ever; or else the so-called buds were so brown they did not show up from this distance. Perhaps the shedding of the branch had been its finish. And a good job too.

He turned away from the window and set about rearranging the room to his taste, spreading his things about. He liked pottering, opening drawers, taking things out and putting them back again. There was a red pencil in one of the side tables that must have slipped down behind a pile of books and been found during the turn-out. He sharpened it, gave it a sleek fine point. He found a new film in another drawer, and kept it out to put in his camera in the morning. There were a number of papers and old photographs in the drawer, heaped in a jumble, and snapshots too, dozens of them. Midge used to look after these things at one time and put them in albums; then during the war she must have lost interest, or had too many other things to do.

All this junk could really be cleared away. It would have made a fine fire the other night, and might have got even the apple logs to burn. There was little sense in keeping any of it. This appalling photo of Midge, for instance, taken heaven knows how many years ago, not long after their marriage, judging from the style of it. Did she really wear her hair that way? That fluffy mop, much too thick and bushy for her face, which was long and narrow even then. The low neck, pointing to a V, and the dangling earrings, and the smile, too eager, making her mouth seem larger than it was. In the left-hand corner she had written 'To my own darling Buzz, from his loving Midge'. He had completely forgotten his old nickname. It had been dropped years back, and he seemed to remember he had never cared for it: he had found it ridiculous and embarrassing and had chided her for using it in front of people.

He tore the photograph in half and threw it on the fire. He watched it curl up upon itself and burn, and the last to go was that vivid smile. My own darling Buzz . . . Suddenly he remembered the evening dress in the photograph. It was green, not her colour ever, turning her sallow; and she had bought it for some special occasion, some big dinner party with friends who were celebrating their wedding anniversary. The idea of the dinner had been to invite all those friends and neighbours who had been married roughly around the same time, which was the reason Midge and he had gone.

There was a lot of champagne, and one or two speeches, and much conviviality, laughter, and joking – some of the joking rather broad – and he remembered that when the evening was over, and they were climbing into the car to drive away, his host, with a gust of laughter, said, 'Try paying your addresses in a top hat, old boy, they say it never fails!' He had been aware of Midge beside him, in that green evening frock, sitting very straight and still, and on her face that same smile which she had worn in the photograph just destroyed, eager yet uncertain, doubtful of the meaning of the words that her host, slightly intoxicated, had let fall upon the evening air, yet wishing to seem advanced, anxious to please, and more than either of these things desperately anxious to attract.

When he had put the car away in the garage and gone into the house he had found her waiting there, in the living-room, for no reason at all. Her coat was thrown off to show the evening dress, and the smile, rather uncertain, was on her face.

He yawned, and settling himself down in a chair picked up a book. She waited a little while, then slowly took up her coat and went upstairs. It must have been shortly afterwards that she had that photograph taken. 'My own darling Buzz, from his loving Midge.' He threw a great handful of dry sticks on to the fire. They crackled and split and turned the photograph to ashes. No damp green logs tonight . . .

It was fine and warm the following day. The sun shone, and the birds sang. He had a sudden impulse to go to London. It was a day for sauntering along Bond Street, watching the passing crowds. A day for calling in at his tailors, for having a hair-cut, for eating a dozen oysters at his favourite bar. The chill had left him. The pleasant hours stretched before him. He might even look in at a matinée.

The day passed without incident, peaceful, untiring, just as he had planned, making a change from day-by-day country routine. He drove home about seven o'clock, looking forward to his drink and to his dinner. It was so warm he did not need his overcoat, not even now, with the sun gone down. He waved a hand to the farmer, who happened to be passing the gate as he turned into the drive.

'Lovely day,' he shouted.

The man nodded, smiled. 'Can do with plenty of these from now on,' he shouted back. Decent fellow. They had always been very matey since those war days, when he had driven the tractor.

He put away the car and had a drink, and while waiting for supper took a stroll around the garden. What a difference those hours of sunshine had made to everything. Several daffodils were out, narcissi too, and the green hedgerows fresh and sprouting. As for the apple trees, the buds had burst, and they were all of them in flower. He went to his little favourite and touched the blossom. It felt soft to his hand and he gently shook a bough. It was firm, well-set, and would not fall. The scent was scarcely perceptible as yet, but in a day or two, with a little more sun, perhaps a shower or two, it would come from the open flower and softly fill the air, never pungent, never strong, a modest scent. A scent which you would have to find for yourself, as the bees did. Once found it stayed with you, it lingered always, alluring, comforting, and sweet. He patted the little tree, and went down the steps into the house.

Next morning, at breakfast, there came a knock on the dining-room window, and the daily woman said that Willis was outside and wanted to have a word with him. He asked Willis to step in.

The gardener looked aggrieved. Was it trouble, then?

'I'm sorry to bother you, sir,' he said, 'but I had a few words with Mr Jackson this morning. He's been complaining.'

Jackson was the farmer, who owned the neighbouring fields.

'What's he complaining about?'

'Says I've been throwing wood over the fence into his field, and the young foal out there, with the mare, tripped over it and went lame. I've never thrown wood over the fence in my life, sir. Quite nasty he was, sir. Spoke of the value of the foal, and it might spoil his chances to sell it.'

'I hope you told him, then, it wasn't true.'

'I did, sir. But the point is someone has been throwing wood over the fence. He showed me the very spot. Just behind the garage. I went with Mr Jackson, and there they were. Logs had been tipped there, sir. I thought it best to come to you about it before I spoke in the kitchen, otherwise you know how it is, there would be unpleasantness.'

He felt the gardener's eye upon him. No way out, of course. And it was Willis's fault in the first place.

'No need to say anything in the kitchen, Willis,' he said. 'I threw the logs there myself. You brought them into the house, without my asking you to do so, with the result that they put out my fire, filled the room with smoke, and ruined an evening. I chucked them over the fence in a devil of a temper, and if they have damaged Jackson's foal you can apologize for me, and tell him I'll pay him compensation. All I ask is that you don't bring any more logs like those into the house again.'

'No sir, I understood they had not been a success. I didn't think, though, that you would go so far as to throw them out.'

'Well, I did. And there's an end to it.'

'Yes, sir.' He made as if to go, but before he left the dining-room he paused and said, 'I can't understand about the logs not burning, all the same. I took a small piece back to the wife, and it burnt lovely in our kitchen, bright as anything.'

'It did not burn here.'

'Anyway, the old tree is making up for one spoilt branch, sir. Have you seen her this morning?'

'No.'

'It's yesterday's sun that has done it, sir, and the warm night. Quite a treat she is, with all the blossom. You should go out and take a look at her directly.'

Willis left the room, and he continued his breakfast.

Presently he went out on to the terrace. At first he did not go up on to the lawn; he made a pretence of seeing to other things, of getting the heavy garden seat out, now that the weather was set fair. And then, fetching a pair of clippers, he did a bit of pruning to the few roses, under the windows. Yet, finally, something drew him to the tree.

It was just as Willis said. Whether it was the sun, the warmth, the mild still night, he could not tell; but the small brown

178

buds had unfolded themselves, had ripened into flower, and now spread themselves above his head into a fantastic cloud of white, moist blossom. It grew thickest at the top of the tree, the flowers so clustered together that they looked like wad upon wad of soggy cotton wool, and all of it, from the topmost branches to those nearer to the ground, had this same pallid colour of sickly white.

It did not resemble a tree at all; it might have been a flapping tent, left out in the rain by campers who had gone away, or else a mop, a giant mop, whose streaky surface had been caught somehow by the sun, and so turned bleached. The blossom was too thick, too great a burden for the long thin trunk, and the moisture clinging to it made it heavier still. Already, as if the effort had been too much, the lower flowers, those nearest the ground, were turning brown; yet there had been no rain.

Well, there it was. Willis had been proved right. The tree had blossomed. But instead of blossoming to life, to beauty, it had somehow, deep in nature, gone awry and turned a freak. A freak which did not know its texture or its shape, but thought to please. Almost as though it said, self-conscious, with a smirk, 'Look. All this is for you.'

Suddenly he heard a step behind him. It was Willis.

'Fine sight, sir, isn't it?'

'Sorry, I don't admire it. The blossom is far too thick.'

The gardener stared at him and said nothing. It struck him that Willis must think him very difficult, very hard, and possibly eccentric. He would go and discuss him in the kitchen with the daily woman.

He forced himself to smile at Willis.

'Look here,' he said, 'I don't mean to damp you. But all this blossom doesn't interest me. I prefer it small and light and colourful, like the little tree. But you take some of it back home, to your wife. Cut as much of it as you like, I don't mind at all. I'd like you to have it.'

He waved his arm, generously. He wanted Willis to go now, and fetch a ladder, and carry the stuff away.

The man shook his head. He looked quite shocked.

'No, thank you, sir, I wouldn't dream of it. It would spoil the tree. I want to wait for the fruit. That's what I'm banking on, the fruit.'

There was no more to be said.

'All right, Willis. Don't bother, then.'

He went back to the terrace. But when he sat down there in the sun, looking up the sloping lawn, he could not see the little tree at all, standing modest and demure above the steps, her soft flowers lifting to the sky. She was dwarfed and hidden by the freak, with its great cloud of sagging petals, already wilting, dingy white, on to the grass beneath. And whichever way he turned his chair, this way or that upon the terrace, it seemed to him that he could not escape the tree, that it stood there above him, reproachful, anxious, desirous of the admiration that he could not give.

That summer he took a longer holiday than he had done for many years − a bare ten days with his old mother in Norfolk, instead of the customary month that he had been used to spend with Midge, and the rest of August and the whole of September in Switzerland and Italy.

He took his car, and so was free to motor from place to place as the mood inclined. He cared little for sight-seeing or excursions, and was not much of a climber. What he liked most was to come upon a little town in the cool of the evening, pick out a small but comfortable hotel, and then stay there, if it pleased him, for two or three days at a time, doing nothing, mooching.

He liked sitting about in the sun all morning, at some café or restaurant, with a glass of wine in front of him, watching the people; so many gay young creatures seemed to travel nowadays. He enjoyed the chatter of conversation around him, as long as he did not have to join in; and now and again a smile would come his way, a word or two of greeting from some guest in the same hotel, but nothing to commit him, merely a sense of being in the swim, of being a man of leisure on his own, abroad.

The difficulty in the old days, on holiday anywhere with Midge, would be her habit of striking up acquaintance with people, some other couple who struck her as looking 'nice' or, as she put it, 'our sort'. It would start with conversation over coffee, and then pass on to mutual planning of shared days, car drives in foursomes – he could not bear it, the holiday would be ruined.

Now, thank heaven, there was no need for this. He did what he liked, in his own time. There was no Midge to say, 'Well, shall we be moving?' when he was still sitting contentedly over his wine, no Midge to plan a visit to some old church that did not interest him.

He put on weight during his holiday, and he did not mind. There was no one to suggest a good long walk to keep fit after the rich food, thus spoiling the pleasant somnolence that comes with coffee and dessert; no one to glance, surprised, at the sudden wearing of a jaunty shirt, a flamboyant tie.

Strolling through the little towns and villages, hatless, smoking a cigar, receiving smiles from the jolly young folk around him, he felt himself a dog. This was the life, no worries, no cares. No 'We have to be back on the fifteenth because of that committee meeting at the hospital'; no 'We can't possibly leave the house shut up for longer than a fortnight, something might happen'. Instead, the bright lights of a little country fair, in a village whose name he did not even bother to find out; the tinkle of music, boys and girls laughing, and he himself, after a bottle of the local wine, bowing to a young thing with a gay handkerchief round her head and sweeping her off to dance under the hot tent. No matter if her steps did not harmonize with his – it was years since he had danced – this was the thing, this was it. He released her when the music stopped, and off she ran, giggling, back to her young friends, laughing at him no doubt. What of it? He had had his fun.

He left Italy when the weather turned, at the end of September, and was back home the first week in October. No problem to it. A telegram to the daily woman, with the probable date of arrival, and that was all. Even a brief holiday with Midge and the return meant complications. Written instructions about groceries, milk, and bread; airing of beds, lighting of fires, reminders about the delivery of the morning papers. The whole business turned into a chore.

He turned into the drive on a mellow October evening and there was smoke coming from the chimneys, the front door open, and his pleasant home awaiting him. No rushing through to the back regions to learn of possible plumbing disasters, breakages, water shortages, food difficulties; the daily woman knew better than to bother him with these. Merely, 'Good evening, sir. I hope you had a good holiday. Supper at the usual time?' And then silence. He could have his drink, light his pipe, and relax; the small pile of letters did not matter. No feverish tearing of them open, and then the start of the telephoning, the hearing of those endless one-sided conversations between women friends. 'Well? How are things? Really? My dear . . . And what did you say to that? . . . She did? . . . I can't possibly on Wednesday . . .'

He stretched himself contentedly, stiff after his drive, and gazed comfortably around the cheerful, empty living-room.

He was hungry, after his journey up from Dover, and the chop seemed rather meagre after foreign fare. But there it was, it wouldn't hurt him to return to plainer food. A sardine on toast followed the chop, and then he looked about him for dessert.

There was a plate of apples on the sideboard. He fetched them and put them down in front of him on the dining-room table. Poor-looking things. Small and wizened, dullish brown in colour. He bit into one, but as soon as the taste of it was on his tongue he spat it out. The thing was rotten. He tried another. It was just the same. He looked more closely at the pile of apples. The skins were leathery and rough and hard; you would expect the insides to be sour. On the contrary they were pulpy soft, and the cores were yellow. Filthy-tasting things. A stray piece stuck to his tooth and he pulled it out. Stringy, beastly . . .

He rang the bell, and the woman came through from the kitchen.

'Have we any other dessert?' he said.

'I am afraid not, sir. I remembered how fond you were of apples, and Willis brought in these from the garden. He said they were especially good, and just ripe for eating.'

'Well, he's quite wrong. They're uneatable.'

'I'm very sorry, sir. I wouldn't have put them through had I known. There's a lot more outside, too. Willis brought in a great basketful.'

'All the same sort?'

'Yes, sir. The small brown ones. No other kind, at all.'

'Never mind, it can't be helped. I'll look for myself in the morning.'

He got up from the table and went through to the living-room. He had a glass of port to take away the taste of the apples, but it seemed to make no difference, not even a biscuit with it. The pulpy rotten tang clung to his tongue and the roof of his mouth, and in the end he was obliged to go up to the bathroom and clean his teeth. The maddening thing was that he could have done with a good clean apple, after that rather indifferent supper: something with a smooth clear skin, the inside not too sweet, a little sharp in flavour. He knew the kind. Good biting texture. You had to pick them, of course, at just the right moment.

He dreamt that night he was back again in Italy, dancing under the tent in the little cobbled square. He woke with the tinkling music in his ear, but he could not recall the face of the peasant girl or remember the feel of her, tripping against his feet. He tried to recapture the memory, lying awake, over his morning tea, but it eluded him.

He got up out of bed and went over to the window, to glance at the weather. Fine enough, with a slight nip in the air.

Then he saw the tree. The sight of it came as a shock, it was so unexpected. Now he realized at once where the apples had come from the night before. The tree was laden, bowed down, under her burden of fruit. They clustered, small and brown, on every branch, diminishing in size as they reached the top, so that those on the high boughs, not grown yet to full size, looked like nuts. They weighed heavy on the tree, and because of this it seemed bent and twisted out of shape, the lower branches nearly sweeping the ground; and on the grass, at the foot of the tree, were more and yet more apples, windfalls, the first-grown, pushed off by their clamouring brothers and sisters. The ground was covered with them, many split open and rotting where the wasps had been. Never in his life had he seen a tree so laden with fruit. It was a miracle that it had not fallen under the weight.

He went out before breakfast – curiosity was too great – and stood beside the tree, staring at it. There was no mistake about it, these were the same apples that had been put in the

184

dining-room last night. Hardly bigger than tangerines, and many of them smaller than that, they grew so close together on the branches that to pick one you would be forced to pick a dozen.

There was something monstrous in the sight, something distasteful; yet it was pitiful too that the months had brought this agony upon the tree, for agony it was, there could be no other word for it. The tree was tortured by fruit, groaning under the weight of it, and the frightful part about it was that not one of the fruit was eatable. Every apple was rotten through and through. He trod them underfoot, the windfalls on the grass, there was no escaping them; and in a moment they were mush and slime, clinging about his heels – he had to clean the mess off with wisps of grass.

It would have been far better if the tree had died, stark and bare, before this ever happened. What use was it to him or anyone, this load of rotting fruit, littering up the place, fouling the ground? And the tree itself humped, as it were, in pain, and yet he could almost swear triumphant, gloating.

Just as in spring, when the mass of fluffy blossom, colourless and sodden, dragged the reluctant eye away from the other trees, so it did now. Impossible to avoid seeing the tree, with its burden of fruit. Every window in the front part of the house looked out upon it. And he knew how it would be. The fruit would cling there until it was picked, staying upon the branches through October and November, and it never would be picked, because nobody could eat it. He could see himself being bothered with the tree throughout the autumn. Whenever he came out on to the terrace there it would be, sagging and loathsome.

It was extraordinary the dislike he had taken to the tree. It was a perpetual reminder of the fact that he . . . well, he was blessed if he knew what . . . a perpetual reminder of all the things he most detested, and always had, he could not put a name to them. He decided then and there that Willis should pick the fruit and take it away, sell it, get rid of it, anything, as long as he did not have to eat it, and as long as he was not forced to watch the tree drooping there, day after day, throughout the autumn.

He turned his back upon it and was relieved to see that none of the other trees had so degraded themselves to excess. They carried a fair crop, nothing out of the way, and as he might have known the young tree, to the right of the old one, made a brave little show on its own, with a light load of medium-sized, rosy-looking apples, not too dark in colour, but freshly reddened where the sun had ripened them. He would pick one now, and take it in, to eat with breakfast. He made his choice, and the apple fell at the first touch into his hand. It looked so good that he bit into it with appetite. That was it, juicy, sweet-smelling, sharp, the dew upon it still. He did not look back at the old tree. He went indoors, hungry, to breakfast.

It took the gardener nearly a week to strip the tree, and it was plain he did it under protest.

'I don't care what you do with them,' said his employer. 'You can sell them and keep the money, or you can take them home and feed them to your pigs. I can't stand the sight of them, and that's all there is to it. Find a long ladder, and start on the job right away.'

It seemed to him that Willis, from sheer obstinacy, spun out the time. He would watch the man from the windows act as though in slow motion. First the placing of the ladder. Then the laborious climb, and the descent to steady it again. After that the performance of plucking off the fruit, dropping them, one by one, into the basket. Day after day it was the same. Willis was always there on the sloping lawn with his ladder, under the tree, the branches creaking and groaning, and beneath him on the grass baskets, pails, basins, any receptacle that would hold the apples.

At last the job was finished. The ladder was removed, the baskets and pails also, and the tree was stripped bare. He looked out at it, the evening of that day, in satisfaction. No more rotting fruit to offend his eye. Every single apple gone.

Yet the tree, instead of seeming lighter from the loss of its burden, looked, if it were possible, more dejected than ever. The branches still sagged, and the leaves, withering now to the cold autumnal evening, folded upon themselves and shivered. 'Is this my reward?' it seemed to say. 'After all I've done for you?'

As the light faded, the shadow of the tree cast a blight upon the dank night. Winter would soon come. And the short, dull days.

He had never cared much for the fall of the year. In the old days, when he went up to London every day to the office, it had meant that early start by train, on a nippy morning. And then, before three o'clock in the afternoon, the clerks were turning on the lights, and as often as not there would be fog in the air, murky and dismal, and a slow chugging journey home, daily bread-ers like himself sitting five abreast in a carriage, some of them with colds in their heads. Then the long evening followed, with Midge opposite him before the living-room fire, and he listening, or feigning to listen, to the account of her days and the things that had gone wrong.

If she had not shouldered any actual household disaster, she would pick upon some current event to cast a gloom. 'I see fares are going up again, what about your season ticket?', or 'This business in South Africa looks nasty, quite a long bit about it on the six o'clock news', or yet again 'Three more cases of polio over at the isolation hospital. I don't know, I'm sure, what the medical world thinks it's doing . . .'

Now, at least, he was spared the role of listener, but the memory of those long evenings was with him still, and when the lights were lit and the curtains were drawn he would be reminded of the click-click of the needles, the aimless chatter, and the 'Heigh-ho' of the yawns. He began to drop in, sometimes before supper, sometimes afterwards, at the Green Man, the old public house a quarter of a mile away on the main road. Nobody bothered him there. He would sit in a corner, having said good evening to genial Mrs Hill, the proprietress, and then, with a cigarette and a whisky-and-soda, watch the local inhabitants stroll in to have a pint, to throw a dart, to gossip.

In a sense it made a continuation of his summer holiday. It bore resemblance, admittedly slight, to the care-free atmosphere of the cafés and the restaurants; and there was a kind of warmth about the bright smoke-filled bar, crowded with working men who did not bother him, which he found pleasant, comforting. These visits cut into the length of the dark winter evenings, making them more tolerable.

A cold in the head, caught in mid-December, put a stop to this for more than a week. He was obliged to keep to the house. And it was odd, he thought to himself, how much he missed the Green Man, and how sick to death he became of sitting about in the living-room or in the study, with nothing to do but read or listen to the wireless. The cold and the boredom made him morose and irritable, and the enforced inactivity turned his liver sluggish. He needed exercise. Whatever the weather, he decided towards the end of yet another cold grim day, he would go out tomorrow. The sky had been heavy from mid-afternoon and threatened snow, but no matter, he could not stand the house for a further twenty-four hours without a break.

The final edge to his irritation came with the fruit tart at supper. He was in that final stage of a bad cold when the taste is not yet fully returned, appetite is poor, but there is a certain emptiness within that needs ministration of a particular kind. A bird might have done it. Half a partridge, roasted to perfection, followed by a cheese soufflé. As well ask for the moon. The daily woman, not gifted with imagination, produced plaice, of all fish the most tasteless, the most dry. When she had borne the remains of this away – he had left most of it upon his plate – she returned with a tart, and because hunger was far from being satisfied he helped himself to it liberally.

One taste was enough. Choking, spluttering, he spat out the contents of his spoon upon the plate. He got up and rang the bell.

The woman appeared, a query on her face, at the unexpected summons.

'What the devil is this stuff?'

'Jam tart, sir.'

'What sort of jam?'

'Apple jam, sir. Made from my own bottling.'

He threw down his napkin on the table.

'I guessed as much. You've been using some of those apples that I complained to you about months ago. I told you and Willis quite distinctly that I would not have any of those apples in the house.'

The woman's face became tight and drawn.

'You said, sir, not to cook the apples, or to bring them in for dessert. You said nothing about not making jam. I thought they would taste all right as jam. And I made some myself, to try. It was perfectly all right. So I made several bottles of jam from the apples Willis gave me. We always made jam here, madam and myself.'

'Well, I'm sorry for your trouble, but I can't eat it. Those apples disagreed with me in the autumn, and whether they are made into jam or whatever you like they will do so again. Take the tart away, and don't let me see it, or the jam, again. I'll have some coffee in the living-room.'

He went out of the room, trembling. It was fantastic that such a small incident should make him feel so angry. God! What fools people were. She knew, Willis knew, that he disliked the apples, loathed the taste and smell of them, but in their cheese-paring way they decided that it would save money if he was given home-made jam, jam made from the apples he particularly detested.

He swallowed down a stiff whisky and lit a cigarette.

In a moment or two she appeared with the coffee. She did not retire immediately on putting down the tray.

'Could I have a word with you, sir?'

'What is it?'

'I think it would be for the best if I gave in my notice.'

Now this, on top of the other. What a day, what an evening.

'What reason? Because I can't eat apple-tart?'

'It's not just that, sir. Somehow I feel things are very different from what they were. I have meant to speak several times.'

'I don't give much trouble, do I?'

'No, sir. Only in the old days, when madam was alive, I felt my work was appreciated. Now it's as though it didn't matter one way or the other. Nothing's ever said, and although I try to do my best I can't be sure. I think I'd be happier if I went where there was a lady again who took notice of what I did.'

'You are the best judge of that, of course. I'm sorry if you haven't liked it here lately.'

'You were away so much too, sir, this summer. When madam was alive it was never for more than a fortnight. Everything seems so changed. I don't know where I am, or Willis either.'

'So Willis is fed up too?'

'That's not for me to say, of course. I know he was upset about the apples, but that's some time ago. Perhaps he'll be speaking to you himself.'

'Perhaps he will. I had no idea I was causing so much concern to you both. All right, that's quite enough. Goodnight.'

She went out of the room. He stared moodily about him. Good riddance to them both, if that was how they felt. Things aren't the same. Everything so changed. Damned nonsense. As for Willis being upset about the apples, what infernal impudence. Hadn't he a right to do what he liked with his own tree? To hell with his cold and with the weather. He couldn't bear sitting about in front of the fire thinking about Willis and the cook. He would go down to the Green Man and forget the whole thing.

He put on his overcoat and muffler and his old cap and walked briskly down the road, and in twenty minutes he was sitting in his usual corner in the Green Man, with Mrs Hill pouring out his whisky and expressing her delight to see him back. One or two of the habitués smiled at him, asked after his health.

'Had a cold, sir? Same everywhere. Everyone's got one.'

'That's right.'

'Well, it's the time of year, isn't it?'

'Got to expect it. It's when it's on the chest it's nasty.'

'No worse than being stuffed up, like, in the head.'

'That's right. One's as bad as the other. Nothing to it.'

Likeable fellows. Friendly. Not harping at one, not bothering.

'Another whisky, please.'

'There you are, sir. Do you good. Keep out the cold.'

Mrs Hill beamed behind the bar. Large, comfortable old soul. Through a haze of smoke he heard the chatter, the deep laughter, the click of the darts, the jocular roar at a bull's eye.

'. . . and if it comes on to snow, I don't know how we shall

191

manage,' Mrs Hill was saying, 'them being so late delivering the coal. If we had a load of logs it would help us out, but what do you think they're asking? Two pounds a load. I mean to say . . .'

He leant forward and his voice sounded far away, even to himself.

'I'll let you have some logs,' he said.

Mrs Hill turned round. She had not been talking to him.

'Excuse me?' she said.

'I'll let you have some logs,' he repeated. 'Got an old tree, up at home, needed sawing down for months. Do it for you tomorrow.'

He nodded, smiling.

'Oh no, sir. I couldn't think of putting you to the trouble. The coal will turn up, never fear.'

'No trouble at all. A pleasure. Like to do it for you, the exercise, you know, do me good. Putting on weight. You count on me.'

He got down from his seat and reached, rather carefully, for his coat.

'It's apple wood,' he said. 'Do you mind apple wood?'

'Why no,' she answered, 'any wood will do. But can you spare it, sir?'

He nodded, mysteriously. It was a bargain, it was a secret.

'I'll bring it down to you in my trailer tomorrow night,' he said.

'Careful, sir,' she said, 'mind the step . . .'

He walked home, through the cold crisp night, smiling to himself. He did not remember undressing or getting into bed, but when he woke the next morning the first thought that came to his mind was the promise he had made about the tree.

It was not one of Willis's days, he realized with satisfaction.

There would be no interfering with his plan. The sky was heavy and snow had fallen in the night. More to come. But as yet nothing to worry about, nothing to hamper him.

He went through to the kitchen garden, after breakfast, to the tool shed. He took down the saw, the wedges, and the axe. He might need all of them. He ran his thumb along the edges. They would do. As he shouldered his tools and walked back to the front garden he laughed to himself, thinking that he must resemble an executioner of old days, setting forth to behead some wretched victim in the Tower.

He laid his tools down beneath the apple tree. It would be an act of mercy, really. Never had he seen anything so wretched, so utterly woebegone, as the apple tree. There couldn't be any life left in it. Not a leaf remained. Twisted, ugly, bent, it ruined the appearance of the lawn. Once it was out of the way the whole setting of the garden would change.

A snow-flake fell on to his hand, then another. He glanced down past the terrace to the dining-room window. He could see the woman laying his lunch. He went down the steps and into the house. 'Look,' he said, 'if you like to leave my lunch ready in the oven, I think I'll fend for myself today. I may be busy, and I don't want to be pinned down for time. Also it's going to snow. You had better go off early today and get home, in case it becomes really bad. I can manage perfectly well. And I prefer it.'

Perhaps she thought his decision came through offence at her giving notice the night before. Whatever she thought, he did not mind. He wanted to be alone. He wanted no face peering from the window.

She went off at about twelve-thirty, and as soon as she had gone he went to the oven and got his lunch. He meant to get it over, so that he could give up the whole short afternoon to the felling of the tree.

No more snow had fallen, apart from a few flakes that did not lie. He took off his coat, rolled up his sleeves, and seized the saw. With his left hand he ripped away the wire at the base of the tree. Then he placed the saw about a foot from the bottom and began to work it, backwards, forwards.

For the first dozen strokes all went smoothly. The saw bit into the wood, the teeth took hold. Then after a few moments the saw began to bind. He had been afraid of that.

He tried to work it free, but the opening that he had made was not yet large enough, and the tree gripped upon the saw and held it fast. He drove in the first wedge, with no result. He drove in the second, and the opening gaped a little wider, but still not wide enough to release the saw.

He pulled and tugged at the saw, to no avail. He began to lose his temper. He took up his axe and started hacking at the tree, pieces of the trunk flying outwards, scattering on the grass.

That was more like it. That was the answer.

Up and down went the heavy axe, splitting and tearing at the tree. Off came the peeling bark, the great white strips of underwood, raw and stringy. Hack at it, blast at it, gouge at the tough tissue, throw the axe away, claw at the rubbery flesh with the bare hands. Not far enough yet, go on, go on.

There goes the saw, the wedge, released. Now up with the axe again. Down there, heavy, where the stringy threads cling so steadfast. Now she's groaning, now she's splitting, now she's rocking and swaying, hanging there upon one bleeding strip. Boot her, then. That's it, kick her, kick her again, one final blow, she's over, she's falling . . . she's down . . . damn her, blast her . . . she's down, splitting the air with sound, and all her branches spread about her on the ground.

He stood back, wiping the sweat from his forehead, from his chin. The wreckage surrounded him on either side, and below him, at his feet, gaped the torn, white, jagged stump of the axed tree.

It began snowing.

His first task, after felling the apple tree, was to hack off the branches and the smaller boughs, and so to grade the wood in stacks, which made it easier to drag away.

The small stuff, bundled and roped, would do for kindling; Mrs Hill would no doubt be glad of that as well. He brought the car, with the trailer attached, to the garden gate, hard by the terrace. This chopping up of the branches was simple work; much of it could be done with a hook. The fatigue came with bending and tying the bundles, and then heaving them down past the terrace and through the gate up on to the trailer. The thicker branches he disposed of with the axe, then split them into three or four lengths, which he could also rope and drag, one by one, to the trailer.

He was fighting all the while against time. The light, what there was of it, would be gone by half past four, and the snow went on falling. The ground was already covered, and when he paused for a moment in his work, and wiped the sweat away from his face, the thin frozen flakes fell upon his lips and made their way, insidious and soft, down his collar to his neck and body. If he lifted his eyes to the sky he was blinded at once. The flakes came thicker, faster, swirling about his head, and it was as though the heaven had turned itself into a canopy of snow, ever descending, coming nearer, closer, stifling the earth. The snow fell upon the torn boughs and the hacked branches, hampering his work. If he rested but an instant to draw breath and renew his strength, it seemed to throw a protective cover, soft and white, over the pile of wood.

He could not wear gloves. If he did so he had no grip upon his hook or his axe, nor could he tie the rope and drag the branches. His fingers were numb with cold, soon they would be too stiff to bend. He had a pain now, under the heart, from the strain of dragging the stuff on to the trailer; and the work never seemed to lessen. Whenever he returned to the fallen tree the pile of wood would appear as high as ever, long boughs, short boughs, a heap of kindling there, nearly covered with the snow, which he had forgotten: all must be roped and fastened and carried or pulled away.

It was after half past four, and almost dark, when he had disposed of all the branches, and nothing now remained but to drag the trunk, already hacked into three lengths, over the terrace to the waiting trailer.

He was very nearly at the point of exhaustion. Only his will to be rid of the tree kept him to the task. His breath came slowly, painfully, and all the while the snow fell into his mouth and into his eyes and he could barely see.

He took his rope and slid it under the cold slippery trunk, knotting it fiercely. How hard and unyielding was the naked wood, and the bark was rough, hurting his numb hands.

'That's the end of you,' he muttered, 'that's your finish.'

Staggering to his feet he bore the weight of the heavy trunk over his shoulder, and began to drag it slowly down over the slope to the terrace and to the garden gate. It followed him, bump . . . bump . . . down the steps of the terrace. Heavy and lifeless, the last bare limbs of the apple tree dragged in his wake through the wet snow.

It was over. His task was done. He stood panting, one hand upon the trailer. Now nothing more remained but to take the stuff down to the Green Man before the snow made the drive impossible. He had chains for the car, he had thought of that already.

He went into the house to change the clothes that were clinging to him and to have a drink. Never mind about his fire, never mind about drawing curtains, seeing what there might be for supper, all the chores the daily woman usually did – that would come later. He must have his drink and get the wood away.

His mind was numb and weary, like his hands and his whole body. For a moment he thought of leaving the job until the following day, flopping down into the armchair, and closing his eyes. No, it would not do. Tomorrow there would be more snow, tomorrow the drive would be two or three feet deep. He knew the signs. And there would be the trailer, stuck outside the garden gate, with the pile of wood inside it, frozen white. He must make the effort and do the job tonight.

He finished his drink, changed, and went out to start the car. It was still snowing, but now that darkness had fallen a colder, cleaner feeling had come into the air, and it was freezing. The dizzy, swirling flakes came more slowly now, with preci-sion.

The engine started and he began to drive downhill, the trailer in tow. He drove slowly, and very carefully, because of the heavy load. And it was an added strain, after the hard work of the afternoon, peering through the falling snow, wiping the windscreen. Never had the lights of the Green Man shone more cheerfully as he pulled up into the little yard.

He blinked as he stood within the doorway, smiling to himself.

'Well, I've brought your wood,' he said.

Mrs Hill stared at him from behind the bar, one or two fellows turned and looked at him, and a hush fell upon the dart-players.

'You never . . .' began Mrs Hill, but he jerked his head at the door and laughed at her.

'Go and see,' he said, 'but don't ask me to unload it tonight.'

He moved to his favourite corner, chuckling to himself, and

there they all were, exclaiming and talking and laughing by the door, and he was quite a hero, the fellows crowding round with questions, and Mrs Hill pouring out his whisky and thanking him and laughing and shaking her head. 'You'll drink on the house tonight,' she said.

'Not a bit of it,' he said, 'this is my party. Rounds one and two to me. Come on, you chaps.'

It was festive, warm, jolly, and good luck to them all, he kept saying, good luck to Mrs Hill, and to himself, and to the whole world. When was Christmas? Next week, the week after? Well, here's to it, and a merry Christmas. Never mind the snow, never mind the weather. For the first time he was one of them, not isolated in his corner. For the first time he drank with them, he laughed with them, he even threw a dart with them, and there they all were in that warm stuffy smoke-filled bar, and he felt they liked him, he belonged, he was no longer 'the gentleman' from the house up the road.

The hours passed, and some of them went home, and others took their place, and he was still sitting there, hazy, comfortable, the warmth and the smoke blending together. Nothing of what he heard or saw made very much sense but somehow it did not seem to matter, for there was jolly, fat, easy-going Mrs Hill to minister to his needs, her face glowing at him over the bar.

Another face swung into his view, that of one of the labourers from the farm, with whom, in the old war days, he had shared the driving of the tractor. He leant forward, touching the fellow on the shoulder.

'What happened to the little girl?' he said.

The man lowered his tankard. 'Beg pardon, sir?' he said.

'You remember. The little land-girl. She used to milk the cows, feed the pigs, up at the farm. Pretty girl, dark curly hair, always smiling.'

Mrs Hill turned round from serving another customer.

'Does the gentleman mean May, I wonder?' she asked.

'Yes, that's it, that was the name, young May,' he said.

'Why, didn't you ever hear about it, sir?' said Mrs Hill, filling up his glass. 'We were all very much shocked at the time, everyone was talking of it, weren't they, Fred?'

'That's right, Mrs Hill.'

The man wiped his mouth with the back of his hand.

'Killed,' he said, 'thrown from the back of some chap's motor-bike. Going to be married very shortly. About four years ago, now. Dreadful thing, eh? Nice kid too.'

'We all sent a wreath, from just around,' said Mrs Hill. 'Her mother wrote back, very touched, and sent a cutting from the local paper, didn't she, Fred? Quite a big funeral they had, ever so many floral tributes. Poor May. We were all fond of May.'

'That's right,' said Fred.

'And fancy you never hearing about it, sir!' said Mrs Hill.

'No,' he said, 'no, nobody ever told me. I'm sorry about it. Very sorry.'

He stared in front of him at his half-filled glass.

The conversation went on around him but he was no longer part of the company. He was on his own again, silent, in his corner. Dead. That poor, pretty girl was dead. Thrown off a motor-bike. Been dead for three or four years. Some careless, bloody fellow, taking a corner too fast, the girl behind him, clinging on to his belt, laughing probably in his ear, and then crash . . . finish. No more curling hair, blowing about her face, no more laughter.

May, that was the name; he remembered clearly now. He could see her smiling over her shoulder, when they called to her. 'Coming,' she sang out, and put a clattering pail down in the yard and went off, whistling, with big clumping boots. He had put his arm about her and kissed her for one brief, fleeting moment. May, the land-girl, with the laughing eyes.

'Going, sir?' said Mrs Hill.

'Yes. Yes, I think I'll be going now.'

He stumbled to the entrance and opened the door. It had frozen hard during the past hour and it was no longer snowing. The heavy pall had gone from the sky and the stars shone.

'Want a hand with the car, sir?' said someone.

'No, thank you,' he said, 'I can manage.'

He unhitched the trailer and let it fall. Some of the wood lurched forward heavily. That would do tomorrow. Tomorrow, if he felt like it, he would come down again and help to unload the wood. Not tonight. He had done enough. Now he was really tired; now he was spent.

It took him some time to start the car, and before he was halfway up the side-road leading to his house he realized that he had made a mistake to bring it at all. The snow was heavy all about him, and the track he had made earlier in the evening was now covered. The car lurched and slithered, and suddenly the right wheel dipped and the whole body plunged sideways. He had got into a drift.

He climbed out and looked about him. The car was deep in the drift, impossible to move without two or three men to help him, and even then, if he went for assistance, what hope was there of trying to continue further, with the snow just as thick ahead? Better leave it. Try again in the morning, when he was fresh. No sense in hanging about now, spending half the night pushing and shoving at the car, all to no purpose. No harm would come to it, here on the side-road; nobody else would be coming this way tonight.

He started walking up the road towards his own drive. It was bad luck that he had got the car into the drift. In the centre of the road the going was not bad and the snow did not come above his ankles. He thrust his hands deep in the pockets of his overcoat and ploughed on, up the hill, the countryside a great white waste on either side of him.

He remembered that he had sent the daily woman home at midday and that the house would strike cheerless and cold on his return. The fire would have gone out, and in all probability the furnace too. The windows, uncurtained, would stare bleakly down at him, letting in the night. Supper to get into the bargain. Well, it was his own fault. No one to blame but himself. This was the moment when there should be someone waiting, someone to come running through from the living-room to the hall, opening the front-door, flooding the hall with light. 'Are you all right, darling? I was getting anxious.'

He paused for breath at the top of the hill and saw his home, shrouded by trees, at the end of the short drive. It looked dark and forbidding, without a light in any window. There was more friendliness in the open, under the bright stars, standing on the crisp white snow, than in the sombre house.

He had left the side-gate open, and he went through that way to the terrace, shutting the gate behind him. What a hush had fallen upon the garden – there was no sound at all. It was as though some spirit had come and put a spell upon the place, leaving it white and still.

He walked softly over the snow towards the apple trees.

Now the young one stood alone, above the steps, dwarfed no longer; and with her branches spread, glistening white, she belonged to the spirit world, a world of fantasy and ghosts. He wanted to stand beside the little tree and touch the branches, to make certain she was still alive, that the snow had not harmed her, so that in the spring she would blossom once again.

She was almost within his reach when he stumbled and fell, his foot twisted underneath him, caught in some obstacle hidden by the snow. He tried to move his foot but it was jammed, and he knew suddenly, by the sharpness of the pain biting his ankle, that what had trapped him was the jagged split stump of the old apple tree he had felled that afternoon.

He leant forward on his elbows, in an attempt to drag himself along the ground, but such was his position, in falling, that his leg was bent backwards, away from his foot, and every effort that he made only succeeded in imprisoning the foot still more firmly in the grip of the trunk. He felt for the ground, under the snow, but where he felt his hands touched the small broken twigs from the apple tree that had scattered there, when the tree fell, and then were covered by the falling snow. He shouted for help, knowing in his heart no one could hear.

'Let me go,' he shouted, 'let me go,' as though the thing that held him there in its mercy had the power to release him, and as he shouted tears of frustration and of fear ran down his face. He would have to lie there all night, held fast in the clutch of the old apple tree. There was no hope, no escape, until they came to find him in the morning, and supposing it was then too late, that when they came he was dead, lying stiffly in the frozen snow?

Once more he struggled to release his foot, swearing and sobbing as he did so. It was no use. He could not move. Exhausted, he laid his head upon his arms, and wept. He sank deeper, ever deeper into the snow, and when a stray piece of brushwood, cold and wet, touched his lips, it was like a hand, hesitant and timid feeling its way towards him in the darkness.

The Birds

On December the third the wind changed overnight and it was winter. Until then the autumn had been mellow, soft. The leaves had lingered on the trees, golden red, and the hedgerows were still green. The earth was rich where the plough had turned it.

Nat Hocken, because of a war-time disability, had a pension and did not work full-time at the farm. He worked three days a week, and they gave him the lighter jobs: hedging, thatching, repairs to the farm buildings.

Although he was married, with children, his was a solitary disposition; he liked best to work alone. It pleased him when he was given a bank to build up, or a gate to mend at the far end of the peninsula, where the sea surrounded the farm land on either side. Then, at midday, he would pause and eat the pasty that his wife had baked for him, and sitting on the cliff's edge would watch the birds. Autumn was best for this, better than spring. In spring the birds flew inland, purposeful, intent;

they knew where they were bound, the rhythm and ritual of their life brooked no delay. In autumn those that had not migrated overseas but remained to pass the winter were caught up in the same driving urge, but because migration was denied them followed a pattern of their own. Great flocks of them came to the peninsula, restless, uneasy, spending themselves in motion; now wheeling, circling in the sky, now settling to feed on the rich new-turned soil, but even when they fed it was as though they did so without hunger, without desire. Restlessness drove them to the skies again.

Black and white, jackdaw and gull, mingled in strange partnership, seeking some sort of liberation, never satisfied, never still. Flocks of starlings, rustling like silk, flew to fresh pasture, driven by the same necessity of movement, and the smaller birds, the finches and the larks, scattered from tree to hedge as if compelled.

Nat watched them, and he watched the sea-birds too. Down in the bay they waited for the tide. They had more patience. Oyster-catchers, redshank, sanderling, and curlew watched by the water's edge; as the slow sea sucked at the shore and then withdrew, leaving the strip of seaweed bare and the shingle churned, the sea-birds raced and ran upon the beaches. Then that same impulse to flight seized upon them too. Crying, whistling, calling, they skimmed the placid sea and left the shore. Make haste, make speed, hurry and begone: yet where, and to what purpose? The restless urge of autumn, unsatisfying, sad, had put a spell upon them and they must flock, and wheel, and cry; they must spill themselves of motion before winter came.

Perhaps, thought Nat, munching his pasty by the cliff's edge, a message comes to the birds in autumn, like a warning. Winter is coming. Many of them perish. And like people who, apprehensive of death before their time, drive themselves to work or folly, the birds do likewise.

204

The Birds

The birds had been more restless than ever this fall of the year, the agitation more marked because the days were still. As the tractor traced its path up and down the western hills, the figure of the farmer silhouetted on the driving-seat, the whole machine and the man upon it would be lost momentarily in the great cloud of wheeling, crying birds. There were many more than usual, Nat was sure of this. Always, in autumn, they followed the plough, but not in great flocks like these, nor with such clamour.

Nat remarked upon it, when hedging was finished for the day. 'Yes,' said the farmer, 'there are more birds about than usual; I've noticed it too. And daring, some of them, taking no notice of the tractor. One or two gulls came so close to my head this afternoon I thought they'd knock my cap off! As it was, I could scarcely see what I was doing, when they were overhead and I had the sun in my eyes. I have a notion the weather will change. It will be a hard winter. That's why the birds are restless.'

Nat, tramping home across the fields and down the lane to his cottage, saw the birds still flocking over the western hills, in the last glow of the sun. No wind, and the grey sea calm and full. Campion in bloom yet in the hedges, and the air mild. The farmer was right, though, and it was that night the weather turned. Nat's bedroom faced east. He woke just after two and heard the wind in the chimney. Not the storm and bluster of a sou'westerly gale, bringing the rain, but east wind, cold and dry. It sounded hollow in the chimney, and a loose slate rattled on the roof. Nat listened, and he coud hear the sea roaring in the bay. Even the air in the small bedroom had turned chill: a draught came under the skirting of the door, blowing upon the bed. Nat drew the blanket round him, leant closer to the back of his sleeping wife, and stayed wakeful, watchful, aware of misgiving without cause.

Then he heard the tapping on the window. There was no creeper on the cottage walls to break loose and scratch upon the pane. He listened, and the tapping continued until, irritated by the sound, Nat got out of bed and went to the window. He opened it, and as he did so something brushed his hand, jabbing at his knuckles, grazing the skin. Then he saw the flutter of the wings and it was gone, over the roof, behind the cottage.

It was a bird, what kind of bird he could not tell. The wind must have driven it to shelter on the sill.

He shut the window and went back to bed, but feeling his knuckles wet put his mouth to the scratch. The bird had drawn blood. Frightened, he supposed, and bewildered, the bird, seeking shelter, had stabbed at him in the darkness. Once more he settled himself to sleep.

Presently the tapping came again, this time more forceful, more insistent, and now his wife woke at the sound, and turning in the bed said to him, 'See to the window, Nat, it's rattling.'

'I've already seen to it,' he told her, 'there's some bird there, trying to get in. Can't you hear the wind? It's blowing from the east, driving the birds to shelter.'

'Send them away,' she said, 'I can't sleep with that noise.'

He went to the window for the second time, and now when he opened it there was not one bird upon the sill but half a dozen; they flew straight into his face, attacking him.

He shouted, striking out at them with his arms, scattering them; like the first one, they flew over the roof and disappeared. Quickly he let the window fall and latched it.

'Did you hear that?' he said. 'They went for me. Tried to peck my eyes.' He stood by the window, peering into the darkness, and could see nothing. His wife, heavy with sleep, murmured from the bed.

'I'm not making it up,' he said, angry at her suggestion. 'I tell you the birds were on the sill, trying to get into the room.'

Suddenly a frightened cry came from the room across the passage where the children slept.

'It's Jill,' said his wife, roused at the sound, sitting up in bed. 'Go to her, see what's the matter.'

Nat lit the candle, but when he opened the bedroom door to cross the passage the draught blew out the flame.

There came a second cry of terror, this time from both children, and stumbling into their room he felt the beating of wings about him in the darkness. The window was wide open. Through it came the birds, hitting first the ceiling and the walls, then swerving in mid-flight, turning to the children in their beds.

'It's all right, I'm here,' shouted Nat, and the children flung themselves, screaming, upon him, while in the darkness the birds rose and dived and came for him again.

'What is it, Nat, what's happened?' his wife called from the further bedroom, and swiftly he pushed the children through the door to the passage and shut it upon them, so that he was alone now, in their bedroom, with the birds.

He seized a blanket from the nearest bed, and using it as a weapon flung it to right and left about him in the air. He felt the thud of bodies, heard the fluttering of wings, but they were not yet defeated, for again and again they returned to the assault, jabbing his hands, his head, the little stabbing beaks sharp as a pointed fork. The blanket became a weapon of defence; he wound it about his head, and then in greater darkness beat at the birds with his bare hands. He dared not stumble to the door and open it, lest in doing so the birds should follow him.

How long he fought with them in the darkness he could not tell, but at last the beating of the wings about him lessened and then withdrew, and through the density of the blanket he was aware of light. He waited, listened; there was no sound except the fretful crying of one of the children from the bedroom beyond. The fluttering, the whirring of the wings had ceased.

He took the blanket from his head and stared about him. The cold grey morning light exposed the room. Dawn, and the open window, had called the living birds; the dead lay on the floor. Nat gazed at the little corpses, shocked and horrified. They were all small birds, none of any size; there must have been fifty of them lying there upon the floor. There were robins, finches, sparrows, blue tits, larks and bramblings, birds that by nature's law kept to their own flock and their own territory, and now, joining one with another in their urge for battle, had destroyed themselves against the bedroom walls, or in the strife had been destroyed by him. Some had lost feathers in the fight, others had blood, his blood, upon their beaks.

Sickened, Nat went to the window and stared out across his patch of garden to the fields.

It was bitter cold, and the ground had all the hard black look of frost. Not white frost, to shine in the morning sun, but the black frost that the east wind brings. The sea, fiercer now with the turning tide, white-capped and steep, broke harshly in the bay. Of the birds there was no sign. Not a sparrow chattered in the hedge beyond the garden gate, no early missel-thrush or blackbird pecked on the grass for worms. There was no sound at all but the east wind and the sea.

Nat shut the window and the door of the small bedroom, and went back across the passage to his own. His wife sat up in bed, one child asleep beside her, the smaller in her arms, his face bandaged. The curtains were tightly drawn across the window, the candles lit. Her face looked garish in the yellow light. She shook her head for silence.

'He's sleeping now,' she whispered, 'but only just. Something must have cut him, there was blood at the corner of his eyes. Jill said it was the birds. She said she woke up, and the birds were in the room.'

His wife looked up at Nat, searching his face for confirmation. She looked terrified, bewildered, and he did not want her to know that he was also shaken, dazed almost, by the events of the past few hours.

'There are birds in there,' he said, 'dead birds, nearly fifty of them. Robins, wrens, all the little birds from hereabouts. It's as though a madness seized them, with the east wind.' He sat down on the bed beside his wife, and held her hand. 'It's the weather,' he said, 'it must be that, it's the hard weather. They aren't the birds, maybe, from here around. They've been driven down, from up country.'

'But Nat,' whispered his wife, 'it's only this night that the weather turned. There's been no snow to drive them. And they can't be hungry yet. There's food for them, out there, in the fields.'

'It's the weather,' repeated Nat. 'I tell you, it's the weather.'

His face too was drawn and tired, like hers. They stared at one another for a while without speaking.

'I'll go downstairs and make a cup of tea,' he said.

The sight of the kitchen reassured him. The cups and saucers, neatly stacked upon the dresser, the table and chairs, his wife's roll of knitting on her basket chair, the children's toys in a corner cupboard.

He knelt down, raked out the old embers and relit the fire. The glowing sticks brought normality, the steaming kettle and the brown teapot comfort and security. He drank his tea, carried a cup up to his wife. Then he washed in the scullery, and, putting on his boots, opened the back door.

The sky was hard and leaden, and the brown hills that had

gleamed in the sun the day before looked dark and bare. The east wind, like a razor, stripped the trees, and the leaves, crackling and dry, shivered and scattered with the wind's blast. Nat stubbed the earth with his boot. It was frozen hard. He had never known a change so swift and sudden. Black winter had descended in a single night.

The children were awake now. Jill was chattering upstairs and young Johnny crying once again. Nat heard his wife's voice, soothing, comforting. Presently they came down. He had breakfast ready for them, and the routine of the day began.

'Did you drive away the birds?' asked Jill, restored to calm because of the kitchen fire, because of day, because of breakfast.

'Yes, they've all gone now,' said Nat. 'It was the east wind brought them in. They were frightened and lost, they wanted shelter.'

'They tried to peck us,' said Jill. 'They went for Johnny's eyes.'

'Fright made them do that,' said Nat. 'They didn't know where they were, in the dark bedroom.'

'I hope they won't come again,' said Jill. 'Perhaps if we put bread for them outside the window they will eat that and fly away.'

She finished her breakfast and then went for her coat and hood, her school books and her satchel. Nat said nothing, but his wife looked at him across the table. A silent message passed between them.

'I'll walk with her to the bus,' he said, 'I don't go to the farm today.'

And while the child was washing in the scullery he said to his wife, 'Keep all the windows closed, and the doors too. Just to be on the safe side. I'll go to the farm. Find out if they heard anything in the night.' Then he walked with his small daughter up the lane. She seemed to have forgotten her experience of the night before. She danced ahead of him, chasing the leaves, her face whipped with the cold and rosy under the pixie hood.

'Is it going to snow, Dad?' she said. 'It's cold enough.'

He glanced up at the bleak sky, felt the wind tear at his shoulders.

'No,' he said, 'it's not going to snow. This is a black winter, not a white one.'

All the while he searched the hedgerows for the birds, glanced over the top of them to the fields beyond, looked to the small wood above the farm where the rooks and jackdaws gathered. He saw none.

The other children waited by the bus-stop, muffled, hooded like Jill, the faces white and pinched with cold.

Jill ran to them, waving. 'My Dad says it won't snow,' she called, 'it's going to be a black winter.'

She said nothing of the birds. She began to push and struggle with another little girl. The bus came ambling up the hill. Nat saw her on to it, then turned and walked back towards the farm. It was not his day for work, but he wanted to satisfy himself that all was well. Jim, the cowman, was clattering in the yard.

'Boss around?' asked Nat.

'Gone to market,' said Jim. 'It's Tuesday, isn't it?'

He clumped off round the corner of a shed. He had no time for Nat. Nat was said to be superior. Read books, and the like. Nat had forgotten it was Tuesday. This showed how the events of the preceding night had shaken him. He went to the back door of the farm-house and heard Mrs Trigg singing in the kitchen, the wireless making a background to her song.

'Are you there, missus?' called out Nat.

She came to the door, beaming, broad, a good-tempered woman.

'Hullo, Mr Hocken,' she said. 'Can you tell me where this

211

cold is coming from? Is it Russia? I've never seen such a change. And it's going on, the wireless says. Something to do with the Arctic circle.'

'We didn't turn on the wireless this morning,' said Nat. 'Fact is, we had trouble in the night.'

'Kiddies poorly?'

'No . . .' He hardly knew how to explain it. Now, in daylight, the battle of the birds would sound absurd.

He tried to tell Mrs Trigg what had happened, but he could see from her eyes that she thought his story was the result of a nightmare.

'Sure they were real birds,' she said, smiling, 'with proper feathers and all? Not the funny-shaped kind, that the men see after closing hours on a Saturday night?'

'Mrs Trigg,' he said, 'there are fifty dead birds, robins, wrens, and such, lying low on the floor of the children's bedroom. They went for me; they tried to go for young Johnny's eyes.'

Mrs Trigg stared at him doubtfully.

'Well there, now,' she answered, 'I suppose the weather brought them. Once in the bedroom, they wouldn't know where they were to. Foreign birds maybe, from that Arctic circle.'

'No,' said Nat, 'they were the birds you see about here every day.'

'Funny thing,' said Mrs Trigg, 'no explaining it, really. You ought to write up and ask the *Guardian*. They'd have some answer for it. Well, I must be getting on.'

She nodded, smiled, and went back into the kitchen.

Nat, dissatisfied, turned to the farm-gate. Had it not been for those corpses on the bedroom floor, which he must now collect and bury somewhere, he would have considered the tale exaggeration too.

Jim was standing by the gate.

'Had any trouble with the birds?' asked Nat.

'Birds? What birds?'

'We got them up our place last night. Scores of them, came in the children's bedroom. Quite savage they were.'

'Oh?' It took time for anything to penetrate Jim's head. 'Never heard of birds acting savage,' he said at length. 'They get tame, like, sometimes. I've seen them come to the windows for crumbs.'

'These birds last night weren't tame.'

'No? Cold maybe. Hungry. You put out some crumbs.'

Jim was no more interested than Mrs Trigg had been. It was, Nat thought, like air-raids in the war. No one down this end of the country knew what the Plymouth folk had seen and suffered. You had to endure something yourself before it touched you. He walked back along the lane and crossed the stile to his cottage. He found his wife in the kitchen with young Johnny.

'See anyone?' she asked.

'Mrs Trigg and Jim,' he answered. 'I don't think they believed me. Anyway, nothing wrong up there.'

'You might take the birds away,' she said. 'I daren't go into the room to make the beds until you do. I'm scared.'

'Nothing to scare you now,' said Nat. 'They're dead, aren't they?'

He went up with a sack and dropped the stiff bodies into it, one by one. Yes, there were fifty of them, all told. Just the ordinary common birds of the hedgerow, nothing as large even as a thrush. It must have been fright that made them act the way they did. Blue tits, wrens, it was incredible to think of the power of their small beaks, jabbing at his face and hands the night before. He took the sack out into the garden and was faced now with a fresh problem. The ground was too hard to dig. It was frozen solid, yet no snow had fallen, nothing had happened in the past hours but the coming of the east

213

wind. It was unnatural, queer. The weather prophets must be right. The change was something connected with the Arctic circle.

The wind seemed to cut him to the bone as he stood there, uncertainly, holding the sack. He could see the white-capped seas breaking down under in the bay. He decided to take the birds to the shore and bury them.

When he reached the beach below the headland he could scarcely stand, the force of the east wind was so strong. It hurt to draw breath, and his bare hands were blue. Never had he known such cold, not in all the bad winters he could remember. It was low tide. He crunched his way over the shingle to the softer sand and then, his back to the wind, ground a pit in the sand with his heel. He meant to drop the birds into it, but as he opened up the sack the force of the wind carried them, lifted them, as though in flight again, and they were blown away from him along the beach, tossed like feathers, spread and scattered, the bodies of the fifty frozen birds. There was something ugly in the sight. He did not like it. The dead birds were swept away from him by the wind.

'The tide will take them when it turns,' he said to himself.

He looked out to sea and watched the crested breakers, combing green. They rose stiffly, curled, and broke again, and because it was ebb tide the roar was distant, more remote, lacking the sound and thunder of the flood.

Then he saw them. The gulls. Out there, riding the seas.

What he had thought at first to be the white caps of the waves were gulls. Hundreds, thousands, tens of thousands . . . They rose and fell in the trough of the seas, heads to the wind, like a mighty fleet at anchor, waiting on the tide. To eastward, and to the west, the gulls were there. They stretched as far as his eye could reach, in close formation, line upon line. Had the sea been still they would have covered the bay like a white cloud, head to head, body packed to body. Only the east wind, whipping the sea to breakers, hid them from the shore.

Nat turned, and leaving the beach climbed the steep path home. Someone should know of this. Someone should be told. Something was happening, because of the east wind and the weather, that he did not understand. He wondered if he should go to the call-box by the bus-stop and ring up the police. Yet what could they do? What could anyone do? Tens and thousands of gulls riding the sea there, in the bay, because of storm, because of hunger. The police would think him mad, or drunk, or take the statement from him with great calm. 'Thank you. Yes, the matter has already been reported. The hard weather is driving the birds inland in great numbers.' Nat looked about him. Still no sign of any other bird. Perhaps the cold had sent them all from up country? As he drew near to the cottage his wife came to meet him, at the door. She called to him, excited. 'Nat,' she said, 'it's on the wireless. They've just read out a special news bulletin. I've written it down.'

'What's on the wireless?' he said.

'About the birds,' she said. 'It's not only here, it's everywhere. In London, all over the country. Something has happened to the birds.'

Together they went into the kitchen. He read the piece of paper lying on the table.

'Statement from the Home Office at eleven a.m. today. Reports from all over the country are coming in hourly about the vast quantity of birds flocking above towns, villages, and outlying districts, causing obstruction and damage and even attacking individuals. It is thought that the Arctic air stream, at present covering the British Isles, is causing birds to migrate south in immense numbers, and that intense hunger may drive these birds to attack human beings. Householders are warned

215

to see to their windows, doors, and chimneys, and to take reasonable precautions for the safety of their children. A further statement will be issued later.'

A kind of excitement seized Nat; he looked at his wife in triumph.

'There you are,' he said, 'let's hope they'll hear that at the farm. Mrs Trigg will know it wasn't any story. It's true. All over the country. I've been telling myself all morning there's something wrong. And just now, down on the beach, I looked out to sea and there are gulls, thousands of them, tens of thousands, you couldn't put a pin between their heads, and they're all out there, riding on the sea, waiting.'

'What are they waiting for, Nat?' she asked.

He stared at her, then looked down again at the piece of paper.

'I don't know,' he said slowly. 'It says here the birds are hungry.'

He went over to the drawer where he kept his hammer and tools.

'What are you going to do, Nat?'

'See to the windows and the chimneys too, like they tell you.'

'You think they would break in, with the windows shut? Those sparrows and robins and such? Why, how could they?'

He did not answer. He was not thinking of the robins and the sparrows. He was thinking of the gulls . . .

He went upstairs and worked there the rest of the morning, boarding the windows of the bedrooms, filling up the chimney bases. Good job it was his free day and he was not working at the farm. It reminded him of the old days, at the beginning of the war. He was not married then, and he had made all the blackout boards for his mother's house in Plymouth. Made the shelter too. Not that it had been of any use, when the moment came. He wondered if they would take these precautions up at the farm. He doubted it. Too easy-going, Harry Trigg and his missus. Maybe they'd laugh at the whole thing. Go off to a dance or a whist drive.

'Dinner's ready.' She called him, from the kitchen.

'All right. Coming down.'

He was pleased with his handiwork. The frames fitted nicely over the little panes and at the base of the chimneys.

When dinner was over and his wife was washing up, Nat switched on the one o'clock news. The same announcement was repeated, the one which she had taken down during the morning, but the news bulletin enlarged upon it. 'The flocks of birds have caused dislocation in all areas,' read the announcer, 'and in London the sky was so dense at ten o'clock this morning that it seemed as if the city was covered by a vast black cloud.

'The birds settled on roof-tops, on window ledges and on chimneys. The species included blackbird, thrush, the common house-sparrow, and, as might be expected in the metropolis, a vast quantity of pigeons and starlings, and that frequenter of the London river, the black-headed gull. The sight has been so unusual that traffic came to a standstill in many thoroughfares, work was abandoned in shops and offices, and the streets and pavements were crowded with people standing about to watch the birds.'

Various incidents were recounted, the suspected reason of cold and hunger stated again, and warnings to householders repeated. The announcer's voice was smooth and suave. Nat had the impression that this man, in particular, treated the whole business as he would an elaborate joke. There would be others like him, hundreds of them, who did not know what it was to struggle in darkness with a flock of birds. There would be parties tonight in London, like the ones they gave on election nights. People standing about, shouting and laughing, getting drunk. 'Come and watch the birds!'

Nat switched off the wireless. He got up and started work on the kitchen windows. His wife watched him, young Johnny at her heels.

'What, boards for down here too?' she said. 'Why, I'll have to light up before three o'clock. I see no call for boards down here.'

'Better be sure than sorry,' answered Nat. 'I'm not going to take any chances.'

'What they ought to do,' she said, 'is to call the army out and shoot the birds. That would soon scare them off.'

'Let them try,' said Nat. 'How'd they set about it?'

'They have the army to the docks,' she answered, 'when the dockers strike. The soldiers go down and unload the ships.'

'Yes,' said Nat, 'and the population of London is eight million or more. Think of all the buildings, all the flats, and houses. Do you think they've enough soldiers to go round shooting birds from every roof?'

'I don't know. But something should be done. They ought to do something.'

Nat thought to himself that 'they' were no doubt considering the problem at that very moment, but whatever 'they' decided to do in London and the big cities would not help the people here, three hundred miles away. Each householder must look after his own.

'How are we off for food?' he said.

'Now, Nat, whatever next?'

'Never mind. What have you got in the larder?'

'It's shopping day tomorrow, you know that. I don't keep uncooked food hanging about, it goes off. Butcher doesn't call till the day after. But I can bring back something when I go in tomorrow.'

Nat did not want to scare her. He thought it possible that she might not go to town tomorrow. He looked in the larder for himself, and in the cupboard where she kept her tins. They would do, for a couple of days. Bread was low.

'What about the baker?'

'He comes tomorrow too.'

He saw she had flour. If the baker did not call she had enough to bake one loaf.

'We'd be better off in the old days,' he said, 'when the women baked twice a week, and had pilchards salted, and there was food for a family to last a siege, if need be.'

'I've tried the children with tinned fish, they don't like it,' she said.

Nat went on hammering the boards across the kitchen windows. Candles. They were low in candles too. That must be another thing she meant to buy tomorrow. Well, it could not be helped. They must go early to bed tonight. That was, if . . .

He got up and went out of the back door and stood in the garden, looking down towards the sea. There had been no sun all day, and now, at barely three o'clock, a kind of darkness had already come, the sky sullen, heavy, colourless like salt. He could hear the vicious sea drumming on the rocks. He walked down the path, half-way to the beach. And then he stopped. He could see the tide had turned. The rock that had shown in mid-morning was now covered, but it was not the sea that held his eyes. The gulls had risen. They were circling, hundreds of them, thousands of them, lifting their wings against the wind. It was the gulls that made the darkening of the sky. And they were silent. They made not a sound. They just went on soaring and circling, rising, falling, trying their strength against the wind.

Nat turned. He ran up the path, back to the cottage.

'I'm going for Jill,' he said. 'I'll wait for her, at the bus-stop.'

'What's the matter?' asked his wife. 'You've gone quite white.'

'Keep Johnny inside,' he said. 'Keep the door shut. Light up now, and draw the curtains.'

'It's only just gone three,' she said.

'Never mind. Do what I tell you.'

He looked inside the toolshed, outside the back door. Nothing there of much use. A spade was too heavy, and a fork no good. He took the hoe. It was the only possible tool, and light enough to carry.

He started walking up the lane to the bus-stop, and now and again glanced back over his shoulder.

The gulls had risen higher now, their circles were broader, wider, they were spreading out in huge formation across the sky.

He hurried on; although he knew the bus would not come to the top of the hill before four o'clock he had to hurry. He passed no one on the way. He was glad of this. No time to stop and chatter.

At the top of the hill he waited. He was much too soon. There was half an hour still to go. The east wind came whipping across the fields from the higher ground. He stamped his feet and blew upon his hands. In the distance he could see the clay hills, white and clean, against the heavy pallor of the sky. Something black rose from behind them, like a smudge at first, then widening, becoming deeper, and the smudge became a cloud, and the cloud divided again into five other clouds, spreading north, east, south and west, and they were not clouds at all; they were birds. He watched them travel across the sky, and as one section passed overhead, within two or three hundred feet of him, he knew from their speed, they were bound inland, up country, they had no business with the people here on the peninsula. They were rooks, crows, jackdaws, magpies, jays, all birds that usually preyed upon the smaller species; but this afternoon they were bound on some other mission.

'They've been given the towns,' thought Nat, 'they know what they have to do. We don't matter so much here. The gulls will serve for us. The others go to the towns.'

He went to the call-box, stepped inside and lifted the receiver. The exchange would do. They would pass the message on.

'I'm speaking from Highway,' he said, 'by the bus-stop. I want to report large formations of birds travelling up country. The gulls are also forming in the bay.'

'All right,' answered the voice, laconic, weary.

'You'll be sure and pass this message on to the proper quarter?'

'Yes . . . yes . . .' Impatient now, fed-up. The buzzing note resumed.

'She's another,' thought Nat, 'she doesn't care. Maybe she's had to answer calls all day. She hopes to go to the pictures tonight. She'll squeeze some fellow's hand, and point up at the sky, and say "Look at all them birds!" She doesn't care.'

The bus came lumbering up the hill. Jill climbed out and three or four other children. The bus went on towards the town.

'What's the hoe for, Dad?'

They crowded around him, laughing, pointing.

'I just brought it along,' he said. 'Come on now, let's get home. It's cold, no hanging about. Here, you. I'll watch you across the fields, see how fast you can run.'

He was speaking to Jill's companions who came from different families, living in the council houses. A short cut would take them to the cottages.

'We want to play a bit in the lane,' said one of them.

'No, you don't. You go off home, or I'll tell your mammy.'

They whispered to one another, round-eyed, then scuttled off across the fields. Jill stared at her father, her mouth sullen.

'We always play in the lane,' she said.

'Not tonight, you don't,' he said. 'Come on now, no dawdling.'

He could see the gulls now, circling the fields, coming in towards the land. Still silent. Still no sound.

'Look, Dad, look over there, look at all the gulls.'

'Yes. Hurry, now.'

'Where are they flying to? Where are they going?'

'Up country, I dare say. Where it's warmer.'

He seized her hand and dragged her after him along the lane.

'Don't go so fast. I can't keep up.'

The gulls were copying the rooks and crows. They were spreading out in formation across the sky. They headed, in bands of thousands, to the four compass points.

'Dad, what is it? What are the gulls doing?'

They were not intent upon their flight, as the crows, as the jackdaws had been. They still circled overhead. Nor did they fly so high. It was as though they waited upon some signal. As though some decision had yet to be given. The order was not clear.

'Do you want me to carry you, Jill? Here, come pick-a-back.'

This way he might put on speed; but he was wrong. Jill was heavy. She kept slipping. And she was crying too. His sense of urgency, of fear, had communicated itself to the child.

'I wish the gulls would go away. I don't like them. They're coming closer to the lane.'

He put her down again. He started running, swinging Jill after him. As they went past the farm turning he saw the farmer backing his car out of the garage. Nat called to him.

'Can you give us a lift?' he said.

'What's that?'

Mr Trigg turned in the driving seat and stared at them. Then a smile came to his cheerful, rubicund face.

'It looks as though we're in for some fun,' he said. 'Have you seen the gulls? Jim and I are going to take a crack at them. Everyone's gone bird crazy, talking of nothing else. I hear you were troubled in the night. Want a gun?'

Nat shook his head.

The small car was packed. There was just room for Jill, if she crouched on top of petrol tins on the back seat.

'I don't want a gun,' said Nat, 'but I'd be obliged if you'd run Jill home. She's scared of the birds.'

He spoke briefly. He did not want to talk in front of Jill.

'OK,' said the farmer, 'I'll take her home. Why don't you stop behind and join the shooting match? We'll make the feathers fly.'

Jill climbed in, and turning the car the driver sped up the lane. Nat followed after. Trigg must be crazy. What use was a gun against a sky of birds?

Now Nat was not responsible for Jill he had time to look about him. The birds were circling still, above the fields. Mostly herring gull, but the black-headed gull amongst them. Usually they kept apart. Now they were united. Some bond had brought them together. It was the black-backed gull that attacked the smaller birds, and even new-born lambs, so he'd heard. He'd never seen it done. He remembered this now, though, looking above him in the sky. They were coming in towards the farm. They were circling lower in the sky, and the black-backed gulls were to the front, the black-backed gulls were leading. The farm, then, was their target. They were making for the farm.

Nat increased his pace towards his own cottage. He saw the farmer's car turn and come back along the lane. It drew up beside him with a jerk.

'The kid has run inside,' said the farmer. 'Your wife was watching for her. Well, what do you make of it? They're saying in town the Russians have done it. The Russians have poisoned the birds.'

'How could they do that?' asked Nat.

'Don't ask me. You know how stories get around. Will you join my shooting match?'

'No, I'll get along home. The wife will be worried else.'

'My missus says if you could eat gull, there'd be some sense in it,' said Trigg, 'we'd have roast gull, baked gull, and pickle 'em into the bargain. You wait until I let off a few barrels into the brutes. That'll scare 'em.'

'Have you boarded your windows?' asked Nat.

'No. Lot of nonsense. They like to scare you on the wireless. I've had more to do today than to go round boarding up my windows.'

'I'd board them now, if I were you.'

'Garn. You're windy. Like to come to our place to sleep?'

'No, thanks all the same.'

'All right. See you in the morning. Give you a gull breakfast.'

The farmer grinned and turned his car to the farm entrance.

Nat hurried on. Past the little wood, past the old barn, and then across the stile to the remaining field.

As he jumped the stile he heard the whirr of wings. A black-backed gull dived down at him from the sky, missed, swerved in flight, and rose to dive again. In a moment it was joined by others, six, seven, a dozen, black-backed and herring mixed. Nat dropped his hoe. The hoe was useless. Covering his head with his arms he ran towards the cottage. They kept coming at him from the air, silent save for the beating wings. The terrible, fluttering wings. He could feel the blood on his hands, his wrists, his neck. Each stab of a swooping beak tore his flesh. If only he could keep them from his eyes. Nothing else mattered. He must keep them from his eyes. They had not learnt yet how to cling to a shoulder, how to rip clothing, how to dive in mass upon the head, upon the body. But with each dive, with each attack, they became bolder. And they had no thought for themselves. When they dived low and missed, they crashed, bruised and broken, on the ground. As Nat ran he stumbled, kicking their spent bodies in front of him.

He found the door, he hammered upon it with his bleeding hands. Because of the boarded windows no light shone. Everything was dark.

'Let me in,' he shouted, 'it's Nat. Let me in.'

He shouted loud to make himself heard above the whirr of the gulls' wings.

Then he saw the gannet, poised for the dive, above him in the sky. The gulls circled, retired, soared, one with another, against the wind. Only the gannet remained. One single gannet, above him in the sky. The wings folded suddenly to its body. It dropped like a stone. Nat screamed, and the door opened. He stumbled across the threshold, and his wife threw her weight against the door.

They heard the thud of the gannet as it fell.

His wife dressed his wounds. They were not deep. The backs of his hands had suffered most, and his wrists. Had he not worn a cap they would have reached his head. As to the gannet . . . the gannet could have split his skull.

The children were crying, of course. They had seen the blood on their father's hands.

'It's all right now,' he told them. 'I'm not hurt. Just a few scratches. You play with Johnny, Jill. Mammy will wash these cuts.'

He half shut the door to the scullery, so that they could

not see. His wife was ashen. She began running water from the sink.

'I saw them overhead,' she whispered. 'They began collecting just as Jill ran in with Mr Trigg. I shut the door fast, and it jammed. That's why I couldn't open it at once, when you came.'

'Thank God they waited for me,' he said. 'Jill would have fallen at once. One bird alone would have done it.'

Furtively, so as not to alarm the children, they whispered together, as she bandaged his hands and the back of his neck.

'They're flying inland,' he said, 'thousands of them. Rooks, crows, all the bigger birds. I saw them from the bus-stop. They're making for the towns.'

'But what can they do, Nat?'

'They'll attack. Go for everyone out in the streets. Then they'll try the windows, the chimneys.'

'Why don't the authorities do something? Why don't they get the army, get machine-guns, anything?'

'There's been no time. Nobody's prepared. We'll hear what they have to say on the six o'clock news.'

Nat went back into the kitchen, followed by his wife. Johnny was playing quietly on the floor. Only Jill looked anxious.

'I can hear the birds,' she said. 'Listen, Dad.'

Nat listened. Muffled sounds came from the windows, from the door. Wings brushing the surface, sliding, scraping, seeking a way of entry. The sound of many bodies, pressed together, shuffling on the sills. Now and again came a thud, a crash, as some bird dived and fell. 'Some of them will kill themselves that way,' he thought, 'but not enough. Never enough.'

'All right,' he said aloud, 'I've got boards over the windows, Jill. The birds can't get in.'

He went and examined all the windows. His work had been thorough. Every gap was closed. He would make extra certain, however. He found wedges, pieces of old tin, strips of wood and metal, and fastened them at the sides to reinforce the boards. His hammering helped to deafen the sound of the birds, the shuffling, the tapping, and more ominous – he did not want his wife or the children to hear it – the splinter of cracked glass.

'Turn on the wireless,' he said, 'let's have the wireless.'

This would drown the sound also. He went upstairs to the bedrooms and reinforced the windows there. Now he could hear the birds on the roof, the scraping of claws, a sliding, jostling sound.

He decided they must sleep in the kitchen, keep up the fire, bring down the mattresses and lay them out on the floor. He was afraid of the bedroom chimneys. The boards he had placed at the chimney bases might give way. In the kitchen they would be safe, because of the fire. He would have to make a joke of it. Pretend to the children they were playing at camp. If the worst happened, and the birds forced an entry down the bedroom chimneys, it would be hours, days perhaps, before they could break down the doors. The birds would be imprisoned in the bedrooms. They could do no harm there. Crowded together, they would stifle and die.

He began to bring the mattresses downstairs. At sight of them his wife's eyes widened in apprehension. She thought the birds had already broken in upstairs.

'All right,' he said cheerfully, 'we'll all sleep together in the kitchen tonight. More cosy here by the fire. Then we shan't be worried by those silly old birds tapping at the windows.'

He made the children help him rearrange the furniture, and he took the precaution of moving the dresser, with his wife's help, across the window. It fitted well. It was an added safeguard. The mattresses could now be lain, one beside the other, against the wall where the dresser had stood.

'We're safe enough now,' he thought, 'we're snug and tight, like an air-raid shelter. We can hold out. It's just the food that worries me. Food, and coal for the fire. We've enough for two or three days, not more. By that time . . .'

No use thinking ahead as far as that. And they'd be giving directions on the wireless. People would be told what to do. And now, in the midst of many problems, he realized that it was dance music only coming over the air. Not Children's Hour, as it should have been. He glanced at the dial. Yes, they were on the Home Service all right. Dance records. He switched to the Light programme. He knew the reason. The usual programmes had been abandoned. This only happened at exceptional times. Elections, and such. He tried to remember if it had happened in the war, during the heavy raids on London. But of course. The BBC was not stationed in London during the war. The programmes were broadcast from other, temporary quarters. 'We're better off here,' he thought, 'we're better off here in the kitchen, with the windows and the doors boarded, than they are up in the towns. Thank God we're not in the towns.'

At six o'clock the records ceased. The time signal was given. No matter if it scared the children, he must hear the news. There was a pause after the pips. Then the announcer spoke. His voice was solemn, grave. Quite different from midday.

'This is London,' he said. 'A National Emergency was proclaimed at four o'clock this afternoon. Measures are being taken to safeguard the lives and property of the population, but it must be understood that these are not easy to effect immediately, owing to the unforeseen and unparalleled nature of the present crisis. Every householder must take precautions to his own building, and where several people live together, as in flats and apartments, they must unite to do the utmost they can to prevent entry. It is absolutely imperative that every individual stays indoors tonight, and that no one at all remains

228

on the streets, or roads, or anywhere without doors. The birds, in vast numbers, are attacking anyone on sight, and have already begun an assault upon buildings; but these, with due care, should be impenetrable. The population is asked to remain calm, and not to panic. Owing to the exceptional nature of the emergency, there will be no further transmission from any broadcasting station until seven a.m. tomorrow.'

They played the National Anthem. Nothing more happened. Nat switched off the set. He looked at his wife. She stared back at him.

'What's it mean?' said Jill. 'What did the news say?'

'There won't be any more programmes tonight,' said Nat. 'There's been a breakdown at the BBC.'

'Is it the birds?' asked Jill. 'Have the birds done it?'

'No,' said Nat, 'it's just that everyone's very busy, and then of course they have to get rid of the birds, messing everything up, in the towns. Well, we can manage without the wireless for one evening.'

'I wish we had a gramophone,' said Jill, 'that would be better than nothing.'

She had her face turned to the dresser, backed against the windows. Try as they did to ignore it, they were all aware of the shuffling, the stabbing, the persistent beating and sweeping of wings.

'We'll have supper early,' suggested Nat, 'something for a treat. Ask Mammy. Toasted cheese, eh? Something we all like?'

He winked and nodded at his wife. He wanted the look of dread, of apprehension, to go from Jill's face.

He helped with the supper, whistling, singing, making as much clatter as he could, and it seemed to him that the shuffling and the tapping were not so intense as they had been at first. Presently he went up to the bedrooms and listened, and he no longer heard the jostling for place upon the roof.

'They've got reasoning powers,' he thought, 'they know it's hard to break in here. They'll try elsewhere. They won't waste their time with us.'

Supper passed without incident, and then, when they were clearing away, they heard a new sound, droning, familiar, a sound they all knew and understood.

His wife looked up at him, her face alight. 'It's planes,' she said, 'they're sending out planes after the birds. That's what I said they ought to do, all along. That will get them. Isn't that gun-fire? Can't you hear guns?'

It might be gun-fire, out at sea. Nat could not tell. Big naval guns might have an effect upon the gulls out at sea, but the gulls were inland now. The guns couldn't shell the shore, because of the population.

'It's good, isn't it,' said his wife, 'to hear the planes?'

And Jill, catching her enthusiasm, jumped up and down with Johnny. 'The planes will get the birds. The planes will shoot them.'

Just then they heard a crash about two miles distant, followed by a second, then a third. The droning became more distant, passed away out to sea.

'What was that?' asked his wife. 'Were they dropping bombs on the birds?'

'I don't know,' answered Nat, 'I don't think so.'

He did not want to tell her that the sound they had heard was the crashing of aircraft. It was, he had no doubt, a venture on the part of the authorities to send out reconnaissance forces, but they might have known the venture was suicidal. What could aircraft do against birds that flung themselves to death against propeller and fuselage, but hurtle to the ground themselves? This was being tried now, he supposed, over the whole country. And at a cost. Someone high up had lost his head.

'Where have the planes gone, Dad?' asked Jill.

'Back to base,' he said. 'Come on, now, time to tuck down for bed.'

It kept his wife occupied, undressing the children before the fire, seeing to the bedding, one thing and another, while he went round the cottage again, making sure that nothing had worked loose. There was no further drone of aircraft, and the naval guns had ceased. 'Waste of life and effort,' Nat said to himself. 'We can't destroy enough of them that way. Cost too heavy. There's always gas. Maybe they'll try spraying with gas, mustard gas. We'll be warned first, of course, if they do. There's one thing, the best brains of the country will be on to it tonight.'

Somehow the thought reassured him. He had a picture of scientists, naturalists, technicians, and all those chaps they called the back-room boys, summoned to a council; they'd be working on the problem now. This was not a job for the government, for the chiefs-of-staff – they would merely carry out the orders of the scientists.

'They'll have to be ruthless,' he thought. 'Where the trouble's worst they'll have to risk more lives, if they use gas. All the livestock, too, and the soil – all contaminated. As long as everyone doesn't panic. That's the trouble. People panicking, losing their heads. The BBC was right to warn us of that.'

Upstairs in the bedrooms all was quiet. No further scraping and stabbing at the windows. A lull in battle. Forces regrouping. Wasn't that what they called it, in the old war-time bulletins? The wind hadn't dropped, though. He could still hear it, roaring in the chimneys. And the sea breaking down on the shore. Then he remembered the tide. The tide would be on the turn. Maybe the lull in battle was because of the tide. There was some law the birds obeyed, and it was all to do with the east wind and the tide.

He glanced at his watch. Nearly eight o'clock. It must have

gone high water an hour ago. That explained the lull: the birds attacked with the flood tide. It might not work that way inland, up country, but it seemed as if it was so this way on the coast. He reckoned the time limit in his head. They had six hours to go, without attack. When the tide turned again, around one-twenty in the morning, the birds would come back . . .

There were two things he could do. The first to rest, with his wife and the children, and all of them snatch what sleep they could, until the small hours. The second to go out, see how they were faring at the farm, see if the telephone was still working there, so that they might get news from the exchange.

He called softly to his wife, who had just settled the children. She came half-way up the stairs and he whispered to her.

'You're not to go,' she said at once, 'you're not to go and leave me alone with the children. I can't stand it.'

Her voice rose hysterically. He hushed her, calmed her.

'All right,' he said, 'all right. I'll wait till morning. And we'll get the wireless bulletin then too, at seven. But in the morning, when the tide ebbs again, I'll try for the farm, and they may let us have bread and potatoes, and milk too.'

His mind was busy again, planning against emergency. They would not have milked, of course, this evening. The cows would be standing by the gate, waiting in the yard, with the household inside, battened behind boards, as they were here at the cottage. That is, if they had time to take precautions. He thought of the farmer, Trigg, smiling at him from the car. There would have been no shooting party, not tonight.

The children were asleep. His wife, still clothed, was sitting on her mattress. She watched him, her eyes nervous.

'What are you going to do?' she whispered.

He shook his head for silence. Softly, stealthily, he opened the back door and looked outside.

It was pitch dark. The wind was blowing harder than ever, coming in steady gusts, icy, from the sea. He kicked at the step outside the door. It was heaped with birds. There were dead birds everywhere. Under the windows, against the walls. These were the suicides, the divers, the ones with broken necks. Wherever he looked he saw dead birds. No trace of the living. The living had flown seaward with the turn of the tide. The gulls would be riding the seas now, as they had done in the forenoon.

In the far distance, on the hill where the tractor had been two days before, something was burning. One of the aircraft that had crashed; the fire, fanned by the wind, had set light to a stack.

He looked at the bodies of the birds, and he had a notion that if he heaped them, one upon the other, on the window sills they would make added protection for the next attack. Not much, perhaps, but something. The bodies would have to be clawed at, pecked, and dragged aside, before the living birds gained purchase on the sills and attacked the panes. He set to work in the darkness. It was queer; he hated touching them. The bodies were still warm and bloody. The blood matted their feathers. He felt his stomach turn, but he went on with his work. He noticed, grimly, that every window-pane was shattered. Only the boards had kept the birds from breaking in. He stuffed the cracked panes with the bleeding bodies of the birds.

When he had finished he went back into the cottage. He barricaded the kitchen door, made it doubly secure. He took off his bandages, sticky with the birds' blood, not with his own cuts, and put on fresh plaster.

His wife had made him cocoa and he drank it thirstily. He was very tired.

'All right,' he said, smiling, 'don't worry. We'll get through.'

He lay down on his mattress and closed his eyes. He slept at once. He dreamt uneasily, because through his dreams there ran a thread of something forgotten. Some piece of work, neglected, that he should have done. Some precaution that he had known well but had not taken, and he could not put a name to it in his dreams. It was connected in some way with the burning aircraft and the stack upon the hill. He went on sleeping, though; he did not awake. It was his wife shaking his shoulder that awoke him finally.

'They've begun,' she sobbed, 'they've started this last hour, I can't listen to it any longer, alone. There's something smelling bad too, something burning.'

Then he remembered. He had forgotten to make up the fire. It was smouldering, nearly out. He got up swiftly and lit the lamp. The hammering had started at the windows and the doors, but it was not that he minded now. It was the smell of singed feathers. The smell filled the kitchen. He knew at once what it was. The birds were coming down the chimney, squeezing their way down to the kitchen range.

He got sticks and paper and put them on the embers, then reached for the can of paraffin.

'Stand back,' he shouted to his wife, 'we've got to risk this.'

He threw the paraffin on to the fire. The flame roared up the pipe, and down upon the fire fell the scorched, blackened bodies of the birds.

The children woke, crying, 'What is it?' said Jill. 'What's happened?'

Nat had no time to answer. He was raking the bodies from the chimney, clawing them out on to the floor. The flames still roared, and the danger of the chimney catching fire was one he had to take. The flames would send away the living birds from the chimney top. The lower joint was the difficulty, though. This was choked with the smouldering helpless bodies of the birds caught by fire. He scarcely heeded the attack on the windows and the door: let them beat their wings, break their beaks, lose their lives, in the attempt to force an entry into his home. They would not break in. He thanked God he had one of the old cottages, with small windows, stout walls. Not like the new council houses. Heaven help them up the lane, in the new council houses.

'Stop crying,' he called to the children. 'There's nothing to be afraid of, stop crying.'

He went on raking at the burning, smouldering bodies as they fell into the fire.

'This'll fetch them,' he said to himself, 'the draught and the flames together. We're all right, as long as the chimney doesn't catch. I ought to be shot for this. It's all my fault. Last thing I should have made up the fire. I knew there was something.'

Amid the scratching and tearing at the window boards came the sudden homely striking of the kitchen clock. Three a.m. A little more than four hours yet to go. He could not be sure of the exact time of high water. He reckoned it would not turn much before half past seven, twenty to eight.

'Light up the primus,' he said to his wife. 'Make us some tea, and the kids some cocoa. No use sitting around doing nothing.'

That was the line. Keep her busy, and the children too. Move about, eat, drink; always best to be on the go.

He waited by the range. The flames were dying. But no more blackened bodies fell from the chimney. He thrust his poker up as far as it could go and found nothing. It was clear. The chimney was clear. He wiped the sweat from his forehead.

'Come on now, Jill,' he said, 'bring me some more sticks. We'll have a good fire going directly.' She wouldn't come near him, though. She was staring at the heaped singed bodies of the birds.

'Never mind them,' he said, 'we'll put those in the passage when I've got the fire steady.'

The danger of the chimney was over. It could not happen again, not if the fire was kept burning day and night.

'I'll have to get more fuel from the farm tomorrow,' he thought. 'This will never last. I'll manage, though. I can do all that with the ebb tide. It can be worked, fetching what we need, when the tide's turned. We've just got to adapt ourselves, that's all.'

They drank tea and cocoa and ate slices of bread and Bovril. Only half a loaf left, Nat noticed. Never mind though, they'd get by.

'Stop it,' said young Johnny, pointing to the windows with his spoon, 'stop it, you old birds.'

'That's right,' said Nat, smiling, 'we don't want the old beggars, do we? Had enough of 'em.'

They began to cheer when they heard the thud of the suicide birds.

'There's another, Dad,' cried Jill, 'he's done for.'

'He's had it,' said Nat, 'there he goes, the blighter.'

This was the way to face up to it. This was the spirit. If they could keep this up, hang on like this until seven, when the first news bulletin came through, they would not have done too badly.

'Give us a fag,' he said to his wife. 'A bit of a smoke will clear away the smell of the scorched feathers.'

'There's only two left in the packet,' she said. 'I was going to buy you some from the Co-op.'

'I'll have one,' he said, 't'other will keep for a rainy day.'

No sense trying to make the children rest. There was no rest to be got while the tapping and the scratching went on at the windows. He sat with one arm round his wife and the other round Jill, with Johnny on his mother's lap and the blankets heaped about them on the mattress.

'You can't help admiring the beggars,' he said, 'they've got persistence. You'd think they'd tire of the game, but not a bit of it.'

Admiration was hard to sustain. The tapping went on and on and a new rasping note struck Nat's ear, as though a sharper beak than any hitherto had come to take over from its fellows. He tried to remember the names of birds, he tried to think which species would go for this particular job. It was not the tap of the woodpecker. That would be light and frequent. This was more serious, because if it continued long the wood would splinter as the glass had done. Then he remembered the hawks. Could the hawks have taken over from the gulls? Were there buzzards now upon the sills, using talons as well as beaks? Hawks, buzzards, kestrels, falcons – he had forgotten the birds of prey. He had forgotten the gripping power of the birds of prey. Three hours to go, and while they waited the sound of the splintering wood, the talons tearing at the wood.

Nat looked about him, seeing what furniture he could destroy to fortify the door. The windows were safe, because of the dresser. He was not certain of the door. He went upstairs, but when he reached the landing he paused and listened. There was a soft patter on the floor of the children's bedroom. The birds had broken through . . . He put his ear to the door. No mistake. He could hear the rustle of wings, and the light patter as they searched the floor. The other bedroom was still clear. He went into it and began bringing out the furniture, to pile at the head of the stairs should the door of the children's bedroom go. It was a preparation. It might never be needed. He could not stack the furniture against the door, because it opened inward. The only possible thing was to have it at the top of the stairs.

'Come down, Nat, what are you doing?' called his wife.

'I won't be long,' he shouted. 'Just making everything ship-shape up here.'

He did not want her to come; he did not want her to hear the pattering of the feet in the children's bedroom, the brushing of those wings against the door.

At five-thirty he suggested breakfast, bacon and fried bread, if only to stop the growing look of panic in his wife's eyes and to calm the fretful children. She did not know about the birds upstairs. The bedroom, luckily, was not over the kitchen. Had it been so she could not have failed to hear the sound of them, up there, tapping the boards. And the silly, senseless thud of the suicide birds, the death-and-glory boys, who flew into the bedroom, smashing their heads against the walls. He knew them of old, the herring gulls. They had no brains. The black-backs were different, they knew what they were doing. So did the buzzards, the hawks . . .

He found himself watching the clock, gazing at the hands that went so slowly round the dial. If his theory was not correct, if the attack did not cease with the turn of the tide, he knew they were beaten. They could not continue through the long day without air, without rest, without more fuel, without . . . his mind raced. He knew there were so many things they needed to withstand siege. They were not fully prepared. They were not ready. It might be that it would be safer in the towns after all. If he could get a message through, on the farm telephone, to his cousin, only a short journey by train up country they might be able to hire a car. That would be quicker – hire a car between tides . . .

His wife's voice, calling his name, drove away the sudden, desperate desire for sleep.

'What is it? What now?' he said sharply.

'The wireless,' said his wife. 'I've been watching the clock. It's nearly seven.'

'Don't twist the knob,' he said, impatient for the first time, 'it's on the Home where it is. They'll speak from the Home.'

They waited. The kitchen clock struck seven. There was no sound. No chimes, no music. They waited until a quarter past, switching to the Light. The result was the same. No news bulletin came through.

'We've heard wrong,' he said, 'they won't be broadcasting until eight o'clock.'

They left it switched on, and Nat thought of the battery, wondered how much power was left in it. It was generally recharged when his wife went shopping in the town. If the battery failed they would not hear the instructions.

'It's getting light,' whispered his wife, 'I can't see it, but I can feel it. And the birds aren't hammering so loud.'

She was right. The rasping, tearing sound grew fainter every moment. So did the shuffling, the jostling for place upon the step, upon the sills. The tide was on the turn. By eight there was no sound at all. Only the wind. The children, lulled at last by the stillness, fell asleep. At half past eight Nat switched the wireless off.

'What are you doing? We'll miss the news,' said his wife.

'There isn't going to be any news,' said Nat. 'We've got to depend upon ourselves.'

He went to the door and slowly pulled away the barricades. He drew the bolts, and kicking the bodies from the step outside the door breathed the cold air. He had six working hours before him, and he knew he must reserve his strength for the right things, not waste it in any way. Food, and light, and fuel; these were the necessary things. If he could get them in sufficiency, they could endure another night.

He stepped into the garden, and as he did so he saw the living birds. The gulls had gone to ride the sea, as they had done before; they sought sea food, and the buoyancy of the

239

tide, before they returned to the attack. Not so the land birds. They waited and watched. Nat saw them, on the hedgerows, on the soil, crowded in the trees, outside in the field, line upon line of birds, all still, doing nothing.

He went to the end of his small garden. The birds did not move. They went on watching him.

'I've got to get food,' said Nat to himself, 'I've got to go to the farm to find food.'

He went back to the cottage. He saw to the windows and the doors. He went upstairs and opened the children's bedroom. It was empty, except for the dead birds on the floor. The living were out there, in the garden, in the fields. He went downstairs.

'I'm going to the farm,' he said.

His wife clung to him. She had seen the living birds from the open door.

'Take us with you,' she begged, 'we can't stay here alone. I'd rather die than stay here alone.'

He considered the matter. He nodded.

'Come on, then,' he said, 'bring baskets, and Johnny's pram. We can load up the pram.'

They dressed against the biting wind, wore gloves and scarves. His wife put Johnny in the pram. Nat took Jill's hand.

'The birds,' she whimpered, 'they're all out there, in the fields.'

'They won't hurt us,' he said, 'not in the light.'

They started walking across the field towards the stile, and the birds did not move. They waited, their heads turned to the wind.

When they reached the turning to the farm, Nat stopped and told his wife to wait in the shelter of the hedge with the two children.

'But I want to see Mrs Trigg,' she protested. 'There are lots of things we can borrow, if they went to market yesterday; not only bread, and . . .'

'Wait here,' Nat interrupted. 'I'll be back in a moment.'

The cows were lowing, moving restlessly in the yard, and he could see a gap in the fence where the sheep had knocked their way through, to roam unchecked in the front garden before the farm-house. No smoke came from the chimneys. He was filled with misgivings. He did not want his wife or the children to go down to the farm.

'Don't jib now,' said Nat, harshly, 'do what I say.'

She withdrew with the pram into the hedge, screening herself and the children from the wind.

He went down alone to the farm. He pushed his way through the herd of bellowing cows, which turned this way and that, distressed, their udders full. He saw the car standing by the gate, not put away in the garage. The windows of the farm-house were smashed. There were many dead gulls lying in the yard and around the house. The living birds perched on the group of trees behind the farm and on the roof of the house. They were quite still. They watched him.

Jim's body lay in the yard . . . what was left of it. When the birds had finished, the cows had trampled him. His gun was beside him. The door of the house was shut and bolted, but as the windows were smashed it was easy to lift them and climb through. Trigg's body was close to the telephone. He must have been trying to get through to the exchange when the birds came for him. The receiver was hanging loose, the instrument torn from the wall. No sign of Mrs Trigg. She would be upstairs. Was it any use going up? Sickened, Nat knew what he would find.

'Thank God,' he said to himself, 'there were no children.'

He forced himself to climb the stairs, but half-way he turned and descended again. He could see her legs, protruding from the open bedroom door. Beside her were the bodies of the black-backed gulls, and an umbrella, broken.

'It's no use,' thought Nat, 'doing anything. I've only got five hours, less than that. The Triggs would understand. I must load up with what I can find.'

He tramped back to his wife and children.

'I'm going to fill up the car with stuff,' he said. 'I'll put coal in it, and paraffin for the primus. We'll take it home and return for a fresh load.'

'What about the Triggs?' asked his wife.

'They must have gone to friends,' he said.

'Shall I come and help you, then?'

'No; there's a mess down there. Cows and sheep all over the place. Wait, I'll get the car. You can sit in it.'

Clumsily he backed the car out of the yard and into the lane. His wife and the children could not see Jim's body from there.

'Stay here,' he said, 'never mind the pram. The pram can be fetched later. I'm going to load the car.'

Her eyes watched his all the time. He believed she understood, otherwise she would have suggested helping him to find the bread and groceries.

They made three journeys altogether, backwards and forwards between their cottage and the farm, before he was satisfied they had everything they needed. It was surprising, once he started thinking, how many things were necessary. Almost the most important of all was planking for the windows. He had to go round searching for timber. He wanted to renew the boards on all the windows at the cottage. Candles, paraffin, nails, tinned stuff; the list was endless. Besides all that, he milked three of the cows. The rest, poor brutes, would have to go on bellowing.

On the final journey he drove the car to the bus-stop, got

out, and went to the telephone box. He waited a few minutes, jangling the receiver. No good, though. The line was dead. He climbed on to a bank and looked over the countryside, but there was no sign of life at all, nothing in the fields but the waiting, watching birds. Some of them slept — he could see the beaks tucked into the feathers.

'You'd think they'd be feeding,' he said to himself, 'not just standing in that way.'

Then he remembered. They were gorged with food. They had eaten their fill during the night. That was why they did not move this morning . . .

No smoke came from the chimneys of the council houses. He thought of the children who had run across the fields the night before.

'I should have known,' he thought, 'I ought to have taken them home with me.'

He lifted his face to the sky. It was colourless and grey. The bare trees on the landscape looked bent and blackened by the east wind. The cold did not affect the living birds, waiting out there in the fields.

'This is the time they ought to get them,' said Nat, 'they're a sitting target now. They must be doing this all over the country. Why don't our aircraft take off now and spray them with mustard gas? What are all our chaps doing? They must know, they must see for themselves.'

He went back to the car and got into the driver's seat.

'Go quickly past that second gate,' whispered his wife. 'The postman's lying there. I don't want Jill to see.'

He accelerated. The little Morris bumped and rattled along the lane. The children shrieked with laughter.

'Up-a-down, up-a-down,' shouted young Johnny.

It was a quarter to one by the time they reached the cottage. Only an hour to go.

'Better have cold dinner,' said Nat. 'Hot up something for yourself and the children, some of that soup. I've no time to eat now. I've got to unload all this stuff.'

He got everything inside the cottage. It could be sorted later. Give them all something to do during the long hours ahead. First he must see to the windows and the doors.

He went round the cottage methodically, testing every window, every door. He climbed on to the roof also, and fixed boards across every chimney, except the kitchen. The cold was so intense he could hardly bear it, but the job had to be done. Now and again he would look up, searching the sky for aircraft. None came. As he worked he cursed the inefficiency of the authorities.

'It's always the same,' he muttered, 'they always let us down. Muddle, muddle, from the start. No plan, no real organization. And we don't matter, down here. That's what it is. The people up country have priority. They're using gas up there, no doubt, and all the aircraft. We've got to wait and take what comes.'

He paused, his work on the bedroom chimney finished, and looked out to sea. Something was moving out there. Something grey and white amongst the breakers.

'Good old Navy,' he said, 'they never let us down. They're coming down channel, they're turning in the bay.'

He waited, straining his eyes, watering in the wind, towards the sea. He was wrong, though. It was not ships. The Navy was not there. The gulls were rising from the sea. The massed flocks in the fields, with ruffled feathers, rose in formation from the ground, and wing to wing soared upwards to the sky.

The tide had turned again.

Nat climbed down the ladder and went inside the kitchen. The family were at dinner. It was a little after two. He bolted the door, put up the barricade, and lit the lamp.

'It's night-time,' said young Johnny.

His wife had switched on the wireless once again, but no sound came from it.

'I've been all round the dial,' she said, 'foreign stations, and that lot. I can't get anything.'

'Maybe they have the same trouble,' he said, 'maybe it's the same right through Europe.'

She poured out a plateful of the Triggs' soup, cut him a large slice of the Triggs' bread, and spread their dripping upon it.

They ate in silence. A piece of the dripping ran down young Johnny's chin and fell on to the table.

'Manners, Johnny,' said Jill, 'you should learn to wipe your mouth.'

The tapping began at the windows, at the door. The rustling, the jostling, the pushing for position on the sills. The first thud of the suicide gulls upon the step.

'Won't America do something?' said his wife. 'They've always been our allies, haven't they? Surely America will do something?'

Nat did not answer. The boards were strong against the windows, and on the chimneys too. The cottage was filled with stores, with fuel, with all they needed for the next few days. When he had finished dinner he would put the stuff away, stack it neatly, get everything shipshape, handy-like. His wife could help him, and the children too. They'd tire themselves out, between now and a quarter to nine, when the tide would ebb; then he'd tuck them down on their mattresses, see that they slept good and sound until three in the morning.

He had a new scheme for the windows, which was to fix barbed wire in front of the boards. He had brought a great roll of it from the farm. The nuisance was, he'd have to work at this in the dark, when the lull came between nine and three. Pity he had not thought of it before. Still, as long as the wife slept, and the kids, that was the main thing.

The smaller birds were at the window now. He recognized the light tap-tapping of their beaks, and the soft brush of their wings. The hawks ignored the windows. They concentrated their attack upon the door. Nat listened to the tearing sound of splintering wood, and wondered how many million years of memory were stored in those little brains, behind the stabbing beaks, the piercing eyes, now giving them this instinct to destroy mankind with all the deft precision of machines.

'I'll smoke that last fag,' he said to his wife. 'Stupid of me, it was the one thing I forgot to bring back from the farm.'

He reached for it, switched on the silent wireless. He threw the empty packet on the fire, and watched it burn.

Monte Verità

They told me afterwards they had found nothing. No trace of anyone, living or dead. Maddened by anger, and I believe by fear, they had succeeded at last in breaking into those forbidden walls, dreaded and shunned through countless years – to be met by silence. Frustrated, bewildered, frightened, driven to fury at the sight of those empty cells, that bare court, the valley people resorted to the primitive methods that have served so many peasants through so many centuries: fire and destruction.

It was the only answer, I suppose, to something they did not understand. Then, their anger spent, they must have realized that nothing of any purpose had been destroyed. The smouldering and blackened walls that met their eyes in the starry, frozen dawn had cheated them in the end.

Search parties were sent out, of course. The more experienced climbers amongst them, undaunted by the bare rock of the mountain summit, covered the whole ridge, from north to south, from east to west, with no result.

And that is the end of the story. Nothing more is known.

Two men from the village helped me to carry Victor's body to the valley, and he was buried at the foot of Monte Verità. I think I envied him, at peace there. He had kept his dream.

As to myself, my old life claimed me again. The second war churned up the world once more. Today, approaching seventy, I have few illusions; yet often I think of Monte Verità and wonder what could have been the final answer.

I have three theories, but none of them may be true.

The first, and the most fantastic, is that Victor was right, after all, to hold to his belief that the inhabitants of Monte Verità *had* reached some strange state of immortality which gave them power when the hour of need arrived, so that, like the prophets of old, they vanished into the heavens. The ancient Greeks believed this of their gods, the Jews believed it of Elijah, the Christians of their Founder. Throughout the long history of religious superstition and credulity runs this ever-recurrent conviction that some persons attain such holiness and power that death can be overcome. This faith is strong in eastern countries, and in Africa; it is only to our sophisticated western eyes that the disappearance of things tangible, of persons of flesh and blood, seems impossible.

Religious teachers disagree when they try to show the difference between good and evil: what is a miracle to one becomes black magic to another. The good prophets have been stoned, but so have the witch-doctors. Blasphemy in one age becomes holy utterance in the next, and this day's heresy is tomorrow's credo.

I am no great thinker, and never have been. But this I do know, from my old climbing days: that in the mountains we come closest to whatever Being it is that rules our destiny.

The great utterances of old were given from the mountain tops: it was always to the hills that the prophets climbed. The saints, the messiahs, were gathered to their fathers in the clouds. It is credible to me, in my more solemn moods, that the hand of magic reached down that night to Monte Verità and plucked those souls to safety.

Remember, I myself saw the full moon shining upon that mountain. I also, at midday, saw the sun. What I saw and heard and felt was not of this world. I think of the rock-face, with the moon upon it; I hear the chanting from the forbidden walls; I see the crevasse, cupped like a chalice between the twin peaks of the mountain; I hear the laughter; I see the bare bronzed arms outstretched to the sun.

When I remember these things, I believe in immortality . . .

Then – and this is perhaps because my climbing days are over, and the magic of the mountains loses its grip over old memories, as it does over old limbs – I remind myself that the eyes I looked into that last day on Monte Verità were the eyes of a living, breathing person, and the hands I touched were flesh.

Even the spoken words belonged to a human being. 'Please do not concern yourself with us. We know what we must do.' And then that final, tragic word, 'Let Victor keep his dream.'

So my second theory comes into being, and I see nightfall, and the stars, and the courage of that soul which chose the wisest way for itself and for the others; and while I returned to Victor, and the people from the valley gathered themselves together for the assault, the little band of believers, the last company of those seekers after Truth, climbed to that crevasse, between the peaks, and so were lost.

My third theory is one that comes to me in moods more cynical, more lonely, when, having dined well with friends who mean little to me, I take myself home to my apartment in New York. Looking from the window at the fantastic light and colour of my glittering fairy-world of fact that holds no tenderness, no quietude, I long suddenly for peace, for understanding. Then, I tell myself, perhaps the inhabitants of Monte Verità had long prepared themselves against departure, and when the moment came it found them ready, neither for immortality nor for death, but for the world of men and women. In stealth, in secret, they came down into the valley unobserved, and, mingling with the people, went their separate ways. I wonder, looking down from my apartment into the hub and hustle of my world, if some of them wander there, in the crowded streets and subways, and whether, if I went out and searched the passing faces, I should find such a one and have my answer.

Sometimes, when travelling, I have fancied to myself, in coming upon a stranger, that there is something exceptional in the turn of a head, in the expression of an eye, that is at once compelling and strange. I want to speak, and hold such a person instantly in conversation, but – possibly it is my fancy – it is as though some instinct warns them. A momentary pause, a hesitation, and they are gone. It might be in a train, or in some crowded thoroughfare, and for one brief moment I am aware of someone with more than earthly beauty and human grace, and I want to stretch out my hand and say, swiftly, softly, 'Were you among those I saw on Monte Verità?' But there is never time. They vanish, they are gone, and I am alone again, with my third theory still unproven.

As I grow older – nearly seventy, as I have said, and memory shortens with the lengthening years – the story of Monte Verità becomes more dim to me, and more improbable, and because of this I have a great urge to write it down before memory fails me altogether. It may be that someone reading it will have the love of mountains that I had once, and so bring his own understanding to the tale, his own interpretation.

One word of warning. There are many mountain peaks in

Europe, and countless numbers may bear the name of Monte Verità. They can be found in Switzerland, in France, in Spain, in Italy, in the Tyrol. I prefer to give no precise locality to mine. In these days, after two world wars, no mountain seems inaccessible. All can be climbed. None, with due caution, need be dangerous. My Monte Verità was never shunned because of difficulties of height, of ice and snow. The track leading to the summit could be followed by anyone of sure and certain step, even in late autumn. No common danger kept the climber back, but awe and fear.

I have little doubt that today my Monte Verità has been plotted upon the map with all the others. There may be resting camps near the summit, even an hotel in the little village on the eastern slopes, and the tourist lifted to the twin peaks by electric cable. Even so, I like to think there can be no final desecration, that at midnight, when the full moon rises, the mountain face is still inviolate, unchanged, and that in winter, when snow and ice, great wind and drifting cloud make the climb impassable to man, the rock-face of Monte Verità, her twin peaks lifted to the sun, stares down in silence and compassion upon a blinded world.

We were boys together, Victor and I. We were both at Marlborough, and went up to Cambridge the same year. In those days I was his greatest friend, and if we did not see so much of each other after we left the Varsity it was only because we moved in rather different worlds: my work took me much abroad, while he was busily employed running his own estate up in Shropshire. When we saw each other, we resumed our friendship without any sense of having grown apart.

My work was absorbing, so was his; but we had money enough, and leisure too, to indulge in our favourite pastime, which was climbing. The modern expert, with his equipment

251

and his scientific training, would think our expeditions amateur in the extreme − I am talking of the idyllic days before the First World War − and, looking back on them, I suppose they were just that. Certainly there was nothing professional about the two young men who used to cling with the hands and feet to those projecting rocks in Cumberland and Wales, and later, when some experience was gained, tried the more hazardous ascents in southern Europe.

In time we became less foolhardy and more weather-wise, and learnt to treat our mountains with respect − not as an enemy to be conquered, but as an ally to be won. We used to climb, Victor and I, from no desire for danger or because we wanted to add mountain peaks to our repertoire of achievement. We climbed from desire, because we loved the thing we won.

The moods of a mountain can be more varying, more swiftly-changing, than any woman's, bringing joy, and fear, and also great repose. The urge to climb will never be explained. In olden days, perhaps, it was a wish to reach the stars. Today, anyone so minded can buy a seat on a plane and feel himself master of the skies. Even so, he will not have rock under his feet, or air upon his face; nor will he know the silence that comes only on the hills.

The best hours of my life were spent, when I was young, upon the mountains. That urge to spill all energy, all thought, to be as nothing, blotted against the sky − we called it mountain-fever, Victor and I. He used to recover from the experience more quickly than I did. He would look about him, method-ical, careful, planning the descent, while I was lost in wonder, locked in a dream I could not understand. Endurance had been tested, the summit was ours, but something indefinable waited to be won. Always it was denied to me, the experience I desired, and something seemed to tell me the fault was in myself. But they were good days. The finest I have known . . .

One summer, shortly after I returned to London from a business trip to Canada, a letter arrived from Victor, written in tremendous spirits. He was engaged to be married. He was, in fact, to be married very soon. She was the loveliest girl he had ever seen, and would I be his best man? I wrote back, as one does on these occasions, expressing myself delighted and wishing him all the happiness in the world. A confirmed bachelor myself, I considered him yet another good friend lost, the best of all, bogged down in domesticity.

The bride-to-be was Welsh and lived just over the border from Victor's place in Shropshire. 'And would you believe it,' said Victor in a second letter, 'she has never as much as set foot on Snowdon! I am going to take her education in hand.' I could imagine nothing I should dislike more than trailing an inexperienced girl after me on any mountain.

A third letter announced Victor's arrival in London, and hers too, in all the bustle and preparation of the wedding. I invited both of them to luncheon. I don't know what I expected. Someone small, I think, and dark and stocky, with handsome eyes. Certainly not the beauty that came forward, putting out her hand to me and saying, 'I am Anna.'

In those days, before the First World War, young women did not use make-up. Anna was free of lipstick, and her gold hair was rolled in great coils over her ears. I remember staring at her, at her incredible beauty, and Victor laughed, very pleased, and said, 'What did I tell you?' We sat down to lunch, and the three of us were soon at ease and chatting comfortably. A certain reserve was part of her charm, but because she knew I was Victor's greatest friend I felt myself accepted, and liked into the bargain.

Victor certainly was lucky, I said to myself, and any doubt I might have felt about the marriage went on sight of her. Inevitably, with Victor and myself, the conversation turned to mountains, and to climbing, before lunch was half-way through.

'So you are going to marry a man whose hobby is climbing mountains,' I said to her, 'and you've never even gone up your own Snowdon.'

'No,' she said, 'no, I never have.'

Some hesitation in her voice made me wonder. A little frown had come between those two very perfect eyes.

'Why?' I asked. 'It's almost criminal to be Welsh, and know nothing of your highest mountain.'

Victor interrupted. 'Anna is scared,' he said. 'Every time I suggest an expedition she thinks out an excuse.'

She turned to him swiftly. 'No, Victor,' she said, 'it's not that. You just don't understand. I'm not afraid of climbing.'

'What is it, then?' he said.

He put out his hand and held hers on the table. I could see how devoted he was to her, and how happy they were likely to become. She looked across at me, feeling me, as it were, with her eyes, and suddenly I knew instinctively what she was going to say.

'Mountains are very demanding,' she said. 'You have to give everything. It's wiser, for someone like myself, to keep away.'

I understood what she meant, at least I thought then that I did; but because Victor was in love with her, and she was in love with him, it seemed to me that nothing could be better than the fact that they might share the same hobby, once her initial awe was overcome.

'But that's splendid,' I said, 'you've got just the right approach to mountain climbing. Of course you have to give everything, but together you can achieve that. Victor won't let you attempt anything beyond you. He's more cautious than I am.'

Anna smiled, and then withdrew her hand from Victor's on the table.

'You are both very obstinate,' she said, 'and you neither of you understand. I was born in the hills. I know what I mean.'

254

And then some mutual friend of Victor's and my own came up to the table to be introduced, and there was no more talk of mountains.

They were married about six weeks later, and I have never seen a lovelier bride than Anna. Victor was pale with nerves, I remember well, and I thought what a responsibility lay on his shoulders, to make this girl happy for all time.

I saw much of her during the six weeks of their engagement, and, though Victor never realized it for one instant, came to love her as much as he did. It was not her natural charm, nor yet her beauty, but a strange blending of both, a kind of inner radiance, that drew me to her. My only fear for their future was that Victor might be a little too boisterous, too light-hearted and cheerful – his was a very open, simple nature – and that she might withdraw into herself because of it. Certainly they made a handsome pair as they drove off after the reception – given by an elderly aunt of Anna's, for her parents were dead – and I sentimentally looked forward to staying with them in Shropshire, and being godfather to the first child.

Business took me away shortly after the wedding, and it was not until the following December that I heard from Victor, asking me down for Christmas. I accepted gladly.

They had then been married about eight months. Victor looked fit and very happy, and Anna, it seemed to me, more beautiful than ever. It was hard to take my eyes off her. They gave me a great welcome, and I settled down to a peaceful week in Victor's fine old home, which I knew well from previous visits. The marriage was almost definitely a success, that I could tell from the first. And if there appeared to be no heir on the way, there was plenty of time for that.

We walked about the estate, shot a little, read in the evenings, and were a most contented trio.

I noticed that Victor had adapted himself to Anna's quieter personality, though quiet, perhaps, is hardly the right definition for her gift of stillness. This stillness — for there is no other word for it — came from some depth within her and put a spell upon the whole house. It had always been a pleasant place in which to stay, with its lofty rambling rooms and mullioned windows; but now the peaceful atmosphere was somehow intensified and deepened, and it was as though every room had become impregnated with a strange brooding silence, to my mind quite remarkable, and much more than merely restful, as it had been before.

It is odd, but looking back to that Christmas week I can recollect nothing of the traditional festivity itself. I don't remember what we ate or drank, or whether we set foot inside the church, which surely we must have done, with Victor as the local squire. I can only remember the quite indescribable peace of the evenings, when the shutters had been fastened and we sat before the fire in the great hall. My business trip must have tired me more than I realized, for sitting there, in Victor and Anna's home, I had no desire to do anything but relax and give myself up to this blessed, healing silence.

The other change that had come upon the house, which I did not fully take in until I had been there a few days, was that it was much barer than it had been before. The multiple odds and ends, and the collection of furniture handed down from Victor's forebears, seemed to have disappeared. The big rooms were now sparse and the great hall, where we sat, had nothing in it but a long refectory table and the chairs before the open fire. It seemed very right that it should be so, yet, thinking about it, it was an odd change for a woman to make. The usual habit of a bride is to buy new curtains and carpets, to bring the feminine touch into a bachelor house. I ventured to remark upon it to Victor.

'Oh yes,' he said, looking about him vaguely, 'we have cleared out a lot of stuff. It was Anna's idea. She doesn't believe in possessions, you know. No, we didn't have a sale, or anything like that. We gave them all away.'

The spare room allotted to me was the one I had always used in the past, and this was pretty much as it had been before. And I had the same old comforts − cans of hot water, early tea, biscuits by my bed, cigarette box filled, all the touches of a thoughtful hostess.

Yet once, passing down the long corridor to the stair-head, I noticed that the door of Anna's room, which was usually closed, was open; and knowing it to have been Victor's mother's room in former days, with a fine old four-poster bed and several pieces of heavy solid furniture, all in keeping with the style of the house, ordinary curiosity made me glance over my shoulder as I passed the open door. The room was bare of furniture. There were no curtains to the windows, and no carpet on the floor. The wooden boards were plain. There was a table and a chair, and a long trestle bed with no covering upon it but a blanket. The windows were wide open to the dusk, which was then falling. I turned away and walked down the stairs, and as I did so came face to face with Victor, who was ascending. He must have seen me glance into the room and I did not wish to appear furtive in any way.

'Forgive the trespass,' I said, 'but I happened to notice the room looked very different from your mother's day.'

'Yes,' he said briefly, 'Anna hates frills. Are you ready for dinner? She sent me to find you.'

And we went downstairs together without further conversation. Somehow I could not forget that bare sparse bedroom, comparing it with the soft luxury of my own, and I felt oddly inferior that Anna should consider me as someone who could not dispense with ease and elegance, which she, for some reason, did so well without.

That evening I watched her as we sat beside the fire. Victor had been called from the hall on some business, and she and I were alone for a few moments. As usual I felt the still, soothing peace of her presence come upon me with the silence; I was wrapped about with it, enfolded, as it were, and it was unlike anything I knew in my ordinary humdrum life; this stillness came out of her, yet from another world. I wanted to tell her about it but could not find the words. At last I said, 'You have done something to this house. I don't understand it.'

'Don't you?' she said. 'I think you do. We are both in search of the same thing, after all.'

For some reason I felt afraid. The stillness was with us just the same, but intensified, almost overpowering.

'I am not aware,' I said, 'that I am in search of anything.'

My words fell foolishly on the air and were lost. My eyes, that had drifted to the fire, were drawn, as if compelled, to hers.

'Aren't you?' she said.

I remember being swept by a feeling of profound distress. I saw myself, for the first time, as a very worthless, very trivial human being, travelling here and there about the world to no purpose, doing unnecessary business with other human beings as worthless as myself, and to no other end but that we should be fed and clothed and housed in adequate comfort until death.

I thought of my own small house in Westminster, chosen after long deliberation and furnished with great care. I saw my books, my pictures, my collection of china, and the two good servants who waited upon me and kept the house spotless always, in preparation for my return. Up to this moment my house and all it held had given me great pleasure. Now I was not sure that it had any value.

'What would you suggest?' I heard myself saying to Anna. 'Should I sell everything I have and give up my work? What then?'

Thinking back on the brief conversation that passed between us, nothing that she said warranted this sudden question on my part. She implied that I was in search of something, and instead of answering her directly, yes or no, I asked her if I must give up all I had? The significance of this did not strike me at the time. All I knew then was that I was profoundly moved, and whereas a few moments before I had been at peace, I was now troubled.

'Your answer may not be the same as mine,' she said, 'and anyway, I am not certain of my own, as yet. One day I shall know.'

Surely, I thought to myself in looking upon her, she has the answer now, with her beauty, her serenity, her understanding. What more can she possibly achieve, unless it is that up to the present she lacks children, and so feels unfulfilled?

Victor came back into the hall, and it seemed to me his presence brought solidity and warmth to the atmosphere; there was something familiar and comfortable about his old smoking jacket worn with his evening trousers.

'It's freezing hard,' he said. 'I went outside to see. The thermometer is down to thirty. Lovely night, though. Full moon.' He drew up his chair before the fire and smiled affectionately at Anna. 'Almost as cold as the night we spent on Snowdon,' he said. 'Heavens above, I shan't forget that in a hurry.' And turning to me with a laugh he added, 'I never told you, did I, that Anna condescended to come climbing with me after all?'

'No,' I said, astonished. 'I thought she had set herself against it.'

I looked across at Anna, and I noticed that her eyes had grown strangely blank, without expression. I felt instinctively that the subject brought up by Victor was one she would not have chosen. Victor, insensitive to this, went prattling on.

'She's a dark horse,' he said. 'She knows just as much about climbing mountains as you or I. In fact, she was ahead of me the whole time, and I lost her.'

He continued, half-laughing, half-serious, giving me every detail of the climb, which seemed hazardous in the extreme, as they had left it much too late in the year.

It seemed that the weather, which had promised well in the morning for their start, had turned by mid-afternoon, bringing thunder and lightning and finally a blizzard; so that darkness overtook them in the descent, and they were forced to spend the night in the open.

'The thing I shall never understand,' said Victor, 'is how I came to miss her. One moment she was by my side, and the next she had gone. I can tell you I had a very bad three hours, in pitch darkness and half a gale.'

Anna never said a word while he told the story. It was as though she withdrew herself completely. She sat in her chair, motionless. I felt uneasy, anxious. I wanted Victor to stop.

'Anyway,' I said, to hasten him, 'you got down all right, and none the worse for it.'

'Yes,' he said ruefully, 'at about five in the morning, thoroughly wet and thoroughly frightened. Anna came up to me out of the mist not even damp, surprised that I was angry. Said she had been sheltered by a piece of rock. It was a wonder she had not broken her neck. Next time we go mountain climbing, I've told her that she can be the guide.'

'Perhaps,' I said, with a glance at Anna, 'there won't be a next time. Once was enough.'

'Not a bit of it,' said Victor cheerfully, 'we are all set, you know, to go off next summer. The Alps, or the Dolomites, or the Pyrenees, we haven't decided yet on the objective. You had better come with us and we'll have a proper expedition.'

I shook my head, regretfully.

'I only wish I could,' I said, 'but it's impossible. I must be in New York by May and shan't be home again until September.'

'Oh, that's a long way ahead,' said Victor, 'anything may happen by May. We'll talk of it again, nearer the time.'

Still Anna said no word, and I wondered why Victor saw nothing strange in her reticence. Suddenly she said good night and went upstairs. It was obvious to me that all this chatter of mountain climbing had been unwelcome to her. I felt an urge to attack Victor on the subject.

'Look here,' I said, 'do think twice about this holiday in the mountains. I am pretty sure Anna isn't for it.'

'Not for it?' said Victor, surprised. 'Why, it was her idea entirely.'

I stared at him.

'Are you sure?' I asked.

'Of course I'm sure. I tell you, old fellow, she's crazy about mountains. She had a fetish about them. It's her Welsh blood, I suppose. I was being light-hearted just now about that night on Snowdon, but between ourselves I was quite amazed at her courage and her endurance. I don't mind admitting that what with the blizzard, and being frightened for her, I was dead beat by morning; but she came out of that mist like a spirit from another world. I've never seen her like it. She went down that blasted mountain as if she had spent the night on Olympus, while I limped behind her like a child. She is a very remarkable person: you realize that, don't you?'

'Yes,' I said slowly, 'I do agree. Anna is very remarkable.'

Shortly afterwards we went upstairs to bed, and as I undressed and put on my pyjamas, which had been left to warm for me before the fire, and noticed the thermos flask of hot milk on the bedside table, in case I should be wakeful, and padded about the thick carpeted room in my soft slippers, I thought once again of that strange bare room where Anna slept, and of the narrow trestle bed. In a futile, unnecessary gesture, I threw aside the heavy satin quilt that lay on top of my blankets, and before getting into bed opened my windows wide.

I was restless, though, and could not sleep. My fire sank low and the cold air penetrated the room. I heard my old worn travelling clock race round the hours through the night. At four I could stand it no longer and remembered the thermos of milk with gratitude. Before drinking it I decided to pamper myself still further and close the window.

I climbed out of bed and, shivering, went across the room to do so. Victor was right. A white frost covered the ground. The moon was full. I stood for a moment by the open window, and from the trees in shadow I saw a figure come and stand below me on the lawn. Not furtive, as a trespasser, not creeping, as a thief. Whoever it was stood motionless, as though in meditation, with face uplifted to the moon.

Then I perceived that it was Anna. She wore a dressing-gown, with a cord about it, and her hair was loose on her shoulders. She made no sound as she stood there on the frosty lawn, and I saw, with a shock of horror, that her feet were bare. I stood watching, my hand on the curtain, and suddenly I felt that I was looking upon something intimate and secret, which concerned me not. So I shut my window and returned to bed. Instinct told me that I must say nothing of what I had seen to Victor, or to Anna herself; and because of this I was filled with disquiet, almost with apprehension.

Next morning the sun shone and we were out about the grounds with the dogs, Anna and Victor both so normal and cheerful that I told myself I had been overwrought the previous night. If Anna chose to walk bare-foot in the small hours it was her business, and I had behaved ill in spying upon her. The rest of my visit passed without incident; we were all three happy and content, and I was very loath to leave them.

262

I saw them again for a brief moment, some months later, before I left for America. I had gone into the Map House, in St James's, to buy myself some half-dozen books to read on that long thrash across the Atlantic – a journey one took with certain qualms in those days, the *Titanic* tragedy still fresh in memory – and there were Victor and Anna, poring over maps, which they had spread out over every available space.

There was no chance of a real meeting. I had engagements for the rest of the day, and so had they, so it was hail and farewell.

'You find us,' said Victor, 'getting busy about the summer holiday. The itinerary is planned. Change your mind and join us.'

'Impossible,' I said. 'All being well, I should be home by September. I'll get in touch with you directly I return. Well, where are you making for?'

'Anna's choice,' said Victor. 'She's been thinking this out for weeks, and she's hit on a spot that looks completely inaccessible. Anyway, it's somewhere you and I have never climbed.'

He pointed down to the large-scale map in front of them. I followed his finger to a point that Anna had already marked with a tiny cross.

'Monte Verità,' I read.

I looked up and saw that Anna's eyes were upon me.

'Completely unknown territory, as far as I'm concerned,' I said. 'Be sure and have advice first, before setting forth. Get hold of local guides, and so on. What made you choose that particular ridge of mountains?'

Anna smiled, and I felt a sense of shame, of inferiority beside her.

'The Mountain of Truth,' she said. 'Come with us, do.'

I shook my head and went off upon my journey.

During the months that followed I thought of them both, and envied them too. They were climbing, and I was hemmed in, not by the mountains that I loved but by hard business. Often I wished I had the courage to throw my work aside, turn my back on the civilized world and its dubious delights, and go seeking after truth with my two friends. Only convention deterred me, the sense that I was making a successful career for myself, which it would be folly to cut short. The pattern of my life was set. It was too late to change.

I returned to England in September, and I was surprised, in going through the great pile of letters that awaited me, to have nothing from Victor. He had promised to write and give me news of all they had seen and done. They were not on the telephone, so I could not get in touch with them direct, but I made a note to write to Victor as soon as I had sorted out my business mail.

A couple of days later, coming out of my club, I ran into a man, a mutual friend of ours, who detained me a moment to ask some question about my journey, and then, just as I was going down the steps, called over his shoulder, 'I say, what a tragedy about poor Victor. Are you going to see him?'

'What do you mean? What tragedy?' I asked. 'Has there been an accident?'

'He's terribly ill in a nursing-home, here in London,' came the answer. 'Nervous breakdown. You know his wife has left him?'

'Good God, no,' I exclaimed.

'Oh, yes. That's the cause of all the trouble. He's gone quite to pieces. You know he was devoted to her.'

I was stunned. I stood staring at the fellow, my face blank.

'Do you mean,' I said, 'that she has gone off with somebody else?'

'I don't know. I assume so. No one can get anything out of Victor. Anyway, there he has been for several weeks, with this breakdown.'

I asked for the address of the nursing-home, and at once, without further delay, jumped into a cab and was driven there.

At first I was told, on making inquiry, that Victor was seeing no visitors, but I took out my card and scribbled a line across the back. Surely he would not refuse to see me? A nurse came, and I was taken upstairs to a room on the first floor.

I was horrified, when she opened the door, to see the haggard face that looked up at me from the chair beside the gas-fire, so frail he was, so altered.

'My dear old boy,' I said, going towards him, 'I only heard five minutes ago that you were here.'

The nurse closed the door and left us together.

To my distress Victor's eyes filled with tears.

'It's all right,' I said, 'don't mind me. You know I shall understand.'

He seemed unable to speak. He just sat there, hunched in his dressing-gown, the tears running down his cheeks. I had never felt more helpless. He pointed to a chair, and I drew it up beside him. I waited. If he did not want to tell me what had happened I would not press him. I only wanted to comfort him, to be of some assistance.

At last he spoke, and I hardly recognized his voice.

'Anna's gone,' he said. 'Did you know that? She's gone.'

I nodded. I put my hand on his knee, as though he were a small boy again and not a man past thirty, of my own age.

'I know,' I said gently, 'but it will be all right. She will come back again. You are sure to get her back.'

He shook his head. I had never seen such despair, and such complete conviction.

'Oh no,' he said, 'she will never come back. I know her too well. She's found what she wants.'

It was pitiful to see how completely he had given in to what had happened. Victor, usually so strong, so well-balanced.

'Who is it?' I said. 'Where did she meet this other fellow?' Victor stared at me, bewildered.

'What do you mean?' he said. 'She hasn't met anyone. It's not that at all. If it were, that would be easy . . .'

He paused, spreading out his hands in a hopeless gesture. And suddenly he broke down again, but this time not with weakness but with a more fearful sort of stifled rage, the impotent, useless rage of a man who fights against something stronger than himself. 'It was the mountain that got her,' he said, 'that God-damned mountain, Monte Verità. There's a sect there, a closed order, they shut themselves up for life – there, on that mountain. I never dreamed there could be such a thing. I never knew. And she's there. On that damned mountain. On Monte Verità . . .'

I sat there with him in the nursing-home all afternoon, and little by little had the whole story from him.

The journey itself, Victor said, had been pleasant and uneventful. Eventually they reached the centre from which they proposed to explore the terrain immediately below Monte Verità, and here they met with difficulties. The country was unknown to Victor, and the people seemed morose and unfriendly, very different, he said, to the sort of folk who had welcomed us in the past. They spoke in a patois hard to understand, and they lacked intelligence.

'At least, that's how they struck me,' said Victor. 'They were very rough and somehow undeveloped, the sort of people who might have stepped out of a former century. You know how, when we climbed together, the people could not do enough to help us, and we always managed to find guides. Here, it was different. When Anna and I tried to find out the best approach to Monte Verità, they would not tell us. They just stared at us in a stupid sort of way, and shrugged their shoulders. They had no guides, one fellow said; the mountain was — savage, unexplored.'

Victor paused, and looked at me with that same expression of despair.

'You see,' he said, 'that's when I made my mistake. I should have realized the expedition was a failure — to that particular spot at any rate — and suggested to Anna that we turned back and tackled something else, something nearer to civilization anyhow, where the people were more helpful and the country more familiar. But you know how it is. You get a stubborn feeling inside you, on the mountains, and any opposition somehow rouses you.

'And Monte Verità itself . . .' he broke off and stared in front of him. It was as though he was looking upon it again in his own mind. 'I've never been one for lyrical description, you know that,' he said. 'On our finest climbs I was always the practical one and you the poet. For sheer beauty, I have never seen anything like Monte Verità. We have climbed many higher peaks, you and I, and far more dangerous ones, too; but this was somehow . . . sublime.'

After a few moments' silence he continued talking. 'I said to Anna, "What shall we do?", and she answered me without hesitation, "We must go on." I did not argue, I knew perfectly well that would be her wish. The place had put a spell on both of us.'

They left the valley, and began the ascent.

'It was a wonderful day,' said Victor, 'hardly a breath of wind, and not a cloud in the sky. Scorching sun, you know how it can be, cut the air clean and cold. I chaffed Anna about that other climb, up Snowdon, and made her promise not to leave me behind this time. She was wearing an open shirt, and a brief kilted skirt, and her hair was loose. She looked . . . quite beautiful.'

As he talked, slowly, quietly, I had the impression that it must surely be an accident that had happened, but that his mind, unhinged by tragedy, baulked at Anna's death. It must be so. Anna had fallen. He had seen her fall and had been powerless to help her. He had then returned, broken in mind and spirit, telling himself she still lived on Monte Verità.

'We came to a village an hour before sundown,' said Victor.

'The climb had taken us all day. We were still about three hours from the peak itself, or so I judged. The village consisted of some dozen dwellings or so, huddled together. And as we walked towards the first one, a curious thing happened.'

He paused and stared in front of him.

'Anna was a little ahead of me,' he said, 'moving swiftly with those long strides of hers, you know how she does. I saw two or three men, with some children and goats, come on to the track from a piece of pasture land to the right of us. Anna raised her hand in salute, and at sight of her the men started, as if terrified, and snatching up the children ran to the nearest group of hovels, as if all the fiends in hell were after them. I heard them bolt the doors and shutter the windows. It was the most extraordinary thing. The goats went scattering down the track, equally scared.'

Victor said he had made some joke to Anna about a charming welcome, and that she seemed upset; she did not know what she could have done to frighten them. Victor went to the first hut and knocked upon the door.

Nothing happened at all, but he could hear whispers inside and a child crying. Then he lost patience and began to shout. This had effect, and after a moment one of the shutters was removed and a man's face appeared at the gap and stared at him. Victor, by way of encouragement, nodded and smiled. Slowly the man withdrew the whole of the shutter and Victor spoke to him. At first the man shook his head, then he seemed to change his mind and came and unbolted the door. He stood in the entrance, peering nervously about him, and, ignoring Victor, looked at Anna. He shook his head violently and, speaking very quickly and quite unintelligibly, pointed towards the summit of Monte Verità. Then from the shadows of the small room came an elderly man, leaning on two sticks, who motioned aside the terrified children and moved past them to the door. He, at least, spoke a language that was not entirely patois.

'Who is that woman?' he asked. 'What does she want with us?'

Victor explained that Anna was his wife, that they had come from the valley to climb the mountain, that they were tourists on holiday, and they would be glad of shelter for the night. He said the old man stared away from him to Anna.

'She is your wife?' he said. 'She is not from Monte Verità?'

'She is my wife,' repeated Victor. 'We come from England. We are in this country on holiday. We have never been here before.'

The old man turned to the younger and they muttered together for a few moments. Then the younger man went back inside the house, and there was further talk from the interior. A woman appeared, even more frightened than the younger man. She was literally trembling, Victor said, as she looked out of the doorway towards Anna. It was Anna who disturbed them.

'She is my wife,' said Victor again, 'we come from the valley.'

Finally the old man made a gesture of consent, of understanding.

'I believe you,' he said. 'You are welcome to come inside. If you are from the valley, that is all right. We have to be careful.'

Victor beckoned to Anna, and slowly she came up the track and stood beside Victor, on the threshold of the house. Even now the woman looked at her with timidity, and she and the children backed away.

The old man motioned his visitors inside. The living-room was bare but clean, and there was a fire burning.

'We have food,' said Victor, unshouldering his pack, 'and mattresses too. We don't want to be a nuisance. But if we could eat here, and sleep on the floor, it will do very well indeed.'

The old man nodded. 'I am satisfied,' he said, 'I believe you.'

Then he withdrew with his family.

Victor said he and Anna were both puzzled at their reception, and could not understand why the fact of their being married, and coming from the valley, should have gained them admittance, after that first odd show of terror. They ate, and unrolled their packs, and then the old man appeared again with milk for them, and cheese. The woman remained behind, but the younger man, out of curiosity, accompanied the elder.

Victor thanked the old fellow for his hospitality, and said that now they would sleep, and in the morning, soon after sunrise, they would climb to the summit of the mountain.

'Is the way easy?' he asked.

'It is not difficult,' came the reply. 'I would offer to send someone with you, but no one cares to go.'

His manner was diffident, and Victor said he glanced again at Anna.

'Your wife will be all right in the house here,' he said. 'We will take care of her.'

'My wife will climb with me,' said Victor. 'She won't want to stay behind.'

A look of anxiety came into the old man's face.

'It is better that your wife does not go up Monte Verità,' he said. 'It will be dangerous.'

'Why is it dangerous for me to go up to Monte Verità?' asked Anna.

The old man looked at her, his anxiety deepening.

'For girls,' he said, 'for women, it is dangerous.'

'But how?' asked Anna. 'Why? You told my husband the path is easy.'

'It is not the path that is dangerous,' he answered; 'my son can set you on the path. It is because of the . . .' and Victor said he used a word that neither he nor Anna understood, but that it sounded like *sacerdotessa*, or *sacerdozio*.

'That's priestess, or priesthood,' said Victor. 'It can't be that. I wonder what on earth he means?'

The old man, anxious and distressed, looked from one to the other of them.

'It is safe for you to climb Monte Verità, and to descend again,' he repeated to Victor, 'but not for your wife. They have great power, the *sacerdotesse*. Here in the village we are always in fear for our young girls, for our women.'

Victor said the whole thing sounded like an African travel tale, where a tribe of wild men pounced out of the jungle and carried off the female population into captivity.

'I don't know what he's talking about,' he said to Anna, 'but I suppose they are riddled with some sort of superstition, which will appeal to you, with your Welsh blood.'

He laughed, he told me, making light of it, and then, being confoundedly sleepy, arranged their mattresses in front of the fire. Bidding the old man good evening, he and Anna settled themselves for the night.

He slept soundly, in the profound sleep that comes after climbing, and woke suddenly, just before daybreak, to the sound of a cock crowing in the village outside.

He turned over on his side to see if Anna was awake.

The mattress was thrown back, and bare. Anna had gone . . .

271

No one was yet astir in the house, Victor said, and the only sound was the cock crowing. He got up and put on his shoes and coat, went to the door and stepped outside.

It was the cold, still moment that comes just before sunrise. The last few stars were paling in the sky. Clouds hid the valley, some thousands of feet below. Only here, near the summit of the mountain, was it clear.

At first Victor felt no misgiving. He knew by this time that Anna was capable of looking after herself, and was as sure-footed as he — more so, possibly. She would take no foolish risks, and anyway the old man had told them that the climb was not dangerous. He felt hurt, though, that she had not waited for him. It was breaking the promise that they should always climb together. And he had no idea how much of a start she had in front of him. The only thing he could do was to follow her as swiftly as he could.

He went back into the room to collect their rations for the day — she had not thought of that. Their packs they could fetch later, for the descent, and they would probably have to accept hospitality here for another night.

His movements must have roused his host, for suddenly the old man appeared from the inner room and stood beside him. His eyes fell on Anna's empty mattress, then he searched Victor's eyes, almost in accusation.

'My wife has gone on ahead,' Victor said. 'I am going to follow her.'

The old man looked very grave. He went to the open door and stood there, staring away from the village, up the mountain.

'It was wrong to let her go,' he said, 'you should not have permitted it.' He appeared very distressed, Victor said, and shook his head to and fro, murmuring to himself.

'It's all right,' said Victor. 'I shall soon catch her up, and we shall probably be back again, soon after midday.'

He put his hand on the old fellow's arm, to reassure him.

'I fear very much that it will be too late,' said the old man. 'She will go to them, and once she is with them she will not come back.'

Once again he used the word *sacerdotesse*, the power of the *sacerdotesse*, and his manner, his state of apprehension, now communicated itself to Victor, so that he too felt a sense of urgency, and of fear.

'Do you mean that there are living people at the top of Monte Verità?' he said. 'People who may attack her, and harm her bodily?'

The old man began to talk rapidly, and it was difficult to make any sense out of the torrent of words that now sprang from him. No, he said, the *sacerdotesse* would not hurt her, they hurt no one; it was that they would take her to become one of them. Anna would go to them, she could not help herself, the power was so strong. Twenty, thirty years ago, the old man said, his daughter had gone to them: he had never seen her again. Other young women from the village, and from down below, in the valley, were called by the *sacerdotesse*. Once they were called they had to go, no one could keep them back. No one saw them again. Never, never. It had been so for many years, in his father's time, his father's father's time, before that, even.

It was not known now when the *sacerdotesse* first came to Monte Verità. No man living had set eyes upon them. They lived there, enclosed, behind their walls, but with power, he kept insisting, with magic. 'Some say they have this from God, some from the Devil,' he said, 'but we do not know, we cannot tell. It is rumoured that the *sacerdotesse* on Monte Verità never grow old, they stay for ever young and beautiful, and that it is from the moon they draw their power. It is the moon they worship, and the sun.'

Victor gathered little from this wild talk. It must all be legend, superstition.

The old man shook his head and looked towards the mountain track. 'I saw it in her eyes last night,' he said, 'I was afraid of it. She had the eyes they have, when they are called. I have seen it before. With my own daughter, with others.'

By now the rest of the family had woken and had come by turn into the room. They seemed to sense what had happened. The younger man, and the woman, even the children, looked at Victor with anxiety and a strange sort of compassion. He said the atmosphere filled him not so much with alarm as with anger and irritation. It made him think of cats, and broomsticks, and sixteenth-century witchcraft.

The mist was breaking slowly, down in the valley, and the clouds were going. The soft glow in the sky, beyond the range of mountains to the eastward, heralded the rising sun.

The old man said something to the younger, and pointed with his stick.

'My son will put you on the track,' he said, 'he will come part of the way only. Further he does not care to go.'

Victor said he set off with all their eyes upon him; and not only from this first hut, but from the other dwellings in the little village, he was aware of faces looking from drawn shutters, and faces peering from half-open doors. The whole village was astir now and intent upon watching him, held by a fearful fascination.

His guide made no attempt to talk to him. He walked ahead, his shoulders bent, his eyes on the ground. Victor felt that he went only on command of the old man, his father.

The track was rough and stony, broken in many places, and was, Victor judged, part of an old water-course that would be impassable when the rains came. Now, in full summer, it was easy enough to climb. Verdure, thorn, and scrub they left behind them, after climbing steadily for an hour, and the summit of the mountain pierced the sky directly above their heads, split into two like a divided hand. From the depths of the valley, and from the village even, this division could not be seen; the two peaks seemed as one.

The sun had risen with them as they climbed, and now shone in full upon the south-eastern face, turning it to coral. Great banks of clouds, soft and rolling, hid the world below. Victor's guide stopped suddenly and pointed ahead, where a jutting lip of rock wound in a razor's edge and curved south-ward out of sight.

'Monte Verità,' he said, and then repeated it again, 'Monte Verità.'

Then he turned swiftly and began scrambling back along the way that they had come.

Victor called to him, but the man did not answer; he did not even bother to turn his head. In a moment he was out of sight. There was nothing for it but to go on alone, round the lip of the escarpment, Victor said, and trust that he found Anna waiting for him on the further side.

It took him another half-hour to encircle the projecting shoulder of the mountain, and with every step he took his anxiety deepened, because now, on the southward side, there was no gradual incline – the mountain face was sheer. Soon further progress would be impossible.

'Then,' Victor said, 'I came out through a sort of gully-way, over a ridge about three hundred feet only from the summit; and I saw it, the monastery, built out of the rock between the two peaks, absolutely bare and naked; a steep rock wall enclosing it, a drop of a thousand feet beneath the wall to the next ridge, and above, nothing but the sky and the twin peaks of Monte Verità.'

It was true, then. Victor had not lost his mind. The place existed. There had been no accident. He sat there, in his chair by the gas-fire, in the nursing-home; and this had happened, it was not fantasy, born out of tragedy.

He seemed calm, now that he had told me so much. A great part of the strain had gone, his hands no longer trembled. He looked more like the old Victor, and his voice was steady.

'It must have been centuries old,' he said, after a moment or two. 'God knows how long it must have taken to build, hewn out of the rock-face like that. I have never seen anything more stark and savage, nor, in a strange way, more beautiful. It seemed to hang there, suspended, between the mountain and the sky. There were many long narrow slits, for light and air. No real windows, in the sense we know them. There was a tower, looking west, with a sheer drop below. The great wall encircled the whole place, making it impregnable, like a fortress. I could see no way of entrance. There was no sign of life. No sign of anyone. I stood there staring at the place, and the narrow window slits stared back at me. There was nothing I could do but wait there until Anna showed herself. Because now, you see, I was convinced the old man had been right, and I knew what must have happened. The inhabitants had seen Anna, from behind those slit windows, and had called to her. She was with them now, inside. She must see me, standing outside the wall, and presently would come out to me. So I waited there, all day . . .'

His words were simple. Just a plain statement of fact. Any husband might have waited thus for a wife who had, during their holiday, ventured forth one morning to call upon friends. He sat down, and later ate his lunch, and watched the rolling banks of cloud that hid the world below move, and disperse, and form again; and the sun, in all its summer strength, beat down upon the unprotected face of Monte Verità, on the tower and the narrow window-slits, and the great encircling wall, from whence came no movement and no sound.

276

'I sat there all the day,' said Victor, 'but she did not come. The force of the sun was blinding, scorching, and I had to go back to the gully-way for shelter. There, lying under the shadow of a projecting rock, I could still watch that tower and those window slits. You and I in the past have known silence on the mountains, but nothing like the silence beneath those twin peaks of Monte Verità.

'The hours dragged by and I went on waiting. Gradually it grew cooler, and then, as my anxiety increased, time raced instead. The sun went too fast into the west. The colour of the rock-face was changing. There was no longer any glare. I began to panic then. I went to the wall and shouted. I felt along the wall with my hands, but there was no entrance, there was nothing. My voice echoed back to me, again and again. I looked up, and all I could see were those blind slits of windows. I began to doubt everything, the old man's story, all that he had said. This place was uninhabited, no one had lived there for a thousand years. It was something built long ago in time, and now deserted. And Anna had never come to it at all. She had fallen, on that narrow lip-way where the track ended and the man had left me. She must have fallen into the sheer depths where the southern shoulder of the mountain ridge began. And this is what had happened to the other women who had come this way, the old man's daughter, the girls from the valleys; they had all fallen, none of them had ever reached the ultimate rock-face, here between the peaks.'

The suspense would have been easier to bear if the first strain and sign of breakdown had come back into Victor's voice. As it was, sitting there in the London nursing-home, the room impersonal and plain, the routine bottles of medicines and pills on the table by his side, and the sound of traffic coming from Wigmore Street, his voice took on a steady monotonous quality, like a clock ticking; it would have been more natural had he turned suddenly, and screamed.

'Yet I dared not go back,' he said, 'unless she came. I was compelled to go on waiting there, beneath the wall. The clouds banked up towards me and turned grey. All the warning evening shadows that I knew too well crept into the sky. One moment the rock-face, and the wall, and the slit windows were golden; then, suddenly, the sun was gone. There was no dusk at all. It was cold, and it was night.'

Victor told me that he stayed there against the wall until daybreak. He did not sleep. He paced up and down to keep warm. When dawn came he was chilled and numb, faint, too, from want of food. He had brought with him only the rations for their midday meal.

Sense told him that to wait now, through another day, was madness. He must return to the village for food and drink, and if possible enlist the help of the men there to form a search-party. Reluctantly, when the sun rose, he left the rock-face. Silence enwrapped it still. He was certain now there was no life behind the walls.

He went back, round the shoulder of the mountain, to the track; and so down into the morning mist, and to the village.

Victor said they were waiting there for him. It was as though he was expected. The old man was standing at the entrance of his home, and gathered about him were neighbours, mostly men and children.

Victor's first question was, 'Has my wife returned?' Somehow, descending from the summit, hope had come to him again – that she had never climbed the mountain track, that she had walked another way, and had come back to the village by a different path. When he saw their faces his hope went.

'She will not come back,' said the old man, 'we told you she would not come back. She has gone to them, on Monte Verità.'

278

Victor had wisdom enough to ask for food and drink before entering into argument. They gave him this. They stood beside him, watching him with compassion. Victor said the greatest agony was the sight of Anna's pack, her mattress, her drinking bottle, her knife; the little personal possessions she had not taken with her.

When he had eaten they continued to stand there, waiting for him to speak. He told the old man everything. How he had waited all day, and through the night. How there was never a sound, or a sign of life, from those slit windows on the rock-face on Monte Verità. Now and again the old man translated what Victor said to the neighbours.

When Victor had finished the old man spoke.

'It is as I said. Your wife is there. She is with them.'

Victor, his nerves to pieces, shouted aloud.

'How can she be there? There is no one alive in that place. It's dead, it's empty. It's been dead for centuries.'

The old man leant forward and put his hand on Victor's shoulder. 'It is not dead. That is what many have said before. They went and waited, as you waited. Twenty-five years ago I did the same. This man here, my neighbour, waited three months, day after day, night after night, many years ago, when his wife was called. She never came back. No one who is called to Monte Verità returns.'

She had fallen, then. She had died. It was that after all. Victor told them this, he insisted upon it, he begged that they would go now, with him, and search the mountain for her body.

Gently, compassionately, the old man shook his head. 'In the past we did that too,' he said. 'There are those among us who climb with great skill, who know the mountain, every inch of it, and who have descended the southern side even, to the edge of the great glacier, beyond which no one can live. There

279

are no bodies. Our women never fell. They were not there. They are in Monte Verità, with the *sacerdotesse.*'

It was hopeless, Victor said. It was no use to try argument. He knew that he must go down to the valley, and if he could not get help there go further yet, back to some part of the country that was familiar to him, where he could find guides who would be willing to return with him.

'My wife's body is somewhere on this mountain,' he said. 'I must find it. If your people won't help me, I will get others.'

The old man looked over his shoulder and spoke a name. From the little crowd of silent spectators came a child, a small girl of about nine years old. He laid his hand upon her head.

'This child,' he said to Victor, 'has seen and spoken with the *sacerdotesse*. Other children, in the past, have seen them too. Only to children, and then rarely, do they show themselves. She will tell you what she saw.'

The child began her recitation, in a high sing-song voice, her eyes fixed upon Victor; and he could tell, he said, that it was a tale she had repeated so many times, to the same listeners, that it was now a chant, a lesson learnt by heart. And it was all in patois. Not one word could Victor understand.

When she had finished the old man acted as interpreter; and from force of habit he too declaimed as the child had done, his tone taking that same sing-song quality.

'I was with my companions on Monte Verità. A storm came, and my companions ran away. I walked, and lost myself, and came to the place where the wall is, and the windows. I cried; I was afraid. She came out of the wall, the tall and splendid one, and another with her, also young and beautiful. They comforted me and I wanted to go inside the walls with them, when I heard the singing from the tower, but they told me it was forbidden. When I was thirteen years old I could return to live with them. They wore white raiment to the knees, their arms and legs were bare, the hair close to the head. They were more beautiful than the people of this world. They led me back from Monte Verità, down the track where I could find my way. Then they went from me. I have told all I know.'

The old man watched Victor's face when he had finished his recital. Victor said the faith that must have been put in the child's statement astounded him. It was obvious, he thought, that the child had fallen asleep, and dreamt, and translated her dream into reality.

'I am sorry,' he told his interpreter, 'but I can't believe the child's tale. It is imagination.'

Once again the child was called and spoken to, and she at once ran out of the house and disappeared.

'They gave her a circlet of stones on Monte Verità,' said the old man. 'Her parents keep it locked up, in case of evil. She has gone to ask for it, to show you.'

In a few moments the child returned, and she put into Victor's hand a girdle, small enough to encompass a narrow waist, or else to hang about the neck. The stones, which looked like quartz, were cut and shaped by hand, fitting into one another in hollowed grooves. The craftsmanship was fine, even exquisitely done. It was not the rude handiwork of peasants, done of a winter's evening, to pass the time. In silence Victor handed the circlet back to the child.

'She may have found it on the mountain side,' he said.

'We do not work thus,' answered the old man, 'nor the people in the valley, nor even in the cities of this country, where I have been. The child was given the circlet, as she has told us, by those who inhabit Monte Verità.'

Victor knew then that further argument was useless. Their obstinacy was too strong, and their superstition proof against all worldly sense. He asked if he might remain in the house another day and night.

'You are welcome to stay,' said the old man, 'until you know the truth.'

One by one the neighbours dispersed, the routine of the quiet day was resumed. It was as though nothing had happened. Victor went out again, this time towards the northern shoulder of the mountain. He had not gone far before he realized that this ridge was unclimbable, at any rate without skilled help and equipment. If Anna had gone that way she had found certain death.

He came back to the village, which, situated as it was on the eastern slopes, had already lost the sun. He went into the living-room, and saw that there was a meal there prepared for him, and his mattress lay on the floor before the hearth.

He was too exhausted to eat. He flung himself down on the mattress and slept. Next morning he rose early, and climbed once more to Monte Verità, and sat there all the day. He waited, watching the slit windows, while the hot sun scorched the rock-face through the long hours and then sank down into the western sky; and nothing stirred, and no one came.

He thought of that other man from the village who some years ago had waited there three months, day after day, night after night; and Victor wondered what limitation time would put to his endurance, and whether he would equal the other in fortitude.

On the third day, at that moment of midday when the sun was strongest, he could bear the heat no longer and went to lie in the gully-way, in the shadow and blessed coolness of the projecting rock. Worn with the strain of watching, and with the despair that now filled his entire being, Victor slept.

He awoke with a start. The hands of his watch pointed to five o'clock, and it was already cold inside the gully. He climbed out and looked towards the rock-face, golden now in the setting sun. Then he saw her. She was standing beneath the

282

wall, but on a ledge only a few feet in circumference, and below her the rock-face fell away sheer, a thousand feet or more.

She waited there, looking towards him, and he ran towards her shouting 'Anna . . . Anna . . .' And he said that he heard himself sobbing, and he thought his heart would burst.

When he drew closer he saw that he could not reach her. The great drop to the depths below divided them. She was a bare twelve feet away from him, and he could not touch her.

'I stood where I was, staring at her,' said Victor. 'I did not speak. Something seemed to choke my voice. I felt the tears running down my face. I was crying. I had made up my mind that she was dead, you see, that she had fallen. And she was there, she was alive. Ordinary words wouldn't come. I tried to say 'What has happened? Where have you been?' – but it wasn't any use. Because as I looked at her I knew in one moment, with terrible blinding certainty, that it was all true, what the old man had said, and the child; it wasn't imagination, it wasn't superstition. Though I saw no one but Anna, the whole place suddenly became alive. From behind those window slits above me there were God knows how many eyes, watching, looking down on me. I could feel the nearness of them, beyond those walls. And it was uncanny, and horrible, and real.'

Now the strain had come back into Victor's voice, now his hands trembled once again. He reached out for a glass of water and drank thirstily.

'She was not wearing her own clothes,' he said. 'She had a kind of shirt, like a tunic, to her knees, and round her waist a circlet of stones, like the one the child had shown me. Nothing on her feet, and her arms bare. What frightened me most was that her hair was cut quite short, as short as yours or mine. It altered her strangely, made her look younger, but in some way terribly austere. Then she spoke to me. She said

283

quite naturally, as if nothing had happened, "I want you to go
back home, Victor darling. You mustn't worry about me any
more."'

Victor told me he could hardly credit it, at first, that she
could stand there and say this to him. It reminded him of
those so-called psychic messages that mediums give out to
relatives at a spiritualistic séance. He could hardly trust himself
to answer. He thought that perhaps she had been hypnotized
and was speaking under suggestion.

'Why do you want me to go home?' he said, very gently,
not wanting to damage her mind, which these people might
have destroyed.

'It's the only thing to do,' she answered. And then, Victor
said, she smiled, normally, happily, as if they were at home
discussing plans. 'I'm all right, darling,' she said. 'This isn't
madness, or hypnotism, or any of the things you imagine it
to be. They have frightened you in the village, and it's understandable. This thing is so much stronger than most people.
But I must have always known it existed, somewhere; and I've
been waiting all these years. When men go into monasteries,
and women shut themselves up in convents, their relatives
suffer very much, I know, but in time they come to bear it. I
want you to do the same, Victor, please. I want you, if you
can, to understand.'

She stood there, quite calm, quite peaceful, smiling down
at him.

'You mean,' he said, 'you want to stay in this place always?'

'Yes,' she said, 'there can be no other life for me, any more,
ever. You must believe this. I want you to go home, and live
as you have always done, and look after the house and the
estate, and if you fall in love with anyone to marry and be
happy. Bless you for your love and kindness and devotion,
darling, which I shall never forget. If I were dead, you would

284

want to think of me at peace, in paradise. This place, to me, is paradise. And I would rather jump now, to those rocks hundreds of feet below me, than go back to the world from Monte Verità.'

Victor said he went on staring at her as she spoke, and he said there was a radiance about her there had never been before, even in their most contented days.

'You and I,' he said to me, 'have both read of transfiguration in the Bible. That is the only word I can use to describe her face. It was not hysteria, it was not emotion; it was just that. Something – out of this world of ours – had put its hand upon her. To plead with her was useless, to attempt force impossible. Anna, rather than go back to the world, would throw herself off the rock-face. I should achieve nothing.'

He said the feeling of utter helplessness was overwhelming, the knowledge that there was nothing he could do. It was as if he and she were standing on a dockway, and she was about to set foot in a ship, bound to an unknown destination, and the last few minutes were passing by before the ship's siren blew, warning him the gangways would be withdrawn and she must go.

He asked her if she had all she needed, if she would be given sufficient food, enough covering, and whether there were any facilities should she fall ill. He wanted to know if there was anything she wanted that he could send to her. And she smiled back at him, saying she had everything, within those walls, that she would ever need.

He said to her, 'I shall return every year, at this time, to ask you to come back. I shall never forget.'

She said, 'It will be harder for you if you do that. Like putting flowers on a grave. I would rather you stayed away.'

'I can't stay away,' he said, 'with the knowledge you are here, behind these walls.'

'I won't be able to come to you again,' she said, 'this is the last time you will see me. Remember, though, that I shall go on looking like this, always. That is part of the belief. Carry me with you.'

Then, Victor said, she asked him to go. She could not return inside the walls until he had gone. The sun was low in the sky and already the rock-face was in shadow.

Victor looked at Anna a long time; then he turned his back on her, standing by the ledge, and walked away from the wall towards the gully, without looking over his shoulder. When he came to the gully he waited there a few minutes, then looked out again towards the rock-face. Anna was no longer standing on the ledge. There was nothing there but the wall and the slit windows, and above, not yet in shadow, the twin peaks of Monte Verità.

I managed to spare half an hour or so, every day, to go and visit Victor in the nursing-home. Each day he appeared stronger, more himself. I spoke to the doctor attending him, to the matron and the nurses. They told me there was no question of a deranged mind; he came to them suffering from severe shock and nervous collapse. It had already done him immense good to see me and to talk to me. In a fortnight he was well enough to leave the nursing-home, and he came to stay with me in Westminster.

During those autumn evenings we went over all that had happened again and again. I questioned him more closely than I had done before. He denied that there had ever been anything abnormal about Anna. Theirs had been a normal, happy marriage. Her dislike of possessions, her spartan way of living, was, he agreed, unusual; but it had not struck him as peculiar – it was Anna. I told him of the night I had seen her standing with bare feet in the garden, on the frosted lawn. Yes, he said, that was the sort of thing she did. But she had a fastidiousness, a certain personal reticence, that he respected. He never intruded upon it.

I asked him how much he knew of her life before he married her. He told me there was very little to know. Her parents had died when she was young, and she had been brought up in Wales by an aunt. There was no peculiar background, no skeletons in the cupboard. Her upbringing had been entirely ordinary in every way.

'It's no use,' said Victor, 'you can't explain Anna. She is just herself, unique. You can't explain her any more than you can explain the sudden phenomenon of a musician, born to ordinary parents, or a poet, or a saint. There is no accounting for them. They just appear. It was my great fortune, praise God, to find her, just as it is my own personal hell, now, to have lost her. Somehow I shall continue living, as she expected me to do. And once a year I shall go back to Monte Verità.'

His acquiescence to the total break-up of his life astounded me. I felt that I could not have overcome my own despair, had the tragedy been mine. It seemed to me monstrous that an unknown sect, on a mountain side, could, in the space of a few days, have such power over a woman, a woman of intelligence and personality. It was understandable that ignorant peasant girls could be emotionally misled and their relatives, blinded by superstition, do nothing about it. I told Victor this. I told him that it should be possible, through the ordinary channels of our embassy, to approach the government of that country, to have a nation-wide inquiry, to get the Press on to it, the backing of our own government. I told him I was prepared, myself, to set all this in motion. We were living in the twentieth century, not in the Middle Ages. A place like Monte Verità should not be permitted to exist. I would arouse the whole country with the story, create an international situation.

'But why,' said Victor quietly, 'to what end?'

'To get Anna back,' I said, 'and to free the rest. To prevent the break-up of other people's lives.'

'We don't,' said Victor, 'go about destroying monasteries or convents. There are hundreds of them, all over the world.'

'That is different,' I argued. 'They are organized bodies of religious people. They have existed for centuries.'

'I think, very probably, Monte Verità has too.'

'How do they live, how do they eat, what happens when they fall ill, when they die?'

'I don't know. I try not to think about it. All I cling to is that Anna said she had found what she was searching for, that she was happy. I'm not going to destroy that happiness.'

Then he looked at me, in a way half puzzled, half wise, and said, 'It's odd, your talking in this way. Because by rights you should understand Anna's feelings more than I do. You were always the one with mountain fever. You were the one, in old climbing days, to have your head in the clouds and quote to me —

The world is too much with us; late and soon,
Getting and spending, we lay waste our powers.'

I remember getting up and going over to the window and looking out over the foggy street, down to the embankment. I said nothing. His words had moved me very much. I could not answer them. And I knew, in the depths of my heart, why I hated the story of Monte Verità and wanted the place to be destroyed. It was because Anna had found her Truth, and I had not . . .

That conversation between Victor and myself made, if not a division in our friendship, at least a turning-point. We had reached a half-way mark in both our lives. He went back to his home in Shropshire, and later wrote to me that he intended making over the property to a young nephew, still at school, and during the next few years intended having the lad to stay with him in the holidays, to get him acquainted with the place. After that, he did not know. He would not commit himself to plans. My own future, at this time, was full with change. My work necessitated living in America for a period of two years.

Then, as it turned out, the whole tenor of the world became disrupted. The following year was 1914.

Victor was one of the first to join up. Perhaps he thought this would be his answer. Perhaps he thought he might be killed. I did not follow his example until my period in America was over. It was certainly not my answer, and I disliked every moment of my army years. I saw nothing of Victor during the whole of the war; we fought on different fronts, and did not even meet on leave. I did hear from him, once. And this is what he said:

In spite of everything, I have managed to get to Monte Verità each year, as I promised to do. I stayed a night with the old man in the village, and climbed on to the mountain top the following day. It looked exactly the same. Quite dead, and silent. I left a letter for Anna beneath the wall and sat there, all the day, looking at the place, feeling her near. I knew she would not come to me. The next day I went again, and was overjoyed to find a letter from her in return. If you can call it a letter. It was cut on flat stone, and I suppose this is the only method they have of communication. She said she was well, and strong, and very happy. She gave me her blessing, and you also. She told me never to be anxious for her. That was all. It was, as I told you at the nursing-home, like a spirit message from the dead. With this I have to be content, and am. If I survive this war,

I shall probably go out and live somewhere in that country, so that I can be near her, even if I never see her again, or hear nothing of her but a few words scrawled on a stone once a year.

Good luck to yourself, old fellow. I wonder where you are.

Victor

When the Armistice came, and I got myself demobilized and set about the restoration of my normal life, one of the first things I did was to inquire for Victor. I wrote to him, in Shropshire. I had a courteous reply from the nephew. He had taken over the house and the estate. Victor had been wounded, but not badly. He had now left England and was somewhere abroad, either in Italy or Spain, the nephew was not sure which. But he believed his uncle had decided to live out there for good. If he had news of him, he would let me know. No further news came. As to myself, I decided I disliked post-war London and the people who lived there. I cut myself loose from home ties too, and went to America.

I did not see Victor again for nearly twenty years.

It was not chance that brought us together again. I am sure of that. These things are predestined. I have a theory that each man's life is like a pack of cards, and those we meet and sometimes love are shuffled with us. We find ourselves in the same suit, held by the hand of Fate. The game is played, we are discarded, and pass on. What combination of events brought me to Europe again at the age of fifty-five, two or three years before the Second World War, does not matter to this story. It so happened that I came.

I was flying from one capital city to another – the names of both are immaterial – and the aeroplane in which I travelled made a forced landing, luckily without loss of life, in desolate mountainous country. For two days the crew and passengers, myself amongst them, held no contact with the outer world. We camped in the partially wrecked machine and waited for rescue. This adventure made headlines in the world Press at the time, even taking precedence, for a few days, over the simmering European situation.

Hardship, for those forty-eight hours, was not acute. Luckily there were no women or children passengers travelling, so we men put the best face on it we could, and waited for rescue. We were confident that help would reach us before long. Our wireless had functioned until the moment of the forced landing, and the operator had given our position. It was all a matter of patience, and of keeping warm.

For my part, with my mission in Europe accomplished and no ties strong enough back in the States to believe myself anxiously awaited, this sudden plunging into the sort of country that years ago I had most passionately loved was a strange experience. I had become so much a man of cities, and a creature of comfort. The high pulse of American living, the pace, the vitality, the whole breathless energy of the New World, had combined to make me forget the ties that still bound me to the Old.

Now, looking about me in the desolation and the splendour, I knew what I had lacked all these years. I forgot my fellow-travellers, forgot the grey fuselage of the crippled plane – an anachronism, surely, amid the wilderness of centuries – and forgot too my grey hair, my heavy frame, and all the burden of my five-and-fifty years. I was a boy again, hopeful, eager, seeking an answer to eternity. Surely it was there, waiting, beyond the further peaks. I stood there, incongruous in my city clothes, and the mountain fever raced back into my blood.

I wanted to get away from the wrecked plane and the

pinched faces of my companions; I wanted to forget the waste of the years between. What I would have given to be young again, a boy, and, reckless of the consequences, set forth towards those peaks and climb to glory. I knew how it would feel, up there on the higher mountains. The air keener and still more cold, the silence deeper. The strange burning quality of ice, the penetrating strength of the sun, and that moment when the heart misses a beat as the foot, momentarily slipping on the narrow ledge, seeks safety; the hand's clutch to the rope.

I gazed up at them, the mountains that I loved, and felt a traitor. I had betrayed them for baser things, for comfort, ease, security. When rescue came to me and to my fellow-travellers, I would make amends for the time that had been lost. There was no pressing hurry to return to the States. I would take a vacation, here in Europe, and go climbing once again. I would buy proper clothes, equipment, set myself to it. This decision taken, I felt light-hearted, irresponsible. Nothing seemed to matter any more. I returned to my little party, sheltering beside the plane, and laughed and joked through the remaining hours.

Help reached us on the second day. We had been certain of rescue when we had sighted an aeroplane, at dawn, hundreds of feet above us. The search party consisted of true mountaineers and guides, rough fellows but likeable. They had brought clothing, kit, and food for us, and were astonished, they admitted, that we were all in condition to make use of them. They had thought to find none of us alive.

They helped us down to the valley in easy stages, and it took us until the following day. We spent the night encamped on the north side of the great ridge of mountains that had seemed to us, beside the useless plane, so remote and so inaccessible. At daybreak we set forth again, a splendid clear day, and the whole of the valley below our camp lay plain to the eye. Eastward the mountain range ran sheer, and as far as I could judge impassable, to a snow-capped peak, or possibly two, that pierced the dazzling sky like the knuckles on a closed hand.

I said to the leader of the rescue expedition, just as we were starting out on the descent, 'I used to climb much, in old days, when I was young. I don't know this country at all. Do many expeditions come this way?'

He shook his head. He told me conditions were difficult. He and his companions came from some distance away. The people in the valley to the eastward there were backward and ignorant; there were few facilities for tourists or for strangers. If I cared about climbing he could take me to other places, where I should find good sport. It was already rather late in the year, though, for expeditions.

I went on looking at that eastward ridge, remote and strangely beautiful.

'What do they call them,' I said, 'those twin peaks, to the east?'

He answered, 'Monte Verità.'

I knew then what had brought me back to Europe . . .

We parted, my fellow-travellers and I, at a little town some twenty miles from the spot where the aeroplane had crashed. Transport took them on to the nearest railway line, and to civilization. I remained behind. I booked a room at the small hotel and deposited my luggage there. I bought myself strong boots, a pair of breeches, a jerkin, and a couple of shirts. Then I turned my back upon the town and climbed.

It was, as the guide had told me, late in the year for expeditions. Somehow I did not care. I was alone, and on the mountains once again. I had forgotten how healing solitude could be. The old strength came back to my legs and to my lungs, and the cold air bit into the whole of me. I could have shouted with delight, at fifty-five. Gone was the turmoil and the stress, the anxious stir of many millions; gone were the lights, and the vapid city smells. I had been mad to endure it for so long.

In a mood of exaltation I came to the valley that lies at the eastern foot of Monte Verità. It had not changed much, it seemed to me, from the description Victor gave of it, those many years ago before the war. The little town was small and primitive, the people dull and dour. There was a rough sort of inn – one could not grace it by the name of hotel – where I proposed to stay the night.

I was received with indifference, though not discourtesy. After supper I asked if the track was still passable to the summit of Monte Verità. My informant behind his bar – for bar and café were in one, and I ate there, being the only visitor – regarded me without interest as he drank the glass of wine I offered him.

'It is passable, I believe, as far as the village. Beyond that I do not know,' he said.

'Is there much coming and going between your people in the valley here and those in the village on the mountain?' I asked.

'Sometimes. Perhaps. Not at this time of year,' he answered.

'Do you ever have tourists here?'

'Few tourists. They go north. It is better in the north.'

'Is there any place in the village where I could sleep tomorrow night?'

'I do not know.'

I paused a moment, watching his heavy sullen face, then I said to him, 'And the *sacerdotesse*, do they still live on the rock-face on the summit of Monte Verità?'

He started. He turned his eyes full upon me, and leant over the bar. 'Who are you, then? What do you know of them?'

'Then they do exist still?' I said.

He watched me, suspicious. Much had happened to his country in the past twenty years, violence, revolution, hostility between father and son, and even this remote corner must have had its share. It may have been this that made reserve.

'There are stories,' he said, slowly. 'I prefer not to mix myself up in such matters. It is dangerous. One day there will be trouble.'

'Trouble for whom?'

'For those in the village, for those who may live on Monte Verità – I know nothing of them – for us here in the valley. I do not know. If I do not know, no harm can come to me.'

He finished his wine, and cleaned his glass, and wiped the bar with a cloth. He was anxious to be rid of me.

'At what time do you wish for your breakfast in the morning?' he said.

I told him seven, and went up to my room.

I opened the double windows and stood out on the narrow balcony. The little town was quiet. Few lights winked in the darkness. The night was clear and cold. The moon had risen and would be full tomorrow or the day after. It shone upon the dark mountain mass in front of me. I felt oddly moved, as though I had stepped back into the past. This room, where I should pass the night, might have been the same one where Victor and Anna slept, all those years ago, in the summer of 1913. Anna herself might have stood here, on the balcony, gazing up at Monte Verità, while Victor, unconscious of the tragedy so few hours distant, called to her from within.

And now, in their footsteps, I had come to Monte Verità.

The next morning I took my breakfast in the café-bar, and my landlord of the night before was absent. My coffee and bread were brought to me by a girl, perhaps his daughter. Her manner was quiet and courteous, and she wished me a pleasant day.

295

'I am going to climb,' I said, 'the weather seems set fair. Tell me, have you ever been to Monte Verità?'

Her eyes flickered away from mine instantly.

'No,' she said, 'no, I have never been away from the valley.'

My manner was matter-of-fact, and casual. I said something about friends of mine having been here, some while ago – I did not say how long – and that they had climbed to the summit, and had found the rock-face there, between the peaks, and had been much interested to learn about the sect who lived enclosed within the walls.

'Are they still there, do you know?' I asked, lighting a cigarette, elaborately at ease.

She glanced over her shoulder nervously, as though conscious that she might be overheard.

'It is said so,' she answered. 'My father does not discuss it before me. It is a forbidden subject to young people.'

I went on smoking my cigarette.

'I live in America,' I said, 'and I find that there, as in most places, when the young people get together there is nothing they like discussing so well as forbidden subjects.'

She smiled faintly but said nothing.

'I dare say you and your young friends often whisper together about what happens on Monte Verità,' I said.

I felt slightly ashamed of my duplicity, but I felt that this method of attack was the most likely one to produce information.

'Yes,' she said, 'that is true. But we say nothing out loud. But just lately . . .' Once again she glanced over her shoulder, and then resumed, her voice pitched lower, 'A girl I knew quite well, she was to marry shortly, she went away one day, she has not come back, and they are saying she has been called to Monte Verità.'

'No one saw her go?'

'No. She went by night. She left no word, nothing.'

'Could she not have gone somewhere quite different, to a large town, to one of the tourist centres?'

'It is believed not. Besides, just before, she had acted strangely. She had been heard talking in her sleep about Monte Verità.'

I waited for a moment, then continued my inquiry, still nonchalant, still casual.

'What is the fascination in Monte Verità?' I asked. 'The life there must be unbearably harsh, and even cruel?'

'Not to those who are called,' she said, shaking her head. 'They stay young always, they never grow old.'

'If nobody has ever seen them, how can you know?'

'It has always been so. That is the belief. That is why here, in the valley, they are hated and feared, and also envied. They have the secret of life, on Monte Verità.'

She looked out of the window towards the mountain. There was a wistful expression in her eyes.

'And you?' I said. 'Do you think you will ever be called?'

'I am not worthy,' she said. 'Also, I am afraid.'

She took away my coffee and offered me some fruit.

'And now,' she said, her voice still lower, 'since this last disappearance, there is likely to be trouble. The people are angry, here in the valley. Some of the men have climbed to the village and are trying to rouse them there, to get force of numbers, and then they will attack the rock. Our men will go wild. They will try to kill those who live there. Then there will be more trouble, we shall get the army here, there will be inquiries, punishments, shooting; it will all end badly. So it is not pleasant at the moment. Everyone goes about afraid. Everybody is whispering in secret.'

A footstep outside sent her swiftly behind the bar. She busied herself there, her head low, as her father came into the room.

He glanced at both of us, suspiciously. I put out my cigarette and rose from the table.

'So you are still intent to climb?' he asked me.

'Yes,' I said. 'I shall be back in a day or two.'

'It would be imprudent to stay there longer,' he said.

'You mean the weather will break?'

'The weather will break, yes. Also, it might not be safe.'

'In what way might it not be safe?'

'There may be disturbance. Things are unsettled just now. Men are out of temper. When they are out of temper, they lose their heads. And strangers, foreigners, can come to harm at such a time. It would be better if you gave up your idea of climbing Monte Verità and turned northwards. There is no trouble there.'

'Thank you. But I have set my heart on climbing Monte Verità.'

He shrugged his shoulders. He looked away from me.

'As you will,' he said, 'it is not my affair.'

I walked out of the inn, down to the street, and crossing the little bridge above the mountain stream I set my face to the track through the valley that led me to the eastern face of Monte Verità.

At first the sounds from the valley were distinct. The barking of dogs, the tinkle of cow bells, the voices of men calling to one another, all these rose clearly to me in the still air. Then the blue smoke from the houses merged and became one misty haze, and the houses themselves took on a toy-town quality. The track wound above me and away, ever deeper into the heart of the mountain itself, until by midday the valley was lost in the depths and I had no other thought in my mind but to climb upwards, higher, always higher, win my way beyond that first ridge to the left, leave it behind me and gain the second, forget both in turn to achieve the third, steeper yet and overshadowed. My progress was slow, with untuned muscles and imperfect wind, but exhilaration of spirit kept me going and I was in no way tired, rather the reverse. I could have gone on for ever.

It was with a shock of surprise that I came finally upon the village, for I had pictured it at least another hour away. I must have climbed at a great pace, for it was barely four o'clock. The village wore a forlorn, almost deserted appearance, and I judged that today there were few remaining inhabitants. Some of the dwellings were boarded up, others fallen in and partly destroyed. Smoke came only from two or three of them, and I saw no one working in the pasture-land around. A few cows, lean-looking and unkempt, grazed by the side of the track, the jangling bells around their necks sounding hollow somehow in the still air. The place had a sombre, depressing effect, after the stimulation of the climb. If this was where I must spend the night I did not think much of it.

I went to the door of the first dwelling that had a thin wisp of smoke coming from the roof and knocked upon the door. It was opened, after some time, by a lad of about fourteen, who after one look at me called over his shoulder to somebody within. A man of about my own age, stupid-looking and heavy, came to the door. He said something to me in patois, then staring a moment, and realizing his mistake, he broke, even more haltingly than I, into the language of the country.

'You are the doctor from the valley?' he said to me.

'No,' I replied, 'I am a stranger on vacation, climbing in the district. I want a bed for the night, if you can give me one.'

His face fell. He did not reply directly to my request.

'We have someone here very sick,' he said, 'I do not know what to do. They said a doctor would come from the valley. You met no one?'

'I'm afraid not. No one climbed from the valley except myself. Who is ill? A child?'

The man shook his head. 'No, no, we have no children here.'

299

He went on looking at me, in a dazed, helpless sort of way, and I felt sorry for his trouble, but I did not see what I could do. I had no sort of medicines upon me but a first-aid packet and a small bottle of aspirin. The aspirin might be of use, if there was fever. I undid it from my pack and gave a handful to the man.

'These may help,' I said, 'if you care to try them.'

He beckoned me inside. 'Please to give them yourself,' he said.

I had some reluctance to step within and be faced with the grim spectacle of a dying relative, but plain humanity told me I could hardly do otherwise. I followed him into the living-room. There was a trestle bed against the wall and lying upon it, covered with two blankets, was a man, his eyes closed. He was pale and unshaven, and his features had that sharp pointed look about them that comes upon the face when near to death. I went close to the bed and gazed down upon him. He opened his eyes. For a moment we stared at one another, unbelieving. Then he put out his hand to me, and smiled. It was Victor . . .

'Thank God,' he said.

I was too much moved to speak. I saw him beckon to the fellow, who stood apart, and speak to him in the patois, and he must have told him we were friends, for some sort of light broke in the man's face and he withdrew. I went on standing by the trestle bed, with Victor's hand in mine.

'How long have you been like this?' I asked at length.

'Nearly five days,' he said. 'Touch of pleurisy; I've had it before. Rather worse this time. I'm getting old.'

Once again he smiled, and although I guessed him to be desperately ill, he was little changed, he was the same Victor still.

'You seem to have prospered,' he said to me, still smiling, 'you have all the sleek appearance of success.'

I asked him why he had never written, and what he had been doing with himself for twenty years.

'I cut myself adrift,' he said. 'I gather you did the same, but in a different way. I haven't been back to England since I left. What is it that you're holding there?'

I showed him the bottle of aspirin.

'I'm afraid that's no use to you,' I said. 'The best thing I can suggest is for me to stay here tonight, and then first thing in the morning get the chap here, and one or two others, to help me carry you down to the valley.'

He shook his head. 'Waste of time,' he said. 'I'm done for. I know that.'

'Nonsense. You need a doctor, proper nursing. That's impossible in this place.' I looked around the primitive living-room, dark and airless.

'Never mind about me,' he said. 'Someone else is more important.'

'Who?'

'Anna,' he said, and then as I answered nothing, at a loss for words, he added, 'She's still here, you know, on Monte Verità.'

'You mean,' I said, 'that she's in that place, enclosed, she's never left it?'

'That's why I'm here,' said Victor. 'I come every year, and have done, since the beginning. I wrote and told you, surely, after the war? I live in a little fishing port all the year round, very isolated and quiet, and then come here once in twelve months. I left it later this year, because I had been ill.'

It was incredible. What an existence, all these years, without friends, without interests, enduring the long months until the time came for this hopeless annual pilgrimage.

'Have you ever seen her?' I asked.

'Never.'

'Do you write to her?'

'I bring a letter every year. I take it up with me and leave it beneath the wall, and then return the following day.'

'The letter gets taken?'

'Always. And in its place there is a slab of stone, with writing scrawled upon it. Never more than a few words. I take the stones away with me. I have them all down on the coast, where I live.'

It was heart-rending, his faith in her, his fidelity through the years.

'I've tried to study it,' he said, 'this religion, belief. It's very ancient, way back before Christianity. There are old books that hint at it. I've picked them up from time to time, and I've spoken to people, scholars, who have made a study of mysticism and the old rites of ancient Gaul, and the Druids; there's a strong link between all mountain folk of those times. In every instance that I have read there is this insistence on the power of the moon and the belief that the followers stay young and beautiful.'

'You talk, Victor, as if you believe that too,' I said.

'I do,' he answered. 'The children believe it, here in the village, the few that remain.'

Talking to me had tired him. He reached out for a pitcher of water that stood beside the bed.

'Look here,' I said, 'these aspirins can't hurt you, they can only help, if you have fever. And you might get some sleep.'

I made him swallow three, and drew the blankets closer round him.

'Are there any women in the house?' I asked.

'No,' he said, 'I've been puzzled about that, since I've been here this time. The village is pretty much deserted. All the women and children have shifted to the valley. There are about twenty men and boys left, all told.'

'Do you know when the women and children went?'

'I gather they left a few days before I came. This fellow here

– he's the son of the old man who used to live here, who died many years ago – is such a fool that he never knows anything. He just looks vague if you question him. But he's competent, in his own way. He'll give you food, and find bedding for you, and the little chap is bright enough.'

Victor closed his eyes, and I hoped that he might sleep. I thought I knew why the women and children had left the village. It was since the girl from the valley had disappeared. They had been warned that trouble might come to Monte Verità. I did not dare tell Victor this. I wished I could persuade him to be carried down into the valley.

By this time it was quite dark, and I was hungry. I went through a sort of recess to the back. There was no one there but the boy. I asked him for something to eat and drink, and he understood. He brought me bread, and meat, and cheese, and I ate it in the living-room, with the boy watching me. Victor's eyes were still closed and I believed he slept.

'Will he get better?' asked the boy. He did not speak in patois.

'I think so,' I answered, 'if I can get help to carry him to a doctor in the valley.'

'I will help you,' said the boy, 'and two of my companions. We should go tomorrow. After that, it will be difficult.'

'Why?'

'There will be coming and going the day after. Men from the valley, much excitement, and my companions and I will join them.'

'What is going to happen?' He hesitated. He looked at me with quick bright eyes.

'I do not know,' he said. He slipped away, back to the recess.

Victor's voice came from the trestle bed.

'What did the boy say?' he asked. 'Who is coming from the valley?'

'I don't know,' I said casually, 'some expedition, perhaps. But he has offered to help take you down the mountain tomorrow.'

'No expeditions ever come here,' said Victor, 'there must be some mistake.' He called to the boy, and when the lad reappeared spoke to him in the patois. The boy was ill at ease, and diffident; he seemed reluctant now to answer questions. Several times I heard the words Monte Verità repeated, both by him and Victor. Presently he went back to the inner room and left us alone.

'Did you understand any of that?' asked Victor.

'No,' I replied.

'I don't like it,' he said, 'there's something queer. I've felt it, since I've lain here these last few days. The men look furtive, odd. He tells me there's been some disturbance in the valley, and the people there are very angry. Did you hear anything about it?'

I did not know what to say. He was watching me closely.

'The fellow in the inn was not very forthcoming,' I said, 'but he did advise against coming to Monte Verità.'

'What reason did he give?'

'No particular reason. He just said there might be trouble.'

Victor was silent. I could feel him thinking there beside me.

'Have any of the women disappeared from the valley?' he said.

It was useless to lie. 'I heard something about a missing girl,' I told him, 'but I don't know if it's true.'

'It will be true. That is it, then.'

He said nothing for a long while, and I could not see his face – it was in shadow. The room was lit by a single lamp, giving a pallid glow.

'You must climb tomorrow and warn Anna at Monte Verità,' he said at last.

I think I had expected this. I asked him how it could be done.

'I can sketch the track for you,' he said, 'you can't go wrong. It's straight up the old water-course, heading south all the while. The rains haven't made it impassable yet. If you leave before dawn you'll have all day before you.'

'What happens when I get there?'

'You must leave a letter, as I do, and then come away. They won't fetch it while you are there. I will write, also. I shall tell Anna that I am ill here, and that you've suddenly appeared, after nearly twenty years. You know, I was thinking, just now, while you were talking to the boy, it's like a miracle. I have a strange sort of feeling Anna brought you here.'

His eyes were shining with that old boyish faith that I remembered.

'Perhaps,' I said. 'Either Anna, or what you used to call my mountain fever.'

'Isn't that the same thing?' he said to me.

We looked at one another in the silence of that small dark room, and then I turned away and called the boy to bring me bedding and a pillow. I would sleep the night on the floor by Victor's bed.

He was restless in the night, and breathed with difficulty. Several times I got up to him and gave him more aspirin and water. He sweated much, which might be a good thing or a bad, I did not know. The night seemed endless, and for myself, I barely slept at all. We were both awake when the first darkness paled.

'You should start now,' he said, and going to him I saw with apprehension that his skin had gone clammy cold. He was worse, I was certain, and much weaker.

'Tell Anna,' he said, 'that if the valley people come she and the others will be in great danger. I am sure of it.'

'I will write all that,' I said.

'She knows how much I love her. I tell her that always in

305

my letters, but you could say so, once again. Wait in the gully. You may have to wait two hours, or even three, or longer still. Then go back to the wall and look for the answer on the slab of stone. It will be there.'

I touched his cold hand and went out into the chill morning air. Then, as I looked about me, I had my first misgiving. There was cloud everywhere. Not only beneath me, masking the track from the valley where I had come the night before, but here in the silent village, wreathing in mist the roofs of the huts, and also above me, where the path wound through scrub and disappeared upon the mountain side.

Softly, silently, the clouds touched my face and drifted past, never dissolving, never clearing. The moisture clung to my hair and to my hands, and I could taste it on my tongue. I looked this way and that, in the half light, wondering what I should do. All the old instinct of self-preservation told me to return. To set forth, in breaking weather, was madness, to my remembered mountain lore. Yet to stay there, in the village, with Victor's eyes upon me, hopeful, patient, was more than I could stand. He was dying, we both knew it. And I carried in my breast pocket his last letter to his wife.

I turned to the south, and still the clouds came travelling past, slowly, relentlessly, down from the summit of Monte Verità.

I began to climb . . .

Victor had told me that I should reach the summit in two hours. Less than that, with the rising sun behind me. I had also a guide, the rough sketch map that he had drawn.

In the first hour after leaving the village I realized my error. I should never see the sun that day. The clouds drove past me, vapour in my face, clammy and cold. They hid the winding water-course up which I had climbed five minutes since, down which already came the mountain springs, loosening the earth and stones.

By the time the contour changed, and I was free of roots and scrub and feeling my way upon bare rock, it was past midday. I was defeated. Worse still, I was lost. I turned back and could not find the water-course that had brought me so far. I approached another, but it ran north-east and had already broken for the season; a torrent of water washed away down the mountain-side. One false move, and the current would have borne me away, tearing my hands to pieces as I sought for a grip among the stones,

Gone was my exultation of the day before. I was no longer in the thrall of mountain fever but held instead by the equally well-remembered sense of fear. It had happened in the past, many a time, the coming of cloud. Nothing renders a man so helpless, unless he can recognize every inch of the way by which he has come, and so descend. But I had been young in those days, trained, and climbing fit. Now I was a middle-aged city dweller, alone on a mountain I had never climbed before, and I was scared.

I sat down under the lee of a great boulder, away from the drifting cloud, and ate my lunch – the remainder of sandwiches packed at the valley inn – and waited. Then, still waiting, I got up and stamped about for warmth. The air was not penetrating yet but seeping cold, the moist chill cold that always comes with cloud.

I had this one hope, that with the coming of darkness, and with a fall in temperature, the cloud would lift. I remembered it would be full moon, a great point to my advantage, for cloud rarely lingers at these times, but tends to break up and dissolve. I welcomed, therefore, the coming of a sharper cold into the atmosphere. The air was perceptibly keener, and looking out towards the south, from which direction the cloud had drifted all the day, I could now see some ten feet ahead. Below me it was still as thick as ever. A wall of impenetrable mist hid the descent. I went on waiting. Above me, always to the south, the distance that I could see increased from a dozen feet to fifteen, from fifteen to twenty. The cloud was cloud no longer, but vapour only, thin, and vanishing; and suddenly the whole contour of the mountain came into view, not the summit as yet, but the great jutting shoulder, leaning south, and beyond it my first glimpse of the sky.

I looked at my watch again. It was a quarter to six. Night had fallen on Monte Verità.

Vapour came again, obscuring that clear patch of sky that I had seen, and then it drifted, and the sky was there once more. I left my place of shelter where I had been all day. For the second time I was faced with a decision. To climb, or to descend. Above me, the way was clear. There was the shoulder of the mountain, described by Victor; I could even see the ridge along it running to the south, which was the way I should have taken twelve hours before. In two or three hours the moon would have risen and would give me all the light I needed to reach the rock-face of Monte Verità. I looked east, to the descent. The whole of it was hidden in the same wall of cloud. Until the cloud dissolved I should still be in the same position I had been all day, uncertain of direction, helpless in visibility that was never more than three feet.

I decided to go on, and to climb to the summit of the mountain with my message.

Now the cloud was beneath me my spirits revived. I studied the rough map drawn by Victor, and set out towards the southern shoulder. I was hungry, and would have given much to have back the sandwiches I had eaten at midday. A roll of bread was all that remained to me. That, and a packet of cigarettes.

Cigarettes were not helpful to the wind, but at least they staved off the desire for food.

Now I could see the twin peaks themselves, clear and stark against the sky. And a new excitement came to me, as I looked up at them, for I knew that when I had rounded the shoulder and had come to the southern face of the mountain, I should have reached my journey's end.

I went on climbing; and I saw how the ridge narrowed and how the rock steepened, becoming more sheer as the southern slopes opened up to view, and then, over my shoulder, rose the first tip of the moon's great face, out of the misty vapour to the east. The sight of it stirred me to a new sense of isolation. It was as though I walked alone on the earth's rim, the universe below me and above. No one trod this empty discus but myself, and it spun its way through space to ultimate darkness.

As the moon rose, the man that climbed with it shrank to insignificance. I was no longer aware of personal identity. This shell, in which I had my being, moved forward without feeling, drawn to the summit of the mountain by some name- less force which seemed to hold suction from the moon itself. I was impelled, like the flow and ebb of tide upon water. I could not disobey the law that urged me on, any more than I could cease to breathe. This was not mountain fever in my blood, but mountain magic. It was not nervous energy that drove me, but the tug of the full moon.

The rock narrowed and closed above my head, making an arch, a gully, so that I had to stoop and feel my way; then I emerged from darkness into light, and there before me, silver-white, were the twin peaks and the rock face of Monte Verità.

For the first time in my life I looked on beauty bare. My mission was forgotten, my anxiety for Victor, my own fear of cloud that had clamped me through the day. This indeed was journey's end. This was fulfilment. Time did not matter. I had no thought of it. I stood there staring at the rock-face under the moon.

How long I remained motionless I do not know, nor do I remember when the change came to the tower and the walls; but suddenly the figures were there, that had not been before. They stood one behind the other on the walls, silhouetted against the sky, and they might have been stone images, carved from the rock itself, so still they were, so motionless.

I was too distant from them to see their faces or their shape. One stood alone, within the open tower; this one alone was shrouded, in a garment reaching from head to foot. Suddenly there came to my mind old tales of ancient days, of Druids, of slaughter, and of sacrifice. These people worshipped the moon, and the moon was full. Some victim was going to be flung to the depths below, and I would witness the act.

I had known fear in my life before, but never terror. Now it came upon me in full measure. I knelt down, in the shadow of the gully, for surely they must see me standing there, in the moon's path. I saw them raise their arms above their heads, and slowly a murmur came from them, low and indistinct at first, then swelling louder, breaking upon the silence that hitherto had been profound. The sound echoed from the rock-face, rose and fell upon the air, and I saw them one and all turn to the full moon. There was no sacrifice. No act of slaughter. This was their song of praise.

I hid there, in the shadows, with all the ignorance and shame of one who stumbles into a place of worship alien to his knowledge, while the chanting rang in my ears, unearthly, terrifying, yet beautiful in a way impossible to bear. I clasped my hands over my head, I shut my eyes, I bent low until my forehead touched the ground.

Then slowly, very slowly, the great hymn of praise faded in strength. It sank lower to a murmur, to a sigh. It hushed and died away. Silence came back to Monte Verità.

Still I dared not move. My hands covered my head. My face was to the ground. I am not ashamed of my terror. I was lost between two worlds. My own was gone, and I was not of theirs. I longed for the sanctuary of the drifting clouds again.

I waited, still upon my knees. Then furtive, creeping, I lifted up my head and looked towards the rock-face. The walls and the tower were bare. The figures had vanished. And a cloud, dark and ragged, hid the moon.

I stood up, but I did not move. I kept my eyes fixed upon the tower and the walls. Nothing stirred, now that the moon was masked. They might never have been, the figures and the chanting. Perhaps my own fear and imagination had created them.

I waited until the cloud that hid the moon's face passed away. Then I took courage and felt for the letters in my pocket. I do not know what Victor had written, but my own ran thus:

Dear Anna,

Some strange providence brought me to the village on Monte Verità. I found Victor there. He is desperately ill, and I think dying. If you have a message to send him, leave it beneath the wall. I will carry it to him. I must warn you also that I believe your community to be in danger. The people from the valley are frightened and angry because one of their women has disappeared. They are likely to come to Monte Verità, and do damage.

In parting, I want to tell you that Victor has never stopped loving you and thinking about you.

311

And I signed my name at the bottom of the page.

I started walking towards the wall. As I drew close I could see the slit windows, described to me long ago by Victor, and it came to me that there might be eyes behind them, watching, that beyond each narrow opening there could be a figure, waiting.

I stooped and put the letters on the ground beneath the wall. As I did so, the wall before me swung back suddenly and opened. Arms stretched forth from the yawning gap and seized me, and I was flung to the ground, with hands about my throat.

The last thing I heard, before losing consciousness, was the sound of a boy, laughing.

I awoke with violence, jerked back into reality from some great depth of slumber, and I knew that a moment before I had not been alone. Someone had been beside me, kneeling, peering down into my sleeping face.

I sat up and looked about me, cold and numb. I was in a cell about ten foot long, and the daylight, ghostly pale, filtered through the narrow slit in the stone wall. I glanced at my watch. The hands pointed to a quarter to five. I must have lain unconscious for a little over four hours, and this was the false light that comes before dawn.

My first feeling now, on waking, was one of anger. I had been fooled. The people in the village below Monte Verità had lied to me, and to Victor too. The rough hands that had seized me, and the boy's laugh that I heard, these had belonged to the villagers themselves. That man, and his son, had preceded me up the mountain track, and had lain in wait for me. They knew a way of entry through the walls. They had fooled Victor through the years, and thought to fool me too. God alone knew their motive. It could not be robbery. We neither of us had anything but the clothes we wore. This cell into which they had thrust me was quite bare. No sign of human habitation, not even a board on which to lie. A strange thing, though – they had not bound me. And there was no door to the cell. The entry was open, a long slit, like the window, but large enough to permit the passage of a single form.

I sat waiting for the light to strengthen and for the feeling, too, to come back to my shoulders, arms and legs. My sense of caution told me this was wise. If I ventured through the opening now, I might in the dim light stumble, and fall, and be lost in some labyrinth of passage-way or stair.

My anger grew with the daylight, yet with it also a feeling of despair. I longed more than anything to get hold of the fellow and his son, threaten them both, fight them if necessary – I would not be thrown to the ground a second time unawares. But what if they had gone away and left me in this place, without means of exit? Supposing this, then, was the trick they played on strangers, and had done so through countless years, the old man before them, and others before him, luring the women from the valley too, and once inside these walls leaving the victims to starvation and death? The uneasiness mounting in me would turn to panic if I thought too far ahead, and to calm myself I felt in my pocket for my cigarette case. The first few puffs steadied me, the smell and the taste of the smoke belonged to the world I knew.

Then I saw the frescoes. The growing light betrayed them to me. They covered the walls of the cell, and were drawn upon the ceiling too. Not the rough primitive efforts of uncultured peasants, nor yet the saintly scrawling of religious artists, deeply moved by faith. These frescoes had life and vigour, colour and intensity, and whether they told a story or not I did not know, but the motif was clearly worship of the moon. Some figures knelt, others stood; one and all had their arms up, raised to the full moon traced upon the ceiling. Yet in

313

some strange fashion the eyes of the worshippers, drawn with uncanny skill, looked down upon me, not upwards to the moon. I smoked my cigarette and looked away, but all the time I felt their eyes fasten on me, as the daylight grew, and it was like being back outside the walls again, aware of silent watchers from behind the slit windows.

I got up, stamping on my cigarette, and it seemed to me that anything would be better than to remain there in the cell, alone with those figures on the painted walls. I moved to the opening, and as I did so I heard the laughter once again. Softer this time, as though subdued, but mocking and youthful still. That damned boy . . .

I plunged through the opening, cursing him and shouting. He might have a knife upon him but I didn't care. And there he was, flattened against the wall, waiting for me. I could see the gleam of his eyes, and I saw his close-cropped hair. I struck at his face, and missed. I heard him laughing as he slipped to one side. Then he wasn't alone any more; there was another just behind, and a third. They threw themselves upon me and I was borne to the ground as though I had no strength at all, and the first one knelt with his knee on my chest and his hands about my throat, and he was smiling at me.

I lay fighting for breath, and he relaxed his grip, and the three of them watched me, with that same mocking smile upon their lips. I saw then that none of them was the boy from the village, nor was the father there, and they did not have the faces of village people or of the valley people: their faces were like the painted frescoes on the wall.

Their eyes were heavy-lidded, slanting, without mercy, like the eyes I had seen once long ago on an Egyptian tomb, and on a vase long hidden and forgotten under the dust and rubble of a buried city. Each wore a tunic to his knees, with bare arms, bare legs and hair cropped close to the head, and there was a strange austere beauty about them, and a devilish grace as well. I tried to raise myself from the ground, but the one who had his hand upon my throat pressed me back, and I knew I was no match for him or his companions, and if they wanted to they could throw me from the walls down to the depths below Monte Verità. This was the end, then. It was only a matter of time, and Victor would die alone, back in the hut on the mountain-side.

'Go ahead,' I said, 'have done with it,' resigned, caring no longer. I expected the laughter again, mocking and youthful, and the sudden seizing of my body with their hands, and the savage thrusting of me through the slit window to darkness and to death. I closed my eyes, and with nerves taut braced myself for horror. Nothing happened. I felt the boy touch my lips. I opened my eyes and he was smiling still, and he had a cup in his hands, with milk in it, and he was urging me to drink, but he did not speak. I shook my head but his companions came and knelt behind me, supporting my shoulders and my back, and I began to drink, foolishly, gratefully, like a child. The fear went as they held me, and the horror too, and it was as though strength passed from their hands to mine, and not only to my hands but to the whole of me.

When I had finished drinking the first one took the cup from me and put it on the ground, then he placed his two hands on my heart, his fingers touching, and the feeling that came to me was something I had never experienced in my life before. It was as if the peace of God came upon me, quiet and strong, and, with the touch of hands, took from me all anxiety and fear, all the fatigue and terror of the preceding night; and my memory of the cloud and mist on the mountain, and Victor dying on his lonely bed, became suddenly things of no importance. They shrank into insignificance beside this feeling of strength and beauty that I knew now. If Victor died it would not matter. His body would be a shell lying there in the peasant hut, but his heart would be beating here, as mine was beating, and his mind would come to us too.

I say 'to us' because it seemed to me, sitting there in the narrow cell, that I had been accepted by my companions and made one of them. This, I thought to myself, still wondering but bewildered, happy, this is what I always hoped that death would be. The negation of all pain and all distress, and the centre of life flowing, not from the quibbling brain, but from the heart.

The boy took his hands from me, still smiling, but the feeling of strength, of power, was with me still. He rose to his feet and I did the same, and I followed him and the two others through the gap in the cell. There was no honeycomb of twisting corridors, no dark cloisters, but a great open court on to which the cells all gave, and the fourth side of the court led upwards to the twin peaks of Monte Verità, ice-capped, beautiful, caught now in the rose light of the rising sun. Steps cut in the ice led to the summit, and now I knew the reason for the silence within the walls and in the court as well, for there were the other ones, ranged upon the steps, dressed in those same tunics with bare arms and legs, girdles about the waist, and the hair cropped close to the head.

We passed through the court and up the steps beside them. There was no sound: they did not speak to me or to one another, but they smiled as the first three had done; and their smile was neither courteous nor tender, as we know it in the world, but had a strange exulting quality, as if wisdom and triumph and passion were all blended into one. They were ageless, they were sexless, they were neither male nor female, old or young, but the beauty of their faces, and of their bodies too, was more stirring and exciting than anything I had ever seen or known, and with a sudden longing I wanted to be one of them, to be dressed as they were dressed, to love as they must love, to laugh and worship and be silent.

I looked down at my coat and shirt, my climbing breeches, my thick socks and shoes, and suddenly I hated and despised them. They were like grave clothes covering the dead, and I flung them off, in haste to have them gone, throwing them over my shoulder down to the court below; and I stood naked under the sun. I was without embarrassment or shame. I was quite unconscious how I looked and I did not care. All I knew was that I wanted to have done with the trappings of the world, and my clothes seemed to symbolize the self I had once been.

We climbed the steps and reached the summit, and now the whole world lay before us, without mist or cloud, the lesser peaks stretching away into infinity, and far below, concerning us not at all, hazy and green and still, were the valleys and the streams and the little sleeping towns. Then, turning from the world below, I saw that the twin peaks of Monte Verità were divided by a great crevasse, narrow yet impassable, and standing on the summit, gazing downwards, I realized with wonder, and with awe as well, that my eyes could not penetrate the depths. The ice-blue walls of the crevasse descended smooth and hard without a break to some great bottomless chasm, hidden for ever in the mountain heart. The sun that rose to bathe the peaks at midday would never touch the depths of that crevasse, nor would the rays of the full moon come to it, but it seemed to me, between the peaks, that the shape of it was like a chalice held between two hands.

Someone was standing there, dressed in white from head to foot, on the very brink of the chasm, and although I could not see her features, for the cowl of the white robe concealed them, the tall upright figure, with head thrown back and arms outstretched, caught at my heart with sudden tense excitement.

317

I knew it was Anna. I knew that no one else would stand in just that way. I forgot Victor, I forgot my mission, I forgot time and place and all the years between. I remembered only the stillness of her presence, the beauty of her face, and that quiet voice saying to me, 'We are both in search of the same thing, after all.' I knew then that I had loved her always, and that though she had met Victor first, and chosen him, and married him, the ties and ceremony of marriage concerned neither of us, and never had. Our minds had met and crossed and understood from the first moment when Victor introduced us in my club, and that queer, inexplicable bond of the heart, breaking through every barrier, every restraint, had kept us close to one another always, in spite of silence, absence, and long years of separation.

The mistake was mine from the beginning in letting her go alone to find her mountain. Had I gone with them, she and Victor, when they asked me that day in the Map House long ago, intuition would have told me what was in her mind and the spell would have come upon me as well. I would not have slept on in the hut, as Victor had slept, but would have woken and gone with her, and the years that I had wasted and thrown away, futile and mis-spent, would have been our years, Anna's and mine, shared here on the mountain, cut off from the world.

Once again I looked about me and at the faces of those who stood beside me, and I guessed dimly, with a sort of hunger near to pain, what ecstasy of love they knew, that I had never known. Their silence was not a vow, condemning them to darkness, but a peace that the mountain gave to them, merging their minds in tune. There was no need for speech, when a smile, a glance, conveyed a message and a thought; while laughter, triumphant always, sprang from the heart's centre, never to be suppressed. This was no closed order, gloomy, sepulchral, denying all that

318

instinct gave the heart. Here Life was fulfilled, clamouring, intense, and the great heat of the sun seeped into the veins, becoming part of the blood stream, part of the living flesh; and the frozen air, merging with the direct rays of the sun, cleansed the body and the lungs, bringing power and strength – the power I had felt when the fingers touched my heart.

In the space of so short a while my values had all changed, and the self who had climbed the mountain through the mist, fearful, anxious and angry too, but a little while ago, seemed to exist no more. I was grey-haired, past middle age, a madman to the world's eyes if they could see me now, a laughing-stock, a fool; and I stood naked with the rest of them on Monte Verità and held up my arms to the sun. It rose now in the sky and shone upon us, and the blistering of my skin was pain and pleasure blended, and the heat drove through my heart and through my lungs.

I kept my eyes fixed on Anna, loving her with such intensity that I heard myself calling aloud, 'Anna . . . Anna . . .' And she knew that I was there, for she lifted her hand in signal. None of them minded, none of them cared. They laughed with me, they understood.

Then from the midst of us came a girl, walking. She was dressed in a simple village frock, with stockings and shoes, and her hair hung loose on her shoulders. I thought her hands were folded together, as though in prayer, but they were not. She held them to her heart, the fingers touching.

She went to the brink of the crevasse, where Anna stood. Last night, beneath the moon, I should have been gripped by fear, but not now. I had been accepted. I was one of them. For one instant, in its space of time above us in the sky, the sun's ray touched the lip of the crevasse, and the blue ice shone. We knelt with one accord, our faces to the sun, and I heard the hymn of praise.

'This,' I thought, 'was how men worshipped in the beginning, how they will worship in the end. Here is no creed, no saviour, and no deity. Only the sun, which gives us light and life. This is how it has always been, from the beginning of time.'

The sun's ray lifted and passed on, and then the girl, rising to her feet, threw off her stockings and her shoes and her dress also, and Anna, with a knife in her hand, cut off her hair, cropping it close above the ears. The girl stood before her, her hands upon her heart.

'Now she is free,' I thought. 'She won't go back to the valley again. Her parents will mourn her, and her young man too, and they'll never discover what she has found, here on Monte Verità. In the valley there would have been feasting and celebration, and then dancing at the wedding, and afterwards the turmoil of a brief romance turning to humdrum married life, the cares of her house, the cares of children, anxiety, fret, illness, trouble, the day-by-day routine of growing old. Now she is spared all that. Here, nothing once felt is lost. Love and beauty don't die or fade away. Living's hard, because Nature's hard, and Nature has no mercy; but it was this she wanted in the valley, it was for this she came. She will know everything here that she never knew before and would not have discovered, below there in the world. Passion and joy and laughter, the heat of the sun, the tug of the moon, love without emotion, sleep with no waking dream. And that's why they hate it, in the valley, that's why they're afraid of Monte Verità. Because here on the summit is something they don't possess and never will, so they are angry and envious and unhappy.'

Then Anna turned, and the girl who had thrown her sex away with her past life and her village clothes followed barefoot, bare armed, cropped-haired like the others; and she was radiant, smiling, and I knew that nothing would ever matter to her again.

They descended to the court, leaving me alone on the summit, and I felt like an outcast before the gates of heaven. My brief moment had come and gone. They belonged here, and I did not. I was a stranger from the world below.

I put on my clothes again, restored to a sanity I did not want, and remembering Victor and my mission I too went down the steps to the court, and looking upwards I saw that Anna was waiting for me in the tower above.

The others flattened themselves against the wall to let me pass, and I saw that Anna alone amongst them wore the long white robe and the cowl. The tower was lofty, open to the sky, and characteristically, with that same gesture I remembered when she used to sit on the low stool before the fire in the great hall, Anna sat down now, on the topmost step of the tower, one knee raised and elbow on that knee. Today was yesterday, today was six-and-twenty years ago, and we were alone once more in the manor house in Shropshire; and the peace she had brought to me then she brought me now. I wanted to kneel beside her and take her hand. Instead I went and stood beside the wall, my arms folded.

'So you found it at last,' she said. 'It took a little time.'

The voice was soft and still and quite unchanged.

'Did you bring me here?' I asked. 'Did you call me when the aircraft crashed?'

She laughed, and I had never been away from her. Time stood still on Monte Verità.

'I wanted you to come long before that,' she said, 'but you shut your mind away from me. It was like clamping down a receiver. It always took two to make a telephone call. Does it still?'

'It does,' I answered, 'and our more modern inventions need valves for contact. Not the mind, though.'

'Your mind has been a box for so many years,' she said. 'It was a pity – we could have shared so much. Victor had to tell

321

me his thoughts in letters, which wouldn't have been necessary with you.'

It was then, I think, that the first hope came to me. I must feel my way towards it, though, with care.

'You've read his letter,' I asked, 'and mine as well? You know that he's dying?'

'Yes,' she said, 'he's been ill for many weeks. That's why I wanted you to be here at this time, so that you could be with him when he died. And it will be all right for him, now, when you go back to him and tell him that you've spoken to me. He'll be happy then.'

'Why not come yourself?'

'Better this way,' she said. 'Then he can keep his dream.'

His dream? What did she mean? They were not, then, all-powerful here on Monte Verità? She understood the danger in which they stood.

'Anna,' I said, 'I'll do what you want me to do. I'll return to Victor and be with him at the last. But time is very short. More important still is the fact that you and the others here are in great danger. Tomorrow, tonight even, the people from the valley are going to climb here to Monte Verità, and they'll break into this place and kill you. It's imperative that you get away before they come. If you have no means of saving yourselves, then you must allow me to do something to help you. We are not so far from civilization as to make that impossible. I can get down to the valley, find a telephone, get through to the police, to the army, to some authority in charge . . .'

My words trailed off, because although my plans were not clear in my own mind I wanted her to have confidence in me, to feel that she could trust me.

'The point is,' I told her, 'that life is going to be impossible for you here, from now on. If I can prevent the attack this time, which is doubtful, it will happen next week, next month.

Your days of security are numbered. You've lived here shut away so long that you don't understand the state of the world as it is now. Even this country here is torn in two with suspicion, and the people in the valley aren't superstitious peasants any longer; they're armed with modern weapons, and they've got murder in their hearts. You won't stand a chance, you and the rest, here on Monte Verità.'

She did not answer. She sat there on the step, listening, a remote and silent figure in her white robe and cowl.

'Anna,' I said, 'Victor's dying. He may be already dead. When you leave here he can't help you, but I can. I've loved you always. No need to tell you that, you must have guessed it. You destroyed two men, you know, when you came to live on Monte Verità six-and-twenty years ago. But that doesn't matter any more. I've found you again. And there are still places far away, inaccessible to civilization, where we could live, you and I — and the others with you here, if they wished to come with us. I have money enough to arrange all that; you won't have to worry about anything.'

I saw myself discussing practicalities with consuls, embassies, going into the question of passports, papers, clothing.

I saw too, in my mind's eye, the map of the world. I ranged in thought from a ridge of mountains in South America to the Himalayas, from the Himalayas to Africa. Or the northern wastes of Canada were still vast and unexplored, and stretches of Greenland. And there were islands, innumerable, countless islands, where no man ever trod, visited only by sea-birds, washed by the lonely sea. Mountain or island, scrubby wilderness or desert, impenetrable forest or Arctic waste, I did not care which she chose; but I had been without sight of her for so long, and now all I wanted was to be with her always.

This was now possible, because Victor, who would have claimed her, was going to die. I was blunt. I was truthful. I told her this as well. And then I waited, to hear what she would say.

She laughed, that warm, much loved and well-remembered laugh, and I wanted to go to her and put my arms round her, because the laugh held so much life in it, and so much joy and promise.

'Well?' I said.

Then she got up from the step and came and stood beside me, very still.

'There was once a man,' she said, 'who went to the booking office at Waterloo and said to the clerk eagerly, hopefully, 'I want a ticket to Paradise. A single ticket. No return.' And when the clerk told him there was no such place the man picked up the ink-well and threw it in the clerk's face. The police were summoned, and took the man away and put him in prison. Isn't that what you're asking of me now, a ticket to Paradise? This is the mountain of truth, which is very different.'

I felt hurt, irritated even. She hadn't taken a word of my plans seriously and was making fun of me.

'What do you propose, then?' I asked. 'To wait here, behind these walls, for the people to come and break them down?'

'Don't worry about us,' she said. 'We know what we shall do.'

She spoke with indifference, as if the matter was of no importance, and in agony I saw the future, that I had begun to plan for us both, slip away from me.

'Then you do possess some secret?' I asked, almost in accusation. 'You can work some miracle, and save yourself and the others, too? What about me? Can't you take me with you?'

'You wouldn't want to come,' she said. She put her hand on my arm. 'It takes time, you know, to build a Monte Verità. It isn't just doing without clothes and worshipping the sun.'

'I realize that,' I told her. 'I'm prepared to begin all over again, to learn new values, to start from the beginning. I know that nothing I've done in the world is any use. Talent, hard work, success, all those things are meaningless. But if I could be with you . . .'

'How? With me?' she said.

And I did not know what to answer, because it would be too sudden and too direct, but I knew in my heart that what I wanted was everything that could be between a woman and a man; not at first, of course, but later, when we had found our other mountain, or our wilderness, or wherever it was we might go to hide ourselves from the world. There was no need to rehearse all that now. The point was that I was prepared to follow her anywhere, if she would let me.

'I love you, and have always loved you. Isn't that enough?' I asked.

'No,' she said, 'not on Monte Verità.'

And she threw back her cowl and I saw her face.

I gazed at her in horror . . . I could not move, I could not speak. It was as though all feeling had been frozen. My heart was cold . . . One side of her face was eaten quite away, ravaged, terrible. The disease had come upon her brow, her cheek, her throat, blotching, searing the skin. The eyes that I had loved were blackened, sunk deep into the sockets.

'You see,' she said, 'it isn't Paradise.'

I think I turned away. I don't remember. I know I leant against the rock of the tower and stared down into the depths below, and saw nothing but the great bank of cloud that hid the world.

'It happened to others,' Anna said, 'but they died. If I survived longer, it was because I was hardier than they. Leprosy can come to anyone, even to the supposed immortals of Monte Verità. It hasn't really mattered, you know. I regret nothing. Long ago I remember telling you that those who go to the mountain must give everything. That's all there is to it. I no longer suffer, so there's no need to suffer for me.'

I said nothing. I felt the tears run down my face. I didn't bother to wipe them away.

'There are no illusions and no dreams on Monte Verità,' she said. 'They belong to the world, and you belong there too. If I've destroyed the fantasy you made of me, forgive me. You've lost the Anna you knew once, and found another one instead. Which you will remember longer rather depends upon yourself. Now go back to your world of men and women and build yourself a Monte Verità.'

Somewhere there was scrub and grass and stunted trees; somewhere there was earth and stones and the sound of running water. Deep in the valley there were homes, where men lived with their women, reared their children. They had firelight, curling smoke and lighted windows. Somewhere there were roads, there were railways, there were cities. So many cities, so many streets. And all with crowded buildings, lighted windows. They were there, beneath the cloud, beneath Monte Verità.

'Don't be anxious or afraid,' said Anna, 'and as for the valley people, they can't harm us. One thing only . . .' She paused, and although I did not look at her I think she smiled. 'Let Victor keep his dream,' she said.

Then she took my hand, and we went down the steps of the tower together, and through the court and to the walls of the rock-face. They stood there watching us, those others, with their bare arms and legs, their close-cropped hair, and I saw too the little village girl, the proselyte, who had renounced the world and was now one of them. I saw her turn and look at Anna, and I saw the expression in her eyes; there was no horror there, no fear and no revulsion. One and all they looked at Anna with triumph, with exultation, with all knowledge and all understanding. And I knew that what she felt and what she endured they felt also, and shared with her, and accepted. She was not alone.

They turned their eyes to me, and their expression changed; instead of love and knowledge I read compassion.

Anna did not say goodbye. She put her hand an instant on my shoulder. Then the wall opened, and she was gone from me. The sun was no longer overhead. It had started its journey in the western sky. The great white banks of cloud rolled upward from the world below. I turned my back on Monte Verità.

It was evening when I came to the village. The moon had not yet risen. Presently, within two hours or less, it would top the eastern ridge of the further mountains and give light to the whole sky. They were waiting, the people from the valley. There must have been three hundred or more, waiting there in groups beside the huts. All of them were armed, some with rifles, with grenades, others, more primitive, with picks and axes. They had kindled fires, on the village track between the huts, and had brought provisions too. They stood or sat before the fires eating and drinking, smoking and talking. Some of them had dogs, held tightly on a leash.

The owner of the first hut stood by the door with his son. They too were armed. The boy had a pick and a knife thrust in his belt. The man watched me with his sullen, stupid face.

'Your friend is dead,' he said. 'He has been dead these many hours.'

I pushed past him and went into the living-room of the hut. Candles had been lit. One at the head of the bed, one at the foot. I bent over Victor and took his hand. The man had lied to me. Victor was breathing still. When he felt me touch his hand, he opened his eyes.

'Did you see her?' he asked.

'Yes,' I answered.

'Something told me you would,' he said. 'Lying here, I felt that it would happen. She's my wife, and I've loved her all

327

these years, but you only have been allowed to see her. Too late, isn't it, to be jealous now?'

The candlelight was dim. He could not see the shadows by the door, nor hear the movement and the whispering without.

'Did you give her my letter?' he said.

'She has it,' I answered. 'She told you not to worry, not to be anxious. She is all right. Everything is well with her.'

Victor smiled. He let go my hand.

'So it's true,' he said, 'all the dreams I had of Monte Verità. She is happy and contented and she will never grow old, never lose her beauty. Tell me, her hair, her eyes, her smile – were they still the same?'

'Just the same,' I said. 'Anna will always be the most beautiful woman you or I have ever known.'

He did not answer. And as I waited there, beside him, I heard the sudden blowing of a horn, echoed by a second and a third. I heard the restless movement of the men outside in the village, as they shouldered their weapons, kicked out the fires and gathered together for the climb. I heard the dogs barking and the men laughing, ready now, excited. When they had gone I went and stood alone in the deserted village, and I watched the full moon rising from the dark valley.

The Pool

The children ran out on to the lawn. There was space all around them, and light, and air, with the trees indeterminate beyond. The gardener had cut the grass. The lawn was crisp and firm now, because of the hot sun through the day; but near the summer-house where the tall grass stood there were dew-drops like frost clinging to the narrow stems.

The children said nothing. The first moment always took them by surprise. The fact that it waited, thought Deborah, all the time they were away; that day after day while they were at school, or in the Easter holidays with the aunts at Hunstanton being blown to bits, or in the Christmas holidays with their father in London riding on buses and going to theatres – the fact that the garden waited for them was a miracle known only to herself. A year was so long. How did the garden endure the snows clamping down upon it, or the chilly rain that fell in November? Surely sometimes it must mock the slow steps of Grandpapa pacing up and down the terrace in front of the windows, or Grandmama calling to Patch? The garden had to endure month after month of silence, while the children were gone. Even the spring and the days of May and June were wasted, all those mornings of butterflies and darting birds, with no one to watch but Patch gasping for breath on a cool stone slab. So wasted was the garden, so lost.

'You must never think we forget,' said Deborah in the silent voice she used to her own possessions. 'I remember, even at school, in the middle of French' – but the ache then was unbearable, that it should be the hard grain of a desk under her hands, and not the grass she bent to touch now. The children had had an argument once about whether there was more grass in the world or more sand, and Roger said that of course there must be more sand, because of under the sea; in every ocean all over the world there would be sand, if you looked deep down. But there could be grass too, argued Deborah, a waving grass, a grass that nobody had ever seen, and the colour of that ocean grass would be darker than any grass on the surface of the world, in fields or prairies or people's gardens in America. It would be taller than trees and it would move like corn in a wind.

They had run in to ask somebody adult, 'What is there most of in the world, grass or sand?', both children hot and passionate from the argument. But Grandpapa stood there in his old panama hat looking for clippers to trim the hedge – he was rummaging in the drawer full of screws – and he said, 'What? What?' impatiently.

The boy turned red – perhaps it was a stupid question – but the girl thought, he doesn't know, they never know, and she made a face at her brother to show that she was on his side. Later they asked their grandmother, and she, being practical, said briskly, 'I should think sand. Think of all the grains,' and

330

Roger turned in triumph, 'I told you so!' The grains. Deborah had not considered the grains. The magic of millions and millions of grains clinging together in the world and under the oceans made her sick. Let Roger win, it did not matter. It was better to be in the minority of the waving grass.

Now, on this first evening of summer holiday, she knelt and then lay full-length on the lawn, and stretched her hands out on either side like Jesus on the Cross, only face downwards, and murmured over and over again the words she had memorized from Confirmation preparation. 'A full, perfect and sufficient sacrifice . . . a full, perfect and sufficient sacrifice . . . satisfaction, and oblation, for the sins of the whole world.' To offer herself to the earth, to the garden, the garden that had waited patiently all these months since last summer, surely this must be her first gesture.

'Come on,' said Roger, rousing himself from his appreciation of how Willis the gardener had mown the lawn to just the right closeness for cricket, and without waiting for his sister's answer he ran to the summer-house and made a dive at the long box in the corner where the stumps were kept. He smiled as he lifted the lid. The familiarity of the smell was satisfying. Old varnish and chipped paint, and surely that must be the same spider and the same cobweb? He drew out the stumps one by one, and the bails, and there was the ball – it had not been lost after all, as he had feared. It was worn, though, a greyish red – he smelt it and bit it, to taste the shabby leather. Then he gathered the things in his arms and went out to set up the stumps.

'Come and help me measure the pitch,' he called to his sister, and looking at her, squatting in the grass with her face hidden, his heart sank, because it meant that she was in one of her absent moods and would not concentrate on the cricket.

'Deb?' he called anxiously. 'You are going to play?'

331

Deborah heard his voice through the multitude of earth sounds, the heartbeat and the pulse. If she listened with her ear to the ground there was a humming much deeper than anything that bees did, or the sea at Hunstanton. The nearest to it was the wind, but the wind was reckless. The humming of the earth was patient. Deborah sat up, and her heart sank just as her brother's had done, for the same reason in reverse. The monotony of the game ahead would be like a great chunk torn out of privacy.

'How long shall we have to be?' she called.

The lack of enthusiasm damped the boy. It was not going to be any fun at all if she made a favour of it. He must be firm, though. Any concession on his part she snatched and turned to her advantage.

'Half-an-hour,' he said, and then, for encouragement's sake, 'You can bat first.'

Deborah smelt her knees. They had not yet got the country smell, but if she rubbed them in the grass, and in the earth too, the white London look would go.

'All right,' she said, 'but no longer than half-an-hour.'

He nodded quickly, and so as not to lose time measured out the pitch and then began ramming the stumps in the ground. Deborah went into the summer-house to get the bats. The familiarity of the little wooden hut pleased her as it had her brother. It was a long time now, many years, since they had played in the summer-house, making yet another house inside this one with the help of broken deck-chairs; but, just as the garden waited for them a whole year, so did the summer-house, the windows on either side, cobweb-wrapped and stained, gazing out like eyes. Deborah did her ritual of bowing twice. If she should forget this, on her first entrance, it spelt ill-luck.

She picked out the two bats from the corner, where they were stacked with old croquet-hoops, and she knew at once that Roger would choose the one with the rubber handle, even though they could not bat at the same time, and for the whole of the holidays she must make do with the smaller one, that had half the whipping off. There was a croquet clip lying on the floor. She picked it up and put it on her nose and stood a moment, wondering how it would be if forever more she had to live thus, nostrils pinched, making her voice like Punch. Would people pity her?

'Hurry,' shouted Roger, and she threw the clip into the corner, then quickly returned when she was halfway to the pitch, because she knew the clip was lying apart from its fellows, and she might wake in the night and remember it. The clip would turn malevolent, and haunt her. She replaced him on the floor with two others, and now she was absolved and the summer-house at peace.

'Don't get out too soon,' warned Roger as she stood in the crease he had marked for her, and with a tremendous effort of concentration Deborah forced her eyes to his retreating figure and watched him roll up his sleeves and pace the required length for his run-up. Down came the ball and she lunged out, smacking it in the air in an easy catch. The impact of ball on bat stung her hands. Roger missed the catch on purpose. Neither of them said anything.

'Who shall I be?' called Deborah.

The game could only be endured, and concentration kept, if Roger gave her a part to play. Not an individual, but a country.

'You're India,' he said, and Deborah felt herself grow dark and lean. Part of her was tiger, part of her was sacred cow, the long grass fringing the lawn was jungle, the roof of the summer-house a minaret.

Even so, the half-hour dragged, and, when her turn came to bowl, the ball she threw fell wider every time, so that Roger, flushed and self-conscious because their grandfather had come out on to the terrace and was watching them, called angrily, 'Do try.'

Once again the effort of concentration, the figure of their grandfather – a source of apprehension to the boy, for he might criticize them – acting as a spur to his sister. Grandpapa was an Indian God, and tribute must be paid to him, a golden apple. The apple must be flung to slay his enemies. Deborah muttered a prayer, and the ball she bowled came fast and true and hit Roger's off-stump. In the moment of delivery their grandfather had turned away and pottered back again through the french windows of the drawing-room.

Roger looked round swiftly. His disgrace had not been seen. 'Jolly good ball,' he said. 'It's your turn to bat again.'

But his time was up. The stable clock chimed six. Solemnly Roger drew stumps.

'What shall we do now?' he asked.

Deborah wanted to be alone, but if she said so, on this first evening of the holiday, he would be offended.

'Go to the orchard and see how the apples are coming on,' she suggested, 'and then round by the kitchen-garden in case the raspberries haven't all been picked. But you have to do it all without meeting anyone. If you see Willis or anyone, even the cat, you lose a mark.'

It was these sudden inventions that saved her. She knew her brother would be stimulated at the thought of outwitting the gardener. The aimless wander round the orchard would turn into a stalking exercise.

'Will you come too?' he asked.

'No,' she said, 'you have to test your skill.'

He seemed satisfied with this and ran off towards the orchard, stopping on the way to cut himself a switch from the bamboo.

As soon as he had disappeared Deborah made for the trees

fringing the lawn, and once in the shrouded wood felt herself safe. She walked softly along the alley-way to the pool. The late sun sent shafts of light between the trees and on to the alley-way, and a myriad insects webbed their way in the beams, ascending and descending like angels on Jacob's ladder. But were they insects, wondered Deborah, or particles of dust, or even split fragments of light itself, beaten out and scattered by the sun?

It was very quiet. The woods were made for secrecy. They did not recognize her as the garden did. They did not care that for a whole year she could be at school, or at Hunstanton, or in London. The woods would never miss her: they had their own dark, passionate life.

Deborah came to the opening where the pool lay, with the five alley-ways branching from it, and she stood a moment before advancing to the brink, because this was holy ground and required atonement. She crossed her hands on her breast and shut her eyes. Then she kicked off her shoes. 'Mother of all things wild, do with me what you will,' she said aloud. The sound of her own voice gave her a slight shock. Then she went down on her knees and touched the ground three times with her forehead.

The first part of her atonement was accomplished, but the pool demanded sacrifice, and Deborah had come prepared. There was a stub of pencil she had carried in her pocket throughout the school term which she called her luck. It had teeth marks on it, and a chewed piece of rubber at one end. This treasure must be given to the pool just as other treasures had been given in the past, a miniature jug, a crested button, a china pig. Deborah felt for the stub of pencil and kissed it. She had carried and caressed it for so many lonely months, and now the moment of parting had come. The pool must not be denied. She flung out her right hand, her eyes still shut, and heard the faint plop as the stub of pencil struck the water. Then she opened her eyes, and saw in mid-pool a ripple. The pencil had gone, but the ripple moved, gently shaking the water-lilies. The movement symbolized acceptance.

Deborah, still on her knees and crossing her hands once more, edged her way to the brink of the pool and then, crouching there beside it, looked down into the water. Her reflection wavered up at her, and it was not the face she knew, not even the looking-glass face which anyway was false, but a disturbed image, dark-skinned and ghostly. The crossed hands were like the petals of the water-lilies themselves, and the colour was not waxen white but phantom green. The hair too was not the live clump she brushed every day and tied back with ribbon, but a canopy, a shroud. When the image smiled it became more distorted still. Uncrossing her hands, Deborah leant forward, took a twig, and drew a circle three times on the smooth surface. The water shook in ever widening ripples, and her reflection, broken into fragments, heaved and danced, a sort of monster, and the eyes were there no longer, nor the mouth.

Presently the water became still. Insects, long-legged flies and beetles with spread wings hummed upon it. A dragon-fly had all the magnificence of a lily leaf to himself. He hovered there, rejoicing. But when Deborah took her eyes off him for a moment he was gone. At the far end of the pool, beyond the clustering lilies, green scum had formed, and beneath the scum were rooted, tangled weeds. They were so thick, and had lain in the pool so long, that if a man walked into them from the bank he would be held and choked. A fly, though, or a beetle, could sit upon the surface, and to him the pale green scum would not be treacherous at all, but a resting-place, a haven. And if someone threw a stone, so that the ripples formed, eventually they came to the scum, and rocked it, and the whole of the mossy surface moved in rhythm, a dancing-floor for those who played upon it.

There was a dead tree standing by the far end of the pool. He could have been fir or pine, or even larch, for time had stripped him of identity. He had no distinguishing mark upon his person, but with grotesque limbs straddled the sky. A cap of ivy crowned his raked head. Last winter a dangling branch had broken loose, and this now lay in the pool half-submerged, the green scum dripping from the withered twigs. The soggy branch made a vantage-point for birds, and as Deborah watched a nestling suddenly flew from the undergrowth enveloping the dead tree, and perched for an instant on the mossy filigree. He was lost in terror. The parent bird cried warningly from some dark safety, and the nestling, pricking to the cry, took off from the branch that had offered him temporary salvation. He swerved across the pool, his flight mistimed, yet reached security. The chitter from the undergrowth told of his scolding. When he had gone silence returned to the pool.

It was, so Deborah thought, the time for prayer. The water-lilies were folding upon themselves. The ripples ceased. And that dark hollow in the centre of the pool, that black stillness where the water was deepest, was surely a funnel to the kingdom that lay below. Down that funnel had travelled the discarded treasures. The stub of pencil had lately plunged the depths. He had now been received as an equal among his fellows. This was the single law of the pool, for there were no other commandments. Once it was over, that first cold headlong flight, Deborah knew that the softness of the welcoming water took away all fear. It lapped the face and cleansed the eyes, and the plunge was not into darkness at all but into light. It did not become blacker as the pool was penetrated, but paler, more golden-green, and the mud that people told themselves was there was only a defence against strangers. Those who belonged, who knew, went to the source at once, and there were caverns and fountains and rainbow-coloured seas. There were shores of the whitest sand. There was soundless music.

Once again Deborah closed her eyes and bent lower to the pool. Her lips nearly touched the water. This was the great silence, when she had no thoughts, and was accepted by the pool. Waves of quiet ringed themselves about her, and slowly she lost all feeling, and had no knowledge of her legs, or of her kneeling body, or of her cold, clasped hands. There was nothing but the intensity of peace. It was a deeper acceptance than listening to the earth, because the earth was of the world, the earth was a throbbing pulse, but the acceptance of the pool meant another kind of hearing, a closing in of the waters, and just as the lilies folded so did the soul submerge.

'Deborah . . . ? Deborah . . . ?' Oh, no! Not now, don't let them call me back now! It was as though someone had hit her on the back, or jumped out at her from behind a corner, the sharp and sudden clamour of another life destroying the silence, the secrecy. And then came the tinkle of the cowbells. It was the signal from their grandmother that the time had come to go in. Not imperious and ugly with authority, like the clanging bell at school summoning those at play to lessons or chapel, but a reminder, nevertheless, that Time was all-important, that life was ruled to order, that even here, in the holiday home the children loved, the adult reigned supreme.

'All right, all right,' muttered Deborah, standing up and thrusting her numbed feet into her shoes. This time the rather raised tone of 'Deborah?', and the more hurried clanging of the cowbells, brought long ago from Switzerland, suggested a more imperious Grandmama than the tolerant one who seldom questioned. It must mean their supper was already laid, soup perhaps getting cold, and the farce of washing hands, of tidying, of combing hair, must first be gone through.

'Come on, Deb,' and now the shout was close, was right at hand, privacy lost forever, for her brother came running down the alley-way swishing his bamboo stick in the air.

'What *have* you been doing?' The question was an intrusion and a threat. She would never have asked him what he had been doing, had he wandered away wanting to be alone, but Roger, alas, did not claim privacy. He liked companionship, and his question now, asked half in irritation, half in resentment, came really from the fear that he might lose her.

'Nothing,' said Deborah.

Roger eyed her suspiciously. She was in that morning mood. And it meant, when they went to bed, that she would not talk. One of the best things, in the holidays, was having the two adjoining rooms and calling through to Deb, making her talk.

'Come on,' he said, 'they've rung,' and the making of their grandmother into 'they', turning a loved individual into something impersonal, showed Deborah that even if he did not understand he was on her side. He had been called from play, just as she had.

They ran from the woods to the lawn, and on to the terrace. Their grandmother had gone inside, but the cowbells hanging by the french window were still jangling.

The custom was for the children to have their supper first, at seven, and it was laid for them in the dining-room on a hot-plate. They served themselves. At a quarter-to-eight their grandparents had dinner. It was called dinner, but this was a concession to their status. They ate the same as the children, though Grandpapa had a savoury which was not served to the children. If the children were late for supper then it put out Time, as well as Agnes, who cooked for both generations, and it might mean five minutes' delay before Grandpapa had his soup. This shook routine.

The children ran up to the bathroom to wash, then downstairs to the dining-room. Their grandfather was standing in the hall. Deborah sometimes thought that he would have enjoyed sitting with them while they ate their supper, but he never suggested it. Grandmama had warned them, too, never to be a nuisance, or indeed to shout, if Grandpapa was near. This was not because he was nervous, but because he liked to shout himself.

'There's going to be a heat-wave,' he said. He had been listening to the news.

'That will mean lunch outside tomorrow,' said Roger swiftly. Lunch was the meal they took in common with the grandparents, and it was the moment of the day he disliked. He was nervous that his grandfather would ask him how he was getting on at school.

'Not for me, thank you,' said Grandpapa. 'Too many wasps.'

Roger was at once relieved. This meant that he and Deborah would have the little round garden-table to themselves. But Deborah felt sorry for her grandfather as he went back into the drawing-room. Lunch on the terrace could be gay, and would liven him up. When people grew old they had so few treats.

'What do you look forward to most in the day?' she once asked her grandmother.

'Going to bed,' was the reply, 'and filling my two hot water bottles.' Why work through being young, thought Deborah, to this?

Back in the dining-room the children discussed what they should do during the heat-wave. It would be too hot, Deborah said, for cricket. But they might make a house, suggested Roger, in the trees by the paddock. If he got a few old boards from Willis, and nailed them together like a platform, and borrowed the orchard ladder, then they could take fruit and bottles of orange squash and keep them up there, and it would be a camp from which they could spy on Willis afterwards.

Deborah's first instinct was to say she did not want to play, but she checked herself in time. Finding the boards and fixing them would take Roger a whole morning. It would keep him employed. 'Yes, it's a good idea,' she said, and to foster his spirit of adventure she looked at his notebook, as they were drinking their soup, and approved of items necessary for the camp while he jotted them down. It was all part of the day-long deceit she practised to express understanding of his way of life.

When they had finished supper they took their trays to the kitchen and watched Agnes, for a moment, as she prepared the second meal for the grandparents. The soup was the same, but garnished. Little croûtons of toasted bread were added to it. And the butter was made into pats, not cut in a slab. The savoury tonight was to be cheese straws. The children finished the ones that Agnes had burnt. Then they went through to the drawing-room to say good night. The older people had both changed. Grandpapa was in a smoking-jacket, and wore soft slippers. Grandmama had a dress that she had worn several years ago in London. She had a cardigan round her shoulders like a cape.

'Go carefully with the bath-water,' she said. 'We'll be short if there's no rain.'

They kissed her smooth, soft skin. It smelt of rose leaves. Grandpapa's chin was sharp and bony. He did not kiss Roger.

'Be quiet overhead,' whispered their grandmother. The children nodded. The dining-room was underneath their rooms, and any jumping about or laughter would make a disturbance.

Deborah felt a wave of affection for the two old people. Their lives must be empty and sad. 'We *are* glad to be here,' she said. Grandmama smiled. This was how she lived, thought Deborah, on little crumbs of comfort.

Once out of the room their spirits soared, and to show relief Roger chased Deborah upstairs, both laughing for no reason. Undressing, they forgot the instructions about the bath, and when they went into the bathroom – Deborah was to have first go – the water was gurgling into the overflow. They tore out the plug in a panic, and listened to the waste roaring down the pipe to the drain below. If Agnes did not have the wireless on she would hear it.

The children were too old now for boats or play, but the bathroom was a place for confidences, for a sharing of those few tastes they agreed upon, or, after quarrelling, for moody silence. The one who broke silence first would then lose face.

'Willis has a new bicycle,' said Roger. 'I saw it propped against the shed. I couldn't try it because he was there. But I shall tomorrow. It's a Raleigh.'

He liked all practical things, and the trying of the gardener's bicycle would give an added interest to the morning of next day. Willis had a bag of tools in a leather pouch behind the saddle. These could all be felt and the spanners, smelling of oil, tested for shape and usefulness.

'If Willis died,' said Deborah, 'I wonder what age he would be.'

It was the kind of remark that Roger resented always. What had death to do with bicycles? 'He's sixty-five,' he said, 'so he'd be sixty-five.'

'No,' said Deborah, 'what age when he got *there*.'

Roger did not want to discuss it. 'I bet I can ride it round the stables if I lower the seat,' he said. 'I bet I don't fall off.'

But if Roger would not rise to death, Deborah would not rise to the wager. 'Who cares?' she said.

The sudden streak of cruelty stung the brother. Who cared indeed . . . The horror of an empty world encompassed him, and to give himself confidence he seized the wet sponge and flung it out of the window. They heard it splosh on the terrace below.

'Grandpapa will step on it, and slip,' said Deborah, aghast.

The image seized them, and choking back laughter they covered their faces. Hysteria doubled them up. Roger rolled over and over on the bathroom floor. Deborah, the first to recover, wondered why laughter was so near to pain, why Roger's face, twisted now in merriment, was yet the same crumpled thing when his heart was breaking.

'Hurry up,' she said briefly, 'let's dry the floor,' and as they wiped the linoleum with their towels the action sobered them both.

Back in their bedrooms, the door open between them, they watched the light slowly fading. But the air was warm like day. Their grandfather and the people who said what the weather was going to be were right. The heat-wave was on its way. Deborah, leaning out of the open window, fancied she could see it in the sky, a dull haze where the sun had been before; and the trees beyond the lawn, day-coloured when they were having their supper in the dining-room, had turned into night-birds with outstretched wings. The garden knew about the promised heat-wave, and rejoiced: the lack of rain was of no consequence yet, for the warm air was a trap, lulling it into a drowsy contentment.

The dull murmur of their grandparents' voices came from the dining-room below. What did they discuss, wondered Deborah. Did they make those sounds to reassure the children, or were their voices part of their unreal world? Presently the voices ceased, and then there was a scraping of chairs, and voices from a different quarter, the drawing-room now, and a faint smell of their grandfather's cigarette.

Deborah called softly to her brother but he did not answer. She went through to his room, and he was asleep. He must have fallen asleep suddenly, in the midst of talking. She was relieved. Now she could be alone again, and not have to keep up the pretence of sharing conversation. Dusk was everywhere, the sky a deepening black. 'When they've gone up to bed,' thought Deborah, 'then I'll be truly alone.' She knew what she was going to do. She waited there, by the open window, and the deepening sky lost the veil that covered it, the haze disintegrated, and the stars broke through. Where there had been nothing was life, dusty and bright, and the waiting earth gave off a scent of knowledge. Dew rose from the pores. The lawn was white.

Patch, the old dog, who slept at the end of Grandpapa's bed on a plaid rug, came out on to the terrace and barked hoarsely. Deborah leant out and threw a piece of creeper on to him. He shook his back. Then he waddled slowly to the flower-tub above the steps and cocked his leg. It was his nightly routine. He barked once more, staring blindly at the hostile trees, and went back into the drawing-room. Soon afterwards, someone came to close the windows – Grandmama, thought Deborah, for the touch was light. 'They are shutting out the best,' said the child to herself, 'all the meaning, and all the point.' Patch, being an animal, should know better. He ought to be in a kennel where he could watch, but instead, grown fat and soft, he preferred the bumpiness of her grandfather's bed. He had forgotten the secrets. So had they, the old people.

Deborah heard her grandparents come upstairs. First her grandmother, the quicker of the two, and then her grandfather, more laboured, saying a word or two to Patch as the little dog wheezed his way up. There was a general clicking of lights and shutting of doors. Then silence. How remote, the world of the grandparents, undressing with curtains closed. A pattern of life unchanged for so many years. What went on without would never be known. 'He that has ears to hear, let him hear,' said Deborah, and she thought of the callousness of Jesus which no priest could explain. Let the dead bury their dead. All the people in the world, undressing now, or sleeping, not just in the village but in cities and capitals, they were shutting out the truth, they were burying their dead. They wasted silence.

The stable clock struck eleven. Deborah pulled on her clothes. Not the cotton frock of the day, but her old jeans that Grandmama disliked, rolled up above her knees. And a jersey. Sandshoes with a hole that did not matter. She was cunning enough to go down by the back stairs. Patch would bark if she tried the front stairs, close to the grandparents' rooms. The backstairs led past Agnes' room, which smelt of apples though she never ate fruit. Deborah could hear her snoring. She would not even wake on Judgement Day. And this led her to wonder on the truth of that fable too, for there might be so many millions by then who liked their graves – Grandpapa, for instance, fond of his routine, and irritated at the sudden riot of trumpets.

Deborah crept past the pantry and the servants' hall – it was only a tiny sitting-room for Agnes, but long usage had given it the dignity of the name – and unlatched and unbolted the heavy back door. Then she stepped outside, on to the gravel, and took the long way round by the front of the house so as not to tread on the terrace, fronting the lawns and the garden.

The warm night claimed her. In a moment it was part of her. She walked on the grass, and her shoes were instantly soaked. She flung up her arms to the sky. Power ran to her fingertips. Excitement was communicated from the waiting trees, and the orchard, and the paddock; the intensity of their secret life caught at her and made her run. It was nothing like the excitement of ordinary looking forward, of birthday presents, of Christmas stockings, but the pull of a magnet – her grandfather had shown her once how it worked, little needles springing to the jaws – and now night and the sky above were a vast magnet, and the things that waited below were needles, caught up in the great demand.

Deborah went to the summer-house, and it was not sleeping like the house fronting the terrace but open to understanding, sharing complicity. Even the dusty windows caught the light, and the cobwebs shone. She rummaged for the old lilo and the moth-eaten car rug that Grandmama had thrown out two summers ago, and bearing them over her shoulder she made her way to the pool. The alley-way was ghostly, and Deborah knew, for all her mounting tension, that the test was hard. Part of her was still body-bound, and afraid of shadows. If anything stirred she would jump and know true terror. She must show defiance, though. The woods expected it. Like old wise lamas they expected courage.

She sensed approval as she ran the gauntlet, the tall trees watching. Any sign of turning back, of panic, and they would crowd upon her in a choking mass, smothering protest. Branches would become arms, gnarled and knotty, ready to strangle, and the leaves of the higher trees fold in and close like the sudden furling of giant umbrellas. The smaller undergrowth, obedient to the will, would become a briary of a million thorns where animals of no known world crouched snarling, their eyes on fire. To show fear was to show misunderstanding. The woods were merciless.

Deborah walked the alley-way to the pool, her left hand holding the lilo and the rug on her shoulder, her right hand raised in salutation. This was a gesture of respect. Then she paused before the pool and laid down her burden beside it. The lilo was to be her bed, the rug her cover. She took off her shoes, also in respect, and lay down upon the lilo. Then, drawing the rug to her chin, she lay flat, her eyes upon the sky. The gauntlet of the alley-way over, she had no more fear.

The woods had accepted her, and the pool was the final resting-place, the doorway, the key.

'I shan't sleep,' thought Deborah. 'I shall just lie awake here all the night and wait for morning, but it will be a kind of introduction to life, like being confirmed.'

The stars were thicker now than they had been before. No space in the sky without a prick of light, each star a sun. Some, she thought, were newly born, white-hot, and others wise and colder, nearing completion. The law encompassed them, fixing the riotous path, but how they fell and tumbled depended upon themselves. Such peace, such stillness, such sudden quietude, excitement gone. The trees were no longer menacing but guardians, and the pool was primeval water, the first, the last.

Then Deborah stood at the wicket-gate, the boundary, and there was a woman with outstretched hand, demanding tickets. 'Pass through,' she said when Deborah reached her. 'We saw you coming.' The wicket-gate became a turnstile. Deborah pushed against it and there was no resistance, she was through.

'What is it?' she asked. 'Am I really here at last? Is this the bottom of the pool?'

'It could be,' smiled the woman. 'There are so many ways. You just happened to choose this one.'

Other people were pressing to come through. They had no faces, they were only shadows. Deborah stood aside to let them by, and in a moment they had gone, all phantoms.

'Why only now, tonight?' asked Deborah. 'Why not in the afternoon, when I came to the pool?'

'It's a trick,' said the woman. 'You seize on the moment in time. We were here this afternoon. We're always here. Our life goes on around you, but nobody knows it. The trick's easier by night, that's all.'

'Am I dreaming, then?' asked Deborah.

347

'No,' said the woman, 'this isn't a dream. And it isn't death, either. It's the secret world.'

The secret world . . . It was something Deborah had always known, and now the pattern was complete. The memory of it, and the relief, were so tremendous that something seemed to burst inside her heart.

'Of course . . .' she said, 'of course . . .' and everything that had ever been fell into place. There was no disharmony. The joy was indescribable, and the surge of feeling, like wings about her in the air, lifted her away from the turnstile and the woman, and she had all knowledge. That was it – the invasion of knowledge.

'I'm not myself, then, after all,' she thought. 'I knew I wasn't. It was only the task given,' and, looking down, she saw a little child who was blind trying to find her way. Pity seized her. She bent down and put her hands on the child's eyes, and they opened, and the child was herself at two years old. The incident came back. It was when her mother died and Roger was born.

'It doesn't matter after all,' she told the child. 'You are not lost. You don't have to go on crying.' Then the child that had been herself melted, and became absorbed in the water and the sky, and the joy of the invading flood intensified so that there was no body at all but only being. No words, only movements. And the beating of wings. This above all, the beating of wings.

'Don't let me go!' It was a pulse in her ear, and a cry, and she saw the woman at the turnstile put up her hands to hold her. Then there was such darkness, such dragging, terrible darkness, and the beginning of pain all over again, the leaden heart, the tears, the misunderstanding. The voice saying 'No!' was her own harsh, worldly voice, and she was staring at the restless trees, black and ominous against the sky. One hand trailed in the water of the pool.

Deborah sat up, sobbing. The hand that had been in the pool was wet and cold. She dried it on the rug. And suddenly she was seized with such fear that her body took possession, and throwing aside the rug she began to run along the alley-way, the dark trees mocking and the welcome of the woman at the turnstile turned to treachery. Safety lay in the house behind the closed curtains, security was with the grandparents sleeping in their beds, and like a leaf driven before a whirlwind Deborah was out of the woods and across the silver soaking lawn, up the steps beyond the terrace and through the garden-gate to the back door.

The slumbering solid house received her. It was like an old staid person who, surviving many trials, had learnt experience. 'Don't take any notice of them,' it seemed to say, jerking its head – did a house have a head? – towards the woods beyond. 'They've made no contribution to civilization. I'm man-made and different. This is where you belong, dear child. Now settle down.'

Deborah went back again upstairs and into her bedroom. Nothing had changed. It was still the same. Going to the open window she saw that the woods and the lawn seemed unaltered from the moment, how long back she did not know, when she had stood there, deciding upon the visit to the pool. The only difference now was in herself. The excitement had gone, the tension too. Even the terror of those last moments, when her flying feet had brought her to the house, seemed unreal.

She drew the curtains, just as her grandmother might have done, and climbed into bed. Her mind was now preoccupied with practical difficulties, like explaining the presence of the lilo and the rug beside the pool. Willis might find them, and tell her grandfather. The feel of her own pillow, and of her own blankets, reassured her. Both were familiar. And being tired was familiar too, it was a solid bodily ache, like the tiredness after too much jumping or cricket. The thing was, though — and the last remaining conscious thread of thought decided to postpone conclusion until the morning — which was real? This safety of the house, or the secret world?

2

When Deborah woke next morning she knew at once that her mood was bad. It would last her for the day. Her eyes ached, and her neck was stiff, and there was a taste in her mouth like magnesia. Immediately Roger came running into her room, his face refreshed and smiling from some dreamless sleep, and jumped on her bed.

'It's come,' he said, 'the heat-wave's come. It's going to be ninety in the shade.'

Deborah considered how best she could damp his day. 'It can go to a hundred for all I care,' she said. 'I'm going to read all morning.'

His face fell. A look of bewilderment came into his eyes. 'But the house?' he said. 'We'd decided to have a house in the trees, don't you remember? I was going to get some planks from Willis.'

Deborah turned over in bed and humped her knees. 'You can, if you like,' she said. 'I think it's a silly game.'

She shut her eyes, feigning sleep, and presently she heard his feet patter slowly back to his own room, and then the thud of a ball against the wall. If he goes on doing that, she thought maliciously, Grandpapa will ring his bell, and Agnes will come panting up the stairs. She hoped for destruction, for grumbling and snapping, and everyone falling out, not speaking. That was the way of the world.

The kitchen, where the children breakfasted, faced west, so

it did not get the morning sun. Agnes had hung up fly-papers to catch wasps. The cereal, puffed wheat, was soggy. Deborah complained, mashing the mess with her spoon.

'It's a new packet,' said Agnes. 'You're mighty particular all of a sudden.'

'Deb's got out of bed the wrong side,' said Roger.

The two remarks fused to make a challenge. Deborah seized the nearest weapon, a knife, and threw it at her brother. It narrowly missed his eye, but cut his cheek. Surprised, he put his hand to his face and felt the blood. Hurt, not by the knife but by his sister's action, his face turned red and his lower lip quivered. Deborah ran out of the kitchen and slammed the door. Her own violence distressed her, but the power of the mood was too strong. Going on to the terrace, she saw that the worst had happened. Willis had found the lilo and the rug, and had put them to dry in the sun. He was talking to her grandmother. Deborah tried to slip back into the house, but it was too late.

'Deborah, how very thoughtless of you,' said Grandmama. 'I tell you children every summer that I don't mind your taking the things from the hut into the garden if only you'll put them back.'

Deborah knew she should apologize, but the mood forbade it. 'That old rug is full of moth,' she said contemptuously, 'and the lilo has a rainproof back. It doesn't hurt them.'

They both stared at her, and her grandmother flushed, just as Roger had done when she had thrown the knife at him. Then her grandmother turned her back and continued giving some instructions to the gardener.

Deborah stalked along the terrace, pretending that nothing had happened, and skirting the lawn she made her way towards the orchard and so to the fields beyond. She picked up a windfall, but as soon as her teeth bit into it the taste was green.

She threw it away. She went and sat on a gate and stared in front of her, looking at nothing. Such deception everywhere. Such sour sadness. It was like Adam and Eve being locked out of paradise. The Garden of Eden was no more. Somewhere, very close, the woman at the turnstile waited to let her in, the secret world was all about her, but the key was gone. Why had she ever come back? What had brought her?

People were going about their business. The old man who came three days a week to help Willis was sharpening his scythe behind the toolshed. Beyond the field where the lane ran towards the main road she could see the top of the post-man's head. He was pedalling his bicycle towards the village. She heard Roger calling, 'Deb? Deb . . . ?', which meant that he had forgiven her, but still the mood held sway and she did not answer. Her own dullness made her own punishment. Presently a knocking sound told her that he had got the planks from Willis and had embarked on the building of his house. He was like his grandfather; he kept to the routine set for himself.

Deborah was consumed with pity. Not for the sullen self humped upon the gate, but for all of them going about their business in the world who did not hold the key. The key was hers, and she had lost it. Perhaps if she worked her way through the long day the magic would return with evening and she would find it once again. Or even now, by the pool, there might be a clue, a vision.

Deborah slid off the gate and went the long way round. By skirting the fields, parched under the sun, she could reach the other side of the wood and meet no one. The husky wheat was stiff. She had to keep close to the hedge to avoid brushing it, and the hedge was tangled. Foxgloves had grown too tall and were bending with empty sockets, their flowers gone. There were nettles everywhere. There was no gate into the wood, and she had to climb the pricking hedge with the barbed wire tearing her knickers. Once in the wood some measure of peace returned, but the alley-ways this side had not been scythed, and the grass was long. She had to wade through it like a sea, brushing it aside with her hands.

She came upon the pool from behind the monster tree, the hybrid whose naked arms were like a dead man's stumps, projecting at all angles. This side, on the lip of the pool, the scum was carpet-thick, and all the lilies, coaxed by the risen sun, had opened wide. They basked as lizards bask on hot stone walls. But here, with stems in water, they swung in grace, cluster upon cluster, pink and waxen white. 'They're asleep,' thought Deborah. 'So is the wood. The morning is not their time,' and it seemed to her beyond possibility that the turnstile was at hand and the woman waiting, smiling. 'She said they were always there, even in the day, but the truth is that being a child I'm blinded in the day. I don't know how to see.'

She dipped her hands in the pool, and the water was tepid brown. She tasted her fingers, and the taste was rank. Brackish water, stagnant from long stillness. Yet beneath . . . beneath, she knew, by night the woman waited, and not only the woman but the whole secret world. Deborah began to pray. 'Let it happen again,' she whispered. 'Let it happen again. Tonight. I won't be afraid.'

The sluggish pool made no acknowledgement, but the very silence seemed a testimony of faith, of acceptance. Beside the pool, where the imprint of the lilo had marked the moss, Deborah found a kirby-grip, fallen from her hair during the night. It was proof of visitation. She threw it into the pool as part of the treasury. Then she walked back into the ordinary day and the heat-wave, and her black mood was softened. She went to find Roger in the orchard. He was busy with the platform. Three of the boards were fixed, and the noisy hammering was something that had to be borne. He saw her coming, and as always, after trouble, sensed that her mood had changed and mention must never be made of it. Had he called, 'Feeling better?', it would have revived the antagonism, and she might not play with him all the day. Instead, he took no notice. She must be the first to speak.

Deborah waited at the foot of the tree, then bent, and handed him up an apple. It was green, but the offering meant peace. He ate it manfully. 'Thanks,' he said. She climbed into the tree beside him and reached for the box of nails. Contact had been renewed. All was well between them.

3

The hot day spun itself out like a web. The heat haze stretched across the sky, dun-coloured and opaque. Crouching on the burning boards of the apple-tree, the children drank ginger-beer and fanned themselves with dock-leaves. They grew hotter still. When the cowbells summoned them for lunch they found that their grandmother had drawn the curtains of all the rooms downstairs, and the drawing-room was a vault and strangely cool. They flung themselves into chairs. No one was hungry. Patch lay under the piano, his soft mouth dripping saliva. Grandmama had changed into a sleeveless linen dress never before seen, and Grandpapa, in a dented panama, carried a fly-whisk used years ago in Egypt.

'Ninety-one,' he said grimly, 'on the Air Ministry roof. It was on the one o'clock news.'

Deborah thought of the men who must measure heat, toiling up and down on this Ministry roof with rods and tapes and odd-shaped instruments. Did anyone care but Grandpapa?

'Can we take our lunch outside?' asked Roger.

His grandmother nodded. Speech was too much effort, and she sank languidly into her chair at the foot of the dining-room table. The roses she had picked last night had wilted.

The children carried chicken drumsticks to the summer-house. It was too hot to sit inside, but they sprawled in the shadow it cast, their heads on faded cushions shedding kapok. Somewhere, far above their heads, an aeroplane climbed like a small silver fish, and was lost in space.

'A Meteor,' said Roger. 'Grandpapa says they're obsolete.'

Deborah thought of Icarus, soaring towards the sun. Did he know when his wings began to melt? How did he feel? She stretched out her arms and thought of them as wings. The fingertips would be the first to curl, and then turn cloggy soft, and useless. What terror in the sudden loss of height, the drooping power . . .

Roger, watching her, hoped it was some game. He threw his picked drumstick into a flower-bed and jumped to his feet.

'Look,' he said, 'I'm a Javelin,' and he too stretched his arms and ran in circles, banking. Jet noises came from his clenched teeth. Deborah dropped her arms and looked at the drumstick. What had been clean and white from Roger's teeth was now earth-brown. Was it offended to be chucked away? Years later, when everyone was dead, it would be found, moulded like a fossil. Nobody would care.

'Come on,' said Roger.

'Where to?' she asked.

'To fetch the raspberries,' he said.

'You go,' she told him.

Roger did not like going into the dining-room alone. He was self-conscious. Deborah made a shield from the adult eyes. In the end he consented to fetch the raspberries without her on condition that she played cricket after tea. After tea was a long way off.

She watched him return, walking very slowly, bearing the plates of raspberries and clotted cream. She was seized with sudden pity, that same pity which, earlier, she had felt for all people other than herself. How absorbed he was, how intent on the moment that held him. But tomorrow he would be some old man far away, the garden forgotten, and this day long past.

'Grandmama says it can't go on,' he announced. 'There'll have to be a storm.'

But why? Why not forever? Why not breathe a spell so that all of them could stay locked and dreaming like the courtiers in the *Sleeping Beauty*, never knowing, never waking, cobwebs in their hair and on their hands, tendrils imprisoning the house itself?

'Race me,' said Roger, and to please him she plunged her spoon into the mush of raspberries but finished last, to his delight.

No one moved during the long afternoon. Grandmama went upstairs to her room. The children saw her at her window in her petticoat drawing the curtains close. Grandpapa put his feet up in the drawing-room, a handkerchief over his face. Patch did not stir from his place under the piano. Roger, undefeated, found employment still. He first helped Agnes to shell peas for supper, squatting on the back-door step while she relaxed on a lop-sided basket chair dragged from the servants' hall. This task finished, he discovered a tin-bath, put away in the cellar, in which Patch had been washed in younger days. He carried it to the lawn and filled it with water. Then he stripped to bathing-trunks and sat in it solemnly, an umbrella over his head to keep off the sun.

Deborah lay on her back behind the summer-house, wondering what would happen if Jesus and Buddha met. Would there be discussion, courtesy, an exchange of views like politicians at summit talks? Or were they after all the same person, born at separate times? The queer thing was that this topic, interesting now, meant nothing in the secret world. Last night, through the turnstile, all problems disappeared. They were non-existent. There was only the knowledge and the joy.

She must have slept, because when she opened her eyes she saw to her dismay that Roger was no longer in the bath but was hammering the cricket-stumps into the lawn. It was a quarter-to-five.

'Hurry up,' he called, when he saw her move. 'I've had tea.'

She got up and dragged herself into the house, sleepy still, and giddy. The grandparents were in the drawing-room, refreshed from the long repose of the afternoon. Grandpapa smelt of eau-de-cologne. Even Patch had come to and was lapping his saucer of cold tea.

'You look tired,' said Grandmama critically. 'Are you feeling all right?'

Deborah was not sure. Her head was heavy. It must have been sleeping in the afternoon, a thing she never did.

'I think so,' she answered, 'but if anyone gave me roast pork I know I'd be sick.'

'No one suggested you should eat roast pork,' said her grandmother, surprised. 'Have a cucumber sandwich, they're cool enough.'

Grandnapa was lying in wait for a wasp. He watched it hover over his tea, grim, expectant. Suddenly he slammed at the air with his whisk. 'Got the brute,' he said in triumph. He ground it into the carpet with his heel. It made Deborah think of Jehovah.

'Don't rush around in the heat,' said Grandmama. 'It isn't wise. Can't you and Roger play some nice, quiet game?'

'What sort of game?' asked Deborah.

But her grandmother was without invention. The croquet

mallets were all broken. 'We might pretend to be dwarfs and use the heads,' said Deborah, and she toyed for a moment with the idea of squatting to croquet. Their knees would stiffen, though, it would be too difficult.

'I'll read aloud to you, if you like,' said Grandmama.

Deborah seized upon the suggestion. It delayed cricket. She ran out on to the lawn and padded the idea to make it acceptable to Roger.

'I'll play afterwards,' she said, 'and that ice-cream that Agnes has in the fridge, you can eat all of it. I'll talk tonight in bed.'

Roger hesitated. Everything must be weighed. Three goods to balance evil.

'You know that stick of sealing-wax Daddy gave you?' he said.

'Yes.'

'Can I have it?'

The balance for Deborah too. The quiet of the moment in opposition to the loss of the long thick stick so brightly red.

'All right,' she grudged.

Roger left the cricket stumps and they went into the drawing-room. Grandpapa, at the first suggestion of reading aloud, had disappeared, taking Patch with him. Grandmama had cleared away the tea. She found her spectacles and the book. It was *Black Beauty*. Grandmama kept no modern children's books, and this made common ground for the three of them. She read the terrible chapter where the stable-lad lets Beauty get overheated and gives him a cold drink and does not put on his blanket. The story was suited to the day. Even Roger listened entranced. And Deborah, watching her grandmother's calm face and hearing her careful voice reading the sentences, thought how strange it was that Grandmama could turn herself into Beauty with such ease. She *was* a horse, suffering there with pneumonia in the stable, being saved by the wise coachman.

After the reading, cricket was anti-climax, but Deborah must keep her bargain. She kept thinking of Black Beauty writing the book. It showed how good the story was, Grandmama said, because no child had ever yet questioned the practical side of it, or posed the picture of a horse with a pen in its hoof.

'A modern horse would have a typewriter,' thought Deborah, and she began to bowl to Roger, smiling to herself as she did so because of the twentieth-century Beauty clacking with both hoofs at a machine.

This evening, because of the heat-wave, the routine was changed. They had their baths first, before their supper, for they were hot and exhausted from the cricket. Then, putting on pyjamas and cardigans, they ate their supper on the terrace. For once Grandmama was indulgent. It was still so hot that they could not take chill, and the dew had not yet risen. It made a small excitement, being in pyjamas on the terrace. Like people abroad, said Roger. Or natives in the South Seas, said Deborah. Or beachcombers who had lost caste. Grandpapa, changed into a white tropical jacket, had not lost caste.

'He's a white trader,' whispered Deborah. 'He's made a fortune out of pearls.'

Roger choked. Any joke about his grandfather, whom he feared, had all the sweet agony of danger.

'What's the thermometer say?' asked Deborah.

Her grandfather, pleased at her interest, went to inspect it.

'Still above eighty,' he said with relish.

Deborah, when she cleaned her teeth later, thought how pale her face looked in the mirror above the wash-basin. It was not brown, like Roger's, from the day in the sun, but wan and yellow. She tied back her hair with a ribbon, and the nose and chin were peaky sharp. She yawned largely, as Agnes did in the kitchen on Sunday afternoons.

'Don't forget you promised to talk,' said Roger quickly.

Talk . . . That was the burden. She was so tired she longed for the white smoothness of her pillow, all blankets thrown aside, bearing only a single sheet. But Roger, wakeful on his bed, the door between them wide, would not relent. Laughter was the one solution, and to make him hysterical, and so exhaust him sooner, she fabricated a day in the life of Willis, from his first morning kipper to his final glass of beer at the village inn. The adventures in between would have tried Gulliver. Roger's delight drew protests from the adult world below. There was the sound of a bell, and then Agnes came up the stairs and put her head round the corner of Deborah's door.

'Your Granny says you're not to make so much noise,' she said.

Deborah, spent with invention, lay back and closed her eyes. She could go no further. The children called good night to each other, both speaking at the same time, from age-long custom, beginning with their names and addresses and ending with the world, the universe, and space. Then the final main 'Good night', after which neither must ever speak, on pain of unknown calamity.

'I must try and keep awake,' thought Deborah, but the power was not in her. Sleep was too compelling, and it was hours later that she opened her eyes and saw her curtains blowing and the forked flash light the ceiling, and heard the trees tossing and sobbing against the sky. She was out of bed in an instant. Chaos had come. There were no stars, and the night was sulphurous. A great crack split the heavens and tore them in two. The garden groaned. If the rain would only fall there might be mercy, and the trees, imploring, bowed themselves this way and that, while the vivid lawn, bright in expectation, lay like a sheet of metal exposed to flame. Let the waters break. Bring down the rain.

Suddenly the lightning forked again, and standing there,

alive yet immobile, was the woman by the turnstile. She stared up at the windows of the house, and Deborah recognized her. The turnstile was there, inviting entry, and already the phantom figures, passing through it, crowded towards the trees beyond the lawn. The secret world was waiting. Through the long day, while the storm was brewing, it had hovered there unseen beyond her reach, but now that night had come, and the thunder with it, the barriers were down. Another crack, mighty in its summons, the turnstile yawned, and the woman with her hand upon it smiled and beckoned.

Deborah ran out of the room and down the stairs. Somewhere somebody called – Roger, perhaps, it did not matter – and Patch was barking; but caring nothing for concealment she went through the dark drawing-room and opened the french window on to the terrace. The lightning searched the terrace and lit the paving, and Deborah ran down the steps on to the lawn where the turnstile gleamed.

Haste was imperative. If she did not run the turnstile might be closed, the woman vanish, and all the wonder of the sacred world be taken from her. She was in time. The woman was still waiting. She held out her hand for tickets, but Deborah shook her head. 'I have none.' The woman, laughing, brushed her through into the secret world where there were no laws, no rules, and all the faceless phantoms ran before her to the woods, blown by the rising wind. Then the rain came. The sky, deep brown as the lightning pierced it, opened, and the water hissed to the ground, rebounding from the earth in bubbles. There was no order now in the alley-way. The ferns had turned to trees, the trees to Titans. All moved in ecstasy, with sweeping limbs, but the rhythm was broken up, tumultuous, so that some of them were bent backwards, torn by the sky, and others dashed their heads to the undergrowth where they were caught and beaten.

In the world behind, laughed Deborah as she ran, this would be punishment, but here in the secret world it was a tribute. The phantoms who ran beside her were like waves. They were linked one with another, and they were, each one of them, and Deborah too, part of the night force that made the sobbing and the laughter. The lightning forked where they willed it, and the thunder cracked as they looked upwards to the sky.

The pool had come alive. The water-lilies had turned to hands, with palms upraised, and in the far corner, usually so still under the green scum, bubbles sucked at the surface, steaming and multiplying as the torrents fell. Everyone crowded to the pool. The phantoms bowed and crouched by the water's edge, and now the woman had set up her turnstile in the middle of the pool, beckoning them once more. Some remnant of a sense of social order rose in Deborah and protested.

'But we've already paid,' she shouted, and remembered a second later that she had passed through free. Must there be duplication? Was the secret world a rainbow, always repeating itself, alighting on another hill when you believed yourself beneath it? No time to think. The phantoms had gone through. The lightning, streaky white, lit the old dead monster tree with his crown of ivy, and because he had no spring now in his joints he could not sway in tribute with the trees and ferns, but had to remain there, rigid, like a crucifix.

'And now . . . and now . . . and now . . .' called Deborah.

The triumph was that she was not afraid, was filled with such wild acceptance . . . She ran into the pool. Her living feet felt the mud and the broken sticks and all the tangle of old weeds, and the water was up to her armpits and her chin. The lilies held her. The rain blinded her. The woman and the turnstile were no more.

'Take me too,' cried the child. 'Don't leave me behind!' In

362

her heart was a savage disenchantment. They had broken their promise, they had left her in the world. The pool that claimed her now was not the pool of secrecy, but dank, dark, brackish water choked with scum.

4

'Grandpapa says he's going to have it fenced round,' said Roger. 'It should have been done years ago. A proper fence, then nothing can ever happen. But barrow-loads of shingle tipped in it first. Then it won't be a pool, but just a dewpond. Dewponds aren't dangerous.'

He was looking at her over the edge of her bed. He had risen in status, being the only one of them downstairs, the bearer of tidings good or ill, the go-between. Deborah had been ordered two days in bed.

'I should think by Wednesday,' he went on, 'you'd be able to play cricket. It's not as if you're hurt. People who walk in their sleep are just a bit potty.'

'I did not walk in my sleep,' said Deborah.

'Grandpapa said you must have done,' said Roger. 'It was a good thing that Patch woke him up and he saw you going across the lawn . . .' Then, to show his release from tension, he stood on his hands.

Deborah could see the sky from her bed. It was flat and dull. The day was a summer day that had worked through storm. Agnes came into the room with junket on a tray. She looked important.

'Now run off,' she said to Roger. 'Deborah doesn't want to talk to you. She's supposed to rest.'

Surprisingly, Roger obeyed, and Agnes placed the junket on the table beside the bed. 'You don't feel hungry, I expect,' she

363

said. 'Never mind, you can eat this later, when you fancy it. Have you got a pain? It's usual, the first time.'

'No,' said Deborah.

What had happened to her was personal. They had prepared her for it at school, but nevertheless it was a shock, not to be discussed with Agnes. The woman hovered a moment, in case the child asked questions; but, seeing that none came, she turned and left the room.

Deborah, her cheek on her hand, stared at the empty sky. The heaviness of knowledge lay upon her, a strange, deep sorrow.

'I won't come back,' she thought. 'I've lost the key.'

The hidden world, like ripples on the pool so soon to be filled in and fenced, was out of her reach for ever.

The Doll

Foreword.

The following pages were found in a shabby pocket book, very much sodden and discoloured by salt water, tucked away between the crevices of a rock in — Bay.

Their owner has never been traced, and the most diligent enquiries have failed to discover his identity. Either the wretched man drowned himself near the spot where he hid his pocket book, and his body has been lost at sea; or he is still wandering about the world trying to forget himself and his tragedy.

Some of the pages of his story were so damaged by exposure as to render them completely illegible; thus there are many gaps, and much of it seems without sequence, including the abrupt and unsatisfactory termination.

I have placed three dots between sentences when words or lines were undecipherable. Whether the wild improbabilities of the story are true, or whether the whole is but the hysterical product of a diseased mind, we shall never know. My sole reason for publishing these pages is to satisfy the entreaties of many friends who have been interested in my discovery.

Signed. DR E. STRONGMAN.

— BAY,

   S. ENGLAND.

I want to know if men realise when they are insane. Sometimes I think that my brain cannot hold together, it is filled with too much horror − too great a despair.

And there is no one; I have never been so unutterably alone. Why should it help me to write this? . . . Vomit forth the poison in my brain.

For I am poisoned, I cannot sleep, I cannot close my eyes without seeing his damned face . . .

If only it had been a dream, something to laugh over, a festered imagination.

It's easy enough to laugh, who wouldn't crack their sides and split their tongues with laughing. Let's laugh till the blood runs from our eyes − there's fun, if you like. No, it's the emptiness that hurts, the breaking up of everything inside me.

If I could feel, I should have followed her to the ends of the earth, no matter how she pleaded or how she loathed me. I should have taught her what it is to be loved by a man − yes − a man, and I would have thrown his filthy battered body from the window, watched him disappear for ever, his evil scarlet mouth distorted . . .

It's the hot feeling that has filled me, the utter incapacity to reason.

And I am deceiving myself when I say she would have come to me. I did not follow her because I knew that it was hopeless. She would never have loved me − she will never love any man.

366

Sometimes I can think of it all dispassionately, and I pity her. She misses so much – so much – and no one will ever know the truth. What was her life before I knew her, what is it now?

Rebecca – Rebecca, when I think of you with your pale earnest face, your great wide fanatical eyes like a saint, the narrow mouth that hid your teeth, sharp and white as ivory, and your halo of savage hair, electric, dark, uncontrolled – there has never been anyone more beautiful. Who will ever know your heart, who will ever know your mind?

Intense, restrained, and soul-less; for you must be soul-less to have done what you have done. You have that fatal quality of silence – of a tight repression that suggests a hidden fire – yes, a burning fire unquenchable. What have I not done with you in dreams, Rebecca?

You would be fatal to any man. A spark that lights, and does not burn itself, a flame fanning other flames.

What did I love in you but your indifference, and the suggestions that lay beneath your indifference?

I loved you too much, wanted you too much, had for you too great a tenderness. Now all of this is like a twisted root in my heart, a deadly poison in my brain. You have made of me a madman. You fill me with a kind of horror, a devastating hate that is akin to love – a hunger that is nausea. If only I could be calm and clear for one moment – one moment only . . .

I want to make a plan – an orderly arrangement of dates.

It was at Olga's studio first, I think. I can remember how it rained outside, and the rain made dirty streaks on the window-pane. The room was full, a lot of people were talking by the piano – Vorki was there, they were trying to make him sing, and Olga was screaming with laughter.

I always hated the hard thin reed of her laugh. You were sitting – Rebecca was sitting on a stool by the fire.

367

Her legs were twisted under her, and she looked like an elf, a sort of boy.

Her back was turned to me, and she wore a funny little fur cap on her head. I remember being amused at her position, I wanted to see her face. I called out to Olga to introduce me.

'Rebecca,' she said, 'Rebecca, show yourself.' . . . flinging off her cap as she turned. Her hair sprung from her head like a savage, her eyes opened wide – and she smiled at me, biting her lip.

I can remember sitting down on the floor beside her, and talking, talking – what does it matter what I said, dull stuff, nonsense of course, but she spoke breathlessly, with a sort of constrained eagerness. She did not say much, she smiled . . . eyes of a visionary, of a fanatic – they saw too much, demanded too much – one lost oneself in them, and became incapable of resistance. It was like drowning. From the moment I saw her then I was doomed. I left her, and came away, and walked down the embankment like a drunkard. Faces spluttered up at me, and shoulders brushed me, I was aware of dim lights reflected on wet pavements, and the hazy throb of traffic – through it all were her eyes and her wild impossible hair, her slim body like a boy . . . all coming clear now, I can see each event as it happened, each moment of the game. I went to Olga's again and she was there.

She came right up to me and said 'Do you care for music?' gravely, like a child. Why did she say this, I don't know, there was no one at the piano – I answered vaguely, and noticed the colour of her skin, pale coffee, and clear, clear as water.

She was dressed in brown, some sort of velvet I think, with a red scarf round her neck.

Her throat was very long and thin, like a swan's. I remember thinking how easy it would be to tighten the scarf and strangle her. I imagined her face when dying – her lips parted, and the enquiring look in her eyes – they would show white, but she would not be afraid. All this in the space of a moment, and while she was talking to me. I could drag very little from her. She was a violinist apparently, an orphan, and lived alone in Bloomsbury.

Yes, she had travelled much, she said, and especially in Hungary. She had lived in Budapest for three years, studying music. She did not care for England, she wanted to go back to Budapest. It was the only city in the world.

'Rebecca,' someone called, and she glanced over her shoulder with a smile. How much could I write about Rebecca's smile! It was so vivid, so intensely alive, and yet apart, unearthly, it had no relation to anything one said. Her eyes would be transfigured as if by a shaft of silver.

She left early that day, and I crossed the room to ask Olga about her. I was in an agony of impatience to know everything. Olga could tell me little. 'She comes from Hungary,' she said, 'no one knows who were her parents, Jewish, I imagine. Vorki brought her here. He found her in Paris, playing the violin in one of those Russian cafés. She won't have anything to do with him though, she lives entirely alone. Vorki says her talent is marvellous, if she only goes on there will be no one to touch her. But she won't work, she doesn't seem to care. I heard her at Vorki's flat – it sent cold shivers down my spine. She stood at the end of the room, looking like something off another planet, – her hair sticking out, a sort of fur bush round her head, and she played. The notes were weird, haunting, I've never known anything quite like it, it's impossible to describe.'

Once again I left Olga's studio in a dream, with Rebecca's face dancing before my eyes. I too could see her playing the violin – she would stand straight and firm as a child, her eyes wide open, her lips parted in a smile.

She was to play at Vorki's flat the following evening, and

I went to hear her. Olga had not exaggerated, with all her palpable, shallow insincerity. I sat like a drugged man, incapable of movement. I don't know what she played, but it was shattering – stupendous. I was not aware of anything but that I and Rebecca were together – out of the world, away, lost – lost in unutterable bliss. We were climbing, then flying, higher – higher.

At one time the violin seemed to protest, and it was as if she were refusing me, and I were pursuing her – then there came a torrent of sound, a medley of acceptance and denial, a confusion of notes in which were mingled desire and sweetness, and intolerable pleasure. I could feel my heart beating like the throb of some mighty vessel, and the blood pounded in my temples.

Rebecca was part of me, she was myself – it was too much, it was too glorious. We had reached the summit, we could go no farther, the sun seemed to strike into my eyes. I looked up – Rebecca was smiling at me, the violin broke on a note of exquisite beauty – it was fulfilment.

I leant back exhausted on the sofa, my senses swimming – it was too wonderful, too wonderful. Three minutes passed before I came fully conscious again. I felt as if I had plunged in the black abyss of eternity to sleep – and had come awake once more.

No one had noticed me, Vorki was handing round drinks, and Rebecca was sitting by the piano turning over some music. When they asked her to play again, she refused, she was tired, she said. They implored her so she took up her violin and played once more – something quite short, but very lovely and pure, like a child's prayer.

Later in the evening she came and sat beside me, for a few moments I was too moved to speak. Then I cursed myself for a fool, and turned to her, and looked into her face.

'You gave me a marvellous sensation when you played,' I told her, 'it was beautiful, intoxicating, I shall never forget it. You have a rare – no – a very dangerous talent.' She was silent, and then spoke in her restrained, breathless little voice. 'I played for you,' she said, 'I wanted to see what it was like to play to a man.' Her words bewildered me, they seemed utterly inexplicable. She was not lying, her eyes looked straight into mine, and she was smiling.

'What do you mean?' I asked her. 'Have you never played for anyone before, do you use your gift just to satisfy yourself? I don't understand.'

'Perhaps,' she said slowly, 'perhaps, it's like that, I can't explain.'

'I want to see you again,' I told her, 'I'd like to come and see you alone, where we can talk, really talk. I've thought about you ever since I saw you in Olga's studio, you knew that, didn't you? That's why you played to me tonight, wasn't it?'

I wanted to drag the answer from her lips, I wanted to force her to say yes. She shrugged her shoulders, she refused to be definite, it was exasperating.

'I don't know,' she said, 'I don't know.' Then I asked for her address, and she gave it to me. She was busy, she would not be able to see me until the end of the week. The party broke up soon after and she disappeared.

The days that passed seemed interminable, I could not wait to see her again. I thought about her ceaselessly.

On Friday I could stand it no longer, so I went to her. She lived in an odd sort of a house somewhere in Bloomsbury. She rented the top floor as a flat. The outlook was dull and dreary, I wondered how she could bear to live there.

She opened the door to me herself, and took me into a large bare room like a studio, with an oil-stove burning. I was struck by the cheerlessness of it, but she did not seem to notice anything, and made me sit down in a shabby arm-chair.

'This is where I practise,' Rebecca told me, 'and have my meals. It's a bright room, don't you think?' I said nothing to this and then she went to a cupboard and brought out some drinks, and a few stale biscuits. She took nothing herself.

I found her strange, detached – she seemed bored at my being there. Our conversation was forced and there were pauses. I found it impossible to say any of the things I wanted to say. She played to me for a while, but they were all classical things that I knew, and quite different from what she had played that evening at Vorki's.

Before I left she showed me round her tiny flat. There was a little scullery place she used for a kitchen, a poky bathroom, and her own small bedroom which was furnished like a nun's cell, quite plain and bare. There was another room leading from the studio, but she did not show me this. It was obviously a fair-sized room, as I saw the window from the street afterwards, and watched her draw the heavy curtains across it . . .

(*Note.* Here some pages were completely illegible, covered with blots, and discoloured. The narrative appears to continue in the middle of a sentence. Dr Strongman)

. . . 'not really cold,' she insisted, 'I've tried to explain to you that I'm odd in some ways, I've never met anyone to care for, I've never been in love. I've always disliked people rather than been attracted by them.' 'That doesn't explain your music.' I broke in impatiently. 'You play as if you knew everything – everything.'

I was becoming maddened by her indifference, it was not natural but calculated; she always gave me the impression of concealment. I felt I should never discover what was in her mind, whether she was like a child asleep, a flower before it has blossomed – or whether she was lying to me throughout, in which case every man would have been her lover – every man.

I was tortured by doubt and jealousy, the thought of other

men was driving me insane. And she gave me no relief, she would look at me with her great pale eyes, pure as water, until I could swear that she was untouched – and yet, and yet? A look, a smile, and back would come my torture and my misery. She was impossible, she evaded everything, and yet it was this fatal quality of restraint that tore at me and broke at me, until my love for her became an obsession, a terrible driving force.

I asked Olga about her, asked Vorki, asked everyone who knew her. No one could tell me anything, anything.

I'm forgetting days and weeks as I write this, nothing seems to have any sequence for me, it's like rising from the dead, it's like being reincarnated from dust and ashes to live it again, to live my whole cursed life again – for what was my life before I loved Rebecca, where was I, who was I?

I had better write that Sunday now, Sunday that was really the end; and I didn't know it, I thought it was the beginning. I was like someone walking in the dark, no, walking in the light with his eyes open and not seeing – deliberately blinding himself.

Sunday, day of hollow and mistaken happiness. I went to her flat about nine in the evening. She was waiting for me. She was dressed in scarlet – like Mephistopheles, odd strange clothes, that only Rebecca could wear. She seemed excited, intoxicated – she ran about the room like an elf.

Then she sat down at my feet with her legs tucked under her, and held out her thin brown hands to the stove. She laughed and giggled childishly, she reminded me of a mischievous child planning some naughtiness.

Then all at once she turned to me, her face pale, her eyes strangely alight. She said, 'Is it possible to love someone so much, that it gives one a pleasure, an unaccountable pleasure to hurt them? To hurt them by jealousy I mean, and to hurt oneself at the same time. Pleasure and pain, an equal mingling of pleasure and pain, just as an experiment, a rare sensation?'

She puzzled me, but I tried to explain to her what was meant by Sadism. She seemed to understand, and nodded her head thoughtfully once or twice.

Then she rose and went slowly across the room to the door I had never yet seen opened. She looked oddly pale as she stood there, her mass of queer savage hair springing from her head, her hand on the knob of the door. 'I want to introduce you to Julio,' she said. I left my chair and went towards her, I had no idea of what she was talking about. She took my hand and then opened the door. I saw a low round-shaped room, whose walls were draped with some sort of velvet hangings as if to deaden any sound, and long thick curtains were drawn across the window. There was a log fire, but it had burnt very low. Near the fireplace was a divan, covered with cushions thrown anyhow, and the only light came from a small shaded lamp, thus leaving the room in a half darkness.

There was one chair in the room, and this was facing the divan.

Something was sitting in the chair. I felt an eerie cold feeling in my heart, as if the room were haunted. 'What is it?' I whispered.

Rebecca took the lamp and held it over the chair. 'This is Julio,' she said softly. I stepped closer, and saw what I took to be a boy of about sixteen, dressed in a dinner jacket, shirt and waistcoat, and long Spanish trousers.

His face was the most evil thing I have ever seen. It was ashen pale in colour, and the mouth was a crimson gash, sensual and depraved. The nose was thin, with curved nostrils, and the eyes were cruel, gleaming and narrow, and curiously still. They seemed to stare right through one – the eyes of a hawk. The hair was sleek and dark, brushed right back from the white forehead.

It was the face of a satyr, a grinning hateful satyr.

Then I was aware of a strange feeling of disappointment, a helpless sensation of not understanding, of dumb incredulity.

There was no boy sitting in the chair. It was a doll. Human enough, damnably lifelike, with a foul distinctive personality, but a doll.

Only a doll. The eyes stared into mine without recognition, the mouth leered foolishly.

I looked at Rebecca, she was watching my face.

'I don't see,' I said, 'what's the point of all this? Where did you get this loathsome toy? Are you having a joke with me?' I spoke sharply, I felt uneasy and cold. The next moment the room was in darkness, she had turned out the lamp. I felt her arms round my neck, and her mouth upon mine.

'Now shall I tell you I love you?' she whispered, 'shall I?'

A hot wave of something swept over me, the floor seemed to swing beneath my feet. She clung to me and kissed my throat, I could feel her fingers at the back of my neck. I let her hands wander over my body, and she kissed me again. It was devastating – it was madness – it was like death.

I don't know how long we stood there, I don't remember anything, words, or thoughts, or dreams – only the silence of that dark room, the feeble glow of the fire, the beating of my heart – the singing in my ears – and Rebecca – Rebecca—. When, – and whether hours had passed or years I cannot tell – when I raised my eyes above her head I looked straight into his eyes – his damned doll's eyes.

They seemed to squint at me and leer, one eyebrow was cocked, and his crimson treacherous mouth was twisted at the corner. I wanted to leap at it, and smash its beastly grinning face, trample on its sordid human body. Was Rebecca mad to keep such a toy, what was her motive, where had she found it? But she would not answer my questions.

'Come away,' she said, and dragged me from the room, back

once more into the hard glaring light of the bare studio. 'You must go now,' she said breathlessly, 'it's late – I had forgotten.' I tried to take hold of her, once more, I wanted to kiss her again and again, she surely did not mean me to go now.

'Tomorrow,' she said impatiently, 'I promise you tomorrow, but not at the moment. I'm tired and bewildered – don't you see? Let me alone just for tonight, it's been too strong, I can't realise anything.'

She stamped her foot with impatience, she looked ill. I saw it was hopeless. I took my things and went – and walked, and walked – all night I think.

I watched the dawn break on Hampstead Heath, grey and sunless; heavy rain fell from a leaden sky.

My body was cold, but my brain was on fire. Once more I was certain that Rebecca had lied to me – from the moment she kissed me I knew that she had lied to me.

She had known five, ten, what matter the number, twenty lovers – and I was not one of them.

No, I was not one of them.

I found myself near Camden Town, buses rumbled along the streets; it was still raining, people straggled past me, their figures bent under umbrellas.

I found a taxi somewhere, and went home. I got into bed without undressing, and slept. I slept for hours. When I awoke it was dark once more; it must have been about six in the evening. I remember washing mechanically, and then once more walking in the direction of Bloomsbury.

I reached the flat and rang at her bell.

She let me in without a word, and then sat down in the studio before the oil stove. I told her I was going to be her lover. She said nothing. There were red rims under her eyes as if she had been crying, and thin lines round her mouth. I bent towards her to kiss her, but she pushed me away.

She began to speak rapidly.

'You must forget what happened last night. Today I realise I made a mistake. I'm not well, I haven't slept. All this has worried me considerably. You must leave me alone.'

I tried to seize her, and break down her iron restraint. It was like hammering at an iron wall. She lay cold and still in my arms. Her mouth was icy. I left her in despair. Then followed a week of doubt and torture. Sometimes she sat apart from me without a word, sometimes I could have sworn that she loved me. And she would not let me touch her, she was not in the mood she said. I must wait until she wanted me again. I must wait in suspense, in agony. She never mentioned Julio. We never went into that room again. I asked her what she had done with him. I wanted to know what was at the back of it all. She would answer evasively and change the subject. It was useless to press her. She was maddening. She was intolerable.

And yet I could not keep away from her. I could not live without her.

One evening she would be gentle and affectionate. She would sit at my feet and talk about her music, about her future plans. She was always changing. She was never the same.

I felt hopeless. My position was ridiculous – but what was I to do? She had become a madness to me – an obsession.

I've now come to the last evening, the very last. Then crash – blankness – the depths of hell – and desolation – utter desolation.

Let me get it clear – when was it, what time was it? Seven, eight perhaps. I can't remember. I was leaving the flat and she came to the door with me.

She suddenly put her arms round me and kissed me. . . .There have been men in arid deserts where the sun has so disfigured them that they have become things of horror – parched and blackened, twisted and torn. Their eyes run blood, their tongues are bitten through – and then they come upon water.

I know, because I was one of their number.

Laugh at all these comparisons, call me a madman, but the laugh is on my side.

There are women – but you have not kissed Rebecca, you cannot know.

You are a fool asleep. You have never begun to imagine . . .

(*Note*. Much of this seems completely unintelligible, and the quarter page that follows consists of nothing but broken sentences and half formed ideas. Then the narrative continues.)

It was shattering. She let me kiss her again and again. I took her face in my hands and looked down into her eyes.

'Who were your lovers?' I said. 'How often did you kiss them like that? Who taught you to kiss them like that? Who was the first, the very first? Tell me.'

A haze of fury was before my eyes, my hands shook.

'I swear to you that you are the first man I have ever kissed. I swear to you there has been no man before you. Never. Never.'

She looked straight at me. Her voice was firm. I saw that she was speaking the truth.

'Now you must go,' she said, 'tomorrow you shall come, and then we shall have so much to tell each other, so much.'

She smiled at me. I saw right through her wall of restraint, right through ice to the flame, the hidden fire.

I remember leaving the flat, and having dinner somewhere. My head was on fire. I seemed to walk among the gods. It was incredible that Rebecca should love me, it was incredible that I should know such happiness. I wanted to shout. I wanted to chuck myself off a roof.

I went home, and paced up and down the room. I couldn't sleep, every nerve in my body seemed alive.

Then suddenly, at midnight, I could stand it no longer. I had to go to Rebecca, I had to.

I felt my love for her was so strong that she would know. She would wait for me. She would understand. She would have to understand.

I don't know how I got to her flat. Seconds seemed to flash by, and I was standing outside in the street, gazing up at the windows.

I persuaded the night porter to let me in, he was half asleep and he let me pass upstairs. I listened outside her door – not a sound came from within. It might have been the entrance to a tomb.

I put my hand on the door knob, and turned it slowly. To my surprise it was not locked – Rebecca must have forgotten to turn the key after I left.

I stepped inside, everything was in darkness. 'Rebecca,' I called softly, 'Rebecca.' No answer.

The door of her bedroom was open, there was no one inside.

Then I went into the kitchen and the bathroom, both were empty.

Then I knew. Something gripped my heart, cold, clammy fear.

I looked towards that other room – his room – Julio's room.

I knew that Rebecca was in there, with the doll – with Julio.

I felt my way across the room and beat against the door. It was locked. I kicked against the panel, and tore at it with my nails. It gave way beneath my weight. I heard a cry of fury from Rebecca, and she turned on the lamp.

Oh! Christ, I shall never forget her eyes, the terrible light – the unholy rapture in her eyes, and her ashen – ashen face.

I saw everything – the room, the divan – I knew everything. I was seized with deadly sickness – a terrible despair.

And all the time his vile filthy face was looking at me. His eyes never left me, staring with a lifeless, glassy immobility.

The wet crimson mouth was sneering – the sleek dark hair hung in streaks across his cheek. He was a machine – something worked by screws – he was not alive, not human – but terrible, ghastly.

And Rebecca turned to me. Her voice was cold – apart – unearthly.

'And you expect me to love you. Don't you see that I can't – I can't? How can I care for you, or any man? Go away, leave me. I loathe you. I loathe you all. I don't need you. I don't want you.'

Something cracked inside my heart. I turned away. I left them. I left them alone. I ran into the street – tears were pouring down my face – I sobbed aloud – I shook my fist at the stars . . .

And that is all, there is no more to say, no more to tell. I went the next day and she had gone, they had both gone. No one knew where she was. I asked everyone I saw – no one could tell me.

Everything is dim, everything is useless. I shall never see Rebecca again – no one will see her again. It will always be Rebecca and Julio. Days will come, and nights, and nothing – they will haunt me – I shall never sleep – I'm cursed. I don't know what I'm saying, what I'm writing. What am I going to do? Oh! God, what am I going to do? I can't live – I can't cope . . .

Ganymede

They call it Little Venice. That was what drew me here in the first place. And you have to admit that there is a curious resemblance – at least for people like myself, with imagination. There is a corner, for instance, where the canal takes a bend, fronted by a row of terraced houses, and the water itself has a particular stillness, especially at night, and the glaring discordancies that are noticeable during the day, like the noise of the shunting from Paddington Station, the rattle of the trains, the ugliness, all that seems to vanish. Instead . . . the yellow light from the street lamps might be the mysterious glow you get from those old lanterns set in brackets on the corner of some crumbling palazzo, whose shuttered windows look blindly down upon the stagnant sweetness of a side-canal.

It is, and I must repeat this, essential to have imagination, and the house-agents are clever – they frame their advertisements to catch the eye of waverers like myself. 'Two-roomed flat, with balcony, overlooking canal, in the quiet backwater known as Little Venice,' and instantly, to the famished mind, the aching heart, comes a vision of another two-roomed flat, another balcony, where at the hour of waking the sun makes patterns on a flaking ceiling, water patterns, and the sour Venetian smell comes through the window with the murmur of Venetian voices, the poignant 'Ohé!' as the gondola rounds the bend and disappears.

In Little Venice we have traffic too. Not sharp-nosed gondolas, of course, gently rocking from side to side, but barges pass my window carrying bricks, and sometimes coal – the coal-dust dirties the balcony; and if I shut my eyes, surprised by the sudden hooting, and listen to the rapid chug-chug of the barge's engine, I can fancy myself, with my same shut eyes, waiting for a *vaporetto* at one of the landing-stages. I stand on the wooden planking, hemmed in by a chattering crowd, and there is a great surge and throbbing as the vessel goes hard astern. Then the *vaporetto* is alongside, and I, with my chattering crowd, have gone on board and we are off again, churning the water into wavelets with our wash, and I am trying to make up my mind whether to go direct to San Marco, and so to the piazza and my usual table, or to leave the *vaporetto* higher up the Grand Canal and thus prolong exquisite anticipation.

The hooting stops. The barge passes. I cannot tell you where they go. There is a junction, close to Paddington, where the canal splits. This does not interest me; all that interests me is the echo of the barge's hooter, the echo of the engine, and – if I am walking – the barge's wake in the canal water, so that, glancing down the bank, I can see a film of oil amongst the bubbles, and then the oil disperses, and the bubbles too, and the water becomes still.

Come with me, and I'll show you something. You see the

street across the canal, that one there, with the shops, going towards Paddington Station; and you see the bus stop, halfway down, and the board with blue letters on it. Your eyes won't be able to pick it up at this distance, but I can tell you that it reads MARIO, and it's the name of a small restaurant, an Italian restaurant, hardly more than a bar. They know me there. I go there every day. You see, the lad there — he's training to be a waiter — reminds me of Ganymede . . .

2

I am a classical scholar. I suppose that was really the trouble. Had my interests been scientific, or geographical, or even historical — though history has associations enough, heaven knows — then I don't believe anything would have happened. I could have gone to Venice, and enjoyed my holiday, and come away again, without losing myself to such an extent that . . . Well, what occurred there meant a total break with everything that had gone before.

You see, I've given up my job. My superior was exceedingly nice about it all, most sympathetic in fact, but, as he said, they really couldn't afford to take risks, they couldn't permit one of their employees — and, naturally, that applied to me — to continue working for them if he had been connected . . . that was the word he used, not mixed-up but connected . . . with what he called unsavoury practices.

Unsavoury is a hideous word. It's the most hideous word in the dictionary. It conjures up, to my mind, all that is ugly in life, yes, and in death too. The savoury is the joy, the élan, the zest that goes with mind and body working in unison; the unsavoury is the malodorous decay of vegetation, the rotted flesh, the mud beneath the water of the canal. And another

383

thing. The word unsavoury suggests a lack of personal cleanliness: unchanged linen, bed-sheets hanging to dry, the fluff off combs, torn packets in waste-paper baskets. None of this can I abide. I am fastidious. Above all things I am fastidious. So that when my superior mentioned the word unsavoury I knew I had to go. I knew I could never allow him, or anyone, so to misinterpret my actions that they could consider what had taken place as, to put it bluntly, nauseous. So I resigned. Yes, I resigned. There was nothing else for it. I just cut myself loose. And I saw the advertisement in the house-agent's column, and here I am in Little Venice . . .

I took my holiday late that year because my sister, who lives in Devon, and with whom I usually spend three weeks in August, suddenly had domestic trouble. A favourite cook left after a lifetime of devotion, and the household was disorganized. My nieces wanted to hire a caravan, my sister wrote me: they were all determined to go camping in Wales, and although I would be welcome she was sure it was not the sort of break that would appeal to me. She was right. The idea of hammering tent-pegs into the ground in a tearing wind, or sitting humped four abreast in a tiny space while my sister and her daughters produced luncheon out of a tin, filled me with misgiving. I cursed the cook whose departure had put an end to the pleasurable series of long, lazy days to which I had been accustomed, when, relaxing in a chaise-longue, favourite book in hand, and most delightfully fed, I had idled away my Augusts for many years.

When I protested over a series of trunk calls that I had nowhere to go, my sister said, or rather shouted over the muffled line, 'Get abroad for a change. It would do you a world of good to break routine. Try France, or Italy.' She even suggested a cruise, which frightened me even more than a caravan.

'Very well,' I told her coldly, for in a sense I blamed her for the cook's departure and the cessation of my comfort, 'I will go to Venice,' thinking that, if I was obliged to get myself out of the rut, then I would at least be obvious. I would go, guidebook in hand, to a tourist's paradise. But not in August. Definitely not in August. I would wait until my compatriots and my friends across the Atlantic had been and gone again. Only then would I venture forth, when the heat of the day was done, and some measure of peace had returned to the place I believed was beautiful.

I arrived the first week in October . . . You know how sometimes a holiday, even a brief one, a visit to friends for the week-end, can go wrong from the start. One departs in rain, or misses a connexion, or wakes with a chill, and the thread of ill-luck laced with irritation continues to mar every hour. Not so with Venice. The very fact that I had left it late, that the month was October, that the people I knew were now back again at office desks, made me more aware of my own good fortune.

I reached my destination just before dusk. Nothing had gone amiss. I had slept in my sleeper. I had not been annoyed by my fellow travellers. I had digested my dinner of the preceding night and my luncheon of the day. I had not been obliged to over-tip. Venice with all its glories lay before me. I collected my baggage and stepped out of the train, and there was the Grand Canal at my feet, the thronging gondolas, the lapping water, the golden *palazzi*, the dappled sky.

A fat porter from my hotel who had come to meet the train, so like a deceased member of the royal family that I dubbed him Prince Hal on the spot, seized my trappings from me. I was wafted, as so many travellers have been wafted before me, through the years and centuries, from the prosaic rattle of the tourist train to an instant dream world of romance.

To be met by boat; to travel by water; to loll upon cushions, swaying from side to side, even with a Prince Hal shouting the sights in one's ear in appalling English – all this makes for a loosening of restraint. I eased my collar. I threw off my hat. I averted my eyes from my walking-stick and my umbrella and my burberry tucked in the hold-all – I invariably travel with a hold-all. Lighting a cigarette, I was aware, surely for the first time in my life, of a sense of abandon, of belonging – certainly not to the present, nor to the future, nor even to the past, but to a period in time that was changeless and was Venetian time, that was outside the rest of Europe and even the world, and existed, magically, for myself alone.

Mark you, I realized there must be others. In that dark gondola floating by, at that wide window, even on the bridge from which, as we passed underneath, a figure peering down suddenly withdrew, I knew there must be others who, like myself, found themselves suddenly enchanted, not by the Venice they perceived, but by the Venice they felt within themselves. That uncelestial city from which no traveller returns . . .

What am I saying, though? I anticipate events and thoughts which no doubt I could not have had during that first half-hour from station to hotel. It is only now, in retrospect, that I realize there must be others like myself who, with the first glimpse, become enchanted, damned. Oh yes, indeed, we know all about the rest, the obvious rest. The people clicking cameras, the hubbub of nationalities, the students, the schoolmistresses, the artists. And the Venetians themselves – the Prince Hal porter, for instance, and the fellow who steered the gondola and was thinking of his pasta supper and his wife and children and the lire I would give him, and all those homeward bounders in the *vaporetti* no different from other homeward bounders at home who go by bus or tube – those people are part of the Venice of today, just as their forebears were part of the Venice that is past: dukes, and merchants, and lovers, and ravished maidens. No, we have a different key. A different secret. It is what I said before, the Venice within ourselves.

'To ze right,' shouted Prince Hal, 'famous palazzo now belonging to American gentleman.' Foolish and useless as his information was, it did at least suggest that some tycoon, weary of making money, had created an illusion, and, stepping into the speed-boat I saw tethered at the steps, believed himself immortal.

That was what I felt, you see. I had the sense of immortality, the knowledge, instantaneous as I left the station and heard the lapping water, that time contained me. I was not imprisoned. I was held. And then we left the Grand Canal and were in the backwaters, and Prince Hal fell silent, and there was no sound except the stroke of the long oar as we were propelled along the narrow stream. I remember thinking – curious, wasn't it? – of the waters that usher us into this life at birth, of the waters that contain us in the womb. Somehow they must have the same stillness, the same force.

We came out of darkness into light, we shot under a bridge – it was only later that I realized it was the Bridge of Sighs – and there was the lagoon in front of us, and a hundred stabbing, flickering lights, and a great jostle of figures, of people walking up and down. I had to cope at once with my unaccustomed lire, with the gondolier, with Prince Hal, before being swallowed up in the hotel and the paraphernalia of desk-clerk, keys, and page showing me to my room. Mine was one of the smaller hotels, basking in the proximity of the more famous, yet comfortable enough at first glance, though a little stuffy perhaps – odd how they keep a room tight closed before a guest arrives. As I threw open the shutters the warm damp air from the lagoon infiltrated slowly, and the laughter and footsteps of the promenaders floated upwards while I unpacked.

I changed and descended, but one glance at the half-empty dining-room decided me against dining there, although my pension terms permitted it, and I went out and joined the promenaders by the lagoon.

The sensation I had was strange, and never experienced before. Not the usual anticipation of the traveller on the first evening of his holiday, who looks forward to his dinner and the pleasure of new surroundings. After all, in spite of my sister's mockery I was no John Bull. I used to know Paris quite well. I had been to Germany. I had toured the Scandinavian countries before the war. I had spent an Easter in Rome. It was only that I had been idle of late years, without initiative, and to take my annual holiday in Devon saved planning and, incidentally, my purse.

No, the sensation I had now, as inevitably I walked past the Doge's palace – which I recognized from postcards – and into the Piazza San Marco, was one of . . . I hardly know how to describe it . . . recognition. I don't mean the feeling 'I have been here before'. I don't mean the romantic dream 'This is re-incarnation'. Neither of those things. It was as though, intuitively, I had become, at last, myself. I had arrived. This particular moment in time had been waiting for me, and I for it. Curiously, it was like the first flavour of intoxication, but more heightened, more acute. And deeply secret. It is important to remember that; deeply secret. This sensation was somehow palpable, invading the whole of me, the palms of my hands, my scalp. My throat was dry. Physically, I felt I was infused with electricity, that I had become some sort of power-house radiating, into the damp atmosphere of this Venice I had never seen, currents which, becoming charged with other currents, returned to me again. The excitement was intense, almost unbearable. And, to look at me, nobody would guess anything. I was just another Englishman at the fag-end of the tourist season, strolling, walking-stick in hand, on his first night in Venice.

Although it was nearly nine o'clock the crowd was still dense on the piazza. I wondered how many amongst them felt the same current, the same intuition. Nevertheless, I must dine, and to escape the crowd I chose a turning to the right halfway down the piazza which brought me to one of the side-canals, very dark and still, and as luck had it to a restaurant nearby. I dined well, with excellent wine, at far less expense than I had feared, and lighting a cigar — one of my small extravagances, a really good cigar — I strolled back again to the piazza, that same electric current with me still.

The crowd had thinned, and instead of strolling had concentrated into two marked groups before two separate orchestras. These orchestras — rivals, so it appeared — had their stance in front of a couple of cafés, also rivals. Separated by perhaps some seventy yards, they played against one another with gay indifference. Tables and chairs were set out about the orchestras, and the café clientèle drank and gossiped and listened to the music in a semi-circle, backs turned to the rival orchestra whose beat and rhythm made discord to the ear. I happened to be closest to the orchestra in mid-piazza. I found an empty table and sat down. A burst of applause from the second audience nearer the church gave warning that the rival orchestra had come to a breathing-space in its repertoire. This was the signal for ours to play louder still. It was Puccini, of course. As the evening progressed there came the songs of the day, the hit tunes of the moment, but as I sat down and looked about for a waiter to bring me a liqueur, and accepted — at a price — the rose offered to me by an ancient crone in a black shawl, the orchestra was playing *Madame Butterfly*. I felt relaxed, amused. And then I saw him.

I told you I was a classical scholar. Therefore you will understand — you should understand — that what happened in that second was transformation. The electricity that had charged me all evening focused on a single point in my brain to the exclusion of all else; the rest of me was jelly. I could sense the man at my table raise his hand and summon the lad in the white coat carrying a tray, but I myself was above him, did not exist in his time; and this self who was non-existent knew with every nerve fibre, every brain-cell, every blood corpuscle that he was indeed Zeus, the giver of life and death, the immortal one, the lover; and that the boy who came towards him was his own beloved, his cup-bearer, his slave, his Ganymede. I was poised, not in the body, not in the world, and I summoned him. He knew me, and he came.

Then it was all over. The tears were pouring down my face and I heard a voice saying, 'Is anything wrong, *signore*?'

The lad was watching me with some concern. Nobody had noticed anything; they were all intent upon their drinks, or their friends, or the orchestra, and I fumbled for my handkerchief and blew my nose and said, 'Bring me a curaçao.'

3

I remember sitting staring at the table in front of me, still smoking my cigar, not daring to raise my head, and I heard his quick footstep beside me. He put down the drink and went away again, and the question uppermost in my mind was, 'Does he know?'

You see, the flash of recognition was so swift, so overwhelming, that it was like being jerked into consciousness from a lifetime of sleep. The absolute certainty of who I was and where I was, and the bond between us, possessed me just as Paul was possessed on the Damascus road. Thank heaven I was not blinded by my visions; no one would have to lead

me back to the hotel. No, I was just another tourist come to
Venice, listening to a little string band and smoking a cigar.

I let five minutes or so go by, and then I lifted my head
and casually, very casually, looked over the heads of the people
towards the café. He was standing alone, his hands behind his
back, watching the orchestra. He seemed to me about fifteen,
not more, and he was small for his age, and slight, and his
white mess jacket and dark trousers reminded me of an officer's
kit in Her Majesty's Mediterranean fleet. He did not look
Italian. His forehead was high, and he wore his light brown
hair *en brosse*. His eyes were not brown but blue, and his
complexion was fair, not olive. There were two other waiters
hovering between the tables, one of them about eighteen or
nineteen and both of them obvious Italians, the eighteen-
year-old swarthy and fat. You could tell at a glance they were
born to be waiters, they would never rise to anything else, but
my boy, my Ganymede, the very set of his proud head, the
expression on his face, the air of grave tolerance with which
he regarded the orchestra, showed him to be of a different
stamp . . . my stamp, the stamp of the immortals.

I watched him covertly, the small clasped hands, the small
foot in its black shoe tapping time to the music. If he recognized me, I said to myself, he will look at me. This evasion,
this play of watching the orchestra, is only a pretext, because
what we have felt together, in that moment out of time, has
been too strong for both of us. Suddenly – and with an exquisite feeling of delight and apprehension in one – I knew what
was going to happen. He made a decision. He looked away
from the orchestra and directly across to my table, and still
grave, still thoughtful, walked up to me and said,

'Do you wish for anything more, *signore*?'

It was foolish of me, but, do you know, I could not speak.
I could only shake my head. Then he took away the ash-tray

and put a clean one in its place. The very gesture was somehow thoughtful, loving, and my throat tightened and I was reminded of a biblical expression surely used by Joseph about Benjamin. I forget the context, but it says somewhere in the Old Testament, 'for his bowels did yearn upon his brother'. I felt that, exactly.

I went on sitting there until midnight, when the great bells sounded and filled the air, and the orchestras – both of them – put away their instruments, and the straggling listeners melted away. I looked down at the scrap of paper, the bill, which he had brought me and put beside the ash-tray, and, as I glanced at the scribbled figures and paid, it seemed to me that the smile he gave me, and the little bow of deference, were the answer I had been seeking. He knew. Ganymede knew.

I went off alone across the now deserted piazza, and passed under the colonnade by the Doge's palace where an old hunched man was sleeping. The lights were no longer bright but dim, the damp wind troubled the water and rocked the rows of gondolas on the black lagoon, but my boy's spirit was with me, and his shadow too.

I awoke to brilliance. The long day to be filled, and what a day! So much to experience and to see, from the obvious interiors of San Marco and the Doge's palace to a visit to the Accademia and an excursion up and down the Grand Canal. I did everything the tourist does except feed the pigeons; too fat, too sleek as they were, I picked my way amongst them with distaste. I had an ice at Florians. I bought picture postcards for my nieces. I leant over the Rialto bridge. And the happy day, of which I enjoyed every moment, was only a preliminary to the evening. Deliberately I had avoided the café on the right-hand side of the piazza. I had walked only on the opposite side.

I remember I got back to my hotel about six, and lay down on my bed and read Chaucer for an hour – the *Canterbury*

Tales in a Penguin edition. Then I had a bath and changed. I went to the same restaurant to dine where I had dined the night before. The dinner was equally good and equally cheap. I lit my cigar and strolled to the piazza. The orchestras were playing. I chose a table on the fringe of the crowd, and as I put down my cigar for a moment I noticed that my hand was trembling. The excitement, the suspense, were unbearable. It seemed to me impossible that the family group at the table beside me should not perceive my emotion. Luckily I had an evening paper with me. I opened it and pretended to read. Someone flicked a cloth on my table, and it was the swarthy waiter, the ungainly youth, asking for my order. I motioned him away. 'Presently,' I said, and went on reading, or rather going through the motions of reading. The orchestra began to play a little jigging tune, and looking up I saw that Ganymede was watching me. He was standing by the orchestra, his hands clasped behind his back. I did nothing, I did not even move my head, but in a moment he was at my side.

'A curaçao, *signore*?' he said.

Tonight recognition went beyond the first instantaneous flash. I could feel the chair of gold, and the clouds above my head, and the boy was kneeling beside me, and the cup he offered me was gold as well. His humility was not the shamed humility of a slave, but the reverence of a loved one to his master, to his god. Then the flash was gone and, thank heaven, I was in control of emotion. I nodded my head and said, 'Yes, please,' and ordered half a bottle of Evian water to be brought to me with the curaçao.

As I watched him slip past the tables towards the café, I saw a large man in a white raincoat and a broad-brimmed trilby hat step out from the shadows beneath the colonnade and tap him on the shoulder. My boy raised his head and smiled. In that brief moment I experienced evil. A premonition of disaster.

393

The man, like a great white slug, smiled back at Ganymede and gave him an order. The boy smiled again, and disappeared.

The orchestra swung out of the jigging tune and ceased, with a flourish, to a burst of applause. The violinist wiped the perspiration from his forehead and laughed at the pianist. The swarthy waiter brought them drinks. The old woman in the shawl came to my table as she had done the night before and offered me a rose. This time I was wiser: I refused. And I became aware that the man in the white mackintosh was watching me from behind a column . . .

Do you know anything of Greek mythology? I only mention the fact because Poseidon, the brother of Zeus, was also his rival. He was especially associated with the horse; and a horse – unless it is winged – symbolizes corruption. The man in the white mackintosh was corrupt. I knew it instinctively. Intuition bade me beware. When Ganymede returned with my curaçao and my Evian I did not even look up, but continued reading the newspaper. The orchestra, refreshed, took the air once more. The strains of 'Softly Awakes my Heart' strove for supremacy with the 'Colonel Bogey' march from its rival near the church. The woman with the shawl, her roses all unsold, came back to my table in desperation. Brutally I shook my head, and in doing so saw that the man in the white mackintosh and the trilby hat had moved from the column and was now standing beside my chair.

The aroma of evil is a deadly thing. It penetrates, and stifles, and somehow challenges at the same time. I was afraid. Most definitely I was afraid, but determined to give battle, to prove that I was the stronger. I relaxed in my chair, and, inhaling the last breath of my cigar before laying it in the ash-tray, puffed the smoke full in his face. An extraordinary thing happened. I don't know whether the final inhalation turned me giddy, but for an instant my head swam, and the smoke made rings before my eyes, and I saw his hideous, grinning face subside into what seemed to be a trough of sea and foam. I could even feel the spray. When I had recovered from the attack of coughing brought on by my cigar the air cleared: the man in the white mackintosh had disappeared, and I found that I had knocked over and smashed my half-bottle of Evian water. It was Ganymede himself who picked up the broken pieces, it was Ganymede who wiped the table with his cloth, it was Ganymede who suggested, without my ordering it, a fresh half-bottle.

'The *signore* has not cut himself?' he said.

'No.'

'The *signore* will have another curaçao. There may be some pieces of glass in this. There will be no extra charge.'

He spoke with authority, with quiet confidence, this child of fifteen who had the grace of a prince, and then, with exquisite hauteur, he turned to the swarthy youth who was his companion-at-arms, and handed him my debris with a flow of Italian. Then he brought me the second half-bottle of Evian, and the second glass of curaçao.

'*Un sedativo,*' he said, and smiled.

He was not cocky. He was not familiar. He knew, because he had always known, that my hands were trembling and my heart was beating, and I wanted to be calm, to be still.

'*Piove,*' he said, lifting his face and holding up his hand, and indeed it was beginning to rain, suddenly, for no reason, out of a star-studded sky. But a black straggling cloud like a gigantic hand blotted out the stars as he spoke, and down came the rain on to the piazza. Umbrellas went up like mushrooms, and those without them spread across the piazza and away home like beetles to their lair.

Desolation was instant. The tables were bare, the chairs upturned against them. The piano was covered with a tarpaulin, the music-stands were folded, the lights inside the café became dim. Everyone melted away. It was as though there had never been an orchestra, never been an audience of clapping people. The whole thing was a dream.

I was not dreaming, though. I had come out, like a fool, without my umbrella. I waited under the colonnade beside the now deserted café, with the rain from a nearby spout spattering the ground in front of me. I could hardly believe it possible that five minutes ago all had been gay and crowded, and now this wintered gloom.

I turned up the collar of my coat, trying to make up my mind whether to venture forth across the streaming piazza, and then I heard a quick brisk footstep leave the café and trot away under the colonnade. It was Ganymede, his small upright figure still clad in his white mess jacket, his large umbrella held above him like a pennant.

My way was to the left, towards the church. He was walking to the right. In a moment or two he might turn away altogether, and disappear. It was a moment of decision. You will say I made the wrong one. I turned to the right, I followed him.

It was a strange and mad pursuit. I had never done such a thing in my life before. I could not help myself. He trotted ahead, his footsteps loud and clear, along the tortuous narrow passages winding in and out beside silent, dark canals, and there was no other sound at all except his footsteps and the rain, and he never once looked back to see who followed him. Once or twice I slipped: he must have heard me. On, on he went, over bridges, into the shadows, his umbrella bobbing up and down above his head, and a glimpse of his white mess jacket showing now and then as he lifted the umbrella higher. And the rain still sluiced from the roofs of the silent houses, down to the cobbles and the pavings below, down to the Styx-like canals.

Then I missed him. He had turned a corner sharply. I began to run. I ran into a narrow passage, where the tall houses almost touched their neighbours opposite, and he was standing in front of a great door with an iron grille before it, pulling a bell. The door opened, he folded his umbrella and went inside. The door clanged behind him. He must have heard me running, he must have seen me brought up short when I turned the corner into the passage. I stood for a moment staring at the iron grille above the heavy oak door. I looked at my watch: it wanted five minutes to midnight. The folly of my pursuit struck me in all its force. Nothing had been achieved but to get very wet, to have caught a chill in all probability, and to have lost my way.

I turned to go, and a figure stepped out of a doorway opposite the house with the grille and came towards me. It was the man in the white mackintosh and the broad-brimmed trilby hat.

He said, with a bastard American accent, 'Are you looking for somebody, *signore*?'

4

I ask you, what would you have done in my position? I was a stranger in Venice, a tourist. The alleyway was deserted. One had read stories of Italians and vendettas, of knives, of stabs in the back. One false move, and this might happen to me.

'I was taking a walk,' I replied, 'but I seem to have missed my way.'

He was standing very close to me, much too close for comfort. 'Ah! you missa your way,' he repeated, the American accent blending with music-hall Italian. 'In Venice, that happens all the time. I see you home.'

The lantern light above his head turned his face yellow under the broad-brimmed hat. He smiled as he spoke, showing teeth full of gold stoppings. The smile was sinister.

'Thank you,' I said, 'but I can manage very well.'

I turned and began to walk back to the corner. He fell into step beside me.

'No trouble,' he said, 'no trouble at all-a.'

He kept his hands in the pockets of his white mackintosh, and his shoulder brushed mine as we walked side by side. We moved out of the alleyway into the narrow street by the side-canal. It was dark. Drips of water fell from the roof-gutters into the canal.

'You like Venice?' he asked.

'Very much,' I answered; and then – foolishly, perhaps – 'It's my first visit.'

I felt like a prisoner under escort. The tramp-tramp of our feet echoed in hollow fashion. And there was no one to hear us. The whole of Venice slept. He gave a grunt of satisfaction.

'Venice very dear,' he said. 'In the hotels, they robba you always. Where are you staying?'

I hesitated. I did not want to give my address, but if he insisted on coming with me what could I do?

'The Hotel Byron,' I said.

He laughed in scorn. 'They putta twenty per cent on the bill,' he said. 'You ask for a cup of coffee, twenty per cent. It's always the same. They robba the tourist.'

'My terms are reasonable,' I said. 'I can't complain.'

'Whatta you pay them?' he asked.

The cheek of the man staggered me. But the path by the canal was very narrow, and his shoulder still touched mine as we walked. I told him the price of my room at the hotel, and the pension terms. He whistled.

'They take the skin off your back,' he said. 'Tomorrow you

senda them to hell. I find you little apartment. Very cheap, very OK.'

I did not want a little apartment. All I wanted was to be rid of the man, and back in the comparative civilization of the Piazza San Marco. 'Thank you,' I replied, 'but I'm quite comfortable at the Hotel Byron.'

He edged even closer to me, and I found myself nearer still to the black waters of the canal. 'In little apartment,' he said, 'you do as you like-a. You see your friends. Nobody worry you.'

'I'm not worried at the Hotel Byron,' I said.

I began to walk faster, but he kept pace with me, and suddenly he withdrew his right hand from his pocket and my heart missed a beat. I thought he had a knife. But it was to offer me a tattered packet of Lucky Strikes. I shook my head. He lit one for himself.

'I finda you little apartment,' he persisted.

We passed over a bridge and plunged into yet another street, silent, ill-lit, and as we walked he told me the names of people for whom he had found apartments.

'You English?' he asked. 'I thought-a so. I found apartment last year for Sir Johnson. You know Sir Johnson? Very nice man, very discreet. I find apartment too for film-star Bertie Poole. You know Bertie Poole? I save him five hundred thousand lire.'

I had never heard of Sir Johnson or Bertie Poole. I became more and more angry, but there was nothing I could do. We crossed a second bridge, and to my relief I recognized the corner near the restaurant where I had dined. The canal here formed, as it were, a bay, and there were gondolas moored side by side.

'Don't bother to come any further,' I said. 'I know my way now.'

The unbelievable happened. We had turned the corner together, marching as one man, and then, because the narrow path could not hold us two abreast, he dropped a pace behind, and, in doing so, slipped. I heard him gasp, and a second later he was in the canal, the white mackintosh splaying about him like a canopy, the splash of his great body rocking the gondolas. I stared for a moment, too surprised to take action. And then I did a terrible thing. I ran away. I ran into the passage that I knew would lead me finally into the Piazza San Marco, and, when I came to it, walked across it briskly, and so past the Doge's palace and back to my hotel. I encountered no one. As I said before, the whole of Venice slept. At the Hotel Byron, Prince Hal was yawning behind the desk. Rubbing the sleep from his eyes, he took me up in the lift. As soon as I entered my room I went straight to the wash-basin and took the small bottle of medicinal brandy with which I invariably travelled. I swallowed the contents at a single draught.

5

I slept badly and had appalling dreams, which did not surprise me. I saw Poseidon, the god Poseidon, rising from an angry sea, and he shook his trident at me, and the sea became the canal, and then Poseidon himself mounted a bronze horse, the bronze horse of Colleoni, and rode away, with the limp body of Ganymede on the saddle before him.

I swallowed a couple of aspirin with my coffee, and rose late. I don't know what I expected to see when I went out. Knots of people reading newspapers, or the police – some intimation of what had happened. Instead, it was a bright October day, and the life of Venice continued.

I took a steamer to the Lido and lunched there. I deliberately idled away the day at the Lido in case of trouble. What was worrying me was that, should the man in the white mackintosh have survived his ducking of the night before and bear malice towards me for leaving him to his plight, he might have informed the police – perhaps hinting, even, that I had pushed him in. And the police would be waiting for me at the hotel when I returned.

I gave myself until six o'clock. Then, a little before sunset, I took the steamer back. No cloudbursts tonight. The sky was a gentle gold, and Venice basked in the soft light, painfully beautiful.

I entered the hotel and asked for my key. It was handed to me by the clerk with a cheerful, 'Buona sera, signore,' together with a letter from my sister. Nobody had inquired for me. I went upstairs and changed, came down again, and had dinner in the hotel restaurant. The dinner was not in the same class as the dinner in the restaurant the two preceding nights, but I did not mind. I was not very hungry. Nor did I fancy my usual cigar. I lit a cigarette instead. I stood for about ten minutes outside the hotel, smoking and watching the lights on the lagoon. The night was balmy. I wondered if the orchestra was playing in the piazza, and if Ganymede was serving drinks. The thought of him worried me. If he was in any way connected with the man in the white mackintosh, he might suffer for what had happened. The dream could have been a warning – I was a great believer in dreams. Poseidon carrying Ganymede astride his horse . . . I began to walk towards the Piazza San Marco. I told myself I would just stand near the church and see if both orchestras were playing.

When I came to the piazza I saw that all was as usual. There were the same crowds, the same rival orchestras, the same repertoires played against each other. I moved slowly across the piazza towards the second orchestra, and I put on my dark glasses as a form of protection. Yes, there he was. There was Ganymede. I spotted his brush of light hair and his white mess jacket almost immediately. He and his swarthy companion were very busy. The crowd around the orchestra was thicker than usual because of the warm night. I scanned the audience, and the shadows behind the colonnade. There was no sign of the man in the white mackintosh. The wisest thing, I knew, was to leave, return to the hotel, go to bed, and read my Chaucer. Yet I lingered. The old woman selling roses was making her rounds. I drew nearer. The orchestra was playing the theme-song from a Chaplin film. Was it *Limelight*? I did not remember. But the song was haunting, and the violinist drew every ounce of sentiment from it. I decided to wait until the end of the song and then return to the hotel.

Someone snapped his fingers to give an order, and Ganymede turned to take it. As he did so he looked over the heads of the seated crowd straight at me. I was wearing the dark glasses, and I had a hat. Yet he knew me. He gave me a radiant smile of welcome, and ignoring the client's order darted forward, seized a chair, and placed it beside an empty table.

'No rain tonight,' he said. 'Tonight everybody is happy. A curaçao, *signore*?'

How could I refuse him, the smile, the almost pleading gesture? If anything had been wrong, if he had been anxious about the man in the white mackintosh, surely, I thought, there would have been some sort of hint, some warning glance? I sat down. A moment later he was back again with my curaçao.

Perhaps it was more potent than the night before, or perhaps, in my disturbed mood, it had a greater effect on me. Whatever it was, the curaçao went to my head. My nervousness vanished. The man in the white mackintosh and his evil influence no longer troubled me. Perhaps he was dead. What of it? Ganymede remained unharmed. And to show his favour he stood only a few feet away from my table, hands clasped behind his back, on the alert to serve my instant whim.

'Do you never get tired?' I said boldly.

He whisked away my ash-tray and flicked the table.

'No, *signore*,' he answered, 'for my work is a pleasure. This sort of work.' He gave me a little bow.

'Don't you go to school?'

'School?' He jerked his thumb in a gesture of dismissal. '*Finito*, school. I am a man. I work for my living. To keep my mother and my sister.'

I was touched. He believed himself a man. And I had an instant vision of his mother, a sad, complaining woman, and of a little sister. They all of them lived behind the door with the grille.

'Do they pay you well here in the café?' I asked.

He shrugged his shoulders.

'In the season, not so bad,' he said, 'but the season is over. Two more weeks, and it is finished. Everyone goes away.'

'What will you do?'

He shrugged again.

'I have to find work somewhere else,' he said. 'Perhaps I go to Rome. I have friends in Rome.'

I did not like to think of him in Rome – such a child in such a city. Besides, who were his friends?

'What would you like to do?' I inquired.

He bit his lips. For a moment he looked sad. 'I should like to go to London,' he said. 'I should like to go to one of your big hotels. But that is impossible. I have no friends in London.'

I thought of my own immediate superior, who happened to be a director, amongst his other activities, of the Majestic in Park Lane.

'It might be arranged,' I said, 'with a little pulling of strings.'

He smiled, and made an amusing gesture of manipulating

with both hands. 'It is easy, if you know how,' he said, 'but if you don't know how, better to . . .' and he smacked his lips and raised his eyes. The expression implied defeat. Forget about it.

'We'll see,' I said. 'I have influential friends.'

He made no attempt to seize advantage.

'You are kind to me, *signore*,' he murmured, 'very kind indeed.'

At that moment the orchestra stopped, and as the crowd applauded he clapped with them, his condescension perfect.

'Bravo . . . bravo . . .' he said. I almost wept.

When later I paid my bill, I hesitated to over-tip in case he was offended. Besides, I did not want him to look upon me merely as a tourist client. Our relationship went deeper.

'For your mother and your little sister,' I said, pressing five hundred lire into his hand, seeing, in my mind's eye, the three of them tip-toeing to Mass in St Mark's, the mother voluminous, Ganymede in his Sunday black, and the little sister veiled for her first Communion.

'Thank you, thank you, *signore*,' he said, and added, '*A domani*.'

'*A domani*,' I echoed, touched that he should already be looking forward to our next encounter. As for the wretch in the white mackintosh, he was already feeding the fishes in the Adriatic.

The following morning I had a shock. The reception clerk telephoned my room to ask whether I would mind leaving it vacant by midday. I did not know what he meant. The room had been booked for a fortnight. He was full of excuses. There had been a misunderstanding, he said; this particular room had been engaged for many weeks, he thought the travel agent had explained the fact. Very well, I said, huffed, put me somewhere else. He expressed a thousand regrets. The hotel was full. But he could recommend a very comfortable little flat that the management used from time to time

as an annexe. And there would be no extra charge. My breakfast would be brought to me just the same, and I should even
have a private bath.

'It's very upsetting,' I fumed. 'I have all my things unpacked.'

Again a thousand regrets. The porter would move my
luggage. He would even pack for me. I need not stir hand
or foot myself. Finally I consented to the new arrangement,
though I certainly would not permit anyone but myself to
touch my things. Then I went downstairs and found Prince
Hal, with a barrow for my luggage, awaiting me below. I was
in a bad humour, with my arrangements upset, and quite
determined to refuse the room in the annexe on sight, and
demand another.

We skirted the lagoon. Prince Hal trundling the baggage,
and I felt something of a fool stalking along behind him,
bumping into the promenaders, and cursed the travel agent
who had presumably made the muddle about the room in the
hotel.

When we arrived at our destination, though, I was obliged
to change my tune. Prince Hal entered a house with a fine,
even beautiful façade, whose spacious staircase was spotlessly
clean. There was no lift, and he carried my luggage on his
shoulder. He stopped on the first floor, took out a key, fitted
it to the left-hand door, and threw it open. 'Please to enter,'
he said.

It was a charming apartment, and must have been at some
time or other the salon of a private *palazzo*. The windows,
instead of being closed and shuttered like the windows in the
Hotel Byron, were wide open to a balcony, and to my delight
the balcony looked out upon the Grand Canal. I could not
be better placed.

'Are you sure,' I inquired, 'that this room is the same price
as the room in the hotel?'

Prince Hal stared. He obviously did not understand my question.

'Please?' he said.

I left it. After all, the reception clerk had said so. I looked about me. A bathroom led out of the apartment. There were even flowers by the bed.

'What do I do about breakfast?' I asked.

Prince Hal pointed to the telephone. 'You ring,' he said, 'they answer below. They bring it.' Then he handed over the key.

When he had gone I went once more to the balcony and looked out. The canal was full of bustle and life. All Venice was below me. The speed-boats and the *vaporetti* did not worry me, the changing animated scene was one of which I felt I could never grow tired. Here I could sit and laze all day if I so desired. My luck was incredible. Instead of cursing the travel agent I blessed him. I unpacked my things for the second time in three days, but this time, instead of being a number on the third floor of the Hotel Byron, I was lord and master of my own minute *palazzo*. I felt like a king. The great Campanile bell sounded midday and, since I had breakfasted early, I was in the mood for more coffee. I lifted the telephone. I heard a buzz in answer, and then a click. A voice said, 'Yes?'

'*Café complet*,' I ordered.

'At once,' replied the voice. Was it . . . could it be . . . that too-familiar American accent?

I went into the bathroom to wash my hands, and when I returned there was a knock at the door. I called out, '*Avanti!*' The man who bore in the tray was not wearing a white mackintosh or a trilby hat. The light-grey suit was carefully pressed. The terrible suède shoes were yellow. And he had a piece of sticking plaster on his forehead. 'What did I tell you?' he said. 'I arrange-a everything. Very nice. Very OK.'

6

He put the tray down on the table near the window and waved his hand at the balcony and the sounds from the Grand Canal.

'Sir Johnson spend-a the day here,' he said. 'All the day he lie on the balcony with his, how-do-you-call-them?'

He raised his hands in the gesture of field-glasses, and swerved from side to side. His gold-filled teeth showed as he smiled.

'Mr Bertie Poole, different altogether,' he added. 'A speed-boat to the Lido, and back here after dark. Little dinners, little parties, with his friends. He made-a de whoopee.'

The knowing wink filled me with disgust. Officiously he began to pour out the coffee for me. It was too much.

'Look here,' I said, 'I don't know your name, and I don't know how this business has come about. If you have come to an understanding with the clerk at the Hotel Byron it's nothing to do with me.'

He opened his eyes in astonishment.

'You don't like-a the apartment?' he said.

'Of course I like it,' I replied. 'That's not the point. The point is, I made my own arrangements and now . . .'

But he cut me short. 'Don't worry, don't worry,' he said, waving his hand. 'You pay here less than you pay at Hotel Byron, I see to it. And nobody come to disturb you. Nobody at all-a.' He winked again, and moved heavily towards the door. 'If there is anything you want,' he said, 'just ring-a the bell. OK?'

He left the room. I poured the coffee into the Grand Canal. For all I knew it might be poisoned. Then I sat down to think out the situation.

I had been in Venice for three days. I had booked, as I

thought, my room at the Hotel Byron for a fortnight. I had, therefore, ten days left of my holiday. Was I prepared to spend the ten days in this delicious apartment, at what I had been assured was no extra expense, under the aegis of this tout? He apparently bore no malice towards me for his tumble in the canal. The sticking plaster bore evidence to his fall, but the subject had not been mentioned. He looked less sinister in his light-grey suit than he had done in the white mackintosh. Perhaps I had let my imagination run away with me. And yet . . . I dipped my finger in the coffee-pot, and raised it to my lips. It tasted all right. I glanced at the telephone. If I lifted it his odious American voice would answer. I had better telephone the Hotel Byron from outside, or, better still, make my inquiry in person.

I locked the cupboards and the chest-of-drawers, and my suitcases too, and pocketed the keys. I left the room, locking the door of the apartment. No doubt he would have a pass-key, but it could not be helped. Then I went downstairs, walking-stick at the ready in case of attack, and so out into the street. No sign of the enemy anywhere below. The building appeared uninhabited. I went back to the Hotel Byron and tried to get some information from the staff, but my luck was out. The clerk at the reception desk was not the one who had tele-phoned me in the morning about the change of room. Some new arrival was waiting to check in, and the clerk was impa-tient. Because I was no longer under the roof I did not interest him. 'Yes, yes,' he said, 'it's all right, when we are full here we make arrangements to board our guests outside. We have had no complaints.' The couple waiting to check in sighed heavily. I was holding them up.

Frustrated, I left the desk and walked away. There seemed nothing to be done. The sun was shining, a light breeze rippled the water of the lagoon, and the promenaders, without coats and hats, strolled peacefully, taking the air. I supposed I could do the same. After all, nothing very grave had happened. I was the temporary owner of an apartment overlooking the Grand Canal, a matter to strike envy into the breasts of all these tourists. Why should I worry? I boarded a *vaporetto*, and went and sat in the church by the Accademia to gaze at the Bellini Madonna and Child. It calmed my nerves.

I spent the afternoon sleeping and reading upon my balcony without benefit of field-glasses – unlike Sir Johnson, whoever he might be – and nobody came near me. As far as I could see none of my things had been touched. The little trap I had set – a hundred lire note between two ties – was still in place. I breathed a sigh of relief. Possibly, after all, things would work out well.

Before going out to dinner I wrote a letter to my superior. He was always inclined to patronize me, and it was something of a coup to tell him that I had found myself a delightful apartment with quite the finest view in Venice. 'By the way,' I said, 'what chance is there at the Majestic for young waiters to train? There is a very good lad here, of excellent appearance and manners, just the right type for the Majestic. Can I give him any hope? He is the sole support of a widowed mother and orphan sister.'

I dined in my favourite restaurant – I was *persona grata* by now, in spite of the lapse of the night before – and strolled on to the Piazza San Marco without a qualm. The tout might appear, white mackintosh and all, but I had dined too well to care. The orchestra was surrounded by sailors from a destroyer which had anchored in the lagoon. There was much changing of hats, and laughter, and demanding of popular tunes, and the audience entered into the fun, clapping the sailor who pretended to seize the fiddle. I laughed uproariously with the rest of them, Ganymede by my side. How right my sister had been to encourage me to go to Venice instead of to Devon. How I blessed the vagaries of her cook!

It was in mid-laughter that I was carried out of myself. There were clouds above my head and below me, and my right arm, outstretched on the empty chair beside me, was a wing. Both arms were wings, and I was soaring above the earth. Yet I had claws too. The claws held the lifeless body of the boy. His eyes were closed. The wind currents bore me upward through the clouds, and my triumph was such that the still body of the boy only seemed to me more precious and more mine. Then I heard the sound of the orchestra again, and with it laughter and clapping, and I saw that I had put out my hand and gripped Ganymede's, and he had not withdrawn it, but had let it remain there.

I was filled with embarrassment. I snatched mine away and joined in the applause. Then I picked up my glass of curaçao.

'Fortune,' I said, raising my glass to the crowd, to the orchestra, to the world at large. It would not do to single out the child.

Ganymede smiled. 'The *signore* enjoys himself,' he said.

Just that, and no more. But I felt he shared my mood. An impulse made me lean forward. 'I have written to a friend in London,' I said, 'a friend who is a director of a big hotel. I hope to have an answer from him in a few days' time.'

He showed no surprise. He bowed, then clasped his hands behind his back and looked over the heads of the crowd.

'It is very kind of the *signore*,' he said.

I wondered how much faith he had in me, and whether it exceeded that which he put in his friends in Rome.

'You will have to give me your name and all particulars,' I told him, 'and I suppose a reference from the proprietor here.'

A brief nod of the head showed that he understood. 'I have my papers,' he said proudly, and I could not help smiling, thinking of the dossier that probably contained a report from his school and a recommendation to whoever might employ him. 'My uncle too will speak for me,' he added. 'The *signore* has only to ask my uncle.'

'And who is your uncle?' I inquired.

He turned to me, looking for the first time a little modest, a little shy. 'The *signore* has moved to his apartment in the Via Goldoni, I believe,' he said. 'My uncle is a great man of business in Venice.'

His uncle . . . the appalling tout was his uncle. All was explained. It was a family relationship. I need never have worried. Instantly I placed the man as the brother of the nagging mother, both of them, no doubt, playing on the feelings of my Ganymede, who wished to show his independence and get away from them. Still, it had been a narrow escape. I might have offended the man mortally when he took his tumble into the canal.

'Of course, of course,' I said, pretending I had known all the time, for he seemed to take it for granted that this was the case and I had no desire to seem a fool. Then I went on, 'A very comfortable apartment. Do you know it?'

'Naturally I know it, *signore*,' he said, smiling. 'It is I who will bring you your breakfast every morning.'

I nearly fainted. Ganymede bring my breakfast . . . It was too much to absorb in one moment. I concealed my emotion by ordering another curaçao, and he darted off to obey me. I was, as the French say, *bouleversé*. To be tenant of the delicious apartment was one thing – and at no extra cost – but to have Ganymede thrown in, as it were, with my breakfast was almost more than flesh and blood could stand. I made an effort to compose myself before he returned, but his announcement had thrown me into such a flutter that I could hardly sit in my seat. He was back, with the glass of curaçao.

'Pleasant dreams, *signore*,' he said.

Pleasant dreams, indeed . . . I had not the courage to look

at him. And when I had swallowed my curaçao I took advantage of his temporary summons by another client to slip away, although it was long before midnight. I got back to the apartment by instinct rather than by conscious thought – I had not seen where I was going – and then noticed, on the table, the still unposted letter to London. I could have sworn I had taken it with me when I went out to dinner. However, the morning would do. I was too agitated to go out again tonight.

I stood on the balcony and smoked another cigar, an unheard-of excess, and then went through my small store of books with the idea of presenting one to Ganymede when he brought me my breakfast. His English was so good that it needed a tribute, and the idea of a tip was somehow distasteful. Trollope was not right for him, nor Chaucer either. And the volume of Edwardian memoirs would be quite beyond his understanding. Could I bear to part with my well-worn Shakespeare Sonnets? Impossible to come to a decision. I would sleep on it – if I could sleep, which seemed very doubtful. I took two soneryl tablets, and passed out.

When I awoke it was past nine o'clock. The traffic on the Canal might have indicated high noon. The day was brilliantly fine. I rushed from my bed to the bathroom and shaved, a thing I usually did after breakfast, and then, putting on my dressing-gown and slippers, moved the table and the chair on to the balcony. Then, in trepidation, I went to the telephone and lifted the receiver. There came the buzz and the click, and with a rush of blood to the heart I recognized his voice.

'*Buon giorno, signore.* You slept well?'

'Very well,' I answered. 'Will you bring me a *café complet?*'

'*Café complet,*' he repeated.

I hung up and went and sat on the balcony. Then I remembered I had not unlocked the door. I did this, and returned to the balcony. My excitement was intense, and irrational. I even felt a trifle sick. Then, after five minutes that seemed eternity, came the knock on the door. He entered, tray poised high at shoulder level, and his bearing was so regal, his carriage so proud that he might have been bringing me ambrosia or a swan instead of coffee and a roll and butter. He was wearing a morning coat with thin black stripes, the type of jacket worn by valets at a club.

'A good appetite, *signore*,' he said.

'Thank you,' I replied.

I had my small present ready on my knee. The Shakespeare Sonnets must be sacrificed. They were irreplaceable in that particular edition, but no matter. Nothing else would do. First, though, before the presentation, I would sound him.

'I want to make you a little present,' I told him.

He bowed in courtesy. 'The *signore* is too good,' he murmured.

'You speak English so well,' I continued, 'that you need to hear only the best. Now, tell me, who do you think has been the greatest Englishman?'

He considered the matter gravely. And he stood, as he did on the Piazza San Marco, with his hands clasped behind his back.

'Winston Churchill,' he said.

I might have known it. Naturally the boy lived in the present, or it would be more correct to say, in this instance, the immediate past.

'A good answer,' I said, smiling, 'but I want you to think again. No, I'll put my question another way. If you had some money to spend, and you could spend it on anything you wanted connected with the English language, what would be the first thing you would buy?'

This time there was no hesitation. 'I would buy a long-playing gramophone record,' he said, 'a long-playing gramophone record of Elvis Presley or Johnnie Ray.'

413

I was disappointed. It was not the answer I had hoped for. Who were these creatures? Crooners? Ganymede must be educated to better things. On second thoughts, I would not part with the Sonnets.

'Very well,' I said, hoping I did not sound offhand, and I put my hand in my pocket and took out a thousand-lire note, 'but I suggest you buy Mozart instead.'

The note disappeared, crumpled out of sight in his hand. It was discreetly done, and I wondered if he had been able to glimpse the figure. After all, a thousand lire is a thousand lire. I asked him how he managed to evade his duties at the café to bring me my breakfast, and he explained that his work did not begin there until just before midday. And, anyway, there was an understanding between the proprietor of the café and his uncle.

'Your uncle,' I said, 'seems to have an understanding with many people.' I was thinking of the reception clerk at the Hotel Byron.

Ganymede smiled. 'In Venice,' he said, 'everybody knows everybody.'

I noticed that he glanced with admiration at my dressing-gown, which, when I had bought it for travelling, I had thought a shade too bright. Remembering the gramophone records, I reminded myself that he was, after all, nothing but a child, and one should not expect too much.

'Do you ever have a day off?' I asked him.

'On Sundays,' he said. 'I take it in turn with Beppo.'

Beppo must be the unsuitable name of the swarthy youth at the café.

'And what do you do on your day off?' I inquired.

'I go out with my friends,' he replied.

I poured myself more coffee, and wondered if I dared. A rebuff would be so hurtful.

'If you have nothing better to do,' I said, 'and should be free next Sunday, I will take you for a trip to the Lido.' I felt myself blush, and bent over the coffee-pot to hide it.

'In a speed-boat?' he asked quickly.

I was rather nonplussed. I had visualized the usual *vaporetto*. A speed-boat would be very expensive.

'That would depend,' I hedged. 'Surely on a Sunday they would all be booked?'

He shook his head firmly. 'My uncle knows a man who has speed-boats for hire,' he said. 'They can be hired for the whole day.'

Heavens above, it would cost a fortune! It would not do to commit myself. 'We'll see,' I said. 'It would depend upon the weather.'

'The weather will be fine,' he said, smiling. 'It will stay fine now for the rest of the week.'

His enthusiasm was infectious. Poor child, he must have few treats. On his feet all day and half the night serving tourists. A breath of air in a speed-boat would seem like paradise.

'Very well, then,' I said. 'If it's fine, we'll go.'

I stood up, brushing the crumbs off my dressing-gown. He took my gesture as one of dismissal, and seized the tray.

'Can I do anything else for the *signore*?' he asked.

'You can post my letter,' I said. 'It's the one I told you about, to the friend who is a director of a hotel.'

He lowered his eyes modestly, and waited for me to hand him the letter.

'Shall I see you this evening?' I asked.

'Of course, *signore*,' he said. 'I will keep a table for you, at the usual time.'

I let him go and went to run my bath, and it was only when I lay soaking in the hot water that an unpleasant thought occurred to me. Was it possible that Ganymede had also brought breakfast for Sir Johnson, and had gone to the Lido in a speed-boat with Bertie Poole? I dismissed the thought. It was far too offensive . . .

The week remained fine, as he had foretold, and each day I became more entranced with my surroundings. No sign of anyone in the apartment. My bed was made as if by magic. The uncle remained *perdu*. And in the morning, as soon as I touched the telephone, Ganymede replied, and brought my breakfast. Every evening the table at the café awaited me, the chair upturned, the glass of curaçao and the half-bottle of Evian in their place. If I had no more strange visions, and no more dreams, at least I found myself in happy holiday mood, without a care in the world, and with what I can only call a telepathic understanding, an extraordinary sympathy, between Ganymede and myself. No other client existed but me. He did his duty, but remained at my beck and call. And the morning breakfasts on the balcony were the high peak of the day.

Sunday dawned fine. The high wind that might have meant a *vaporetto* was not forthcoming, and when he bore in my coffee and roll the smile on his face betrayed his excitement.

'The *signore* will come to the Lido?' he asked.

I waved my hand. 'Of course,' I said. 'I never break a promise.'

'I will make arrangements,' he said, 'if the *signore* will be at the first landing-stage to the apartment by half-past eleven.'

And for the first time since bringing my breakfast he vanished without further conversation, such was his haste. It was a little alarming. I had not even inquired about the price.

I attended Mass in St Mark's, a moving experience, and one that put me in a lofty mood. The setting was magnificent, and the singing could not have been bettered. I looked around for Ganymede, half expecting to see him enter leading a little sister by the hand, but there was no sign of him in the vast crowd. Oh well, the excitement of the speed-boat had proved too much for him.

I came out of the church into the dazzling sunshine, and put on my dark glasses. There was scarcely a ripple on the lagoon. I wished he had chosen a gondola. In a gondola I could have lain full-length, stretched at my ease, and we could have gone to Torcello. I might even have brought the Shakespeare Sonnets with me, and read one or two of them aloud to him. Instead, I must indulge his youthful whim and enter the age of speed. Blow the expense! It would never happen again.

I saw him standing by the water's edge, changed into brief shorts and a blue shirt. He looked very much younger, a complete child. I waved my walking-stick and smiled.

'All aboard?' I called gaily.

'All board, *signore*,' he replied.

I made for the landing-stage and saw, drawn up to it, a magnificent varnished speed-boat complete with cabin, a small pennant at the prow, a large ensign at the stern. And standing by the controls, in a flaming orange shirt open at the neck, betraying his hairy chest, was a great ungainly figure I recognized with dismay. At sight of me he touched the klaxon, and revved up the engine so that it roared.

'We go places,' he said, with a revolting smile. 'We hit-a the headlines. We have fun.'

7

I stepped aboard, my heart like lead, and was instantly thrown off balance as our horrible mechanic thrust the engine into gear. I clutched at his ape-like arm, to save myself from falling, and he steadied me into the seat beside him, at the same time opening the throttle to such an extent that I feared for my eardrums. We bounced across the lagoon at a fearful speed, hitting the surface every moment with a crash that nearly split the craft in two, and nothing could be seen of the grace and colour of Venice because of the wall of water that rose on either side of us.

'Must we go so fast?' I screamed, endeavouring to make myself heard above the deafening roar of the engine. The tout grinned at me, showing his gold-filled teeth, and shouted back, 'We break-a the records. This most powerful boat in Venice.'

I resigned myself to doom. I was not only ill-prepared for the ordeal, but ill-dressed. My dark blue coat was already spattered with salt-water, and there was a smear of oil on my trouser-leg. The hat I had brought to protect me against the sun was useless. I needed a flying helmet and a pair of goggles. To leave my exposed seat and crawl to the cabin would be risking certain injury to my limbs. Besides, I should get claustrophobia, and the noise inside a confined space would be even worse. On, on we sped, rocking every craft in sight, heading for the Adriatic, and to show off his skill as a helmsman the monster beside me began to perform acrobatics, making great circles and heading into our own wash.

'You watch-a her rise,' he bellowed in my ear, and rise we did, to such an extent that my stomach turned over with the inevitable thud of our descent, and the spray that we had not left behind us trickled over my collar and down my back. Standing in the prow, revelling in every moment, his light hair tossed about in the breeze we were making, stood Ganymede, a sea-sprite, joyous and free. He was my only consolation, and the sight of him there, turning now and again to smile, prevented me from ordering an instant return to Venice.

When we reached the Lido, a pleasant enough trip by *vaporetto*, I was not only wet but deaf into the bargain, the spray and the roar of the engine combined having successfully blocked my right ear. I stepped ashore shaken and silent, and it was odious when the tout took my arm in a familiar gesture and shepherded me into a waiting taxi, while Ganymede leapt in front beside the driver. Where to now, I asked myself? How fatal to make a picture of one's day in fantasy. In the church, during the singing of Mass, I had seen myself landing with Ganymede from some smooth craft piloted by a discreet nonentity, and then the two of us strolling to a little restaurant I had marked down on my previous visit. How delightful, I had thought, to sit at a corner table with him, choosing the menu, watching his happy face, seeing it colour, perhaps, with the wine, and getting him to talk about himself, about his life, about the complaining mother and little sister. Then, with the liqueurs, we would make plans for the future, should my letter to my London superior prove successful.

None of this happened. The taxi drew up with a swerve before a modern hotel facing the Lido bathing-beach. The place was crammed, despite the lateness of the season, and the tout, known apparently to the maître d'hôtel, thrust his way through the chattering crowd into the airless restaurant. To follow in his wake was bad enough, the flaming orange shirt making him conspicuous, but worse was to come. The table in the centre was already filled with hilarious Italians talking at the tops of their voices, who at sight of us rose in unison, pushing back their chairs to make room. A dyed blonde with enormous ear-rings and reeking of scent swooped upon me with a flow of Italian.

'My sister, *signore*,' said the tout, 'she make-a you welcome. She no speak-a the English.'

Was this Ganymede's mother? And the full-bosomed young woman beside her with scarlet fingernails and jangling bangles, was this the little sister? My head whirled.

'It is a great honour, *signore*,' Ganymede murmured, 'that you invite my family to lunch.'

I sat down, defeated. I had invited nobody. But the matter was out of my hands. The uncle – if uncle indeed he was, the monster, the tout – was handing round to everyone menus the size of placards. The maître d'hôtel was bending himself in two in his effort to please. And Ganymede . . . Ganymede was smiling into the eyes of some loathsome cousin who, with clipped moustache and crew-cut, was making the motions of a speed-boat going through the water with a pudgy, olive hand.

I turned to the tout in desperation. 'I had not expected a party,' I said. 'I am afraid I may not have brought enough money.'

He broke off his discussion with the maître d'hotel.

'Don't worry . . . don't worry . . .' he said, waving the air. 'You leave'a the bill to me. We settle later.'

Settle later . . . It was all very well. By the time the day was over I should not be in a position to settle anything. An enormous plate of noodles was set before me, topped with a rich meat sauce, and I saw that my glass was being filled with a particular barolo that, taken in the middle of the day, means certain death.

'You 'avin' fun?' said Ganymede's sister, pressing my foot with hers.

Hours later I found myself on the beach, still seated between her and her mother, both of them changed into bikinis, lying on either side of me like porpoises, while the cousins, the uncles, the aunts splashed into the sea and back again, shrieking and laughing, and Ganymede, beautiful as an angel from heaven, presided at the gramophone that had suddenly materialized from outer space, repeating again and again the long-playing record that he had bought with my thousand lire.

'My mother wants so much to thank you,' said Ganymede,

'for writing to London. If I go, she will come too, and my sister.'

'We all go,' said his uncle. 'We make one big party. We all go to London and set-a the Thames on fire.'

It was over at last. The final splashing in the sea, the final poke from the scarlet toe of the sister, the final bottle of wine. I had a splitting head, and my inside had turned on me. One by one the relations came to shake me by the hand. The mother, voluble with thanks, embraced me. That none of them were to accompany us back to Venice in the speed-boat and continue the party there was the one measure of solace left to me at the end of the disastrous day.

We climbed aboard. The engine started. We were away. And this should have been the return journey I had already made in fantasy – the smooth, rather idling return over limpid water, Ganymede at my side, a new intimacy having grown up between us because of the hours spent in each other's company, the sun, low on the horizon, turning the island that was Venice into a rose façade.

Halfway across, I saw that Ganymede was struggling with a rope that lay coiled across the stern of our craft, and the uncle, easing the throttle so that our progress was suddenly slowed, left the controls to help him. We began to rock from side to side in a sickly fashion.

'What is going to happen now?' I called.

Ganymede shook the hair out of his eyes and smiled. 'I water-ski,' he said. 'I follow you home to Venice on my skis.'

He dived into the cabin and came out again with the skis. Together the uncle and nephew fixed the rope and the skis, and then Ganymede flung off his shirt and his shorts and stood upright, a small bronzed figure in bathing slip.

The uncle beckoned me. 'You sit-a here,' he said. 'You pay out the rope so.'

He secured the rope to a bollard in the stern and put the end into my hands, then rushed forward to the driving seat and started to roar the engine.

'What do you mean?' I cried. 'What do I have to do?'

Ganymede was already over the side and in the water, fixing his bare feet into the slots of the skis, and then, unbelievably, pulling himself up into a standing position while the craft began to race ahead. The uncle sounded the klaxon with an ear-splitting screech, and the craft, gathering momentum, sped over the water at top speed. The rope, made fast to the bollard, held, though I still clung to the end, while in our wake, steady as a rock on his dancing skis, the small figure of Ganymede was silhouetted against the already vanishing Lido.

I seated myself in the stern of the boat and watched him. He might have been a charioteer, and the two skis his racing steeds. His hands were stretched before him, holding the guide-rope as a charioteer would gather his reins, and as we circled once, twice, and he swung out in an arc on his corresponding course, he raised his hand to me in salutation, a smile of triumph on his face.

The sea was the sky, the ripple on the water wisps of cloud, and heaven knows what meteors we drove and scattered, the boy and I, soaring towards the sun. I know that at times I bore him on my shoulders, and at others he slipped away, and once it was as though both of us plunged headlong into a molten mist which was neither sea nor sky, but the luminous rings encircling a star.

As the craft swung into the straight again and bounced away on its course, he signalled to me with one hand, pointing to the rope on the bollard. I did not know whether he meant me to loosen it or make it more secure, and I did the wrong thing, jerked it, for he over-balanced instantly and was flung into the water. He must have hurt himself, for I saw that he made no attempt to swim.

Flustered, I shouted to the uncle, 'Stop the engine! Go astern!'

Surely the right thing to do was to bring the boat to a stand-still? The uncle, startled, seeing nothing but my agitated face, put the engine hard into reverse. His action threw me off my feet, and by the time I had scrambled up again we were almost on top of the boy. There was a mass of churning water, of tangled rope, of sudden, splintering wood, and leaning over the side of the boat I saw the slim body of Ganymede drawn into the suction of the propeller, his legs enmeshed, and I bent down to lift him clear. I put out my hands to grip his shoulders.

'Watch the rope,' yelled the uncle. 'Pull it clear.'

But he did not know that the boy was beside us, was beneath us, and that already he had slipped from my hands which struggled to hold him, to bear him aloft, that already . . . God, already . . . the water was beginning to colour crimson with his blood.

8

Yes, yes, I told the uncle. Yes, I would pay compensation, I would pay anything they asked. It had been my fault, an error of judgement. I had not understood. Yes, I would pay any and every item he liked to put down on his list. I would telegraph to my bank in London, and perhaps the British Consul would help me, would give advice. If I could not raise the money immediately I would pay so much a week, so much a month, so much a year. Indeed, the rest of my life I would continue to pay, I would continue to support the bereaved, because it was my fault, I agreed that it was all my fault.

An error of judgement on my part had been the cause of the accident. The British Consul sat by my side, and he listened to the explanations of the uncle, who produced his notebook and his sheaf of bills.

'This gentleman take-a my apartment for two weeks, and my nephew he bring-a him his breakfast every day. He bring-a flowers. He bring-a coffee and rolls. He insists my nephew look after him and no one else. This gentleman take great fancy to the boy.'

'Is that true?'

'Yes, it's true.'

The lighting of the apartment was extra, it seemed. And the heating for the bath. The bath had to be heated from below in a special way. There was a man's time for coming in to repair a shutter. The boy's time, he told the Consul, for bringing my breakfast, for not going to the café before midday. And the time for taking a Sunday off that was not the regular Sunday. He did not know if the gentleman was prepared to pay for these items.

'I have already said that I will pay for everything.'

The notebook was consulted again, and there was the damage to the engines of the speed-boat, the cost of the water-skis that were smashed beyond repair, the charge for the craft that had been hailed to tow us back to Venice, to tow the speed-boat back to Venice with Ganymede unconscious in my arms, and the telephone call from the quayside for the ambulance. One by one he read out the items from the notebook. The hospital charges, the doctor's fees, the surgeon's fees.

'This gentleman, he insist he pay for everything.'

'Is that true?'

'Yes, it's true.'

The yellow face against the dark suit seemed fatter than before, and the eyes, puffy with weeping, looked sideways at the Consul.

'This gentleman, he write to his friend in London about my nephew. Perhaps already there is a job waiting for the boy, a job he can no longer take. I have a son, Beppo, my son also a very good boy, known to the gentleman here. Beppo and my nephew they both work at the café every night, and serve the gentleman. The gentleman so fond of these boys, he follow them home. Yes, I see it with my own eyes, he follow them home. Beppo would like to go to London in place of his poor cousin. This gentleman arrange it, perhaps? He write again to his friend in London?'

The Consul coughed discreetly. 'Is that true? Did you follow them home?'

'Yes, it's true.'

The uncle took out a large handkerchief and blew his nose.

'My nephew very well brought-up boy. My son the same. Never give any trouble. All the money they earn they give to their family. My nephew he had very great trust in this gentleman, and he tell me, he tell all the family, his mother, his sister, that this gentleman will take him back to London. His mother, she buy a new dress, and his sister too, she buy new clothes for the boy to go to London. Now, she ask-a herself, what happens to the clothes, they cannot be worn, they are no use.'

I said to the Consul that I would pay for everything.

'His poor mother, she break-a her heart,' the voice continued, 'and his sister too, she lose-a all interest in her work, she become nervous, ill. Who is to pay for the funeral of my nephew? Then this gentleman, he kindly say, no expense to be spared.'

No expense to be spared, and let that go too for the mourning, and the veils, and the wreaths, and the music, and the weeping, and the procession, the endless long procession. And I would pay, too, for the tourists clicking cameras and feeding pigeons who knew nothing of what had happened, and for those lovers lying in each other's arms in gondolas, and for the echo of the Angelus sounding from the Campanile, and the lapping water from the lagoon, and the chug-chug of the *vaporetto* leaving the landing-stage which turns into the chug-chug of a coal barge in the Paddington canal.

It passes, of course – not the coal barge over there, I mean, but the horror. The horror of accident, of sudden death. You see, as I told myself afterwards, if it had not been an accident it would have been a war. Or he would have come to London and grown up, grown fat, turned into a tout like the uncle, grown ugly, old. I don't want to make excuses for anything. I don't want to make excuses for anything at all. But – because of what happened – my life has become rather different. As I said before, I've moved my quarters in London to this district. I've given up my job. I've dropped my friends, in a word . . . I've changed. I still see my sister and my nieces from time to time. No, I don't possess any other family. There was a younger brother who died when I was five, but I don't remember him at all: I've never given him a thought. My sister has been my only living relative for years.

Now, if you will excuse me, I see by my watch it is nearly seven o'clock. The restaurant down the road will be open. And I like to be there on time. The fact is, the boy who is training there as a waiter celebrates his fifteenth birthday this evening, and I have a little present for him. Nothing very much, you understand – I don't believe in spoiling these lads – but it seems there is a singer called Perry Como much in favour amongst the young. I have the latest record here. He likes bright colours, too – I rather thought this blue and gold cravat might catch his eye . . .

Leading Lady

He stood in the passage, his hat on the back of his head, a cigar hanging from his mouth. He pulled out an enormous watch and stamped his foot impatiently.

'Look here,' he shouted, for all the world to hear, 'I'm not accustomed to be kept waiting. Doesn't Miss Fabian know I've arrived? What the hell is everybody doing?'

The doorkeeper peered at him timidly. 'I'm sorry, sir; it will only be a few moments. What name was it, sir?'

Damn it all, this fellow hadn't even recognised him! He looked at the doorkeeper steadily, waited so that he should grasp the full significance of his reply.

'Paul Haynes,' he said superbly, and turned away. A frightened dresser appeared at the bottom of the stairs.

'Will you please come this way, sir?' She knew who he was all right. Hers was the proper subservient attitude to take. Good God, once he got this theatre under his control he'd change the whole damn staff. The doorkeeper would be the first to get the sack.

He strode after the dresser along the passage, swaying from side to side like a turkey-cock, spilling ash as he went. He stood on the threshold of the dressing-room, his legs wide apart, his hat still on the back of his head.

She was sitting before the looking-glass, patting her hair into place. She turned round with a little cry of distress.

'Oh, but can you ever forgive me for having kept you waiting? Those appalling film people never leave me alone for a moment – keep pestering me to go to Hollywood and offering me stupendous sums. Lewisheim has been on the telephone for twenty minutes.' She waited a moment to allow her words to sink into the man's brain. She murmured something unnecessary to her dresser, and then turned back to him with a smile. 'However, let's forget about that – it's something quite apart. Now, please sit down – forgive this untidiness everywhere, but you know what it is, the last few days of a long run. First of all, I must tell you, I went yesterday afternoon to see your new revue. Oh, it's the most marvellous thing I've ever seen – but the most. I can't speak about it. I've never enjoyed anything so much. Those girls – the whole production! Of course you're an absolute genius; there's no one to touch you!' She shrugged her shoulders almost impatiently.

He did not attempt to conceal his smile of satisfaction. So she liked it? H'm. Lewisheim's productions would never hold a candle to his. This woman had sense, after all. She was looking more beautiful than ever, too. Pity, perhaps, she wore so little jewellery. Only a chain round her neck. It wasn't impressive; much too simple altogether. He would like to see her in a mass of diamonds.

'Yes, it's a good show, and I don't mind admitting it,' he said loudly, blowing a great cloud of smoke into her face.

Her manners were exquisite; she didn't even wave it away with her hand.

'I spend more money on my productions than any other manager in London,' he went on. 'None of your skimpy, shoddy stuff for me. No painted scenery.'

She made a little sound in her throat and shook her head for sympathy.

'Where you spend money you draw money,' he announced, 'and that's always the way I do things. If you and I put on this play of yours together, I'm going to see that you have the very best of everything. No – don't thank me.' He spread out his large fat hand. 'You're a business woman, you know what you're about when you join forces with me. My dear, you're going to have a real big success, and you're going to make a packet of money.'

She said nothing for a moment. What a conceited fool the man was! Talking to her as if she were some pathetic little actress striking out on her first venture. He didn't know anything about the theatre either. Because he was rich he managed to surround himself with people who did, that was all. He was lucky, and they flattered him, but it was only his money they wanted. Then she leant back in her chair, as if defeated.

'I think you are quite the most wonderful man I know,' she said softly. He looked at her, and put away his cigar. Once more he bent towards her.

'I'm going to tell you something,' he began in a slow, impressive tone, 'and it's something that I don't say to many people, because I'm a very difficult man.' He waited a moment as though to prepare her for some stupendous announcement. Then: 'I like you,' he said. 'I like you very much,' he went on. 'There's no nonsense about you. You look a man straight in the face and tell him the truth. I'm a great believer in truth myself. If I say a thing I mean it. If I didn't like you, I'd be perfectly frank and tell you so. My frankness brings me many enemies, but I'm not afraid of any of 'em. They know what to expect. In fact, the words "to be frank as Paul Haynes" have become a common expression, so they tell me. If a fellow wants to hear the truth about himself, or someone else, let him come along to me.'

'Oh, but I admire you for that,' she broke in impulsively. 'It shows such strength of mind, and such a superb indifference to what the world thinks of you. They matter so little, don't they? – all the people we meet in this profession. I have my few friends – my books, my child.' She turned with a wistful smile at the photograph on her dressing-table. Half-unconsciously she pushed the snapshot of a famous boxer out of sight behind a powder-box.

'You are quite unique, my dear,' he continued. 'If you were not, I shouldn't be sitting here now. You know I've got a whole lot of ideas about the theatre that I think would interest you. I'm a bit of an idealist in my way, you know.'

The fatuity of this man! She glanced at her watch, shading her eyes with her hand.

'Tell me about yourself,' she begged.

'I want to change the present conditions,' he shouted. 'I want to get a different atmosphere into the theatre altogether, and by heaven I'm going to do it. I've started with my own revues, and I want to do the same with the straight plays. Do you know my revues are the cleanest in England? There's not a single line in my new show that would make a man blush. But that's not the point; that's not what I'm getting at. I'm going to put a stop to what goes on behind the scenes – all these dirty little love affairs, all this promiscuous stuff in dressing-rooms. I'm going to make it my business to find out the private life of every actor and actress who works for me. I'll make a clean sweep of the rotters. I'm a powerful man. If I find out

430

that any man or woman hasn't got a fit record, I'll see to it they don't get another job on a London stage.'

He leant back, exhausted with his eloquence.

'Of course, you're quite right,' she said, without hesitating. 'I suppose I'm weak. But I shut my eyes to things. And I hate to get anyone into trouble.'

He went on, pleased with her reply. 'Do you know, you are one of the few actresses who have never been divorced. Of course, you're a widow, but even if your husband had lived, it would have made no difference. Someone told me that five years ago, when you went about a lot with John What's-his-name – the fellow who left his wife and went out to Australia. Whether it's true or not, you showed great wisdom in cutting him out of your life. They tell me he's gone entirely to pieces – out of work, drinks like a fish. Now that's the type of thing I'm going to put a stop to; and I want you on my side. You and I together, my dear, will be practically an unbreakable force. What do you think?'

She looked him straight in the eyes. 'I agree with every word you say,' she told him.

He took her hand and patted it. 'Partners – what?' he said, controlling his smile. 'About the cast,' he went on, clearing his throat. 'We've decided on everyone, I think, except the other man. Is there anyone you fancy for that part?'

She began to polish her nails carelessly.

'You know Bobby Carson, the boy who has been playing my brother in the present play? He's really charming, and very capable. Not a bit expensive either.'

'H'm. It requires more than capability, you know. It's a striking emotional part. The second act is almost entirely in his hands, if you remember. I don't care a damn about the expense. Now, the chap I want in the part is this young Martin Wilton. Have you seen him?'

431

'No.' She turned to the dressing-table, frowning ever so slightly.

'His play comes off next week, so we might be able to get him. Come along Friday afternoon; they have a matinée. I think he's the finest natural actor I've seen for years. Quite young, quite unspoilt. Doesn't know how good he is. See what you think of him, anyway. He can rehearse the part on trial.'

'Yes, yes, of course.' She had heard too much already of this Martin Wilton. People were raving about him. The critics were almost nauseating in their praise.

'Friday, then,' she smiled. 'How exciting! I shall adore it.'

A few minutes later, Haynes leant back in his taxi with a smile of satisfaction. He decided he had made a great impression on her. Well, it was not surprising. After all, he was rich; he had brains; he was under sixty. He felt that she had probably never met anyone quite like him before. He admitted that her husband had been a remarkable man, but no doubt very dull to live with, always wrapped up in his work, seeing her only as a character in one of his plays. He couldn't have known how to make a woman happy. Good thing he had died when he did.

Idly he wondered whether she was lonely. You never heard her name coupled with anyone – not since that fellow went to Australia, all of which was undoubtedly malicious gossip. Well, she had seen eye to eye with him over his ideas for the theatre. It was a wonderful scheme of his, to launch a great purity campaign. With the *Daily Recorder* to back him up, he would get tremendous publicity. He would be known as the Man Who Cleaned Up the English Stage. And Mary Fabian would help. Her beauty and his brains would make a great combination. He supposed she must be well in the thirties by now, with a child growing big. She wasn't everybody's money.

Jove, what a figure, though! He would like to see her in a diamond necklace and with a little less on. This next play was going to be enjoyable in many ways . . .

Back in the dressing-room, Mary Fabian was cursing him for having kept her so long after the performance. He hadn't even apologised. What an appalling man! All that frightful twaddle about his clean revues, while he smacked his lips at her as though she were butchers' meat.

'Tell Mr Carson I'm alone now,' she said to her dresser.

It was past midnight, and she wanted her supper. She threw off her clothes impatiently, and began brushing her hair behind her ears.

'Bobby,' she called through the wall. 'Bobby, my sweet.'

She sat in the stalls on Friday afternoon without moving a muscle of her face. She was alone, after all; Paul Haynes had been called to Manchester. She thanked heaven for his absence. She could not have borne with his enthusiastic remarks, his eager concentration upon the stage. She drew her fur coat more closely around her; she buried herself in it as though she did not wish to be seen.

This Martin Wilton was good, far too good. His personality stuck out a mile, with his vivid face and tawny hair. Not her type at all, of course; but that was not the point. Even had he been attractive to her, she would not have considered him. Not for a moment. It was much too dangerous. It would be fatal to have him in the new play; he would run away with it entirely. She would become a secondary figure, her part would not matter at all.

And she had reached an awkward moment in her career. The slightest slip, the smallest mistake, and attention would be drawn away from her. People would say she was becoming monotonous, she was overplaying herself. No, this boy was too good. Already she could imagine the first night, with Martin Wilton getting the applause. She would have to stand in the background and efface herself, pushing him forward with a smile. And the papers next morning would be a paean of praise. 'Mr Martin Wilton gave the finest performance of the evening.' And so on, and so on . . .

Something had got to be done. He must be prevented at all costs from playing the part. She would have to be careful, though; it was not going to be easy.

Mechanically she wrote a note to Martin Wilton after the matinée.

'Your performance quite marvellous. Never seen anything like it. I want you to come and be with me in my next play. Will send it along for you to read tonight. Wonderful part for you. Forgive me for not coming round. I've got to dash away.'

She felt she could not face that boy now, and his probable insufferable conceit. She drove home, racking her brains for some solution to the problem.

On the morning of the first rehearsal, when Martin Wilton was to read the part for the first time, she received a wire from Haynes. 'Detained Manchester. Impossible to attend rehearsal. Rely on judgment entirely *re* Wilton.'

She crushed the wire in her hand and went on to the stage, sensing victory.

'Mr Haynes is in Manchester, and can't get away for the rehearsal. Is everybody here? Then we'll begin at once.'

At eight o'clock, when they had finished for the day, she flung herself down in her chair, exhausted. Things had gone exactly as she had feared; the boy had been wonderful – never seemed to make a mistake, and his technique was uncanny. How she hated him!

She sat in front of the mirror and began to make up her

face very carefully. She cast her mind back to the night last week when Paul Haynes had voiced his grotesque plans for delving into the private lives of actors and actresses, and the germ of an idea came into her mind. 'Will you tell Mr Wilton I should like to see him?' she said to her dresser.

In a few minutes the boy knocked at her door. 'May I come in?' he said shyly. She gave him a dazzling smile; she held out her hands. 'We've got so much to discuss,' she told him. 'Are you doing anything this evening?'

The boy flushed all over his face. 'As a matter of fact, I was going back to my wife, but if it's important I can easily ring her up.'

She gave a little cry of astonishment. 'Married! – but you're far too young. What do you mean by it?' She shook her head at him in mock reproof. 'Ask her to spare you for a few hours,' she pleaded. 'We've got to talk about this second act.'

In half-an-hour they were having dinner together in her flat. At first he was painfully shy, he would scarcely say a word. Completely unselfconscious on the stage, in private life he was nervous, clumsy, aware of his hands and feet. She pretended not to notice; she smiled encouragement, she spoke softly, using all her old tricks mechanically. Soon he began to warm to the influence of the room, her voice, the excellent food, and his second glass of burgundy. He could scarcely believe he was sitting here alone with Mary Fabian.

She sat with her face in her hands, a cigarette between her lips. The fire cast great shadows on the ceiling, and played about her profile. Her hair shone dully like an old coin. She was so human, so open with him; and he loved the room, with the heavy curtains, the shaded light, and the smell of the queer stuff she burnt on the fire. He was happy and at peace; she seemed to understand him so well. He had never found anyone who could listen to him like this, not even his wife.

'I want you to sit by the fire, and smoke a cigarette, and tell me all about yourself,' she had said.

He found himself speaking to her as if he had known her for years, explaining all the worry of those early years, how he had fought and struggled with his family.

'You seem to understand things about me that nobody else has ever dreamt existed,' he said. 'The serious side of me. What I really feel about life. Because I do feel things, you know, tremendously. People have often told me that when they first meet me I seem horribly shy. All my life it's been the same. My mother, bless her, could never understand my passion for the stage. You're so awfully sympathetic.' He gazed at her with worship in his eyes. 'You'll think me absurd,' he went on, gaining confidence, 'but the one ambition of my life, ever since I first went on the stage, was to act with you. I've dreamt of it for years, grinding away in the provinces.'

'No, no – you're joking!' she smiled.

'I promise you it's absolutely true. I saw you first about five years ago, and I remember thinking to myself: 'There is some-body worth while, who spends her time giving happiness to other people.' Oh, you were simply wonderful. You became my ideal, my sort of guiding star, my good angel. I judged everything by what I imagined your standard to be. I guessed you would never put up with the second-rate in life, or in acting. You would only accept the best. I love it more than anything in the world – the theatre, I mean.'

She stirred slightly, and reached for his hand. 'You dear,' she murmured; 'you dear quixotic person.' Then she leant back in her chair, pillowing her cheek against a cushion.

If he went on much longer she felt she would scream. It was incredible that anyone should talk so much. What a fool he was! She turned her rising yawn into a smile. 'You know, you remind me of myself,' she told him. 'Oh yes, quite a lot.

All your ideals and beliefs. I so appreciate your outlook on life. All for Art, and the world well lost. Ah, how well I understand! I adore my work passionately. I couldn't live without it. One doesn't care about money, people, or success – it's just the longing to achieve something, isn't it?'

'Yes, yes!' he said eagerly, the light of a fanatic in his eyes.

'To create a living character out of a mass of words, to breathe life into it, to – to—' She made a little gesture with her hands, uncertain how to continue. 'Oh, how marvellously you understand!' she ended, and: 'We're going to be such friends, you and I.'

She slipped from her chair to the floor, crouching, her hands spread to the blaze of the fire. Her head was aching; she had had a tiring day. She was longing to go to bed and to sleep. What on earth was he talking about now?

'Hamlet,' he was saying. 'I want to play Hamlet as no one has ever dared to play it before. There is something terrific about him, misunderstood, suppressed. You remember, in the beginning of Act Three, when he is with Ophelia, when she starts, "My lord, I have remembrances of yours," you know . . .'

'Yes, wonderful, wonderful!' she murmured. O God, not Shakespeare, not at this hour! She made no attempt to listen. She was wondering what time Paul Haynes arrived back from Manchester. He was certain to ring her up. The boy mustn't be here then.

'It will almost break my heart if I don't play this part with you,' said Martin Wilton. 'It's the chance of a lifetime. It's going to be hell until it's settled. Supposing Haynes thinks I'm no good?'

She broke from her thoughts with an effort. 'Of course, you are young,' she said gently, 'a little too young. Personally, I think it makes the part all the more sympathetic, and I shall tell him so. Paul Haynes is a very difficult man, but I think

I can persuade him. Unless he gets some absurd idea into his head. He's very thick-headed and obstinate, and once he has made up his mind, nothing in the world will make him change it. But I am sure he will like you; he is bound to agree with me.'

He seized hold of her hands and kissed them. 'You are being an angel to me,' he said, flushing. 'I can't ever forget this.'

She smiled at him sadly; she ran her hand through his hair. 'You remind me of someone I used to be fond of . . .' she began, and then broke off, as though emotionally moved. He cursed himself for his lack of tact. Of course, her husband was dead. It must be terrible for her. How brave she was, facing life alone like that! No one to look after her.

'You must go soon,' she whispered. 'It's getting late. And I've got to say good-night to my little girl. She won't sleep until I've tucked her up myself.' The child was with a nurse in lodgings on the East Coast, but he would never know that. He had probably seen pictures of her soon after she was widowed, holding the child in her arms. When she had appeared the first time after her husband's death, in one of his plays, carefully made up, allowing herself to look a little wan and pale, the audience had gone nearly mad. The publicity had helped her enormously at the time.

'She is the only thing I have left,' she said gently.

He stroked her hand awkwardly, like a clumsy animal. 'I wish I could help,' he began. 'I hate to think of you like this . . . I had no idea . . .' He fumbled with the bangle on her wrist. She seemed very young suddenly, very pathetic. He wished he knew how to comfort her. The world who watched her act would never guess that off the stage she was this sweet, simple woman, broken-hearted, her life empty.

'It's all right,' she was saying, 'but sometimes one gets so frightfully lonely . . .'

Awkwardly he put his arm round her, patting her shoulder as though she was a child. She reached for her scrap of a handkerchief, turning her face from him, blowing her nose and laughing shakily.

'I feel so ashamed,' she said. 'I've never let this happen before.'

He brushed the top of her head with his lips, at a loss for words, and then, impulsively, 'Look here – you ought to meet my wife; she's the most sympathetic person in the world. I know you'd like her; she has a sort of gift for killing depression; she's an absolute angel. We've only got a tiny flat in a mews, but she'd adore to meet you. Come round now – it's not too late. She said she would go to a film when I rang her before dinner, but she'll be back by twelve. And we've got some wonderful records I'd love you to hear. A Beethoven concerto, Cesar Franck . . .'

'No, no, you mustn't tempt me like that; it isn't fair. I've been foolish tonight. I can't understand myself. And I should love to meet your wife, some other time . . . But I'm tired now; we are both tired; and you must go. Bless you for being so sweet to me.'

'Good Lord! I've done nothing. I've just blundered on about myself. It's been the most marvellous evening. You've brought back all my old ideals and faith in the theatre; you've made me feel that everything's worth while. Any success I make I shall owe to you.'

He stumbled out of the flat, not looking where he was going, his head in the clouds, his mind filled with the glorious, impossible future.

Thanking God she was alone at last, she sank into a chair, a cushion behind her head, a cigarette between her lips. Five minutes after he had gone the telephone rang. It was Paul Haynes.

'Hullo,' he said. 'I'm only this minute back from Manchester. Have you gone to bed or can I slip round for two minutes?'

'No, I'd love to see you,' she lied. 'Come along at once.'

She powdered her face a little whiter than usual, using no colour, but shadowing her eyes. She looked very beautiful, but tired, strained.

'Now, I'm not going to keep you up,' he said, as soon as he came into the room. 'You've had a long day, and so have I. We can't afford to burn the candle at both ends in our profession, eh? Got to have beauty sleep.' He smiled broadly, showing large gums. 'Well, just tell me how it went. Everything go off all right without me?'

'Marvellous – considering. You know what first rehearsals are.'

'Tell me – how did they all seem?'

'Splendid, on the whole. I don't think we need make any change.'

'And what about young Martin Wilton? Is he going to be good?'

'He was very much all there. Knew exactly what to do. He won't require much producing. His technique is marvellous in anyone so young. I can't understand where he's learnt it all.'

'He's not too young, is he?'

'No – not really, I don't think. I hope not. We don't want to make a blunder, though. Oh, how I wish you'd been there!'

'Yes. I could have told you what I thought as soon as I'd clapped eyes on him. How did he strike you personally? Did he seem a nice chap? – not conceited? Will you like having him in the theatre?'

She did not reply for a moment, and then laughed a little self-consciously. 'He's very good at his job – I've said so already. What more can I say?'

'Look here, you're keeping something back. Don't pretend with me. Part of our bargain is to tell the truth. Martin Wilton was rude, bad-mannered?'

'No, no. Please don't ask me any more. Let's forget about him.'

'I don't forget, and I shall worry you until I've had this out with you. Come on, my dear; what was the trouble?'

'It's so unfair to the boy,' she protested. 'He probably didn't realise what he was doing. He's young, and I suppose mixes with a crowd of awful people. I know the type – half-drunk and very promiscuous.'

'What are you driving at? Wasn't he sober? What did he do to upset you?'

'Well, he – he tried to make the most violent love to me, that's all.' She laughed and shrugged her shoulders.

Paul Haynes looked at her in amazement. 'Good God! what on earth do you mean?'

'My dear, I assure you I was never more embarrassed in my life. Those sort of things don't happen to me. However, let's forget it.'

'No, by heaven, we won't forget it,' he said savagely. 'I want to get to the bottom of this. What did he do, the little swine?'

'I asked him back here to talk over the second act and he stayed on and seemed to expect dinner. Perhaps he drank a little too much – I don't know. But he started talking the most frightful nonsense about being here alone with me, and said he'd been waiting for this for years. He tried to kiss me, and was, well, rather rough. I was so surprised that I wasn't prepared, you see, and – Oh, I hate telling you all this!'

'Go on,' he said.

'I think he must be very unbalanced and rather peculiar. So many young men are, nowadays, don't you think? I feel so sorry for his poor little wife.'

'Do you mean the little rat is married?'

'Yes – that's the awful part about it. He seized hold of me and said would I go to his flat – his wife was out – wouldn't

441

be back till late. He was quite uncontrolled; it was revolting. Finally, I quietened him down and managed to get him away. He'd been gone only a few minutes when you rang up. That's why I'm looking so exhausted. I suppose he lost his head for the moment – probably took advantage of my being here alone. Promise me not to think any more about it.'

'I'm very sorry,' he said slowly. 'But you remember what I told you the other day? It's just that type of thing I'm out to smash. It's vicious and disgusting. How he dared try it on with you, that's what gets me! He's probably stiff with drugs. An out-and-out rotter. And to think I was going to offer him the chance of his life! But, my dear, you weren't going to tell me. That's carrying chivalry a bit too far, isn't it?'

'But I hate making trouble,' she broke in.

'Trouble? Don't talk such nonsense. If I let that boy play the part it would go against all my principles; it's one of my great ambitions to break up that gang of degenerates and I'm going to start right now. Young Mr Wilton is going to get the surprise of his life. He'll be finished in six months. As for the part, I'd rather give it to a stage-hand than to him.'

She shook her head hopelessly. He moved towards the door.

'Well, you're dead-beat, my dear, and must go to bed. You've been through a very trying time.'

Then, as he reached for his hat, 'What's the name of the chap who played your brother?'

'What?' she said carelessly. 'Oh, Bobby Carson. Why?'

'We'll get on to him in the morning. Tell him to be down at the theatre for rehearsal at eleven o'clock sharp. Good-night, my dear.'

Not After Midnight

I am a schoolmaster by profession. Or was. I handed in my resignation to the Head before the end of the summer term in order to forestall inevitable dismissal. The reason I gave was true enough – ill-health, caused by a wretched bug picked up on holiday in Crete, which might necessitate a stay in hospital of several weeks, various injections, etc. I did not specify the nature of the bug. He knew, though, and so did the rest of the staff. And the boys. My complaint is universal, and has been so through the ages, an excuse for jest and hilarious laughter from earliest times, until one of us oversteps the mark and becomes a menace to society. Then we are given the boot. The passer-by averts his gaze, and we are left to crawl out of the ditch alone, or stay there and die.

If I am bitter, it is because the bug I caught was picked up in all innocence. Fellow-sufferers of my complaint can plead predisposition, poor heredity, family trouble, excess of the good life, and, throwing themselves on a psychoanalyst's couch, spill

443

out the rotten beans within and so effect a cure. I can do none
of this. The doctor to whom I endeavoured to explain what
had happened listened with a superior smile, and then murmured
something about emotionally destructive identification coupled
with repressed guilt, and put me on a course of pills. They
might have helped me if I had taken them. Instead I threw
them down the drain and became more deeply imbued with
the poison that seeped through me, made worse of course by
the fatal recognition of my condition by the youngsters I had
believed to be my friends, who nudged one another when I
came into class, or, with stifled laughter, bent their loathsome
little heads over their desks – until the moment arrived when
I knew I could not continue, and took the decision to knock
on the headmaster's door.

Well, that's over, done with, finished. Before I take myself
to hospital or alternatively, blot out memory, which is a second
possibility, I want to establish what happened in the first place.
So that, whatever becomes of me, this paper will be found,
and the reader can make up his mind whether, as the doctor
suggested, some want of inner balance made me an easy victim
of superstitious fear, or whether, as I myself believe, my down-
fall was caused by an age-old magic, insidious, evil, its origins
lost in the dawn of history. Suffice to say that he who first
made the magic deemed himself immortal, and with unholy
joy infected others, sowing in his heirs, throughout the world
and down the centuries, the seeds of self-destruction.

To return to the present. The time was April, the Easter
holidays. I had been to Greece twice before, but never Crete.
I taught classics to the boys at the preparatory school, but my
reason for visiting Crete was not to explore the sites of Knossos
or Phaestus but to indulge a personal hobby. I have a minor
talent for painting in oils, and this I find all-absorbing, whether
on free days or in the school holidays. My work has been

444

praised by one or two friends in the art world, and my ambition was to collect enough paintings to give a small exhibition. Even if none of them sold, the holding of a private show would be a happy achievement.

Here, briefly, a word about my personal life. I am a bachelor. Age forty-nine. Parents dead. Educated at Sherborne and Brasenose, Oxford. Profession, as you already know, schoolmaster. I play cricket and golf, badminton, and rather poor bridge. Interests, apart from teaching, art, as I have already said, and occasional travel, when I can afford it. Vices, up to the present, literally none. Which is not being self-complacent, but the truth is that my life has been uneventful by any standard. Nor has this bothered me. I am probably a dull man. Emotionally I have had no complications. I was engaged to a pretty girl, a neighbour, when I was twenty-five, but she married somebody else. It hurt at the time, but the wound healed in less than a year. One fault, if fault it is, I have always had, which perhaps accounts for my hitherto monotonous life. This is an aversion to becoming involved with people. Friends I possess, but at a distance. Once involved, trouble occurs, and too often disaster follows.

I set out for Crete in the Easter holidays with no encumbrance but a fair-sized suitcase and my painting gear. A travel agent had recommended a hotel overlooking the Gulf of Mirabello on the eastern coast, after I had told him I was not interested in archaeological sights but wanted to paint. I was shown a brochure which seemed to meet my requirements. A pleasantly situated hotel close to the sea, and chalets by the water's edge where one slept and breakfasted. Clientèle well-to-do, and although I count myself no snob I cannot abide paper bags and orange-peel. A couple of pictures painted the previous winter – a view of St Paul's Cathedral under snow, and another one of Hampstead Heath, both sold to an obliging

445

female cousin – would pay for my journey, and I permitted myself an added indulgence, though it was really a necessity – the hiring of a small Volkswagen on arrival at the airport of Herakleion.

The flight, with an overnight stop in Athens, was pleasant and uneventful, the forty-odd miles' drive to my destination somewhat tedious, for being a cautious driver I took it slowly, and the twisting road, once I reached the hills, was decidedly hazardous. Cars passed me, or swerved towards me, hooting loudly. Also, it was very hot, and I was hungry. The sight of the blue Gulf of Mirabello and the splendid mountains to the east acted as a spur to sagging spirits, and once I arrived at the hotel, set delightfully in its own grounds, with lunch served to me on the terrace despite the fact that it was after two in the afternoon – how different from England! – I was ready to relax and inspect my quarters. Disappointment followed. The young porter led me down a garden path flagged on either side by brilliant geraniums to a small chalet bunched in by neighbours on either side, and overlooking, not the sea, but a part of the garden laid out for mini-golf. My next-door neighbours, an obviously English mother and her brood, smiled in welcome from their balcony, which was strewn with bathing-suits drying under the sun. Two middle-aged men were engaged in mini-golf. I might have been in Maidenhead.

'This won't do,' I said, turning to my escort. 'I have come here to paint. I must have a view of the sea.'

He shrugged his shoulders, murmuring something about the chalets beside the sea being fully booked. It was not his fault, of course. I made him trek back to the hotel with me, and addressed myself to the clerk at the reception desk.

'There has been some mistake,' I said. 'I asked for a chalet overlooking the sea, and privacy above all.'

The clerk smiled, apologised, began ruffling papers, and the inevitable excuses followed. My travel agent had not specifically booked a chalet overlooking the sea. These were in great demand, and were fully booked. Perhaps in a few days there might be some cancellations, one never could tell, in the meantime he was sure I should be very comfortable in the chalet that had been allotted to me. All the furnishings were the same, my breakfast would be served me, etc., etc.

I was adamant. I would not be fobbed off with the English family and the mini-golf. Not having flown all those miles at considerable expense. I was bored by the whole affair, tired, and considerably annoyed.

'I am a professor of art,' I told the clerk. 'I have been commissioned to execute several paintings while I am here, and it is essential that I should have a view of the sea, and neighbours who will not disturb me.'

(My passport states my occupation as professor. It sounds better than schoolmaster or teacher, and usually arouses respect in the attitude of reception clerks.)

The clerk seemed genuinely concerned, and repeated his apologies. He turned again to the sheaf of papers before him. Exasperated, I strode across the spacious hall and looked out of the door on to the terrace down to the sea.

'I cannot believe,' I said, 'that every chalet is taken. It's too early in the season. In summer, perhaps, but not now.' I waved my hand towards the western side of the bay. 'That group over there,' I said, 'down by the water's edge. Do you mean to say every single one of them is booked?'

He shook his head and smiled. 'We do not usually open those until mid-season. Also, they are more expensive. They have a bath as well as a shower.'

'How much more expensive?' I hedged.

He told me. I made a quick calculation. I could afford it if I cut down on all other expenses. Had my evening meal in the hotel, and went without lunch. No extras in the bar, not even mineral water.

'Then there is no problem,' I said grandly. 'I will willingly pay more for privacy. And, if you have no objection, I should like to choose the chalet which would suit me best. I'll walk down to the sea now and then come back for the key, and your porter can bring my things.'

I gave him no time to reply, but turned on my heel and went out on to the terrace. It paid to be firm. One moment's hesitation, and he would have fobbed me off with the stuffy chalet overlooking the mini-golf. I could imagine the consequences. The chattering children on the balcony next door, the possibly effusive mother, and the middle-aged golfers urging me to have a game. I could not have borne it.

I walked down through the garden to the sea, and as I did so my spirits rose. For this, of course, was what had been so highly coloured on the agent's brochure, and why I had flown so many miles. No exaggeration, either. Little whitewashed dwellings, discreetly set apart from one another, the sea washing the rocks below. There was a beach, from which doubtless people swam in high season, but no one was on it now, and, even if they should intrude, the chalets themselves were well to the left, inviolate, private. I peered at each in turn, mounting the steps, standing on the balconies. The clerk must have been telling the truth about none of them being let before full season, for all had their windows shuttered. All except one. And directly I mounted the steps and stood on the balcony I knew that it must be mine. This was the view I had imagined. The sea beneath me, lapping the rocks, the bay widening into the gulf itself, and beyond the mountains. It was perfect. The chalets to the east of the hotel, which was out of sight anyway, could be ignored. One, close to a neck of land, stood on its own like a solitary outpost with a landing-stage below, but this would only enhance my picture when I came to paint it. The rest were mercifully hidden by rising ground. I turned, and looked through the open windows to the bedroom within. Plain whitewashed walls, a stone floor, a comfortable divan bed with rugs upon it. A bedside table with a lamp and telephone. But for these last it had all the simplicity of a monk's cell, and I wished for nothing more.

I wondered why this chalet, and none of its neighbours, was unshuttered, and stepping inside I heard from the bathroom beyond the sound of running water. Not further disappointment, and the place booked after all? I put my head round the open door, and saw that it was a little Greek maid swabbing the bathroom floor. She seemed startled at the sight of me. I gestured, pointed, said, 'Is this taken?' She did not understand, but answered me in Greek. Then she seized her cloth and pail and, plainly terrified, brushed past me to the entrance, leaving her work unfinished.

I went back into the bedroom and picked up the telephone, and in a moment the smooth voice of the reception clerk answered.

'This is Mr Grey,' I told him, 'Mr Timothy Grey. I was speaking to you just now about changing my chalet.'

'Yes, Mr Grey,' he replied. He sounded puzzled. 'Where are you speaking from?'

'Hold on a minute,' I said. I put down the receiver and crossed the room to the balcony. The number was above the open door. It was 62. I went back to the telephone. 'I'm speaking from the chalet I have chosen,' I said. 'It happened to be open – one of the maids was cleaning the bathroom, and I'm afraid I scared her away. This chalet is ideal for my purpose. It is No. 62.'

He did not answer immediately, and when he did he sounded doubtful. 'No. 62?' he repeated. And then, after a moment's hesitation, 'I am not sure if it is available.'

Daphne du Maurier

'Oh, for heaven's sake . . .' I began, exasperated, and I heard him talking in Greek to someone beside him at the desk. The conversation went back and forth between them; there was obviously some difficulty, which made me all the more determined.

'Are you there?' I said. 'What's the trouble?'

More hurried whispers, and then he spoke to me again. 'No trouble, Mr Grey. It is just that we feel you might be more comfortable in No. 57, which is a little nearer to the hotel.'

'Nonsense,' I said, 'I prefer the view from here. What's wrong with No. 62? Doesn't the plumbing work?'

'Certainly the plumbing works,' he assured me, while the whispering started again. 'There is nothing wrong with the chalet. If you have made up your mind I will send down the porter with your luggage and the key.'

He rang off, possibly to finish his discussion with the whisperer at his side. Perhaps they were going to step up the price. If they did, I would have further argument. The chalet was no different from its empty neighbours, but the position, dead centre to sea and mountains, was all I had dreamed and more. I stood on the balcony, looking out across the sea and smiling. What a prospect, what a place! I would unpack and have a swim, then put up my easel and do a preliminary sketch before starting serious work in the morning.

I heard voices, and saw the little maid staring at me from halfway up the garden path, cloth and pail still in hand. Then, as the young porter advanced downhill bearing my suitcase and painting gear, she must have realised that I was to be the occupant of No. 62, for she stopped him midway, and another whispered conversation began. I had evidently caused a break in the smooth routine of the hotel. A few moments later they climbed the steps to the chalet together, the porter to set down my luggage, the maid doubtless to finish her swabbing of the bathroom floor. I had no desire to be on awkward terms with

450

either of them, and, smiling cheerfully, placed coins in both their hands.

'Lovely view,' I said loudly, pointing to the sea. 'Must go for a swim,' and made breast-stroke gestures to show my intent, hoping for the ready smile of the native Greek, usually so responsive to goodwill.

The porter evaded my eyes and bowed gravely, accepting my tip nevertheless. As for the little maid, distress was evident in her face, and forgetting about the bathroom floor she hurried after him. I could hear them talking as they walked up the garden path together to the hotel.

Well, it was not my problem. Staff and management must sort out their troubles between them. I had got what I wanted, and that was all that concerned me. I unpacked and made myself at home. Then, slipping on bathing trunks, I stepped down to the ledge of rock beneath the balcony, and ventured a toe into the water. It was surprisingly chill, despite the hot sun that had been upon it all day. Never mind. I must prove my mettle, if only to myself. I took the plunge and gasped, and being a cautious swimmer at the best of times, especially in strange waters, swam round and round in circles rather like a sea-lion pup in a zoological pool.

Refreshing, undoubtedly, but a few minutes were enough, and as I climbed out again on to the rocks I saw that the porter and the little maid had been watching me all the time from behind a flowering bush up the garden path. I hoped I had not lost face. And anyway, why the interest? People must be swimming every day from the other chalets. The bathing-suits on the various balconies proved it. I dried myself on the balcony, observing how the sun, now in the western sky behind my chalet, made dappled patterns on the water. Fishing-boats were returning to the little harbour port a few miles distant, the chug-chug engines making a pleasing sound.

I dressed, taking the precaution of having a hot bath, for the first swim of the year is always numbing, and then set up my easel and instantly became absorbed. This was why I was here, and nothing else mattered. I worked for a couple of hours, and as the light failed, and the colour of the sea deepened and the mountains turned a softer purple blue, I rejoiced to think that tomorrow I should be able to seize this after-glow in paint instead of charcoal, and the picture would begin to come alive.

It was time to stop. I stacked away my gear, and before changing for dinner and drawing the shutters – doubtless there were mosquitoes, and I had no wish to be bitten – watched a motor-boat with gently purring engine draw in softly to the eastward point with the landing-stage away to my right. Three people aboard, fishing enthusiasts no doubt, a woman amongst them. One man, a local, probably, made the boat fast, and stepped on the landing-stage to help the woman ashore. Then all three stared in my direction, and the second man, who had been standing in the stern, put up a pair of binoculars and fixed them on me. He held them steady for several minutes, focusing, no doubt, on every detail of my personal appearance, which is unremarkable enough, heaven knows, and would have continued had I not suddenly become annoyed and withdrawn into the bedroom, slamming the shutters to. How rude can you get, I asked myself. Then I remembered that these western chalets were all unoccupied, and mine was the first to open for the season. Possibly this was the reason for the intense interest I appeared to cause, beginning with members of the hotel staff and now embracing guests as well. Interest would soon fade. I was neither pop star nor millionaire. And my painting efforts, however pleasing to myself, were hardly likely to draw a fascinated crowd.

Punctually at eight o'clock I walked up the garden path to the hotel and presented myself in the dining-room for dinner.

It was moderately full and I was allotted a table in the corner, suitable to my single status, close to the screen dividing the service entrance from the kitchens. Never mind. I preferred this position to the centre of the room, where I could tell immediately that the hotel clientele were on what my mother used to describe as an 'all fellows to football' basis.

I enjoyed my dinner, treated myself – despite my de luxe chalet – to half a bottle of domestica wine, and was peeling an orange when an almighty crash from the far end of the room disturbed us all. Waiters hurried to the scene. Heads turned, mine amongst them. A hoarse American voice, hailing from the deep South, called loudly, 'For God's sake clear up this God-darn mess!' It came from a square-shouldered man of middle age, whose face was so swollen and blistered by exposure to the sun that he looked as if he had been stung by a million bees. His eyes were sunk into his head, which was bald on top, with a grizzled thatch on either side, and the pink crown had the appearance of being tightly stretched, like the skin of a sausage about to burst. A pair of enormous ears the size of clams gave further distortion to his appearance, while a drooping wisp of moustache did nothing to hide the protruding underlip, thick as blubber and about as moist. I have seldom set eyes on a more unattractive individual. A woman, I suppose his wife, sat beside him, stiff and bolt upright, apparently unmoved by the debris on the floor, which appeared to consist chiefly of bottles. She was likewise middle-aged, with a mop of tow-coloured hair turning white, and a face as sunburnt as her husband's, but mahogany brown instead of red.

'Let's get the hell out of here and go to the bar!' The hoarse strains echoed across the room. The guests at the other tables turned discreetly back to their own dinner, and I must have been the only one to watch the unsteady exit of the bee-stung spouse and his wife – I could see the deaf-aid in her ear, hence possibly her husband's rasping tones – as he literally rolled past me to the bar, a lurching vessel in the wake of his steady partner. I silently commended the efficiency of the hotel staff, who made short work of clearing the wreckage.

The dining-room emptied. 'Coffee in the bar, sir,' murmured my waiter. Fearing a crush and loud chatter I hesitated before entering, for the camaraderie of hotel bars has always bored me, but I hate going without my after-dinner coffee. I need not have worried. The bar was empty, apart from the white-coated server behind the bar, and the American sitting at a table with his wife. Neither of them was speaking. There were three empty beer bottles already on the table before him. Greek music played softly from some lair behind the bar. I sat myself on a stool and ordered coffee.

The bar-tender, who spoke excellent English, asked if I had spent a pleasant day. I told him yes. I had had a good flight, found the road from Herakleion hazardous, and my first swim rather cold. He explained that it was still early in the year. 'In any case,' I told him, 'I have come to paint, and swimming will take second place. I have a chalet right on the water-front, No. 62, and the view from the balcony is perfect.'

Rather odd. He was polishing a glass, and his expression changed. He seemed about to say something, then evidently thought better of it, and continued with his work.

'Turn that God-damn record off!'

The hoarse, imperious summons filled the empty room. The bar-man made at once for the gramophone in the corner and adjusted the switch. A moment later the summons rang forth again.

'Bring me another bottle of beer!'

Now, had I been the bar-tender I should have turned to the man and, like a parent to a child, insisted that he said please. Instead, the brute was promptly served, and I was just downing my coffee when the voice from the table echoed through the room once more.

'Hi, you there, chalet No. 62. You're not superstitious?'

I turned on my stool. He was staring at me, glass in hand. His wife looked straight in front of her. Perhaps she had removed her deaf-aid. Remembering the maxim that one must humour madmen and drunks, I replied courteously enough.

'No,' I said, 'I'm not superstitious. Should I be?'

He began to laugh, his scarlet face creasing into a hundred lines.

'Well, God darn it, I would be,' he answered. 'The fellow from that chalet was drowned only two weeks ago. Missing for two days, and then his body brought up in a net by a local fisherman, half-eaten by octopuses.'

He began to shake with laughter, slapping his hand on his knee. I turned away in disgust, and raised my eyebrows in inquiry to the bar-tender.

'An unfortunate accident,' he murmured. 'Mr Gordon such a nice gentleman. Interested in archaeology. It was very warm the night he disappeared, and he must have gone swimming after dinner. Of course the police were called. We were all most distressed here at the hotel. You understand, sir, we don't talk about it much. It would be bad for business. But I do assure you that bathing is perfectly safe. This is the first accident we have ever had.'

'Oh, quite,' I said.

Nevertheless . . . It was rather off-putting, the fact that the poor chap had been the last to use my chalet. However, it was not as though he had died in the bed. And I was not superstitious. I understood now why the staff had been reluctant to let the chalet again so soon, and why the little maid had been upset.

'I tell you one thing,' boomed the revolting voice. 'Don't go swimming after midnight, or the octopuses will get you too.' This statement was followed by another outburst of laughter. Then he said, 'Come on, Maud. We're for bed,' and he noisily shoved the table aside.

I breathed more easily when the room was clear and we were alone.

'What an impossible man,' I said. 'Can't the management get rid of him?'

The bar-tender shrugged. 'Business is business. What can they do? The Stolls have plenty of money. This is their second season here, and they arrived when we opened in March. They seem to be crazy about the place. It's only this year, though, that Mr Stoll has become such a heavy drinker. He'll kill himself if he goes on at this rate. It's always like this, night after night. Yet his day must be healthy enough. Out at sea fishing from early morning until sundown.'

'I dare say more bottles go over the side than he catches fish,' I observed.

'Could be,' the bar-tender agreed. 'He never brings his fish to the hotel. The boatman takes them home, I dare say.'

'I feel sorry for the wife.'

The bar-tender shrugged. 'She's the one with the money,' he replied sotto voce, for a couple of guests had just entered the bar, 'and I don't think Mr Stoll has it all his own way. Being deaf may be convenient to her at times. But she never leaves his side, I'll grant her that. Goes fishing with him every day. Yes, gentlemen, what can I get for you?'

He turned to his new customers, and I made my escape. The cliché that it takes all sorts to make a world passed through my head. Thank heaven it was not my world, and Mr Stoll and his deaf wife could burn themselves black under the sun all day at sea as far as I was concerned, and break beer bottles every evening into the bargain. In any event, they were not neighbours. No. 62 may have had the unfortunate victim of a drowning accident for its last occupant, but at least this had insured privacy for its present tenant.

I walked down the garden path to my abode. It was a clear starlit night. The air was balmy, and sweet with the scent of the flowering shrubs planted thickly in the red earth. Standing on my balcony I looked out across the sea towards the distant shrouded mountains and the harbour lights from the little fishing port. To my right winked the lights of the other chalets, giving a pleasing, almost fairy impression, like a clever back-cloth on a stage. Truly a wonderful spot, and I blessed the travel agent who had recommended it.

I let myself in through my shuttered doorway and turned on the bedside lamp. The room looked welcoming and snug; I could not have been better housed. I undressed, and before getting into bed remembered I had left a book I wanted to glance at on the balcony. I opened the shutters and picked it up from the deck-chair where I had thrown it, and once more, before turning in, glanced out at the open sea. Most of the fairy lights had been extinguished, but the chalet that stood on its own on the extreme point still had its light burning on the balcony. The boat, tied to the landing-stage, bore a riding-light. Seconds later I saw something moving close to my rocks. It was the snorkel of an under-water swimmer. I could see the narrow pipe, like a minute periscope, move steadily across the still, dark surface of the sea. Then it disappeared to the far left out of sight. I drew my shutters and went inside.

I don't know why it was, but the sight of that moving object was somehow disconcerting. It made me think of the unfortunate man who had been drowned during a midnight swim. My predecessor. He too, perhaps, had sallied forth one balmy evening such as this, intent on under-water exploration, and by so doing lost his life. One would imagine the unhappy accident would scare off other hotel visitors from swimming alone at night. I made a firm decision never to bathe except in broad daylight, and – chicken-hearted, maybe – well within my depth.

I read a few pages of my book, then, feeling ready for sleep, turned to switch out my light. In doing so I clumsily bumped the telephone, which fell to the floor. I bent over, picked it up, luckily no damage done, and saw that the small drawer that was part of the fixture had fallen open. It contained a scrap of paper, or rather card, with the name Charles Gordon upon it, and an address in Bloomsbury. Surely Gordon had been the name of my predecessor? The little maid, when she cleaned the room, had not thought to open the drawer. I turned the card over. There was something scrawled on the other side, the words 'Not after midnight'. And then, maybe as an afterthought, the figure 38. I replaced the card in the drawer and switched off the light. Perhaps I was overtired after the journey, but it was well past two before I finally got off to sleep. I lay awake for no rhyme or reason, listening to the water lapping against the rocks beneath my balcony.

I painted solidly for three days, never quitting my chalet except for the morning swim and my evening meal at the hotel. Nobody bothered me. An obliging waiter brought my breakfast, from which I saved rolls for midday lunch, the little maid made my bed and did her chores without disturbing me, and when I had finished my impressionistic scene on the afternoon of the third day I felt quite certain it was one of the best things I had ever done. It would take pride of place in the planned exhibition of my work. Well satisfied, I could now relax, and I determined to explore along the coast the following day, and discover another view to whip up inspiration. The weather was glorious. Warm as a good English June. And the best thing about the whole site was the total absence of neighbours. The other guests kept to their side of the domain, and, apart from bows and nods from adjoining tables as one entered the dining-room for dinner, no one attempted to strike up acquaintance. I took good care to drink my coffee in the bar before the obnoxious Mr Stoll had left his table.

I realised now that it was his boat which lay anchored off the point. They were away too early in the morning for me to watch their departure, but I used to spot them returning in the late afternoon; his square, hunched form was easily recognisable, and the occasional hoarse shout to the man in charge of the boat as they came to the landing-stage. Theirs, too, was the isolated chalet on the point, and I wondered if he had picked it purposely in order to soak himself into oblivion out of sight and earshot of his nearest neighbours. Well, good luck to him, as long as he did not obtrude his offensive presence upon me.

Feeling the need of gentle exercise, I decided to spend the rest of the afternoon taking a stroll to the eastern side of the hotel grounds. Once again I congratulated myself on having escaped the cluster of chalets in this populated quarter. Mini-golf and tennis were in full swing, and the little beach was crowded with sprawling bodies on every available patch of sand. But soon the murmur of the world was behind me, and screened and safe behind the flowering shrubs I found myself on the point near to the landing-stage. The boat was not yet at its mooring, nor even in sight out in the gulf.

A sudden temptation to peep at the unpleasant Mr Stoll's chalet swept upon me. I crept up the little path, feeling as furtive as a burglar on the prowl, and stared up at the shuttered windows. It was no different from its fellows, or mine for that matter, except for a tell-tale heap of bottles lying in a corner of the balcony. Brute . . . Then something else caught my eye. A pair of frog-feet, and a snorkel. Surely, with all that liquor inside him, he did not venture his carcass under water? Perhaps he sent the local Greek whom he employed as crew to seek for crabs. I remembered the snorkel on my first evening, close to the rocks, and the riding-light in the boat.

I moved away, for I thought I could hear someone coming down the path and did not want to be caught prying, but before doing so I glanced up at the number of the chalet. It was 38. The figure had no particular significance for me then, but later on, changing for dinner, I picked up the tie-pin I had placed on my bedside table, and on sudden impulse opened the drawer beneath the telephone to look at my predecessor's card again. Yes, I thought so. The scrawled figure *was* 38. Pure coincidence, of course, and yet . . . 'Not after midnight'. The words suddenly had meaning. Stoll had warned me about swimming late on my first evening. Had he warned Gordon too? And Gordon had jotted down the warning on his card with Stoll's chalet-number underneath? It made sense, but obviously poor Gordon had disregarded the advice. And so, apparently, did one of the occupants of Chalet 38.

I finished changing, and instead of replacing the card in the telephone drawer put it in my wallet. I had an uneasy feeling that it was my duty to hand it in to the reception desk in case it threw any light on my unfortunate predecessor's demise. I toyed with the thought through dinner, but came to no decision. The point was, I might become involved, questioned by the police. And as far as I knew the case was closed. There was little point in my suddenly coming forward with a calling-card lying forgotten in a drawer that probably had no significance at all.

It so happened that the people seated to the right of me in the dining-room appeared to have gone, and the Stolls' table in the corner now came into view without my being obliged to turn my head. I could watch them without making it too obvious, and I was struck by the fact that he never once addressed a word to her. They made an odd contrast. She stiff as a ramrod, prim-looking, austere, forking her food to her mouth like a Sunday school teacher on an outing, and he, more scarlet than ever, like a great swollen sausage, pushing aside most of what the waiter placed before him after the first mouthful, and reaching out a pudgy, hairy hand to an ever-emptying glass.

I finished my dinner and went through to the bar to drink my coffee. I was early, and had the place to myself. The bar-tender and I exchanged the usual pleasantries and then, after an allusion to the weather, I jerked my head in the direction of the dining-room.

'I noticed our friend Mr Stoll and his lady spent the whole day at sea as usual,' I said.

The bar-tender shrugged. 'Day after day, it never varies,' he replied, 'and mostly in the same direction, westward out of the bay into the gulf. It can be squally, too, at times, but they don't seem to care.'

'I don't know how she puts up with him,' I said. 'I watched them at dinner – he didn't speak to her at all. I wonder what the other guests make of him.'

'They keep well clear, sir. You saw how it was for yourself. If he ever does open his mouth it's only to be rude. And the same goes for the staff. The girls dare not go in to clean the chalet until he's out of the way. And the smell!' He grimaced, and leant forward confidentially. 'The girls say he brews his own beer. He lights the fire in the chimney, and has a pot standing, filled with rotting grain, like some sort of pig swill! Oh, yes, he drinks it right enough. Imagine the state of his liver, after what he consumes at dinner and afterwards here in the bar!'

'I suppose,' I said, 'that's why he keeps his balcony light on so late at night. Drinking pig-swill until the small hours. Tell

461

me, which of the hotel visitors is it who goes under-water swimming?'

The bar-tender looked surprised. 'No one, to my knowledge. Not since the accident, anyway. Poor Mr Gordon liked a night swim, at least so we supposed. He was one of the few visitors who ever talked to Mr Stoll, now I think of it. They had quite a conversation here one evening in the bar.'

'Indeed?'

'Not about swimming, though, or fishing either. They were discussing antiquities. There's a fine little museum here in the village, you know, but it's closed at present for repairs. Mr Gordon had some connection with the British Museum in London.'

'I wouldn't have thought,' I said, 'that would interest friend Stoll.'

'Ah,' said the bar-tender, 'you'd be surprised. Mr Stoll is no fool. Last year he and Mrs Stoll used to take the car and visit all the famous sites, Knossos, Mallia, and other places not so well known. This year it's quite different. It's the boat and fishing every day.'

'And Mr Gordon,' I pursued, 'did he ever go fishing with them?'

'No, sir. Not to my knowledge. He hired a car, like you, and explored the district. He was writing a book, he told me, on archaeological finds in eastern Crete, and their connection with Greek mythology.'

'Mythology?'

'Yes, I understood him to tell Mr Stoll it was mythology, but it was all above my head, you can imagine, nor did I hear much of the conversation – we were busy that evening in the bar. Mr Gordon was a quiet sort of gentleman, rather after your own style, if you'll excuse me, sir, seeming very interested in what they were discussing, all to do with the old gods. They were at it for over an hour.'

H'm . . . I thought of the card in my wallet. Should I, or should I not, hand it over to the reception clerk at the desk? I said goodnight to the bar-tender and went back through the dining-room to the hall. The Stolls had just left their table and were walking ahead of me. I hung back until the way was clear, surprised that they had turned their backs upon the bar and were making for the hall. I stood by the rack of postcards, to give myself an excuse for loitering, but out of their range of vision, and watched Mrs Stoll take her coat from a hook in the lobby near the entrance, while her unpleasant husband visited the cloakroom, and then the pair of them walked out of the front door which led direct to the car park. They must be going for a drive. With Stoll at the wheel in his condition?

I hesitated. The reception clerk was on the telephone. It wasn't the moment to hand over the card. Some impulse, like that of a small boy playing detective, made me walk to my own car, and when Stoll's tail-light was out of sight – he was driving a Mercedes – I followed in his wake. There was only the one road, and he was heading east towards the village and the harbour lights. I lost him, inevitably, on reaching the little port, for, instinctively making for the quayside opposite what appeared to be a main café, I thought he must have done the same. I parked the Volkswagen, and looked around me. No sign of the Mercedes. Just a sprinkling of other tourists like myself, and local inhabitants, strolling, or drinking in front of the café.

Oh well, forget it, I'd sit and enjoy the scene, have a lemonade. I must have sat there for over half an hour, savouring what is known as 'local colour', amused by the passing crowd, Greek families taking the air, pretty, self-conscious girls eyeing the youths, who appeared to stick together, practising a form of segregation, a bearded Orthodox priest who smoked incessantly at the table next to me, playing some game of dice with a

463

couple of very old men, and of course the familiar bunch of hippies from my own country, considerably longer-haired than anybody else, dirtier, and making far more noise. When they switched on a transistor and squatted on the cobbled stones behind me, I felt it was time to move.

I paid for my lemonade, and strolled to the end of the quay and back – the line upon line of fishing-boats would be colourful by day, and possibly the scene worth painting – and then I crossed the street, my eye caught by a glint of water inland, where a side-road appeared to end in a cul-de-sac. This must be the feature mentioned in the guidebook as the Bottomless Pool, much frequented and photographed by tourists in the high season. It was larger than I had expected, quite a sizeable lake, the water full of scum and floating debris, and I did not envy those who had the temerity to use the diving-board at the further end of it by day.

Then I saw the Mercedes. It was drawn up opposite a dimly-lit café, and there was no mistaking the hunched figure at the table, beer-bottles before him, the upright lady at his side, but to my surprise, and I may add disgust, he was not imbibing alone but appeared to be sharing his after-dinner carousal with a crowd of raucous fishermen at the adjoining table.

Clamour and laughter filled the air. They were evidently mocking him, Greek courtesy forgotten in their cups, while strains of song burst forth from some younger member of the clan, and suddenly he put out his hand and swept the empty bottles from his table on to the pavement, with the inevitable crash of broken glass and the accompanying cheers of his companions. I expected the local police to appear at any moment and break up the party, but there was no sign of authority. I did not care what happened to Stoll – a night in gaol might sober him up – but it was a wretched business for his wife. However, it wasn't my affair, and I was turning to go back to the quay when he staggered to his feet, applauded by the fishermen, and, lifting the remaining bottle from his table, swung it over his head. Then, with amazing dexterity for one in his condition, he pitched it like a discus-thrower into the lake. It must have missed me by a couple of feet, and he saw me duck. This was too much. I advanced towards him, livid with rage.

'What the hell are you playing at?' I shouted.

He stood before me, swaying on his feet. The laughter from the café ceased as his cronies watched with interest. I expected a flood of abuse, but Stoll's swollen face creased into a grin, and he lurched forward and patted me on the arm.

'Know something?' he said. 'If you hadn't been in the way I could have lobbed it into the centre of the God-damn pool. Which is more than any of those fellows could. Not a pure-blooded Cretan amongst them. They're all of them God-damn Turks.'

I tried to shake him off, but he clung on to me with the effusive affection of the habitual drunkard who has suddenly found, or imagines he has found, a life-long friend.

'You're from the hotel, aren't you?' he hiccoughed. 'Don't deny it, buddy boy, I've got a good eye for faces. You're the fellow who paints all day on his God-damn porch. Well, I admire you for it. Know a bit about art myself. I might even buy your picture.'

His bonhomie was offensive, his attempt at patronage intolerable.

'I'm sorry,' I said stiffly, 'the picture is not for sale.'

'Oh, come off it,' he retorted. 'You artists are all the same. Play hard to get until someone offers 'em a darn good price. Take Charlie Gordon now . . .' He broke off, peering slyly into my face. 'Hang on, you didn't meet Charlie Gordon, did you?'

'No,' I said shortly, 'he was before my time.'

465

'That's right, that's right,' he agreed, 'poor fellow's dead. Drowned in the bay there, right under your rocks. At least, that's where they found him.'

His slit eyes were practically closed in his swollen face, but I knew he was watching for my reaction.

'Yes,' I said, 'so I understand. He wasn't an artist.'

'An artist?' Stoll repeated the word after me, then burst into a guffaw of laughter. 'No, he was a connoisseur, and I guess that means the same God-damn thing to a chap like me. Charlie Gordon, connoisseur. Well, it didn't do him much good in the end, did it?'

'No,' I said, 'obviously not.'

He was making an effort to pull himself together, and still rocking on his feet he fumbled for a packet of cigarettes and a lighter. He lit one for himself, then offered me the packet. I shook my head, telling him I did not smoke. Then, greatly daring, I observed, 'I don't drink either.'

'Good for you,' he answered astonishingly, 'neither do I. The beer they sell you here is all piss anyway, and the wine is poison.' He looked over his shoulder to the group at the café and with a conspiratorial wink dragged me to the wall beside the pool.

'I told you all those bastards are Turks, and so they are,' he said, 'wine-drinking, coffee-drinking Turks. They haven't brewed the right stuff here for over five thousand years. They knew how to do it then.'

I remembered what the bar-tender had told me about the pigswill in his chalet. 'Is that so?' I enquired.

He winked again, and then his slit eyes widened, and I noticed that they were naturally bulbous and protuberant, a discoloured muddy brown with the whites red-flecked. 'Know something?' he whispered hoarsely. 'The scholars have got it all wrong. It was beer the Cretans drank here in the mountains, brewed from spruce and ivy, long before wine. Wine was discovered centuries later by the God-damn Greeks.'

He steadied himself, one hand on the wall, the other on my arm. Then he leant forward and was sick into the pool. I was very nearly sick myself.

'That's better,' he said, 'gets rid of the poison. Doesn't do to have poison in the system. Tell you what, we'll go back to the hotel and you shall come along and have a night-cap at our chalet. I've taken a fancy to you, Mr What's-your-Name. You've got the right ideas. Don't drink, don't smoke, and you paint pictures. What's your job?'

It was impossible to shake myself clear, and I was forced to let him tow me across the road. Luckily the group at the café had now dispersed, disappointed, no doubt, because we had not come to blows, and Mrs Stoll had climbed into the Mercedes and was sitting in the passenger seat in front.

'Don't take any notice of her,' he said. 'She's stone-deaf unless you bawl at her. Plenty of room at the back.'

'Thank you,' I said, 'I've got my own car on the quay.'

'Suit yourself,' he answered. 'Well, come on, tell me, Mr Artist, what's your job? An academician?'

I could have left it at that, but some pompous strain in me made me tell the truth, in the foolish hope that he would then consider me too dull to cultivate.

'I'm a teacher,' I said, 'in a boys' preparatory school.'

He stopped in his tracks, his wet mouth open wide in a delighted grin. 'Oh my God,' he shouted, 'that's rich, that's really rich. A God-damn tutor, a nurse to babes and sucklings. You're one of us, my buddy, you're one of us. And you've the nerve to tell me you've never brewed spruce and ivy!'

He was raving mad, of course, but at least this sudden burst of hilarity had made him free my arm, and he went on ahead of me to his car, shaking his head from side to side, his legs

467

bearing his cumbersome body in a curious jog-trot, one-two
. . . one-two . . . like a clumsy horse.

I watched him climb into the car beside his wife, and then
I moved swiftly away to make for the safety of the quayside,
but he had turned his car with surprising agility, and had
caught up with me before I reached the corner of the street.
He thrust his head out of the window, smiling still.

'Come and call on us, Mr Tutor, any time you like. You'll
always find a welcome. Tell him so, Maud. Can't you see the
fellow's shy?'

His bawling word of command echoed through the street.
Strolling passers-by looked in our direction. The stiff, impassive
face of Mrs Stoll peered over her husband's shoulder. She
seemed quite unperturbed, as if nothing was wrong, as if driving
in a foreign village beside a drunken husband was the most
usual pastime in the world.

'Good evening,' she said in a voice without any expression.
'Pleased to meet you, Mr Tutor. Do call on us. Not after
midnight. Chalet 38 . . .'

Stoll waved his hand, and the car went roaring up the street
to cover the few kilometres to the hotel, while I followed
behind, telling myself that this was one invitation I should
never accept if my life depended on it.

It would not be true to say the encounter cast a blight on
my holiday and put me off the place. A half-truth, perhaps.
I was angry and disgusted, but only with the Stolls. I awoke
refreshed after a good night's sleep to another brilliant day,
and nothing seems so bad in the morning. I had only the one
problem, which was to avoid Stoll and his equally half-witted
wife. They were out in their boat all day, so this was easy. By
dining early I could escape them in the dining-room. They
never walked about the grounds, and meeting them face to

face in the garden was not likely. If I happened to be on my balcony when they returned in the evening from fishing, and he turned his field-glasses in my direction, I would promptly disappear inside my chalet. In any event, with luck, he might have forgotten my existence, or, if that was too much to hope for, the memory of our evening's conversation might have passed from his mind. The episode had been unpleasant, even, in a curious sense, alarming, but I was not going to let it spoil the days that remained to me.

The boat had left its landing-stage by the time I came on to my balcony to have breakfast, and I intended to carry out my plan of exploring the coast with my painting gear, and, once absorbed in my hobby, could forget all about them. And I would not pass on to the management poor Gordon's scribbled card. I guessed now what had happened. The poor devil, without realising where his conversation in the bar would lead him, had been intrigued by Stoll's smattering of mythology and nonsense about ancient Crete, and, as an archaeologist, had thought further conversation might prove fruitful. He had accepted an invitation to visit Chalet 38 – the uncanny similarity of the words on the card and those spoken by Mrs Stoll still haunted me – though why he had chosen to swim across the bay instead of walking the slightly longer way by the rock path was a mystery. A touch of bravado, perhaps? Who knows? Once in Stoll's chalet he had been induced, poor victim, to drink some of the hell-brew offered by his host, which must have knocked all sense and judgement out of him, and when he took to the water once again, the carousal over, what followed was bound to happen. I only hoped he had been too far gone to panic, and sank instantly. Stoll had never come forward to give the facts, and that was that. Indeed, my theory of what had happened was based on intuition alone, coincidental scraps that appeared to fit, and prejudice. It was time to dismiss the whole thing from my mind and concentrate on the day ahead.

Or rather, days. My exploration along the coast westward, in the opposite direction from the harbour, proved even more successful than I had anticipated. I followed the winding road to the left of the hotel, and having climbed for several kilometres descended again from the hills to sea level, where the land on my right suddenly flattened out to what seemed to be a great stretch of dried marsh, sun-baked, putty-coloured, the dazzling blue sea affording a splendid contrast as it lapped the stretch of land on either side. Driving closer I saw that it was not marsh at all but salt flats, with narrow causeways running between them, the flats themselves contained by walls intersected by dykes to allow the sea-water to drain, leaving the salt behind. Here and there were the ruins of abandoned windmills, their rounded walls like castle keeps, and in a rough patch of ground a few hundred yards distant, and close to the sea, was a small church – I could see the minute cross on the roof shining in the sun. Then the salt flats ended abruptly, and the land rose once more to form the long, narrow isthmus of Spinalongha beyond.

I bumped the Volkswagen down to the track leading to the flats. The place was quite deserted. This, I decided, after viewing the scene from every angle, would be my pitch for the next few days. The ruined church in the foreground, the abandoned windmills beyond, the salt-flats on the left, and blue water rippling to the shore of the isthmus on my right.

I set up my easel, planted my battered felt hat on my head, and forgot everything but the scene before me. Those three days on the salt-flats – for I repeated the expedition on successive days – were the high-spot of my holiday. Solitude and peace were absolute. I never saw a single soul. The occasional car wound its way along the coast road in the distance and

470

then vanished. I broke off for sandwiches and lemonade, which I'd brought with me, and then, when the sun was hottest, rested by the ruined windmill. I returned to the hotel in the cool of the evening, had an early dinner, and then retired to my chalet to read until bedtime. A hermit at his prayers could not have wished for greater seclusion.

The fourth day, having completed two separate paintings from different angles, yet loath to leave my chosen territory, which had now become a personal stamping ground, I stacked my gear in the car and struck off on foot to the rising terrain of the isthmus, with the idea of choosing a new site for the following day. Height might give an added advantage. I toiled up the hill, fanning myself with my hat, for it was extremely hot, and was surprised when I reached the summit to find how narrow was the isthmus, no more than a long neck of land with the sea immediately below me. Not the calm water that washed the salt-flats I had left behind, but the curling crests of the outer gulf itself, whipped by a northerly wind that nearly blew my hat out of my hand. A genius might have caught those varying shades on canvas – turquoise blending into Aegean blue with wine-deep shadows beneath – but not an amateur like myself. Besides, I could hardly stand upright. Canvas and easel would have instantly blown away.

I climbed downwards towards a clump of broom affording shelter, where I could rest for a few minutes and watch that curling sea, and it was then that I saw the boat. It was moored close to a small inlet where the land curved and the water was comparatively smooth. There was no mistaking the craft: it was theirs all right. The Greek they employed as crew was seated in the bows, with a fishing-line over the side, but from his lounging attitude the fishing did not seem to be serious, and I judged he was taking his siesta. He was the only occupant of the boat. I glanced directly beneath me to the spit

471

of sand along the shore, and saw there was a rough stone building, more or less ruined, built against the cliff-face, possibly used at one time as a shelter for sheep or goats. There was a haversack and a picnic-basket lying by the entrance, and a coat. The Stolls must have landed earlier from the boat, although nosing the bows of the craft on to the shore must have been hazardous in the running sea, and were now taking their ease out of the wind. Perhaps Stoll was even brewing his peculiar mixture of spruce and ivy, with some goat-dung added for good measure, and this lonely spot on the isthmus of Spinalongha was his 'still'.

Suddenly the fellow in the boat sat up, and winding in his line he moved to the stern and stood there, watching the water. I saw something move, a form beneath the surface, and then the form itself emerged, head-piece, goggles, rubber suiting, aqualung and all. Then it was hidden from me by the Greek bending to assist the swimmer to remove his top-gear, and my attention was diverted to the ruined shelter on the shore. Something was standing in the entrance. I say 'something' because, doubtless owing to a trick of light, it had at first the shaggy appearance of a colt standing on its hind legs. Legs and even rump were covered with hair, and then I realised that it was Stoll himself, naked, his arms and chest as hairy as the rest of him. Only his swollen scarlet face proclaimed him for the man he was, with the enormous ears like saucers standing out from either side of his bald head. I had never in all my life seen a more revolting sight. He came out into the sunlight and looked towards the boat, and then, as if well pleased with himself and his world, strutted forward, pacing up and down the spit of sand before the ruined shelter with that curious movement I had noticed earlier in the village, not the rolling gait of a drunken man but a stumping jog-trot, arms akimbo, his chest thrust forward, his backside prominent behind him.

The swimmer, having discarded goggles and aqualung, was now coming in to the beach with long leisurely strokes, still wearing flippers – I could see them thrash the surface like a giant fish. Then, flippers cast aside on the sand, the swimmer stood up, and despite the disguise of the rubber suiting I saw, with astonishment, that it was Mrs Stoll. She was carrying some sort of bag around her neck, and advancing up the sand to meet her strutting husband she lifted it over her head and gave it to him. I did not hear them exchange a word, and they went together to the hut and disappeared inside. As for the Greek, he had gone once more to the bows of the boat to resume his idle fishing.

I lay down under cover of the broom and waited. I would give them twenty minutes, half an hour, perhaps, then make my way back to the salt-flats and my car. As it happened, I did not have to wait so long. It was barely ten minutes before I heard a shout below me on the beach, and peering through the broom I saw that they were both standing on the spit of sand, haversack, picnic-basket, and flippers in hand. The Greek was already starting the engine, and immediately afterwards he began to pull up the anchor. Then he steered the boat slowly inshore, touching it beside a ledge of rock where the Stolls had installed themselves. They climbed aboard, and in another moment the Greek had turned the boat, and it was heading out to sea away from the sheltered inlet and into the gulf. Then it rounded the point and was out of my sight.

Curiosity was too much for me. I scrambled down the cliff on to the sand and made straight for the ruined shelter. As I thought, it had been a haven for goats; the muddied floor reeked, and their droppings were everywhere. In a corner, though, a clearing had been made, and there were planks of wood, forming a sort of shelf. The inevitable beer bottles were stacked beneath this, but whether they had contained the local brew or Stoll's own poison I could not tell. The shelf itself held odds and ends of pottery, as though someone had been digging in a rubbish dump and had turned up broken pieces of discarded household junk. There was no earth upon them, though; they were scaled with barnacles, and some of them were damp, and it suddenly occurred to me that these were what archaeologists call 'sherds', and came from the sea-bed. Mrs Stoll had been exploring, and exploring under-water, whether for shells or for something of greater interest I did not know, and these pieces scattered here were throwouts, of no use, and so neither she nor her husband had bothered to remove them. I am no judge of these things, and after looking around me, and finding nothing of further interest, I left the ruin.

The move was a fatal one. As I turned to climb the cliff I heard the throb of an engine, and the boat had returned once more, to cruise along the shore, so I judged from its position. All three heads were turned in my direction, and inevitably the squat figure in the stern had field-glasses poised. He would have no difficulty, I feared, in distinguishing who it was that had just left the ruined shelter and was struggling up the cliff to the hill above.

I did not look back but went on climbing, my hat pulled down well over my brows in the vain hope that it might afford some sort of concealment. After all, I might have been any tourist who had happened to be at that particular spot at that particular time. Nevertheless, I feared recognition was inevitable. I tramped back to the car on the salt-flats, tired, breathless and thoroughly irritated. I wished I had never decided to explore the further side of the peninsula. The Stolls would think I had been spying upon them, which indeed was true. My pleasure in the day was spoilt. I decided to pack it in and go back to the hotel. Luck was against me, though, for I had hardly turned on to the track leading from the marsh to the road when I noticed that one of my tyres was flat. By the time I had put on the spare wheel – for I am ham-fisted at all mechanical jobs – forty minutes had gone by.

My disgruntled mood did not improve, when at last I reached the hotel, to see that the Stolls had beaten me to it. Their boat was already at its moorings beside the landing-stage, and Stoll himself was sitting on his balcony with field-glasses trained upon my chalet. I stumped up the steps feeling as self-conscious as someone under a television camera and went into my quarters, closing the shutters behind me. I was taking a bath when the telephone rang.

'Yes?' Towel round the middle, dripping hands, it could not have rung at a more inconvenient moment.

'That you, Mr Tutor-boy?'

The rasping, wheezing voice was unmistakable. He did not sound drunk though.

'This is Timothy Grey,' I replied stiffly.

'Grey or Black, it's all the same to me,' he said. His tone was unpleasant, hostile. 'You were out on Spinalongha this afternoon. Correct?'

'I was walking on the peninsula,' I told him. 'I don't know why you should be interested.'

'Oh, stuff it up,' he answered, 'you can't fool me. You're just like the other fellow. You're nothing but a God-damn spy. Well, let me tell you this. The wreck was clean-picked centuries ago.'

'I don't know what you're talking about,' I said. 'What wreck?'

There was a moment's pause. He muttered something under his breath, whether to himself or to his wife I could not tell, but when he resumed speaking his tone had moderated, something of pseudo-bonhomie had returned.

'O.K. . . . O.K., Tutor-boy,' he said. 'We won't argue the point. Let us say you and I share an interest. Schoolmasters,

475

university professors, college lecturers, we're all alike under the skin, and above it too sometimes.' His low chuckle was offensive. 'Don't panic, I won't give you away,' he continued. 'I've taken a fancy to you, as I told you the other night. You want something for your God-darn school museum, correct? Something you can show the pretty lads and your colleagues, too? Fine. Agreed. I've got just the thing. You call round here later this evening, and I'll make you a present of it. I don't want your God-damn money. . .' He broke off, chuckling again, and Mrs Stoll must have made some remark, for he added, 'That's right, that's right. We'll have a cosy little party, just the three of us. My wife's taken quite a fancy to you too.'

The towel round my middle slipped to the floor, leaving me naked. I felt vulnerable for no reason at all. And the patronising, insinuating voice infuriated me.

'Mr Stoll,' I said, 'I'm not a collector for schools, colleges, or museums. I'm not interested in antiquities. I am here on holiday to paint, for my own pleasure, and quite frankly I have no intention of calling upon you or any other visitor at the hotel. Good evening.'

I slammed down the receiver and went back to the bathroom. Infernal impudence. Loathsome man. The question was, would he now leave me alone, or would he keep his glasses trained on my balcony until he saw me go up to the hotel for dinner, and then follow me, wife in tow, to the dining-room? Surely he would not dare to resume the conversation in front of waiters and guests? If I guessed his intentions aright, he wanted to buy my silence by fobbing me off with some gift. Those day-long fishing expeditions of his were a mask for under-water exploration – hence his allusion to a wreck – during which he hoped to find, possibly had found already, objects of value that he intended to smuggle out of Crete. Doubtless he had succeeded in doing this the preceding year, and the Greek boatman would be well paid for holding his tongue.

This season, however, it had not worked to plan. My unfortunate predecessor at Chalet 62, Charles Gordon, himself an expert in antiquities, had grown suspicious. Stoll's allusion, 'You're like the other fellow. Nothing but a God-damn spy', made this plain. What if Gordon had received an invitation to Chalet 38, not to drink the spurious beer but to inspect Stoll's collection and be offered a bribe for keeping silent? Had he refused, threatening to expose Stoll? Did he really drown accidentally, or had Stoll's wife followed him down into the water in her rubber suit and mask and flippers, and then, once beneath the surface . . . ?

My imagination was running away with me. I had no proof of anything. All I knew was that nothing in the world would get me to Stoll's chalet, and indeed, if he attempted to pester me again, I should have to tell the whole story to the management.

I changed for dinner, then opened my shutters a fraction and stood behind them, looking out towards his chalet. The light shone on his balcony, for it was already dusk, but he himself had disappeared. I stepped outside, locking the shutters behind me, and walked up the garden to the hotel.

I was just about to go through to the reception hall from the terrace when I saw Stoll and his wife sitting on a couple of chairs inside, guarding, as it were, the passage-way to lounge and dining-room. If I wanted to eat I had to pass them. Right, I thought. You can sit there all evening waiting. I went back along the terrace, and circling the hotel by the kitchens went round to the car park and got into the Volkswagen. I would have dinner down in the village, and damn the extra expense. I drove off in a fury, found an obscure taverna well away from the harbour itself, and instead of the three-course hotel meal I had been looking forward to on my *en pension* terms – for

477

I was hungry after my day in the open and meagre sandwiches on the salt-flats — I was obliged to content myself with an omelette, an orange and a cup of coffee.

It was after ten when I arrived back in the hotel. I parked the car, and skirting the kitchen quarters once again made my way furtively down the garden path to my chalet, letting myself in through the shutters like a thief. The light was still shining on Stoll's balcony, and by this time he was doubtless deep in his cups. If there was any trouble with him the next day I would definitely go to the management.

I undressed and lay reading in bed until after midnight, then, feeling sleepy, switched out my light and went across the room to open the shutters, for the air felt stuffy and close. I stood for a moment looking out across the bay. The chalet lights were all extinguished except for one. Stoll's, of course. His balcony light cast a yellow streak on the water beside his landing-stage. The water rippled, yet there was no wind. Then I saw it. I mean, the snorkel. The little pipe was caught an instant in the yellow gleam, but before I lost it I knew that it was heading in a direct course for the rocks beneath my chalet. I waited. Nothing happened, there was no sound, no further ripple on the water. Perhaps she did this every evening. Perhaps it was routine, and while I was lying on my bed reading, oblivious of the world outside, she had been treading water close to the rocks. The thought was discomforting, to say the least of it, that regularly after midnight she left her besotted husband asleep over his hell-brew of spruce and ivy and came herself, his under-water-partner, in her black-seal rubber suit, her mask, her flippers, to spy upon Chalet 62. And on this night in particular, after the telephone conversation and my refusal to visit them, coupled with my new theory as to the fate of my predecessor, her presence in my immediate vicinity was more than ominous, it was threatening.

Suddenly, out of the dark stillness to my right, the snorkel-pipe was caught in a finger-thread of light from my own balcony. Now it was almost immediately below me. I panicked, turned, and fled inside my room, closing the shutters fast. I switched off the balcony light and stood against the wall between my bedroom and bathroom, listening. The soft air filtered through the shutters beside me. It seemed an eternity before the sound I expected, dreaded, came to my ears. A kind of swishing movement from the balcony, a fumbling of hands, and heavy breathing. I could see nothing from where I stood against the wall, but the sounds came through the chinks in the shutters, and I knew she was there. I knew she was holding on to the hasp, and the water was dripping from the skin-tight rubber suit, and that even if I shouted, 'What do you want?' she would not hear. No deaf-aids under water, no mechanical device for soundless ears. Whatever she did by night must be done by sight, by touch.

She began to rattle on the shutters. I took no notice. She rattled again. Then she found the bell, and the shrill summons pierced the air above my head with all the intensity of a dentist's drill upon a nerve. She rang three times. Then silence. No more rattling of the shutters. No more breathing. She might yet be crouching on the balcony, the water dripping from the black rubber suit, waiting for me to lose patience, to emerge.

I crept away from the wall and sat down on the bed. There was not a sound from the balcony. Boldly I switched on my bedside light, half expecting the rattling of the shutters to begin again, or the sharp ping of the bell. Nothing happened, though. I looked at my watch. It was half-past twelve. I sat there hunched on my bed, my mind that had been so heavy with sleep now horribly awake, full of foreboding, my dread of that sleek black figure increasing minute by minute so that all sense and reason seemed to desert me, and my dread was

479

the more intense and irrational because the figure in the rubber suit was female. What did she want?

I sat there for an hour or more until reason took possession once again. She must have gone. I got up from the bed and went to the shutters and listened. There wasn't a sound. Only the lapping of water beneath the rocks. Gently, very gently, I opened the hasp and peered through the shutters. Nobody was there. I opened them wider and stepped on to the balcony. I looked out across the bay, and there was no longer any light shining from the balcony of No. 38. The little pool of water beneath my shutters was evidence enough of the figure that had stood there an hour ago, and the wet footmarks leading down the steps towards the rocks suggested she had gone the way she came. I breathed a sigh of relief. Now I could sleep in peace.

It was only then that I saw the object at my feet, lying close to the shutter's base. I bent and picked it up. It was a small package, wrapped in some sort of waterproof cloth. I took it inside and examined it, sitting on the bed. Foolish suspicions of plastic bombs came to my mind, but surely a journey under-water would neutralise the lethal effect? The package was sewn about with twine, criss-crossed. It felt quite light. I remembered the old classical proverb, 'Beware of the Greeks when they bear gifts'. But the Stolls were not Greeks, and, whatever lost Atlantis they might have plundered, explosives did not form part of the treasure-trove of that vanished continent.

I cut the twine with a pair of nail-scissors, then unthreaded it piece by piece and unfolded the waterproof wrapping. A layer of finely-meshed net concealed the object within, and, this unravelled, the final token itself lay in my open hand. It was a small jug, reddish in colour, with a handle on either side for safe holding. I had seen this sort of object before – the correct name, I believe, is rhyton – displayed behind glass cases in museums. The body of the jug had been shaped cunningly and brilliantly into a man's face, with upstanding ears like scallop-shells, while protruding eyes and bulbous nose stood out above the leering, open mouth, the moustache drooping to the rounded beard that formed the base. At the top, between the handles, were the upright figures of three strutting men, their faces similar to that upon the jug, but here human resemblance ended, for they had neither hands nor feet but hooves, and from each of their hairy rumps extended a horse's tail.

I turned the object over. The same face leered at me from the other side. The same three figures strutted at the top. There was no crack, no blemish that I could see, except a faint mark on the lip. I looked inside the jug and saw a note lying on the bottom. The opening was too small for my hand, so I shook it out. The note was a plain white card, with words typed upon it. It read: 'Silenos, earth-born satyr, half-horse, half-man, who, unable to distinguish truth from falsehood, reared Dionysus, god of intoxication, as a girl in a Cretan cave, then became his drunken tutor and companion.'

That was all. Nothing more. I put the note back inside the jug, and the jug on the table at the far end of the room. Even then the lewd mocking face leered back at me, and the three strutting figures of the horse-men stood out in bold relief across the top. I was too weary to wrap it up again. I covered it with my jacket and climbed back into bed. In the morning I would cope with the laborious task of packing it up and getting my waiter to take it across to Chalet 38. Stoll could keep his rhyton – heaven knew what the value might be – and good luck to him. I wanted no part of it.

Exhausted, I fell asleep, but, oh God, to no oblivion. The dreams which came, and from which I struggled to awaken, but in vain, belonged to some other unknown world horribly intermingled with my own. Term had started, but the school

481

in which I taught was on a mountain top hemmed in by forest, though the school buildings were the same and the classroom was my own. My boys, all of them familiar faces, lads I knew, wore vine-leaves in their hair, and had a strange, unearthly beauty both endearing and corrupt. They ran towards me, smiling, and I put my arms about them, and the pleasure they gave me was insidious and sweet, never before experienced, never before imagined, the man who pranced in their midst and played with them was not myself, not the self I knew, but a demon shadow emerging from a jug, strutting in his conceit as Stoll had done upon the spit of sand at Spinalongha.

I awoke after what seemed like centuries of time, and indeed broad daylight seeped through the shutters, and it was a quarter to ten. My head was throbbing. I felt sick, exhausted. I rang for coffee, and looked out across the bay. The boat was at its moorings. The Stolls had not gone fishing. Usually they were away by nine. I took the jug from under my coat, and with fumbling hands began to wrap it up in the net and waterproof packing. I had made a botched job of it when the waiter came on to the balcony with my breakfast tray. He wished me good morning with his usual smile.

'I wonder,' I said, 'if you would do me a favour.'

'You are welcome, sir,' he replied.

'It concerns Mr Stoll,' I went on. 'I believe he has Chalet 38 across the bay. He usually goes fishing every day, but I see his boat is still at the landing-stage.'

'That is not surprising,' the waiter smiled. 'Mr and Mrs Stoll left this morning by car.'

'I see. Do you know when they will be back?'

'They will not be back, sir. They have left for good. They are driving to the airport en route for Athens. The boat is probably vacant now if you wish to hire it.'

He went down the steps into the garden, and the jar in its waterproof packing was still lying beside the breakfast tray.

The sun was already fierce upon my balcony. It was going to be a scorching day, too hot to paint. And anyway, I wasn't in the mood. The events of the night before had left me tired, jaded, with a curious sapped feeling due not so much to the intruder beyond my shutters as to those interminable dreams. I might be free of the Stolls themselves, but not of their legacy.

I unwrapped it once again and turned it over in my hands. The leering, mocking face repelled me; its resemblance to the human Stoll was not pure fancy but compelling, sinister, doubtless his very reason for palming it off on me − I remembered the chuckle down the telephone − and if he possessed treasures of equal value to this rhyton, or even greater, then one object the less would not bother him. He would have a problem getting them through Customs, especially in Athens. The penalties were enormous for this sort of thing. Doubtless he had his contacts, knew what to do.

I stared at the dancing figures near the top of the jar, and once more I was struck by their likeness to the strutting Stoll on the shore of Spinalongha, his naked, hairy form, his protruding rump. Part man, part horse, a satyr . . . 'Silenos, drunken tutor to the god Dionysus.'

The jar was horrible, evil. Small wonder that my dreams had been distorted, utterly foreign to my nature. But not perhaps to Stoll's? Could it be that he too had realised its bestiality, but not until too late? The bar-tender had told me that it was only this year he had gone to pieces, taken to drink. There must be some link between his alcoholism and the finding of the jar. One thing was very evident, I must get rid of it − but how? If I took it to the management questions would be asked. They might not believe my story about its being dumped on my balcony the night before; they might

483

suspect that I had taken it from some archaeological site, and then had second thoughts about trying to smuggle it out of the country or dispose of it somewhere on the island. So what? Drive along the coast and chuck it away, a rhyton centuries old and possibly priceless?

I wrapped it carefully in my jacket pocket and walked up the garden to the hotel. The bar was empty, the bar-tender behind his counter polishing glasses. I sat down on a stool in front of him and ordered a mineral water.

'No expedition today, sir?' he enquired.

'Not yet,' I said. 'I may go out later.'

'A cool dip in the sea and a siesta on the balcony,' he suggested, 'and by the way, sir, I have something for you.'

He bent down and brought out a small screw-topped bottle filled with what appeared to be bitter lemon.

'Left here last evening with Mr Stoll's compliments,' he said. 'He waited for you in the bar until nearly midnight, but you never came. So I promised to hand it over when you did.'

I looked at it suspiciously. 'What is it?' I asked.

The bar-tender smiled. 'Some of his chalet home-brew,' he said. 'It's quite harmless, he gave me a bottle for myself and my wife. She says it's nothing but lemonade. The real smelling stuff must have been thrown away. Try it.' He had poured some into my mineral water before I could stop him.

Hesitant, wary, I dipped my finger into the glass and tasted it. It was like the barley-water my mother used to make when I was a child. And equally tasteless. And yet . . . it left a sort of aftermath on the palate and the tongue. Not as sweet as honey nor as sharp as grapes, but pleasant, like the smell of raisins under the sun, curiously blended with the ears of ripening corn.

'Oh well,' I said, 'here's to the improved health of Mr Stoll,' and I drank my medicine like a man.

'I know one thing,' said the bar-tender, 'I've lost my best customer. They went away early this morning.'

'Yes,' I said, 'so my waiter informed me.'

'The best thing Mrs Stoll could do would be to get him into hospital,' the bar-tender continued. 'Her husband's a sick man, and it's not just the drink.'

'What do you mean?'

He tapped his forehead. 'Something wrong up here,' he said. 'You could see for yourself how he acted. Something on his mind. Some sort of obsession. I rather doubt we shall see them again next year.'

I sipped my mineral water, which was undoubtedly improved by the barley taste.

'What was his profession?' I asked.

'Mr Stoll? Well, he told me he had been professor of classics in some American university, but you never could tell if he was speaking the truth or not. Mrs Stoll paid the bills here, hired the boatman, arranged everything. Though he swore at her in public he seemed to depend on her. I sometimes wondered, though . . .'

He broke off.

'Wondered what?' I enquired.

'Well . . . She had a lot to put up with. I've seen her look at him sometimes, and it wasn't with love. Women of her age must seek some sort of satisfaction out of life. Perhaps she found it on the side while he indulged his passion for liquor and antiques. He had picked up quite a few items in Greece, and around the islands and here in Crete. It's not too difficult if you know the ropes.'

He winked. I nodded, and ordered another mineral water. The warm atmosphere in the bar had given me a thirst.

'Are there any lesser known sites along the coast?' I asked. 'I mean, places they might have gone ashore to from the boat?'

485

It may have been my fancy, but I thought he avoided my eye.

'I hardly know, sir,' he said. 'I dare say there are, but they would have custodians of some sort. I doubt if there are any places the authorities don't know about.'

'What about wrecks?' I pursued. 'Vessels that might have been sunk centuries ago, and are now lying on the sea bottom?'

He shrugged his shoulders. 'There are always local rumours,' he said casually, 'stories that get handed down through generations. But it's mostly superstition. I've never believed in them myself, and I don't know anybody with education who does.'

He was silent for a moment, polishing a glass. I wondered if I had said too much. 'We all know small objects are discovered from time to time,' he murmured, 'and they can be of great value. They get smuggled out of the country, or if too much risk is involved they can be disposed of locally to experts and a good price paid. I have a cousin in the village connected with the local museum. He owns the café opposite the Bottomless Pool. Mr Stoll used to patronise him. Papitos is the name. As a matter of fact, the boat hired by Mr Stoll belongs to my cousin; he lets it out on hire to the visitors here at the hotel.'

'I see.'

'But there . . . You are not a collector, sir, and you're not interested in antiques.'

'No,' I said, 'I am not a collector.'

I got up from the stool and bade him good morning. I wondered if the small package in my pocket made a bulge.

I went out of the bar and strolled on to the terrace. Nagging curiosity made me wander down to the landing-stage below the Stolls' chalet. The chalet itself had evidently been swept and tidied, the balcony cleared, the shutters closed. No trace remained of the last occupants. Before the day was over, in all probability, it would be opened for some English family who would strew the place with bathing-suits.

The boat was at its moorings, and the Greek hand was swabbing down the sides. I looked out across the bay to my own chalet on the opposite side and saw it, for the first time, from Stoll's viewpoint. As he stood there, peering through his field-glasses, it seemed clearer to me than ever before that he must have taken me for an interloper, a spy – possibly, even, someone sent out from England to enquire into the true circumstances of Charles Gordon's death. Was the gift of the jar, the night before departure, a gesture of defiance? A bribe? Or a curse?

Then the Greek fellow on the boat stood up and faced towards me. It was not the regular boatman, but another one. I had not realised this before when his back was turned. The man who used to accompany the Stolls had been younger, dark, and this was an older chap altogether. I remembered what the bar-tender had told me about the boat belonging to his cousin, Papitos, who owned the café in the village by the Bottomless Pool.

'Excuse me,' I called, 'are you the owner of the boat?'

The man climbed on to the landing-stage and stood before me.

'Nicolai Papitos is my brother,' he said. 'You want to go for trip round the bay? Plenty good fish outside. No wind today. Sea very calm.'

'I don't want to fish,' I told him. 'I wouldn't mind an outing for an hour or so. How much does it cost?'

He gave me the sum in drachmae, and I did a quick reckoning and made it out to be not more than two pounds for the hour, though it would doubtless be double that sum to round the point and go along the coast as far as that spit of sand on the isthmus of Spinalongha. I took out my wallet to see if I had the necessary notes or whether I should have to return to the reception desk and cash a traveller's cheque.

'You charge to hotel,' he said quickly, evidently reading my thoughts. 'The cost go on your bill.'

This decided me. Damn it all, my extras had been moderate to date.

'Very well,' I said, 'I'll hire the boat for a couple of hours.'

It was a curious sensation to be chug-chugging across the bay as the Stolls had done so many times, the line of chalets in my wake, the harbour astern on my right and the blue waters of the open gulf ahead. I had no clear plan in mind. It was just that, for some inexplicable reason, I felt myself drawn towards that inlet near the shore where the boat had been anchored on the previous day. 'The wreck was picked clean centuries ago . . .' Those had been Stoll's words. Was he lying? Or could it be that day after day, through the past weeks, that particular spot had been his hunting-ground, and his wife, diving, had brought the dripping treasure from its sea-bed to his grasping hands? We rounded the point, and inevitably, away from the sheltering arm that had hitherto encompassed us, the breeze appeared to freshen, the boat became more lively as the bows struck the short curling seas.

The long isthmus of Spinalongha lay ahead of us to the left, and I had some difficulty in explaining to my helmsman that I did not want him to steer into the comparative tranquillity of the waters bordering the salt-flats, but to continue along the more exposed outward shores of the isthmus bordering the open sea.

'You want to fish?' he shouted above the roar of the engine. 'You find very good fish in there,' pointing to my flats of yesterday.

'No, no,' I shouted back, 'further on along the coast.'

He shrugged. He couldn't believe I had no desire to fish,

and I wondered, when we reached our destination, what possible excuse I could make for heading the boat inshore and anchoring, unless – and this seemed plausible enough – I pleaded that the motion of the boat was proving too much for me.

The hills I had climbed yesterday swung into sight above the bows, and then, rounding a neck of land, the inlet itself, the ruined shepherd's hut close to the shore.

'In there,' I pointed. 'Anchor close to the shore.'

He stared at me, puzzled, and shook his head. 'No good,' he shouted, 'too many rocks.'

'Nonsense,' I yelled. 'I saw some people from the hotel anchored here yesterday.'

Suddenly he slowed the engine, so that my voice rang out foolishly on the air. The boat danced up and down in the troughs of the short seas.

'Not a good place to anchor,' he repeated doggedly. 'Wreck there, fouling the ground.'

So there was a wreck. . . . I felt a mounting excitement, and I was not to be put off.

'I don't know anything about that,' I replied, with equal determination, 'but this boat did anchor here, just by the inlet, I saw it myself.'

He muttered something to himself, and made the sign of the cross.

'And if I lose the anchor?' he said. 'What do I say to my brother Nicolai?'

He was nosing the boat gently, very gently, towards the inlet, and then, cursing under his breath, he went forward to the bows and threw the anchor overboard. He waited until it held, then returned and switched off the engine.

'If you want to go in close, you must take the dinghy,' he said sulkily. 'I blow it up for you, yes?'

He went forward once again, and dragged out one of those inflatable rubber affairs they use on air-sea rescue craft.

'Very well,' I said, 'I'll take the dinghy.'

In point of fact, it suited my purpose better. I could paddle close inshore, and would not have him breathing over my shoulder. At the same time, I couldn't forbear a slight prick to his pride.

'The man in charge of the boat yesterday anchored further in without mishap,' I told him.

My helmsman paused in the act of inflating the dinghy.

'If he like to risk my brother's boat that is his affair,' he said shortly. 'I have charge of it today. Other fellow not turn up for work this morning, so he lose his job. I do not want to lose mine.'

I made no reply. If the other fellow had lost his job it was probably because he had pocketed too many tips from Stoll.

The dinghy inflated and in the water, I climbed into it gingerly and began to paddle myself towards the shore. Luckily there was no run upon the spit of sand, and I was able to land successfully and pull the dinghy after me. I noticed that my helmsman was watching me with some interest from his safe anchorage, then, once he perceived that the dinghy was unlikely to come to harm, he turned his back and squatted in the bows of the boat, shoulders humped in protest, meditating, no doubt, upon the folly of English visitors.

My reason for landing was that I wanted to judge, from the shore, the exact spot where the boat had anchored yesterday. It was as I thought. Perhaps a hundred yards to the left of where we had anchored today, and closer inshore. The sea was smooth enough, I could navigate it perfectly in the rubber dinghy. I glanced towards the shepherd's hut, and saw my footprints of the day before. There were other footprints too. Fresh ones. The sand in front of the hut had been disturbed.

It was as though something had lain there, and then been dragged to the water's edge where I stood now. The goatherd himself, perhaps, had visited the place with his flock earlier that morning.

I crossed over to the hut and looked inside. Curious . . . The little pile of rubble, odds and ends of pottery, had gone. The empty bottles still stood in the far corner, and three more had been added to their number, one of them half-full. It was warm inside the hut, and I was sweating. The sun had been beating down on my bare head for nearly an hour – like a fool I had left my hat back in the chalet, not having prepared myself for this expedition – and I was seized with an intolerable thirst. I had acted on impulse, and was paying for it now. It was, in retrospect, an idiotic thing to have done. I might become completely dehydrated, pass out with heat-stroke. The half-bottle of beer would be better than nothing.

I did not fancy drinking from it after the goatherd, if it was indeed he who had brought it here; these fellows were none too clean. Then I remembered the jar in my pocket. Well, it would at least serve a purpose. I pulled the package out of its wrappings and poured the beer into it. It was only after I had swallowed the first draught that I realised it wasn't beer at all. It was barley-water. It was the same home-brewed stuff that Stoll had left for me in the bar. Did the locals, then, drink it too? It was innocuous enough. I knew that; the bar-tender had tasted it himself, and so had his wife.

When I had finished the bottle I examined the jar once again. I don't know how it was, but somehow the leering face no longer seemed so lewd. It had a certain dignity that had escaped me before. The beard, for instance. The beard was shaped to perfection around the base – whoever had fashioned it was a master of his craft. I wondered whether Socrates had looked thus when he strolled in the Athenian agora with his

491

pupils and discoursed on life. He could have done. And his pupils may not necessarily have been the young men whom Plato said they were, but of a tenderer age, like my lads at school, like those youngsters of eleven and twelve who had smiled upon me in my dreams last night.

I felt the scalloped ears, the rounded nose, the full soft lips of the tutor Silenos upon the jar, the eyes no longer protruding but questioning, appealing, and even the naked horse-men on the top had grown in grace. It seemed to me now they were not strutting in conceit but dancing with linked hands, filled with a gay abandon, a pleasing, wanton joy. It must have been my fear of the midnight intruder that had made me look upon the jar with such distaste.

I put it back in my pocket, and walked out of the hut and down the spit of beach to the rubber dinghy. Supposing I went to the fellow Papitos who had connections with the local museum, and asked him to value the jar? Supposing it was worth hundreds, thousands, and he could dispose of it for me, or tell me of a contact in London? Stoll must be doing this all the time, and getting away with it. Or so the bar-tender had hinted . . . I climbed into the dinghy and began to paddle away from the shore, thinking of the difference between a man like Stoll, with all his wealth, and myself. There he was, a brute with a skin so thick you couldn't pierce it with a spear, and his shelves back at home in the States loaded with loot. Whereas I . . . Teaching small boys on an inadequate salary, and all for what? Moralists said that money made no difference to happiness, but they were wrong. If I had a quarter of the Stolls' wealth I could retire, live abroad, on a Greek island, perhaps, and winter in some studio in Athens or Rome. A whole new way of life would open up, and just at the right moment too, before I touched middle-age.

I pulled out from the shore and made for the spot where I judged the boat to have anchored the day before. Then I let the dinghy rest, pulled in my paddles and stared down into the water. The colour was pale green, translucent, yet surely fathoms deep, for, as I looked down to the golden sands beneath, the sea-bed had all the tranquillity of another world, remote from the one I knew. A shoal of fish, silver-bright and gleaming, wriggled their way towards a tress of coral hair that might have graced Aphrodite, but was seaweed moving gently in whatever currents lapped the shore. Pebbles that on land would have been no more than rounded stones were brilliant here as jewels. The breeze that rippled the gulf beyond the anchored boat would never touch these depths, but only the surface of the water, and as the dinghy floated on, circling slowly without pull of wind or tide, I wondered whether it was the motion in itself that had drawn the unhearing Mrs Stoll to under-water swimming. Treasure was the excuse, to satisfy her husband's greed, but down there, in the depths, she would escape from a way of life that must have been unbearable.

Then I looked up at the hills above the retreating spit of sand, and I saw something flash. It was a ray of sunlight upon glass, and the glass moved. Someone was watching me through field-glasses. I rested upon my paddles and stared. Two figures moved stealthily away over the brow of the hill, but I recog-nised them instantly. One was Mrs Stoll, the other the Greek fellow who had acted as their crew I glanced over my shoulder to the anchored boat. My helmsman was still staring out to sea. He had seen nothing.

The footsteps outside the hut were now explained. Mrs Stoll, the boatman in tow, had paid a final visit to the hut to clear the rubble, and now, their mission accomplished, they would drive on to the airport to catch the afternoon plane to Athens, their journey made several miles longer by the detour along the coast road. And Stoll himself? Asleep, no doubt, at the back of the car upon the salt-flats, awaiting their return.

The sight of that woman once again gave me a profound distaste for my expedition. I wished I had not come. And my helmsman had spoken the truth; the dinghy was now floating above rock. A ridge must run out here from the shore in a single reef. The sand had darkened, changed in texture, become grey. I peered closer into the water, cupping my eyes with my hands, and suddenly I saw the vast encrusted anchor, the shells and barnacles of centuries upon its spokes, and as the dinghy drifted on the bones of the long-buried craft itself appeared, broken, sparless, her decks, if decks there had been, long since dismembered or destroyed.

Stoll had been right: her bones had been picked clean. Nothing of any value could now remain upon that skeleton. No pitchers, no jars, no gleaming coins. A momentary breeze rippled the water, and when it became clear again and all was still I saw the second anchor by the skeleton bows, and a body, arms outstretched, legs imprisoned in the anchor's jaws. The motion of the water gave the body life, as though, in some desperate fashion, it still struggled for release, but, trapped as it was, escape would never come. The days and nights would follow, months and years, and slowly the flesh would dissolve, leaving the frame impaled upon the spikes.

The body was Stoll's, head, trunk, limbs grotesque, inhuman, as they swayed backwards and forwards at the bidding of the current.

I looked up once more to the crest of the hill, but the two figures had long since vanished, and in an appalling flash of intuition a picture of what had happened became vivid: Stoll strutting on the spit of sand, the half-bottle raised to his lips, and then they struck him down and dragged him to the water's edge, and it was his wife who towed him, drowning, to his final resting-place beneath the surface, there below me, impaled on the crusted anchor. I was sole witness to his fate, and no matter what lies she told to account for his disappearance I would remain silent; it was not my responsibility; guilt might increasingly haunt me, but I must never become involved.

I heard the sound of something choking beside me — I realise now it was myself, in horror and in fear — and I struck at the water with my paddles and started pulling away from the wreck back to the boat. As I did so my arm brushed against the jar in my pocket, and in sudden panic I dragged it forth and flung it overboard. Even as I did so, I knew the gesture was in vain. It did not sink immediately but remained bobbing on the surface, then slowly filled with that green translucent sea, pale as the barley liquid laced with spruce and ivy. Not innocuous but evil, stifling conscience, dulling intellect, the hell-brew of the smiling god Dionysus, which turned his followers into drunken sots, would claim another victim before long. The eyes in the swollen face stared up at me, and they were not only those of Silenos the satyr tutor, and of the drowned Stoll, but my own as well, as I should see them soon reflected in a mirror. They seemed to hold all knowledge in their depths, and all despair.

Split Second

Mrs Ellis was methodical and tidy. Unanswered letters, unpaid bills, the litter and rummage of a slovenly writing-desk were things that she abhorred. Today, more than usual, she was in what her late husband used to call her 'clearing' mood. She had wakened to this mood; it remained with her throughout breakfast and lasted the whole morning. Besides, it was the first of the month, and as she ripped off the page of her daily calendar and saw the bright clean 1 staring at her, it seemed to symbolise a new start to her day.

The hours ahead of her must somehow seem untarnished like the date; she must let nothing slide.

First she checked the linen. The smooth white sheets lying in rows upon their shelves, pillow slips beside, and one set still in its pristine newness from the shop, tied with blue ribbon, waiting for a guest who never came.

Next, the store cupboard. The stock of homemade jam pleased her, the labels, and the date in her own handwriting. There were also bottled fruit, and tomatoes, and chutney to her own recipe. She was sparing of these, keeping them in reserve for the holidays when Susan should be home, and even then, when she brought them down and put them proudly on the table, the luxury of the treat was spoilt by a little stab of disappointment; it would mean a gap upon the store cupboard shelf.

When she had closed the store cupboard and hidden the key (she could never be quite certain of Grace, her cook), Mrs Ellis went into the drawing-room and settled herself at her desk. She was determined to be ruthless. The pigeonholes were searched, and those old envelopes that she had kept because they were not torn and could be used again (to tradesmen, not to friends) were thrown away. She would buy fresh buff envelopes of a cheap quality instead.

Here were some receipts of two years back. Unnecessary to keep them now. Those of a year ago were filed, and tied with tape. A little drawer, stiff to open, she found crammed with old counterfoils from her chequebook. This was wasting space. Instead, she wrote in her clear handwriting, 'Letters to Keep'. In the future, the drawer would be used for this purpose.

She permitted herself the luxury of filling her blotter with new sheets of paper. The pen tray was dusted. A new pencil sharpened. And, steeling her heart, she threw the stub of the little old one, with worn rubber at the base, into the waste-paper basket.

She straightened the magazines on the side table, pulled the books to the front on the shelf beside the fire – Grace had an infuriating habit of pushing them all to the back – and filled the flower vases with clean water. Then with a bare ten minutes before Grace popped her head round the door and said, 'Lunch is in,' Mrs Ellis sat down, a little breathless, before the fire, and smiled in satisfaction. Her morning had been very full indeed. Happy, well spent.

She looked about her drawing-room (Grace insisted on calling it the lounge and Mrs Ellis was forever correcting her) and thought how comfortable it was, and bright, and how wise they had been not to move when poor Wilfred suggested it a few months before he died. They had so nearly taken that house in the country, because of his health, and his fad that vegetables should be picked fresh every morning, and then luckily — well, hardly luckily, it was most terribly sad and a fearful shock to her — but before they had signed the lease Wilfred had a heart attack and died. Mrs Ellis was able to stay on in the home she knew and loved, and where she had first come as a bride ten years before.

People were inclined to say the locality was going downhill, that it had become worse than suburban. Nonsense. The blocks of flats that were going up at the top of the road could not be seen from her windows, and the houses, solid like her own, standing in a little circle of front garden, were quite unspoilt.

Besides, she liked the life. Her mornings, shopping in the town, her basket over her arm. The tradesmen knew her, treated her well. Morning coffee at eleven, at the Cosy Café opposite the bookshop, was a small pleasure she allowed herself on cold mornings — she could not get Grace to make good coffee — and in the summer the Cosy Café sold ice cream. Childishly, she would hurry back with this in a paper bag and eat it for lunch; it saved thinking of a sweet.

She believed in a brisk walk in the afternoons, and the heath was so close to hand it was just as good as the country; and in the evenings she read, or sewed, or wrote to Susan.

Life, if she thought deeply about it, which she did not, because to think deeply made her uncomfortable, was really built round Susan. Susan was nine years old, and her only child.

Because of Wilfred's ill-health and, it must be confessed, his irritability, Susan had been sent to boarding school at an early

499

age. Mrs Ellis had passed many sleepless nights before making this decision, but in the end she knew it would be for Susan's good. The child was healthy and high-spirited, and it was impossible to keep her quiet and subdued in one room with Wilfred fractious in another. It meant sending her down to the kitchen with Grace, and that, Mrs Ellis decided, did not do.

Reluctantly, the school was chosen, some thirty miles away. It was easily reached within an hour-and-a-half by Green Line bus, the children seemed happy and well cared for, the principal was grey-haired and sympathetic, and as the prospectus described it, the place was a 'home from home'.

Mrs Ellis left Susan, on the opening day of her first term, in agony of mind, but constant telephone calls between herself and the headmistress during the first week reassured her that Susan had settled placidly to her new existence.

When her husband died, Mrs Ellis thought Susan would want to return home and go to a day school, but to her surprise and disappointment the suggestion was received with dismay, and even tears.

'But I love my school,' said the child. 'We have such fun, and I have lots of friends.'

'You would make other friends at a day school,' said her mother, 'and think, we would be together in the evenings.'

'Yes,' answered Susan doubtfully, 'but what would we do?'

Mrs Ellis was hurt, but she did not permit Susan to see this. 'Perhaps you are right,' she said. 'You are contented and happy where you are. Anyway, we shall always have the holidays.'

The holidays were like brightly coloured beads on a frame, and stood out with significance in Mrs Ellis's engagement diary, throwing the weeks between into obscurity.

How leaden was February, in spite of its twenty-eight days; how blue and interminable was March, for all that morning coffee at the Cosy Café, the choosing of library books, the visits with friends to the local cinema, or sometimes, more dashing, a matinée 'in town'.

Then April came, and danced its flowery way across the calendar. Easter, and daffodils, and Susan with glowing cheeks whipped by a spring wind, hugging her once again; honey for tea, scones baked by Grace ('You've been and grown again'), those afternoon walks across the heath, sunny and gay because of the figure running on ahead. May was quiet, and June pleasant because of wide-flung windows, and the snapdragons in the front garden; June was leisurely. Besides, there was the school play on Parents' Day, and Susan, with bright eyes, surely much the best of the pixies, and although she did not speak her actions were so good.

July dragged until the twenty-fourth, and then the weeks spun themselves into a sequence of glory until the last week in September. Susan at the sea . . . Susan on a farm . . . Susan on Dartmoor . . . Susan just at home, licking an ice cream, leaning out of a window.

'She swims quite well for her age,' thus, casually, to a neighbour on the beach. 'She insists on going in, even when it's cold.'

'I don't mind saying,' this to Grace, 'that I hated going through that field of bullocks, but Susan didn't mind a scrap. She has a way with animals.'

Bare scratched legs in sandals, summer frocks outgrown, a sunhat, faded, lying on the floor. October did not bear thinking about . . . But, after all, there was always plenty to do in the house. Forget November, and the rain, and the fogs that turned white upon the heath. Draw the curtains, poke the fire, settle to something, the *Weekly Home Companion*, Fashions for Young Folk. Not that pink, but the green with the smocked top and a wide sash would be just the thing for Susan at parties in the Christmas holidays. December . . . Christmas . . .

501

This was the best, this was the height of home enjoyment. As soon as Mrs Ellis saw the first small trees standing outside the florist's and those orange boxes of dates in the grocer's window, her heart would give a little leap of excitement. Susan would be home in three weeks now. Then the laughter and the chatter. The nods between herself and Grace. The smiles of mystery. The furtiveness of wrappings.

All over in one day like the bursting of a swollen balloon; paper ribbon, cracker novelties, even presents, chosen with care, thrown aside. But no matter. It was worth it. Mrs Ellis, looking down upon a sleeping Susan tucked in with a doll in her arms, turned down the light and crept off to her own bed, sapped, exhausted. The egg cosy, Susan's handiwork at school, hastily stitched, stood on her bedside table. Mrs Ellis never ate boiled eggs, but, as she said to Grace, there is such a gleam in the hen's eye; it's very cleverly done.

The fever, the pace of the New Year. The Circus, the pantomime. Mrs Ellis watched Susan, never the performers. 'You should have seen her laugh when the seal blew the trumpet; I've never known a child with such a gift for enjoyment.'

And how she stood out at parties, in the green frock, with her fair hair and blue eyes. Other children were so stumpy. Ill-made little bodies or big shapeless mouths. 'She said, "Thank you for a lovely time," when we left, which was more than most of them did. And she won at musical chairs.'

There were bad moments too, of course. The restless night, the high spot of colour, the sore throat, the temperature of 102. Shaking hands on the telephone. The doctor's reassuring voice. And his footsteps on the stairs, a steady, reliable man. 'We had better take a swab, in case.' A swab? That meant diphtheria, scarlet fever? A little figure being carried down in blankets, an ambulance, hospital . . . ?

Thank God, it proved to be a relaxed throat. Lots of them

about. Too many parties, keep her quiet for a few days. Yes, Doctor, yes. The relief from dread anxiety, and on and on without a stop, the reading to Susan from her *Playbook Annual*, story after story, terrible and trite, 'and so Nicky Nod *did* lose his treasure after all, which just served him right, didn't it, children?'

'All things pass,' thought Mrs Ellis, 'pleasure and pain, and happiness and suffering, and I suppose my friends would say my life is a dull one, rather uneventful, but I am grateful for it, and contented, and although sometimes I feel I did not do my utmost for poor Wilfred – his was a difficult nature, luckily Susan has not inherited it – at least I believe I have succeeded in making a happy home for Susan.' She looked about her, that first day of the month, and noticed with affection and appreciation those bits and pieces of furniture, the pictures on the walls, the ornaments on the mantelpiece, all the things she had gathered about her during ten years of marriage, which meant herself, her home.

The sofa and two chairs, part of an original suite, were worn but comfortable. The pouf by the fire, she had covered it herself. The fire irons, not quite so polished as they should be, she must speak to Grace. The rather melancholy portrait of Wilfred in that dark corner behind the bookshelf, at least he looked distinguished. And was, thought Mrs Ellis to herself, hastily. The flower picture showed more to advantage over the mantel-piece; the green foliage harmonised so well with the green coat of the Staffordshire figure who stood with his lady beside the clock.

'I could do with new covers,' thought Mrs Ellis, 'and curtains too, but they must wait. Susan has grown so enormously the last few months. Her clothes are more important. The child is tall for her age.'

Grace looked round the door. 'Lunch is in,' she said.

'If she would open the door outright,' thought Mrs Ellis, 'and come right into the room, I have mentioned it a hundred times. It's the sudden thrust of the head that is so disconcerting, and if I have anyone to lunch . . .'

She sat down to guinea-fowl and apple charlotte, and wondered if they were remembering to give Susan extra milk at school this term, and the Minidex tonic; the matron was inclined to be forgetful.

Suddenly, for no reason, she laid her spoon down on the plate, swept with a wave of such intense melancholy as to be almost unbearable. Her heart was heavy. Her throat tightened. She could not continue her lunch.

'Something is wrong with Susan,' she thought. 'This is a warning that she wants me.'

She rang for coffee and went into the drawing-room. She crossed to the window and stood looking at the back of the house opposite. From an open window sagged an ugly red curtain, and a lavatory brush hung from a nail.

'The district *is* losing class,' thought Mrs Ellis. 'I shall have lodging-houses for neighbours soon.'

She drank her coffee, but the feeling of uneasiness, of apprehension, did not leave her. At last she went to the telephone and rang up the school.

The secretary answered. Surprised, and a little impatient, surely. Susan was perfectly all right. She had just eaten a good lunch. No, she had no sign of a cold. No one was ill in the school. Did Mrs Ellis want to speak to Susan? The child was outside with the others, playing, but could be called in if necessary.

'No,' said Mrs Ellis, 'it was just a foolish notion on my part that Susan might not be well. I am so sorry to have bothered you.'

She hung up the receiver, and went to her bedroom to put

on her outdoor clothes. A good walk would do her good. She gazed in satisfaction upon the photograph of Susan on the dressing table. The photographer had caught the expression in her eyes to perfection. Such a lovely light on the hair too.

Mrs Ellis hesitated. Was it really a walk she needed? Or was this vague feeling of distress a sign that she was overtired, that she had better rest? She looked with inclination at the downy quilt upon her bed. Her hot-water bottle, hanging by the washstand, would take only a moment to fill. She could loosen her girdle, throw off her shoes, and lie down for an hour on the bed, warm with the bottle under the downy quilt. No. She decided to be firm with herself. She went to the wardrobe and got out her camel coat, wound a scarf round her head, pulled on a pair of gauntlet gloves and walked downstairs.

She went into the drawing-room, made up the fire and put the guard in front of it. Grace was apt to be forgetful of the fire. She opened the window at the top so that the room should not strike stuffy when she came back. She folded the daily papers ready to read when she returned, and replaced the marker in her library book.

'I'm going out for a little while. I shan't be long,' she called down to the basement to Grace.

'All right, ma'am,' came the answer.

Mrs Ellis caught the whiff of cigarette, and frowned. Grace could do as she liked in the basement, but there was something not quite right about a maidservant smoking.

She shut the front door behind her, went down the steps and into the road, and turned left towards the heath. It was a dull, grey day. Mild for the time of year, almost to oppression. Later, there would be fog, perhaps, rolling up from London the way it did, in a great wall, stifling the clean air.

Mrs Ellis made her 'short round', as she always called it.

Eastward, to the Viaduct ponds, and then back, circling, to the Vale of Health.

It was not an inviting afternoon, and she did not enjoy her walk. She kept wishing she was home again, in bed with a hot-water bottle, or sitting in the drawing-room beside the fire, soon to shut out the muggy, murky sky, and draw the curtains. She walked swiftly past nurses pushing prams, two or three of them in groups chatting together, their charges running ahead. Dogs barked beside the ponds. Solitary men in macintoshes stared into vacancy. An old woman on a seat threw crumbs to chirping sparrows. The sky took on a darker, olive tone. Mrs Ellis quickened her steps. The fairground by the Vale of Health looked sombre, the merry-go-round shrouded in its winter wrappings of canvas, and two lean cats stalked each other in and out of the palings. A milkman, whistling, clanked his tray of bottles and, lifting them to his cart, urged the pony to a trot.

'I must,' thought Mrs Ellis inconsequently, 'get Susan a bicycle for her birthday. Nine is a good age for a first bicycle.'

She saw herself choosing one, asking advice, feeling the handle-bars. The colour red, perhaps. Or a good blue. A little basket on the front and a leather bag, for tools, strapped to the back of the seat. The brakes must be sound but not too gripping, otherwise Susan would topple headfirst over the handle-bars and graze her face.

Hoops were out of fashion, which was a pity. When she had been a child there had been no fun like a good springy hoop, struck smartly with a little stick, bowling its way ahead of you. Quite an art to it, too. Susan would have been good with a hoop.

Mrs Ellis came to the junction of two roads and crossed to the opposite side; the second road was her own, and her house the last one on the corner.

As she did so she saw the laundry van swinging down towards her, much too fast. She saw it swerve, heard the screech of its brakes. She saw the look of surprise on the face of the laundry boy. 'I shall speak to the driver next time he calls,' she said to herself. 'One of these days there will be an accident.' She thought of Susan on the bicycle, and shuddered. Perhaps a note to the manager of the laundry would do more good. 'If you could possibly give a word of warning to your driver, I should be grateful. He takes his corners much too fast.' And she would ask to remain anonymous. Otherwise the man might complain about carrying the heavy basket down the steps each time.

She had arrived at her own gate. She pushed it open, and noticed with annoyance that it was nearly off its hinges. The men calling for the laundry must have wrenched at it in some way and done the damage. The note to the manager would be stronger still. She would write immediately after tea. While it was on her mind.

She took out her key and put it in the Yale lock of the front door. It stuck. She could not turn it. How very irritating. She rang the bell. This would mean bringing Grace up from the basement, which she did not like. Better to call down, perhaps, and explain the situation. She leant over the steps and called down to the kitchen. 'Grace, it's only me,' she said, 'my key has jammed in the door; could you come up and let me in?'

She paused. There was no sound from below. Grace must have gone out. This was sheer deceit. It was an agreed bargain between them that when Mrs Ellis was out Grace must stay in. The house must not be left. But sometimes Mrs Ellis suspected that Grace did not keep to the bargain. Here was proof.

She called once again, rather more sharply this time. 'Grace?'

There was a sound of a window opening below, and a man thrust his head out of the kitchen. He was in his shirt sleeves. And he had not shaved.

'What are you bawling your head off about?' he said.

Mrs Ellis was too stunned to answer. So this was what happened when her back was turned. Grace, respectable, well over thirty, had a man in the house. Mrs Ellis swallowed, but kept her temper.

'Perhaps you will have the goodness to ask Grace to come upstairs and let me in,' she said.

The sarcasm was wasted, of course. The man blinked at her, bewildered. 'Who's Grace?' he said.

This was too much. So Grace had the nerve to pass under another name. Something fanciful, no doubt. Shirley, or Marlene. She was pretty sure now what must have happened. Grace had slipped out to the public house down the road to buy this man beer. The man was left to loll in the kitchen. He might even have been poking his fingers in the larder. Now she knew why there was so little left on the joint two days ago.

'If Grace is out,' said Mrs Ellis, and her voice was icy, 'kindly let me in yourself. I prefer not to use the back entrance.'

That would put him in his place. Mrs Ellis trembled with rage. She was seldom angry; she was a mild, even-tempered woman. But this reception, from a lout in shirt sleeves at her own kitchen window, was rather more than she could bear. It was going to be unpleasant, the interview with Grace. Grace would give notice, in all probability. But some things could not be allowed to slide, and this was one of them.

She heard shuffling footsteps coming along the hall. The man had mounted from the basement. He opened the front door and stood there, staring at her.

'Who is it you want?' he said.

Mrs Ellis heard the furious yapping of a little dog from the drawing-room. Callers . . . This was the end. How perfectly frightful, how really overwhelmingly embarrassing. Someone had called and Grace had let them in, or, worse still, this man in his shirt sleeves had done so. What would people think?

'Who is in the drawing-room, do you know?' she murmured swiftly.

'I think Mr and Mrs Bolton are in, but I'm not sure,' he said. 'I can hear the dog yapping. Was it them you wanted to see?'

Mrs Ellis did not know a Mr and Mrs Bolton. She turned impatiently towards the drawing-room, first whipping off her coat and putting her gloves in her pocket.

'You had better go down to the basement again,' she said to the man, who was still staring at her. 'Tell Grace not to bring tea until I ring. These people may not stay.'

The man appeared bewildered. 'All right,' he said, 'I'm going down. But if you want Mr and Mrs Bolton again, ring twice.'

He shuffled off down the basement stairs. He was drunk, no doubt. He meant to be insulting. If he proved difficult, later in the evening, after dark, it would mean ringing for the police.

Mrs Ellis slipped into the lobby to hang up her coat. No time to go upstairs if callers were in the drawing-room. She fumbled for the switch but the bulb had gone. Another pinprick. Now she could not see herself in the mirror.

She stumbled over something, and bent to see what it was. It was a man's boot. And here was another, and a pair of shoes, and beside them a suitcase and an old rug. If Grace had allowed that man to put his things in her lobby, then Grace would go tonight. Crisis had come. High crisis.

Mrs Ellis opened the drawing-room door, forcing a smile of welcome, not too warm, upon her lips. A little dog rushed towards her, barking furiously.

'Quiet, Judy,' said a man, grey-haired, with horn spectacles, sitting before the fire. He was clicking a typewriter.

Something had happened to the room. It was covered with books and papers. Odds and ends of junk littered the floor. A parrot, in a cage, hopped on its perch and screeched a welcome. Mrs Ellis tried to speak, but her voice would not come. Grace had gone raving mad. She had let that man into the house, and this one too, and they had brought the most terrible disorder; they had turned the room upside down; they had deliberately, maliciously, set themselves to destroy her things.

No. Worse. It was part of a great thieving plot. She had heard of such things. Gangs went about breaking into houses. Grace, perhaps, was not at fault. She was lying in the basement, gagged and bound. Mrs Ellis felt her heart beating much too fast. She also felt a little faint.

'I must keep calm,' she said to herself, 'whatever happens, I must keep calm. If I can get to the telephone, to the police, it is the only hope. This man must not see that I am planning what to do.'

The little dog kept sniffing at her heels. 'Excuse me,' said the intruder, pushing his horn spectacles on to his forehead, 'but do you want anything? My wife is upstairs.'

The diabolic cunning of the plot. The cool bluff of his sitting there, the typewriter on his knees. They must have brought all this stuff in through the door to the back garden; the french window was ajar. Mrs Ellis glanced swiftly at the mantelpiece. It was as she feared. The Staffordshire figures had been removed, and the flower picture too. There must be a car, a van, waiting down the road . . . Her mind worked quickly. It might be that the man had not guessed her identity. Two could play at bluff. Memories of amateur theatricals flashed through her mind. Somehow she must detain these people until the police arrived. How fast they had worked. Her desk was gone, the bookshelves too, nor could she see her armchair.

But she kept her eyes steadily on the stranger. He must not notice her brief glance round the room.

'Your wife is upstairs?' said Mrs Ellis, her voice strained, yet calm.

'Yes,' said the man, 'if you've come for an appointment, she always makes them. You'll find her in the studio. Room in the front.'

Steadily, softly, Mrs Ellis left the drawing-room, but the wretched little dog had followed her.

One thing was certain. The man had not realised who she was. They believed the householder out of the way for the afternoon, and that she, standing now in the hall, listening, her heart beating, was some caller to be fobbed off with a lie about appointments.

She stood silently by the drawing-room door. The man had resumed typing on his machine. She marvelled at the coolness of it, the drawn-out continuity of the bluff. There had been nothing in the papers very recently about large-scale robberies. This was something new, something outstanding. It was extraordinary that they should pick on her house. But they must know she was a widow, on her own, with one maidservant. The telephone had already been removed from the stand in the hall. There was a loaf of bread on it instead, and something that looked like meat wrapped up in newspaper. So they had brought provisions . . . There was a chance that the telephone in her bedroom had not yet been taken away, nor the wires cut. The man had said his wife was upstairs. It may have been part of his bluff, or it might be that he worked with a woman accomplice. This woman, even now, was probably turning out Mrs Ellis's wardrobe, seizing her fur coat, ramming the single string of cultured pearls into a pocket.

Mrs Ellis thought she could hear footsteps in her bedroom. Her anger overcame her fear. She had not the strength to do

511

battle with the man, but she could face the woman. And if the worst came to the worst, she would run to the window, put her head out, and scream. The people next door would hear. Or someone might be passing in the street.

Stealthily, Mrs Ellis crept upstairs. The little dog led the way with confidence. She paused outside her bedroom door. There was certainly movement from within. The dog waited, his eyes fixed upon her with intelligence.

At that moment the door of Susan's small bedroom opened, and a fat elderly woman looked out, blowzy and red in the face. She had a tabby cat under her arm. As soon as the dog saw the cat it started a furious yapping.

'Now that's torn it,' said the woman. 'What do you want to bring the dog upstairs for? They always fight when they meet. Do you know if the post's been yet? Oh, sorry. I thought you were Mrs Bolton.' She brought an empty milk bottle from under her other arm and put it down on the landing. 'I'm blowed if I can manage the stairs today,' she said, 'somebody else will have to take it down for me. Is it foggy out?'

'No,' said Mrs Ellis, shocked into a natural answer, and then, feeling the woman's eyes upon her, hesitated between entering her bedroom door and withdrawing down the stairs. This evil-looking old woman was part of the gang and might call the man from below.

'Got an appointment?' said the other. 'She won't see you if you haven't booked an appointment.'

A tremor of a smile appeared on Mrs Ellis's lips. 'Thank you,' she said, 'yes, I have an appointment.'

She was amazed at her own steadiness, and that she could carry off the situation with such aplomb. An actress on the London stage could not have played her part better.

The elderly woman winked and, drawing nearer, plucked Mrs Ellis by the sleeve. 'Is she going to do you straight or fancy?' she whispered. 'It's the fancy ones that get the men. You know what I mean!' She nudged Mrs Ellis and winked again. 'I see by your ring you're married,' she said. 'You'd be surprised – even the quietest husbands like their pictures fancy. Take a tip from an old pro. Get her to do you fancy.'

She lurched back into Susan's room, the cat under her arm, and shut the door.

'It's possible,' thought Mrs Ellis, the faint feeling coming over her once again, 'that a group of lunatics have escaped from an asylum, and in their terrible, insane fashion they have broken into my house not to thieve, not to destroy my belongings, but because in some crazed, deluded fashion they believe themselves to be at home.'

The publicity would be frightful once it became known. Headlines in the papers. Her photograph taken. So bad for Susan. Susan . . . That horrible, disgusting old woman in Susan's bedroom.

Emboldened, fortified, Mrs Ellis opened her own bedroom door. One glance revealed the worst. The room was bare, stripped. There were several lights at various points, and a camera on a tripod. A divan was pushed against the wall. A young woman, with a crop of thick fuzzy hair, was kneeling on the floor, sorting papers.

'Who is it?' she said. 'I don't see anyone without an appointment. You've no right to come in here.'

Mrs Ellis, calm, resolute, did not answer. She had made certain that the telephone, though it had been moved like the rest of her things, was still in the room. She went to it and lifted the receiver.

'Leave my telephone alone,' cried the shock-haired girl, and she began to struggle to her knees.

'I want the police,' said Mrs Ellis firmly to the exchange, 'I want them to come at once to 17 Elmhurst Road. I am in great danger. Please report this message to the police at once.'

The girl was beside her now, taking the receiver from her. 'Who's sent you here?' said the girl, her face sallow, colourless, against the fuzzy hair. 'If you think you can come in snooping, you're mistaken. You won't find anything. Nor the police, neither. I have a trade licence for the work I do.'

Her voice had risen, and the dog, alarmed, joined her with high-pitched barks. The girl opened the door and called down the stairs. 'Harry?' she shouted. 'Come here and throw this woman out.'

Mrs Ellis remained quite calm. She stood with her back to the wall, her hands folded. The exchange had taken her message. It would not be long now before the police arrived.

She heard the drawing-room door open from below and the man's voice called up, petulant, irritated. 'What's the matter?' he shouted. 'You know I'm busy. Can't you deal with the woman? She probably wants a special pose.'

The girl's eyes narrowed. She looked closely at Mrs Ellis. 'What did my husband say to you?' she said.

Ah, thought Mrs Ellis triumphantly, they're getting frightened. It's not such an easy game as they think. 'I had no conversation with your husband,' she said quietly; 'he merely told me I should find you upstairs. In this room. Don't try any bluff with me. It's too late. I can see what you have been doing.' She gestured at the room.

The girl stared at her. 'You can't put any phony business over on me,' she said. 'This studio is decent, respectable, everyone knows that. I take camera studies of children. Plenty of clients can testify to that. You've got no proof of anything else. Show me a negative, and then I might believe you?'

Mrs Ellis wondered how long it would be before the police came. She must continue to play for time. Later, she might even feel sorry, perhaps, for this wretched deluded girl who had wrought such havoc in the bedroom, believing herself to be a photographer; but this moment, now, she must be calm, calm.

'Well?' said the girl. 'What are you going to say when the police come? What's your story?'

It did not do to antagonise lunatics. Mrs Ellis knew that. They must be humoured. She must humour this girl until the police came. 'I shall tell them that I live here,' she said gently. 'That is all they will need to know. Nothing further.'

The girl looked at her, puzzled, and lit a cigarette. 'Then it is a pose you want?' she said. 'That call was just a bluff? Why don't you come clean and say why you're here?'

The sound of their voices had attracted the attention of the old woman in Susan's room. She tapped on the door, which was already open, and stood on the threshold.

'Anything wrong, dear?' she said slyly to the girl.

'Push on out of it,' said the girl impatiently, 'this is none of your business. I don't interfere with you, and you don't interfere with me.'

'I'm not interfering, dear,' said the woman, 'I only wanted to know if I could help. Difficult client, eh? Wants something outsize?'

'Oh, shut your mouth,' said the girl.

The girl's husband, Bolton or whatever his name was, the spectacled man from the drawing-room, came upstairs and into the bedroom.

'Just what's going on?' he said.

The girl shrugged her shoulders and glanced at Mrs Ellis. 'I don't know,' she said, 'but I think it's blackmail.'

'Has she got any negatives?' said the man swiftly.

'Not that I know of. Never seen her before.'

'She might have got them from another client,' said the elderly woman, watching.

The three of them stared at Mrs Ellis. She was not afraid. She had the situation well in hand.

'I think we've all become a little overwrought,' she said, 'and much the best thing to do would be to go downstairs, sit quietly by the fire, and have a little chat, and you can talk to me about your work. Tell me, are you all three photographers?'

As she spoke, half of her mind was wondering where they had managed to hide her things. They must have bundled her bed into Susan's room; the wardrobe was in two parts, of course, and could be taken to pieces very soon; but her clothes . . . her ornaments . . . these must have been concealed in a lorry. Somewhere, there was a lorry filled with all her things. It might be parked down another road, or might have been driven off already by yet another accomplice. The police were good at tracing stolen goods, she knew that, and everything was insured; but such a mess had been made of the house; insurance would never cover that, unless there was some clause, some proviso against damage by lunatics; surely the insurance people would not call that an act of God . . . Her mind ran on and on, taking in the mess, the disorder, these people had created, and how many days and weeks would it take for her and Grace to get everything straight again?

Poor Grace. She had forgotten Grace. Grace must be shut up somewhere in that basement with that dreadful man in shirt sleeves, another of the gang, not a follower at all.

'Well,' said Mrs Ellis with the other half of her mind, the half that was acting so famously, 'shall we do as I suggest and go downstairs?' She turned and led the way, and to her surprise they followed her, the man and his wife, not the horrible old woman. She remained above, leaning over the banisters.

'Call me if you want me,' she said.

Mrs Ellis could not bear to think of her fingering Susan's things in the little bedroom. 'Won't you join us?' she said, steeling herself to courtesy. 'It's far more cheerful down below.'

The old woman smirked. 'That's for Mr and Mrs Bolton to say,' she said, 'I don't push myself.'

'If I can get all three of them pinned into the drawing-room,' thought Mrs Ellis, 'and somehow lock the door, and make a tremendous effort at conversation, I might possibly keep their attention until the police arrive. There is, of course, the door into the garden, but then they will have to climb the fence, fall over that potting shed next door. The old woman, at least, would never do it.'

'Now,' said Mrs Ellis, her heart turning over inside at the havoc of the drawing-room, 'shall we sit down and recover ourselves, and you shall tell me all about this photography.'

But she had scarcely finished speaking before there was a ring at the front door and a knock, authoritative, loud. The relief sent her dizzy. She steadied herself against the door. It was the police. The man looked at the girl, a question in his eye.

'Better have 'em in,' he said, 'she's got no proof.' He crossed the hall and opened the front door. 'Come in, officer,' he said. 'There's two of you, I see.'

'We had a telephone call,' Mrs Ellis heard the constable say, 'some trouble going on, I understand.'

'I think there must be some mistake,' said Bolton. 'The fact is, we've had a caller and I think she got hysterical.'

Mrs Ellis walked into the hall. She did not recognise the constable, nor the young policeman from the beat. It was unfortunate, but it did not really matter. Both were stout, well-built men.

'I am not hysterical,' she said firmly, 'I am perfectly all right. I put the telephone call through the exchange.'

The constable took out a notebook and a pencil. 'What's the trouble?' he said. 'But give me first your name and address.'

Mrs Ellis smiled patiently. She hoped he was not going to be a stupid man. 'It's hardly necessary,' she said, 'but my name is Mrs Wilfred Ellis of this address.'

'Lodge here?' asked the constable.

Mrs Ellis frowned. 'No,' she said, 'this is my house, I live here.' And then, because she saw a look flash from Bolton to his wife, she knew the time had come to be explicit. 'I must speak to you alone, Constable,' she said, 'the matter is terribly urgent; I don't think you quite understand.'

'If you have any charge to bring, Mrs Ellis,' said the officer, 'you can bring it at the police station at the proper time. We were informed that somebody lodging here at Number 17 was in danger. Are you, or are you not, the person who gave that information to the exchange?'

Mrs Ellis began to lose control.

'Of course I am that person,' she said. 'I returned home to find that my house had been broken into by thieves, these people here, dangerous thieves, lunatics, I don't know what they are, and my things carried away, the whole of my house turned upside down, the most terrible disorder everywhere.' She talked so rapidly, her words fell over themselves.

The man from the basement had now joined them in the hall. He stared at the two policemen, his eyes goggling. 'I saw her come to the door,' he said. 'I thought she was balmy. Wouldn't have let her in if I had known.'

The constable, a little nettled, turned to the interrupter. 'Who are you?' he said.

'Name of Upshaw,' said the man, 'William Upshaw. Me and my missus has the basement flat here.'

'That man is lying,' said Mrs Ellis, 'he does not live here; he belongs to this gang of thieves. Nobody lives in the basement except my maid – perhaps I should say cook-general – Grace Jackson, and if you will search the premises you will probably find her gagged and bound somewhere, and by that ruffian.' She had now lost all restraint. She could hear her voice, usually low and quiet, rising to a hysterical pitch.

'Balmy,' said the man from the basement, 'you can see the straw in her hair.'

'Quiet, please,' said the constable, and turned to the young policeman, who murmured something in his ear. 'Yes, yes,' he said, 'I've got the directory here.'

He consulted another book. Mrs Ellis watched him feverishly. Never had she seen such a stupid man. Why had they sent out such a slow-witted fool from the police station?

The constable now turned to the man in the horn spectacles. 'Are you Henry Bolton?' he asked.

'Yes, officer,' replied the man eagerly, 'and this is my wife. We have the ground floor here. She uses an upstairs room for a studio. Camera portraits, you know.'

There was a shuffle down the stairs, and the evil old woman came to the foot of the banisters. 'My name's Baxter,' she said, 'Billie Baxter they used to call me in my old stage days. Used to be in the profession, you know. I have the first-floor back here at Number 17. I can witness this woman came as a sort of Paul Pry, and up to no good. I saw her looking through the keyhole of Mrs Bolton's studio.'

'Then she doesn't lodge here?' asked the constable. 'I didn't think she did; the name isn't in the directory.'

'We have never seen her before, officer,' said Bolton. 'Mr Upshaw let her into the house through some error; she walked into our living-room, and then forced her way into my wife's studio, threatened her, and in hysterical fashion rang for the police.'

The constable looked at Mrs Ellis. 'Anything to say?' he said.

Mrs Ellis swallowed. If only she could keep calm, if only her heart would not beat so dreadfully fast, and the terrible desire to cry would not rise in her throat.

'Constable,' she said, 'there has been some terrible mistake. You are new to the district, perhaps, and the young policeman too – I don't seem to recognise him – but if you would kindly get through to your headquarters, they must know all about me; I have lived here for years. My maid Grace has been with me a very long time; I am a widow; my husband, Wilfred Ellis, has been dead two years; I have a little girl of nine at school. I went out for a walk on the heath this afternoon, and during my absence these people have broken into my house, seized or destroyed my belongings – the whole place is upside down; if you would please get through immediately to your head-quarters . . .'

'There, there,' said the constable, putting his notebook away, 'that's all right; we can go into all that quietly down at the station. Now do any of you want to charge Mrs Ellis with trespassing?'

There was silence. Nobody said anything.

'We don't wish to be unkind,' said Bolton diffidently. 'I think my wife and I are quite willing to let the matter pass.'

'I think it should be clearly understood,' interposed the shock-haired girl, 'that anything this woman says about us at the police station is completely untrue.'

'Quite,' said the officer. 'You will both be called, if needed, but I very much doubt the necessity. Now, Mrs Ellis' – he turned to her, not harshly in any way, but with authority – 'we have a car outside, and we can run you down to the station, and you can tell your story there. Have you a coat?'

Mrs Ellis turned blindly to the lobby. She knew the police station well; it was barely five minutes away. It was best to go there direct. See someone in authority, not this fool, this hope-less, useless fool. But in the meantime, these people were getting away with their criminal story. By the time she and an addi-tional police force returned, they would have fled. She groped for her coat in the dark lobby, stumbling again over the boots, the suitcases. 'Constable,' she said softly, 'here, one minute.'

He moved towards her. 'Yes?' he said.

'They've taken away the electric bulb,' she said rapidly in a low whisper. 'It was perfectly all right this afternoon, and these boots, and this pile of suitcases, all these have been brought in, and thrown here; the suitcases are probably filled with my ornaments. I must ask you most urgently to leave the policeman in charge here until we return, to see that these people don't escape.'

'That's all right, Mrs Ellis,' said the officer. 'Now, are you ready to come along?'

She saw a look pass between the constable and the young policeman. The young policeman was trying to hide his smile. Mrs Ellis felt certain that the constable was *not* going to remain in the house. And a new suspicion flashed into her mind. Could this officer and his subordinate be genuine members of the police force? Or were they, after all, members of the gang? This would explain their strange faces, their obvious mishandling of the situation. In which case they were now going to take her away to some lair, drug her, kill her possibly.

'I'm not going with you,' she said swiftly.

'Now, Mrs Ellis,' said the constable, 'don't give any trouble. You shall have a cup of tea down at the station, and no one is going to hurt you.'

He seized her arm. She tried to shake it off. The young policeman moved closer.

'Help,' she shouted, 'help . . . help . . .'

There must be someone. Those people from next door, she barely knew them, but no matter, if she raised her voice loud enough . . .

'Poor thing,' said the man in shirt sleeves, 'seems sad, don't it? I wonder how she got like it.'

Mrs Ellis saw his bulbous eyes fixed on her with pity, and she nearly choked.

'You rogue,' she said, 'how dare you, how dare you!' But she was being bundled down the steps, through the front garden and into the car, and there was another policeman at the wheel of the car; and she was thrust at the back, the constable keeping a steady hold upon her arm. The car turned downhill, past the stretch of heath; she tried to see out of the windows where they were going, but the bulk of the constable prevented her. After twisting and turning the car stopped, to her great surprise, in front of the police station. Then these men were genuine, after all. They were not members of the gang. Stupefied for a moment, but relieved, thankful, Mrs Ellis stumbled from the car. The constable, still holding her arm, led her inside.

The hall was not unfamiliar; she remembered coming once before, years ago, when the ginger cat was lost; there was somebody in charge always, sitting at a sort of desk, everything very official, very brisk. She supposed she would stop here in the hall, but the constable led her on to an inner room, and here was another officer seated at a large desk, a more superior type altogether, thank heaven, and he looked intelligent.

She was determined to get her word in before the constable spoke. 'There has been great confusion,' she began. 'I am Mrs Ellis, of 17 Elmhurst Road, and my house has been broken into, robbery is going on at this moment on a huge scale; I believe the thieves to be very desperate and extraordinarily cunning; they have completely taken in the constable here, and the other policeman . . .'

To her indignation this superior officer did not look at her. He raised his eyebrows at the constable, and the constable, who had taken off his hat, coughed and approached the desk. A policewoman, appearing from nowhere, stood beside Mrs Ellis and held her arm.

The constable and the superior officer were talking together in low tones. Mrs Ellis could not hear what they were saying. Her legs trembled with emotion. She felt her head swim. Thankfully, she accepted the chair dragged forward by the policewoman, and in a few moments she was given a cup of tea. She did not want it, though. Precious time was being lost.

'I must insist that you hear what I have to say,' she said, and the policewoman tightened her grip on Mrs Ellis's arm. The officer behind the desk motioned her forward, and she was assisted to another chair, the policewoman remaining beside her all the while.

'Now,' he said, 'what is it you want to tell me?'

Mrs Ellis gripped her hands together. She had a premonition that this man, in spite of his superior face, was going to prove as great a fool as the constable.

'My name is Ellis,' she said, 'Mrs Wilfred Ellis, of 17 Elmhurst Road. I am in the telephone book. I am very well known in the district, and have lived at Elmhurst Road for ten years. I am a widow, and I have one little girl of nine years at present at school. I employ one maidservant, Grace Jackson, who cooks for me and does general work. This afternoon I went for a short walk on the heath, round by the Viaduct and the Vale of Health ponds, and when I returned home I found my house had been broken into, my maid had disappeared; the rooms were already stripped of my belongings and the thieves were in possession of my home, putting up a stupendous act of bluff that deceived even the constable here. I put the call through to the exchange, which frightened the thieves, and I endeavoured to keep them pinned in my drawing-room until help arrived.'

Mrs Ellis paused for breath. She saw that the officer was paying attention to her story, and kept his eyes fixed upon her.

'Thank you,' he said, 'that is very helpful, Mrs Ellis. Now, have you anything you can show me to prove your identity?'

She stared at him. Prove her identity? Well, of course. But not here, not actually on her person. She had come away without her handbag, and her calling cards were in the writing desk, and her passport – she and Wilfred had been to Dieppe once – was, if she remembered rightly, in the left-hand pigeon-hole of the small writing desk in her bedroom.

But she suddenly remembered the havoc of the house. Nothing would be found . . .

'It's very unfortunate,' she said to the officer, 'but I didn't take my handbag with me when I went out for my walk this afternoon. I left it in the chest-of-drawers in the bedroom. My calling-cards are in the desk in the drawing-room, and there is a passport – rather out of date; my husband and I did not travel much – in a pigeonhole in a small desk in my bedroom. But everything has been upset, taken by these thieves. The house is in utter chaos.'

The officer made a note on the pad beside him. 'You can't produce your identity card or your ration book?' he asked.

'I have explained,' said Mrs Ellis, governing her temper. 'My calling-cards are in my writing-desk. I don't know what you mean by ration book.'

The officer went on writing on his pad. He glanced at the policewoman, who began feeling Mrs Ellis's pockets, touching her in a familiar way. Mrs Ellis tried to think which of her friends could be telephoned to, who could vouch for her, who could come at once by car and make these idiots, these stone-witted fools, see sense. 'I must keep calm,' she told herself again, 'I must keep calm.' The Collins were abroad; they would have been the best, but Netta Draycott should be at home; she was usually at home about this time because of the children.

'I have asked you,' said Mrs Ellis, 'to verify my name and address in the telephone book. If you refuse to do that, ask the postmaster, or the manager of my bank, a branch of which is in the High Street, where I cashed a cheque on Saturday. Finally, would you care to ring up Mrs Draycott, a friend of mine, 21 Charlton Court, the block of flats in Charlton Avenue, who will vouch for me?'

She sat back in the chair, exhausted. No nightmare, she told herself, could ever have the horror, the frustrated hopelessness, of her present plight. Little incident piled on little incident. If she had only remembered to bring her handbag, there was a calling-card case in her handbag. And all the while those thieves, those devils, breaking up her home, getting away with her precious things, her belongings . . .

'Now, Mrs Ellis,' said the officer, 'we have checked up on your statements, you know, and they won't do. You are not in the telephone book, nor in the local directory.'

'I assure you I am,' said Mrs Ellis with indignation. 'Give me the books and I'll show you.'

The constable, still standing, placed the books before her. She ran her finger down the name of Ellis to the position on the left-hand page where she knew it would be. The name Ellis was repeated, but not hers. And none with her address or number. She looked in the directory and saw that beside 17 Elmhurst Road were the names of Bolton, of Upshaw, of Baxter . . . She pushed both books away from her. She stared at the officer.

'There is something wrong with these books,' she said, 'they are not up to date, they are false, they are not the books I have at home.'

The officer did not answer. He closed the books. 'Now, Mrs Ellis,' he said, 'I can see you are tired, and a rest would do you good. We will try to find your friends for you. If you will go along now, we will get in touch with them as soon as possible. I will send a doctor to you, and he may chat with you a little and give you a sedative, and then, after some rest, you will feel better in the morning and we may have news for you.'

The policewoman helped Mrs Ellis to her feet. 'Come along now,' she said.

'But my house?' said Mrs Ellis. 'Those thieves, and my maid Grace, Grace may be lying in the basement. Surely you are going to do something about the house? You won't permit them to get away with this monstrous crime? Even now we have wasted a precious half-hour—'

'That's all right, Mrs Ellis,' said the officer, 'you can leave everything in our hands.'

The policewoman led her away, still talking, still protesting, and now she was being taken down a corridor, and the police-woman kept saying: 'Now, don't fuss, take it calmly; no one's going to hurt you,' and she was in a little room with a bed; heavens . . . it was a cell, a cell where they put the prisoners, and the policewoman was helping her off with her coat, unpin-ning the scarf that was still tied round her hair, and because Mrs Ellis felt so faint the policewoman made her lie down on the bed, covered her with the coarse grey blanket, placed the little hard pillow under her head.

Mrs Ellis seized the woman's hands. Her face, after all, was not unkind. 'I beg of you,' she said, 'ring up Hampstead 4072, the number of my friend Mrs Draycott, and ask her to come here. The officer won't listen to me. He won't hear my story.'

'Yes, yes, that will be all right,' said the policewoman.

Now somebody else was coming into the room, the cell. Cleanshaven, alert, he carried a case in his hands. He said good evening to the policewoman, and opened his case. He took out a stethoscope and a thermometer. He smiled at Mrs Ellis. 'Feeling a little upset, I hear,' he said. 'Well, we'll soon put that to rights. Now, will you give me your wrist?'

Mrs Ellis sat up on the hard narrow bed, pulling the blanket close. 'Doctor,' she said, 'there is nothing whatever the matter with me. I admit I have been through a terrible experience, quite enough to unnerve anyone; my house has been broken into; no one here will listen to my story, but I am Mrs Ellis, Mrs Wilfred Ellis, if you can possibly persuade the authorities here . . .'

He was not listening to her. With the assistance of the policewoman he was taking her temperature, under her arm, not in the mouth, treating her like a child; and now he was feeling her pulse, dragging down her eyelids, listening to her chest . . . Mrs Ellis went on talking.

'I realise this is a matter of routine. You are obliged to do this. But I want to warn you that my whole treatment, since I have been brought here, since the police came to my house before that, has been infamous, scandalous. I don't personally know our M.P., but I sincerely believe that when he hears my story he will take the matter up, and someone is going to answer for the consequences. Unfortunately I am a widow, no immediate relatives, my little daughter is away at school; my closest friends, a Mr and Mrs Collins, are abroad, but my bank manager . . .'

He was dabbing her arm with spirit; he was inserting a needle, and with a whimper of pain Mrs Ellis fell back on to the hard pillow. The doctor went on holding her arm, and Mrs Ellis, her head going round and round, felt a strange numb sensation as the injection worked into her bloodstream. Tears ran down her cheeks. She could not fight. She was too weak.

'How is that?' said the doctor. 'Better, eh?'

Her throat was parched, her mouth without saliva. It was one of those drugs that paralysed you, made you helpless. But the emotion bubbling within her was eased, was still. The anger, the fear and frustration that had keyed her nerves to a point of contraction seemed to die away. She had explained things badly.

527

The folly of coming out without her handbag had caused half the trouble. And the terrible, wicked cunning of those thieves. 'Be still,' she said to her mind, 'be still. Rest now.'

'Now,' said the doctor, letting go her wrist, 'supposing you tell me your story again. You say your name is Mrs Ellis?'

Mrs Ellis sighed and closed her eyes. Must she go into it all again? Had they not got the whole thing written down in their notebooks? What was the use, when the inefficiency of the whole establishment was so obvious? Those telephone books, directories, with wrong names, wrong addresses. Small wonder there were burglaries, murders, every sort of crime, with a police force that was obviously rotten to the core. What was the name of the Member? It was on the tip of her tongue. A nice man, sandy-haired, always looked so trustworthy on a poster. Hampstead was a safe seat, of course. He would take up her case . . .

'Mrs Ellis,' said the doctor, 'do you think you can remember now your real address?'

Mrs Ellis opened her eyes. Wearily, patiently, she fixed them upon the doctor. 'I live at 17 Elmhurst Road,' she said mechanically. 'I am a widow, my husband has been dead for two years. I have a little girl of nine at school. I went for a short walk on the heath this afternoon after lunch, and when I returned—'

He interrupted her. 'Yes,' he said, 'we know that. We know what happened after your walk. What we want you to tell us is what happened before.'

'I had lunch,' said Mrs Ellis. 'I remember perfectly well what I ate. Guinea fowl and apple charlotte, followed by coffee. Then I nearly decided to take a nap upstairs on my bed, because I was not feeling very well, but decided the air would do me good.'

As soon as she said this, she regretted it. The doctor looked at her keenly. 'Ah!' he said. 'You weren't feeling very well. Can you tell me what the trouble was?'

Mrs Ellis knew what he was after. He and the rest of the police force at the station wanted to certify her as insane. They would make out that she had suffered from some brainstorm, that her whole story was fabrication.

'There was nothing much the matter,' she said quickly. 'I was rather tired from sorting things during the morning. I tidied the linen, cleared out my desk in the drawing-room – all that took time.'

'Can you describe your house, Mrs Ellis?' he said. 'The furniture, for instance, of your bedroom, your drawing-room?'

'Very easily,' she answered, 'but you must remember that the thieves who broke into the house this afternoon have done what I begin to fear is irreparable damage. Everything had been seized, hidden away. The rooms were strewn with rubbish, and there was a young woman upstairs in my bedroom pretending to be a photographer.'

'Yes,' he said, 'don't worry about that. Just tell me about your furniture, how the various things were placed, and so on.'

He was more sympathetic than she had thought. Mrs Ellis launched into a description of every room in her house. She named the ornaments, the pictures, the position of the chairs and tables.

'And you say your cook is called Grace Jackson?'

'Yes, Doctor, she has been with me several years. She was in the kitchen when I left this afternoon; I remember most distinctly calling down to the basement and saying that I was going for a short walk and would not be long. I am extremely worried about her, Doctor. Those thieves will have got hold of her, perhaps kidnapped her.'

'We'll see to that,' said the doctor. 'Now, Mrs Ellis, you have been very helpful, and you have given such a clear account of your home that I think we shan't be long in tracing it, and your relations. You must stay here tonight, and I hope in the morning we shall have news for you. Now, you say your small daughter is at school? Can you remember the address?'

'Of course,' said Mrs Ellis, 'and the telephone number too. The school is High Close, Bishops' Lane, Hatchworth, and the telephone number is Hatchworth 202. But I don't understand what you mean about tracing my home.'

'There is nothing to worry about,' said the doctor. 'You are not ill, and you are not lying, I quite realise that. You are suffering from a temporary loss of memory that often happens to all sorts of people, and it quickly passes. We've had many cases before.' He smiled. He stood up, his case in his hand.

'But it isn't true,' said Mrs Ellis, trying to raise herself from the pillow. 'My memory is perfectly all right. I have given you every detail I can think of; I have told you my name, where I live, a description of my home, the address of my daughter at school . . .'

'All right,' he said. 'Now, don't worry. Just try to relax and have a little sleep. We shall find your friends for you.'

He murmured something to the policewoman and left the cell. The policewoman came over to the bed and tucked in the blanket.

'Now, cheer up,' she said, 'do as the doctor said. Get a little rest. Everything will be all right, you'll see.'

Rest . . . but how? Relax . . . But to what purpose? Even now her house was being looted, sacked, every room stripped. The thieves getting clear away with their booty, leaving no trace behind them. They would take Grace with them; poor Grace could not come down to the police station to give witness to her identity. But the people next door, the Furbers, surely they would be good enough; it would not be too much trouble . . . Mrs Ellis supposed she should have called, been more friendly, had them to tea, but after all, people did not expect that unless they lived in the country, it was out of date.

If the police officer had not got hold of Netta Draycott then the Furbers must be got in touch with at once . . .

Mrs Ellis plucked at the policewoman's sleeve. 'The Furbers,' she said, 'next door, at number 19, they will vouch for me. They are not friends of mine, but they know me well by sight. We have been neighbours for quite six years. The Furbers.'

'Yes,' said the policewoman, 'try to get some sleep.'

Oh, Susan, my Susan, if this had happened in the holidays, how much more fearful; what would we have done? Coming back from an afternoon walk to find those devils in the house, and then, who knows, that dreadful photographer woman and her husband taking a fancy to Susan, so pretty, so fair, and wanting to kidnap her . . . At least the child was safe, knew nothing of what was happening, and if only the story could be kept out of the newspapers, she need never know. So shameful, so degrading, a night spent in a prison cell through such crass stupidity, such appalling blunders . . .

'You've had a good sleep, then,' said the policewoman, handing her a cup of tea.

'I don't know what you mean,' said Mrs Ellis. 'I haven't slept at all.'

'Oh, yes, you have.' The woman smiled. 'They all say that.'

Mrs Ellis blinked, sat up on the narrow bed. She had been speaking to the policewoman only a moment before. Her head ached abominably. She sipped at the tea, tasteless, unrefreshing. She yearned for her bed at home, for Grace coming in noiselessly, drawing the curtains.

'You're to have a wash,' said the policewoman, 'and I'll give you a comb through, and then you are to see the doctor again.'

Mrs Ellis suffered the indignity of washing under supervision, of having her hair combed; then her scarf and coat and gloves were given to her again and she was taken out of the cell, along the corridor, back through the hall to the room where they had questioned her the night before. This time a different officer sat at the desk, but she recognised the police constable, and the doctor too.

The last came towards her with that same bland smile on his face. 'How are you feeling today?' he said. 'A little more like your true self?'

'On the contrary,' said Mrs Ellis, 'I am feeling very unwell indeed, and shall continue to do so until I know what has happened at home. Is anyone here prepared to tell me what has happened since last night? Has anything at all been done to safeguard my property?'

The doctor did not answer, but guided her towards the chair at the desk. 'Now,' he said, 'the officer here wants to show you a picture in a newspaper.'

Mrs Ellis sat down in the chair. The officer handed her a copy of the *News of the World* – a paper Grace took on Sundays; Mrs Ellis never looked at it – and there was a photograph of a woman with a scarf round her head and chubby cheeks, wearing some sort of light-coloured coat. The photograph had a red circle round it, and underneath was written: 'Missing from Home, Ada Lewis, aged 36, widow, of 105 Albert Buildings, Kentish Town.' She handed the paper back across the desk. 'I'm afraid I can't help you,' she said. 'I don't know this woman.'

'The name Ada Lewis conveys nothing to you?' said the officer. 'Nor Albert Buildings?'

'No,' said Mrs Ellis, 'certainly not.'

Suddenly she knew the purpose of the interrogation. The police thought that she was this missing woman, this Ada Lewis from Albert Buildings. Simply because she wore a light-coloured coat and had a scarf round her hair. She rose from the chair.

'This is absolutely preposterous,' she said. 'I have told you my name and my address, and you persist in disbelieving me.

532

My detention here is an outrage; I demand to see a lawyer, my own lawyer . . .' But wait, she hadn't needed the services of a lawyer since Wilfred died, and the firm had moved or been taken over by somebody else; better not give the name; they would think she was lying once again; it was safer to give the name of the bank manager . . .

'One moment,' said the officer, and she was interrupted once again, because somebody else came into the room, a seedy, common-looking man in a checked shabby suit, holding his trilby hat in his hand. 'Can you identify this woman as your sister, Ada Lewis?' asked the officer.

A flush of fury swept Mrs Ellis as the man stepped forward and peered into her face. 'No, sir,' he said, 'this isn't Ada. Ada isn't so stout, and this woman's teeth seem to be her own. Ada wore dentures. Never seen this woman before.'

'Thank you,' said the officer, 'that's all. You can go. We will let you know if we find your sister.'

The seedy-looking man left the room. Mrs Ellis turned in triumph to the officer behind the desk. 'Now,' she said, 'perhaps you will believe me?'

The officer considered her for a moment, and then, glancing at the doctor, looked down at some notes on his desk. 'Much as I would like to believe you,' he said, 'for it would save us all a great deal of trouble if I could, unfortunately I can't. Your facts have been proved wrong in every particular. So far.'

'What do you mean?' said Mrs Ellis.

'First, your address. You do not live at 17 Elmhurst Road because the house is occupied by various tenants who have lived there for some time and who are known to us. Number 17 is an apartment house and the floors are let separately. You are not one of the tenants.'

Mrs Ellis gripped the sides of her chair. The obstinate, proud, and completely unmoved face of the officer stared back at her.

'You are mistaken,' she said quietly. 'Number 17 is not a lodging-house. It is a private house. My own.'

The officer glanced down again at his notes. 'There are no people called Furber living at number 19,' he went on. 'Number 19 is also a lodging-house. You are not in the directory under the name of Ellis, nor in the telephone book. There is no Ellis on the register of the branch of the bank you mentioned to us last night. Nor can we trace anyone of the name of Grace Jackson in the district.'

Mrs Ellis looked up at the doctor, at the police constable, at the policewoman, who was still standing by her side. 'Is there some conspiracy?' she said. 'Why are you all against me? I don't understand what I have done . . .' Her voice faltered. She must not break down. She must be firm with them, be brave, for Susan's sake. 'You rang up my friend at Charlton Court?' she she asked. 'Mrs Draycott, that big block of flats?'

'Mrs Draycott is not living at Charlton Court, Mrs Ellis,' said the police officer, 'for the simple reason that Charlton Court no longer exists. It was destroyed by a fire bomb.'

Mrs Ellis stared at him in horror. A fire bomb? But how perfectly terrible! When? How? In the night? Disaster upon disaster . . . Who could have done it, anarchists, strikers, unemployed, gangs of people, possibly those who had broken into her house? Poor Netta and her husband and children; Mrs Ellis felt her head reeling . . .

'Forgive me,' she said, summoning her strength, her dignity, 'I had no idea there had been such a fearful outrage. No doubt part of the same plot, those people in my house . . .'

Then she stopped, because she realised they were lying to her; everything was lies; they were not policemen; they had seized the building; they were spies; the government was to be overthrown; but then why bother with her, with a simple harmless individual like herself; why were they not getting on with the civil war, bringing machine guns into the street, marching to Buckingham Palace; why sit here, pretending to her?

A policeman came into the room and clicked his heels and stood before the desk. 'Checked up on all the nursing homes,' he said, 'and the mental homes, sir, in the district, and within a radius of five miles. Nobody missing.'

'Thank you,' said the officer. Ignoring Mrs Ellis, he looked across at the doctor. 'We can't keep her here,' he said. 'You'll have to persuade them to take her at Moreton Hill. The matron *must* find a room. Say it's a temporary measure. Case of amnesia.'

'I'll do what I can,' said the doctor.

Moreton Hill. Mrs Ellis knew at once what they meant by Moreton Hill. It was a well-known mental home somewhere near Highgate, very badly run, she always heard, a dreadful place.

'Moreton Hill?' she said. 'You can't possibly take me there. It has a shocking reputation. The nurses are always leaving. I refuse to go to Moreton Hill. I demand to see a lawyer – no, my doctor, Dr Godber; he lives in Parkwell Gardens.'

The officer stared at her thoughtfully. 'She must be a local woman,' he said; 'she gets the names right every time. But Godber went to Portsmouth, didn't he? I remember Godber.'

'If he's at Portsmouth,' said Mrs Ellis, 'he would only have gone for a few days. He's most conscientious. But his secretary knows me. I took Susan there last holidays.'

Nobody listened to her, though, and the officer was consulting his notes again. 'By the way,' he said, 'you gave me the name of that school correctly. Wrong telephone number, but right school. Co-educational. We got through to them last night.'

'I'm afraid then,' said Mrs Ellis, 'that you got the wrong school. High Close is most certainly not co-educational, and I should never have sent Susan there if it had been.'

'High Close,' repeated the officer, reading from his notes, 'is a co-educational school, run by a Mr Foster and his wife.'

'It is run by a Miss Slater,' said Mrs Ellis, 'a Miss Hilda Slater.'

'You mean it *was* run by a Miss Slater,' said the officer. 'A Miss Slater had the school and then retired, and it was taken over by Mr and Mrs Foster. They have no pupil there of the name of Susan Ellis.'

Mrs Ellis sat very still in her chair. She looked at each face in turn. None was harsh. None was unfriendly. And the police-woman smiled encouragement. They all watched her steadily. At last she said: 'You are not deliberately trying to mislead me? You do realise that I am anxious, most desperately anxious, to know what has happened? If all that you are saying is some kind of a game, some kind of torture, would you tell me so that I know, so that I can understand?'

The doctor took her hand, and the officer leant forward in his chair. 'We are trying to help you,' he said. 'We are doing everything we can to find your friends.'

Mrs Ellis held tight to the doctor's hand. It had suddenly become a refuge. 'I don't understand,' she said, 'what has happened. If I am suffering from loss of memory, why do I remember everything so clearly? My address, my name, people, the school . . . Where is Susan; where is my little girl?' She looked round her in blind panic. She tried to rise from the chair. 'If Susan is not at High Close, where is she?'

Someone was patting her on the shoulder. Someone was giving her a glass of water.

'If Miss Slater had retired to give place to a Mr and Mrs Foster, I should have heard, they would have told me,' she kept repeating. 'I telephoned the school only yesterday. Susan was quite well, and playing in the grounds.'

'Are you suggesting that Miss Slater answered you herself?' enquired the officer.

'No, the secretary answered. I telephoned because I had . . . what seemed to me a premonition that Susan might not be well. The secretary assured me that the child had eaten a good lunch and was playing. I am not making this up. It happened yesterday. I tell you, the secretary would have told me if Miss Slater was making changes in the school.'

Mrs Ellis searched the doubtful faces fixed upon her. And momentarily her attention was caught by the large 2 on the calendar standing on the desk.

'I *know* it was yesterday,' she said, 'because today is the second of the month, isn't it? And I distinctly remember tearing off the page in my calendar, and because it was the first of the month I decided to tidy my desk, sort out my papers, during the morning.'

The police officer relaxed and smiled. 'You are certainly very convincing,' he said, 'and we can all tell from your appearance, the fact that you have no money on you, that your shoes are polished, and other little signs, that you do definitely belong somewhere in this district; you have not wandered from any great distance. But you do not come from 17 Elmhurst Road, Mrs Ellis, that is quite certain. For some reason, which we hope to discover, that address has become fixed in your mind, and other addresses too. I promise you everything will be done to clear your mind and to get you well again; and you need have no fear about going to Moreton Hill; I know it well, and they will look after you there.'

Mrs Ellis saw herself shut up behind those grey forbidding walls, grimly situated, frowning down upon the further ponds the far side of the heath. She had skirted those walls many times, pitying the inmates within. The man who came with the groceries had a wife who became insane. Mrs Ellis remembered Grace coming to her one morning full of the story, 'and he says they've taken her to Moreton Hill.' Once inside, she

537

would never get out. These men at the police station would not bother with her any more. And now there was this new, hideous misunderstanding about Susan, and the talk of a Mr and Mrs Foster taking over the school.

Mrs Ellis leant forward, clasping her hands together. 'I do assure you,' she said, 'that I don't want to make trouble. I have always been a very quiet, peaceable sort of person, not easily excited, never quarrelsome, and if I have really lost my memory I will do what the doctor tells me, take any drugs or medicines that will help. But I am worried, desperately worried, about my little girl and what you have told me about the school and Miss Slater's having retired. Would you do just one thing for me? Telephone the school and ask them where you can get in touch with Miss Slater. It is just possible that she has taken the house down the road and removed there with some of the children, Susan amongst them; and whoever answered the telephone was new to the work and gave you vague information.'

She spoke clearly, without any sort of hysteria or emotion; they must see that she was in deadly earnest, and this request of hers was not wild fancy.

The police officer glanced at the doctor, then he seemed to make up his mind. 'Very well,' he said, 'we will do that. We will try to contact this Miss Slater, but it may take time. Meanwhile, I think it is best if you wait in another room while we put through the enquiry.'

Mrs Ellis stood up, this time without the help of the police-woman. She was determined to show that she was well, mentally and bodily, and quite capable of managing her affairs without the assistance of anybody, if it could be permitted. She wished she had a hat instead of the scarf, which she knew instinctively was unbecoming, and her hands were lost without her handbag. At least she had gloves. But gloves were not enough. She nodded briskly to the police officer and the doctor – at all costs she must show civility – and followed the policewoman to a waiting room. This time she was spared the indignity of a cell. Another cup of tea was brought to her.

'It's all they think about,' she said to herself, 'cups of tea, instead of getting on with their job.'

Suddenly she remembered poor Netta Draycott and the terrible tragedy of the fire bomb. Possibly she and her family had escaped and were now with friends, but there was no immediate means of finding out. 'Is it all in the morning papers about the disaster?' she asked the policewoman.

'What disaster?' said the woman.

'The fire at Charlton Court the officer spoke to me about.'

The policewoman stared at her with a puzzled expression. 'I don't remember him saying anything about a fire,' she said.

'Oh, yes, he did,' said Mrs Ellis. 'He told me that Charlton Court had been destroyed by fire, by some bomb. I was aghast to hear it because I have friends living there. It must surely be in all the morning papers.'

The woman's face cleared. 'Oh, that,' she said. 'I think the officer was referring to some fire bomb during the war.'

'No, no,' said Mrs Ellis impatiently. 'Charlton Court was built a long time after the war. I remember the block being built when my husband and I first came to Hampstead. No, this accident apparently happened last night, the most dreadful thing.'

The policewoman shrugged her shoulders. 'I think you're mistaken,' she said; 'there's been no talk of any accident or disaster here.'

An ignorant, silly sort of girl, thought Mrs Ellis. It was a wonder she had passed her test into the force. She thought they only employed very intelligent women. She sipped her tea in silence. No use carrying on any sort of conversation with her. It seemed a long while before the door opened, but when it did it was to reveal the doctor, who stood on the threshold with a smile on his face.

'Well,' he said, 'I think we're a little nearer home. We were able to contact Miss Slater.'

Mrs Ellis rose to her feet, her eyes shining. 'Oh, Doctor, thank heaven . . . Have you news of my daughter?'

'Steady a moment now. You mustn't get excited or we shall have all last night's trouble over again, and that would never do. I take it, when you refer to your daughter, you mean someone who is called, or was called, Susan Ellis?'

'Yes, yes, of course,' said Mrs Ellis swiftly. 'Is she all right, is she with Miss Slater?'

'No, she is not with Miss Slater, but she is perfectly well. I have spoken to her on the telephone myself, and I have her present address here in my notebook.' The doctor patted his breast pocket and smiled again.

'Not with Miss Slater?' Mrs Ellis stared in bewilderment. 'Then the school *has* been handed over; you spoke to these people called Foster. Is it next door? Have they moved far? What has happened?'

The doctor took her hand and led her to the seat once more. 'Now,' he said, 'I want you to think quite calmly and quite clearly and not be agitated in any way, and your trouble will be cleared up, your mind will be free again. You remember last night you gave us the name of your maid, Grace Jackson?'

'Yes, Doctor.'

'Now, take your time. Tell us a little about Grace Jackson.'

'Have you found her? Is she at home? Is she all right?'

'Never mind for the moment. Describe Grace Jackson.'

Mrs Ellis was horribly afraid poor Grace had been found murdered, and they were going to ask her to identify the body. 'She is a big girl,' she said, 'at least not really a girl, about my own age, but you know how one is inclined to talk of a servant as a girl; she has a large bust, rather thick ankles, brownish hair, grey eyes, and she would be wearing, let me see, I think she may not have changed into her cap and apron when those thieves arrived; she was still probably in her overalls. She is inclined to change rather late in the afternoon; I have often spoken about it; it looks so bad to open the front door in overalls, slovenly, like a boarding-house. Grace has good teeth and a pleasant expression, though of course if anything has happened to her she would hardly—' Mrs Ellis broke off. Murdered, battered. Grace would not be smiling.

The doctor did not seem to notice this. He was looking closely at Mrs Ellis. 'You know,' he said, 'you have given a very accurate description of yourself.'

'Myself?' said Mrs Ellis.

'Yes. Figure, colouring, and so on. We think, you know, it is just possible that your amnesia has taken the form of mistaken identity and that you are really Grace Jackson, believing yourself to be a Mrs Ellis, and now we are doing our best to trace the relatives of Grace Jackson.'

This was too much. Mrs Ellis swallowed. Outraged pride rose in her. 'Doctor,' she said rapidly, 'you have gone a little too far. I bear no sort of resemblance to my maid, Grace Jackson, and if and when you ever find trace of the unfortunate girl, she would be the first to agree with me. Grace has been in my employment seven years; she came originally from Scotland; her parents were Scottish, I believe – in fact, I know it, because she used to go for her holiday to Aberdeen. Grace is a good, hard-working, and I like to think honest girl; we have had our little ups and downs, but nothing serious; she is inclined to be obstinate; I am obstinate myself – who is not? – but . . .'

If only the doctor would not look at her in that smiling,

patronising way. 'You see,' he said, 'you do know a very great deal about Grace Jackson.'

Mrs Ellis could have hit him. He was so self-assured, so confident. 'I must keep my temper,' she told herself. 'I must, I must . . .' Aloud she said: 'Doctor, I know about Grace Jackson because, as I have told you, she has been in my employment for seven years. If she is found ill or in any way hurt, I shall hold the police force here responsible, because, in spite of my entreaties, I do not believe they kept a watch on my house last night. Now perhaps you will be good enough to tell me where I can find my child. She, at least, will recognise me.'

Mrs Ellis considered she had been very restrained, very calm. In spite of terrible provocation she had not lost control of herself.

'You insist that your age is thirty-five?' said the doctor, switching the subject. 'And that Grace Jackson was approximately the same?'

'I was thirty-five in August last,' said Mrs Ellis. 'I believe Grace to be a year younger, I am not sure.'

'You certainly don't look more,' said the doctor, smiling.

Surely, at such a moment, he was not going to attempt to appease her by gallantry?

'But,' he continued, 'following upon the telephone conversation I have just had, Grace Jackson would be, today, at least fifty-five or fifty-six.'

'There are probably,' said Mrs Ellis icily, 'several persons of the name of Grace Jackson employed as domestic servants. If you propose tracing every one of them, it will take you and the police force a considerable time. I am sorry to insist, but I must know the whereabouts of my daughter Susan before anything else.'

He was relenting; she could see it in his eye. 'As a matter of fact,' he said, 'it happens, very conveniently, that Miss Slater was able to put us in touch with her; we have spoken to her on the telephone, and she is only a short distance away, in St John's Wood. She is not sure, but she thinks she would remember Grace Jackson if she saw her.'

For a moment Mrs Ellis was speechless. What in the world was Susan doing in St John's Wood? And how monstrous to drag the child to the telephone and question her about Grace. Of course she would be bewildered and say she 'thought' she would remember Grace, though goodness only knows it was only two months since Grace was waving her good-bye from the doorstep when she left for school.

Then she suddenly remembered the Zoo. Perhaps, if these changes at school were all being decided upon in a great hurry, one of the junior mistresses had taken a party of children up to London to the Zoo, to be out of the way. The Zoo or Madame Tussaud's.

'Do you know where she spoke from?' asked Mrs Ellis sharply. 'I mean, somebody was in charge, somebody was looking after her?'

'She spoke from 2a Halifax Avenue,' said the doctor, 'and I don't think you will find she needs any looking after. She sounded very capable, and I heard her turn from the telephone and call to a little boy named Keith to keep quiet and not make so much noise, because she couldn't hear herself speak.'

A tremor of a smile appeared on Mrs Ellis's lips. How clever of Susan to have shown herself so quick and lively. It was just like her, though. She was so advanced for her age. Such a little companion. But Keith . . . It sounded very much as though the school *had* suddenly become co-educational; this was a mixed party being taken to the Zoo or Madame Tussaud's. They were all having lunch, perhaps, at Halifax Avenue, relations of Miss Slater's, or these Fosters, but really the whole thing was most inexcusable, that changes should come about like this, and the

543

children be taken backwards and forwards from High Close to London without any attempt to notify the parents. Mrs Ellis would write very strongly to Miss Slater about it, and if the school had changed hands and was to be co-educational, she would remove Susan at the end of the term.

'Doctor,' she said, 'I am ready to go to Halifax Avenue at once, if the authorities here will only permit me to do so.'

'Very well,' said the doctor. 'I am afraid I can't accompany you, but we have arranged for that, and Sister Henderson, who knows all about the matter, will go with you.'

He nodded to the policewoman, who opened the door of the waiting room and admitted a severe middle-aged woman in nurse's uniform. Mrs Ellis said nothing, but her mouth tightened. She was very sure that Sister Henderson had been summoned from Moreton Hill.

'Now, Sister,' said the doctor cheerfully, 'this is the lady, and you know where to take her and what to do; and I think you will only be a few minutes at Halifax Avenue, and then we hope things will be straightened out.'

'Yes, Doctor,' said the nurse. She looked across at Mrs Ellis with a quick professional eye.

'If only I had a hat,' thought Mrs Ellis, 'if only I had not come out with nothing but this wretched scarf, and I can feel bits and pieces of hair straggling at the back of my neck. No powder compact on me, no comb, nothing. Of course I must look terrible to them, ungroomed, common . . .'

She straightened her shoulders, resisted an impulse to put her hands in her pockets. She walked stiffly towards the open door. The doctor, the Sister, and the policewoman conducted her down the steps of the police station to a waiting car. A uniformed chauffeur was to drive, she was thankful to see, and she climbed into the car, followed by the Sister.

The awful thought flashed through her mind that there

might be some charge for the night's lodging in the cell and for the cups of tea; also, should she have tipped the police-woman? But anyway, she had no money. It was impossible. She nodded brightly to the policewoman as a sort of sop, to show she had no ill feeling. She felt rather different towards the doctor. She bowed rather formally, coldly. The car drove away.

Mrs Ellis wondered if she was expected to make conversation with the Sister, who sat stalwart and forbidding at her side. Better not, perhaps. Anything she said might be taken as evidence of mental disturbance. She stared straight in front of her, her gloved hands primly folded on her lap. The traffic jams were very bad, worse than she had ever known. There must be a motor exhibition on. So many American cars on the road. A rally, perhaps . . .

She did not think much of Halifax Avenue when they came to it. Houses very shabby, and quite a number with windows broken. The car drew up at a small house that had 2a written on the pillar outside. Curious place to take a party of children for lunch. A good Lyons café would have been so much better.

The Sister got out of the car and waited to help Mrs Ellis. 'We shan't be long,' she said to the chauffeur.

'That's what you think,' said Mrs Ellis to herself, 'but I shall certainly stay with Susan as long as I please.'

They walked through the piece of front garden to the front door. The Sister rang the bell. Mrs Ellis saw a face looking at them from the front window and then quickly dart behind a curtain. Good heavens . . . It was Dorothy, Wilfred's younger sister, who was a schoolteacher in Birmingham; of course it was, it must be . . . Everything became clearer; the Fosters must know Dorothy; people to do with education always knew each other, but how awkward, what a bore. Mrs Ellis had never cared for Dorothy, had stopped writing to her in fact; Dorothy had been so unpleasant when poor Wilfred died, and had insisted that the writing bureau was hers, and rather a nice piece of jewellery that Mrs Ellis had always understood Wilfred's mother had given to her, Mrs Ellis; and in fact the whole afternoon after the funeral had been spent in such unpleasant argument and discussion that Mrs Ellis had been only too glad to send Dorothy away with the jewellery, and the bureau, and a very nice rug to which she had no right at all. Dorothy was the last person Mrs Ellis wanted to see, and especially in these very trying circumstances, with this Sister at her side, and herself looking so untidy, without a hat or a bag.

There was no time to compose herself because the door opened. No . . . no, it was not Dorothy after all, but . . . how strange, so very like her. That same thin nose and rather peeved expression. A little taller, perhaps, and the hair was lighter. The resemblance, though, was really quite extraordinary.

'Are you Mrs Drew?' asked the Sister.

'Yes,' answered the young woman, and then because a child was calling from an inner room she called back over her shoulder impatiently, 'Oh, be quiet, Keith, do, for heaven's sake.'

A little boy of about five appeared along the hall dragging a toy on wheels. 'Dear little fellow,' thought Mrs Ellis, 'what a tiresome nagging mother. But where are all the children; where is Susan?'

'This is the person I have brought along for you to identify,' said the Sister.

'You had better come inside,' said Mrs Drew rather grudgingly. 'I'm afraid everything's in a fearful mess. I've got no help, and you know how it is.'

Mrs Ellis, whose temper was beginning to rise again, stepped neatly over a broken toy on the door mat and, followed by the Sister, went into what she supposed was this Mrs Drew's living-room. It was certainly a mess. Remains of breakfast not cleared away – or was it lunch? – and toys everywhere, and some material for cutting out spread on a table by the window.

Mrs Drew laughed apologetically. 'What with Keith's toys and my material – I'm a dressmaker in my spare time – and trying to get a decent meal for my husband when he comes home in the evening, life isn't a bed of roses,' she said. Her voice was *so* like Dorothy's. Mrs Ellis could hardly take her eyes off her. The same note of complaint.

'We don't want to take up your time,' said the Sister civilly, 'if you will just say whether this person is Grace Jackson or not.'

The young woman, Mrs Drew, stared at Mrs Ellis thoughtfully. 'No,' she said at length, 'I'm sure she is not. I haven't seen Grace for years, not since I married; I used to look her up in Hampstead occasionally before then; but she had quite a different appearance from this person. She was stouter, darker, older too.'

'Thank you,' said the Sister, 'then you are sure you have never seen this lady before?'

'No, never,' said Mrs Drew.

'Very well then,' said the Sister, 'we needn't detain you any longer.'

She turned, as though to go, but Mrs Ellis was not to be fobbed off with the nonsense that had just passed.

'Excuse me,' she said to Mrs Drew, 'there has been a most unfortunate misunderstanding all round, but I understand you spoke to the doctor at the police station at Hampstead this morning, or someone did from this house, and that you have a party of school children here from High Close, my child amongst them. Can you tell me if she is still here; is anyone from the school in charge?'

The Sister was about to intervene, but Mrs Drew did not notice this, because the little boy had come into the room, dragging his toy. 'Keith, I *told* you to stay outside,' she nagged.

Mrs Ellis smiled at the boy. She loved all children. 'What a pretty boy,' she said, and she held out her hand to him. He took it, holding it tight.

'He doesn't usually take to strangers,' said Mrs Drew, 'he's very shy. It makes me wild at times when he won't speak and hangs his head.'

'I was shy myself as a child, I understand it,' said Mrs Ellis.

Keith looked up at her with confidence and trust. Her heart warmed to him. But she was forgetting Susan . . . 'We were talking about the party from High Close,' she said.

'Yes,' said Mrs Drew, 'but that police officer was rather an idiot, I'm afraid, and got everything wrong. My name was Susan Ellis before I married, and I used to go to school at High Close, and that's where the mistake came in. There are no children from the school here.'

'What a remarkable coincidence,' said Mrs Ellis, smiling, 'because my name is Ellis, and my daughter is called Susan, and an even stranger coincidence is that you are so like a sister of my late husband's.'

'Oh?' said Mrs Drew. 'Well, the name is common enough, isn't it? The butcher is Ellis, down the road.'

Mrs Ellis flushed. Not a very tactful remark. And she felt suddenly nervous, too, because the Sister was advancing and was leaning forward as though to take her by the arm and walk to the front door. Mrs Ellis was determined not to leave the house. Or, at any rate, not to leave it with the Sister.

'I've always found High Close such a homey sort of school,' she said rapidly, 'but I am rather distressed about the changes they are making there, and I am afraid it is going to be on rather a different tone in the future.'

'I don't think they've changed it much,' said Mrs Drew. 'Most small children are horrible little beasts, anyway, and it does them good not to see too much of their parents and to be thoroughly well mixed up with every sort of type.'

'I'm afraid I don't agree with you on that,' said Mrs Ellis. So peculiar. The tone, the expression might have been Dorothy's.

'Of course,' said Mrs Drew, 'I can't help being grateful to old Slaty. She's a funny old stick, but a heart of gold, and she did her best for me, I'll say that, and kept me in the holidays after my mother was killed in a street accident.'

'How good of her,' said Mrs Ellis, 'and what a dreadful thing for you.'

Mrs Drew laughed. 'I was pretty tough, I think,' she said. 'I don't remember much about it. But I do remember my mother was a very kind person, and pretty too. I think Keith takes after her.'

The little boy had not relinquished Mrs Ellis's hand.

'It's time we were getting along,' said the Sister. 'Come now, Mrs Drew has told us all we need to know.'

'I don't want to go,' said Mrs Ellis calmly, 'and you have no right to make me go.'

The Sister exchanged a glance with Mrs Drew. 'I'm sorry,' she said in a low tone, 'I shall have to get the chauffeur. I wanted them to send another nurse with me, but they said it wouldn't be necessary.'

'That's all right,' said Mrs Drew. 'So many people are bats these days, one extra doesn't make much difference. But perhaps I had better remove Keith to the kitchen, or she may kidnap him.'

Keith, protesting, was carried from the room.

Once again the Sister looked at Mrs Ellis. 'Come along now,' she said, 'be reasonable.'

'No,' said Mrs Ellis, and with a quickness that surprised herself she reached out to the table where Mrs Drew had been cutting out material, and seized the pair of scissors. 'If you come near me, I shall stab you,' she said.

The Sister turned and went quickly out of the room and down the steps, calling for the chauffeur. The next few moments passed quickly, but for all this Mrs Ellis had time to realise that her tactics were brilliant, rivalling the heroes of detective fiction. She crossed the room, opened the long french windows that gave on to a back yard. The window of the bedroom was open; she could hear the chauffeur calling.

'Tradesmen's entrance is ajar,' he shouted. 'She must have gone this way.'

'Let them go on with their confusion,' thought Mrs Ellis, leaning against the bed. 'Let them. Good luck to them in their running about. This will take down some of the Sister's weight. Not much running about for her at Moreton Hill. Cups of tea at all hours, and sweet biscuits, while the patients are given bread and water.'

The movement went on for some time. Somebody used the telephone. There was more talk. And then, when Mrs Ellis was nearly dozing off against the bed valance, she heard the car drive away. Everything was silent. Mrs Ellis listened. The only sound was the little boy playing in the hall below. She crept to the door and listened once again. The wheeled toy was being dragged backwards and forwards, up and down the hall. And there was a new sound coming from the living-room. The sound of a sewing-machine going at great speed. Mrs Drew was at work.

The Sister and the chauffeur had gone. An hour, two hours must have passed since they had left. Mrs Ellis glanced at the clock on the mantelpiece. It was two o'clock. What an untidy, scattered sort of room, everything all over the place. Shoes in the middle of the floor, a coat flung down on a chair, and Keith's cot had not been made up; the blankets were rumpled anyhow.

'Badly brought up,' thought Mrs Ellis, 'and such rough, casual manners. But poor girl, if she had no mother . . .'

She took a last glance round the room, and she saw with a shrug of her shoulder that even Mrs Drew's calendar had a printing error. It said 1952 instead of 1932. How careless . . .

She tiptoed to the head of the stairs. The door of the living-room was shut. The sound of the sewing-machine came at breathless speed. 'They must be hard up,' thought Mrs Ellis, 'if she has to do dressmaking. I wonder what her husband does for a living.' Softly she crept downstairs. She made no sound. And if she had, the sound of the sewing-machine would have covered it. As she passed the living-room door it opened. The boy stood there, staring at her. He said nothing. He smiled. Mrs Ellis smiled back at him. She could not help herself. She had a feeling that he would not give her away.

'Shut the door, Keith, *do*,' nagged his mother from within. The door slammed. The sound of the sewing-machine became more distant, muffled. Mrs Ellis let herself out of the house and slipped away . . . She turned northward, like an animal scenting direction, because northward was her home.

She was soon swallowed up in traffic, the buses swinging past her in the Finchley Road. Her feet began to ache and she was tired, but she could not take a bus or summon a taxi because she had no money. No one looked at her; no one bothered with her; they were all intent upon their business, either going from home or returning, and it seemed to Mrs Ellis, as she toiled up the hill towards Hampstead, that for the first time in her life she was friendless and alone. She wanted her house, her home, the consolation of her own surroundings; she wanted to take up her normal, everyday life that had been interrupted in so brutal a fashion. There was so much to straighten out, so much to do, and Mrs Ellis did not know where to begin or whom to ask for help.

'I want everything to be as it was before that walk yesterday,'

551

thought Mrs Ellis, her back aching, her feet throbbing. 'I want my home. I want my little girl.'

And here was the heath once again. This was where she had stood before crossing the road. She even remembered what she had been thinking about. She had been planning to buy a red bicycle for Susan. Something light – but strong, a good make.

The memory of the bicycle made her forget her troubles, her fatigue. As soon as all this muddle and confusion were over, she would buy a red bicycle for Susan.

Why, though, for the second time, that screech of brakes when she crossed the road, and the vacant face of the laundry boy looking down at her?

The Breakthrough

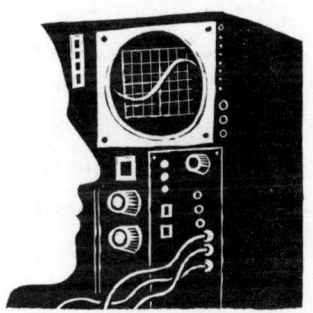

My part in the affair started on September 18th, when my chief sent for me and told me he was transferring me to Saxmere on the east coast. He was sorry about it, he said, but I was the only one with the necessary technical qualifications for the particular work they had on hand. No, he couldn't give me any details; they were an odd lot down there, and shut themselves up behind barbed wire at the slightest provocation. The place had been a radar experimental station a few years back, but this was finished, and any experiments that were going on now were of an entirely different nature, something to do with vibrations and the pitch of sound.

'I'll be perfectly frank with you,' said my chief, removing his horn-rimmed spectacles and waving them in the air apologetically. 'The fact is that James MacLean is a very old friend of mine. We were at Cambridge together and I saw a lot of him then and afterwards, but our paths diverged, and he tied himself up in experimental work of rather a dubious nature. Lost the government a lot of money, and didn't do his own reputation much good either. I gather that's forgotten, and he's been reinstated down at Saxmere with his own hand-picked team of experts and a government grant. They're stuck for an electronics engineer – which is where you come in. MacLean has sent me an S.O.S. for someone I can vouch for personally – in other words, he wants a chap who won't talk. You'd do me a personal favour if you went.'

Put like this, there was little I could do but accept. It was a damned nuisance, all the same. The last thing in the world I wanted to do was to leave Associated Electronics Ltd, and its unique facilities for research, and drift off to the east coast to work for someone who had blotted his copybook once and might do so again.

'When do you want me to go?' I asked.

The chief looked more apologetic than ever.

'As soon as you can make it. The day after tomorrow? I'm really very sorry, Saunders. With any luck you'll be back by Christmas. I've told MacLean I'm lending you to him for this particular project only. No question of a long-term transfer. You're too valuable here.'

This was the sop. The pat on the back. A.E.L. would forget about me for the next three months. I had another question, though.

'What sort of a chap is he?'

'MacLean?' My chief paused before replacing his horn-rims, always a signal of dismissal. 'He's what I'd call an enthusiast, the kind that don't let go. A fanatic in his way. Oh, he won't bore you. I remember at Cambridge he spent most of his time bird-watching. He had some peculiar theory then about migration, but he didn't inflict it on us. He nearly chucked physics for neurology, but thought better of it – the girl he later married persuaded him. Then came the tragedy. She died after they'd only been married a year.'

My chief replaced his spectacles. He had no more to say or, if he had, it was beside the point. As I was leaving the room he called after me, 'You can keep that last piece of information to yourself. About his wife, I mean. His staff down there may not know anything about it.'

It was not until I had actually packed up at A.E.L. and left my comfortable digs, and the train was drawing out of Liverpool Street station, that the full force of my situation hit me. Here I was, lumbered with a job I didn't want in an outfit I knew nothing about, and all as a personal favour to my chief, who obviously had some private reason for obliging his one-time colleague. As I stared moodily out of the carriage window, feeling more bloody-minded every minute, I kept seeing the expression on my successor's face when I told him I was going to Saxmere.

'That dump?' he said. 'Why, it's a joke – they haven't done any serious research there for years. The Ministry have given it over to the crackpots, hoping they'll blow themselves to pieces.'

A few discreet off-hand inquiries in other quarters had brought the same answer. A friend of mine with a sense of humour advised me over the telephone to take golf-clubs and plenty of paperbacks. 'There's no sort of organisation,' he said. 'MacLean works with a handful of chaps who think he's the Messiah. If you don't fall into line he ignores you, and you'll find yourself doing sweet f.a.'

'Fine. That suits me. I need a holiday,' I lied, hanging up with feelings of intense irritation against the world in general.

It was typical, I suppose, of my approach to the whole business that I hadn't checked thoroughly on timetables, and therefore an added annoyance to find that I had to get out at Ipswich, wait forty minutes, and board a slow train to Thirlwall, which was the station for Saxmere. It was raining when I finally descended upon the empty windswept platform, and the porter who took my ticket told me that the taxi which usually waited for this particular train had been snapped up five minutes before.

'There's a garage opposite the Three Cocks,' he added. 'They might still be open and could run you over to Saxmere.'

I walked past the booking office carrying my bags and blaming myself for my bad staff-work. As I stood outside the station wondering whether to brave the doubtful hospitality of the Three Cocks – it was close on seven, and even if a car was not available I could do with a drink – a very ancient Morris came swerving into the station-yard and pulled up in front of me. The driver got out and made a dive for my bags.

'You are Saunders, I take it?' he asked, smiling. He was young, not more than about nineteen, with a shock of fair hair.

'That's right,' I said. 'I was just wondering where the hell I'd raise a taxi.'

'You wouldn't,' he answered. 'On a wet night the Yanks swipe the lot. Anything on wheels that will take 'em out of Thirlwall. Hop in, will you?'

I'd forgotten about Thirlwall being a U.S. air-base, and made a mental note to avoid the Three Cocks in my leisure hours. American personnel on the loose are not among my favourite companions.

'Sorry about the rattle,' apologised the driver as we swerved through the town to the accompaniment of what sounded like a couple of petrol cans rolling under the back seat. 'I keep meaning to fix it, but never find time. My name's Ryan, by the way, Ken Ryan, always known as Ken. We don't go in for surnames at Saxmere.'

I said nothing. My Christian name is Stephen, nor had anyone ever shortened it to Steve. My gloom increased and I lit a cigarette. Already the houses of Thirlwall lay behind us and our road, having traversed a mile or two of flat country-side consisting of turnip fields, suddenly shot up on to a sandy track across a heath, over which we proceeded in a series of bumps until my head nearly hit the roof.

My companion apologised once more.

'I could have taken you in by the main entrance,' he said, 'but this way is so much shorter. Don't worry, the springs are used to it.'

The sandy track topped a rise and there below us, stretching into infinity, lay acre upon acre of waste land, marsh and reed, bounded on the left by sand-dunes with the open sea beyond. The marshes were intersected here and there by dykes, beside which stood clumps of forlorn rushes bending to the wind and rain, the dykes in their turn forming them-selves into dank pools, one or two of them miniature lakes, ringed about with reeds.

Our road, the surface of which was now built up with clinkers and small stones, descended abruptly to this scene of desolation, winding like a narrow ribbon with the marsh on either side. In the far distance a square tower, grey and squat, stood out against the skyline, and as we drew nearer I could see beyond the tower itself the curving spiral of the one-time radar installation, brooding over the waste land like a giant oyster-shell. This, then, was Saxmere. My worst forebodings could not have conjured up a more forbidding place.

My companion, sensing probably from my silence that I lacked enthusiasm, gave me a half-glance.

'It looks a bit grim in this light,' he said, 'but that's the rain. The weather's pretty good on the whole, though the wind is keen. We get some stunning sunsets.'

The laugh with which I greeted his remark was intended to be ironic, but it missed its mark, or was taken as encouragement, for he added, 'If you're keen on birds you've come to the right spot. Avocets breed here in the spring, and last March I heard the bittern boom.'

I choked back the expletive that rose to my lips – his phraseology struck me as naïve – and while admitting indifference to all objects furred or feathered I expressed surprise that anything in such a dreary locality should have a desire to breed at all. My sarcasm was lost, for he said, quite seriously, 'Oh, you'd be surprised,' and ground the Morris to a halt before a gate set in a high wired fence.

'Have to unlock this,' he told me, jumping out of the car, and I saw that now we had come to Saxmere itself. The area ahead was bounded on all sides by this same fence, some ten feet in height, giving the place the look of a concentration camp. This agreeable vista was enhanced by the sudden appearance of an Alsatian dog, who loped out of the marshes to the left, and stood wagging its tail at young Ken as he unlocked the gate.

'Where are the tommy-guns?' I asked, when he climbed back into the driving-seat. 'Or does the dog's handler watch us unseen from some concrete dug-out in the marsh?'

This time he had the grace to laugh as we passed through the barricade. 'No guns, no handlers,' he said. 'Cerberus is as gentle as a lamb. Not that I expected to find him here, but Mac will have him under control.'

He got out once more and locked the gate, while the dog, his head pointing across the marsh, took no more notice of us. Then all at once, pricking his ears, he dived into the reeds, and I watched him running along a narrow muddy track in the direction of the tower.

'He'll be home before we are,' said Ken, letting in the clutch, and the car swerved to the right along a broad asphalt road, the marsh giving place now to scrub and shingle.

The rain had stopped, the clouds had broken into splintered fragments, and the squat tower of Saxmere stood out bold and black against a copper sky. Did this, I wondered, herald one of the famous sunsets? If so, no member of the staff appeared to be taking advantage of it. Road and marsh alike were deserted. We passed the fork to the main entrance and turned left towards the disused radar installation and the tower itself, grouped about with sheds and concrete buildings. The place looked more like a deserted Dachau than ever.

Ken drove past the tower and the main buildings, taking a side road running seaward, at the end of which was a row of prefabricated huts.

'Here we are,' he said, 'and what did I tell you? Cerberus has beaten us to it.'

The dog emerged from a track on the left and ran off behind the huts.

'How is he trained?' I asked. 'A hi-fi whistle?'

'Not exactly,' answered my companion.

I got out of the car and he heaved my bags from the rear seat.

'These are the sleeping-quarters, I suppose?'

I glanced about me. The pre-fabs at least looked wind- and water-tight.

'It's the whole works,' replied Ken. 'We sleep, feed, and do everything here.'

He ignored my stare and led the way ahead. There was a small entrance hall, and a corridor beyond running right and left. Nobody was about. The walls of both hall and corridor were a dull grey, the floor covered with linoleum. The impression was that of a small-town country surgery after hours.

'We feed at eight, but there's loads of time,' said Ken. 'You'd like to see your room and have a bath, perhaps.'

I had no particular desire for a bath, but I badly needed a

drink. I followed him down the left-hand corridor, and he opened a door and switched on the light, then crossed the floor and pulled aside the curtains.

'Sorry about that,' he said. 'Janus likes to bed us down early before going through to the kitchen. Winter or summer, these curtains are drawn at six-thirty, and the covers removed from the beds. He's a stickler for routine.'

I looked around. Whoever designed the room must have had a hospital training all right. It had the bare essentials. Bed, wash-basin, chest-of-drawers, wardrobe, one chair. The window gave on to the entrance front. The blankets on the bed were folded hospital fashion, and a military hospital at that.

'O.K.?' asked Ken. He looked puzzled. Possibly my expression surprised him.

'Fine,' I answered. 'Now what about a drink?'

I followed him up the corridor once more, across the entrance hall, and on through a swing-door at the far end. I heard the light clack-clack of ping-pong balls, and braced myself for frivolity. The room we entered was empty. The sportsmen, whoever they were, were playing in the room beyond. Here there were easy chairs, a table or two, an electric fire and a bar in the far corner, behind which my youthful companion installed himself. I noticed, with misgiving, two enormous urns.

'Coffee or cocoa?' he asked. 'Or do you prefer something cool? I can recommend the orange juice with a splash of soda.'

'I'd like a Scotch,' I said.

He looked distressed. His expression became that of an anxious host whose guest demands fresh strawberries in midwinter.

'I'm frightfully sorry,' he said, 'we none of us touch alcohol. Mac won't have it served, it's one of his things. But of course you can bring your own supply and drink in your room. What a fool I was not to have warned you. We could have stopped at Thirlwall and brought you back a bottle from the Three Cocks.'

His distress was so genuine that I controlled the flood-gates of emotion that threatened to burst from me, and told him I would settle for orange juice. He looked relieved, and splashed the nauseous liquid into a tall glass, deftly sousing it with soda.

I felt the time had come for further explanation, not only about him, the acolyte, but about the rest of the establishment. Was the Order Benedictine or Franciscan, and at what hour would the bell sound for Vespers and Compline?

'Forgive my ignorance,' I said, 'but my briefing before leaving A.E.L. was somewhat short. I don't know the first thing about Saxmere, or what you do here.'

'Oh, don't worry,' he answered, smiling. 'Mac will explain all that.'

He poured some juice into his own glass and said, 'Cheers.' I ignored the toast and listened to the echo of the ping-pong balls.

'You told me,' I continued, 'that all the work was done in this building where we are now.'

'That's right,' he said.

'But where do all the personnel hang out?' I persisted.

'Personnel?' he echoed, frowning. 'There are no personnel. That's to say, there's only Mac, Robbie, Janus — I suppose you'd count Janus — and myself. And now of course you.'

I put down my glass and stared. Was he having me on? No, he seemed perfectly serious. Tossing down his orange juice like a cup-bearer of the gods quaffing ambrosia, he watched me from behind the bar.

'It's O.K., you know,' he said. 'We're a very happy party.'

I did not doubt it. What with cocoa, ping-pong, and the booming bittern, this team of sportsmen would make the members of a Women's Institute seem like trolls.

My baser instincts made me yearn to prick the youngster's pride.

'And what,' I asked, 'is your position on the staff? Ganymede to the professor's Jove?'

To my intense surprise he laughed, and with an ear cocked to the further room, where the sound of balls had ceased, set two more glasses down upon the bar and filled them both with juice.

'How smart of you to guess,' he answered. 'That's roughly the idea . . . to snatch me from this earth to a doubtful heaven. No, seriously, I'm Mac's guinea-pig, along with Janus's daughter and Cerberus the dog.'

At that moment the door opened and two men came into the room.

Instinctively I recognised MacLean. He was fiftyish, craggy, tall, with the pale, rather light blue eyes which I associate with drunkards, criminals and fighter pilots – in my view the three frequently combine. His lightish hair receded from a high forehead, and the prominent nose was matched by a thrusting chin. He wore baggy corduroy trousers and an immense pull-over with a turtle neck.

His companion was sallow, bespectacled and squat. Shorts and a baggy shirt gave him a boy scout appearance, nor did the circular sweat stains under his armpits enhance his charm.

MacLean advanced towards me holding out his hand, the broad smile of welcome suggesting I had already become one of his small band of brothers.

'I'm so very glad to see you,' he said. 'I do hope Ken has been looking after you all right. Such a wretched evening for your first glimpse of Saxmere, but we'll do better for you tomorrow, won't we, Robbie?'

His voice, his manner, was that of an old-fashioned host.

I might have been a late arrival at a country-house shoot. He put his hand on my shoulder and urged me towards the bar.

'Orange juice for all, please, Ken,' he said, and, turning to me, 'We've heard tremendous things about you from A.E.L. I can't tell you how grateful I am to them – to John in particular – for allowing you to come. And above all to yourself. We'll do everything we can to make your visit memorable. Robbie, Ken, I want you to drink to – it's Stephen, isn't it? Shall we say Steve? – and to the success of our joint efforts.'

I forced a smile, and felt it become a fixture on my face. Robbie, the boy scout, blinked at me from behind his spectacles.

'Your very good health,' he said. 'I'm the Johannis factotum here. I do everything from exploding gases to taking Ken's temperature, as well as exercising the dog. When in trouble send for me.'

I laughed, then swiftly realised that the falsetto, music-hall comedian voice was in fact his own, and not assumed for the occasion.

We crossed the corridor to a room facing the front, plain and bare like the one we had left, with a table set for four. A long-faced, saturnine fellow, with close-cropped grizzled hair, stood by the sideboard.

'Meet Janus,' Mac said to me. 'I don't know how they feed you at A.E.L., but Janus sees we none of us starve.'

I favoured the steward with a cheerful nod. He replied to it with a grunt, and I instantly doubted his willingness to run errands for me to the Three Cocks. I waited for MacLean to say grace, which would somehow have seemed in character, but none was forthcoming, and Janus set before him an enormous old-fashioned soup tureen shaped like a jerry, from which my new chief ladled a steaming, saffron-coloured brew. It was surprisingly good. The grilled Dover sole that followed was better still, and the cheese soufflé feather-light. The meal took us some fifty minutes to consume, and by the end of it I was ready to make peace with my fellow-men.

Young Ken – whose conversation during dinner had consisted of a series of private jokes with Robbie, while MacLean discoursed on mountain climbing in Crete, the beauty of flamingos on the wing in the Camargue, and the peculiar composition of Piero della Francesca's 'Flagellation of Christ' – was the first to rise from the table and ask leave to be dismissed.

MacLean nodded. 'Don't read too late,' he said. 'Robbie will turn your light out if you do. Nine-thirty's the limit.'

The youngster smiled, and bade the three of us goodnight. I asked whether Ken was in training to race the dog around the marsh and back.

'No,' answered MacLean abruptly, 'but he needs a lot of sleep. Let's to billiards.'

He led the way from the dining-room back to the so-called bar, while I prepared myself for half an hour or so in the room beyond – nothing loath, for I rather fancied myself with a cue – but as we passed through, and I saw nothing but a ping-pong table and a dart-board, Robbie, noticing my puzzled expression, boomed in my ear, 'A quote from Shakespeare, the Serpent of old Nile. Mac means he wants to brief you.' He pushed me gently forward and then vanished. I followed my leader through yet another door, sound-proofed this time, and we entered the chill atmosphere of what appeared to be half-working lab, half-clinic, streamlined and severe. It even had an operating table under a centre light, and instruments and jars behind glass panels on the walls.

'Robbie's department,' said MacLean. 'He can do anything here from developing a virus to taking out your tonsils.'

I made no comment, having small desire to offer myself as

a potential victim to the boy scout's doubtful ministrations, and we passed from the laboratory to the room adjoining.

'You'll feel more at home here,' observed MacLean, and as he switched on the lights I saw that we had reached the electronics department. The first installation to which we came appeared similar to the one we had built for the G.P.O. some years ago – that is to say, a computer capable of speech, though its vocabulary was limited and the actual 'voice' was far from perfect. MacLean's box of tricks, however, had various accessories, and I went up to examine them closely.

'He's neat, don't you think?' said MacLean, rather like a proud father showing off his new-born infant. 'I call him Charon 1.'

We all have pet names for our inventions, and Hermes had seemed particularly appropriate for the winged messenger we had developed for the G.P.O. Charon, if I remembered rightly, was the ferryman who conveyed the spirits of the dead across the Styx. I supposed this was MacLean's own brand of humour.

'What does it do?' I asked cautiously.

'It has several functions,' answered MacLean, 'which I'll explain later, but your main concern will be the voice mechanism.'

He went through a starting-up procedure, much as we had done at A.E.L., but the result was very different. The voice reproduction was perfect, and he had got rid of all the hesitation.

'I'm using the computer for certain experiments in the field of hypnosis,' he went on. 'These involve programming it with a series of questions. The answers are then fed back into the computer, and are themselves used to modify the questions that follow. What do you think of that?'

'It's fantastic!' I answered. 'You've gone miles beyond what anybody else is doing.'

I was indeed flabbergasted, and wondered just how he had done it – as well as keeping it all so secret. We thought we had achieved all that could be done in this particular field at A.E.L.

'Yes,' said Mac, 'your experts will hardly improve upon it. Charon 1 will have many uses, especially in the medical world. I won't go into any more details tonight, except to say that it is primarily connected with an experiment I'm working on which the Ministry knows nothing whatever about.'

He smiled, and here we go, I thought, now we're coming to the 'experiments of a dubious nature' which my chief had warned me about. I said nothing, and MacLean moved to a different installation.

'This,' he said, 'is what really concerns the government, and the military chaps in particular. You know, of course, that blast is difficult to control. An aeroplane breaking the sound barrier may shatter windows indiscriminately, but not one particular window, or one particular target. Charon 2 can do just that.' He crossed the room to a cabinet, took out a glass jar, and placed it on the working bench by the wall. Then he threw a switch on his second installation, and the glass shivered to fragments.

'Rather neat, don't you think?' said MacLean. 'But of course the point is the long-range use, should you wish to inflict serious damage on specific objects at a distance. I personally don't – blast doesn't interest me – but the Services would find it effective on occasion. It's just a case of a special method of transmission. But my particular concern is high-frequency response between individuals, and between people and animals. I'm keeping this quiet from my masters, who give me a grant.' He put his fingers on another control on the second installation. 'You won't see anything with this one,' he said. 'It's the call-note with which I control Cerberus. Human beings can't pick it up.'

We waited in silence, and a few minutes later I heard the sound of a dog scratching at the further door. MacLean let him in. 'All right. Good boy. Lie down.' He turned to me, smiling. 'Nothing really in that – he was only the other side of the building – but we've got him to obey orders from long distances. It could be quite useful in an emergency.' He glanced at his watch. 'I wonder if Mrs J. will forgive me,' he murmured. 'It's only a quarter-past nine after all. And I do so enjoy showing off.' His schoolboy grin was suddenly infectious.

'What are you going to do?' I asked.

'Bring her small daughter to the telephone, or wake her up if she's asleep.'

He made another adjustment to the apparatus, and once again we waited. In about two minutes the telephone rang. MacLean crossed the room to answer it. 'Hullo?' he said. 'Sorry, Mrs J. Just an experiment. I'm sorry if I've woken her up. Yes, put her on. Hullo, Niki. No, it's all right. You can go back to bed. Sleep tight.' He replaced the receiver, then bent down to pat Cerberus stretched at his feet.

'Children, like dogs, are particularly easy to train,' he said. 'Or put it this way – their sixth sense, the one that picks up these signals, is highly developed. Niki has her own call-note, just as Cerberus does, and the fact that she suffers from retarded development makes her an excellent subject.'

He patted his box of tricks in much the same fashion that he had patted his dog. Then he glanced up at me and smiled.

'Any questions?'

'Obviously,' I replied. 'The first being, what is the exact object of the exercise? Are you trying to prove that certain high-frequency signals have potentialities not only for destruction but also for controlling the receptive mechanism in an animal, and also the human brain?'

I forced a composure I was far from feeling. If these were

the sort of experiments that were going on at Saxmere, small wonder the place had been shrugged aside as a crackpot's paradise.

MacLean looked at me thoughtfully. 'Of course Charon 2 could be said to prove exactly that,' he said, 'though this is not my intention. The Ministry may possibly be very disappointed in consequence. No, I personally am trying to tackle something more far-reaching.' He paused, then put his hand on my shoulder. 'We'll leave Charons 1 and 2 for tonight. Come outside for a breath of air.'

We left by the door which the dog had scratched at. It led to another corridor, and finally to an entrance at the back of the building. MacLean unbolted the door and I followed him through. The rain had ceased and the air was clean and cold, the sky brilliant with stars. In the distance, beyond the line of sand-dunes, I could hear the roar of sea breaking upon shingle.

MacLean inhaled deeply, his face turned seaward. Then he looked upward at the stars. I lit a cigarette and waited for him to speak.

'Have you any experience of poltergeists?' he asked.

'Things that go bump in the night?' I said. 'No, I can't say I have.' I offered him a cigarette, but he shook his head.

'What you watched just now,' said MacLean, 'the glass shivering to pieces, is the same thing. Electrical force, released. Mrs J. had trouble with crashing objects long before I developed Charon. Saucepans, and so on, hurling themselves about at the coastguard's cottage where they live. It was Niki, of course.'

I stared at him, incredulous. 'You mean the child?'

'Yes.'

He thrust his hands in his pockets and began pacing up and down. 'Naturally, she was quite unaware of the fact,' he continued. 'So were her parents. It was only psychic energy

exploding, extra strong in her case because her brain is undeveloped, and since she is the only survivor of identical twins
the force was doubled.'

This was rather too much to swallow, and I laughed. He
swung round and faced me.

'Have you a better solution?' he asked.

'No,' I admitted, 'but surely . . .'

'Exactly,' he interrupted. 'Nobody ever has. There are
hundreds, thousands of cases of these so-called phenomena,
and almost every time they are reported there is evidence to
show that a child, or someone who is regarded as of sub-standard
intelligence, was in the locality at the time.' He resumed his
walk and I beside him, the dog at our heels.

'So what?' I said.

'So that,' he went on, 'it suggests we all possess an untapped
source of energy within us that awaits release. Call it, if you
like, Force Six. It works in the same way as the high-frequency
impulse which I released just now from Charon. Here is the
explanation of telepathy, precognition, and all the so-called
psychic mysteries. The power we develop in any electronic
device is the same as the power that the Janus child possesses
– with one difference, to date: we can control the one but
not the other.'

I saw his meaning, but not where the discussion was leading
us. God knows life is complicated enough without seeking to
probe the unconscious forces that may lie dormant within
man, especially if the connecting link must first be an animal,
or an idiot child.

'All right,' I said, 'so you tap this Force Six, as you call it.
Not only in Janus's daughter, but in all animals, in backward
children, and finally in the human race. You have us breaking
glasses, sending saucepans flying, exchanging messages by telepathic communication, and so on and so forth; but wouldn't

it add immeasurably to our difficulties, so that we ended up in the complete chaos from which we presumably sprang?'

This time it was MacLean who laughed. Our walk had taken us to a ridge of high ground, and we were looking across the sand-dunes to the sea beyond. The long shingle beach seemed to stretch into eternity, as drear and featureless as the marsh behind it. The sea broke with a monotonous roar, sucking at the dragging stones, only to renew the effort and spend itself once more.

'No doubt it would,' he said, 'but that's not what I'm after. Man will find a proper use for Force Six in his own good time. I want to make it work for him after the body dies.'

I threw my cigarette on to the ground and watched it glow an instant before it flickered to a wet stub.

'What on earth do you mean?' I asked him.

He was looking at me, trying to size up my reaction to his words. I could not make up my mind if he was mad or not, but there was something vaguely endearing about him as he stood there, hunched, speculative, like an overgrown schoolboy in his corduroy bags and his old turtle-necked sweater.

'I'm quite serious,' he said. 'The energy is there, you know, when it leaves the body on the point of death. Think of the appalling wastage through the centuries; all that energy escaping as we die, when it might be used for the benefit of mankind. It's the oldest of theories, of course, that the soul escapes through the nostrils or the mouth – the Greeks believed in it, so do certain African tribes today. You and I are not concerned with souls, and we know that our intelligence dies with our body. But not the vital spark. The life-force continues as energy, uncontrolled, and up to the present . . . useless. It's above us and around us as we stand talking here.'

Once again he threw back his head and looked at the stars, and I wondered what deep inner loneliness had driven him to this vain quest after the intangible. Then I remembered that his wife had died. Doubtless this theoretical bunk had saved him.

'I'm afraid it will take you a lifetime to prove,' I said to him.

'No,' he answered. 'At the most a couple of months. You see, Charon 3, which I didn't show you, has a built-in storage unit, to receive and contain power, or, to be exact, to receive and contain Force Six when it is available.' He paused. The glance he threw at me was curious, speculative. I waited for him to continue. 'The ground work has all been done,' he said. 'We are geared and ready for the great experiment, when Charons 1 and 3 will be used in conjunction, but I need an assistant, fully trained to work both installations, when the moment comes. I'll be perfectly frank with you. Your predecessor here at Saxmere wouldn't co-operate. Oh yes, you had one. I asked your chief at A.E.L. not to tell you – I preferred to tell you myself. Your predecessor refused his co-operation for reasons of conscience which I respect.'

I stared. I was not surprised at the other fellow refusing to co-operate, but I did not see where ethics came into it.

'He was a Catholic,' explained MacLean. 'Believing as he did in the survival of the soul and its sojourn in purgatory, he couldn't stomach any idea of imprisoning the life force and making it work for us here on earth. Which, as I have told you, is my intention.'

He turned away from the sea and began walking back the way we had come. The lights were all extinguished in the low line of pre-fabs where presumably we were to eat, work, sleep and have our being during the eight weeks that lay ahead. Behind them loomed the square tower of the disused radar station, a monument to the ingenuity of man.

'They told me at A.E.L. you had no religious scruples,' went on MacLean. 'Neither have the rest of us at Saxmere, though

571

we like to think of ourselves as dedicated men. As young Ken puts it himself, it comes to the same thing as giving your eyes to a hospital, or your kidneys to cold storage. The problem is ours, not his.'

I had a sudden recollection of the youngster at the bar, pouring out the orange juice and calling himself a guinea-pig.

'What's Ken's part in all this, then?' I asked.

MacLean paused in his walk and looked straight at me.

'The boy has leukaemia,' he said. 'Robbie gives him three months at the outside. There'll be no pain. He has tremendous guts, and believes wholeheartedly in the experiment. It's very possible the attempt may fail. If it fails, we lose nothing – his life is forfeit anyway. If we succeed . . .' He broke off, catching his breath as though swept by a sudden deep emotion. 'If we succeed, you see what it will mean?' he said. 'We shall have the answer at last to the intolerable futility of death.'

When I awoke next morning to a brilliant day and looked from my bedroom window along the asphalt road to the disused radar tower, brooding like a sentinel over empty sheds and rusted metal, towards the marsh beyond, I made my decision then and there to go.

I shaved, bathed, and went along to breakfast determined to be courteous to all, and to ask for five minutes alone with MacLean immediately afterwards. I would catch the first available train, and with luck be in London by one o'clock. If there was any unpleasantness with A.E.L. my chief would take the rap for it, not I.

The dining-room was empty except for Robbie, who was attacking an enormous plateful of soused herrings. I bade him a brief good day and helped myself to bacon. I looked round for a morning paper but there was none. Conversation would be forced upon me.

'Fine morning,' I observed.

He did not answer me immediately. He was engaged in dissecting his herring with the finesse of an expert. Then his falsetto voice came at me across the table.

'Are you proposing to back out?' he asked.

His question took me by surprise, and I disliked the note of derision.

'I'm an electronics engineer,' I answered, 'I'm not interested in psychical research.'

'No more were Lister's colleagues concerned with discovering antisepsis,' he rejoined. 'What fools they were made to look later.'

He forked a half-herring into his mouth and proceeded to chew it, watching me from behind his bi-focal specs.

'So you believe all this stuff about Force Six?' I said.

'Don't you?' he parried.

I pushed aside my plate in protest.

'Look here,' I said. 'I can accept this work MacLean has done on sound. He has found the answer to voice production which we failed to do at A.E.L. He has developed a system by which high-frequency waves can be picked up by animals, and also, it seems, by one idiot child. I give him full marks for the first, am doubtful about the potential value of the second, and as to his third project – capturing the life-force, or whatever he calls it, as it leaves the body – if anyone talked to the Ministry about that one, your boss would find himself inside.'

I resumed my bacon feeling I had put Robbie in his place. He finished his herrings, then started on the toast and marmalade.

'Ever watched anyone die?' he asked suddenly.

'As a matter of fact, no,' I answered.

'I'm a doctor, and it's part of my job,' he said, 'in hospitals, in homes, in refugee camps after the war. I suppose I've witnessed scores of deaths during my professional life. It's not a pleasant experience. Here at Saxmere it's become my business to stand by a very plucky, likeable lad, not only during his last hours, but during the few weeks that remain to him. I could do with some help.'

I got up and took my plate to the sideboard. Then I returned and helped myself to coffee.

'I'm sorry,' I said.

He pushed the toast-rack towards me but I shook my head. Breakfast is not my favourite meal, and this morning I lacked appetite. There was a sound of footsteps outside on the asphalt, and a head looked in at the window. It was Ken.

'Hullo,' he said, with a grin, 'what a wonderful morning. If Mac doesn't need you in the control room I'll show you round. We could take a walk up to the coastguard cottages and over Saxmere cliff. Are you game?' He took my hesitation for assent. 'Splendid! It's no use asking Robbie. He'll spend the morning in the lab gloating over specimens of my blood.'

The head vanished, and I heard him call to Janus through the kitchen window alongside. Neither Robbie nor I spoke. The sound of munching toast became unbearable. I stood up.

'Where will I find MacLean?' I asked.

'In the control room,' he answered, and went on eating.

It was best done at once. I went the way I had been shown the night before, through the swing door to the lab. Somehow the operating table under the centre light held more significance this morning, and I avoided looking at it. I went through the door at the far end, and saw MacLean standing by Charon 1. He beckoned me over.

'There's a slight fault in the processing unit,' he said. 'I noticed it last night. I'm sure you'll be able to fix it.'

This was the moment to express my regrets and tell him I

had decided against joining his team and intended to return to London immediately. I did no such thing. Instead I crossed the floor to the computer and stood by while he explained the circuits. Professional pride, professional jealousy, if you will, coupled with intense curiosity to know why this particular apparatus was superior to the one we had built at A.E.L., proved too much for me.

'There are some overalls on the wall,' said MacLean. 'Put 'em on, and we'll fix the fault between us.'

From then onward I was lost, or perhaps it would be more correct to say that I was won. Not to his lunatic theories, not to any future experiment with life and death; I was conquered by the supreme beauty and efficiency of Charon 1 itself. Beauty may be an odd word to use where electronics are concerned. I did not find it so. Herein lay all my passion, all my feelings; from my boyhood I had been involved with the creation of these things. This was my life's work. I was not interested in the uses to which the machines I had helped to develop and perfect were ultimately put. My part was to see that they fulfilled the function for which they were designed. Until arriving at Saxmere I had had no other object, no other aim in life, but to do what I was fitted to do, and do it well.

Charon 1 awakened something else in me, an awareness of power. I had only to handle those controls to know that what I wanted now was to have detailed knowledge of all the working parts, and then be given charge of the whole lay-out. Nothing else mattered. By the end of that first morning I had not only located the fault, a minor one, but had set it right. MacLean had become Mac, the shortening of my name to Steve was something that no longer jarred, and the whole fantastic set-up had ceased to irritate or to dismay; I had become one of the team.

Robbie showed no surprise when I turned up at lunchtime,

nor did he allude to our conversation at breakfast. In the late afternoon, with Mac's permission, I took my suggested walk with Ken. It was impossible to connect approaching death with this irrepressible youngster, and I put it from my mind. It could be that both Mac and Robbie were wrong about it. Anyway, it was not, thank God, my problem.

He showed no sign of fatigue and led the way, laughing and chatting, across the sand-dunes to the sea. The sun was shining, the air felt cold and clean, even the long stretch of shore that had seemed dreary the night before had now a latent charm. The heavy shingle gave place to sand, crisp under our feet; Cerberus, who accompanied us, bounded ahead. We threw sticks for him to retrieve from the pallid, almost effortless, sea, which gently, without menace, broke beside us as we walked. We did not discuss Saxmere, or anything connected with it; instead Ken regaled me with amusing gossip about the U.S. base at Thirlwall, where he had apparently worked as one of the ground staff before Mac arranged his transfer ten months before.

Suddenly Cerberus, barking puppy-fashion for another stick, turned and stood motionless, ears pricked, head to wind. Then he started loping back the way we had come, his lithe black-and-tan form soon lost to sight against the darker shingle and the dunes beyond.

'He's had a signal from Charon,' said Ken.

The night before, watching Mac at the controls, the dog's scratching at the door seemed natural. Here, some three miles distant on the lonely shore, his swift departure was uncanny.

'Effective, isn't it?' said Ken.

I nodded; but somehow, because of what I'd seen, my spirits left me. Enthusiasm for the walk had waned. It would have been different had I been alone. Now, with the boy beside me, I was, as it were, confronted with the future, the project Mac had in mind, the months ahead.

'Want to turn back?' he asked me.

His words reminded me of Robbie's at breakfast, though he meant them otherwise. 'Just as you like,' I said indifferently.

He swung left and we clambered, slipping and sliding with every step, up the steep slope to the cliffs above the beach. I was breathless when I reached the top. Not Ken. Smiling, he lent a hand to pull me up. Heather and scrub lay all about us, and the wind was in our faces, stronger than it had been below. About a quarter of a mile distant, stark and white against the skyline, stood a row of coastguard cottages, bleak windows all aflame with the setting sun.

'Come and pay your respects to Mrs J.,' suggested Ken.

Reluctantly I followed, detesting unpremeditated visits, no matter where. The unprepossessing Janus household did not attract me. As he drew near I saw that only the far cottage was inhabited. The others had the forlorn, lost look of buildings untenanted for years. Two had their windows broken. Gardens, untended, sprawled. Posts, sagging drunkenly from the damp earth, trailed pieces of barbed wire from their rotting stumps. A small girl was leaning over the gate of the occupied cottage. Dark, straight hair framed her pinched face, her eyes were lustreless, and she was wanting a front tooth.

'Hullo, Niki,' called Ken.

The child stared, then slowly removed herself from the gate. Morosely, she pointed at me. 'Who's that?' she asked.

'His name is Steve,' Ken answered her.

'I don't like his shoes,' said the child.

Ken laughed and opened the gate, and as he did so the child attempted to climb upon him. Gently he put her aside, and walking up the path to the open door called, 'Are you there, Mrs J.?'

A woman appeared, pallid and dark like her child. Her anxious face broke into a smile at the sight of Ken. She bade us enter, apologising for the disarray. I was introduced as Steve, and we hovered uncomfortably in the front room, where the child's toys were strewn about the floor.

'We've had tea,' Ken said, in reply to Mrs J.'s question, but, insisting that the kettle had just boiled, the woman vanished to the adjoining kitchen, to reappear at once with a large brown tea-pot and two cups and saucers. There was nothing for it but to swallow the stuff under her watchful eyes, while the child, edging against Ken all the while, stared balefully at my inoffensive canvas shoes.

I gave full marks to my young companion. He exchanged pleasantries with Mrs Janus, and patted the unendearing Niki. I remained silent throughout, and wondered why the child's likeness, framed in place of honour over the fireplace, should be so much more pleasing than the child herself.

'It's very cold here in the winter, but a bracing cold,' said Mrs Janus, fixing me with her own mournful eyes. 'I always say I prefer the frost to the damp.'

I agreed and shook my head at the offer of more tea. At this moment the child stiffened. She stood rigid a moment, her eyes closed. I wondered if she were going to throw a fit. Then very calmly she announced, 'Mac wants me.'

Mrs Janus, with a murmur of apology, went into the hall and I heard her dial. Ken was watching the child, himself unmoved. I felt slightly sick. In a moment I heard Mrs Janus speaking over the telephone and she called, 'Niki, come here and speak to Mac.'

The child ran from the room, and for the first time since our arrival showed animation. She even laughed. Mrs Janus returned and smiled at Ken.

'I think Mac really wants a word with you,' she said.

Ken got up and went into the hall. Alone with the child's mother, I did not know what to say. At last, in desperation, nodding at the photograph above the fireplace, I said, 'What a good likeness of Niki. Taken a few years ago, I suppose?'

To my dismay, the woman's eyes filled with tears.

'That's not Niki, that's her twin,' she answered. 'That's our Penny. We lost her soon after they had both turned five.'

My awkward apology was cut short by the entrance of the child herself. Ignoring my shoes she came straight to me, put her hand on my knee and announced, 'Mac says Cerberus is back. And you and Ken can go home.'

'Thank you,' I said.

As we walked away from the cottages, over scrub and heather, and took a short cut back to Saxmere through the marsh, I asked Ken whether the call-signal from Charon invariably had the effect I had seen, that of awakening latent intelligence in the child.

'Yes,' he said. 'We don't know why. Robbie thinks the ultra-short-wave may have therapeutic value in itself. Mac doesn't agree. He believes that when he puts out the call it connects Niki with what he calls Force Six, which in her case is doubled because of the dead twin.'

Ken spoke as if this fantastic theory was perfectly natural.

'Do you mean,' I asked, 'that when the call goes through the dead twin somehow takes over?'

Ken laughed. He walked so fast it was hard to keep up with him.

'Ghoulies and ghosties?' he queried. 'Good Lord, no! There's nothing left of poor Penny but electric energy, still attached to her living twin. That's why Niki makes such a useful guinea-pig.'

He glanced across at me, smiling.

'When I go,' he said, 'Mac plans to tap my energy too. Don't ask me how. I just don't know. But he's welcome to have a crack at it.'

We went on walking. The sour smell of stagnant water rose from the marsh on either side of us. The wind strengthened, flattening the reeds. The tower of Saxmere loomed ahead, hard and black against a russet sky.

I had the voice production unit functioning to my satisfaction within the next few days. We fed it with tape, programmed in advance as we had done at A.E.L., but the vocabulary was more extensive, consisting of a call signal 'This is Charon speaking . . . this is Charon speaking . . .' followed by a series of numbers, spoken with great clarity. Then came questions, most of them quite simple, such as, 'Are you O.K.?' 'Does anything bother you?', proceeding to statements of fact like, 'You are not with us. You are at Thirlwall. It is two years back. Tell us what you see,' and so on. My job was to control the precision of the voice, the programme was Mac's responsibility, and, if the questions and statements appeared inane to me, doubtless they made sound sense to him.

On Friday he told me that he considered Charon was ready for use the next day, and Robbie and Ken were warned for eleven a.m. Mac himself would be at the controls, and I was to watch. In the light of what I had already witnessed, I should have been fully prepared for what happened. Oddly enough, I was not. I took up my station in the adjoining lab, while Ken stretched himself out on the operating table.

'It's all right,' he said to me with a wink. 'Robbie isn't going to carve me up.'

There was a microphone in position above his head, with a lead going through to Charon 1. A yellow light for 'Stand-by' flashed on the wall. It changed to red. I saw Ken close his eyes. Then a voice came from Charon. 'This is Charon speaking . . . This is Charon speaking.' The series of numbers followed, and, after a pause, the question, 'Are you O.K.?'

When Ken replied, 'Yes, I'm O.K.' I noticed that his voice lacked its usual buoyancy; it was flatter, pitched in a lower key. I glanced at Robbie; he handed me a slip of paper on which were written the words, 'He's under hypnosis'.

The penny dropped, and I realised for the first time the full importance of the sound unit and the reason for perfecting it. Ken had been conditioned to hypnosis by the electronic voice. The questions on the programme were not haphazard, they were taped for him. The implications of this were even more shocking to me than when I had seen the dog and the child obey the call signal from a distance. When Ken, jokingly, had spoken of 'going to work', this was what he had meant.

'Does anything bother you?' asked the voice.

There was a long pause before the answer, and when it came the tone was impatient, almost fretful.

'It's the hanging about. I want it to happen quickly. If it could be over and done with, then I wouldn't give a damn.'

I might have been standing by a confessional, and I understood now why my predecessor had turned in his job. I saw Robbie's eyes upon me; the demonstration had been staged not only to show Ken's co-operation under hypnosis, proved no doubt dozens of times already, but to test my nerve. The ordeal continued. Much of what Ken said made painful hearing. I don't want to repeat it here. It revealed the unconscious strain under which he lived, never outwardly apparent either to us or to himself.

The programme Mac used was not one I had heard before, and it ended with the words, 'You'll be all right, Ken. You aren't alone. We're with you every step of the way. O.K.?'

A faint smile passed over the quiet face.

'O.K.'

Then the numbers were repeated, in swifter sequence, ending with the words 'Wake up, Ken!'

The boy stretched himself, opened his eyes and sat up. He looked first at Robbie, then at me, and grinned.

'Did old Charon do his stuff?' he asked.

'One hundred per cent,' I answered, my voice falsely hearty.

Ken slid off the operating table, his work for the morning done. I went through to Mac, standing by the controls.

'Thanks, Steve,' he said. 'You can appreciate the necessity for Charon 1 now. An electronic voice, plus a planned programme, eliminates emotion on our part, which will be essential when the time comes. That's the reason Ken has been conditioned to the machine. He responds very well. But better, of course, if the child is with him.'

'The child?' I repeated.

'Yes,' he answered. 'Niki is an essential part of the experiment. She is conditioned to the voice too, and the pair of them chat away together as gay as crickets. They know nothing about it afterwards, naturally.' He paused, watching me closely as Robbie had done. 'Ken will almost certainly go into coma at the end. The child will be our only link with him then. Now, I suggest you borrow a car, drive into Thirlwall and buy yourself a drink.'

He turned away, craggy, imperturbable, suggesting a benevolent bird of prey.

I didn't go into Thirlwall. I walked out across the sand-dunes to the sea. There was nothing calm about it today. Turbulent and grey, it sank into troughs before breaking on the shingle with a roar. Miles away along the beach a group of U.S. Air Corps cadets were practising bugle calls. The shrill notes, the discordant sounds, drove towards me down the wind. For no reason at all the half-forgotten lines of a Negro spiritual kept repeating themselves over and over in my mind.

> *'He has the whole world in his hands,*
> *He has the whole world in his hands . . .'*

The demonstration was repeated, with varying programmes, every three days during the weeks that followed. Mac and I took it in turn at the controls. I soon grew accustomed to this, and the bizarre sessions became a matter of routine.

It was, as Mac had said, less painful when the child was present. Her father would bring her to the lab and leave her with us, Ken already in position and under control. The child would sit in a chair beside him, also with a microphone above her head to record her speech. She was told that Ken was asleep. Then, in her turn, she would receive the signal from Charon, and a different series of numbers from Ken's, after which she would be under control. The programme was different when the two were working together. Charon would take Ken back in time, to a period when he was the same age as Niki, saying, 'You are seven years old. Niki has come to play with you. She is your friend,' and a similar message would be given to the child, 'Ken has come to play with you. He is a boy of your age.'

The two would then chat together, without interruption from Charon, with the quite fantastic result – this had been built up during the past months, I gathered – that the pair were now close friends 'in time', hiding nothing from each other, playing imaginary games, exchanging ideas. Niki, backward and morose when conscious, was lively and gay under control. The taped conversations were checked after each session, to record the increasingly closer rapport between the two, and to act as guide for further programmes. Ken, when conscious, looked upon Niki as Janus's backward child, a sad little object of no interest. He was totally ignorant of what happened when under control. I was not so sure about Niki. Intuition seemed to draw her to him. She would hang about him, if given the chance.

I asked Robbie what the Janus parents felt about the sessions.

'They'd do anything for Mac,' he told me, 'and they believe it may help Niki. The other twin was normal, you see.'

'Do they realise about Ken?'

'That he's going to die?' replied Robbie. 'They've been told, but I doubt if they understand. Who would, looking at him now?'

We were at the bar, and from where we stood we could see Ken and Mac engaged in a game of ping-pong in the room beyond.

Early in December we had a scare. A letter came from the Ministry asking how the Saxmere experiments were going, and could they send someone down to have a look round? We had a consultation, the upshot of which was that I undertook to go up to London to choke them off. By this time I was whole-heartedly behind Mac in all he was doing, and during my brief stay in town I succeeded in satisfying the authorities in question that a visit at this moment would be premature, but we hoped to have something to show them before Christmas. Their interest, of course, lay in Charon 2's potentialities for blast; they knew nothing of Mac's intended project.

When I returned, alighting at Saxmere station in a very different mood from that of three months past, the Morris was waiting for me, but without Ken's cheerful face at the wheel. Janus had replaced him. He was never a talkative bloke, and he answered my question with a shrug.

'Ken's got a cold,' he said. 'Robbie's keeping him in bed as a precaution.'

I went straight to the boy's room on arrival. He looked a bit flushed, but was in his usual spirits, full of protests against Robbie.

'There's absolutely nothing the matter,' he said. 'I got wet feet stalking a bird down in the marsh.'

I sat with him awhile, joking about London and the Ministry, then went to report to Mac.

'Ken has some fever,' he said at once. 'Robbie's done a blood test. It's not too good.' He paused. 'This could be it.'

I felt suddenly chilled. After a moment I told him about London. He nodded briefly.

'Whatever happens,' he said, 'we can't have them here now.'

I found Robbie in the lab, busy with slides and a microscope. He was preoccupied, and hadn't much time for me.

'It's too soon to say yet,' he said. 'Another forty-eight hours should show one way or the other. There's an infection in the right lung. With leukaemia that could be fatal. Go and keep Ken amused.'

I took a portable gramophone along to the boy's bedroom. I suppose I put on about a dozen records, and he seemed quite cheerful. Later he dozed off and I sat there, wondering what to do. My mouth felt dry, and I kept swallowing. Something inside me kept saying, 'Don't let it happen.'

Conversation at dinner was forced. Mac talked about under-graduate days at Cambridge, while Robbie reminisced over past Rugby games – he'd played scrum-half for Guy's. I don't think I talked at all. I went along afterwards to say goodnight to Ken, but he was already asleep. Janus was sitting with him. Back in my room I flung myself on my bed and tried to read, but I couldn't concentrate. There was fog at sea, and every few minutes the fog-horn boomed from the lighthouse along the coast. There was no other sound.

Next morning Mac came to my room at a quarter to eight.

'Ken's worse,' he said. 'Robbie's going to try a blood trans-fusion. Janus will assist.' Janus was a trained orderly.

'What do you want me to do?' I asked.

'Help me get Charons 1 and 3 ready for action,' he said. 'If Ken doesn't respond, I may decide to put phase one of Operation Styx into effect. Mrs J. has been warned we may need the child.'

As I finished dressing I kept telling myself that this was the moment we had been training for all through the past two and a half months. It didn't help. I swallowed some coffee and went to the control room. The door to the lab was closed. They had Ken in there, giving him the blood transfusion. Mac and I worked over both Charons, seeing that everything functioned perfectly, and that there could be no hitch when the time came. Programmes, tapes, microphones, all were ready. After that it was a matter of standing by until Robbie came through with his report. We got it at about half-past twelve.

'Slight improvement.' They had taken him back to his room. We all had something to eat while Janus continued his watch over Ken. Today there was no question of forced conversation. The work on hand was the concern of all. I felt calmer, steadier. The morning's work had knocked me into shape. Mac proposed a game of ping-pong after lunch, and whereas the night before I would have felt aghast at the suggestion, today it seemed the right thing to do. Looking from the window, between games, I saw Niki wandering up and down with Mrs Janus, a strange, lost-looking little figure, filling a battered doll's pram with sticks and stones. She had been on the premises since ten o'clock.

At half-past four Robbie came into the sports room. I could tell by his face that it was no good. He shook his head when Mac suggested another transfusion. It would be a waste of time, he told us.

'He's conscious?' asked Mac.

'Yes,' answered Robbie. 'I'll bring him through when you're ready.'

Mac and I went back to the control room. Phase two of Operation Styx consisted of bringing the operating table in here, placing it between the three Charons, and connecting up with an oxygen unit alongside. The microphones were already in position. We had done the manoeuvre often before, in practice runs, but today we beat our fastest time by two minutes.

'Good work,' said Mac.

The thought struck me that he had been looking forward to this moment for months, perhaps for years. He pressed the button to signal that we were ready, and in less than four minutes Robbie and Janus arrived with Ken on the trolley, and lifted him on to the table. I hardly recognised him. The eyes, usually so luminous, had almost disappeared into the sunken face. He looked bewildered. Mac quickly attached electrodes, one against each temple and others to his chest and neck, connecting him to Charon 3. Then he bent over the boy.

'It's all right,' he said. 'We've got you in the lab to do a few tests. Just relax, and you'll be fine.'

Ken stared up at Mac, and then he smiled. We all knew that this was the last we should see of his conscious self. It was, in fact, goodbye. Mac looked at me, and I put Charon 1 into operation, the voice ringing clear and true. 'This is Charon calling . . . This is Charon calling . . .' Ken closed his eyes. He was under hypnosis. Robbie stood beside him, finger on pulse. I set the programme in motion. We had numbered it X in the files, because it was different from the others.

'How do you feel, Ken?'

Even with the microphone close to his lips we could barely hear the answer. 'You know damn well how I feel.'

'Where are you, Ken?'

'I'm in the control room. Robbie's turned the heating off. I've got the idea now. It's to freeze me, like butcher's meat. Ask Robbie to bring back the heat . . .' There was a long pause, and then he said, 'I'm standing by a tunnel. It looks like a tunnel. It could be the wrong end of a telescope, the figures look so small . . . Tell Robbie to bring back the heat.'

Mac, who was beside me at the controls, made an adjustment, and we let the programme run without sound until it reached a certain point, when it was amplified once more to reach Ken.

'You are five years old, Ken. Tell us how you feel.'

There was a long pause and then, to my dismay, though I suppose I should have been prepared for it, Ken whimpered, 'I don't feel well. I don't want to play.'

Mac pressed a button, and the door at the far end opened. Janus pushed his daughter into the room, then closed the door again. Mac had her under control with her call-sign at once, and she did not see Ken on the table. She went and sat down in her chair and closed her eyes.

'Tell Ken you are here, Niki.'

I saw the child clutch the arms of her chair.

'Ken's sick,' she said. 'He's crying. He doesn't want to play.'

The voice of Charon went ruthlessly on.

'Make Ken talk, Niki.'

'Ken won't talk,' said the child. 'He's going to say his prayers.'

Ken's voice came faintly through the microphone to the loudspeakers. The words were gabbled, indistinct.

> *'Gen'ral Jesus, mekan mild,*
> *Look'pon little child,*
> *Pity my simple city,*
> *Sofa me to come to thee . . .'*

There was a long pause after this. Neither Ken nor Niki said anything. I kept my hands on the controls, ready to continue the programme when Mac nodded. Niki began drumming her feet on the floor. All at once she said, 'I shan't go down the tunnel after Ken. It's too dark.'

Robbie, watching his patient, looked up. 'He's gone into coma,' he said.

Mac signalled to me to set Charon 1 in motion again.

'Go after Ken, Niki,' said the voice.

The child protested. 'It's black in there,' she said. She was nearly crying. She hunched herself in her chair and went through crawling motions. 'I don't want to go,' she said. 'It's too long, and Ken won't wait for me.'

She started to tremble all over. I looked across at Mac. He questioned Robbie with a glance.

'He won't come out of it,' Robbie said. 'It may last hours.'

Mac ordered the oxygen apparatus to be put into operation, and Robbie fixed the mask on Ken. Mac went over to Charon 3 and switched on the monitor display screen. He made some adjustments and nodded at me. 'I'll take over,' he said.

The child was still crying, but the next command from Charon 1 gave her no respite. 'Stay with Ken,' it said. 'Tell us what happens.'

I hoped Mac knew what he was doing. Suppose the child went into a coma too? Could he bring her back? Hunched in her chair, she was as still as Ken, and about as lifeless. Robbie told me to put blankets round her and feel her pulse. It was faint, but steady. Nothing happened for over an hour. We watched the flickering and erratic signals on the screen, as the electrodes transmitted Ken's weakening brain impulses. Still the child did not speak.

Later, much later, she stirred, then moved with a strange twisting motion. She crossed her arms over her breast, humping her knees. Her head dropped forward. I wondered if, like Ken, she was engaged in some childish prayer. Then I realised that her position was that of a foetus before birth. Personality had vanished from her face. She looked wizened, old.

Robbie said, 'He's going.'

Mac beckoned me to the controls, and Robbie bent over Ken with fingers on his pulse. The signals on the screen were fainter, and faltering, but suddenly they surged in a strong upward beat, and in the same instant Robbie said, 'It's all over. He's dead.'

The signal was rising and falling steadily now. Mac disconnected the electrodes and turned back to watch the screen. There was no break in the rhythm of the signal, as it moved up and down, up and down, like a heartbeat, like a pulse.

'We've done it!' said Mac. 'Oh, my God . . . we've done it!'

We stood there, the three of us, watching the signal that never for one instant changed its pattern. It seemed to contain, in its confident movement, the whole of life.

I don't know how long we stayed there – it could have been minutes, hours. At last Robbie said, 'What about the child?'

We had forgotten Niki, just as we had forgotten the quiet, peaceful body that had been Ken. She was still lying in her strange, cramped position, her head bowed to her knees. I went to the controls of Charon 1 to operate the voice, but Mac waved me aside.

'Before we wake her, we'll see what she has to say,' he said.

He put through the call signal very faintly, so as not to shock her to consciousness too soon. I followed with the voice, which repeated the final programme command.

'Stay with Ken. Tell us what happens.'

At first there was no response. Then slowly she uncoiled, her gestures odd, uncouth. Her arms fell to her side. She began to rock backwards and forwards as though following the motion on the screen. When she spoke her voice was sharp, pitched high.

'He wants you to let him go,' she said, 'that's what he wants. Let go . . . let go . . . let go . . .' Still rocking she began to gasp for breath, and, lifting her arms, pummelled the air with her fists.

'Let go . . . let go . . . let go . . . let go . . .'

Robbie said urgently, 'Mac, you've got to wake her.'

On the screen the rhythm of the signal had quickened. The

child began to choke. Without waiting for Mac, I set the voice in motion.

'This is Charon speaking . . . This is Charon speaking . . . Wake up, Niki.'

The child shuddered, and the suffused colour drained from her face. Her breathing became normal. She opened her eyes. She stared at each of us in turn in her usual apathetic way, and proceeded to pick her nose.

'I want to go to the toilet,' she said sullenly.

Robbie led her from the room. The signal, which had increased its speed during the child's outburst, resumed its steady rise and fall.

'Why did it alter speed?' I asked.

'If you hadn't panicked and woken her up, we might have found out,' Mac said.

His voice was harsh, quite unlike himself.

'Mac,' I protested, 'that kid was choking to death.'

'No,' he said, 'no, I don't think so.'

He turned and faced me. 'Her movements simulated the shock of birth,' he said. 'Her gasp for air was the first breath of an infant, struggling for life. Ken, in coma, had gone back to that moment, and Niki was with him.'

I knew by this time that almost anything was possible under hypnosis, but I wasn't convinced.

'Mac,' I said, 'Niki's struggle came *after* Ken was dead, *after* the new signal appeared on Charon 3. Ken couldn't have gone back to the moment of birth – he was already dead, don't you see?'

He did not answer at once. 'I just don't know,' he said at last. 'I think we shall have to put her under control again.'

'No,' said Robbie. He had entered the lab while we were talking. 'That child has had enough. I've sent her home, and told her mother to put her to bed.'

I had never heard him speak with authority before. He looked away from the lighted screen back to the still body on the table. 'Doesn't that go for the rest of us?' he said. 'Haven't we all had enough? You've proved your point, Mac. I'll celebrate with you tomorrow, but not tonight.'

He was ready to break. So, I think, were we all. We had barely eaten through the day, and when Janus returned he set about getting us a meal. He had taken the news of Ken's death with his usual calm. The child, he told us, had fallen asleep the moment she was put to bed.

So . . . it was all over. Reaction, exhaustion, numbness of feeling, all three set in, and I yearned, like Niki, for the total release of sleep.

Before dragging myself to bed some impulse, stronger than the aching fatigue that overwhelmed me, urged me back to the control room. Everything was as we had left it. Ken's body lay on the table, covered with a blanket. The screen was lighted still, and the signal was pulsing steadily up and down. I waited a moment, then I bent to the tape-control, setting it to play back that last outburst from the child. I remembered the rocking head, the hands fighting to be free, and switched it on.

'He wants you to let him go,' said the high-pitched voice, 'that's what he wants. Let go . . . let go . . . let go . . .' Then came the gasp for breath, and the words were repeated. 'Let go . . . let go . . . let go . . . let go . . .'

I switched it off. The words did not make sense. The signal was simply electrical energy, trapped at the actual moment of Ken's death. How could the child have translated this into a cry for freedom, unless . . . ?

I looked up. Mac was watching me from the doorway. The dog was with him.

'Cerberus is restless,' he said. 'He keeps padding backwards and forwards in my room. He won't let me sleep.'

'Mac,' I said, 'I've played that recording again. There's something wrong.'

He came and stood beside me. 'What do you mean, something wrong? The recording doesn't affect the issue. Look at the screen. The signal's steady. The experiment has been a hundred per cent successful. We've done what we set out to do. The energy is there.'

'I know it's there,' I replied, 'but is that all?'

I set the recording in motion once again. Together we listened to the child's gasp, and the words 'Let go . . . let go . . .'

'Mac,' I said, 'when the child said that, Ken was already dead. Therefore, there could be no further communication between them.'

'Well?'

'How then, after death, can she still identify herself with his personality – a personality that says "Let go . . . let go . . ." unless—'

'Unless what?'

'Unless something has happened that we know to be impossible, and what we can see, imprisoned on the screen, is the essence of Ken himself?'

He stared at me, unbelieving, and together we looked once more at the signal, which suddenly took on new meaning, new significance, and as it did so became the expression of our dawning sense of anguish and fear.

'Mac,' I said, 'what have we done?'

Mrs Janus telephoned in the morning to say that Niki had woken up and was acting strangely. She kept throwing herself backwards and forwards. Mrs Janus had tried to quieten her, but nothing she said did any good. No, she had no temperature, she was not feverish. It was this queer rocking movement all the time. She would not eat any breakfast, she would not speak.

Could Mac put through the call signal? It might quieten her.

Janus had answered the phone, and we were in the dining-room when he brought us his wife's message. Robbie got up and went to the telephone. He came back again almost immediately.

'I'll go over,' he said. 'What happened yesterday – I should never have allowed it.'

'You knew the risk,' answered Mac. 'We've all known the risk from the very start. You always assured me it would do no harm.'

'I was wrong,' said Robbie. 'Oh, not about the experiment . . . God knows you've done what you wanted to do, and it didn't affect poor Ken one way or the other. He's out of it all now. But I was wrong to let that child become involved.'

'We shouldn't have succeeded without her,' replied Mac.

Robbie went out and we heard him start up the car. Mac and I walked along to the control room. Janus and Robbie had been there before us, and had taken Ken's body away. The room was stripped once more to the essentials of normal routine, with one exception. Charon 3, the storage unit, still functioned as it had done the previous day and through the night, the signal keeping up its steady rise and fall. I found myself glancing at it almost furtively, in the irrational hope that it would cease.

Presently the telephone buzzed, and I answered it. It was Robbie.

'I think we ought to get the child away,' he said at once. 'It looks like catatonic schizophrenia, and whether she becomes violent or not Mrs J. can't cope with it. If Mac will say the word, I could take her up myself to the psychiatric ward at Guy's.'

I beckoned to Mac, explaining the situation. He took the receiver from me.

'Look, Robbie,' he said, 'I'm prepared to take the risk of putting Niki under control. It may work, or it may not.'

The argument continued. I could tell from Mac's gesture of frustration that Robbie would not play. He was surely right. Some irreparable damage might have been done to the child's mind already. Yet, if Robbie did take her up to the hospital, what possible explanation could he give?

Mac waved me over to replace him at the telephone.

'Tell Robbie to stand by,' he said.

I was his subordinate, and could not stop him. He went to the transmitter on Charon 2 and set the control. The call signal was in operation. I lifted the receiver and gave Robbie Mac's message. Then I waited.

I heard Robbie shout to Mrs Janus, 'What's the matter?' – then the sound of the receiver being dropped.

Nothing for a moment or two but distant voices, Mrs Janus, I think, pleading, and then an appeal to Robbie, 'Please, let her try . . .'

Mac went over to Charon 1 and made some adjustments. Then he waved to me to bring the telephone as near to him as it would go, and reached out for the receiver.

'Niki,' he said, 'do you hear me? It's Mac.'

I stood beside him, to catch the whisper from the receiver.

'Yes, Mac.'

She sounded bewildered, even frightened.

'Tell me what's wrong, Niki.'

She began to whimper. 'I don't know. There's a clock ticking somewhere. I don't like it.'

'Where's the clock, Niki?'

She did not answer. Mac repeated his question. I could hear Robbie protest. He must have been standing beside her.

'It's all round,' she said at last. 'It's ticking in my head. Penny doesn't like it either.'

Penny. Who was Penny? Then I remembered. The dead twin.

'Why doesn't Penny like it?'

This was intolerable. Robbie was right. Mac should not put the child through this ordeal. I shook my head at him. He took no notice, but once again repeated his question. I could hear the child burst into tears.

'Penny . . . Ken . . .' she sobbed, 'Penny . . . Ken.'

Instantly Mac switched to the recorded voice of Charon 1 giving the order on yesterday's programme:

'Stay with Ken. Tell us what happens.'

The child gave a piercing cry, and she must have fallen, because I heard Robbie and Mrs Janus exclaim and the telephone crash.

Mac and I looked at the screen. The rhythm was getting faster, the signal moving in quick jerks. Robbie, at his end, picked up the receiver.

'You'll kill her, Mac,' he called. 'For Christ's sake . . .'

'What's she doing?' asked Mac.

'The same as yesterday,' called Robbie. 'Backwards, forwards, rocking all the time. She's suffocating. Wait . . .'

Once again he must have let the receiver go. Mac switched back to the call signal. The pulsing on the screen was steadying. Then, after a long interval, Robbie's voice came through again.

'She wants to speak,' he said.

There was a pause. The child's voice, expressionless and dull, said, 'Let them go.'

'Are you all right now, Niki?' asked Mac.

'Let them go.' she repeated.

Mac deliberately hung up. Together we watched the signal resume its normal speed.

'Well?' I said. 'What does it prove?'

He looked suddenly old, and immeasurably tired, but there was an expression in his eyes that I had never seen before; a curious, baffled incredulity. It was as though everything he possessed, senses, body, brain, protested and denied the thoughts within.

'It could mean you were right,' he said.'It could mean survival of intelligence after the body's death. It could mean we've broken through.'

The thought, staggering in its implications, turned us both dumb. Mac recovered first. He went and stood beside Charon 3, his gaze fixed upon the picture.

'You saw it change when the child was speaking,' he said. 'But Niki by herself could not have caused the variation. The power came from Ken's Force Six, and from the dead twin's too. The power is capable of transmission through Niki, but through no one else. Don't you see . . .' He broke off, and swung round to face me, a new excitement dawning. 'Niki is the only link. We must get her here, programme Charon, and put further questions to her. If we really have got intelligence plus power under control . . .'

'Mac,' I interrupted, 'do you want to kill that child, or, worse, condemn her to a mental institution?'

In desperation he looked once more towards the screen. 'I've got to know, Steve,' he said. 'I've got to find out. If intelligence survives, if Force Six can triumph over matter, then it's not just one man who has beaten death but all mankind from the beginning of time. Immortality in some form or other becomes a certainty, the whole meaning of life on earth is changed.'

Yes, I thought, changed forever. The fusion of science and religion in a partnership at first joyous, then the inevitable disenchantment, the scientist realising, and the priest with him, that, with eternity assured, the human being on earth is more easily expendable. Dispatch the maimed, the old, the weak, destroy the very world itself, for what is the point of life if the promise of fulfilment lies elsewhere?

'Mac,' I said. 'You heard what the child said. The words were, "Let them go".'

The telephone rang again. This time it was not Robbie but Janus, from our own extension in the hall. He apologised for disturbing us, but two gentlemen had arrived from the Ministry. He had told them we were in conference, but they said the business was urgent. They had asked to see Mr MacLean at once.

I went into the bar, and the official I had seen in London was standing there with a companion. This first chap expressed apologies, and said the fact was that my predecessor at Saxmere had been to see them, and admitted that his reason for leaving was because he was doubtful of the work MacLean had in progress. There was some experiment going on of which he did not think the Ministry was aware. They wished to speak to MacLean at once.

'He will be with you shortly,' I said. 'In the meantime, if there is anything you want to know, I can brief you.'

They exchanged glances, and then the second chap spoke.

'You're working on vibrations, aren't you,' he asked, 'and their relation to blast? That was what you said in London.'

'We are,' I replied, 'and we have had some success. But, as I warned you, there is still a lot to do.'

'We're here,' he said, 'to be shown what you've achieved.'

'I'm sorry,' I answered, 'the work has been held up since I returned. We've suffered an unfortunate loss on the staff. Nothing to do with the experiment, or the research connected with it. Young Ken Ryan died yesterday from leukaemia.'

Once again there was the swift exchange of glances.

'We heard he was not well,' said the first man. 'Your predecessor told us. In fact, we were given to understand that the experiment in progress was, without the Ministry being informed, connected with this boy's illness.'

'You've been misinformed,' I said. 'His illness had nothing to do with the experiment. The doctor will be back shortly; he can give you the medical details.'

'We should like to see MacLean,' persisted the second chap, 'and we should like to see the electronics department.'

I went back to the control room. I knew that nothing I had said would prevent them from having their way. We were for it.

MacLean was standing by Charon 2 doing something to the controls. I looked quickly from him to Charon 3 alongside. The screen was still glowing, but the signal had vanished. I did not say anything, I just stared at him.

'Yes,' he said, 'it's dismantled. I've disconnected everything. The force is lost.'

My instantaneous feeling of relief turned to compassion, compassion for the man whose work for months, for years, had gone within five minutes. Destroyed by his own act.

'It isn't finished,' he said, meeting my eyes. 'It's only begun. Oh, one part of it is over. Charon 3 is useless now, and what happened will only be known to the three of us – for Robbie must share our knowledge. We were on the verge of a discovery that no one living would believe. But only on the verge. It could well be that both of us were wrong, that what the child told us last night, and again this morning, was simply some distortion of her unconscious mind – I don't know. I just don't know . . . But, because of what she said, I've released the energy. The child is free. Ken is free. He's gone. Where, to what ultimate destination, we shall probably never know. But – and this includes you, Steve, and Robbie, if he will join us – I am prepared to work to the end of my days to find out.'

Then I told him what the officials from the Ministry had said. He shrugged his shoulders.

'I'll tell them all our experiments have failed,' he said, 'that

599

I want to pack in the job. Henceforth, Steve, we'll be on our own. It's strange – somehow I feel nearer to Ken now than I ever did before. Not only Ken, but everyone who has gone before.' He paused, and turned away. 'The child will be all right,' he said. 'Go to her, will you, and send Robbie to me? I'll deal with those sleuths from the Ministry.'

I slipped out of the door at the back and started walking across the marsh towards the coastguard cottages. Cerberus came with me. He was no longer panting, restless, as he had been the night before, but bounded ahead in tearing spirits, returning now and again to make sure that I was following him.

It seemed to me that I had no feeling left, either for what had happened or for what was yet to come. Mac had destroyed, with his own hands, the single thread of evidence that had brought us, through the whole of yesterday, to this morning's dawn. The ultimate dream of every scientist, to give the first answer to the meaning of death, had belonged to us for a brief few hours. We had captured the energy, the energy had ignited the spark, and from that point on there had appeared to loom world after world of discovery.

Now . . . now, my faith was waning. Perhaps we had been wrong, tricked by our own emotions and the suffering of a frightened, backward child. The ultimate questions would never receive their answer, either from us or from anyone.

The marsh fell back on either side of me, and I climbed the scrubby hill to the coastguard cottages. The dog ran on ahead, barking. Away to the right, outlined on the cliff edge, the damned U.S. cadets were blowing their bugles once again. The raucous, discordant screeches tore the air. They were trying, of all things, to sound the Reveille.

I saw Robbie come out of the Januses' cottage, and the child was with him. She seemed all right. She ran forward to greet the dog. Then she heard the sound of the Reveille, and lifted her arms. As the tempo increased she swayed to the rhythm, and ran out towards the cliffs with her arms above her head, laughing, dancing, the dog barking at her feet. The cadets looked back, laughing with her; and then there was nothing else but the dog barking, the child dancing, and the sound of those thin, high bugles in the air.

VIRAGO MODERN CLASSICS

The Virago Modern Classics launched in 1978 with the radical aim of rewriting the canon, bringing women's voices and stories into the spotlight – and into conversation with each other – and expanding the definition of a classic.

The name Virago means a heroic war-like woman – or, as the thesaurus has it, a dragon, fury, hussy, spitfire or tigress – and signalled the founders' intent to challenge, entertain, enrich, raise eyebrows and revolutionise the literary landscape. Our Modern Classics are chosen with the same ambition, and the list itself continues to evolve, finding new ways to champion works by women and authors of underrepresented genders. With introductions by some of today's very best writers, these are books that speak to each new generation.

'The Virago Modern Classics list contains some of the greatest fiction and non-fiction of the modern age ... Still captivating, still memorable, still utterly essential reading' SARAH WATERS

'The Virago Modern Classics list is wonderful. It's quite simply one of the best and most essential things that has happened in publishing in our time' ALI SMITH

'The Virago Modern Classics have reshaped literary history and enriched the reading of us all. No library is complete without them' MARGARET DRABBLE

VIRAGO MODERN CLASSICS

AUTHORS INCLUDE:

Maya Angelou, Elizabeth von Arnim, Beryl Bainbridge, Pat Barker, Nina Bawden, Caroline Blackwood, Vera Brittain, Angela Carter, Willa Cather, Barbara Comyns, E. M. Delafield, Polly Devlin, Monica Dickens, Elaine Dundy, Nell Dunn, Nora Ephron, Janet Flanner, Janet Frame, Miles Franklin, Marilyn French, Stella Gibbons, Charlotte Perkins Gilman, Rumer Godden, Radclyffe Hall, Helene Hanff, Josephine Hart, Shirley Hazzard, Bessie Head, Patricia Highsmith, Winifred Holtby, Zora Neale Hurston, Elizabeth Jenkins, Susanna Kaysen, Molly Keane, Rosamond Lehmann, Anne Lister, Rose Macaulay, Shena Mackay, Beryl Markham, Daphne du Maurier, Mary McCarthy, Gloria Naylor, Kate O'Brien, Grace Paley, Barbara Pym, Mary Renault, Stevie Smith, Muriel Spark, Elizabeth Taylor, Angela Thirkell, Sylvia Townsend Warner, Mary Webb, Eudora Welty, Rebecca West, Edith Wharton, Antonia White

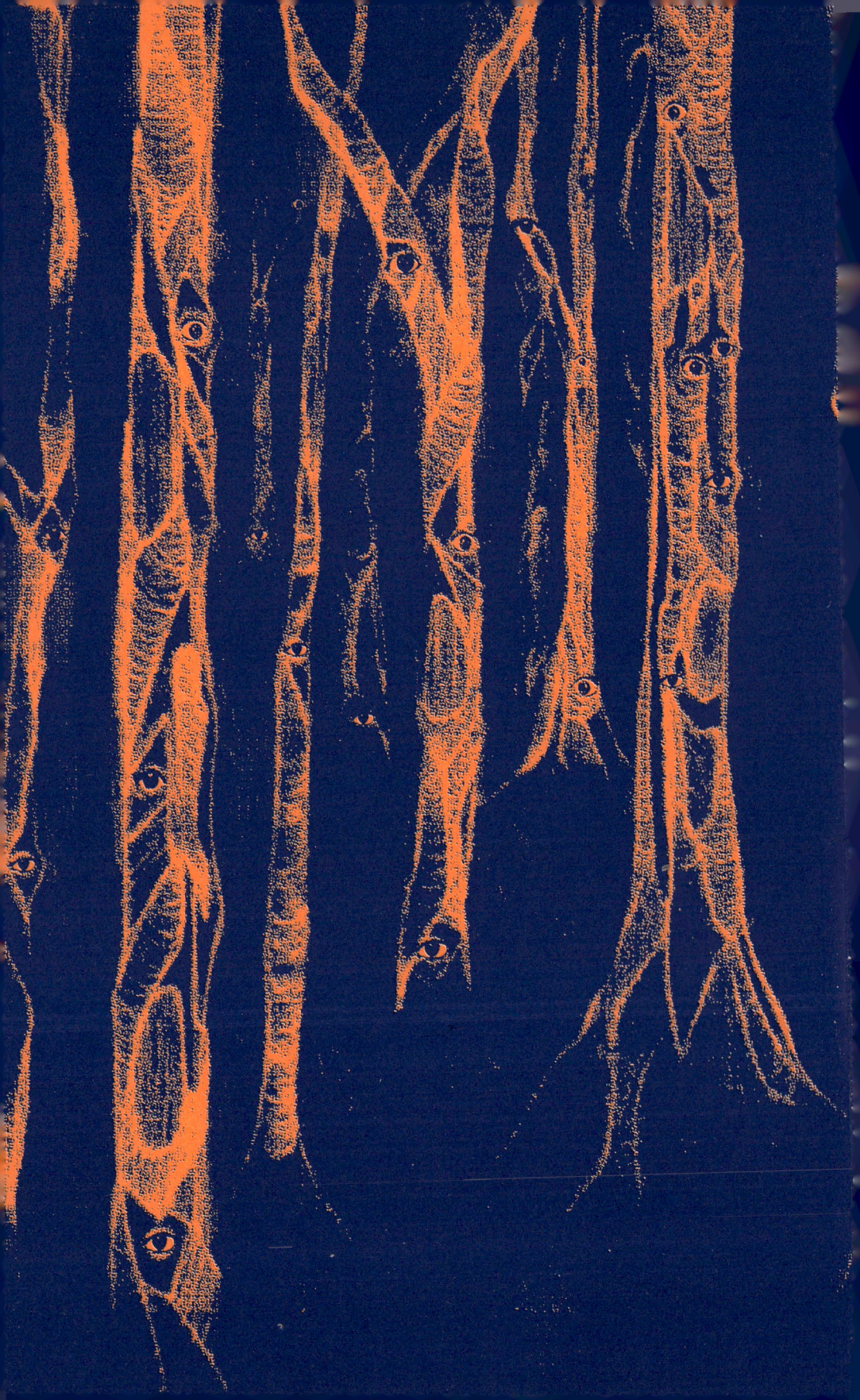